PRAISE FOR

Monica Ferris's Needlecraft Mysteries

"Colorful and humorous . . . perfect."
—*BookBrowser*

"Delightful . . . Monica Ferris is a talented writer who knows how to keep
the attention of her fans."
—*Midwest Book Review*

"A comfortable fit for mystery readers who want to spend an enjoyable
time with interesting characters."
—*St. Paul Pioneer Press*

"Filled with great small town characters. . . . A great time. . . . Fans of
Jessica Fletcher will devour this."
—*Rendezvous*

"Crisp dialogue [and] sharp descriptions."
—*St. Paul Pioneer Press*

"Another treat from Monica Ferris."
—*Mysterious Galaxy*

"A fun read that baffles the reader with mystery and delights with . . . ro-
mance."
—*Romantic Times*

"Fans of Margaret Yorke will relate to Betsy's growth and eventual maturity. . . . You need not be a needlecrafter to enjoy this. . . . Delightful."
—*Mystery Time*

Needlecraft Mysteries by Monica Ferris

CREWEL WORLD

FRAMED IN LACE

A STITCH IN TIME

UNRAVELED SLEEVE

A MURDEROUS YARN

HANGING BY A THREAD

CUTWORK

CREWEL YULE

Patterns of Murder

Monica Ferris

BERKLEY PRIME CRIME, NEW YORK

THE BERKLEY PUBLISHING GROUP
Published by the Penguin Group
Penguin Group (USA) Inc.
375 Hudson Street, New York, New York 10014, USA
Penguin Group (Canada), 10 Alcorn Avenue, Toronto, Ontario M4V 3B2, Canada
(a division of Pearson Penguin Canada Inc.)
Penguin Books Ltd., 80 Strand, London WC2R 0RL, England
Penguin Group Ireland, 25 St. Stephen's Green, Dublin 2, Ireland (a division of Penguin Books Ltd.)
Penguin Group (Australia), 250 Camberwell Road, Camberwell, Victoria 3124, Australia
(a division of Pearson Australia Group Pty. Ltd.)
Penguin Books India Pvt. Ltd., 11 Community Centre, Panchsheel Park, New Delhi—110 017, India
Penguin Group (NZ), Cnr. Airborne and Rosedale Roads, Albany, Auckland 1310, New Zealand
(a division of Pearson New Zealand Ltd.)
Penguin Books (South Africa) (Pty.) Ltd., 24 Sturdee Avenue, Rosebank, Johannesburg 2196,
South Africa

Penguin Books Ltd., Registered Offices: 80 Strand, London WC2R 0RL, England

This book is an original publication of The Berkley Publishing Group.

This is a work of fiction. Names, characters, places, and incidents either are the product of the author's imagination or are used fictitiously, and any resemblance to actual persons, living or dead, business establishments, events, or locales is entirely coincidental.

First edition: July 2005

Library of Congress Cataloging-in-Publication Data

Ferris, Monica.
    Patterns of murder / Monica Ferris.—1st ed.
       p. cm.
    ISBN 0-425-20669-6
    1. Devonshire, Betsy (Fictitious character)—Fiction. 2. Women detectives—Minnesota—Fiction. 3. Detective and mystery stories, American. 4. Needleworkers—Fiction. 5. Needlework—Fiction. 6. Minnesota—Fiction. I. Ferris, Monica. Crewel world. II. Ferris, Monica. Framed in lace. III. Ferris, Monica. Stitch in time. IV. Title.

    PS3566.U47A6 2005
    813'.6—dc22
                                                                                    2005041003

PRINTED IN THE UNITED STATES OF AMERICA

10   9   8   7   6   5   4   3   2   1

CONTENTS

Crewel World
1

Framed in Lace
167

A Stitch in Time
319

Patterns of Murder

Crewel World

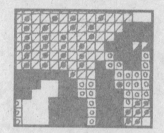

I thought I knew enough about needlework to write this novel. I didn't. Fortunately, people can be generous with their time and talents. Foremost are the owner, staff, and customers of Needle Nest of Minnetonka—particularly Pat Ingle, Sandy Mattson, and the Wednesday Bunch. Denise Williams designed the T'ang horse pattern and told me about painting needlepoint canvases. Elizabeth Proudfit encouraged and advised me and lent generously from her own library of needlework books. And the people of rec.crafts.textile.needlework (an Internet newsgroup) have cheered me on, answered my questions, and continue to be an excellent resource.

To all of you, humble and heartfelt thanks.

One

✦

Nowadays, when she stopped for lunch, Margot sat with her back to her shop's big front window. That gray monstrosity they'd built across the street had taken away her view of the lake. She ate the last Frito and wadded the empty bag into the plastic wrap that had held her sandwich and dropped both into the little wastebasket under the table. She drank the last of the green tea in her pretty porcelain cup—brewed from a bag, but good nevertheless—and took the cup to the back room for a quick rinse.

There were no customers waiting to buy needlework patterns or embroidery floss or knitting yarn when she got back, so she made a quick tour of her shop, rearranging the heap of knitting yarns in a corner, adjusting a display of the new autumn colors of embroidery floss in a basket on a table, and moving a folding knitting stand an inch closer to the traffic lane. Her shop appeared aimlessly cluttered, but every display was calculated to draw customers ever deeper into the room, with items virtually leaping into their hands.

Satisfied, she sat down again and got out her own knitting. She was working on a bolero jacket she intended to wear to a meeting on Saturday. It was a simple pattern, just knit and purl, but she was doing it in quarter-inch ribbon instead of yarn, so the jacket had an interesting depth and texture. It helped that the ribbon blended every few inches from palest pink to soft mauve to gray lavender.

Margot started knitting, her hands moving with swift economy. The jacket was nearly finished—if it wasn't finished already. She was slender enough to look good in a bolero jacket, but short enough that she had to try on everything in clothing stores, even things labeled petite, and nearly always had to adjust knitting patterns. After all these years she should be accustomed to it, but every so often she'd miscalculate or just get carried away with the pleasure of the work, and end up with the voluminous kind of garment teenagers wore. Of all the silliness of the current age, the silliest was a young thug who had to hold up his pants with one hand while he held up a shopkeeper with the other.

Margot Berglund was fifty-three, blond, with kind blue eyes and a bustling but comfortable manner. She had always been happiest with something to keep her busy, and so, when simply doing needlework and teaching her friends to do needlework and organizing expeditions to needlework stores and gatherings wasn't enough, she had opened Crewel World. That was back when crewelwork was the rage; just because it was needlepoint nowadays, she saw no need to change an established name.

The front door went *bing* and a handsome woman whose dark hair was pulled into a fat bun hustled in.

"Sorry I'm late," she said breathlessly. "It's so beautiful out, I found myself walking slowly to enjoy it."

"I don't blame you, Shelly."

Shelly went to hide her purse in the checkout desk's bottom drawer, looked around with a settling-in sigh, and asked, "What's first?"

"The window, I'm afraid," said Margot. The shop was deep but narrow; its front was mostly window, currently ornamented with canvases and patterns featuring brightly colored leaves and one-room schoolhouses.

"What, already? School hasn't even started yet."

Margot smiled. "Our customers are always working in advance of a holiday. Half of them are already making Christmas ornaments. So don't get too elaborate with the window; soon we'll have to advertise Christmas projects for the procrastinators."

Shelly picked up the stack of display items Margot had chosen and went to the front window.

"Ooooh, I think I'd like this one for myself," she said a minute later. Margot looked up to see her holding a counted cross-stitch pattern featuring an enormous pale moon with a silhouetted witch riding her broom across it. In the foreground was a heap of pumpkins out of which rose a windblown scarecrow.

"You'll have to do it on black," warned Margot.

"Yeah, well, I've been thinking of buying one of those Dazor lamps anyway," said Shelly. She traced the tatters of the scarecrow with a finger. "Isn't this just beautiful?"

"Shall I deduct it from your pay?"

"Let me think about it. Maybe I won't have time."

Margot laughed; Shelly sounded almost hopeful.

Shelly Donohue was a schoolteacher who'd taken this part-time job to earn a little spending money over the summer; she'd spent most of it on floss and counted cross-stitch patterns. "How many did you order?" she asked.

"Only three; not many people like working on black."

"Ask me again when there's only one left." Shelly turned to find a place in the window to hang the pattern.

The shop fell silent except for classical music coming from a radio tucked under a table near the back. Mozart's flute concerto, played on a flute for a change.

After a while Margot put down her needles to spread the jacket on the work-table. Was it done? She reached into a basket on the table and among the scissors, marking pencils, knitting needles, and all, found a fabric measuring tape.

"I thought I'd find your sister here when I came in," Shelly said.

"Yes, I've been thinking she might be here today." Margot stretched the tape down the back of the jacket.

"When did you last hear from her?"

"Day before yesterday. She was in Las Vegas." She adjusted the jacket to measure the front.

"Did she win?"

Perhaps just one more row, then she would bind off. "Hmm? Oh, I don't know; she didn't say anything about gambling."

"Is she the sort to gamble?"

"A year ago I would have said yes, definitely. But I'm not so sure now." Margot tucked the tape measure back into the basket and sat down to resume knitting.

Shelly made a concerned face and said, "Oh, Margot; is she coming because she's *broke*?" Shelly had a cousin who mooched.

Margot considered that. "No, I think she's at loose ends right now, and just doesn't know what she wants to do next."

Betsy was Margot's only sibling, her elder by two years. They had been close as children, despite having very different personalities. Margot had been the placid and obedient one; Betsy had been impulsive and adventurous. At eighteen, Betsy had run away to join the navy. A year later she married a sailor in one of those hasty justice-of-the-peace ceremonies, phoning home with the news only afterward. This completed the breach between Betsy and her parents, which was some years healing.

Margot had lived at home until she finished college, then married the boy she'd dated since junior high. The sisters had stayed in touch over the years, but had not seen much of one another. Betsy's first marriage hadn't lasted long. She had moved around a lot, and then wrote of belated plans to get a degree. The Christmas after that she announced her marriage to a college professor. Letters were fewer after that, and less exciting. Margot had thought Betsy settled at last.

Then, just a few weeks ago, Betsy had written a long letter. Her college-professor husband had fallen in love with one of his students and was divorcing Betsy. Apparently there had been a pattern of affairs with students, so Betsy was letting him go. The tone of this letter was very unlike Betsy's normal cheery exuberance. She sounded sad and tired. Margot, worried, wrote back at once and, after an exchange of letters, invited her sister to come for an extended visit. Betsy's reply: *Keep a light on for me, I'll be there in a week or ten days*. That had been just over a week earlier.

". . . funny that," Shelly was saying.

"Funny what?"

Shelly's voice thinned as she strained to put a clear suction cup with a hook on it way up near the top of the window. "It's usually the oldest child who's conservative, more grown-up, the one who helps parent the younger ones."

"You think so? But there was just the two of us, and I'm only twenty-seven months younger. . . ." Her needles slowed as she thought that over. Betsy had been the voice of enthusiasm, the "what if" and "wouldn't it be fun to" child; Margot had been the cautionary, worried "we could get hurt" or "Mama will be mad" child. Each had brought some balance to the tendencies of the other; perhaps that's why they had been so happy together growing up. Perhaps they could recapture some of that balance.

Her musings were interrupted again by the electric *bing* of the door opening. An older woman, tall and very slim, came in. She was wearing a beautiful linen suit in a warm gray a shade darker than her hair.

"Good afternoon, Mrs. Lundgren," said Margot, putting down her knitting.

Mrs. Lundgren loved needlework, but was too busy to do her own. She frequented craft fairs and often came to Margot for bonnets and booties for her granddaughters and needlepoint pictures and pillows for her several homes. Margot rose and went behind the big desk that served as a checkout counter.

"Margot, I've been thinking some more about that T'ang horse," said Mrs. Lundgren.

"It's not for sale, Mrs. Lundgren," said Margot, politely but firmly.

"So you keep telling me." Mrs. Lundgren got just the right light and rueful tone in her voice; Margot relaxed into a smile. "But as I said, I've been thinking. Would it be all right to ask you to make a copy of it for me? It won't be displayed here, but in our winter home."

Margot turned and looked at the wall behind her, where a framed needlepoint picture of a midnight-blue horse hung. The animal had his short tail closely braided, his feet well under him and his neck in a high arch, the head somewhat offset, as if he were looking backward, around his shoulder. He had a white saddle, white stockings, and a golden mane combed flat against his neck. The original was a pottery T'ang Dynasty horse in the Minneapolis art museum.

"Do you know, I should have thought of that," Margot said, surprised at herself. She frowned. "But I threw my old sketches away, so I'd have to start over, take a piece of graph paper, go to the museum and plot the horse on it, and then needlepoint over that."

"I understand. And then could the background be a different color?"

"Of course. Do you know what color?"

Mrs. Lundgren reached into her purse and produced a fabric swatch. "Can you match this?" The color was a faded, dusty red. A trip to the silks rack produced a sample nearly the same color.

"But not quite," said Margot with regret.

"Yes, and not quite won't do. How about this pale olive?" Mrs. Lundgren lifted a skein off its hook.

"Are you sure? I mean, it will look very good as a background color, but you don't want to offend your decor."

"There is a dark olive in the drapes," said Mrs. Lundgren.

"Very well." Margot took the silk from Mrs. Lundgren and the two walked back to her desk.

"How much for the entire project?" asked Mrs. Lundgren.

Margot went to the big desk that was her checkout counter and got out her calculator. "Do you want yours the same size?"

"What is that, fourteen by fourteen?"

"Yes, plus the mat and frame, of course."

"That's what I want, even the same narrow wood frame, please."

Margot began to punch numbers. "I'll have to charge you one hundred and fifty dollars to paint it," she began. That was a very fair price; painting a needlepoint canvas was harder than it looked; not only did the picture have to be artistically done, the curves and lines and color changes had to be worked in a pattern of tiny squares. "Then two dollars a square inch for the stitching, that comes to four hundred dollars; and another hundred and fifty for stretching and framing." Margot punched the total button. "That would be seven hundred dollars."

"How long will it take?"

"I could have it for you by Christmas."

"I'm sure that's a reasonable time allowance, but could it just possibly be sooner than that? We're spending Thanksgiving at our winter home in Honolulu, and I'd like to take it with me."

Margot closed her eyes and thought. As the Christmas season began to loom, her finishers wanted more and more lead time. On the other hand, the bolero jacket was all but done and she had nothing else urgent on her own horizon. If she started right away . . .

"I'll pay you a thousand," coaxed Mrs. Lundgren.

"Yes," Margot said. "Yes, I can do it that quickly for a thousand dollars."

"Oh, wonderful, I'm so pleased! Do you want something down on it?"

"No, but payment in full on delivery."

"Yes, of course. Thank you."

"You're welcome, Mrs. Lundgren."

When the door closed on Mrs. Lundgren, Shelly said, "You were waiting for her to up the offer."

"No, but I should use that tactic more often." Margot touched the frame of the horse, adjusting its position very slightly. It had come back from the framer only four months ago, and was Margot's finest effort at an original needlepoint to date. "Mrs. Lundgren knows a lot of women with time on their hands and money to pay for ways to fill it. She may not hang that picture in her Edina house, but she'll show it around before she takes it to Honolulu. A thousand-dollar price makes the artwork more attractive to some people, who may come in looking for something to hang on their own walls. But it might also bring customers wanting to save money by doing the needlework themselves." Margot smiled and Shelly laughed out loud. There were women, wealthy women, who shorted their families on groceries in order to buy more canvases, more silk floss, more gold thread, more real garnet beads for the endless stream of needle-point and counted cross-stitch work that had become an obsession. Margot sometimes felt like a dope peddler.

When Shelly finished the window, she started dusting. She paused when she came to an old rocking chair with a cushion on it, the cushion almost hidden under an enormous, fluffy white cat with tan and gray patches along its spine, sleeping on the cushion.

"Is Sophie nice and comfy?" cooed Shelly, stroking the animal. Sophie lifted her head to yawn, displaying teeth absurdly small in a cat her size. Then she put her head back down as if to sleep again, but a loud purr could be heard.

Margot had found the cat bedraggled and hungry in her shop doorway one morning and took her in. She had meant for her to live in the apartment over the store, but Sophie had followed her down one morning and been so quietly ornamental—and friendly to anyone who stopped to stroke her—that Margot had allowed her to stay.

Margot picked up her knitting and made an exclamation. She'd done two rows instead of one.

Shelly said, "Do you think Betsy will like it here in Excelsior? This is kind of a quiet place."

"Excelsior has plenty of things going on." People who lived in the small town were gratefully aware of its charms and Margot was among those who worked hard to preserve them. "Anyway, I have a feeling that she was looking for a refuge. Though, of course, how she'll like actually living in one we'll have to see."

Margot began pulling out the extra row. She had carved a safe niche in this small Minnesota town and stayed there content even after her husband died three years earlier.

Now Betsy was seeking a place to be safe in for a while. Apparently she had lost that zest for adventure, perhaps even grown a little afraid. Margot hoped she could give her sister what she needed. She picked up her knitting and began binding off.

Betsy wasn't scared, not really, just . . . nervous. It was one thing to be twenty-five and newly divorced, and not own a home or have a job with medical insurance or a retirement account whose deposits are matched by your employer. It's quite another to be fifty-five and be once again in that same boat.

Betsy wasn't averse to adventure. Crossing the mountains alone in an old car had brought moments that sent the blood rushing along with its old verve.

On the other hand, she'd spent her one night in Las Vegas at the Fremont Street light-and-sound show and having a drink in a beautiful old bar, followed by a phone call to her sister and then turning in early.

When she saw an exit sign pointing to the Grand Canyon, she did give a moment's thought to giving the Japanese tourists a thrill by throwing herself off the rim. But she didn't. In her experience such low thoughts, if not yielded to, tended to be brief and followed by something more interesting.

Later, crossing Iowa, Betsy remembered reading somewhere that while men are scared of birthdays ending in zero, women are frightened by birthdays ending in five. Certainly Betsy was. Fifty-five is no longer young, even when considered while you were in good spirits. Fifty-five can see old age rushing toward it like a mighty tree axed at the root. All too soon it would be *crash*: sixty! And if she reached retirement age with no savings to speak of, she might live out the last years of her life in one small room, fighting off the roaches for her supper of canned cat food.

But Betsy had also read somewhere that there were good jobs going begging in the upper Midwest, and she had her sister who had kindly offered to put her up until she got her feet under her again. Okay, so her sister lived in a small town; that small town was near the Twin Cities. That meant two newspapers, two job markets, right next door to one another. Twice the number of chances to start over.

And a ferocious Minnesota winter might be interesting, another adventure. After all, Betsy had grown up in Milwaukee, where the winters could also be hard.

Betsy pushed the accelerator down a little, and the car responded. Good little car, acting as if it didn't already have a hundred and fifty thousand miles on it. Ahead was the road sign saying WELCOME TO MINNESOTA. She hoped it didn't smell of pig, like Iowa.

Sometime later the freeway forked. Thirty-five-E went to St. Paul, 35W came into Minneapolis. Margot hadn't mentioned this; her directions said to take I-35 into the Cities, and Highway 7 to Excelsior. Betsy chose Minneapolis; she had a notion that Excelsior was west of the Twin Cities and Minneapolis was the western twin. Right? She was pretty sure she hadn't already missed an exit onto Highway 7; certainly she hadn't missed an exit sign saying EXCELSIOR. A pity she had left the road atlas behind in an Omaha motel. She would stop at the next exit and buy a map.

She saw a little strip mall just this side of an exit, featuring a store whose sign advertised GUNS LIQUOR PAWN. Despite this warning that the owner liked to live dangerously, she got off and made her way back to it on a frontage road. She didn't go in; a store next door to it added to the explosive mixture by selling used snowmobiles and those noisy adult tricycles with puffy tires. But people who bought vehicles might also want maps.

They did, and the store sold them. The man behind the counter helped her plan a route to Highway 7. "Thirty-five don't cross 7," he said. "So what you do, you stay on 35W till you get to 494, take 494 west to 100, which only goes north from there, and it'll give you an exit onto 7. Go west and look for a sign." He moved a grubby finger along the map as she watched. It seemed clear enough.

"Thanks," she said, taking the map and folding it on the first try—Betsy was a traveler.

"You bet."

Amazing, they really did say "you bet" in Minnesota, just like in that book on how to speak Minnesotan Margot had sent her one Christmas.

Back on the highway, Betsy drove ten miles over the speed limit—she had to, if she didn't want to be rear ended—and was so excited at the approach of the end of her journey that she didn't really notice that though it was not yet September, the ivy climbing the wooden sound barriers on 35W was turning an autumnal red.

Two

❖

Margot was selecting colored silks for the T'ang horse. She had her original needlepoint of it on the table, still in the frame, which had no glass in it. "I remember it was ten-oh-seven," she murmured to herself.

"What?" asked Shelly.

"The blue color of the horse, I remember it was ten-oh-seven, ten-oh-five, and ten-oh-three." She tried a skein of 1007 Madeira silk, which was a midnight-blue shade, against the neck and shoulder of the horse. "Still is, it seems."

"You have the most amazing memory," remarked Shelly, coming to look.

Margot smiled and preened a little, but said nothing. She had cut a blank canvas to the right size; it was on the table beside the horse, the olive-green skein on it. She put the blue silks beside the green.

But the creamy gold of the mane was harder to match. It was an odd color, not cream, not yellow, not gold. Nothing on her racks came close enough. She closed her eyes, thinking, then said, "I'm going upstairs for a minute."

Shelly waved assent and noticed that Sophie raised her head at the sound of the back door opening. Was it suppertime already? Shelly chuckled; Sophie was fat and cosseted now, but she had a long memory and was determined never to miss a meal again.

Margot was back in three minutes, holding one partly used and two whole skeins of pale gold silk aloft. "I knew I had some left over!" she cheered. She gave Sophie a brisk rub just to share the joy. Sophie raised her rump and her bushy, tan-and-gray tail and purred ecstatically.

Shelly laughed. "You and Sophie are so easy to make happy!" she said.

"If I had gone up there and not found this, we'd all be singing another song," said Margot, but pleasantly, because she had gone up and found it. She put the golden skeins beside the blue on the canvas. "Now we need chalk white for the legs and saddle." She went to the silk rack and began examining the whites.

Highway 7 was a divided highway, mostly under repair. Betsy wove her way among the white and orange pylons, concentrating fiercely in order not to switch lanes in the wrong direction and end up facing an oncoming truck. At the same time she was looking for a sign—and there it was: EXCEL-SIOR, with a warning that it was a left exit. Betsy followed the lane, which led up and over the highway and a railroad bridge. Then there was a thicket of high bushes, a red apartment building, and she pulled up to a stop sign marking an asterisk of intersections.

Ahead were a little post office and the tree-shaded clapboard houses of a small town. Atop a steep hill on her left was a multiroofed Victorian house. A sign said it was the Christopher Inn Bed-and-Breakfast.

On the right was a parking lot with a small carnival Ferris wheel in it, though no other rides were visible.

A block later, at Water Street, was another stop sign. She was supposed to turn here, but which way? To the left the street was lined with old-fashioned, false-front brick stores; to the right, a block away, was a big blue lake with sail-boats on it. Toward the lake, that's what the directions said. She turned right.

Just short of the lake was Lake Street—yes, that checked. A bar and grill with a wharf theme marked the corner. HASKELL'S, said the sign, which also checked. Betsy turned right. Two blocks later the lake disappeared behind a sprawling apartment complex of gray and white clapboards. She pulled over across the street from it, in front of an old, two-story, dark redbrick building. The middle one of the three shops had a pastel-colored sign hanging over the door: CREWEL WORLD, the letters done as if cross-stitched in various colors. From the *D* came an outsized needle pulling yarn in a matching color. She had arrived.

Something made Margot glance up as a car pulled to the curb. It was an older white hatchback, thickly layered with road dust, a woman driving. Margot had a feeling the license plates on it would be Californian.

Shelly said, "Is that her? Is that her?"

But Margot was on her way to the door, and didn't answer, because what if it wasn't? She opened it and watched the woman climb tiredly out on the driver's side. She was about five-three, plumper than Margot remembered, her brown hair well streaked with gray. She was wearing jeans and an ancient green sweatshirt with the sleeves cut off above the elbow.

And no glasses.

"Betsy, how can you drive without your glasses?" she scolded before she could stop herself.

"Contact lenses, of course," replied Betsy, defense at hand, as usual. "Oh, Margot, I am so happy to see you!" She came blundering up onto the sidewalk, blinking away tears, to enter her sister's welcoming embrace.

* * *

An hour later Betsy was in Margot's apartment. It was a nice place, with proportions at once unfamiliar and cozy. The rooms were small, with low ceilings. In an efficient space were two bedrooms and bath, living room, and kitchen. A dining area off the kitchen was too small to be considered a separate room, but it was lit by a window that overlooked a small parking lot behind the building. If Betsy cared to lean sideways, she could see her weary old car pulled up under a lilac bush. Betsy was weary herself, but at the same time wound up tight, her body still swaying to the remembered movements of her car on the highway, her ears a little stopped up.

Last night, in a cheap motel in Omaha, she had been thinking of the ancient fable of the grasshopper and the ant. The prudent ant worked all summer, storing up seeds and dried fruit against the coming winter, while the grasshopper played in the sun. Then winter arrived and the grasshopper came knocking on the ant's door, hoping for shelter. The ant had turned the grasshopper away.

Margot had invited Betsy to come, but in that motel Betsy had worried that her sister might think of her as a grasshopper. What if Margot was critical, or worse, condescending? Betsy wouldn't put up with that. Maybe she should just call tomorrow and say she'd changed her mind, she was going to Chicago.

But Betsy had finished her trip to Minnesota and Margot had indeed seemed very glad to see her. On the other hand, this apartment wasn't exactly the big fancy house Margot used to live in, back when she was married to Aaron Berglund. Betsy had thought Margot had been left a wealthy widow, but apparently not. Did the shop make enough for Betsy to have a lengthy free ride? Maybe she'd better look for a job pretty soon.

Still, "I hope you're planning on a nice, long stay," Margot had said down in the shop, right in front of a witness, a woman with long hair in a knot. Sally was her name, or was it Shelly? Whoever, she unashamedly eavesdropped on everything the sisters said to one another. Margot had finally noticed it was making Betsy uncomfortable, and all three unloaded the car, carrying mismatched suitcases up the stairs.

Margot had given her a quick tour of the apartment, told her to help herself to anything in the kitchen, and went back to work. Betsy had tried lying down on the comfortable bed in the guest room to take a nap, but was too wound up to sleep. She had wandered the apartment awhile, then gone to the refrigerator—eating when she couldn't think of anything else to do was her worst fault—and poured herself a glass of milk, then took a couple of peanut-butter cookies from a cookie jar shaped like a pig—a hint, obviously, but it didn't stop her.

Now she sat at the little table in the dining alcove, trying not to think too much about the suitcases waiting to be unpacked.

The building was only two stories high, so there were no apartments overhead. Margot's apartment took up one end of the second floor, with a stairwell between it and the other apartments. Between its location and the old-fashioned solidness of the building, it was very quiet up here. Of course, it was a quiet little town, too; no fire and police sirens, no traffic's roar. Even the lake's little wavelets could hardly approach the sussurant crash of the Pacific. Oh, dear, she thought as her eyes began to sting, was she going to miss the ocean, too?

No, no, she'd be just fine. She was here, in Excelsior, Minnesota, a nice little town, and welcome. She finished the milk and put one uneaten cookie back in the jar, put the glass into the sink, and as she did noticed the grubbiness of her hands. She went into the bathroom to wash, but when she looked at herself in the mirror, she changed her mind. Just washing her hands and face wasn't going to do.

The tub was a big old-fashioned porcelain one, with claw feet. Real porcelain tubs held the heat much better than fiberglass ones and were therefore great for long soaks. A long soak suddenly seemed very desirable. And here was a jug of bubble bath, herbal-scented, just waiting. So she filled the tub, peeled off her clothes, and sank gratefully into the bubbles. She'd forgotten to go get a paperback, but that was all right; she just closed her eyes and fell into a kind of doze. When she stirred herself half an hour later, and rinsed out her hair, and toweled off with one of the big, thirsty bath towels, she felt a whole lot better.

She had put on fresh clothes and was halfway unpacked when she heard someone come in. "I'm home!" came Margot's voice.

Betsy found Margot in the kitchen. "Early closing tonight," she said. She was measuring out a portion of Iams Less Active for Sophie as the cat watched anxiously.

"Can I help with supper?" asked Betsy.

"No, the kitchen's too small, especially with Sophie in it, too. You sit down and we'll talk."

So Betsy sat at the round table in the dining nook and said, "How's business?"

"Not bad. Would you like to help out in the shop? With school starting, I'll need to replace Shelly."

"Sure. But—um—I mean—" Because she needed a salary.

"I pay six-ten an hour for beginners. Plus room and board, special for you." Margot, gathering things from the refrigerator, chuckled.

"Can you afford to do that?"

"Of course I can. You don't have to worry about that at all." Margot looked around the door, face as surprised as her voice.

"I don't want to be a burden."

"You're not a burden, and even if you were a burden, you wouldn't be a burden, okay?"

"Thanks. When do I start?"

"How about Monday? That will give you tomorrow and the weekend to get settled in."

Supper was a tuna salad made with every kind of lettuce but iceberg, a little sweet onion only on Betsy's salad—"I remember you like onions," Margot said—a sprinkle of herbs, four large croutons, and a dressing that was mostly a flavored vinegar with just a smidge of olive oil. It came with a hot loaf of crusty bread that would have been even better with butter instead of a "lite" margarine that was mostly air and water.

Afterward, over an herbal tea that was supposed to encourage the body to shed fat—Betsy was beginning to see how Margot stayed so trim—Margot said, "Would you like to take a walk and get a look at our city?"

Betsy grinned. "City?"

"It's a legalism. The county passed a law years back that made all the little towns out here incorporate as cities or fold up. Wait till you drive through Navarre, which you must do without blinking or you'll miss it, but it's a city, too. Anyway, come on, I'll show you our famous Lake Minnetonka."

They went back to the corner of Lake and Water, where the lakeshore was marked by small wooden wharves. The sun was bright, but already the sun was well on its southward path, and their shadows pointed north as well as east. Large square-built excursion boats were tied up here, along with one odd little boat whose shape reminded Betsy of an old-fashioned streetcar.

"The *Minnehaha*." Margot nodded. "Built in 1906, sunk in the lake back in 1926, then raised and restored a few years ago. Used to be owned by the public transit company, which explains its shape. It runs on weekends between here and Wayzata."

"Minnetonka, Minnehaha? Do I see a pattern?"

"Indeed you do. The poem 'Hiawatha' was set in Minnesota and was very popular when things were getting named around here."

"Ah."

Beyond the wharves, the lakeshore was marked by a park, where some of the younger maple trees showed traces of orange. Apparently autumn arrived in September here. On their left, away from the lake, the ground swooped up, and was topped by grand old houses with big porches. How pleasant it must be to sit up there and watch the lake in all its moods.

The lake drew away, the park enlarged and grew a hill of its own, marked with big trees, and Lake Street ended at a tennis court. The sisters turned left and Betsy found she was now on *West* Lake Street. Well, okay; the lake itself also turned the corner, she could see it through the trees.

Here the houses were smaller, but still prosperous. None were new but all were in excellent repair, with neatly kept lawns. Some even had picket fences, and from one big tree hung a tire swing.

It was all so charmingly sweet, Betsy remarked, "What is this place, Mayberry-of-the-North?"

Margot laughed. "I'll have to repeat that next time I'm trying to get the city council to understand why it's important we fight to preserve the amenities of Excelsior."

They turned left at the next corner, and there was a quaint little church across the street, with a new, large, and modern church hall attached by a covered walk. "Trinity Episcopal," said Margot. "That's where I go."

"Uh-huh," said Betsy, and pointed to a window on a house on her side of the street where a large brown tabby sat watching them suspiciously. "That cat looks almost as big as Sophie." She didn't want to start a discussion of churchgoing, because she almost never went anymore.

Safely past the church, Margot continued with her tour. "If you look across the parking lot," she said, pointing, "you can see the library, the fire department, and our little city hall on the other side."

Betsy, squinting, nodded. "I see the sign that says CITY HALL," she said, "but it seems to be pointing to the same building that says FIRE DEPARTMENT."

"It is," said Margot. "City Hall is in the basement of the fire department building. I voted against them moving into a building of their own," she added. "Keeps them modest."

They walked to the corner, and found themselves in the heart of the miniature "downtown" of Excelsior. To the left was the movie theater, pet shop, and bookstore, with a gift shop on the corner. Margot turned right and Betsy went with her, past the hardware store, a toy shop, an antique store, and so on. The stores were small, in good repair, apparently prosperous. Delicious smells came from the pizza-by-the-slice shop and the bakery. The wallpaper-and-paint store was having a sale. An art-supply store up the way and across the street had its side painted with a mural of a small cottage and a pond covered with water lilies. In the mural, an artist had set up a large canvas and was painting the water lilies. Betsy saw it and started to laugh. "Monet, I love it!" she said.

They turned and started back, past a dress shop and a florist. "I guess you're farther from the Twin Cities than I thought," remarked Betsy.

"What makes you say that?"

"Well, this isn't a bedroom community, is it? I mean, there are real stores here, open for business."

"Actually, we're very close to Minneapolis. Even back at the turn of the century, people would commute from here to the Cities, using that streetcar boat to get to where the regular streetcars ran. But somewhere, somehow, when a lot of little communities gave up trying to be towns, Excelsior didn't. And the people who live here have decided they wanted to keep the town intact. So they patronize the stores and organize lots of festivals, like Apple Days, which is coming up soon. Excelsior is an old-fashioned word that means 'upward,' and I like to think the name inspires the people who live here."

Betsy said with artful carelessness, "I thought excelsior was wood shavings used to pack fragile items."

Margot looked at Betsy with just the beginning of indignation, then both sisters laughed. Margot said, "All right, I'm a shameless booster. Just you wait, in a few weeks you'll love it here, too. Here's my bank, and up ahead is Haskell's, where we turn to go home."

Back in her cozy living room, Margot sat down in the comfortable chair, opened a kind of wood-framed folding canvas bag at her feet, and took out a large roll of white fabric with needlework on it. She unrolled it to reveal a complex, stylized picture of a field of flowers and small animals, most of which was covered with small stitches. "Last week of the month we work on UFOs," she said.

Betsy, standing behind the chair, said, "That is obviously not a flying saucer, so what does UFO mean in needle talk?"

"Unfinished projects. Like a lot of needleworkers, I'm always buying something new and I get impatient to get started on it and sometimes abandon old projects in the excitement of starting something new. So the last week of every month I've promised to get out something unfinished and work on it. I started this over a year ago and stopped working on it back in February—but now it's going to get finished at last." She smiled up at her sister. "I hope you don't mind if I work while we talk. Is there something you want to work on, too?"

Betsy shook her head. She'd once done quite a bit of embroidery, which had kept her occupied while her husband stayed late on campus. Not, as he'd said, grading papers or attending staff meetings or conferring with colleagues, but making love to various female students. Betsy had not touched an embroidery needle since filing for the divorce, and she had no intention of ever picking one up again.

She went over to the heavily draped window and began lifting layers— drape, sheer, blind—"How big is the lake?" Of course, all she could see was the gray siding of the condominium across the street.

"I think the shoreline is something over four hundred miles."

Betsy dropped the drape's edge and said, surprised, "You must mean forty miles, and I'm surprised it's that big."

"Oh, what you saw today was just one bay. The lake is a collection of bays—a collection of lakes, more like. Very untidy and sprawling. It's hard to describe the shape, but I can show you a map in the store tomorrow. The only way you can see the whole thing is from the air. It's spring-fed and very clean. Big bass-fishing attraction, we have competitions going all summer long. Draws people from all over the country." As she was drawn into her needlework, Margot became telegraphic in her sentences. "You fish?"

"No."

"Sail?"

"Not lately."

"What do you do for fun?"

"Go out with friends to dances and plays and movies. Body-surf. Read a good mystery or something by Terry Pratchett. Margot, how do you stand it?"

"Stand what?"

"It's so quiet and peaceful here. Doesn't it drive you crazy?"

Margot laughed. "I don't think it's so peaceful. In fact, when things get too much for me, I take a week off up in the Boundary Waters. There's peace and quiet for you. Of course, I used to travel all the time, with Aaron. Miami, Cancún, even London and Paris one glorious spring. I've always been glad to get back here, though."

"I don't understand how you can feel a need for someplace even quieter than this."

"After a week or so you'll see how busy I am and you'll understand. There's plenty to do, committees to work on, church business, and of course Crewel World. They tried to get me to run for city council once, but I managed to slip by them that time." She paused to put a new strand of floss into her needle. Betsy noticed she could do it that tricky way involving the edge of her needle.

"That's needlepoint, isn't it, what you're working on."

"Yes, do you like it? I haven't decided if it's going to be a pillow or a wall hanging."

"The colors don't look as if they'd go very well in here."

"It's not for up here, it's going to be a display item in the shop. I have four canvases by this artist and want to encourage my customers to buy them."

"How much does one cost?"

"Three hundred and fifty dollars."

"No, I mean unfinished. Like if I wanted to try one."

"Three hundred and fifty dollars. Plus the yarn, plus finishing." Margot glanced sideways at Betsy, a tiny smile on her face.

"That's ridiculous!"

"No, it isn't. Each canvas is hand-painted, and has to be done in a way so that the stitches that cover the painting will fit. It's a difficult art, trust me. Tomorrow I'll show you some of the really great work done by my customers on these canvases. Fancy stitches, beads, special flosses. Or maybe you'd prefer to take up counted cross-stitch."

"I'm not as fond of needlework as I used to be." A little silence fell. "I have a friend back in San Diego who does counted cross-stitch, but I don't think my eyes could take the strain," amended Betsy. Margot's needle went down and through then up and through. "It's beautiful stuff," further amended Betsy after a while. "She did this angel all in blues and golds that just blew me away." The silence fell again. "But she showed me the pattern and I knew right away that wasn't something I could ever do, not with my eyes." More silence. "I think I'm too tired to keep up my end of this conversation. I'm going to turn in."

But just as Betsy was entering the little hall, Margot said, "Betsy?"

"Yes?"

"I can't tell you how pleased I am that you called on me when you needed someone to take care of you for a while."

"Thanks, Margot. Good night."

"Good night."

Three

It was Saturday, late in the afternoon; the sun was going down, its reddening beams streaming through the open door of the back bedroom. Betsy had spent Friday resting, talking with Margot or her employees down in the shop, unpacking, and going for a brief swim (the water wasn't salty, the waves were nonexistent, and the beach could be walked end to end in about a minute).

Now she was secretly enjoying a cream-filled sweet roll from that very nice little bakery on Water Street in the privacy of the apartment while Margot, unaware, sold floss and evenweave fabric downstairs. She wished you could still see the lake from the living-room window—it really was a pretty lake. But lakeshore property had surged in value, Shelly had told her; new houses were being built that had kitchens bigger than the cottages they replaced. So the little wetland across the street had been filled in and a condominium built on the site.

The price of a condo must be very high if it never occurred to Margot to buy one.

Betsy sat at the small round table in the dining nook drinking a glass of orange juice with her sweet roll, and thinking.

She'd been here three days, if you counted her day of arrival as one, rather than the less-than-half it was. She wasn't sure what she had expected, but Excelsior wasn't a disappointment, yet. If this were still the fifties, Excelsior would be positively typical of a Midwestern country town, down to the lack of used-car lots and warehouse shopping outlets siphoning shoppers from the little downtown. They must have draconian zoning laws around here, she thought.

The people in Excelsior she had met so far were friendly, and the worst teenager she had seen had not been scary, only very oddly dressed. Thoroughly pierced, of course, with hair colored Kool-Aid red. But even he had offered a halfhearted wave.

Crewel World was a going concern, so far as Betsy could tell. Who would have guessed one could make a living selling embroidery floss, hand-spun wool, and bamboo knitting needles? But there had been a steady trickle of customers yesterday while Betsy watched. Two of them had spent lavishly, buying "canvases," stiff white fabric woven so loosely the holes showed, with paintings of dolls, Christmas stockings, cute animals, woodland scenes, or whatever on them. That the customers then also bought yarn and flosses so they could carefully cover every inch of the paintings with wool or cotton or silk only made Betsy sure that they were crazy, especially since the artists who painted the pictures charged so much for their work.

Of course, there was a trick to the store as well, Betsy had learned. Margot had somehow wrangled a lease at an extraordinary rent, even at upper Midwest prices. With the rent so low, it was easier to show a profit. Certainly the furniture in the apartment was of a quality to indicate the opposite of poverty.

There was, of course, a fly in the ointment, and it was, not surprisingly, the landlord. Shelly, who turned out to be friendly and kind, also loved to gossip. She had told Betsy all about him. He was the brother of the original landlord, who had died a year ago, she reported. This brother was by no means the saint the original had been. The new landlord wanted to take advantage of the soaring land values. He proposed tearing down the old brick building and putting up something bigger. .

But Margot, bless her kind but stubborn heart, wanted to stay where she was, where people anxious to buy just the right shade of green silk to complete their counted cross-stitch pattern knew where to find her. And Margot had four years to go on that extraordinary lease.

Shelly had described with awe the one visit she had had from the new land-lord, whose name was a very prosaic Joe. He had come into the shop last Monday, she had said, with fire in his eyes, looking for Margot. Fortunately, Margot had been at the post office and he'd gone away again breathing threats and tucking some kind of paper back into his pocket.

Earlier today, over an incredibly delicious fruit salad bought at the sandwich shop next door, Margot had chuckled at Betsy's alarmed query as to what Joe Mickels was up to.

"Oh, it was probably just another summons."

"Another *what*?"

"Summons. It's a tactic he's come up with. Unlawful detainer of rent, possibly, or some other clause of the lease he's trying to invoke against me. He figures a new one up every few weeks, he's been doing it for the last four or five months. But I have James Penberthy on my side, he's been wonderful." Margot had smiled at Betsy's inquiring face and explained, "He's my attorney. He just laughs and says he'll handle it. And he does. But it's annoying, especially when I have to make a court appearance. I'm so glad Aaron taught me to keep very careful records. The last time, Joe tried to say I hadn't paid my deposit when I first moved in here; but the canceled check was in my files, so I presented it in court and that took care of that. There's no way Joe can run me off with those tricks, so long as Mr. Penberthy represents my interests."

So not everyone who lived in Excelsior was friendly. And Betsy wasn't as sanguine as Margot about legal maneuvers. What if Joe Mickels succeeded in driving Margot out? Where would Margot move her shop? There didn't seem to be many empty stores in Excelsior—Betsy hadn't seen a single one on Water Street, in fact. If Margot had to move to another town, and pay a higher rent, she'd lose customers. Could she then afford to keep Betsy as a guest? When Betsy had tried to talk to Margot about this again, Margot had laughed and waved her hand.

"Oh, for heaven's sake, Betsy, don't worry, we're fine. Anyway, I've already told you: Joe can't possibly do anything, not really."

Sipping her juice, Betsy's frown deepened. Okay, with the low rent and the fact that her customers were faithful, Margot was doing all right here. But if Joe Mickels did succeed in making her move out, then she'd have to start all over again at an unfamiliar address and a much higher rent. If that happened, could she still afford to pay Betsy a salary and at the same time house and feed her?

Maybe Betsy should start right in looking for work somewhere else. Tomorrow was Sunday, she'd take a good look at the employment section of the *Minneapolis Star Tribune*, called by Margot (in that casual way that meant everyone else did, too) "the *Strib*."

There was a sound of a key in a lock. "Hello!" called a chipper voice.

"In here, Margot," called Betsy. "Is it time to close already?"

"Ten minutes past," came the voice, traveling rapidly through the short hall that passed the kitchen and into the living room. "But I had a good customer and I couldn't deny her the chance to spend an extra hundred, could I?"

Betsy got a brief glimpse of her sister as she hurried into the other short hall off which were the bathroom and the bedrooms. From the back one the voice continued, "Are you dressed for the meeting?"

Betsy looked down at herself. She was wearing an ivory knit dress with short, caped sleeves and a moderately low square-cut neck. Her shoes were a trifle clunky, with gold buckles. "Yes," she said.

Something big and furry moved in to block Betsy's view of her shoes: Sophie. When the cat saw she had attracted Betsy's attention, she walked into the kitchen to sit significantly beside her empty food dish.

"I'll feed Sophie," Betsy called, having learned almost as quickly as the cat that if she didn't tell Margot, Sophie would cadge an additional feeding. She took a half scoop of dry food from the big sack under the sink and poured it into Sophie's dish. Iams Less Active certainly described Sophie. *In*active might be even better, but Iams apparently didn't make that variety.

Betsy had gone through boot camp to learn to shower, brush, make up, and dress in an amazingly short time, but somewhere Margot had learned it, too. In just under forty minutes she came into the living room with her hair rearranged, her makeup redone, and wearing a dark sheath dress topped with a short-sleeved sweater that caught the light strangely. Betsy approached her for a closer look.

"Oooooh," she said, fingering the weaving. "Oh, it's that ribbon sweater you were making! It's beautiful!"

"Thank you. Is it too long?"

Betsy stepped back and tilted her head while Margot did a slow pirouette. "N-no," she said. "Actually, it seems just about right. Golly, I like the way it moves. Is there a trick to the way it's knitted?"

"No—Betsy, are you going like that?"

Betsy looked down at herself. "What, am I daringly short for Excelsior?"

"Heavens no; but it cools off quite a bit around here when the sun goes down. You'll want something over that."

Margot went into her closet and brought out a cream-colored shawl with extravagantly long fringe that had been tied into a complex pattern of knots for its first ten inches.

"McNamara lace!" Betsy exclaimed on seeing it, and explained, "In the navy, sailors unlay canvas and tie the fringe into patterns. It's used as trim, on the captain's gig for example."

"Well, the fringe is too long for me, so why don't you keep it?"

Betsy stroked the silky fringe, then looked at her sister, eyes stinging. "Oh, Margot, it's beautiful. Thank you."

"Well, it matches your dress, so you're welcome. Now drape it over your shoulders and let's go. Can you walk in those shoes? We're only a few blocks from the house, it's ridiculous to drive that short a distance."

The house was Christopher Inn, the Victorian bed-and-breakfast Betsy had seen on coming into Excelsior. On the way over, Margot said that the purpose of the gathering was to form a committee to plan a fund-raiser for a child who needed heart surgery. The family had no health insurance and the father was working three jobs to try to raise the money.

It was typical of Excelsior to rise to such an occasion, Margot had told Betsy proudly, noting that there were round plastic coin collectors at nearly every cash register in town supporting some cause or other. But this would be the most important fund-raiser of the year.

They climbed the steps to the house and crossed the big old porch and went inside—the door wasn't locked.

There were eight people attending the meeting, which was to begin with a light supper served by George Anderson, the proprietor of the Christopher Inn. He was a dark, quiet man with a tennis player's build.

Betsy was pleased to note that the house hadn't suffered much remodeling. The front parlor was intact, with two bay windows, and the dining room was large, with a fireplace. Only two of its eight round tables were set for this meal, marked with bouquets of roses and baby's breath—leftovers from a wedding, noted Margot as they greeted Shelly.

Assigned to Betsy and Margot's table were a handsome man with sun-streaked auburn hair and a big young woman with ash-blond hair that looked natural. Betsy had already noticed more natural blonds in Excelsior than anywhere else she had lived.

The man was Hudson Earlie, the assistant curator of Asian art at the Minneapolis Museum of Art; the woman was Jill Cross, a police officer.

"But she comes of a very good family," added Margot while making the introduction.

"I'm sure being a cop is no disgrace," remarked Betsy, a trifle surprised at her sister, taking Jill's proffered hand, which was large and strong. There was an air of calm about Jill that inspired confidence, even while she gave you a look that seemed to read every peccadillo you had ever done. She was wearing a simple frost-blue dress that matched her eyes.

Jill said with patently feigned indifference, "It's okay, even my mother apologizes for me."

"What would she have preferred you to do for a living?" asked Earlie as Betsy and Margot seated themselves.

"Nurse," replied Jill thoughtfully. "Journalist. Business administrator. Stock-car driver. Checkout clerk at a 7-Eleven. Street sweeper. Street*walker*." Though her expression remained impassive, Margot had become helpless with giggles and was waving at her to stop.

Betsy smiled at Hudson Earlie. He was extraordinarily handsome, with an outdoorsman's permanently sunburned skin. "And how about you, Mr. Earlie? What would your mother have preferred you do?"

"Doctor," he said in a good imitation of Jill's smooth, expressionless voice. "Lawyer. Street sweeper. Used-car salesman." He leaned forward and concluded in an undertone aimed at both Betsy and Jill, "Cop." His eyes were a hot blue, his nose short but straight. His mouth, not large, hinted at arrogance, even stubbornness. Then he smiled, a wicked, lusty smile, with laugh lines cut deep. "Call me Hud."

"Sure—Hud," Betsy said, smiling back. As an excuse to tear her eyes away, she arranged her napkin over her lap. "When do we eat?" she asked.

"In a minute," said Margot dryly, and when Betsy looked at her and at Jill, she saw them grinning.

Fine, thought Betsy. "I think you would have made a wonderful policeman," she said to Hud, batting her eyelashes a trifle. "I bet every woman crook in the city would line up to be interrogated by you."

Hud's smile broadened, and he closed one eye in a not-so-surreptitious wink. "You have a right to remain silent," he said in his own voice, a pleasant baritone, "but I hope you continue."

Betsy made a mental note to find out if he was married.

For supper, Anderson served big, locally grown tomatoes stuffed with crab-and-celery salad, and sesame toast. Dessert was devil's-food cake with coconut-caramel icing, cut into generous slabs. Betsy, with the sweet roll still undigested, earned a smile from Margot by taking only two bites. The coffee that came with it was very strong and delicious. Betsy followed Margot's lead and turned down a refill.

But without it, she began to sink into that happy languor that generally follows a generous meal. A thin man with dark hair and eyes rose at the adjoining table and rapped gently on his water glass with his dessert fork. "Let's get started here," he said with a strong Midwest twang. He rapped again, and when he had their attention, he said, "I think first we need a chairman of this committee."

"Who's he?" Betsy murmured in Margot's ear.

"Odell Jamison. He's our mayor." She raised her voice. "How about you, Odell?"

"No, I haven't got time to do a good job," said Odell. "I'm already working with the historical society for their Christmas pageant, playing at being mayor, and remodeling my house—if I don't stay on those painters, they'll never get it finished."

Betsy smiled. Mayor Jamison had listed his profession both second and offhandedly; such a low-key politician couldn't get elected mayor anywhere but in a small town.

"How about you, Paul?" said Shelly, who was sitting next to the mayor.

A young man with a broad, black, closely clipped mustache lifted both hands in protest. "I've got enough on my plate right now," he said.

"How about you, Margot?" suggested Jill.

"No, no, I'm on three committees already, plus the shop. And now my sister is in town, so I'll be busy with her—everyone, this is my sister, Betsy Devonshire, here on an extended visit." She smiled at the mayor's table. "I'd like you to consider her an honorary member of this committee, as she'll be a big help to me on it."

There were polite words of greeting from the other table, and an all-around murmur of agreement that Betsy could be a sort-of member; when it ended, Mayor Jamison said, "How 'bout you, Joe?"

There was a sudden silence during which every head turned, oddly, toward Margot, who became interested in stirring her coffee.

A white-haired man seated across from Jamison said, "No time for that, thanks," in a gruff voice.

The tension eased and Paul said, "Then how about you, Jill?"

"Not till I retire." That brought chuckles; Jill was probably not yet thirty.

Betsy studied Joe curiously. His hair was thick and wavy, and looked as if it might once have been blond—his immense eyebrows were the color of sand, as were his old-fashioned bushy sideburns. He looked immensely strong, with a proud nose, wide mouth, and fierce eyes set well back under those eyebrows. Viking blood there, thought Betsy.

She glanced at Margot, who nodded once. So this was the evil landlord, Joe Mickels.

"How about you, Shelly?" This came from George Anderson, the inn's owner, and Betsy was suddenly aware that he was seated between the two tables in a way that made him one of the group. And on the committee, apparently.

"How about you?" she countered.

"Well . . ." he said, and everyone jumped happily on this sign of weakness. "Oh, all right," he said, and there was applause mixed with laughter.

George proved as deft at running a meeting as he was at serving tables, and soon the committee had agreed to hold the event at the Lafayette Country Club in a month's time, offering a dance, buffet, cash bar, and silent auction.

"These silent auctions can be a big success," said George, "but you've got to deliver the goods." He pointed a finger at every member and asked him or her to pledge something of significant value to the auction and to badger friends and acquaintances to do the same. Margot offered a slash jacket. Shelly groaned with approbation, or acquisitiveness, as Betsy wondered what a "slash jacket" was. Hud offered a Dick Huss glass bowl, and this time the acquisitive sigh came from Margot. Jill offered sailing lessons next summer. The finger wavered, and Betsy, ashamed of being passed over, said she would contribute something, but would need time to think what it might be.

Joe Mickels offered a luxury weekend at a ski lodge; Shelly ten hours of private tutoring; George a getaway weekend at Christopher Inn, "including an afternoon of bass fishing."

When other ideas were solicited, Hud said in his pleasant voice that he had a friend who used to play with Lamont Cranston, and that he would send a request via the friend that they play for this fund-raiser. "I'm sure they'll at least come up with a good excuse for not doing it," he said, with an air of confidence that promised better than that. Betsy wondered who Lamont Cranston was—it was a band, of course, not the man who was the Shadow—but what kind of music did they play? She also wondered what she should do if Joe Mickels said anything to her. He looked easy to offend, but should she let him know that of course she supported her sister in their quarrel?

Betsy was impressed at how Margot gave ideas and recommendations to the committee. She would ask a question or go halfway with an idea so that someone else would answer or complete her thought and so at least share credit for it. At first, Betsy thought nothing of it, but the third time it happened, she realized it was a deliberate and clever ploy.

Later, reluctant to break up, or perhaps just so caffeinated that going home to bed was not an option, the committee stood in couples or trios on the porch, talking and looking at the houses peeping through the trees that lined the lake, or at the restaurant down on the lakeshore. The Ferris wheel in the parking lot, trimmed in moving red lights, spun gently.

For all the summertime appearance of the scene, Betsy was glad for the shawl. The breeze was definitely chilly.

"I don't understand the Ferris wheel," she said.

Margot replied, "There used to be a big amusement park down there, years ago. It sort of commemorates it."

Hud said, "I hear they found a buyer for the restaurant and the new owners are going to sell the Ferris wheel."

Margot smiled at Betsy. "So things do change, even here in Excelsior."

After a little silence, Betsy asked, "How did Joe Mickels get on this committee?"

Margot only shrugged, so Hud replied, "He's turning into a big-time developer; he's got pieces of land working for him all over the state. That ski lodge is his, for example. We can use his money, and his influence."

"If he's what Margot says he is, I'm surprised he's interested in raising money for causes like this."

"Oh, he's a proactive vulture, all right," said Hud, displaying that wicked grin. "But this is a relatively small community, and you have to play along to get ahead. People who don't take part in things like this may find doors closed to them when they want to do business. But I'm surprised he got asked to be part of this fund-raising effort. How about it, Margot; will you be able to work with him?"

Again Margot shrugged. "At this distance, yes. But you could mention to George that he shouldn't assign us to the same subcommittee."

"You're nicer than I'd be about him," said Hud. "But who knows? Maybe this will soften him up. And even if it doesn't, we might find his hardheadedness useful. He's got a good business sense, even if he keeps his heart in cold storage."

Shivering under her shawl, Betsy smiled. "I should think in Minnesota, you don't need cold storage; just put things out on your back porch."

Hud laughed. "Wait till next July, you'll change your tune." He turned to Margot. "That's when we had summer this year, right, Margot? July seventh and eighth, as I recall."

Margot chuckled. "I think you're right; that was the weekend you took your Rolls off its blocks, right? Hud, I'm coming to the art museum on Wednesday to take a new look at the T'ang horse. It's for another needlepoint project. So long as I'm in the city, I'd like to stop by your office and talk about some board business. How's your schedule?"

"Pretty tight, but I can make a hole Wednesday morning, I think. About eleven, say?"

"Thanks. It won't take long."

Mayor Jamison came over then to ask Margot what she had done with the Founders' Day parade sashes, and from there the talk wandered to other things.

Four

✤

Shelly Donohue sat at the white plastic table on a white plastic chair outside the Excelo Bakery shop on Water Street. She was eating a "wicked" sandwich—so designated on a hand-lettered placard—consisting of sprouts, tomato, avocado, two kinds of cheese, and green-goddess dressing on herb-flavored foccacio bread baked on the premises. Her own designation of it was "messy but interesting," as in, "Will you make me one of those messy but interesting veggie sandwiches?" Shelly would not describe anything as wicked except murder and child abuse.

She also had a cup of cranberry juice, not further designated.

She was feeling frazzled, and looking a trifle frazzled as well; her hair was coming out of its bun and tendrils of it were lifted up here and there by a cool, vagrant breeze. An all-day preschool session was under way, and there were new laws and regulations to master, new textbooks (one with several egregious errors of fact) to study, and a new principal full of new ideas. And retirement was twenty years away.

But the morning's harsh edge was being smoothed away by a bit of friendly gossip. She was sharing her table with Irene Potter, a fellow needleworker, who was not drinking her coffee and was pulling fragments off a poppy-seed muffin with her lean, nimble fingers in lieu of eating it.

Irene's shining dark eyes encouraged Shelly to go on with what she was saying.

"You know, you'd hardly think they were sisters at all," Shelly continued. "Margot's such a dainty little thing, so sweet and . . . and . . . oh, I know the word's not considered nice anymore, but she's a *lady*. A real lady. Betsy's nice, too, don't get me wrong. But it's not just that they don't look very much alike; I mean, that sort of thing happens in any family that doesn't marry one another's cousins. But Betsy's . . ." She paused to think of the right words. "She's . . . more so," she said with an air of having at last put her finger on it. "You should have seen her putting the moves on Hudson Earlie Saturday night. And Hud was moving right back—you know Hud—but Margot couldn't say anything right there in front of him."

"Yes, we all know Hud," said Irene, waggling her eyebrows.

"But did you know Margot hired Betsy to work in the store?"

"She did?" Irene had worked a few hours in Crewel World, and wanted to work more.

"And Betsy doesn't know anything about running a store, or all that much about needlework, for that matter. She asked the dumbest questions."

"No!" said Irene.

"Yes. But she's trying really hard to pick up on things. And she's fun to have around, she really seems to like talking with the customers. She sold a whole lot of yarn to this woman by asking her questions about knitting. It was so funny to watch."

By her face, Irene didn't get the joke. "I hear she used to live in *San Francisco*." Her expressive voice turned the name into a synonym for depravity.

Shelly shrugged eloquently. "Yes, she mentioned that. *And* London, *and* New York. As if none of us ever go anywhere. She's been married a few times, too. But no children." Her face was disapproving of both those facts, though she herself was divorced—once—and had no children.

Irene said, "Of course, Margot never had children, either. Though I always *understood* it was Aaron's fault." They shared a slightly different expression this time, then smiled to show it was all just in fun. Each considered herself very close to Margot.

Shelly glanced at her watch then quickly stood and began gathering the remnants of her meal. "Lunch break's about over. I have to get back."

"Yes, you only get forty-five minutes, don't you?" said Irene, also rising. Her job as a supervisor in the shipping department of a local manufacturer wasn't as prestigious as Shelly's, but they gave her an hour for lunch. "So," she went on, walking Shelly to the trash barrel, her voice hopeful, "if Betsy doesn't know much, it seems Margot will still be in the market for a part-timer to help out in the shop?" Irene Potter's ultimate goal in life was to own a needlework shop, and meanwhile to gain full-time employment in Margot's. When she'd heard Margot's sister was coming to stay, she had trembled for the few hours of work Margot would give her.

Shelly, secure in her summer hours in Crewel World, smiled. "Probably not, but why don't you go talk to her? Meet Betsy, too. Maybe you two would get along. Got to run. Bye-bye."

Irene stood on the sidewalk in the bright sunshine, staring after her. Irene had a tendency to see everyone as a rival or potential rival, so Shelly's parting remarks gave her an idea that was positively *brilliant*. Know thine enemy, that was biblical, wasn't it? Or was it Shakespearean? Never mind, if she went over there and made friends, then she might see how to sabotage this Betsy person. Who, after all, knew next to nothing about clerking in a needlework store, while Irene knew everything; that alone might nullify the blood connection.

She hurried to scoop up the remains of her muffin and the paper coffee cup and toss them into the trash container. She dusted crumbs off herself with her napkin, then inspected herself in the window of the bakery. Dark slacks, white blouse, gray vest hand-crocheted herself with cotton thread in a pineapple pattern, and her favorite earrings, shaped like tiny scissors. She patted her dark curly hair, cropped close to her narrow head. She looked neat and competent. She smiled at the reflection, admiring the whiteness of her teeth. Perfect!

She rose onto her toes before stepping off in the direction of Crewel World, a mannerism she had seen in a musical once and copied whenever she was feeling ebullient. She had twenty minutes left of her lunch hour, time enough to get there and start *making friends* with her new rival. What fun!

Betsy sat behind the big old desk that Margot used as a checkout counter. She was biting on her lower lip. In her hands were two metal knitting needles and a ball of cheap purple yarn. Open on the desk was a thin booklet that promised to teach her how to knit in one day.

The reason her lower lip was being held in place was that doing so prevented her from sticking her tongue out.

Betsy considered herself very well coordinated. She could ride, she could shoot, she could thread a needle on the first try. Back when her hair was long, she'd taught herself to French-braid it down the back of her head without looking. But knitting was different.

"Casting on" she could do. She'd cast on twenty-five stitches, as instructed, and on the second try done it loosely enough so that knitting was something she now could also do, after a fashion. She'd proved that by doing about an inch of knitting.

But purling was not possible. The needle went through the knitted stitch, apparently as illustrated, and allowed itself to have a bit of yarn wrapped over it, but it wouldn't capture and bring through the purl stitch. Not without the aid of a third hand, which she didn't have.

Not that she could see why anyone wanted to purl anyhow. It looked like the same thing as knitting, according to the illustration, except up and down instead of across. Which is why it was impossible. One knitted from one side to the other, not upward.

Could it be some kind of secret knitters' thing? They let outsiders try and try to purl while they, the cognoscenti, the in-crowd, the clique, rolled on the floor snorting and giggling? And after a week or two allowed as how there was no such thing as purling? Sure, it was just a hazing thing they did to people who wanted to join the knitting fraternity—er, sorority. Though Betsy knew there were men who knitted. Sorternity?

Wait a second. If she tucked the end of the empty needle under her arm . . . Rats, for a second there she'd thought she'd got it.

She gave up and went back to knitting another row, slowly easing the needle through, wrapping the yarn, lift-twist-tipping it back, slipping the old stitch off.

She remembered how her mother would sit and watch television or her children play in the park, while her hands, as if with an intelligence of their own, moved in a swift, compact pattern and produced sweaters and scarves and mittens by the yard.

And she'd watched Margot do the same on Sunday evening up in the apartment.

While here she struggled slowly, stitch by stitch. Still, she was actually knitting. If she kept this up, in a year she'd have a potholder.

Margot hadn't watched television while she knitted, but talked with Betsy. Of course, there had been the odd pause while Margot counted stitches— knitters were forever losing track, it seemed—but on the whole, Margot had been able to keep up her end of the conversation.

It had been very comfortable up in that apartment, the puddles of yellow light making everything warm and intimate. They'd done some catching up— though now that she thought about it, Betsy had been allowed to do most of the talking, about Professor Hal (the pig), and the cost of living in beautiful San Diego (the sunlight in April on the white buildings and the endless sussurant crashing of the ocean, the dry, harsh, beautiful desert), and the big El Niño of '97 spoiling things.

Margot had said El Niño had even reached as far as Minnesota that year, giving them a very mild winter. Betsy, recalling the news footage of snow up to the eaves of Minnesota houses, decided that mild temperatures were a relative thing. Was she up to a Minnesota winter, she who could not knit well enough to produce a pair of mittens? Maybe she should cut this visit short and be on her way before the hard freeze set in.

She had asked, "Is living in a small town like it is in books, everyone knowing everyone else's business?"

"It is harder to be anonymous, because there is only the one main street where everyone shops, so even if you don't know someone's name, you recognize the face. It's like when you take the bus to and from work; you don't know the people who ride with you, not really, but you recognize their faces. And if someone's been absent for a few days and then gets on with his leg in a cast, you might express concern, even ask him what happened, as if he were a friend."

Betsy had nodded. Okay, living in a small town was like sharing a commute. She could do that.

"And if you get really sick of small-town living there's Minneapolis and St. Paul down the road—and hey, there's the Mall of America, right? Is it as big as they say? How often do you go there?"

"About as often as you visited the Statue of Liberty when you lived in New York City."

"But that was different! You go, you climb, you look out, you go home. At the Mall of America you can . . . *shop*."

"That's true. I went when it first opened, and I've been back, I think, twice. No, three times, twice to take visitors and once because they have a specialty shoe shop. You wouldn't believe it, but I'm hard to fit." Margot had stuck out a small foot complacently. She counted stitches for a bit, then continued, "But you know, there's so much *stuff* there, a great deal of it things you don't really need, like dried flower arrangements and personalized scents for your bath. To be so rich that you can shop as a form of recreation is . . . sinful. Yet people come from all over the world to entertain themselves by buying things they don't really need." She moved her shoulders. "It makes me ashamed somehow." She stopped to count stitches again, and then twinkled over at Betsy. "I know, you want to go glut yourself in all that shopping anyhow, be sinful for a day. Okay, maybe a week from Wednesday?"

And while they had continued talking, about movies and books, Margot's hands performed the same compact dance as Mother's had, and before they stopped to get ready for bed, the sweater she was knitting had become longer and developed a braid pattern.

So if Margot and Mother could do it while talking, by gum Betsy could do it while concentrating. She bit down harder on her captured lip and sped up to three stitches a minute.

She was concentrating so hard that when the door made its electronic sound, she jumped and, dammit, the needle slipped and pulled out of about seven stitches. Before she could figure out what to do, a bony, ice-cold hand covered hers.

She glanced up and saw a stick-thin woman with short dark hair that stuck up in odd-looking curls all over her little head. Like Betty Boop, thought Betsy. Except the face wasn't Boop's merry square, it was long and narrow, with deep lines from nostril to mouth. The eyes were dark and intent. The woman suddenly showed bright, patently false teeth, and Betsy wanted to back away, but was held by the icy grip.

"M-may I help you?" she asked.

"No, my dear, may I help *you*?" said the woman in a chirpy voice that rang as false as the teeth.

"Help me what?" asked Betsy.

"With what you are doing," said the woman, the smile slipping a trifle, looking pointedly at the knitting and back at Betsy.

"Oh, this. Why, do you know how to knit?"

The woman laughed a genuine laugh. "Of course I do! I know how to do every kind of needlework there is, except sewing canvas into sails. What seems to be the problem with your knitting?"

With a small effort, Betsy managed to free her hands. "It's not the knitting, exactly. It's the purling. I just don't get how to do it. And anyhow, now I've spoiled what I was doing, pulling the needle out."

"Oh, that's easy to fix." The woman took the knitting from Betsy's hands and deftly rethreaded the stitches onto the needle. "See? Now, to purl, you hold the needles like this," she said, putting them together in what Betsy was sure was the same way she herself had held them while trying to purl. "See, you go through like this, come around like this and off, and through and around and off, and-through-around-and-off." If she'd continued as slowly as she'd begun, Betsy might have learned something. But she repeated "through and around and off" faster and faster while her hands worked more and more vigorously, until she'd done the row. Then she handed the needles back to Betsy. "Now you try it," she said briskly.

Betsy took the needles, turned the work around to begin the next row and tried to remember where to poke the empty needle through the first stitch. It went in front, she remembered that, but was it through the same direction as the filled needle was pointing, or the other way?

"Here, dear, let me show you again," said the woman impatiently, starting to grab at the needles. Betsy lifted her hands, trying to keep possession.

Bing went the electronic note as the door to the shop opened.

The woman turned toward the door, and Betsy pushed back from the desk, rising.

It was Jill Cross, the police officer, this time in uniform, looking even taller and broader, probably because of that odd hat police officers wear and the thick belt around her hips, laden with gun and flashlight and handcuffs. She looked very authoritarian, and Betsy, who had been growing uneasy about the mad knitter, was glad to see her. But the other woman was already out into the aisle, one hand lifted in greeting.

"Good afternoon, Officer Jill!" she gushed, touching Jill familiarly on the upper arm. "What are we buying today?"

"Good afternoon, Irene." Jill nodded, swinging her elbow forward to free it. "Hi, Betsy," she added. "Did that ultrasuede I ordered come in?" Jill took off her hat, exposing her ash-blond hair, pulled back into a firm knot.

"Let me just check," Irene said, fawning.

"Wait a second, Irene," said Jill. "Margot's trying to bring Betsy up to speed on running the shop, so let's let her find the order for me."

Irene obediently halted and turned toward Betsy, a malicious gleam in her eyes.

Betsy began trying to think where Margot kept incoming orders.

"Shall I show you?" asked Irene.

"No, I remember now," said Betsy, and looked in a cardboard box on the floor under the desk. When she came up with the small package, Irene Potter's superior smile turned into something scary. It may have been a desperate attempt at a broad smile, but there was menace in it. Then she whirled and fled from the shop.

"Is . . . is she all right?" asked Betsy.

"Irene? Sure. Well, maybe she's a hair off center. She's so desperate to buy her own needlework shop that it colors everything she does. It's possible she's been hoping Margot would die of something so she could start her own needlework shop. The town isn't big enough for two of them."

"So why doesn't she move?"

"Because her ancestors were among the first settlers out here, and she would never think of moving away. But now you're here, and it would be too much to hope that both of you die." Jill grinned.

"Both . . ." Betsy hardly knew where to begin her response to that. "She thinks *I'm* going to take over the shop?"

"She probably suspects you and Margot are going to run it together. At the very least, you have put her out of her part-time work here. She just doesn't realize she hasn't a prayer of succeeding on her own, even if this place closes. I mean, would you go into a store a second time to buy something from her?"

Betsy grimaced. "She isn't dangerous, is she?"

Jill said sharply, "Now don't go getting weird ideas! The only thing she's crazy about is needlework. She's actually tremendously talented at it. Most of it is museum quality. She routinely takes first prize in any contest she enters. Her problem is, she was never properly socialized. A few years ago Irene begged and nagged until Margot hired her to teach a class, but Irene has no patience with people not as talented as she is, and every one of her students quit by the fourth lesson."

Betsy nodded. "Yes, she was trying to show me how to purl when you came in, but wouldn't slow down enough for me to catch on. Now let's see if I remember how to open the cash register."

A few minutes later Betsy was handing over the correct change. "Where's Margot?" Jill asked, pocketing her money. "I've got a question for her."

"Upstairs having a bowl of soup. She'll be back any second. Do you want to wait?"

"I can't, I'm on patrol. Tell her I've got a pair of tickets to the Guthrie, and my boyfriend went and switched shifts with someone, so now he can't go. Ask her if she wants to come with me."

A new voice asked, "What's the show?"

They turned; it was Margot, coming in from the back.

"*The Taming of the Shrew.*"

"Oooooh," sighed Margot. "When are the tickets for?"

"Tomorrow. I know Wednesdays are your day off, so I was hoping you could make it."

"The Guthrie!" said Betsy, remembering. "I've heard about the Guthrie. It's been written up in national magazines, hasn't it? It's supposed to be a great place to see good plays. I'd forgotten it was way up here in Minneapolis—or is it in St. Paul?"

"Minneapolis," said Jill, and for some reason there was disapproval again in her voice.

Margot explained, "Minneapolis and St. Paul don't like being mistaken for one another. Jill, I'm sorry, I can't go. I promised to make a presentation at our city-council meeting about next year's art fair tomorrow evening. Debbie Hart's going to be out of town and I promised her I'd do it. I'm really sorry."

"Yeah, well, maybe another time. Though I hate to see this ticket go to waste."

"Why don't you take Betsy?"

"Me?" They looked at her and Betsy tried to explain the tone of voice that had come out in. "I mean, I like Shakespeare very much, but if this is a grand production, you don't want to waste that invitation on someone you hardly know. Surely another friend . . ."

But some signal must have run between Margot and Jill because the latter said, "Betsy, you'll have to take a look at what passes for the big city in this part of the world sooner or later. Might as well be tomorrow. So let's make a night of it; we can have dinner at Buca's, and you can tell me how awful Italian food is in the upper Midwest. Then we'll go see how badly our legitimate theater compares to the stuff on the Great White Way."

Betsy took a breath to say no, but Margot had that look that meant she was hoping Betsy would not be rude, so Betsy turned to Jill and said only a little stiffly, "Well, I've only seen one Broadway production, so I hardly think I'm qualified to compare the Guthrie to the Great White Way. But on the other hand, I lived just two blocks away from the best Italian restaurant in Brooklyn, so I'll be glad to come sneer at what the upper Midwest dares to call Italian food."

Margot laughed, but Betsy wasn't sure Jill was amused. After she left, Betsy asked, "Margot, do you really have to go to a city-council meeting?"

"Yes, why?"

"I'm grateful for the ticket, but I'm not sure Jill and I will get along."

"Oh, nonsense. I'm sure once you get to know her, you'll like her very much."

"Well, there's no need to go out of your way just to be nice to me, when I'm guessing you'd really like to go."

"You're right, I would like to go, but I really do have to attend that meeting. The art show is one of our biggest annual events, thousands of people come here for it, and advance planning is very important. Anyway, I enjoy being nice to you."

"Then I thank you very much."

Margot went behind her desk to check Betsy's entry of the sale to Jill. Betsy followed, asking, "Margot, what are your plans for me?"

"What do you mean?"

"I hope you aren't planning on my being here forever."

"I haven't, but all right, I won't. Why?"

"Irene Potter was in here a little while ago. Don't you find her a little scary? She has the falsest smile I've ever seen. Then Jill came in, and when Irene tried to wait on her, Jill said to let me do it, and when I did it right Irene gave me a look that nearly froze my earlobes off."

"Oh, Irene just has this problem about being nice. She tries, but she doesn't know how."

"No, listen. Jill says that Irene knows you are going to teach me how to run the shop. It seems Irene has her eye on this place, and she's scared you've cut her out entirely by giving me her job."

Margot grimaced. "Hardly. I only hire Irene when all my other part-time help has flu, broken legs, and brain concussions."

Betsy insisted, "Margot, I think Irene Potter seriously hates me."

"How can she hate you? She doesn't know anything about you."

"She thinks I'm taking something that should be hers. And if she hates me for taking her job, I bet she hates you for giving it to me."

But Margot wasn't listening; she was examining Betsy's knitting. "This is very good, Betsy. The knitting is a trifle tight, but this row of purling is really well done!"

Five

❖

Margot woke early the next morning. Her usual first thought presented itself: What day is it?

Ah, Wednesday, her day off. What was on the agenda? Well, there was that art-fair presentation this evening, at seven sharp. Her notes were still on the computer. She'd read them over one more time, then print them out.

Betsy's here, came a sudden memory, almost an interruption. That was something new in her normally predictable life. But not a disruption, came the reassurance, Betsy was all right, Betsy was fitting in fine, Betsy was enjoyable company.

But it did make a difference to have someone else living in the apartment, if only because she had to remember to wear a robe and to check the refrigerator rather than think that just because she had not used the last of the milk that there would be some for the morning coffee.

The question was, was Betsy enjoying herself? Margot hoped so. Because despite what she had said yesterday, this was someone who was not just a weekend guest but a long-term arrangement. All Margot's immediate plans had to be changed, and some of her long-term ones, now that there was another person who had to be considered. It was almost like being married again.

So while it was okay, even enjoyable, to have Betsy here, it was also different. She must decide when she would formally talk to Betsy about her future. Betsy made a nice salesperson, she was interested and friendly; she would make an excellent one once she got up to speed on the terminology and practices of needlework. Yesterday she had sold a beginning inquirer an impressive amount of silks and evenweave fabric and counted cross-stitch patterns, though she knew almost nothing about counted cross-stitch.

But was Betsy really interested in the shop, or was she only "helping out," as any polite guest would? Perhaps it was still too early to get an honest answer. Betsy had always been interested in something new.

But today was not the day to start inquiring. Margot was going to be out all

day today. First, to the Minneapolis art museum, to make a detailed drawing of
the T'ang horse for the canvas.

And about time, too, if she wanted that project finished by Thanksgiving.
She wished she hadn't thrown away the original drawings; then she wouldn't
have to make this trip. No, wait, she was also going to meet with Hudson Earlie at the museum, so she had to go anyway.

She found herself smiling at the memory of Betsy meeting Hud at Christopher Inn. Betsy was attractive and witty and she enjoyed flirting. But twice
burned by bad marriages, what would she do when she found out Hud was
himself a three-time loser? Run? Or make another bad choice?

Probably neither. Betsy wasn't a youngster anymore; she knew better than
to get mixed up with someone like Hud. And she was in the process of sorting
herself out, which was not the time to be starting a courtship, or even an affair.
But what if she was her usual reckless self and got involved, and it turned out
badly? Where would she run to this time? She'd confessed she was here because
she had nowhere else to go, no one else to turn to. Perhaps Margot had better
say something to Hud, though if he got on his high horse about it, she'd warn
Betsy, too.

Margot eased herself out of bed, remembered her robe, and used the bathroom as quietly as she could. Once Betsy had been a morning person, but confessed she had gotten over that. The sunrise over Excelsior still had two hours of
travel before it reached the West Coast; morning would come early until her internal clock adjusted.

Margot went back into her bedroom and booted up her computer, checked
her E-mail, and started to download a couple of newsgroups. RCTN took forever; its thousands of members were incorrigible chatterers. While it was working, she went into the kitchen and started the coffeemaker, then went back to
the computer to scan the messages, reply to a few, and send them. Then she finalized and printed the presentation she was going to make this evening. By
the time that was done, she could hear Betsy in the bathroom.

Betsy sighed and rolled over. Margot hadn't used to be such an
early bird! It was barely light out, and already Margot was putzing around in
the bathroom. Betsy pried an eye open and checked her watch. Six o'clock. God,
these Midwesterners; you'd think they all were farmers. Didn't they know that
early to bed and early to rise means you miss all the parties?

Betsy rolled back onto her side, seeking more sleep. After all, it was only
four A.M. in San Diego; some of last night's parties were just breaking up.

It was awkward living in someone else's home. You had to adjust your sleeping patterns, your TV-watching habits, your eating habits. No more cereal for supper, no more cold pizza for breakfast. And in this place, *lots* more salads.

Which Betsy could use a little of. So okay, bring on the salads.

Very faintly, Betsy heard a series of beeps, and then a chord of music—just the one chord. Ah, Margot was surfing the net. Interesting how her sister, who, back in high school, had difficulty mastering the electric typewriter, was now so proficient on the computer.

Betsy herself was computer literate. A shame she hadn't known Margot had an E-mail address; she could have saved herself this trip. A few weeks of E-mail exchanges and—no, that wouldn't have done it. She had needed to get away, start over.

She had sold her own computer along with most of her other household items when she'd decided to come to Minnesota. Too much trouble hauling a trailer over those mountains, too expensive to put things into storage. And wiping the slate clean was part of the process of starting over.

Should she talk to Margot about her computer? Margot kept it in her bedroom, and had yet to invite Betsy into that sanctum. Margot might think she wanted to pry, though she didn't. Certainly Margot hadn't come into the guest room once she'd turned it over to Betsy. Not that she wasn't welcome.

Margot was a much more private person than Betsy. That could be because Betsy had been such a snoop when they were kids. Margot had had to fight for privacy, and gotten into the habit.

But Betsy was willing to respect that. There were things she didn't want to share with Margot, either. Such as how uncomfortable she felt taking her sister's charity. She wasn't sure whether her sister's offer of a paying job in the shop was a sop to Betsy's pride or because she could really use the help.

But did any of that matter right now? Betsy felt herself sinking into the pillows, a very pleasant sensation. She dozed until the smell of coffee brought her awake again, and had a good breakfast with Margot—mushroom-and-green-pepper omelette with toast—then Margot left for the city and Betsy went down with Sophie to open the shop.

Shelly was somewhat distracted; school was going to start in five days, and she'd just found out that there would be thirty-five children in her fourth-grade class. That was far too many, and with the list of children's names came a little memo saying there would be no teacher's aide until halfway through the semester.

So Betsy's constant stream of questions about Crewel World, its history and profitability, were a nuisance. Shelly made her answers as brief as possible, though she sensed Betsy's growing frustration.

Officer Jill came in around ten-thirty for a cup of coffee and to place an order for more ultrasuede floss. On her way out she said, "Don't forget this evening," and closed the door.

"What about this evening?" Shelly asked Betsy.

"We're going to dinner and the Guthrie."

"Well, isn't that nice! I'm glad you two are going to be friends."

"Us, friends?" said Betsy with a little laugh. "I'm only going because Margot can't go. It was her idea that I take her place."

"What, you don't like Shakespeare?"

"Sure, but I'm not so sure about Jill. Is she always like this?"

"Like what?"

"Frosty."

"She's not frosty, she's just Norwegian. They're not big on showing their feelings. She likes you."

"How can you tell?"

"She came in for coffee, and Wednesday is Margot's day off, everyone knows that. I don't think she knows my schedule, so it wasn't me she came in to see. I think she likes you, or wants to."

"Do you like her?"

Shelly laughed. "Sure, but I've known her since kindergarten."

Betsy wanted to ask more, but a customer came in with a lot of her own questions, and Shelly took her to the back of the store, where a pair of upholstered chairs made answering the questions so comfortable the customer tended to stay a little longer and buy more than she might have otherwise.

Betsy drove to Jill's house about five-thirty. It was time she learned her way around, so she was driving into the city. Jill got in and directed her back down Highway 7, then onto Highway 100 north to 394, then east to Minneapolis. They got off on the Twelfth Street North exit. "When we cross Hennepin it will become South Twelfth," Jill said.

And so it did. Almost immediately, Jill said, "There's Buca's." It was on a corner, marked with an old-fashioned vertical neon sign, showing a wine bottle filling a glass.

The restaurant was in the basement of an apartment building, a series of small rooms. The walls were covered with old photographs of thickly dressed children—presumably the owner's ancestors—and photos of Joe DiMaggio, Yogi Berra, Pope Pius XII, Al Capone, Frank Sinatra, and other notable Italians.

There were the correct checkered tablecloths, and a shabby-friendly atmosphere that felt authentic, down to last Christmas's tinsel still wrapped around the overhead pipes. The plates didn't quite all match, nor did the silverware. The wineglasses were simple tumblers.

Betsy, remembering the shabby little restaurant in Brooklyn, smiled. This was a very authentic look.

And the smell was both authentic and heavenly.

The menu was on the wall, on a big rectangle of whiteboard. Betsy felt alarmed at the prices, which were anything but shabby. A small dinner salad for $6.95? She began to wish she hadn't insisted dinner be dutch treat.

Jill must have read her face, for she said, "We'll get one salad and share—the portions are large."

That was an understatement; the "small" salad came on a platter, a great heap of mixed greens and purple onions, glistening with oil. Dark olives clung precariously to what showed of the rim. The garlic bread they ordered with it was the size and shape of a large pizza, crusted with Parmesan, greening with basil, thickly flecked with slices of roasted garlic.

Betsy had thought it was only New York cops who loved Italian food, but perhaps it was a universal trait; certainly Jill seemed familiar with the menu.

"How long have you known Margot?" asked Betsy as they waited for the entrée.

Jill considered. "Fifteen years, or thereabouts," she replied, and added, "She taught me how to embroider and do crewel. And, more recently, needlepoint."

"Do you knit?"

"No. And neither do you, I guess."

Betsy thought for an instant that this was a witticism, but when she looked up from her second slice of garlic bread, all she saw was that implacable calm and a penetrating pair of eyes.

Jill had the full face the Victorians so admired; not a bone sticking out anywhere. And her eyebrows were so pale they were almost invisible. So there was no quirky eyebrow or quiver of jaw tendon to read in that face.

A little defensively, Betsy said, "Knitting's a dull business, don't you think? It seems so mechanical, knit, purl, knit, purl, on and on—but you have to pay attention, or you end up with a mess."

"You did learn how to purl, then?"

"Yes, Margot showed me. I thought I had taught myself, but Margot looked at it and said she thought I had invented a new stitch."

Was that a glint of amusement in those cool eyes?

Encouraged, Betsy continued, "And while I thought I was dropping stitches, it turned out I had added six. Did you ever notice how knitters have to keep stopping and counting? Always dropping or picking up stitches. Give me the kind of needlework where all I have to do is look and I know where I am."

"Me, too."

The chicken Marsala was to die for. A single serving came as three large chicken breasts in a caramel-brown sauce, covered with big hunks of fresh mushrooms. They shared that, too.

"Well?" said Jill coolly as the meal drew toward its end.

"Well what?" replied Betsy, feeling overfed, and a little fuddled with Chianti. It was too easy to be generous when pouring it into a tumbler.

"Is it as good as that little restaurant in Brooklyn?"

Betsy tried to think. "Frankly, it's been too many years since I was in Brooklyn to remember. But I think so. In any case, it was delicious."

"I'm glad you liked it," said Jill. She looked at her watch. "We don't have time for dessert."

Betsy began to laugh, she couldn't help it.

Jill's inquiring glance had the wintry look in it again, even though she, too, watched as the waitress packed up half a slab of garlic bread and most of the garlic mashed potatoes and one of the chicken breasts. Was it a local custom always to order dessert, even when all you could manage was a polite bite of it? Did Jill think there was an empty refrigerator at home?

But Betsy didn't feel like explaining why she thought Jill had made a joke. She was glad they were going to a play; soon she wouldn't have to try to keep up a conversation with this unreadable ice maiden.

They were well into the first act of the Guthrie production of *The Taming of the Shrew* before enough of the wine wore off that Betsy could look around with appreciation.

The theater was not small enough to be called intimate, but it wasn't a huge cavern by any means. The stage was a thrust, so the audience sat on three sides, but it went well back behind a proscenium as well. The seats were very comfortable. The actors were of the caliber that makes Shakespearean English sound natural, the special effects, while not Broadway spectacular, were well done, and the costuming was beautiful.

It had started raining sometime during the play, and was still raining when they came out of the theater. But the farther west they drove, the lighter the rain became, until out in Excelsior it ceased altogether, leaving platinum puddles as markers of its passing, and tree branches hanging lower, their leaves heavy with water.

They didn't say much on the way home. Betsy dropped Jill off at her house, then drove up Water Street toward the lake. The small downtown was quiet, already mostly asleep. Of course, it was eleven o'clock at night. But there were not the boarded-up windows so sadly evident in many small towns. There was the bakery; Shelly had said they had nice sandwiches. Certainly their sweet rolls were good. And here was Haskell's, where she turned toward home. Interesting, she already thought of it as home. Maybe she would stay and see if she was up to a Minnesota blizzard.

As she pulled up to the curb in front of the dark brick building, her headlights caught the door of Crewel World. It seemed ajar. Probably just the way the lights hit it, thought Betsy.

But when she got out, she went to take a closer look. The door was open a couple of inches. Betsy, sure she had locked it firmly earlier, reached to pull it shut, and saw, dimly, things all over the floor. The drawers of the white dresser were open and canvases were sticking stiffly up and out of them.

She nearly went in, then remembered what she'd been told by a policeman during a National Night Out lecture about coming home to a burglary: *Don't go in; he might still be in there.* A chill ran right down her spine.

She let go the door latch as if it were red-hot and scurried into the little alcove that held the door to the upstairs. It seemed to take forever to locate her key, and it was horribly reluctant to go into the lock. Then it turned and she was inside. She dashed up the thinly carpeted stairs.

She reached the top all out of breath, her hands trembling so that she had to use both of them to unlock the apartment door.

"Margot!" she called, falling into the little entranceway and slamming the door shut behind her. "Margot! There's been a burglary in the shop!"

No answer. Was it possible the meeting at City Hall was still going on?

"Margot?" No reply.

Betsy hastened into the kitchen, flicked on the light. The phone was on the wall. She lifted the receiver and dialed 911.

"This is 911, what is your emergency?" asked a woman's voice.

"A burglar! I'm afraid he might still be in there!"

"Is this burglar in your home?"

"No, in the shop downstairs!"

"Is it your shop?"

"No, my sister's. It's called Crewel World." Betsy gave the address and promised to stay where she was until the police arrived.

Betsy stood by the window, arms folded tightly until, through the closed blinds, she could see the erratic pattern of flashing red and blue lights.

She ran down the stairs and waved to the two husky young men who climbed out of a patrol car, then pointed to the door of Crewel World. They nodded and, with drawn pistols, went inside.

A little later Betsy gave a little shriek and jumped aside, and was surprised to find she had squeezed her eyes shut and stuffed her fingers in her ears against the possible sound of gunfire. The person touching her shoulder was one of the officers.

She sighed with relief. "He's gone, then?"

"Who?"

"The burglar. I was afraid you'd have to shoot him."

"Are you the owner of this store?"

"No, my sister is. I mean, Mr. Joseph Mickels is the owner of the building, and my sister rents from him. I'm just visiting. From California."

They were looking at her in some kind of expectant way, but she'd told them everything she could think of.

"Do you know where your sister is?"

"No. That is, she was here earlier this evening, up in the apartment. That was at about five-thirty, when I left to pick up Jill and we went into Minneapolis for dinner and then to a play. Margot was supposed to go to City Hall for a meeting about the art fair. I can't believe it's still going on. It's after eleven."

"Who's Jill?"

Betsy said, surprised, "She's one of you. A police officer, Jill Cross."

"What's your name?"

"Betsy Devonshire."

"What's your sister's name?"

"Margot Berglund."

"What does she look like?"

"She's about five-feet-one, slim, blond hair—why? Is she—"

A sound that had been growing louder got loud enough to impinge on Betsy's concentration. It was another siren, and it belonged to one of those boxy ambulances that come to the scene of accidents. The officer turned to start toward it.

Betsy called, "Wait, what's going on? Is someone in the store? Is it—is she all right?" She turned toward the shop's entrance, but the officer was in front of her and he put both hands on her shoulders.

"Just take it easy, Ms. Devonshire."

Two people ran from the ambulance into the shop, one carrying a large, square suitcase. Betsy felt her knees growing weak. "What's going on? Is someone in there?"

"Yes, ma'am."

"Who? Is it Margot?"

"We don't know right now who it is."

The door to the upstairs opened and three people came out, a young couple and a middle-aged man, tenants from the other two apartments. Their faces were alarmed, and they stood close together, clutching bathrobes. The older man was wearing unlaced dress shoes. He stared at Betsy.

"Why don't you come with me and sit in the squad car?" said the policeman, taking Betsy by the elbow. "Let's get you out of all this." His voice was kind but firm. In a kind of dream, Betsy allowed herself to be ushered into the backseat of the squad car, whose engine was running, and lights still flashing. The policeman went away.

Except for the radio, it was darkly silent in the car. Everything in it was black—the upholstery, the seats, the shotgun clamped vertically to the black dashboard. Betsy could almost smell the testosterone and suddenly wondered how Jill could stand it.

The radio muttered again, the words too mixed with static to understand. She didn't like being put in the squad car, it indicated her place in this affair was worse than those spectators standing on the sidewalk, merely alarmed.

After a while she noticed raindrops on the windshield; it had started to rain again. The people on the sidewalk went back inside.

After a long while the ambulance people came out. The policeman followed behind them to open the squad car's back door. "Come with me, please," he said, and held out a hand.

"Where are we going?" she asked.

"We want you to look at something," he said, and led her into the store.

Someone had turned on the lights. Betsy could not believe the disarray. The floor was covered with yarn and floss. The spin racks were on their sides, magazines had been crumpled and ripped, baskets that had held knitting yarn had not only been emptied, but stepped on.

The policeman led her past Margot's desk, which was pulled out of place, toward the back of the store. Here shelves came out from the wall on either side. Behind them, on the side where the pretty little upholstered chairs had sat around a little round table, was even wilder disarray. The chairs were overturned. The shelves had been divided vertically into cubes, which had once held yarn and evenweave fabrics; books, magazines, and canvas needlework bags had been emptied onto the floor. Behind the chairs was a big heap of wool and books, and beyond them, as if they had been moved aside to uncover her, was a woman.

She was on her back, her head turned to one side. Her eyes were partly open, as was her mouth. She looked as if she were crying out in pain. Her skin was an odd, pale color. She was wearing a black wool skirt hiked up over one knee and a dark wine sweater, the sleeves pushed up. One of her sensible black shoes was off the heel of her foot and her arms were bent at the elbows, hands clenched. Her blond hair was mussed.

"Do you recognize her?" asked the policeman.

"Margot," whispered Betsy. "It's my sister Margot."

Six

As Jill prepared for bed, she began to smile—though it hardly showed on her face. Betsy Devonshire was an interesting person. And funny; it had been hard to keep from laughing out loud at some of the things she said. On the other hand, Betsy was kind of slow to pick up on a joke. She probably didn't get Jill's crack about knitting, and Jill thought it had been pretty obvious. But never mind; Betsy liked Italian food, complimented Buca's, stayed awake all through the play, and made some intelligent comments on it afterward. And above all, she was the sister of her best friend, Margot Berglund.

She wondered how long it would take Margot to understand the prank of insisting Betsy take home all that garlic-laden food. Margot disliked garlic almost as much as she did onions. Jill snorted softly and climbed between the crisp sheets. She loved jokes whose punch lines went off sometime later.

She was fast asleep when the phone rang, and it took her a minute to understand what the caller was asking her—and why.

"Wait a second, Mike!" she demanded. "Take a breath!" She took one of her own. "Now, what's this about a burglar?"

Betsy sat in the dining nook of the apartment. Jill was in the kitchen and there was the smell of coffee.

"Here, drink this," said Jill, and a mug of coffee appeared in front of Betsy. She put her cold hands around it, burning them. But she left them there; it was an honest, understandable hurt.

"What happens now?" Betsy asked.

"An autopsy. Then the ME—medical examiner—will release the body, and you'll have to make funeral arrangements."

"I don't know how to do that." And she didn't want to learn. She felt sick and weary, all her senses dulled, as if she were coming down with flu. She didn't even have the strength to lift the mug to her mouth. Margot couldn't be dead, Margot had just stayed late at her meeting and would be home any minute, asking what all the fuss was about.

"I assume you want her buried beside her husband?" asked Jill.

"At Aaron's funeral she said something to me about being buried in the same plot. Can you do that?"

"Yes, people do it all the time. Especially if they're cremated. Aaron was cremated. Call Paul Huber, he's good."

"Who's Huber?" asked Betsy wearily.

"The local funeral home. And you should call Reverend John at Trinity."

"Okay. Sure."

"Not this minute, of course."

Betsy, hearing criticism in Jill's voice, looked up. And saw that implacable stare looking back. Suddenly she wanted to punch that smooth face. She wanted to rail, scream, and tear her hair, dress herself in sackcloth and pour ashes on her head, and weep for days, weeks, forever. Margot was dead.

But she didn't scream, or say anything, or do anything, only stared at Jill.

Who looked at her watch, a small, delicate thing, clinging to that sturdy white wrist. "It's very late. You should go to bed."

"I'm tired, but I'm not at all sleepy," said Betsy, looking into the dark liquid in her mug.

"Then just go lie down for an hour."

"I don't want to lie down! Why don't you just go? Go bother someone else!" said Betsy, surprised at the venom escaping through her voice. "You don't understand!"

"Sure I do. Here, let me get you something else." Jill slid the mug out of Betsy's still-clasped hands and went into the kitchen.

Betsy slid back into her felt-lined stupor. She shouldn't shout at Jill, who had gotten out of bed to come and be with her. And there were things that must be done, she knew that. She just wished there could be a period of doing nothing until she could summon some energy.

Margot had been the coping one. She wouldn't be sitting here as if wrapped in thick flannel, her brain turned to oatmeal. Betsy remembered when she herself had seen trouble as a challenge, but that seemed a very long time ago. Why couldn't she be that way now? What was the matter with her? She should be paying attention to Jill, and feeling grateful for her advice. Buck up, she told herself. But her mind replied sullenly that it wanted to be left alone.

"I don't understand why Margot went into the store when you knew enough not to," said Jill from the kitchen, where the refrigerator door was being closed, a pot was being put on the stove.

Betsy pictured Margot walking home—Margot alive and walking!—and seeing the open door. But Margot went in—no, no; don't go in!—but she went in, she went in. While clever Betsy had seen the door open and come running upstairs to call the police. Why had it happened that way?

"Possession," said Betsy. "Territory. You ever read Ardrey's *Territorial Imperative*? Popular sociology, from back in the sixties; forgotten now, probably. He said most animals, including primates, select and defend a territory, whether as an individual or a tribe. That's what we do, and that's why humans fear strangers and fight wars."

Jill said doubtfully, "You think she saw the burglar and went in to run him off?"

"No, of course not! Margot's not an idiot. But she's been having trouble with Joe Mickels trying to throw her out of the shop, so I guess her territorial instincts were all inflamed anyhow. So when she saw the door open she just went in without thinking. I nearly did—" Something like a sob choked Betsy but the relief of tears would not come. "God, I can't bear this."

"Yes, you can," said Jill firmly, coming to put a hand on her shoulder. "You've got to, you're the sole surviving member of your family. But you're not alone. Margot had lots of friends. When they hear about this, you'll have all the help you need." She went back into the kitchen and there was the sound of cabinet doors being opened and closed. "Where's the cocoa?"

"I don't know." The flannel wrapped her again. She didn't care where anything was in a world inexplicably emptied of Margot.

Jill looked everywhere for the cocoa, even, apparently, the bathroom. But she must have found it, because soon a mug of hot cocoa was thrust into Betsy's hands.

"Drink this." It was an order.

Betsy drank. And to her surprise, in a few minutes she was helplessly sleepy. Jill walked her into her bedroom, helped her undress and get into pajamas, tucked her in. Betsy tried to ask a question but instead fell into a black pit.

"She okay alone up there?" asked Mike.

"I put a couple of sleeping pills into her cocoa," said Jill. "She's good for a while. What's the situation?" She shivered against the chill and damp night air—she'd come out only in jeans and a white T-shirt—and glanced into the brightly lit store, where people moved in the routine of a crime-scene investigation.

"It looks like she interrupted a burglar, all right. Cash drawer broken into. And since there's no calculator, I assume it was taken. Did she use a computer?"

"Yes, but it's upstairs," said Jill. "In her bedroom. And she emptied that cash drawer every night."

"Maybe that's why he trashed the place. Pissed because there was nothing of any value to steal."

"Little he knew. Those hand-painted canvases over there cost a lot of money."

The curiosity that'd gotten Mike Malloy promoted from patrol to investigation stirred. He glanced toward where Jill was looking, at the white dresser near the front door. "No kidding?"

"Of course, I don't think there's much call for hot needlepoint canvases; eighty percent of the women who buy them wouldn't know where to find a fence, and the rest don't know what a fence is."

The interest faded. "I wonder why our burglar picked this shop in the first place," grumbled Mike. "It's not like it's a jewelry store, watches in the window, diamonds in the safe. And even more, I wonder why Mrs. Berglund decided to confront him."

"Territorial imperative, maybe."

Mike squinted at Jill, who didn't crack a smile. He gave a dismissive shrug and said, "Well, I better get back to it. You gonna stay?"

"No, I'm back on first watch. Gotta be up pushing my squad first thing in the morning. Mind if I call you about this later?"

"If you got anything of value to tell me, be my guest."

The phone started ringing early Thursday, first a reporter wanting details, then Irene Potter offering to open the shop—which offer Betsy curtly refused—then another reporter, then someone named Alice who went on and on about how everyone who did needlework would miss her, each word scalding Betsy's heart. When the woman slowed enough that Betsy could get a word in, Betsy thanked her through clenched teeth and hung up. Before it could ring again, she took the receiver off the hook. And she discovered that no one buzzed at the door more than three times before going away. She spent the entire day watching television, stupid show after stupid show. She didn't turn the lights on at nightfall, but sat up for hours in the darkness. But she did not cry. At three A.M. she put the phone back on the hook and went to bed.

The Hennepin County Medical Examiner's call woke her early Friday. A woman said they had released Margot's body and someone needed to make arrangements for it to be taken away.

Betsy said she would do so, and wandered the apartment in a mild panic for five minutes. Then she recalled Jill saying there was one funeral home she could trust—but what was its name? She picked up the slim phone directory for Excelsior, Shorewood, Deephaven, and Tonka Bay, and saw there was exactly one funeral home in Excelsior, Huber's. That was it. She phoned and got an answering service, and left an urgent message.

She had just finished brushing her teeth when the phone rang. It was Irene Potter, asking if there was anything Betsy wanted done.

"You want to do me a favor?" said Betsy. "Stay off the phone. I'm waiting for an important call and I don't want the phone tied up."

She was still trying to decipher the coffeemaker's methods when the phone rang again, and it was Paul Huber.

Instead of the oily voice she expected, Huber sounded perfectly ordinary, except he was also brisk, knowledgeable, and efficient. He said he would bring Margot's body to the funeral home; yes, he knew the procedure, it was all routine and she needn't worry. He then made an appointment with her for first thing that afternoon, to discuss the rest of the arrangements.

Betsy sat curled in Margot's chair, sipping coffee and worrying. Didn't funerals cost a great deal of money? Betsy had some money, not much, and most of it was in an IRA, inaccessible.

How was she going to pay for this?

What did other people do?

Betsy knew there were special life-insurance policies people took out to cover final expenses. But Betsy remembered when her father had died; it took weeks for insurance companies to pay off. Betsy needed money by this afternoon.

Maybe funeral homes allowed people to charge funerals.

Betsy had a charge card. She used it sparingly, having learned to fear debt during her first marriage. So it was nowhere near its limit, which on the other hand was a modest five thousand dollars. She had hoped to save it for an emergency—but surely this was an emergency. She couldn't store Margot in the refrigerator until she saved enough money to bury her. Was it bad manners to ask a funeral director if he took Visa?

And was the three thousand seven hundred dollars left in credit enough?

Maybe Margot had cash somewhere. Jill had told her that Margot emptied the cash drawer every night. Where did she put the money? Betsy remembered walking to the bank's night deposit with Margot on Monday evening. But not all the money went into the bank—she needed some to prime the drawer every morning.

Betsy looked toward the little hall that led to Margot's bedroom. Betsy had to go see, go pry. Feeling guilty as a child about to steal a quarter from her mother's purse, she slipped down the short hall to the bedroom door.

Margot's bedroom was beautiful, with designer elements Betsy had not expected. The bed had slim iron pillars and a translucent lace canopy. There was a comforter, all ruffles of ivory lace, a shade lighter than the walls. A thin scent of Margot's perfume lingered on the still air.

The rug on the floor was thick and lush, iron gray with a gold and green fringe. The window had layers of ivory lace curtains pinched and pulled into a complicated pattern. The small, low dresser was wood, stained gray, the low chair in front of it had an iron frame and a plush seat. The mirror over the dresser was round. A pair of badly snagged panty hose draped half out of the otherwise empty wastebasket. The desk in the corner had a modern-looking computer on it, with an ergonomically correct office chair and a two-drawer wooden file cabinet beside it, the bottom drawer not quite shut.

Betsy searched the desk drawers first. She found three checkbooks. One belonged to Crewel World and showed a balance of $2,523.50. The other was a personal checkbook and showed a balance of $372.80. The third was a Piper Jaffray money market account with a balance of close to four thousand dollars. And there was also a savings-account passbook showing a total balance of $3,253.74.

Betsy rubbed her nose, her sign of befuddlement. This was more money than she had expected to find. Why would Margot keep all her money where she could get at it? Didn't she believe in IRAs or certificates of deposit, for heaven's sake? Or was there even more hidden away somewhere? Probably not much— Margot wasn't really wealthy, or she wouldn't be living in a rented apartment.

Not that it mattered in the present emergency. Betsy could not sign Margot's name to anything. What she needed was cash.

The next drawer held sixty dollars in paper and silver, neatly lined up. Is that all it took to prime a cash register?

She could find no more cash, so apparently that was all that was needed. The dresser held perfumes in one drawer, cosmetics in another, and hair curlers, bobby pins, and an electric curling iron in the middle.

Betsy found Margot's plain black purse in the closet and opened it. Inside the wallet were forty-six dollars and ninety-six cents.

That was more than Betsy's wallet, but hardly enough to pay for a funeral.

Now wait, now wait, surely these Huber people were used to this. Unexpected deaths happened all the time; not everyone had access to the cash to pay for a funeral. Doubtless the people at Huber's would know what to do.

Which is exactly the attitude funeral directors enjoy encountering, thought Betsy in a sudden flash: customers coming in all confused and scared. That's how some of those really expensive funerals happen. You go in and hold out all your assets and hope they won't hurt you too badly. But they do, they do.

So it was with her chin firmly set and both hands on the closed top of her purse that Betsy walked up past the post office in the cool morning sunshine, rounded the corner, and crossed Second Street to Huber's, a whited sepulchre with bloodred geraniums in a planter by the entrance.

The lights were dim inside, the carpet soft underfoot. A dark young man with a thick mustache and a Mona Lisa smile stood waiting. Betsy had a vague feeling she'd seen him before.

"Mr. Huber?" said Betsy.

"Ms. Devonshire," said Mr. Huber. "Come with me."

He led her to a small office with dark wood paneling, soft lighting, and samples of ground-level grave markers in the corner. He seated her and went behind the desk.

"I am very saddened by Margot's death," he said.

"You knew her personally?"

"Yes, of course," he replied, by his voice a little puzzled at her tone. "We're both members of Lafayette Country Club, and we worked together on a Habitat for Humanity house in Minneapolis this summer."

That hadn't occurred to Betsy, though it should have. Margot had said that in Excelsior everyone knew everyone else. But Betsy hadn't known her sister was a member of a country club. Of course, that probably didn't mean out here in the wilderness what it did in, say, Rancho Santa Fe.

Still, better tell the bad news up front. "I haven't much money," she said. "What I do have is tied up in an IRA, and of course I don't have any way to access what assets Margot had, so this is going to have to be a . . . an inexpensive funeral. I hope you understand."

Mr. Huber was frowning now, though more in puzzlement than anger. "You haven't spoken with Margot's attorney yet?"

"I haven't talked to anyone, much less Margot's attorney, whose name I don't know. I'm practically a stranger here in town. But there's no time now for that. I know this has to be taken care of promptly, so I want to tell you right now that it can't cost a whole lot."

"What do you consider 'a whole lot'?"

"Why don't you tell me what the very least is I can spend, and we'll see if I can meet even that amount?"

Mr. Huber lifted his hands in a gesture of surrender. "Very well." He helped Betsy fill out a death certificate and write an obituary. He said he'd take care of sending it to the local papers. He was kind and patient through all of this, but then they were back to the big question of the funeral.

"I want her cremated," said Betsy, "so we don't have to do all that chemical stuff, do we? Can you do that right here in your place?"

"No, we don't have the facilities. There are two choices in the area. There's Fairview Cemetery in Minneapolis. They can make it part of a service—"

"No, I want a funeral service in a church."

"Margot was a member of Trinity Episcopal."

Betsy nodded. "Yes. I'm going to call the rector today."

"You'll find Reverend John a pleasure to work with."

He led Betsy upstairs to look at the urns. And here she weakened. She picked a very nice Chinese-vase style in a pearl color with cranberry-colored lotus blossoms on it. Three hundred and forty-nine dollars was the price, which she thought outrageous, but what could she do? The polished wooden box wasn't much less, and it looked like something you keep recipes in.

They went back downstairs to the little office and Mr. Huber got out his calculator. "Two thousand four hundred dollars," he announced with a little sigh.

By now Betsy had a fierce headache. She'd cut every corner she could think of, and it still seemed an enormous sum. She wanted to weep and change her mind about the lotus urn, but she hadn't the strength.

"Do you take Visa?" she asked.

They did.

Seven

Paul Huber sat at his desk for a while after Betsy Devonshire left. It was not uncommon for survivors dealing with unexpected death to look for someone to be angry at. Often they settled on the funeral director. After all, he was doing unknowable . . . *things* to the body, and charging for it besides, which put him right out of the category of friend.

While Betsy Devonshire was not the worst example of this phenomenon, she was one of the saddest he had seen in a very long time.

He wondered if he should have been more persistent in telling her that there really should be a wake of some sort, where all her friends and the many people Margot had touched in her life could get together informally and talk, and pay their last respects.

And that there was no need to be parsimonious about the funeral service.

But Ms. Devonshire was in no mood whatsoever to listen to advice from a funeral director, who, so far as she was concerned, was interested only in lining his pockets.

He shook his head and blew his nose and went to deal with the body of a friend he had long admired.

"Oh, my dear, I tried to call you yesterday, but couldn't get through," said the pleasant voice on the phone. It was Reverend John Rettger. "I'm so sorry about Margot."

"Thank you, Reverend. I'm calling about the funeral."

"Yes, of course. Do you want to come here, or shall I come over there? As it happens, I'm free right now."

"I'll come to you."

Betsy was startled to find that what she had thought was the church hall was, in fact, the church.

"We still use the little church, as a chapel," said Reverend Rettger. He was short, with a broad face, low-set ears that stuck out, and fluffy white hair around a bald spot. He had the kindest blue eyes Betsy had seen in a long while. "It was the first church built in Excelsior, so we want to preserve it," he said in his mild voice. "We use it for early-Sunday services and small weddings and funerals. But of course you'll want to use the big church for Margot." He started to lead her back to his office.

Betsy frowned. "I will?"

"Of course. And the church hall after, for coffee. Half the town will come, and people from all over the area."

"They will?"

The blue eyes twinkled. "You haven't been keeping up with your sister's activities for a while, have you?" He opened the door to an outer office. "Hold my calls, Tracy."

"Yes, Reverend."

He gestured Betsy through the door to his office. "She was a driving force in this town," he continued, following her in and closing the door. "She worked to improve the Common, to run the art fair, to aid the schools, to build this new church and repair the chapel, to get better fireworks for our Fourth of July celebration, to raise money for various fund drives."

Betsy allowed him to seat her in a very comfortable leather chair, one of a pair. His office, while not large, was light and airy. She said, "I went with her to a committee meeting to hold a fund-raiser for a child in need of heart surgery. I didn't realize she did a lot of this sort of thing."

"She wouldn't have thought it a lot, she was always pushing herself to do more. Yet she was very patient with the rest of us, who couldn't keep up."

"Sounds like her eulogy should be given by you."

Rettger gave a little bow from his seat facing her—he hadn't gone behind his desk. "I'd be honored. I have known her a long while, and her husband even longer. Have you spoken with a funeral director?"

"Yes, Mr. Huber. He's taking Margot to be cremated right now. When can you find time in your schedule for the funeral?"

Rettger's white eyebrows lifted. "No visitation?"

"I can't afford it. I want a no-frills funeral service here, and then burial in the same plot as her husband."

Rettger appeared to be about to say something, then visibly repressed whatever it had been and said, "Let me show you the two burial services of the Episcopal church. You have some decisions to make."

It was not unlike selecting a wedding service. There was a framework of ceremony, with options in the hymns and readings. Rettger said, "I want to assure you that there are people in this congregation who are going to insist on having a part in the service. They would be insulted at the notion that you might offer to pay for their efforts." His mild voice and kind eyes took the sting out of his words.

"All right, that's fine," replied Betsy. "Now, I know 'Amazing Grace' is a cliché, but we both loved that hymn." A huge lump suddenly formed in her chest and sought to climb up her throat. But she swallowed it and went on.

Rettger took notes as Betsy made her choices, but had a suggestion of his own for the Old Testament reading, not one of the options. Betsy agreed to it— why not? His intentions seemed at least benign, and surely he knew what he was doing. The funeral was set for Sunday afternoon. "We'll have to form a committee to let people know," he said. "It will be my great honor to take care of that for you."

"Thank you."

Even forewarned by Reverend Rettger, Betsy was astonished at the turnout. She recognized the mayor and decided the people with him must be others from the city government. Shelly was there, with a contingent of women who might be fellow stitchers, or perhaps some of the part-time crew. The crazy lady—what was her name? Potter, Irene Potter—sat behind Betsy, dressed in a shapeless navy-blue dress, dabbing a handkerchief edged in black crochet lace to her eyes and sighing audibly.

There were children and adults and elderly, people dressed beautifully and people dressed very casually, and even some dressed rather shabbily.

Betsy had a black dress, but it was for cocktails, not funerals. So she wore an old purple suit that was too hot.

The music stopped and Reverend Rettger came out. To her astonishment, he was wearing white vestments. Then she noticed he had covered the beautiful funeral urn with a white cloth heavily embroidered in gold. What does he think this is? thought Betsy angrily. We're here to bury Margot, not confirm her.

A small, good choir did a lovely arrangement of "Amazing Grace," which was not spoiled by everyone joining in. Except Betsy, whose breathing had gone all strange, so that she couldn't sing. I'm going to cry at last, she thought. But she didn't.

The first reading, from Proverbs, was done by Mayor Jamison. It was the one suggested by Rettger.

A wife of noble character who can find?
She is worth far more than rubies.
Her husband has full confidence in her. . . .
She selects wool and flax
and works with eager hands. . . .

Some in the congregation began reacting with sounds suspiciously like snickers.

She gets up while it is still dark;
she provides food for her family
and portions for her servant girls. . . .
She sees that her trading is profitable,
and her lamp does not go out at night.
In her hand she holds the distaff
and grasps the spindle with her fingers.

Now Betsy was sure she heard a giggle.

She opens her arms to the poor
and extends her hands to the needy.
When it snows, she has no fear for her household;
for all of them are clothed in scarlet.
She makes coverings for her bed;
she is clothed in fine linen and purple.
Her husband is respected at the city gate,
Where he takes his seat among the elders of the land.
She makes linen garments and sells them.
And supplies the merchants with sashes—

That last line sent everyone over the border and there was audible laughter. The mayor himself was grinning. Betsy felt her cheeks flame. How dare they! And how dare Rettger persuade her to allow this reading! She wanted to crawl under the pew—no, she wanted to stand up on it and shout at them to shut up, shut up! But she sat in shamed silence as the reading went on and on.

She is clothed with strength and dignity;
she can laugh at the days to come.
She speaks with wisdom,
and faithful instruction is on her tongue.

Betsy heard a sound and looked over. She saw Jill and Shelly and some other women. Tears were streaming down their smiling faces. Those tears gave her the courage to sit through the rest of the service.

The urn was carried out in Mayor Jamison's arms like a stiffly wrapped baby, the priest leading the way, the choir singing, "All we go down to the dust; yet even at the grave we make our song: Alleluia, alleluia, alleluia." No, no, no, thought Betsy, her heart a stone in her breast, not alleluia, how can they sing alleluia!

After the ugly work at the cemetery, Betsy sat on a metal folding chair and looked at the raw earth covering the gorgeous urn she'd paid so much money for, that contained all that was left of her beloved sister. Everyone else had gone now, gone to eat and drink and be glad it wasn't they who were reduced to ashes and buried deep underground.

She couldn't stay here, not in a town that turned a funeral into a joke followed by a party.

But what was she going to do? Where was she going to go?

She sat so long that her joints stiffened. It was hard to rise from the chair, and her knees were so stiff she nearly fell making her way to the narrow dirt lane that wound around the hill and down to the street, down which she stumbled, back to the empty apartment, there to fall across her bed and descend immediately into sleep.

Hudson Earlie stood beside the coffee urn, cup and saucer in hand, watching the crowd. Big turnout, which was to be expected, of course. And it had gotten cheerful, as these things tended to do. He hadn't seen the grieving sister, though. Not a bad-looking woman, if you liked them with a little meat on their bones, which he did when no one was looking. She had some intelligence and sophistication to her, too, which he also liked occasionally.

But she was too old, only five or six years younger than he was. He had a strict rule that the women in his string not be older than thirty-five.

Which was too bad in this case, as this one might be the sole heir of her sister's estate, which he knew was considerable.

"Hud, whatever are you thinking about?" said a voice beside him.

"Me? Thinking? You know me better than that," he jested quickly, grinning at Shelly Donohue.

"Seriously," she said.

"I was thinking how the museum would miss Margot. She was on the board, you know, and she brought some good, businesslike attitudes with her to meetings. And I liked her myself—" He had to stop and swallow. That surprised him, and he took a sip of his coffee to clear his throat. "She was a hardworking, capable woman," he concluded.

Shelly nodded. "Yes, she was a terrific friend as well as a good boss. I loved working in her shop. That reading at the funeral had me bawling like a little kid, the one about wool and flax and dressing her servants in scarlet when winter comes. That's from Proverbs, did you know that?"

"No, I didn't."

"I thought Proverbs was all one-liners of advice, like fortune cookies. But that was a long one. And it described Margot so well! Even about the sashes—did you get that?"

"Yes, it came up at Christopher Inn the other night."

They'd held a Founders' Day parade last year, and Margot had helped with costumes. One thing she had done was make sashes for the people who were playing founder George Bertram, and the Reverend Charles Gilpin, and schoolmistress Jane Wolcott, so people would know who they were.

"I don't think her sister is going to be the one to replace her," said Shelly.

"It would take four people to do what she was doing," said Hud.

"Too bad, what happened to her." This was a new voice, and they turned to see Irene Potter in her dark dress and alert face, a cookie stuffed with M&Ms in her slim fingers.

"Terrible," said Shelly.

"What do you suppose he hit her with?" asked Irene.

"Irene!" scolded Shelly.

"Does it matter?" asked Hud.

"Whatever it was, he took it away with him. I was just talking to the detective in the case. He's here, you know. Says it's true murderers always come to the funeral of their victims."

Hud opened his mouth, but Irene talked right over anything he might have said. "I was wondering if maybe Margot didn't bring it down with her, to scare him off with, and he grabbed it away and hit her with it."

"Stop it, Irene!" Shelly turned and walked away and Hud quickly made an excuse to leave her as well. When Irene got into one of her "speculating" moods, there was no talking to her about anything else. You just had to let her get over it.

Reverend Rettger watched this exchange as he sipped the coffee. He was unhappy that Ms. Devonshire had insisted on being left at the cemetery. The manner in which she refused almost made him think she was angry with him, which he knew was impossible. He had thought that when she saw how the congregation reacted to the Proverbs reading, she would understand that everyone present stood eager to give her comfort and aid of any sort. But she seemed to be in a mood to resist any help. He'd seen grief in many forms, but the sort that resisted comfort was the saddest kind.

Of course, she had reason to be angry, her sister being taken from her in such a sudden, dreadful way. Perhaps if the police were to find and arrest her murderer quickly—it was probably one of those teenagers who would be unable to explain himself, unfortunately so common nowadays. It was small satisfaction to a bereaved family, to learn that the captured murderer could only shrug when asked why.

Irene watched Shelly join another group. What was the matter with her? Just a few days ago she'd joined eagerly in speculating about Betsy and Margot. Speculation—Irene didn't call it gossip—was so interesting, and it was great to have found someone who liked it even more than she did. Why did people do what they did? Whatever were they thinking? Irene, perhaps because people were such a mystery to her, never tired of speculating about them.

Why on earth had Margot gone charging into her shop? She hadn't brought a knife, or she would have been stabbed. Irene thought about that, the blood spattering all over the walls—she'd seen a photo once of a crime scene and been quite shocked.

But Margot hadn't been stabbed; she'd been mashed in the head. They'd done an autopsy. But she couldn't speculate on the autopsy, she didn't know how they were done.

So instead she pictured the darkened, ransacked shop, and Margot striding in, hand up, holding a golf club. Margot didn't golf, but her husband had been an avid golfer, which made it kind of strange that he had joined the Lafayette Country Club, with its piddly nine-hole course. Of course, the Lafayette was a very prestigious club, and with such a pretty building. And the setting was quite beautiful, the lake on three sides. Irene had been out there once, as a guest.

But that wasn't relevant. It was the golf club that was relevant. Widows, Irene (who was a spinster) speculated, were inclined to hang on to some of their late husbands' favorite things. So at the back of a closet in that apartment was Aaron's golf bag. What was it Margot had grabbed? A mashie? A nine iron? Irene had heard those were the names of golf clubs. Too bad Shelly—whose former husband was a golfer—didn't want to speculate on this; it would have been very enjoyable.

Joe Mickels drank his coffee and thought. Awful the way Margot had died, he'd agreed six or seven times with people about that. And murder was an ugly thing, to be sure.

But she was gone, really, truly, wholly gone. Forever; and he no longer had to scheme to find ways to make her move out.

How long should he wait before he served notice on the sister to vacate? Not too soon, or the whole town would come down on his neck, and he didn't need any more ill will. But there was a lot to be done, arrangements to be made. Clear the building, remove anything salvageable; find a contractor who wouldn't charge an arm and a leg to tear that old place down. It could be done by Christmas, surely. And maybe by spring the architect's drawings would start coming to life. He meant to put up a high-rise with stores on the ground floor, offices on the second and third, condos above that. First high-rise in Excelsior, a historic building from the git-go. And cut deep in the stone above the entrance: THE MICKELS BUILDING.

And it would make money, more money than he'd made to date, which was already more money than anyone but his accountant knew, more than most people saw in their lifetimes. What a kick it was, making money. The first two million were the hardest, that was what old Aaron Berglund used to say. But he was wrong; what was hardest was parting with hunks of it trying to make more of it. Mickels hated parting with money, even more than he hated pretending he was basically doing good, improving the community, helping his fellowman, and that the money was just sort of a side effect.

As a local radio host liked to say, B as in B, S as in S.

He was making money, first and foremost. If others rode his coattails, or got good out of what he was doing, that was fine, sometimes it was even necessary, but that wasn't what he was doing.

And now the pigheaded impediment to his biggest project was at last out of the way, and he was going to make great heaps of money from that property.

He found himself breathing a little too audibly and buried his nose in the coffee cup. He'd waited for over a year for a way to open and now it had. How long, O Lord, how long did he still have to wait?

Eight

❖

It was just starting to get light when Betsy woke, stiff and grubby from sleeping in her clothes. She'd slept nearly fourteen hours. She rose, got undressed, put on a nightgown, and tried to go back to bed. But though she felt exhausted, she was awake, at least for now.

She went into the kitchen and had another fight with the coffeemaker. This fight was shorter than the first, and more in the nature of a quarrel—after all, the manufacturer hoped people would like its product and recommend it to friends, and so it had to make its features accessible even to people whose sisters had thrown away the manual. Soon a rumble and wakening fragrance filled the kitchen. While it worked, Betsy took a shower. She put on her oldest jeans and sweatshirt, combed her wet hair straight back, and went toward the warm smell of coffee barefoot.

She filled a mug, doctored it shamelessly with milk and sugar, and went into the living room. She went to the front windows and lifted the layers of coverings to peer out. It was raining again, and the sky was that dreary dark color that indicated serious intent to rain all day. She turned away and curled up on the love seat. Time to begin planning.

Mr. Huber at the funeral home had wondered if Betsy had talked yet with Margot's lawyer. And Margot had mentioned him, too, as her ally against Joe Mickels, the evil landlord. What was his name? One of those old-fashioned English names. Penwiper? Wellworthy? Never mind, his name would be around here somewhere. She'd call him today. He could tell her how to access Margot's accounts, close them out. How to get the shop put out of business. How to do a legal going-out-of-business sale.

There were no heirs, except herself. She and Margot had remarked on that one time, how there were no other descendants of this branch of the family. She looked around. All this furniture was hers, and if Margot had paid the September rent, then perhaps Betsy could stay through the month.

But she wouldn't stay here in Excelsior longer than that. And she would probably have to sell the furniture, which was sad, because there were some nice pieces, but they'd bring a good price, and she needed the money.

She tried to think of where she wanted to go. New York City? Like California, it cost the earth to live there. Besides, she was pretty sure she'd outgrown both New York and California.

She needed someplace cheap. She wasn't used to winters anymore, so someplace south. Not Phoenix, too hot. Ditto Florida. Besides, Florida had hurricanes and the people were a little too handy with firearms. Ditto Texas. Arkansas, someone once had said, was very inexpensive. And the Ozarks were both beautiful and relatively cool in the summer. "Not everyone in Arkansas lives in trailer parks," he'd said. "There's a long waiting list." They'd laughed and laughed at that.

But that was where she was going to end up, probably. On that waiting list.

The doorbell rang. Betsy frowned and went to the door of the apartment. There was only a button, not an intercom. Still frowning, she pressed it.

In a minute someone knocked on the door and she opened it a fraction, keeping one set of toes pressed firmly against it.

"Hi, Betsy, it's me, Jill."

"What do you want?"

"To talk to you. Please, it's important."

Reluctantly, Betsy released the door. "Come in," she mumbled, and returned to the love seat.

After shedding a raincoat, Jill detoured into the kitchen and poured herself a cup of coffee, then brought it with her to the comfortable chair. She hesitated very briefly before sitting down in it, and with an almost ceremonial gesture shifted the needlework holder farther out of her way. She was wearing slacks and a soft gray flannel shirt, which made her fair hair look almost silver. "How are you doing?" she asked quietly.

"I don't know. Okay, I guess."

"When are you going to reopen the store?"

"I'm not. I have to get in touch with Margot's lawyer to find out how to get everything shut down and sold off."

"Why?"

"There's a silly question! Because I don't know how to run a business—especially a needlework store!"

"You've done fine the times I've come in and found you behind the counter. Besides, we can help you."

"Who's 'we'?"

"First and foremost, the people Margot hired to work in the shop. Some of them have worked in that place for years and know all about running it. And there's the Monday Bunch."

" 'Monday Bunch'?"

"Today's Monday, so you'll meet them today. They'll turn up around two. They meet to talk and do needlework. Give advice. Help out. Buy supplies. When it's my day off, I join them. Like today. But I decided to come over early to warn you they'll be here, and see if there's anything that needs doing. Have you been into the shop?"

Betsy felt her shoulders tighten. "I don't want to go down there."

"What, you think the police are going to clean up?"

Betsy thought to reply sharply, and instead asked with genuine curiosity, "Who cleans up after a murder?"

"Unfortunately, that's left to the survivors. There are companies you can hire to clean up horrible messes, like after an ax murder or deaths that don't get discovered for weeks and weeks."

"Please!"

"You asked. You don't want to hire someone in this case, unless you can find someone who also knows floss and silk and wool and canvases, so they don't just dump it all in bags and toss it. And, of course, you'd have to supervise them if they do know about it so they don't walk off with the good stuff."

"Sure. Okay."

"You don't have to do it right this minute, of course."

Jill's tone seemed familiar, and Betsy glanced up. Was there the merest hint of a twinkle in those ice-blue eyes?

Still. "I just can't go down there, Jill."

"Sure you can. I'll come with you. Come on, let's go right now and see how bad it is. Up, up, on your feet. Whoops, shoes first, want me to fetch them?"

Jill in this mode was like a bulldozer, and Betsy was too exhausted to resist.

The shop was even worse than Betsy remembered. The damp air seemed to have gotten into all the fibers, dimming their colors and making them sink down on themselves in hopeless tangles. Even turning on all the lights didn't help; it only made the ruin clearer.

The long triple row of wooden stems on the wall that had held skeins of needlepoint wool was nearly empty, and some of the stems were broken. Most of the wool was in a crooked, broken drift along the floor, as if someone had scuffed his feet through it.

Pyramids of knitting yarn had been kicked apart, baskets crushed and broken, magazines torn. The burglar didn't seem to have missed any opportunity to wreak havoc.

"What, was he angry at something?" wondered Betsy aloud.

"Some burglars get upset when there's nothing of value to steal," said Jill, squatting beside a heap of knitting wool and starting to untangle skeins from a webbing of loose yarn.

"Then why did he break in in the first place?" demanded Betsy. Goaded by Jill's labors, she went to the wall where the drift of wool was and stooped to begin sorting by color. The skeins were not actually skeins, but working lengths gently knotted by color. Betsy remembered a customer who had bought a single strand of orange, all she needed to finish a project. The wool was soft in her fingers.

"Because he's a burglar; that's what they do."

They worked in silence for perhaps ten minutes, then Betsy said, "Could it be he was looking for something?"

"For what?"

"I don't know. But the way things are all pulled off the shelves and walls—it's just odd, somehow. It would have to be something small, I guess."

Jill said impatiently, "What could he have been looking for, small *or* big? Nothing in the store is hidden; all the stock is on display." She had found a usable basket, dented on one side, and was putting intact balls of knitting yarn into it.

"Yeah, well, I wonder if anything's missing."

"You'll have to take an inventory."

"I suppose so."

"We'll help," said Jill, apparently sensing her dauntedness.

"Who, you and the Monday ladies? I thought you said not to trust people who knew silk from wool."

Jill did not reply to this, and after a moment's reflection Betsy realized how insulting that sounded, but she did not take it back or say anything more.

They had made barely a dent in the mess by lunchtime, when, prodded by her conscience, Betsy took Jill upstairs and made a tuna salad to share with her.

While putting the plates in the sink, Betsy heard Jill say something and turned off the water to ask, "What was that?"

"I said, where's Sophie?"

Betsy felt a sudden chill. The cat!

"Did she follow us down to the shop?" inquired Jill.

Betsy shook her head. "I haven't seen her for a long time. Days. Since . . . since that night. Since Margot."

"What?" Jill was staring at her.

"I forgot all about her. I'm sorry, but it's true, I haven't seen her since I left that evening to pick you up." She felt stricken.

Jill seemed about to say something, changed her mind, and said instead, "This is very . . . odd. You know how she is when it gets to be suppertime and there's nothing in her dish."

"Indeed, yes. But maybe—does she go off by herself?"

"No; never. I wonder if—no, if she had somehow gotten locked in the shop, she would have come out as soon as we came down there, crying over being left so long." Jill, frowning, began opening floor-level cabinets and looking inside. "Maybe she's scared and hiding because Margot hasn't come home. Have you heard a cat crying?"

"No. I would have been reminded if I heard her, and gone looking."

"Yes, of course you would. Well, this is really strange." Jill closed the last cabinet door, and puffed her cheeks then released the air slowly. "It's darned odd, in fact."

"Maybe she is down there, in the store," Betsy said. "Maybe she got kicked or stepped on or—something."

They hurried down the stairs and through the back hall into the shop. A thorough search proved fruitless.

"Well, I'll be dipped," said Jill.

"Whatever could have happened to her?" Betsy, shying away from worry over Sophie's fate, began instead to consider this as a piece of the greater puzzle. "She was here Wednesday. Margot was out all day, she went to the museum and then somewhere else, she didn't get home until after we closed up, and then she was in a hurry to get changed to go do her presentation at City Hall. So that day I fed Sophie both her breakfast and her supper. I remember Sophie followed me downstairs to the shop in the morning, and came back up with me at lunchtime, hoping for a snack. Which I was told I shouldn't give her, so I didn't. And she came up with me again when the shop closed at five, and I fed her supper."

"And she was in the apartment when you left?"

"Yes, she followed me to the door as I was leaving for your place. Margot was still there." Betsy stooped to pick up the sorted clusters of wool and put them on the table. "Jill, do you know if Margot actually went to City Hall?"

"Yes, that was checked. The council meeting started around seven-fifteen and broke up a little after nine-fifteen. Some members stood around talking with her for half an hour or so, and then Mayor Jamison offered her a ride home; but it had stopped raining and she said she wanted to walk." Jill went to the white dresser and began carefully lifting out painted canvases, shaking her head over the ones badly bent by being caught in a drawer.

"Where else did she go that day? Do you know?"

"She went to the Minneapolis art museum."

"Yes, but would that take all day? How long does it take to make one of those needlepoint canvas paintings?"

Jill shrugged. "I don't think she was going to paint it, just do some sketches, take notes. I don't know how long that takes."

"Not all day. I wonder where else she went? Who else she saw?"

"You can ask around, I guess. Probably Mike has already."

Betsy said, "Well, we know she didn't see someone in the shop on her way home and go in to confront him."

"We do?"

"Yes, because now we know Sophie was with her. She had to go upstairs and then hear something and come down with the cat. Probably she heard the noise he made breaking in."

Jill said, "The lock wasn't forced, or the door broken. The assumption is, he tried the front door and it wasn't locked."

"It was locked, I locked it when I closed up."

Jill didn't say that maybe Betsy only thought she locked it, but her face showed it.

"I did lock it," repeated Betsy stubbornly.

"Okay, you locked it," said Jill. "He picked the lock. But about Sophie: I think you must be right, she came down with Margot. And was frightened by what followed, and ran out the open front door. You said you found it partly open."

"Yes, that's true. But, Jill, if I was going to sneak downstairs to see if there was a burglar, I sure wouldn't bring a cat with me."

Jill shrugged. "Maybe Margot opened the door, and Sophie sort of darted out. And maybe Margot didn't see her."

Betsy snorted. "Not see her? Twenty pounds of white longhair who insists on leading the way? Anyhow, Sophie doesn't dart, she ambles."

Jill shrugged again and returned to lifting out canvases.

"No, listen to me," said Betsy. "I'm trying to picture how this happened. Margot's just gotten home—"

"How do you know that?" interrupted Jill. "Maybe she'd been home an hour."

"Maybe, she got home at ten and I got home at eleven. But she was the kind who takes off her good clothes right away. She would put on something casual to lounge around in, or her pajamas if it was close to bedtime. But she was wearing her good clothes—" Betsy paused to swallow, then shook her head determinedly and continued, "So she hadn't been home more than a couple of minutes. Now, suppose she heard someone breaking in downstairs and decided to go down and get a description for the police. Apart from that being one of the dumber things you can do, it's beyond belief that she'd bring a cat along. Even if she did open the door and Sophie walked out, you'd think she'd have got in front of her and herded her back inside. Sophie's a good cat, she lets herself be herded. Anyone with brains would have done that; you don't want a big white cat going ahead and letting the burglar know someone's coming, *or* hanging around your ankles and tripping you, *or* getting in the way in case you have to hurry back to the apartment and call the cops. *Which* is what she would have done in the first place, so I don't understand why she ended up down here to begin with!" Betsy had been getting more heated in her argument as she became more convinced of its soundness.

She turned away from Jill's doubting look and walked toward the back. She paused by the big heap of yarn, floss, packets of thread wax, yarn organizers, scissors, magnets, and bead nabbers, leavened with counted cross-stitch graphs, needlework books and magazines, then turned to reach for the nearest upholstered chair and put it back on its feet facing the mess. She sat down and reached for a fistful.

"This is just terrible!" she continued in the same angry voice, lifting her arm high and wriggling it to shake a packet of soft thimbles off. Soft thimbles belonged on the other side of the back area, with the counted cross-stitch stuff. So things weren't just tumbled off shelves, they were kicked or even carried around and dropped. "It must have taken the burglar hours to get things this tangled up!" she grumbled.

She looked again at the heap, dropped everything, and said in an entirely different voice, "Now, that's *really* crazy."

"What is?" Jill had come to turn the other chair over.

"All this stuff piled up here." Betsy gestured at the mess in front of her. "If he was doing this for hours before Margot came in and stopped him, why didn't she notice it when she came home? Because there would have been a light on. He couldn't do this thorough a job in the dark."

"Flashlight," said Jill.

Betsy thought, then nodded. "Okay, flashlight. He sees her shape as she passes the window and turns it off. But how about this? When they brought me in to identify Margot, she was there." Betsy pointed toward the back wall, where there was a dark stain on the carpet, which until now she had almost succeeded in not noticing. "And see the edge to the way this stuff is heaped up? It looked that night as if she'd been buried in it, and they had to uncover her."

Jill nodded. "They did, Mike told me that. And?"

"So that would mean he kept on trashing the place *after* he killed her, dumping stuff on top of her. If he was angry there was nothing to steal, wouldn't killing the owner be enough? I mean, doesn't hitting someone over the head sort of take away anger and make you start to worry about going far away really fast?"

For the first time Jill really looked interested.

"No," Betsy continued, "he was looking for something, that's why he tore the place up. I think he came in here specifically looking for something. And he killed Margot and then kept on looking."

"But what?" said Jill. "There isn't anything secret or hidden in the store.

Margot kept her valuables upstairs. Are you telling me she had some kind of secret?"

"If it was a secret, why would she tell me?"

Jill said, mildly exasperated, "If she did have a secret, she wouldn't go hiding an important clue to it in her shop, where people come and go all the time."

"Maybe she didn't know it was a clue."

Now Jill was totally back to disbelief. "Yeah, right; Margot had a secret, and she had a clue to it she didn't know was a clue; nevertheless she hid this clue she didn't know she had in her store. But someone knew she had it and that it was hidden in here. That sounds like a plot for the worst mystery novel ever written."

But Jill's sarcastic tone only fed Betsy's stubborn certainty that there was something wrong with the burglar theory.

On the other hand, she didn't know what else to offer as proof. She said nothing, and got serious about picking up and sorting.

Jill apparently didn't know what else to say, either, and went back out front to work. The two continued sorting wool and cotton yarn, thread, and floss by color, picking up canvases and fabric and smoothing them on the table, finding magazines that were only rumpled instead of torn, putting crushed baskets into a pile, sorting thimbles (soft and metal), knitting needles and crochet hooks on the desk, and wrapping loose yarn around their hands. At two, they heard someone knock at the front door.

Jill went to unlock and open the door, and stand back to let three women and their umbrellas come in. They were middle-aged ladies in slacks, complicated sweaters, and bright head scarves, each carrying a bulging canvas tote bag. They stood inside the shop, staring with dismayed faces at the wreckage.

Jill introduced them as "Patty, Alice, Kate," and said they were from the Monday Bunch.

Betsy came to say an uncomfortable hello. She was in no mood to host a gathering, and in any case didn't know what was expected of her with this group.

"We are so dreadfully sorry about Margot," said one of them, starting them all off on expressions of sympathy.

Betsy didn't know what to say to that, either. "Thank you," was all she could think of, said over and over.

"Well," said the stoutest of them at last, putting her bag and purse on the table. "Where do you want us to start?"

"How about you go up in front, Pat," said Jill immediately, "and pick up all those buttons and the bead packets. Put the whole packets into this basket, and the loose beads into this jar. And you, Kate, sit down here and I'll bring you the loose yarn as I gather it, and you can start making balls. If it's dirty, set it aside—here's a wastebasket. And Alice, come over here, we've got all this perle cotton on the floor, see what you can salvage." Jill went back to rescuing canvases and Betsy to sorting and smoothing graphs. With five people working, in half an hour there was a noticeable difference in the shop.

Betsy was glad she was in the back of the shop so her inability to contribute to the conversation going on up front wasn't as noticeable. The women discussed the best catalog source for patterns, how old the grandchildren had to be before teaching them to stitch, whether or not Aida came in twenty-five count, what to do when your knitting yarn starts to kink, needleworkers who had shamefully messy backs on their projects, overdyed versus watercolors, small laying tools—until Jill (apparently hearing the silence from the back of the room) said, "Can't we talk about something besides needlework?" which surprised them as much as it gratified Betsy.

Obediently, one said, "I saw they caught that man who stole that painting."

"What painting?" asked another.

"A famous one. It was being delivered to Sotheby's New York for an auction, and he took it right off the truck. A Monet?"

"It was a Manet," said Betsy, glad at last to be able to contribute. "And they found the painting first, which led them to the thief. Apparently the buyer reneged."

There was a silence. Betsy looked around the shelves to find them all looking at her inquiringly. "Margot wrote to me about it," said Betsy. "She said that when a valuable painting like that disappears, it very often is stolen to order. When someone with more money than morals wants a Rembrandt or a Monet or a Rubens, he mentions it to the right person, who will arrange to steal it. In this case, the buyer got scared for some reason and backed off. So the thief had to try to get rid of it through a dealer, and the dealer turned him in."

One of the ladies said, "How interesting," but not as if she meant it.

They worked in an uncomfortable silence until Betsy announced she was going to start the coffee urn perking and, for good measure, go upstairs for cookies. When she got back, the women were comfortably deep into a discussion of which was the best evenweave: luguna, jobelan, or jubilee.

Jill saw her coming and gave her an "I tried" shrug, to which Betsy replied with an "I understand" shrug back.

The women broke off their work and came gratefully to the table to drink and eat. "Nice coffee," said one.

"Good cookies," said another—kindly, because they had been bought at the bakery four days ago and there is only so much a cookie jar can do.

"I don't know who was responsible for that funeral, but it was quite, quite wonderful," said one of the women.

"I don't think I ever—" started another.

"Sophie's gone missing," interrupted Jill firmly, her eye caught by a pleading look from Betsy.

"What?"

"Yes, we've looked everywhere and we can't find her," said Betsy.

The ladies stared at Betsy.

"I'm sorry," apologized Betsy, not sure for what.

"Did you call the humane society?" asked one of the ladies, the one who had been rolling yarn. "That's where they take found animals."

"N-no," stammered Betsy, now aware of what she should be ashamed of.

"Of course she didn't, poor thing," said Jill. "She's had far bigger things on her mind."

The lady who had been rolling yarn put it down, went to the checkout desk, found the phone, and dialed a number. "I volunteer over there," she said while waiting for someone to answer. "Hi," she said into the phone. "We're looking for a lost cat—yes, it's me; hi, Merle. A lost cat. Last Wednesday, in Excelsior. A white Persian cross, pastel tortie on top of the head, along the back, and all of the tail. *Big* cat, close to twenty pounds, female spay, no front claws. Very friendly. No collar. Answers to Sophie and any sound that means food. Yes, I'll hold." She smiled at the others, and they all waited in silence. After a while she said, "Thanks," and hung up. "No cat matching that description found."

There was a collective sad sigh from the Monday Bunch.

"We can still get an ad in the weekly paper," said the woman who had been picking up buttons and beads. "And maybe if we put up posters—is there a photo of her?"

Betsy shrugged. "I don't know. I could look, I guess."

"I'm sure there is," said Jill; and to the bunch: "Remember those pictures Margot took at the Christmas party?"

That brought smiles and comments.

The humane-society volunteer said, "Give me the best one. I finally figured out how to use that scanner on my computer, and my son gave me a really nice publishing program for my birthday, so I can make up some attention-getting posters. We'll put them up right away. Why, it wouldn't be the same store without Sophie in it." She looked around, saw the faces looking back, and a little silence fell. It wasn't going to be the same no matter what, they all were thinking.

And Betsy didn't have the heart right then to say there wasn't going to be a shop at all.

Nine

❖

The shop looked almost normal, if you didn't look too close. Jill shut off the vacuum and one of the Monday Bunch pulled the plug. It was close to five o'clock. They had turned away six people; one, a part-time employee, was coming tomorrow to help with inventory.

"Count up what you have left, how much is ruined, and all that," said Jill, with a look in her eye that warned Betsy it still wasn't time to tell anyone she planned to close the shop.

"I think—" Betsy started to say anyway, but was interrupted by another knock at the door.

This time it was a handsome man of about thirty with fine dark eyes. He was standing under a big black umbrella, though it had stopped raining. He was wearing a good gray suit and carrying a large briefcase that looked older than he was.

"Hello, Mr. Penberthy," said Jill.

That was the name, this was Margot's attorney. Betsy had meant to call him today but hadn't gotten around to it.

"Ms. Devonshire?" he said, looking at Betsy.

"Yes?" she said.

"I was out of town, closing our cabin at the lake, and so missed this entire sad business of your sister's death. I was shocked to hear the news, and I hope you will accept my belated condolences." He spoke with a formality that somehow made him seem even younger.

"Thank you," said Betsy.

He made his umbrella collapse. "I hope you don't mind my just stopping by. I've been calling your apartment today without an answer, then someone told me you were in the shop." He put down his briefcase while he fastened the umbrella shut. "I live right across the street from you, so I decided to stop on my way home. Perhaps you know, I was Margot's attorney."

"Yes, I'd heard your name; how do you do, Mr. Penberthy?" Betsy extended her hand.

Penberthy had a nice, warm handclasp. The Monday Bunch began to make

hasty excuses for leaving. Pat—was it Pat?—went out waving the photo of Sophie and promising, "All over town by nightfall!" which made Penberthy blink
after her.

"Sophie's missing. Margot's cat," explained Betsy. "They're going to put up
posters."

"I hope you get her back," said Mr. Penberthy politely, and followed her
through the shop and up the back stairs to the apartment.

The lawyer declined the offer of a cup of coffee or a cookie, saying his supper was waiting.

He took a chair at the little round table in the dining nook and opened his
briefcase.

"How much do you know about your's sister's financial condition?" he
asked.

"Almost nothing," replied Betsy, and when she saw him notice how her fists
were clenched on the table, she dropped them into her lap.

"Do you know the names of any heirs besides yourself?" he asked.

"I don't think there are any."

Penberthy nodded. "Yes, Margot once told me there was only her sister.
That's the reason I could not persuade her to make a will, because everything
was going to come to you in any case." He pulled a thick file folder with the
name Margot Berglund on it from his briefcase. Betsy stared at it, then at Mr.
Penberthy, who was smiling.

"This won't take long," he reassured her. "Most of the papers in here have to
do with her ongoing quarrel with Mr. Mickels, the owner of this building."

"Yes, Margot told me about him, about how he's trying to get her to move
out and suing her for things. She said you were taking care of all that." She
added bitterly, "But I suppose he's won, now."

"That is not the case at all," he said.

Betsy hastily suppressed a triumphant smile. "I don't see how," she said.

"Well, first of all, there is this rather strange lease," said Penberthy, picking
quickly through the documents and finding it. It had been typed as an original on
ordinary typing paper, rather than filled in as a form or properly done on legal-size
paper. "This lease was, I believe, drawn up rather carelessly, probably by the original owner himself. It is my opinion that the lessor at that time felt the lessee
would not stay the full term of the lease." A glance showed she did not understand, and he started again. "That is, I don't think the original Mr. Mickels
thought your sister would stay in business very long. That's why the rent was set
so low, and that's why there are some curious omissions in the terms of the lease.
For example, he failed to include a restriction on the assignment of the lease.
That's where the current situation arises." Again he noticed she didn't understand.

"Normally a lease will state that the lessee—the renter—can't turn the lease over to someone else without the prior, written consent of the lessor—the landlord. This lease does not have that restriction. When your sister incorporated, she assigned the lease to the corporation, so it remains in force."

"What corporation?"

"Crewel World. Your sister incorporated herself, and named two officers, herself as president and you as vice-president."

"She did?"

"She didn't tell you about this?"

"No. When did all this happen?"

"She began the process some weeks ago, and only signed the final papers last Wednesday."

"She came to see you the day she died?"

He raised an eyebrow. "Why, yes, she did die on that Wednesday evening, didn't she? How . . . dreadful."

"I thought you were out of town that day."

"I left right after I finished with her, and didn't get back until late Sunday evening. Long Lake is three hours from here, and my cabin has no phone or electricity. My grandparents bought it in the twenties and added two rooms on to it, but preferred to get right away from modern conveniences. I spent many summers up there as a boy. When I inherited it, I kept it just as they had left it. It's a dozen yards from the lake, and there have been loons nesting near the dock for as long as anyone can remember—" Penberthy brought himself back from his vacation with a little start. "Sorry."

"Margot never mentioned incorporating to me," said Betsy.

"Perhaps she meant to tell you once it was all done, and . . . and never got a chance."

"Yes, that might be. What time did she come to see you?"

Penberthy took a few seconds to think about it. "Her appointment was for two o'clock, but she was about five minutes late, which isn't like her. She apologized, I remember."

"How long was she there?"

"Not very long. Perhaps half an hour. I had closed up and was on the road before three."

"Did she say where she was going next?"

"No, I assumed it was home." Penberthy looked around. "Are you going to keep the apartment, too? It hasn't got the same kind of lease the store has, you know."

"I don't know, yet."

"You are going to keep the shop open, aren't you?"

Betsy started to say no, but instead said, "I haven't finalized my plans. Does Mr. Mickels know about this incorporation?"

"I don't know how he could."

Her voice sharpened. "You mean she didn't tell him?"

"It is not required by law that she inform him ahead of time, if that's what you're asking. And again, I don't think there was time between the signing of the documents and . . . her demise."

"Then I know," she whispered. "I know. Thank you very much for coming by, Mr. Penberthy," she said, rising. "This has been very enlightening."

"But—" he began.

"Good-bye, Mr. Penberthy," she repeated, more firmly, and walked to the door.

He followed unwillingly. "I'll call you tomorrow," he promised. "There are still a great many details you need to be advised of."

"Okay. Or how about I call you later this week?" She all but pushed him out the door, closing it in his face as he turned to say something more.

Betsy slammed the door shut and ran to the phone. Margot had a list of phone numbers taped to the wall beside it, and Jill's number was first under the Cs.

Jill answered on the second ring, and Betsy said, "I got it, I knew there was something, and I've got it!"

"Got what?"

"The proof! Motive! Everything! Margot was murdered, I knew there was something funny about the whole burglary thing, and now I know who did it!"

"What are you talking about?"

"Mr. Penberthy was just here, and he told me about that legal business between Margot and Joe Mickels, over the lease. He wanted her out, she wouldn't go, there's a thick file of all the legal tricks he's been playing trying to get her out. So at last he just killed her!" Betsy made a huge gesture of triumph at the ceiling. "And now there's this incorporation thing! It's clear as daylight!"

"What are you talking about? How could Mr. Penberthy give you proof that Joe Mickels is a *murderer*?"

"Mickels tried every way he could think of to get Margot to give up and move out, but she wouldn't budge. And his threats turned ugly, so she decided to protect herself by incorporating—see, you can't murder a corporation! But she was waiting to sign the final papers before she told him—and he murdered her before she got a chance! Or maybe he somehow found out what she intended to do and tried to kill her before the deal could go through. Penberthy says Joe didn't know, don't you see? I told you that burglar idea was all wrong! And now we know he did it! Who do I tell, how do I get him arrested?"

"Betsy, Betsy, calm down. Take a breath, for heaven's sake. Tell me, exactly what did Mr. Penberthy say?"

"He doesn't know Joe Mickels did it, of course. But he showed me this thick file of legal stuff, the record of the fight Mickels and Margot have been having over the shop. Mickels wanted Margot to move out so he could tear down this building and put up a bigger one."

"Yes, I know. And?"

"Well, don't you see? Murdering Margot didn't do him any good. Margot finished incorporating, you see, and there was something wrong with the lease, some kind of assignment thing, which she did, so I get the shop. So it doesn't mean a thing, not a thing, that he murdered her!"

Jill, trying to understand, said, "So because it doesn't mean a thing, that's proof he murdered her?"

Betsy nearly shouted yes, then swallowed the word whole. Because that wasn't what she meant. What had she meant? Her "proof" that Mickels had murdered her sister was gone as suddenly as a hatful of smoke.

"Betsy?"

"Huh?"

"Are you all right?"

"I guess not." Betsy dropped the receiver back into its cradle and went to sit on the couch in the living room. What was the matter with her?

She remembered back when menopause had started, how she'd suddenly be overcome with some notion: to devote all her spare time to gardening or the study of medieval history, or becoming a vegetarian. She'd start with great determination and energy, only to wake from the vision in a week or a month and wonder what on earth she had been thinking of.

This seemed an echo of that curious time. Where on earth—she suddenly remembered that she was out of estrogen, had been for over two weeks. She'd meant to get here, find a doctor, get a new prescription, but of course all that had flown out of her head because of Margot's death.

So menopause was back. And where some people get hot flashes, Betsy got hot ideas.

She ran the conversation with Mr. Penberthy over in her head, looking for something that might actually point to Joe Mickels as a murderer.

What the attorney had given her was confirmation of the legal battle between her sister and her sister's landlord, and the incorporation trick Margot had pulled on him. Margot hadn't realized it might be important to tell Mickels right away. Well, maybe it wasn't important, maybe he wasn't the murderer. But there was the place Betsy had jumped off, assuming Margot was murdered because she failed to tell Joe Mickels. What had their mother called notions with no substance to them? Snow on your boots. Nothing but snow on her boots, sliding off as soon as you took two steps, melting as soon as you came inside.

No wonder Penberthy had stared at her so strangely. What he must have thought!

She suddenly realized that he had come to tell her about her sister's estate—and that they hadn't gotten to that. She was sure her sister wasn't rich, but maybe there was an IRA or life-insurance policy or something somewhere. And Betsy had wanted to ask what she needed to do to close the shop and turn whatever there was into cash so she could get out of this place.

She would definitely call Penberthy tomorrow. She went to the refrigerator and wrote on Margot's sheet of lined paper under Margot's magnet shaped like a sheep, *Call Penberthy*, and underlined it and put three exclamation marks after it. Then she started looking for something to fix for supper.

She hoped there was enough money to keep her in sandwiches until the closing sale was over. Funny she hadn't told Penberthy she wasn't staying.

Soon she'd have to figure out how to use Margot's computer. Margot had access to the Internet, and surely a search engine could find a Web site that would tell her how to get on that trailer-park waiting list.

J ill tried to lose herself in her current needlepoint project, but her concern about Betsy kept getting in the way of her concentration. The ultrasuede she was using for the horse's hide, not sturdy to begin with, kept getting frailer and frailer because she kept having to unstitch the section she was working on.

When she had first met Margot's sister, she had thought she was a live one, full of wit and good humor, just the kind of person she liked.

Now she was concerned for the woman's sanity. Betsy was shut down tight except for these nutso eruptions—Joe Mickels a murderer, for Pete's sake!

And wanting to close Crewel World. Well, that was more understandable. Betsy wasn't Margot and didn't have Margot's investment in Excelsior, and she didn't know how the store was a warm center of activity for the action-minded. Probably she wasn't a do-gooder like Margot had been in any case. And now the murder had taken away her chance to learn what Margot meant to the town and its people.

Jill put down the needlework. Whenever she was alone and any thought of Margot happened by, she had to stop whatever she was doing because her eyes filled. God, how she missed Margot! All her friends loved Margot's warmth and borrowed from her bottomless store of ideas and energy. But Margot and Jill had become closer than that. Jill was a good little Norwegian. She didn't show her emotions in public, or even to many close friends, but with Margot it had been different. With Margot she could let down all the barriers, talk about how tough it was being a cop, how her boyfriend was pressuring her to quit and start a family with him. And how tempted she was to do just that. Margot had listened, allowed Jill to talk until Jill herself understood that, for now, her sense of duty would not allow her to quit and be happy about it. But she had also nourished Jill's sense of humor until if Jill chose to laugh right out loud, laugh till her sides ached, that was okay, too. With Margot it was all right, with Margot—Jill sobbed once aloud, startling herself. Get a grip, she told herself. Get a grip.

It really wasn't fair that Margot should have died at the hands of someone who could have asked for her help and gotten it, gladly. Margot was always helping— kids with heart problems, people down on their luck, even Prisoner's Aid.

That did it; Jill broke down and wept bitterly. When the storm ended, she went to the bathroom and washed her face.

Back in the living room she picked up her project, found her place, and resolutely stuck the needle in. If she could get into the rhythm of the needlework, she would find peace. That's why she loved needlepoint—it worked like meditation. It was better than meditation, actually, because after a while you found you had both peace of mind and a work of art.

In another minute she was calm and could think some more about what Betsy had asserted. The woman had been right about one thing: Margot had no business sneaking down those stairs to see who was burgling her store. It was a stupid thing to do, and Margot was nobody's fool.

So maybe there was something to Betsy's insistence that there was more to this than Detective Mike Malloy was saying.

But if it wasn't a burglar, then—who? To think Joe Mickels had turned into a murderer in order to break a lease—that was ridiculous!

Yes, yes, Joe wanted Margot out of his building. Jill recalled when Joe had made one of his early moves, thinking that if he got everyone else out, Margot would surrender. So he had sent out eviction notices and soon, except for Margot, the place was empty. Little good it did him. Margot was one of those short, thin women who looked like dandelion fluff, but who was actually made of steel. She wasn't proud or needlessly stubborn, but she knew the real value of Crewel World: what it meant to the stitchers in the area, to the women of Excelsior—to all of Excelsior, really. She had come to her full strength and purpose after her husband died, and Joe had been a fool not to see that. He'd ended up getting new tenants for the other two stores, and new renters for the apartments. None of them seemed very worried about the month-to-month conditions under which they rented, probably because they were locals and knew something about Margot.

But greedy and impatient as Joe Mickels was, Jill couldn't believe he'd resort to murder.

No, this was just Betsy wild to find closure, to get someone arrested. Jill was sure this was some peculiar form of mourning, that what she needed to do was cry her eyes out—Jill had a feeling Betsy hadn't shed any tears over this yet—and then she'd straighten up.

But meanwhile, what if she called Mike?

Or contacted some reporter?

Lord, what a stink that would make!

Jill leaned sideways and lifted the receiver of the phone off its base on the end table. Dialing swiftly, she was rewarded with a busy signal. She disconnected, waited, and tried again. Still busy. She'd better get over there.

Ten

✥

Irene Potter struggled with her harried nerves until finally a good and necessary calm came over her. This was her great opportunity, and she must not, must not, must not mess it up.

She began quite coolly to reason this out, to be sure she was right in her plan of action.

Margot was dead, dead and buried, any quarrel between them gone, forgotten.

Excelsior had had a needlework shop for a very long time, and it was not right to discontinue that tradition.

Betsy Devonshire might be Margot's sister, but she didn't even know how to knit, and Shelly had said she didn't know anything at all about running a needlework shop.

Whereas Irene Potter knew everything about needlework, and almost everything about running a small business.

And she had over sixty thousand dollars in savings.

Therefore it was right, good, and proper that Irene should take over that shop.

Sixty thousand wasn't really enough, of course. Though if Ms. Devonshire was as ignorant as she seemed to be, it might do. If not, then it would serve as a down payment.

With her energy and knowledge, Irene knew she could make a much bigger success of a needlework shop than Margot. After all, Margot hadn't needed to make a living out of it, as Irene did. So it was clear that she, Irene Potter, should take over the needlework shop.

And when she did, then everyone would see that she was good at this! She'd show those people who said she wasn't any good with people! When they had to come to her, then they'd see; the shop would be wonderful, better than before, and everyone would love her for ensuring that the tradition continued.

That thought set off an almost painful excitement, and she had to stop and take several calming breaths. That made her smile. Jill was always saying that: take a breath. Amusement calmed her nerves to steadiness.

Then she got into her raincoat, took up her umbrella, made sure her savings book was in her purse, and left her room. Outside, on the sidewalk, she raised herself onto her toes, pivoted in the direction of the lake, and began walking.

Jill's sharp questioning had brought Betsy to her senses, but she still had felt restless, needing to do something. So she went down to the shop and found the list of employees and their phone numbers, brought it up, and started calling. Before long she found two more of them available to help with inventory tomorrow during the day. Also, Shelly could come after twelve, and another would come by after five to help Shelly take up where the day workers left off.

One of the part-timers who had done inventory before said it would take at least two days, maybe three if it was as bad as Betsy said. This person—a male, oddly enough—recommended she call the insurance agent, which she did (TWENTY-FOUR-HOUR SERVICE his calendar on the kitchen wall advertised). Betsy wasn't up to seeing him tonight, so he would also come by tomorrow.

The phone rang. It seemed as if every time she hung up, it rang again. It was, as before, someone with a cat they thought might be Sophie. This one, by the description, was a kitten.

"No, Sophie's big, really big. Huge," Betsy said. "But thank you for calling, and I hope you find the owner of the kitten."

She had no more than taken her hand off the phone when the doorbell rang. She went to push the button that released the lock. She should go down and unlock it and stick up a note: *Bring Alleged Sophies Up to Apartment One.*

So far two people had come by with cats. The first time, seeing the large heap of white fluff in the woman's arms, her heart had leaped with joy—but it hadn't been Sophie.

The second one, brought in a carrier, hadn't any white on it at all.

It was sad and disturbing to realize how many homeless cats there were in just this small town.

So she was really surprised when she opened the door this time and it was Joe Mickels standing there.

Betsy nearly slammed the door in his face, but restrained herself. Still, she managed a good degree of frost in her voice as she asked, "What do you want?"

"We've got some business to discuss, Ms. Devonshire," he said. His voice was calm, so decided a contrast to his fierce expression that it occurred to her his face looked that way naturally. "May I come in? This won't take long."

"Very well." She stepped back and led him into the living room. Because she did not want him to sit in her sister's chair, she took it, and when she did, he sat on the love seat.

"I understand you are taking inventory in the store."

"We haven't begun yet, we're still cleaning up after—" The words choked her, she could not finish the sentence. "Anyhow how did you find that out?"

He showed a fierce grin. "This is a small town."

"Then perhaps you also know I have spoken with Mr. Penberthy," she said, allowing the ice to show once more, "and he tells me we need to complete an inventory to close the estate."

"Any idea how long that will take?"

"At least three days."

"I can find some helpers if you need them to hurry things along, and to help you set up for the going-out-of-business sale. How about I let you stay in the apartment until everything's finished?"

Something about this offer of a favor got her back up. "What if I decide to keep the shop open?"

"Of course you won't decide that," he said, his certainty now reaching the insufferable stage. "You can't, since the lease ended when your sister died."

"You're wrong. I have the option of continuing the operation of Crewel World."

It was wonderful to see his color change, to watch his eyes widen, then narrow, to see the way the nostrils in that beak of a nose widened. "What idiot told you that?"

"Mr. Penberthy told me that Margot incorporated herself and 'assigned' the lease to the corporation. I was made vice-president of the corporation, and I can keep Crewel World open if I want to."

If she wanted proof that Mickels had not been told about the incorporation, she got it. He jumped to his feet and flung his hands over his head. His raincoat spread itself wide, making him appear enormous in the low-ceilinged room.

"That's not true!" he shouted. "I don't believe Penberthy told you that! This building is mine, this property is mine, and the lease died with your sister! You're out, d'you hear? Out! I'll get an eviction notice on you. You'll be out of that shop in thirty days, and this building will be gone before the ground freezes! I've waited too long for this, and I won't have you start in on me like Margot did!"

Betsy was on her feet now, too. Some little alarm was ringing, but she was beyond hearing it, and was about to make the big accusation when the alarm became a real sound, the sound of the doorbell pealing. It rang in one long noise that continued until she ran to push the door release.

She opened the apartment door to look out and see who had such an urgent need to see her.

In just seconds Irene Potter's excited face appeared in the stairwell, and when she saw Betsy waiting, she raised a thin arm to shake a wet umbrella at her. "I'm so glad to find you at home, Betsy!" she said, rushing up the stairs. "I have something exciting to tell you; I just could not wait!"

Betsy had to step aside or be sluiced down by Irene's wet raincoat as she brushed by.

Irene trotted into the living room, shedding water all the way and exclaiming about the weather and her breathless state. "I hurried over because I was afraid someone else might be talking to you, and I wanted to be the first if I could—" She stopped in mid-sentence to stare. "Why, Mr. Mickels, what are you doing here?"

"This is my building, I can come here if I like," he growled.

"Do you mean to tell me that you often call on your tenants?" Irene demanded, her tone suggesting she had a personal interest in his answer.

"I have business to discuss with Ms. Devonshire," he said, a little more mildly.

"Why, I'm here on business, too." Irene turned to Betsy. "No doubt you have heard that I am quite an expert needleworker," she began in a reasonable tone, but excitement got the better of her and she continued all in a rush, "and I want you to know that I have some private financial resources, and a great deal of experience in running a small business as both an employee of Crewel World and as former manager of Debbie's Gifts, so when you are ready to sell Margot's shop, I know you will give me right of first refusal."

"I'm tearing down the building," announced Mickels.

"What? What? But that would spoil everything!"

"If it spoils some nutty plan you've concocted, then I'm twice as glad I can do what I like with my own property."

Irene approached Mickels like a cat approaching a dog, but the man stood his ground. She came so close her forehead was nearly touching his nose. Then she lifted her face to his—for an instant Betsy was horrified to think she was going to lay a big wet one right on his lips—but she only said with quiet certainty, "I am going to be the new owner of the best needlework shop in this part of the state, maybe in the whole state, and if you get in my way, I'll hurt you!"

This statement was in such marked contrast to Betsy's first thought that she giggled. Both of them turned on her.

"What's so funny?" they asked in near unison.

"The both of you," said Betsy. "You're both hilariously wrong. I don't know what I'm going to do about the shop, but I doubt I will sell it to you, Ms. Potter; and until I decide, and so long as the lease is in effect, you can't evict me, Mr. Mickels."

She walked over to Margot's chair and sat down. "What's more, I am so greatly offended by the two of you squabbling over the shop like vultures that I think I'll do whatever I can to keep either of you from profiting from Margot's death. In fact—"

Again Betsy was interrupted by the doorbell. She rose to answer it.

"Can't you just ignore it?" implored Irene. "I have a great deal to say to you. I'm sure if you'll just listen a minute—"

"It's like goddamn Grand Central Station around here," Mickels growled.

"It may be someone bringing Sophie home," said Betsy, and she pushed the release button.

"Who's Sophie?" she heard Mickels ask.

Irene explained, "It's that nasty cat Margot allowed in her store. I won't have animals in my store."

Betsy opened the door and saw Shelly coming up the stairs. She was carrying something about the size of a large cat wrapped in newspapers.

"What do you have there?" Betsy asked apprehensively.

"A hot dish. I wanted to bring you one last Thursday, but someone said you weren't receiving visitors, so I brought you one tonight. It's diced chicken with onion and celery, mixed with cream of mushroom soup and green beans, and crispy onions on top. I hope you like it. I'll just put it in the kitchen. It's still hot, that's why I wrapped it in newspapers, to keep it hot." Her voice had become less and less certain of her welcome as she approached. "Have I come at a bad time?"

"Uh, well, I do have some people here."

"Then I'll just leave this on the counter."

"Shelly? Is that you?" Irene called.

"Hi, Irene. I brought a hot dish."

"I've already eaten. But come in for a minute, will you?"

Betsy wondered where on earth Irene got the notion the hot dish was for her. She must think Betsy was going to invite her to dinner. As if!

Shelly obeyed. "What's up?"

"I want you to tell Betsy what a good business head I have, and how good my needlework is."

"Her needlework wins blue ribbons all the time," Shelly said obediently, raising her eyebrows at Betsy.

"She wants to buy Crewel World," said Betsy.

"She'll have to find a new place for it," warned Mickels.

"Yes, I was afraid of that," said Shelly to Mickels, coming out of the kitchen. "Are you going to be okay, Betsy?"

"I think so, thanks."

"But I can make the store the talk of the county," Irene insisted, now arguing with all of them. "I've wanted to open my own store for years and years. You know that, Shelly, but Margot got hers started first, so there wasn't anything I could do till she got out of the way."

"That's a strange way of putting it, Irene," Shelly commented. "She didn't exactly decide on her own to step out of anyone's way. She was murdered." Her face was suddenly sad.

Irene shrugged. "Well, it's how I think of it. She wouldn't let me become her partner, so what could I do?"

"What do you mean?" asked Betsy sharply.

"What makes you think Betsy's going to sell Crewel World?" asked Shelly.

Irene turned to Betsy. "Of course you are, everyone knows that. You don't know how to run a store, and you don't know byzantine from basketweave."

Shelly said, "And you don't know how to be nice, Irene."

"I don't have to know how to do needlepoint to sell silk or cotton or metallic thread to people who do," said Betsy, who had been quick to pick up some terminology from her few days in the shop. She turned to include all three of them in her next words. "I think you should know there are some unanswered questions about my sister's death," she began, but before she could continue, the doorbell started ringing again. This time it rang in an urgent series of pulses that continued until she hurried to press the release button by the door.

"What the hell does that mean, there's 'unanswered questions'?" said Mickels from behind her.

"Who knows?" said Shelly. "This whole business is so horrible, we're all acting a little strange."

"I'm not," said Irene.

Betsy heard footsteps coming heavily up the stairs and opened the door.

Jill finished the last steps and hurried toward her. Her light-colored raincoat was rain-spattered and all bundled up in front, as if in her haste she had buttoned it wrong; and she held her arms across her breasts as if she were huddled against the wind or rain. "I found her," she said.

"Who?"

"Let me in, she's hurt."

"Who's hurt? What are you talking about?"

"It's Sophie." Jill brushed by her. "Find something I can put her down on," she ordered. "Quick!"

Betsy ran to the bathroom and brought back a large bath towel. She flipped it open and let it drape across the table in the dining nook. "Here," she said.

Jill ducked and maneuvered something out of her raincoat onto the towel. It was wet, filthy, and made a thin cry of protest.

"Oh, my God," Betsy whispered.

"Take it outside, quick!" cried Irene. "It's sick, it'll give all of us its germs!"

"She was by the Dumpster in back," said Jill. "I had to park back there, and when I got out, I thought I saw something move. I think she's hurt pretty bad."

Betsy bent over the animal. She took up a corner of the towel to wipe its forehead. The backs of her fingers brushed against a small ear. "Hot," she murmured.

"Fever," agreed Jill.

"I'll call her vet," Shelly offered.

The cat hardly looked like Sophie at all, except that it was large and had once, perhaps, been mostly white. The coat was a dirty gray, streaked with mud and dirt, the eyes wide and staring, and one back leg was misshapen in a strange way.

Mickels came to peer over Betsy's shoulder. "It's dying," he pronounced. "All a vet can do is put it to sleep, and he'll charge you money for that. Best just take it back outside and let nature take its course."

But Betsy continued wiping, down her back, on her side, down her front paws. "Oh, Sophie, Sophie," she crooned, wiping gently under the animal's chin. "Poor baby, poor suffering baby." She let the dirty edge of towel slip out of her hand and just used her fingers to stroke. The staring eyes began to close, the head to sink. Tears began gathering in Betsy's eyes; the cat was dying right here in front of her. She could hear Shelly speaking urgently on the phone. Should she stop her?

Her fingers paused.

"Awww, is she dead?" asked Jill.

"No," said Betsy, and burst into tears.

"She's dead, she's dead!" Irene cawed from the living room. "I'm going home, she's dead!" An instant later the door to the apartment slammed.

"I'm so sorry," said Jill, stooping to put a hand on Betsy's knee.

"No, no," said Betsy, through her sobs. "She's not dead, she's purring!"

Jill rose and put two fingers against Sophie's throat. "I'll be dipped," she said. "She *is* purring."

"It's just a damn cat," said Mickels. "It'll cost you plenty no matter what happens."

"Shut up, Joe!" said Jill. "Shelly, what's taking so long in there?"

"Hang on, hang on!" said Shelly. "Yes, I know where you are. About five minutes, I guess. Thanks, doctor." She came over to the table. "He'll meet us at his clinic out on Oak."

Jill carefully picked up Sophie, towel and all, and put her into Betsy's arms. "You're the miracle worker, she didn't purr for me. Let me get my car."

"Mine's out front," said Shelly, "and I know the way."

"Fine."

Shelly drove a big Dodge Caravan with doors that opened when she pushed a device in her pocket. "Slick," approved Jill. "Let's go."

Sophie purred faintly all the way to the vet's office, and continued purring on the examination table. The vet complained, half-amused, that he could not hear her lung sounds very well. She even purred through the pitiful cry she emitted when he tried to work her knee joint. He opened her mouth and said she seemed shocky. But, he also said, she did not seem in imminent danger of dying. She stopped purring only when he administered the anesthetic in order to set her broken hind leg.

Out in the waiting room, Betsy said, "What do you think, she was back there all that while? Why didn't she cry when we were out looking for her?"

"Hurt animals often hole up," said Shelly. "It's instinct for a hurt animal to hide from predators."

"Like we were going to eat her for dinner," snorted Jill. She added, "I wonder how she got hurt. Hit by a car, maybe?"

"Running out the open front door of the shop," Betsy agreed. "This is so wonderful, finding her alive, I was so worried. . . ." She began to cry again.

"Here now, that's enough of that." Jill put an arm around Betsy and rubbed her shoulders briskly. "She's going to be fine. Tell me, who were you on the phone with a while ago?"

"Who not? I've been getting calls all evening from people who thought they'd found Sophie. And people have been coming by with likely candidates." She hiccuped and smiled. "Unlikely ones, too. But now we have her, thanks to you. We'll have to go around tomorrow and take down the posters. And cancel that ad."

Jill said incredulously, "Joe Mickels and Irene Potter brought over some cats for you to look at?"

"No, Joe came to evict me."

Jill leaned in and asked quietly, "You didn't accuse him of murder, did you?"

"I tried to, several times, but kept getting interrupted."

"Good. Say, you didn't tell anyone else about this weird notion you've got, did you? Mike, for instance?"

"Who's Mike?"

Jill sighed in relief. "Never mind." She continued, "But don't go spreading that suspicion about Mr. Mickels around, okay?"

"Irene Potter is just as good a suspect, you know."

"Oh, for heaven's sake, now you're pointing at *two* innocent people! Listen to me, Betsy: it was a burglary that went really wrong. It's a tragedy, an ugly, senseless tragedy, but that's what happened. Please, please, stop making wild accusations. You can get your butt sued, and those two are just the ones to do it."

"You're probably right." Betsy sniffled.

Shelly rummaged in her purse and produced a clean if wrinkled piece of tissue. "Here, kid."

"Thanks." Betsy blew, wiped. "I know I've been acting crazy the last few days. And I want to thank you both for caring about me anyhow."

"That's what friends are for, right?" said Jill.

"That's right," said Shelly, rubbing Betsy on the back. "We're with you, we'll see you through all of this. There are a whole lot of us who want to be your friends, who want to do anything they can, because you're Margot's sister, and we loved her."

"Oh, Margot," Betsy whispered, and this time when she wept, it was for that terrible loss.

Eleven

❖

Betsy had been afraid she'd wake with a sick headache from all the weeping, or emotionally exhausted from all the talking and sharing, of the night before. She also anticipated a state of anxiety over Sophie, who had a badly fractured leg and remained in the care of the vet.

But instead she woke refreshed and lay a minute, stretching slowly, lengthily, enjoying the energy that tickled along her nerves. And also enjoying a new and welcome clarity of thought.

Once upon a time, years ago, Betsy had been a morning person. She had, as she told her sister, "gotten over that." But now she felt almost as if she were back in her twenties, when merely waking up meant a clear mind and high hopes for the new day.

And it was not cockeyed optimism here and now. Terrible as things were, they were not as bad as she had thought. There was hope, there was even a chance for future joy.

What a sad, blind mess she'd been! It was as if Margot's death had plunged her into deep, murky water, where she'd paddled unseeing, unable to find the bottom with her feet, afraid all those around her wished her ill—when all the while the bottom was solid beneath her feet, and she'd been surrounded by people who wanted to be her friends, if only for Margot's sake.

Margot was dead. Her kind and talented sister had been cruelly murdered, reduced to gray ashes, put into a beautiful jar, and buried in the same grave that held her beloved Aaron. Someday the jar would break, and her ashes would wash down through the soil to mingle with Aaron's.

Maybe she could think of an epitaph to put on the stone that would evoke that thought.

Probably she could afford to do that. Shelly and Jill had been emphatically sure of it.

She sat up and fumbled on the floor with her toes for her slippers. According to Jill and Shelly, those few thousand dollars Betsy had found in Margot's checking accounts were small indicators of a sizable money source. Jill said Margot's late husband had left her very well-off. Shelly said she'd chosen to live in this modest apartment because it was convenient to the shop, that she had sold a fine big house because it was too big and too much trouble for just her.

So Penberthy had better be first on the agenda today. He could confirm the size of the estate—and more importantly, how to get hold of some of it, to pay bills and rent and Sophie's medical bills, and buy food. Betsy couldn't live on Shelly's no-longer-hot dish forever.

There was a little bread left, and coffee; she would make toast for breakfast. Then she would call Mr. Penberthy, and apologize for her behavior the other night. And ask how soon she could see him.

And after that, she would go visit Sophie, who was going to be fine. Maybe even bring her home.

Hud Earlie leaned back in the comfortably padded executive chair in his office and thought for a while.

He'd had to resort to a far less reliable source this time. However, she was certain in her assertions that Betsy was a mess. Some things he already knew:

Betsy had shut out people trying to help her and had arranged the cheapest funeral she could for her sister. Now she was hysterical over a sick cat. That wasn't all: she had told her landlord he couldn't reclaim his property and at the same time she refused to listen to an offer that would get her out from under a business she didn't know how to run. And, possibly weirdest of all, Betsy had hinted that her sister's death was not just a burglary gone wrong.

He remembered the witty woman with the happy eyes at Christopher Inn. This sure didn't sound like her.

Though it did kind of sound like the wounded person he had seen at the funeral. Poor broken thing, obviously in need of comfort.

Maybe he should give her a call. They could discuss . . . . the fund-raiser, sure.

To hell with Margot's warning him off—she was dead. And to hell with his rules. What were rules for, if not to be broken?

And maybe he could be of some help to her.

Mickels sat at his desk in his office. He could have afforded a bigger desk in a large, well-lit corner office in a downtown Minneapolis tower. But why spend the money when he was just as comfortable in this little second-floor suite in Excelsior? Here he had three rooms, one with a window that overlooked Water Street. Years ago, at the bankruptcy auction of a business rival, he had bought an old, solid oak desk and matching armchair (on casters, not upholstered) and they had served him ever since. His personal assistant (as she styled herself, though he called her his secretary) had her own small windowless office. The third room, whose only entrance was through his office, was a reinforced and alarmed walk-in closet in which he kept his records. There were other employees, of course, who ran some of his other properties. Many people thought these employees were the owners, which suited Mickels just fine. They never came to this office, and Mickels himself rarely spent an entire day at this desk.

He was there this morning because he needed to think.

He pulled a yellow legal pad from the middle desk drawer and a cheap ballpoint from his pocket. He clicked the point out and drew a dollar sign on the notepad, then a circle around it and a diagonal line through it. If this incorporation business was true, his plans might be in trouble. That Devonshire woman had had that tone of voice people use when they'd won one, but some people were pretty good at faking it. Was she pleased because she was right, or pleased because he'd lost his temper believing her lie? He drew another dollar sign, this one sprouting wings. Was she crazy? She'd acted nuts when Officer Cross brought that hurt cat into the place—but that lady cop and the schoolteacher had been all excited as well. What was that all about?

Okay, okay, he remembered seeing a cat belonging to Margot in the store, a big fat thing, sleeping in a chair. (He was drawing a cat's head, with crosses for eyes, as he thought this.) He didn't remember its name, but it had been white, like the hurt cat might have been under the dirt. So maybe it was Margot's cat. So what? Betsy Devonshire hadn't been in town long enough to get attached to it, had she? All three of those women went hustling it off to the animal doctor like it was a human emergency.

Check cat, he wrote on the pad, because he was a detail person, and it might be useful to know if it still lived.

But that wasn't the real problem here. The real problem was, what if Betsy hadn't been just making idle threats about the corporation? He unlocked his desk and got out a photocopy of the lease, almost illegible with scrawled notes. The original must have been drawn up by his brother from memory, to judge by the semilegal language of the thing. That was what the notes were about: they marked the chinks he'd found in it, hoping one would be the crowbar to pry Margot out of her place. None of them so far had proved strong enough, and now this sister claimed she had a chink of her own that meant she could stay if she wanted to.

"Assigned the lease," that was the term she used, a legalism he was familiar with, being a landlord. It meant that the tenant turned the lease over to a new tenant. In every lease Mickels had ever signed, when assignment wasn't flat forbidden, the landlord's permission was needed for assignment. He glanced over the document, more to refresh his memory than to glean information, because he was already pretty sure the clause forbidding assignment was not in Margot's lease. And it wasn't.

What a jerk his brother had been! On the other hand, as Joe understood it, his brother had been doing a favor for Aaron Berglund, Margot's husband, giving her that lease. He had thought Margot just wanted to play at owning a business, that she would get bored or do something terminally stupid and fold up in six months or a year. Ha! That had been nearly thirteen years ago. He shoved the photocopy back in the drawer and locked it.

Interesting that Betsy Devonshire not only used the right terminology, she was right about the lease not forbidding assignment. Was she brighter than she looked? Or did someone tell her about it?

Wait a second, he hadn't noticed that Margot was arranging to be incorporated! And he kept close check on all his tenants, especially Margot, the fly in his ointment, the bug on his birthday cake.

Margot had been a "d/b/a"—doing business as—back when she started Crewel World, but she'd never incorporated. Never needed to. Never hinted she was thinking about it. He began doodling again, drawing a big threaded needle and then putting a circle with a slash around it. But he added a question mark. Margot was smart enough not to talk about her business to people who didn't need to know. If she had incorporated, it was very recently. And wherever she was, she was laughing up a storm, because he was screwed once again. Dammit, he needed to know!

He reached for his phone, dialed. But Penberthy was still tied up with a client, said his secretary, and could not be interrupted. Mickels left an urgent message and slammed the phone down. Stupid secretary, wouldn't listen when he said he had one question that wouldn't take more than ten seconds!

He settled back to wait, but in a minute he was up and pacing the perimeter of his office, which after four trips put him in mind of a hamster in a cage. He started to reach for the phone to call Penberthy's secretary back and shout at her—but instead did the one thing guaranteed to cool his temper.

He told his own secretary he didn't want to be interrupted for half an hour (she wouldn't let anyone through even for ten seconds, either), locked the door to his office, and went into his strong room. He opened his safe and took out a chipped green metal chest about eighteen inches square, heavy by the way he handled it. He brought it to a small table in the strong room and unlocked its padlock with a key on a ring that was never out of his reach.

The box was nearly full of silver dollars and half-dollars minted in the era when they were all silver, not a base-metal sandwich. The coins were bright and worn from handling, and Mickels plunged his hands into the hoard, rubbing them between his thick fingers, lifting his hands and letting them pour back into the box, then plunging his hands in again. At first energetic in these motions, over the next ten minutes or so he gradually slowed, his actions becoming more playful, then almost sensual; at last holding just one in his palm, and rubbing it over his hands as if it were a sliver of soap. Then he dropped it back in the box with the rest, locked the chest, and put it back in his safe, smiling and calm.

Ms. Devonshire sat very straight and attentive in the big leather chair in Penberthy's office. He was relieved to see her looking far less scattered and unhappy than she had only yesterday. And much more prepared to listen. Poor Huber, he'd had to deal with her when she was truly distraught.

"You know your sister died intestate?" he began.

"Without a will," she replied.

"Yes." He nodded, pleased at this sign of intelligence. "I talked with her on more than one occasion, but she said there was only you and she wanted you to inherit, so there was no need. I believe she was wrong—she had many interests and charities, some of which would have been very glad to be remembered. But it is too late now to know what she might have wished done about that." He gave a subtle shrug. "Of course, she was so active and helpful during her life that perhaps she felt that was enough, and did in fact intend to leave everything to you."

Ms. Devonshire said carefully, "I have been told by two of Margot's friends that there is a rather large estate."

Penberthy replied, "That depends on what you mean by large. I think, when everything has been accounted for, and all debts paid, there should be in the neighborhood of two and a half million."

Ms. Devonshire froze and then her face began to flush. "Two—" she began, but her voice tripped over itself and she fell silent again.

"Two and a half million is only an approximation. And that's before taxes, of course."

"Wow. I mean, Shelly thought five hundred thousand, and Jill said maybe a million; but two and a half million—" She tried a smile, but failed. "That's a lot of money. I had no idea. When I saw how Margot was living, I mean, in that little apartment and running that little shop, and her car is a Volvo—what nationality is a Volvo anyhow?—I thought she wasn't doing as well as it seemed from her letters. What was it, the stock market? Is that where the money was, I mean? That there's so much of it?" She touched her lips with her fingertips to stem the flow of words.

"You, as the personal representative, will conduct a search to discover where and in what form the money presently is held," replied Penberthy. "I know Margot kept good records, so there should be no trouble."

"We're already doing an inventory of the shop." Ms. Devonshire nodded. "But I don't know where to begin looking for anything more."

"I can explain how, if you like. I understand Margot put everything onto her computer. Have you, er, 'logged on' to it as yet?" Penberthy was glad to let his secretary run his computer.

"No. But I guess that has to happen soon."

"Do you know how to operate a computer?"

"Well, I used to own one, when I was living in San Diego, and I kept some records on it, and did my correspondence. I could even surf the net, and send E-mail. But I sold it before I came here." She shivered and rubbed her upper arms with her hands. "This isn't what I wanted to be doing right now," she said. "I came to stay with my sister because I've been having a midlife crisis. I wanted to figure out what to do with the rest of my life, because I didn't like where I was or what I was doing. Margot always had her life together and she seemed so content with herself that when she invited me to come I said yes, gladly. I gave up everything, threw my old life over, left San Diego shaking even the dust of the streets off the soles of my sandals.

"And then when I got here, I worried that Margot couldn't afford to keep me very long, because her shop is just that little place, and her apartment was kind of small. And then she was murdered and I was scared I couldn't even afford to bury her—oh!"

"Something wrong?"

"I was really rude to Mr. Huber at the funeral home. I think he tried to tell me that I didn't have to pinch pennies but I wasn't in a state to listen to him. I'm not sure what I can do about that."

"I don't think it would be a good idea to do the funeral over again."

After a startled moment, this seemed to strike Ms. Devonshire as funny, and when she smiled this time, it worked and she was suddenly very attractive. "No, I suppose that isn't the correct thing to do. But I will have to apologize to him next time I see him. Now, what is the process of transferring Margot's accounts into my name? I will need some money—I'm about broke, and I don't have a job, and I probably won't have a place to stay real soon."

"Then we will begin at once to get the process started—you will need to select a lawyer . . . ?" He paused, hesitating.

And she replied on cue, "I hope you will represent me. If Margot trusted you, then I know I can do the same."

"Thank you. You will need to go through Hennepin County Probate Court. We'll draw up a petition to have you appointed as personal representative. I'll start that at once, and will help you write the announcement you will have to publish in the newspaper, telling people who are owed money to contact you. There will be a brief hearing in court. It will take about a month between the filing of the petition and the hearing." He consulted a leather-bound appointment book. "If I contact them today, we can probably get a hearing around October fifteenth. You must be there to ask the judge to appoint you, and anyone who has any opposition to that will have a chance to be heard. I doubt there will be any trouble of that sort.

"You will gather together all the assets, pay all debts, distribute what's left to heirs—that is, yourself—and close the estate. We'll ask for unsupervised administration, which should be no problem. Then you file a personal-representative statement to close the estate. It will take at least four months before you can do that, to give creditors time to file claims. So six or seven months overall."

Betsy said, "It sounds very complicated."

"It's not, trust me. The procedure is well established and easy to follow. The most complicated part will be computing the taxes, because Congress is reworking the tax codes again. With the old six-hundred-thousand exemption, you can figure a little over two million subject to tax. They are reworking the exemption now, but you'll probably be paying thirty-two percent or more. Minnesota estate tax starts at nine percent."

"So the checks to the state and fed will be dillies."

"Yes, I'm afraid so."

"But what about my living expenses, rent and bills and all, in the meantime?"

"Technically, you are not supposed to give yourself any money from the estate even after you are appointed, not until the period of probate runs out; but you can keep records and reimburse yourself. If you are truly in need, we can petition the court to allow you maintenance."

But Ms. Devonshire obviously didn't like that idea. Penberthy reminded her that Crewel World Incorporated was not included in Margot's personal estate. As the new chief executive and store manager, she could write checks, and pay herself a salary that would let her stay in the apartment and buy groceries.

"Hey, I never thought of that!" she said, and was greatly comforted. Then she sobered again. "I'm afraid Mr. Mickels will continue to make trouble."

"You may be right. You may, of course, call on me when and if he does."

His pleasure at continuing to joust with Mr. Mickels showed in his voice, and she gave him another handsome smile. "Thank you, Mr. Penberthy. I will certainly do that."

Betsy came back to the shop to find Shelly sitting at the table working on a needlepoint canvas that looked, to Betsy, as if it were already finished. A customer was sitting close beside her, watching.

"You got your stitches all nice and even," Shelly was saying. "So I want to be careful to maintain the same tension." Her needle probed from below, came up and went down again. She looked up and said, "Hi, Betsy. My housework's done, so I decided to come in early. This is Mrs. Johnson; she wants this finished and framed."

"What are you doing to it?" asked Betsy.

"Looking for skipped stitches. Everyone has to do this. This is Mrs. Johnson's first big project and she has fewer than a lot of people."

Mrs. Johnson smiled, first at Shelly, then at Betsy, who wondered if that simple remark wasn't good for the sale of at least one more project to Mrs. Johnson.

Betsy nodded, then looked toward the big checkout desk where an exceedingly handsome young man was conferring with a middle-aged man in a black-on-gray houndstooth sports jacket. They both turned to look at her.

"I'm Godwin," said the young man, and Betsy recognized the name and voice as a part-time employee she had called. "I think Mr. Larson came prepared to write us a check." He added in a sweet drawl, one eyebrow raised a little too significantly, "It's a shame we haven't finished taking inventory."

"Yes, I'm afraid we're a little behind where we should be," said Betsy. "I'm Betsy Devonshire," she added, holding out her hand. "You must be Mr. Larson, from the insurance agency."

Taking Godwin's hint, she told the agent that they needed to complete the inventory before they could claim a loss honestly. He was understanding and left.

Two other part-time employees—one barely out of her teens, the other Betsy's age—came from behind the bookshelves where they'd already started counting things. They introduced themselves shyly and went back to work.

Betsy learned a great deal about Crewel World in the next few hours: about stock, about pricing, about storage, about record keeping. Godwin told her he was gay, accepted Betsy's indifference to it, and proved himself very knowledgeable about the workings of the shop.

They were all working in various parts of the shop when Godwin found Betsy's practice knitting in a desk drawer. "What's this?" he called out, holding it up as if it were a dead mouse.

"It's mine," admitted Betsy. "I'm still learning how."

That made him take a second look. He stretched it sideways, examining the stitches. "Not bad for a beginner," he said, "nice and loose. Have you been taking lessons very long?"

"Actually, that's my first try," she said, with less of an air of confessing to a misdemeanor than a moment before.

"Really? Then this is very nice indeed. But of course you're Margot's sister, so I guess a talent for needlework runs in the family. What are you going to make first?"

Betsy hadn't really thought about it. She'd been learning as a show of support for Margot.

"A scarf's easy and useful," Shelly suggested.

"Okay," she said. "A scarf."

They went back to work and continued until lunchtime, when Shelly went next door and bought sandwiches and an herbal iced tea in celebration of the return of mild and sunny weather. Betsy was suddenly hungry and ate quickly.

While waiting for the others to finish, Godwin brought her a skein of bright red wool and showed her a clever way to cast on using two lengths of yarn. Betsy discovered the doubtful pleasures of knit two, purl two, fifty times a row with an additional odd one at each end. Very soon she decided that it wasn't changing from knit to purl that aggravated, but the nuisance of moving the yarn from the front of the knitting to the back with each change. She felt she could make real progress if she could just knit or just purl.

"You could do that, and it would be faster," said Godwin. "But this way it will make such a pretty pattern. You'll see."

Betsy allowed a little additional time for gossip after Godwin and the others had finished their sandwiches. Shelly took out a length of off-white linen on which she was painstakingly cross-stitching an angel in shades of gold, wine, and moss green, consulting a pattern printed in Xs, Os, slashes, and other symbols. Godwin produced a rip-stop nylon sports bag, from which he took his own knitting: a half-finished white cotton sock, done on three small two-ended needles. He worked swiftly with a fourth needle, using tiny gestures, as if he were tickling a kitten.

He paused to look at Shelly's angel. "That is going to be really pretty," he said.

"Yeah, well I started it on forty-count aida, but only got the face done before my eyes crossed and threatened to stay that way if I didn't quit. This twenty-four count is much more comfortable, even if it is linen."

Betsy tried to imagine cross-stitching on fabric woven forty threads to the inch and her own eyes crossed in sympathy.

But soon the talk drifted to Margot.

About how scrupulous she was in sharing out part-time hours.

About how she paid only base wages, but allowed plenty of chat and personal project work—as long as it was needlework—in the shop while waiting for customers.

About how she insisted customers were the most important part of the place and that her employees must always go the extra mile to ensure customer satisfaction, whether it was special orders or returns or private lessons "just to get them started."

About the loyalty felt in return by her customers. "We have several customers who now spend their winters in Arizona or Mexico, but who will buy a winter's worth of projects before they leave rather than buy them from someone else," Godwin said, to LeAnn's emphatic nod.

"And we have some real talented needleworkers in the area," said LeAnn. "For example, Irene Potter—have you seen her work?" she asked Betsy.

"No, but I've heard it's wonderful."

"She's a difficult person, but her work belongs in the Smithsonian, I kid you not."

"Whereas Hud Earlie is a really easy person," said Shelly, exchanging a significant look with Godwin.

"What does that mean?" demanded Betsy.

"He fancies himself a bit, that's all," said Godwin airily. "I mean, where *does* he get that hair dyed? And a matching brass cane, for heaven's sake, *and* a smile that says he's God's gift to the world." Godwin tossed back a lock of his own unnaturally blond hair and Betsy smirked into her knitting—maybe Godwin was miffed that Hud wasn't gay.

"Margot had his number, that's for sure," said the younger of the volunteers. "He never got away with anything when she was around."

"Margot had all our numbers," Shelly put in gently.

The talk went on, and soon there were sniffles. "It was such a beautiful funeral." Godwin sighed. "Didn't you just love that reading about the woman who dresses her servants in scarlet and is always busy with business?" He said to Betsy, "Her Christmas gift to her employees every year is something knitted; year before last it was red mittens, that same shade of red you're working with."

Shelly said, "And that part about the sashes. Wasn't that amazing?"

"But everyone laughed during that!" Betsy protested. "I thought it was a joke!"

"No, no, nooooo." Godwin looked at her, very surprised. "We had a Founders' Day parade last year and Margot made bright green sashes for the people playing the characters so the watchers would know who they were supposed to be. So when that psalm—"

"It was from Proverbs," Shelly corrected.

"Whatever," said Godwin. "When he read that, it was the high point of the whole funeral, if there can be a high point of a *funeral*. I mean, the whole thing was so *apt*. No one will ever forget that reading."

Betsy was working on the fourth row of knitting without seeing any sign of the pattern promised when the door went *bing* and a woman came in. She was tall, about sixty years old, slim, and wearing a heather-blue knit dress.

Betsy put her knitting down and stood. "May I help you?"

"I understand the owner has died," she said. "I had placed an order with her and I wonder what the status of it might be."

Betsy went to the desk. "What is the name, please, and what was it you ordered?"

"I am Mrs. Lundgren. Mrs. Berglund agreed to copy her needlepoint Chinese horse for me for one thousand dollars, to be picked up here before Thanksgiving Day. Since she obviously won't be able to fill that order, I am here to inquire if someone else has taken on the task."

Margot had told Betsy about the commission, and had remarked that Mrs. Lundgren was a longtime customer. Yet the woman standing at the counter did not indicate in the slightest that she was shocked or saddened by the death of Margot.

"I see the framed original has been taken down," said Mrs. Lundgren. "Do you know if it will be for sale?"

"*That's* what's missing!" shouted Godwin.

"What do you mean, it's missing?" Shelly asked. "It was here last Wednesday, I saw Margot matching silks with it. In fact, I hung it back up on the wall myself."

Godwin came around the desk to look on the floor under the wall where the horse had hung. "I wonder where it got to?"

"Broken; stepped on, probably," said Betsy. "Thrown away."

Godwin stared at her. "Did you throw it away?"

"No, of course not. Actually, I don't remember seeing it while we were cleaning up. I know I didn't throw it away. But somebody did. Or else why isn't it here?"

But everyone else emphatically denied that anyone would have thrown away Margot's T'ang horse. They all knew it was Margot's finest original needlepoint piece, that she had loved it. Godwin said there was not a flaw in it, and Shelly said it was very valuable, with a glance at Mrs. Lundgren. They all agreed that even if it had been broken out of its frame and dirtied, it would have been set aside to be cleaned and reframed, not thrown away.

"So it must be here somewhere," Betsy concluded. She began to look through the several boxes of things still waiting to be sorted. Everyone, except Mrs. Lundgren of course, began searching the whole shop.

The search took a long while; they even emptied and sorted through the trash bags. It continued long after Mrs. Lundgren had given up and gone away. But at last Betsy called a halt. "It's gone," she said. "I told the police I thought nothing was taken in that burglary, but it appears I was wrong. Margot's needlepoint T'ang Dynasty horse is missing."

Twelve

❖

"**C**'mon, Mike, at least think about it! Maybe she's got a point!" said Jill, trying to keep her tone light and not sound wheedling or pushy. Which was hard when Detective Mike Malloy was patently not interested in her—or Betsy Devonshire's—thoughts on the case.

"Ah, she's just upset over her sister being murdered by some piece of trash, that's all. Everyone thinks when someone important gets killed it's some kind of plot or something. Even when she's only important to them. But one of these days we'll arrest some druggie or a punk kid and he'll start in crying and tell us all about the store with yarn in it and the woman he offed in there."

Mike wasn't interested in hearing Jill's opinion for two reasons. First, he was sure what he'd just said was correct. Second, he was also sure Jill wanted his job. On a small force like this one, even with only two investigators there was barely enough to do. Uniformed cops with ambition to make detective grade generally moved on to some big city, where openings happened. Cross was ambitious, but she wanted to stay in Excelsior. So naturally she wanted to show she had some ideas of her own.

Mike was ambitious, too—but when he moved up it would be to chief, if not here then in some other small town. Or maybe to sheriff in some out-of-state county.

That meant protecting his turf here and now. Which included not letting some street cop give everyone the idea he was going about this wrong.

On the other hand, Cross was female, so he had to be careful not to give the impression he thought she ought to turn in her badge for a bassinet—though she'd make a better mother than a cop, in his not so humble opinion. She should have a kid balanced on those hips, not a gun.

Jill, watching his eyes wander and thinking she could read his thoughts, tried to stifle a sigh.

Mike saw the sigh and misread it. Sensing victory, he became magnanimous. "How's she doing, the sister?"

"Okay. Better, in fact. You going to talk to her again?"

"Not right now. I got my feelers out all over the area. Something'll turn up soon, you tell her that."

"Sure, Mike. Thanks."

Jill left to go on patrol. She'd done what she told Betsy she'd do, bring Betsy's notions to Mike's attention. Betsy had offered to come in herself if Jill failed to put them across. But if Mike failed to listen to a fellow cop, he'd be even less likely to listen to Betsy, who tended to get excited.

Besides, Mike was awfully sure about the burglar, and he'd busted a small dope ring running right under everyone's noses just last winter. So maybe Betsy was wrong.

"He's the one who's wrong," said Betsy.

"Who died and made you Sherlock Holmes?" asked Jill.

"It doesn't take Sherlock Holmes to see something's wrong," Betsy argued. "Did you do the other thing I asked you to do?"

"Yes, I did," replied Jill, with an air of confessing to a crime, which it probably was. "The preliminary autopsy report says she was struck one time from behind, near the base of her skull, with an instrument that was round or rounded and had a nail or spike on it."

Betsy stared at her. "Round with a spike on it? That sounds like one of those weird medieval weapons you see in museums. Or something Hairless Joe would carry."

"Hairless Joe?"

"A character in an old comic strip called Li'l Abner."

Jill shrugged. "Never heard of it. But that's what the report said. I didn't write down the exact words, I was in a hurry in case Mike came back and caught me. But it was clear enough: she was hit once, with something that gave her a roughly circular depressed fracture with a hole in the middle of it. Killed her instantly." What the report really had said was that Margot had probably lost consciousness immediately and died soon after, but Jill didn't want to distress Betsy with that information.

Betsy sat silent awhile. They were in the shop, which Jill was glad to see was open for business, seated at the table. Betsy had begun knitting something in red yarn, probably a scarf, and while her hands seemed competent, she had the beginner's slow and careful movements. Unless she sped up, that scarf would be ready in time for the Fourth of July.

"They didn't find the murder weapon, did they?" Betsy said, purling twice.

"No. And I can't think of anything in the store that would have made that shape of a wound. Can you?"

"No." Betsy thought awhile, then shook her head in confirmation. "No," she repeated. And after doing that inventory, she knew every item in the store. She looked at her knitting, and knitted the next stitch.

"So he must have brought it with him, and taken it away again," said Jill.

"I remember reading in a book about putting something heavy in a sock and swinging it as a weapon." Knit again.

"Sand," said Jill. "A sockful of sand makes a really nice weapon."

Yarn over. "Yes, but sand hasn't got a spike in it." Purl.

"A long skinny rock can be a kind of spike. And all you have to do after is dump the rock out, run the sock through a washing machine, and nobody's the wiser."

They both glanced toward the store's front window and thought of the lakeshore, a stone's throw away.

* * *

Bing! "Have you had lunch yet, Betsy?" asked a man's voice from the doorway.

Betsy looked up from behind the desk. Hud was standing there in a spice-colored suit and vest, white shirt and no tie, which looked wonderful with his ruddy complexion and streaky hair. He was leaning elegantly on a brass-headed cane and sunlight coming from behind put him in a golden aura.

Betsy smiled, both in admiration and remembering Godwin's sarcastic description. "Well, hi, Hud. As a matter of fact, I haven't yet."

Godwin said, "Bring me back a sandwich. Any kind."

As they left the shop, Betsy teased, "What's that cane for? Did you sprain your ankle?"

He hoisted it, twirled it, set it down again. "What, don't you like it? Then I'll bring another next time. I have a collection." He held it out and she took it.

It was heavy; the shaft was of a dense wood whose color matched his suit, the head was an upright lozenge that on closer examination was seen to be an owl. The barely raised features made it pleasant to grip.

"Is it a sword cane?" she asked, pulling at it.

"Not this one." He took it back. "But I have one with a blade in it, and another that holds about four ounces of whiskey. They look exactly alike; can you imagine me trying to run off a mugger and instead offering him a drink?"

She laughed, then asked, "What are you doing in town?"

"Consulting you. We've been offered a seventeenth-century chatelaine, and I'm wondering if you can tell our European-art curator the uses of the implements in it."

"Why ask me? What's a chatelaine?"

"It's a metal holder for needlework implements. Scissors, thimble, needle pack, like that."

Betsy groaned softly. She was so ignorant!

Hud continued, "But this one has some other things in it that we're not sure of. A tool that looks to me like a really narrow guitar pick, for example. Everything's made of silver and everything matches, but I don't know if that pick really belongs or not."

"We have something like that in the shop. The package it comes in says it's a laying tool, but I have no idea what it's used for. I could ask my Monday Bunch: they know everything."

"No, never mind, one of my staff can look it up. A laying tool, huh? But hey, you want the truth? I've been thinking about you, and I've been looking for an excuse to come and see you. The chatelaine provided me with one." His smile invited her to join the conspiracy. "And now, having asked the question, I have both excused my absence from the office and made my lunch with you a deductible business expense."

"Glad to be of service, sir. Where are we going?" she asked as they rounded the corner that was marked by the post office. "Christopher Inn?"

"No, he doesn't serve lunch. I thought we'd go to Antiquity Rose's."

"Isn't that an antique shop?"

"It's also a very nice place to have lunch."

They had started up Second Street, going past the gas station. Antiquity Rose was just ahead. It had started life as a modest wooden house, and was now painted a blushing pink with maroon shutters. It had retained its front porch and a lawn full of cushion mums and late roses, but now Betsy noticed that the sign announcing its name and advertising antiques also mentioned luncheons.

In the front room were glass cabinets, tables, and shelves of glass dogs, china cats, odd silver spoons, antique jewelry, and collectible dolls. Hud led her to a small table in the next room, obviously converted from a side porch. The air announced fresh-baked bread and hearty soups.

Betsy was not an antiquer, but her eyes couldn't help wandering to the display on the wall over their table. An old poster advertising a black liquid that could cure both cancer and asthma hung between shadow boxes displaying old teacups and miniature Kewpie dolls.

"As the lunches get better here," said Hud, "the antiques get closer to plain secondhand stuff."

"I remember my grandmother sending me a Kewpie doll one Christmas," said Betsy. "I was disappointed that it didn't come with clothes to put on and take off." She smiled at the memory.

"You are looking very well," said Hud.

"Thanks," she said. But then turned to business of her own, for who better to ask about a medieval weapon than a curator?

"Hud, does the museum have antique weapons? I mean really antique, like medieval."

He glanced up from his menu. "No, why?"

"Is there a name for that thing that's a round knob with a spike through it?"

He offered a humorous look of suspicion. "Who are you mad at?"

"Nobody. I was talking with Jill earlier today, and somehow the subject came up. We were trying to think of the name of that kind of thing. Not morning star, not mace, but something in that family."

Hud shrugged and resumed consulting his menu. "Not my area of expertise, sorry. Or the museum's; we collect art, not weapons." He put it down again. "But talk of hurting someone reminds me. How's Sophie?"

"Just fine. She actually gets around despite the cast. They made it longer than her leg to discourage running or jumping, so she kind of paddles with it rather than walking on it. The vet's assistant calls it the square-wheel syndrome. Sophie goes along very smoothly on three legs and then the cast lifts her about two inches." Betsy moved her hand across the table, lifting and dropping it at intervals. "Like a pull toy with one square wheel."

Hud laughed so hard at the image of a cat with a square wheel he had to put the menu down. His voice was a splendid baritone and his laugh matched it; people turned smiling to see who was making that beautiful noise. Betsy wasn't sure whether to feel envied or embarrassed, and so picked up her menu and pretended to read it.

They had corn chowder with hunks of rosemary-flavored chicken in it, and the talk grew so friendly—Hud was familiar with San Diego, Betsy knew something about symbolism in medieval and Renaissance art—that by the end of the meal Hud had to remind her to order a take-out sandwich for Godwin.

Rather than going right to Crewel World with the sandwich, Betsy continued walking with Hud up Lake Street to his car. She had heard you could learn things about a man by the car he drove.

Hud's was a big old black convertible, highly polished but slab-sided. Betsy was startled—she thought Hud was the sports-car type—until she saw the peaked grille with the fey creature perched on top of it. "Oh, my God, Hud; it's a Rolls-Royce! Wow! Say, what kind of salary do they pay you, anyhow?"

"Not enough to buy a car like this." Hud laughed, going to unlock the door. "I bought it seven years ago, used, at a government auction. It probably once belonged to a drug dealer. I paid eighty-two hundred dollars for it." He slid into the tan leather interior and vanished behind darkened glass. When he started the engine, it purred almost inaudibly. Then the passenger-side window rolled silently down and he leaned sideways to look through it at her.

"Like it?"

"What's it like to drive?" she asked.

"Smoooooooth. Would you care to try it out sometime?"

"You'd actually let me?" Betsy had briefly dated a man who owned a Porsche. Nobody drove it but him; he wouldn't even use valet parking.

"Oh, I'm not married to my car like some people are," he said carelessly. "If it wasn't a Rolls, it would be just another ugly car. By the way, there's a dance this Friday, at the Lafayette Club. May I take you?"

She studied him, at first naturally then as a ploy, enjoying the hopeful look on his face. "Yes," she said. "I'd like that."

*   *   *

An order of alpaca wool came in that afternoon, and Betsy had to write a disturbingly large check to pay for it. She was comparing the contents of the box with the order placed by Margot when Irene Potter came in.

"They're rewiring our end of the plant," she said, "so the circuit breakers will stop turning everything off; and they told us to take today and tomorrow off. I decided to stop in and ask—"

"I'm sure we don't have any hours for you to work," Godwin called loudly from the back of the store.

Irene threw a frosty look in his direction and focused her attention more pointedly on Betsy. "—find out if you are getting along all right. I know it must be hard for you to take over a business without warning or preparation."

Betsy said candidly, "Well, it would be nice if I could put everything on hold while I take a semester or two of business courses. Godwin and the others are very helpful, but it's hard to be the boss under these circumstances."

Irene's thin mouth pulled downward. "Margot's death happened at a particularly bad time, just when we're going to be swamped with orders."

"We are?" Betsy noticed the "we"; Irene must still think she was going to own this shop someday.

"Yes, our inventory will be growing quickly toward its peak this month, in time for the holidays. This is when we spend the most, and hope to make it all back and more by the end of December. And, of course, utilities go high during the winter. That front window leaks heat as if it were screen instead of glass— Joe Mickels won't double-glaze it—and with people in and out, the heat just flows like a river through that door. And now, of course, you've got that burglary loss. Have you figured it out yet? How much?"

Betsy was staring at Irene as if she had never seen her before. And, in fact, she hadn't seen this Irene, the competent businesswoman. "Uh, we're pretty sure it's a little over seven thousand, mostly damage to fixtures."

"That's not so bad."

"No, it looked really terrible, but a lot of it we could just pick up and shake out, and there's more I think we can sell after it's been washed. I had wonderful help, they sorted thousands of beads and buttons."

"Getting good help is half the battle." Irene nodded. "I wish I could have been here, too."

"But you have a better job, one that pays more than I can offer."

"Ensuring a computer keyboard gets to Detroit by morning isn't as exciting the thousandth time as it was the first."

Betsy'd had that kind of job, once. Besides, she had a question she wanted to ask Irene. "Would you like a cup of coffee?"

"No, I rather hoped Rosemary would be here. I wanted to ask her about that Appleton wool she bought, if she liked it. Since she isn't, I think I'll just go home—"

Godwin sang "Good Night, Irene!" and this time it was Betsy who glared at him.

"Irene," said Betsy, trying at least to get her to come back soon, "Margot said I should see some of your work, that it was wonderful."

"She said that?"

"People tell me you win prizes with it all the time."

Irene nodded, her dark eyes glowing. "Yes, I do. Very well, I'll bring some to show you, maybe tomorrow. Perhaps you should hire me to teach a course on needlepoint, everyone in the class would end up with a finished project."

"I'm sorry, I can't afford to hire another person right now. And if I could, the person I'd hire is someone to advise me, a consultant, someone to give me more advice like the kind you just gave me."

Irene's dark eyes glittered. "A consultant?"

"Someone like you, who knows how to run a small business, and also knows all about needlework. Look, are you sure you wouldn't like a cup of coffee?"

Irene said slyly, "A consultant's job would pay better than working the register, wouldn't it?"

"Much better, because it's more important. Do you take cream or—"

"Just black," said Irene.

"Fine, I'll be right back."

When Betsy returned, Irene was trying to convince a customer that she could use DMC floss rather than the silks she wanted for a small doorstop canvas, while Godwin made futile attempts to intervene.

"Irene," said Betsy, forcing the smile now, "here's your coffee."

"Just a minute," said Irene. "I'm consulting with this customer."

"Irene," said Betsy, allowing a warning note to creep in, "if you consult with the customers, then I will think you are on their side, not mine."

Irene turned toward her, mouth open, but changed her mind about whatever she was going to say. Instead, she turned back to the customer and said, "But perhaps I am wrong. I think Godwin here can help you. Excuse me?" and went to the table, where Betsy was setting down a pair of pretty china cups.

After the customer left with her selection of silks, Betsy remarked, "I'm surprised Margot didn't think of you as a consultant."

"Oh, Margot thought she knew everything already," said Irene.

"Well, she did know a whole lot more than I do."

"Naturally." Irene shrugged. Then she looked up at Betsy and smiled without a trace of rancor or wickedness in her eyes, and Betsy, with sudden compassion, realized that Irene truly had no understanding of the human heart.

Betsy took a drink of her coffee. "I hope they catch the person who murdered her," she said.

"Well, they probably won't. It was an impulse thing, I'm sure—a burglar who was startled and just swung without meaning to kill. And don't they need fingerprints to solve a murder?" Irene was doing a great deal of stirring and hardly any drinking.

"I should think he'd be sick about it, unable to eat or drink or sleep," said Betsy.

"Probably," agreed Irene, stirring.

Betsy leaned forward, seeking an aura of confidentiality. "You know how you remember what you were doing when something important happens?" she asked.

Irene nodded.

"I was sorting socks from the laundry when the first men landed on the moon."

"I was working on 'Autumn Roses' in crewel for the chair in my living room," said Irene.

"And I was sitting next to Jill Cross in the Guthrie Theatre, watching *The Taming of the Shrew*, when Margot was murdered."

Irene's eyes slid sideways, then back. "I was doing the background of a Kaffe Fassett in basketweave," she said.

"At home?"

"Yes."

"All alone?"

"Yes. I was using Medici wool, which I think works better than Paternayan. That's one of the projects I'll bring in to show you; it came out rather well. Perhaps you'll want to hang it up where Margot's blue horse used to be."

Betsy turned to look at the blank wall behind the checkout desk. "You noticed it was missing?"

"Of course. Was it taken with the rest?"

"Rest?"

"Yes, the Designing Women angel and my Melissa Shirley Christmas stocking and that child-size Irish fisherman sweater. Margot usually kept three or four completed projects on display."

Betsy remembered the sweater, knitted in a beautiful cream-colored wool. "We found the sweater, trampled. I'm going to try washing and reblocking it." She raised her voice. "Godwin, do you remember the other things?"

"What things?" asked Godwin, coming out from behind the shelves where he'd been rearranging instruction books, his eyes suspiciously innocent.

Betsy glanced at Irene for confirmation as she named them, the Designing Women angel and the Melissa Shirley Christmas stocking. He shook his head. "I remember them in the shop, of course, but I don't remember seeing them when we were digging through the trash looking for the T'ang horse, and I think I would have."

"Me, neither." Her eye, too, had been set for finished needlework during the search; she would remember if she'd seen any.

So more than the T'ang horse was missing. What did that mean? She had no idea. She picked up the phone book to look for the police department's number. What was the name of the investigator in charge of her sister's case?

Thirteen

❖

The Excelsior police station was a new, one-story building of brick and dark gray stone. It was on the south edge of town near Highway 7, next door to the McDonald's and across the street from an ice cream shop—perhaps, Irene suggested in a very dry voice, to make up for its being so far from the Excelo Bakery and its wonderful doughnuts.

A thin-mouthed man with dark red hair and a lot of freckles came to the tiny foyer and said he was Detective Sergeant Mike Malloy. He seemed to recognize Irene, and not with pleasure. But he took both of them back to a small office crowded with two messy desks and several filing cabinets.

On one desk was a large paper bag stapled shut, with a big red tag labeled EVIDENCE covering the staples. He pulled a metal chair from the other desk so each woman could sit down.

Malloy broke the seal on the paper bag with professional nonchalance. "I want you first, Betsy, to tell me if you recognize any of this." He upended the bag and wads of colored fabric mixed with the broken sticks of a wooden frame tumbled out.

"May I touch it?" she asked.

"Go ahead."

Betsy picked up a wad of dull green cloth, which unrolled itself into a Christmas stocking. She turned it around to find a needlepoint picture of children looking through a multipaned window at Santa and toys. The stitches were fancy; Santa's beard was done in long curls, his fur trim was really furry, and the toys were crusted with tiny beads. "I think this is ours," said Betsy, looking at Irene for confirmation.

Irene nodded, her eyes sad. "It's mine," she said. "Maybe it can be saved. I won't know until it's been washed and reblocked."

"I think it looks fine, just a little dirt here and there," said Betsy, surprised.

But Irene shook her head. "I don't know if it will ever be the same."

The angel, broken out of its frame, was in much worse shape. It seemed to have been pulled at its opposing corners, distorting the stitches along with the picture, and to have picked up some serious stains along its journey. "Oh, dear." Betsy sighed.

"Yes, quite ruined," said Irene.

Those were the only two pieces of needlework from the bag; there were also pieces of the mat that had enclosed the angel, and fragments of the wooden frame. There was also extraneous paper trash, and an empty plastic pop bottle.

"Is that all you found?" asked Betsy.

"Why, isn't that all that's missing?"

"No, there was also a needlepoint picture of a blue Chinese horse."

"It was in a plain wooden frame, quite narrow," added Irene. "Matted in very pale green."

"That's all that was turned in." Malloy sat back in his chair. "Were there price tags on these items?"

Betsy replied, "No, they weren't for sale. Although there has been a customer who wanted to buy the blue horse. Margot had agreed to make a copy of it for her for a thousand dollars."

Malloy's eyebrows elevated. "A thousand dollars?"

Irene said, "It's quite an art to make a needlepoint project from scratch."

"Would these other two things cost that much if they were for sale?"

Betsy said, "I don't know. An unfinished canvas by the artist who did this stocking sells for three hundred dollars."

Irene said, "If my stocking were for sale, which it is not, I would charge fifteen hundred." Betsy thought it possible that Irene made up that number on the spot, seeking to outdo the value of Margot's work. Certainly she beamed brighter when Malloy wrote that down.

Malloy said, "But people who don't know needlepoint wouldn't know the value of this stuff."

"Probably not," said Betsy. "I didn't before I started helping my sister out in the shop."

"So the fact that a framed horse is missing instead of the stocking tells me the burglar hasn't got a kid, but has got a mother or sweetheart with a birthday coming up."

Betsy stared at him. Malloy laughed, but not unkindly. "Most people don't realize that crooks have a life outside their criminal activities. A lot of burglars are married or have steady girlfriends. And all of them, of course, have mothers. It's not uncommon for a burglar to take something to give as a present. Which is how we catch them, of course."

Irene said, "You mean their own mothers will turn them in?"

Malloy laughed again. "Not very often. But Mom will show off the present, wear the ring or fur coat, hang the painting in her living room, and of course her friends will ask where it came from. 'My son gave it to me,' says Mom, and word gets around, and one of my informants calls me. Then"—Malloy produced a pair of handcuffs—"you're under arrest."

Irene chuckled but Betsy frowned.

"Now, what if it wasn't a burglar who did this," she began.

"I beg your pardon?"

"Suppose someone wanted my sister dead, and came to see her the night I was out, and somehow talked her into going down to the shop, maybe pretending he, or she, wanted to see something. And then murdered her and trashed the shop to make it look as if a burglar had done it."

"Where did you come up with an idea like that?" Malloy asked, his tone patronizing.

"There are a couple of things. For one, the shop was trashed *after* she was murdered."

Malloy nodded. "Yes, we know that. A very cold-blooded individual did this."

"Second, the shop was completely torn apart. Either the thief was angry because there was nothing of value to steal, or he was looking for something."

"Looking for what?"

"I don't know. The blue Chinese horse? It's the only thing missing."

"But that was hanging on the wall in plain sight," said Irene. "And how do you know there's nothing else missing? Have you finished your inventory and compared it to the last inventory and all the orders received since and records of things sold?"

"That's in process. So far nothing important has come up missing. But I don't think the murderer was looking for a pair of bamboo knitting needles; I think it was something else."

"What?" Malloy asked again.

"I don't know. I may be wrong, but maybe he just wanted to make you think he was a burglar, and got carried away."

"Maybe he was angry that he'd broken in and there wasn't anything worth his while to steal."

"You would think killing the owner would be revenge enough," said Betsy, and to her chagrin she sobbed just once.

Malloy sat very still, watching, until he was sure she wasn't going to break down. Then he said, "It's a stinking shame what happened to your sister. This is a quiet town, with a low crime rate. We haven't had a murder here in years. Everyone is angry and upset over it, and I want to assure you that I'm putting in a lot of overtime working the case. Your reporting the missing items really helped, because when someone rummaging in the trash for aluminum cans found this stuff, I got called and here we are. And I appreciate your thoughts as well. I don't want you to think I'm dismissing them just because you aren't a professional like I am." He smiled, stood, and held out his hand.

Betsy, following suit, shook it. Malloy only nodded at Irene, who nodded back. He opened the door to his office.

"I hope you don't mind if I keep working the burglar angle," he said. "After all, the calculator wasn't found in that trash barrel. Maybe he hasn't dropped out of school yet and needs a calculator. But it's that embroidered horse that will identify him as the thief when we catch him, and help us get a confession."

Irene asked eagerly, "You have a suspect?"

"I think I can safely say that significant progress is being made," he said, gesturing her out.

Betsy reluctantly followed. "Who's your suspect?" she asked over her shoulder.

"I don't want to say anything at this point that might jeopardize the case or put an innocent person in a false light," he said, dodging around them and leading the way down the hall. "I will keep you informed, I promise. What I need from you now is a little more patience."

And before Betsy knew it, she was alone with Irene in the little foyer.

Irene thanked Betsy profusely for "this most interesting experience," and went her way. Betsy returned to the shop.

When she walked in, Joe Mickels was waiting for her. "I've come to see who's paying the rent," he said. "Or are you going to make me put in a claim against the estate?"

"I can't do that," she said. "The corporation didn't die; it is an immortal entity." She remembered reading that somewhere and was pleased to note he was familiar enough with the concept to look a trifle diminished. In fact, as she approached him, she saw that he wasn't a whole lot taller than she was. Funny how she remembered him as a big man. Perhaps it was that fierce Viking face, with its bristling sideburns. And the fact that he was a landlord and the bane of Margot's life for many years. His legs, she noticed now, were very short and a little bowed. She wondered if there had been a shortage of milk while he was growing up.

"I assume you want the check sent to the same address where Margot sent it," she said, stepping around him to go behind the desk and opening the center drawer to get out the Crewel World checkbook. "Or, since you're here, shall I just give it to you directly?" She pulled a pen from a small basket of pens, pencils, foot rulers, and scissors and prepared to write.

"The September rent has been paid, so you have a month's grace," he grudged, and handed her a business card with his name and a post office box number on it. "Send October's rent here." Some of his arrogance returned. "And don't be late."

"I won't be," she snapped, and promised herself she'd live on milk and crackers if necessary to make that true.

He turned and looked around the store, nearly restored to its former state. "Not many customers," he noted.

"We're doing fine," she said. "By the way, I've just been talking to the man investigating Margot's murder."

"Yeah?" he grunted, but there was a flicker of interest in his ice-blue eyes.

"He told me he has a suspect in the case."

"Who?" The word came sharply.

"He wouldn't say. I told him—say, would you like a cup of coffee?"

His eyes narrowed suspiciously. "What for?"

She feigned exasperation. "Because I'm having one, and it's only common courtesy to offer. Do you take cream and sugar?"

Wordlessly, he nodded, and wordlessly took the pretty cup when she brought it to him. His fingers were too thick to fit even one through the small handle.

"It was so horrible about Margot," she said, stirring her own sugared cup. "I didn't think things like that happened in small towns."

"It's a city."

"That's right. Margot told me. Something about a law that every town had to reconfigure itself as a city or go out of existence. So why didn't Excelsior make its boundaries city size?"

Mickels shrugged his heavy shoulders. "The town council had a big fight over where to set the borders, either city size, way beyond where the town already was, or just where it was then. They figured that if they expanded the borders, they'd get stuck with high taxes bringing water and sewage to everyone, so they chose to limit the borders. They're still arguing over whether or not it was a good idea."

"What do you think?"

He shrugged again. "It doesn't matter to me. It saved downtown, I guess, but the tax base is too small. There are other towns that had the same choice, and most of them stayed small, too. Then once their borders were settled, Shorewood took the rest. So anytime you're not sure what city you're in out here, you're in Shorewood."

Betsy smiled. "Are you from Excelsior?"

He nodded.

"Do they have a good police department?"

He frowned. "Why do you ask?"

"Because I want to be sure they can find out who murdered my sister, Mr. Mickels."

"I thought you said the police have it solved."

"I said, the detective thinks it was a burglar. But if he has a suspect, why isn't he under arrest? And what if it wasn't a burglar at all?"

His bushy eyebrows met over his nose. "Not a burglar? Then who?"

"Someone who had a reason for wanting the owner of this shop out of the way. Someone, perhaps, like you, Mr. Mickels."

He stared at her for a long moment, then put his cup on the desk, turned, and started for the door.

"Where were you the night she was murdered, Mr. Mickels?" she called after him.

He stopped at the door and there was another long moment of weighty silence. "I was at a business meeting in St. Cloud," he said at last. "Not that it is any business of yours."

"Of course it's my business! She was my sister." Betsy felt her eyes start to sting, and turned away. "Just go," she said, but the door had already closed.

That night up in the apartment, she remained furious at herself for openly accusing Mickels before finding out if he had an alibi. Of course he'd claim to have one, asked the way he had been! And she wasn't sure how to go about proving it false.

She opened a can of soup for supper, watched the early news, then convinced herself she was tired and went to bed.

But she couldn't fall asleep. She got up and dragged on her robe and wandered the apartment for a while, wondering if she might be hungry. But a look in the refrigerator convinced her she wasn't.

Finally she found a radio station that played classical music, sat down in her sister's chair, and took up her knitting.

To her surprise, after ten minutes of it, she felt her mind, like a pond that has been disturbed and then left alone, settle and grow clear.

Mickels's remark notwithstanding, Crewel World had had a good day, saleswise. But there had been more deliveries—most of them, fortunately, with an invoice that gave her thirty or more days to pay. But even ninety days to pay was shorter than the five or six months it was going to take to close the estate. She hoped she could do enough business to make those payments.

Shelly had come back in soon after Joe had left, and said it was time to plan the Christmas display. Shelly and Godwin—who were going to be essential to the continuance of the shop, Betsy was already aware—put their heads together and came up with a design for the front window that looked okay to Betsy.

Later both of them, having apparently discussed it between taking an order for a thousand dollars' worth of silk and metallics for a woman doing an enormous canvas of an Erté-like portrait and explaining the use of an eggbeaterlike device for twisting yarn into braid to a woman who bought two as gifts, had come and sat her down and wanted to know what her plans were. It was obvious they wanted her to keep Crewel World open. She'd been nearly as touched as alarmed. She hadn't agreed—it felt too much like a trap for someone of her ignorance to promise to stay and run a small business in a state notorious for fierce winters. Didn't blizzards close the stores and schools around here for great hunks of the winter?

Hey, she didn't even have a winter coat. And she didn't know how to knit a pair of mittens. She looked down at the red scarf, which was now over a foot in length. She'd put another inch on it sitting here musing, and there was not an error in it, amazingly. So maybe she could do a mitten.

No, wait, mittens had that thumb sticking out. How did one do a thumb? She recalled Godwin knitting his sock. He'd been using four needles, three of them stuck in the project and the fourth used to make and lift off the stitches, around and around, so there was no seam. One set of four to do the hand and another set of littler ones to do the thumb? No, wait, she remembered her mother's hand-knitted mittens. The thumb's stitches weren't smaller than the rest of the mitten. She smirked a little at being able to figure that out. She was learning.

But her ignorance wasn't the main problem. There were people who knew how to run the shop, and they were eager to help. But Betsy needed to decide if she was going to stay, and if not, to decide where she was going to go. And to start making plans to do one or the other.

She turned her knitting around and started back across the row, purl two, knit two. The first three inches of the scarf didn't have the promised welts or ridges or whatever in them, and she had figured out all by herself that when she began a new row, she should do the opposite of what she'd done; that is, where she'd knitted, now she should purl, and vice versa. In two more rows, there were the ribs, boldly standing up. And now that it was long enough to really see, the pattern was very attractive. She had thought about tearing out the beginning, but decided it made an interesting edge, kind of lacy. She'd make the same "mistake" at the other end, if she ever got that far. Shelly had said a good scarf was at least six feet long.

She looked at her knitting. Where was she? Ah, knit two.

First of all, was she going to stay in Excelsior at least until her sister's murder was solved? Yes.

Well then, she'd better make a success of the shop, because she was scared how swiftly the Crewel World bank balance was draining out. She was down to the dregs of what she'd brought with her, and her credit cards were near their limit. It was great that Margot had left so much money, but Betsy couldn't touch any of it for months, according to Mr. Penberthy. And while today's sales were good, Godwin had remarked on the amount that had come in, which meant it was unusual, which meant tomorrow and the day after might not be good at all.

So, maybe she should go ahead and hold that going-out-of-business sale and try to live over at Christopher Inn on the proceeds until Detective Mike Malloy arrested the burglar with a mother who had a birthday coming up.

Because she was not leaving Excelsior until Margot's murderer was behind bars.

But suppose it wasn't a burglar? Suppose she was right and Detective Mike Malloy was wrong, and Margot's murder had been a personal matter? Since her body was found in Crewel World, she probably had been murdered by someone with a connection to the shop. Then, since the motive involved the shop, if Betsy closed the shop, her contacts with people connected with the place ended. And if Joe Mickels's alibi checked out, she might have to look elsewhere for the murderer.

So the shop had to stay open, at least for now.

But on the other hand, Betsy still didn't know what she was doing at Crewel World. Okay, she could write up sales slips, she could read and understand invoices. And she could knit, embroider, and just today she realized she could tell silk from perle cotton from wool at a glance. Just as she could tell at a glance that she had knitted one and needed to knit another. Purl two.

But what about payroll? When were paychecks issued? And in what amount? And how did one figure withholding taxes? And what did one do with the money withheld? She felt the familiar despair come over her. How in the world did she think she was going to do this? She was a fool—an *old* fool! Her fingers cramped and she realized she was gripping the needles too tightly. She forced herself to open them, wriggled them a bit, then slowly knit and purled her way across the rest of the row, waiting for her mind to settle and clear again.

When it did, a memory rose up. Years ago, right out of the Navy, Betsy had worked in a small office, and had helped the office manager do payroll. She remembered it hadn't been all that hard.

And Jill had said that Margot kept all her business information in her computer.

It was time to have a look. Betsy put down her knitting, careful to stick the pointed ends of the needles into the ball of yarn to keep the stitches in place, and marched into Margot's bedroom.

Everything was as it had been, the bed smoothed rather than properly made, Margot's makeup still on the dresser, the scent of her perfume still lingering in the air.

Betsy nearly fled, but told herself not to be an idiot, and went to sit at the computer. She found the power switch and turned it on. The screen flickered, the computer grumbled, and then came the chord of music: ta-dah!

At first Betsy just explored, noting the AOL icon, finding games (FreeCell solitaire and something called You Don't Know Jack, which made her smile wryly) and the word-processing program. Margot had Windows 95, which Betsy had had on her own computer, so it didn't take long to get comfortable.

She began looking for a business program and found Quicken. But when she tried to get into it, it demanded a password. She tried Margot and Berglund and Crewel and World and Crewelworld, and then all the needlework terms she could think of, to no avail. She sat back, frustrated.

She remembered her own computer, and the list of her assets she had kept in a file that required a password. She had used "Margot." She looked at the screen, its cursor flashing impatiently. She typed "B-E-T-S-Y" and hit Enter.

And she was in.

And there she found the business courses she needed to run Crewel World, Inc. In Payroll was a list of employees, their pay scales, their hours (none entered since Margot died, of course, but Betsy knew where the time sheets were kept, so that was all right). Also Social Security paid, and withholding for state and federal income tax, for herself and for each employee. ("That's my first business decision: as CEO, do I get a raise?" she muttered.) The inventory file had a list done in January. And another done a year ago January. And another, and another, going back five years. Taxes, paid and due, the special account it was paid into. A list of suppliers and what was ordered, when it was due, the amounts owed, the amounts paid.

She printed out much, read more. Hours later, heavy-eyed, she could no longer make sense of anything. She shut down the computer and went to bed. She could do this, she was going to stay in business, paying her workers and herself. But she dreamed for the remaining four hours of the night of audits and penalties and bankruptcy.

Fourteen

❖

Late the next morning, she left the shop in Godwin's hands and went to the First State Bank of Excelsior. She found a seat in the little waiting area, feeling important. She was wearing a light gray skirt, white blouse, and jacket-cut gray sweater; she carried an attaché case she'd found in Margot's closet, now weighty with printouts.

The magic word, she had learned, was *line of credit*. Margot had had one, a nice big one. When someone has considerable assets, a bank can issue a line of credit, which is sort of like getting a preapproved series of loans. Betsy was sole heir to two and a half million dollars; surely that was an asset worthy of a considerable line of credit, even if the asset hadn't paid its taxes yet. She had called earlier and gotten a very prompt appointment with the vice-president—okay, *a* vice-president—of the First Bank of Excelsior.

When her name was called, she rose with the air of someone who is about to do a banker a big favor and allowed herself to be shown into a small but nicely decorated office.

And left it half an hour later greatly humbled. The vice-president had read with interest the notes Betsy had written about Margot's estate—but then pointed out that since Margot had banked with First State, the bank was even more cognizant of Margot's financial status than Betsy was.

However.

Bankers were, according to this one, reluctant to make a loan based on an estate that was in the process of being settled. "There is occasionally a slip between the cup and the lip," quoted the vice-president, not quite accurately.

Perhaps when Betsy had been officially named as personal representative, they would consider making a loan against the assets of the shop in order to buy more inventory, because of the fact that the business was of long standing. Perhaps the loan would be as much as one hundred percent of the value of what she was purchasing. They might also lend her money based on the insurance settlement for the burglary.

Even this was not usually done, the banker concluded, but after all, it appeared that Betsy would be coming into a lot of money one of these days, and the bank would love to do business with her, as they had with Margot.

With an effort, Betsy refrained from leaping across the desk and watching the vice-president's pink complexion turn to mauve as she throttled him. Instead, she pointedly snapped the attaché case shut, shook his hand perfunctorily, and left the bank.

First State was on the corner of Water and Second, where she'd almost missed the turn the first time she'd come into Excelsior. She walked toward the lake and reached the tavern, but couldn't make herself turn down Lake Street toward Crewel World. She dreaded going back to the shop. She had been so sure she'd come bursting back in with the glad news that their troubles were over, the shop could keep running, and everyone would be paid. Now . . .

She dithered awhile, and finally crossed Lake Street and walked down to the wharves. They barely met the definition of the word, since no actual ship tied up here, only excursion boats. Still, the boats were large, multidecked objects, painted white, made of Formica. Or was it fiberglass? *Queen of Excelsior*, one was named. Beside them, the streetcar boat *Minnehaha* looked very odd and old-fashioned. Betsy walked out on the wharf it was tied next to.

The *Minnehaha* was made of wood painted a brownish red with mustard-yellow trim. A black metal chimney stuck up from its midsection. Its stern sloped sharply away from the rear, like a warship back in the days of the Great White Fleet.

The lake twinkled in the sunlight. Betsy looked down into the clear water. She could see three good-size crappie swimming among the waving water weeds, into and out of the shadow cast by the *Minnehaha*. How much was a fishing license? Maybe it would be a savings to invest in one, and a cane pole. If she ate fish a few times a week, it would cut back on her grocery bills.

Sophie would probably like that, too. She thought of Sophie, curled on a cushion in the shop, injured leg uppermost so everyone would see her cast and offer sympathy and treats. Sophie, regaining weight almost hourly, had not stopped purring since she'd returned from the hospital.

Some way would have to be found to pay the vet.

She went back up to the corner of Lake and Water. A short block away was Second Street, a little way up that was the entrance to that big parking lot with City Hall on the other side of it. No wonder Margot walked over to the meeting and then home again. It wasn't very far. That's also why she had been wearing those sensible low-heeled pumps instead of her flashy high heels.

Betsy started up Lake Street toward Crewel World. Margot had come home this way on the last night of her life.

Had the murderer been waiting in the shadows for her? Did he come out and introduce himself and find some reason for her to take him up to her apartment?

When did he strike Sophie? Because the vet said he doubted if Sophie had been hit by a car. There was a deep, narrow bruise over the break in Sophie's leg, he said, as if someone had hit her with a rock or club. That confirmed that Sophie and Margot had entered the shop together, where the murderer struck both of them. Perhaps the murderer swung first at Sophie, and Margot could not help crying out, because Margot never struck, nor would she allow anyone else to strike, Sophie. But if he had hit Sophie with the weapon, why didn't Sophie have a hole in the middle of her bruise?

Why wasn't it Sophie who was dead and Margot walking around as if she had a square wheel?

Betsy wished suddenly she had turned down that invitation to go out that evening. She would have been at home with Margot, and the murderer would not have dared to try anything with both of them there.

Say, there was a new thought. Was it possible the murderer knew Margot was home alone?

Who knew Betsy was going out that night? Jill did, Margot did, Shelly did. Did one of them tell Joe?

Without thinking, Betsy put a hand out and opened the door to Crewel World.

"How'd it go?" came Godwin's eager voice.

"Oh!" said Betsy, who, amazingly, had forgotten she was the bearer of bad news. "Not good, I'm afraid. I can borrow against the inventory, he said; and we'll have the insurance money from the burglary claim. And Margot had a life-insurance policy, Mr. Penberthy mentioned it, but I guess it's not very large. We're going to have to work very hard and make this shop pay, not only for itself, but for me, too."

She looked at Godwin's disappointed face. "Sorry," she said, and then she noticed the dark-haired lady standing beside the desk. Irene Potter.

"I brought you something to look at," she said, and unrolled a piece of cloth across the desk.

Betsy came to look. It was a picture of the sun coming up over hills and a river.

"You should get that framed," said Godwin.

It was a stunning work of art, with many subtle changes of color. "Incredible," breathed Betsy. "Tell me, how did you get that misty effect?"

Godwin said over her shoulder, "Oh, my God, she did the *entire thing* in half cross!"

Betsy looked closer; it was true, instead of the X of cross-stitch, here Irene had used only one leg of the cross—and in places, less than that, half of one leg.

The colors shifted constantly, it even appeared that some of the stitches contained more than one color.

"Didn't you get headaches?" asked Betsy.

"Sometimes," Irene admitted. She turned and stared at Godwin until he walked away, then leaned toward Betsy and muttered, "I hear Mr. Mickels told you he was at a business meeting the night your sister was murdered."

"Who told you that?"

Irene hesitated, then lied badly. "I don't remember, exactly. But if that's true, he must have held the meeting on his rowboat. *And* had a for-real battle with his board of directors."

Betsy stared at her. "Why do you say that?"

"Because I saw him walking up Minnetonka Boulevard that Wednesday night with a broken oar in his hand."

Betsy frowned at her. Irene nodded several times. "That's the street that goes out past the old Excelsior Park restaurant—where the Ferris wheel is?"

Betsy nodded wordlessly. You could see the Ferris wheel a long block away from the front porch of Christopher Inn, which was itself barely more than a block from Crewel World.

"What time was this?"

Irene thought briefly. "I'd say around ten-fifteen."

"Could it have been earlier?"

"I don't think so. I started out from my house right about ten, and it usually takes me about ten minutes to walk to the lake. I wasn't walking fast, as I was enjoying the weather. It had stopped raining, and was dark and cool and misty, and as I was coming up the street, he kind of loomed up under a streetlight. He was wearing one of those old-fashioned black rubber raincoats and his hat had the brim turned down, and he was carrying a broken oar. I thought for a second I was seeing a ghost, but then I saw the silver whiskers and I realized it was just Mr. Mickels. I think he saw me the same time I saw him, because he suddenly ducked into the parking lot and went behind this big car."

"A broken oar . . . ?" Betsy prompted.

"Yes, you know." Irene nodded. "The paddle part was gone."

"So how do you know it was an oar?" thrust in Godwin, back like a bad penny. "Without the paddle, it's just a stick, isn't it?"

Irene drew herself up. "The oarlock was still on it."

"Oarlock?" echoed Betsy.

"Yes, you know, oarlock." Impatiently, Irene took up a phone message pad and drew what looked like a capital *U* with a stem growing out of the bottom of it. "You stick the bottom part into a metal holder on the boat so you can row." She looked at Betsy without seeing her, thinking. "Or maybe it's the holder that's the oarlock. Whatever, that's what he was carrying, the handle part of an oar with that metal part dangling. And the paddle part broken off."

Godwin sniggered. "I bet that was a hell of a meeting with his board of directors. I bet they still have headaches."

Betsy cast a quelling look at him and asked, "You're sure this happened last Wednesday?"

"Yes, I'm sure. It had been raining off and on that evening and there was a light fog. Just the right kind of a night to see a ghost. But it wasn't a ghost I saw; it was Mr. Mickels."

"Maybe he didn't duck out of your way," said Betsy. "Maybe he just went to his car." She turned to Godwin. "What kind of car does Joe Mickels drive?"

"Some big old yacht, like a 1973 Cadillac or something."

"See?" said Betsy.

"Is it one of those old cars that has fabric on the roof?" asked Irene. "An imitation convertible. Because this car was like that. And it had a hood ornament, too."

"N-no," said Godwin. "It's a real dark green, I think. And not two-tone, just one solid color."

"This car wasn't two-tone," said Irene. "And it might have been green, though I thought it was black. Those streetlights make it hard to see colors."

Godwin gave Betsy a triumphant look over Irene's head.

"But it did have fabric on the roof," she said. "I know it did. I was there, I saw it."

"Wait a minute, I thought you were at home all that night," said Betsy.

Irene's triumphant glare at Godwin faded abruptly, and her breath snagged in her throat with a sound almost like a snore. "What?"

"I said, I thought you told me you were home, working on a needlework project."

"I was, I was home all evening. But I got hungry, I hadn't had any dinner. And I just love to walk when it's all misty and foggy, so at about ten o'clock I decided to walk to McDonald's and have a hamburger, and I was almost there when I saw Mr. Mickels. And he ran away and hid when he saw me coming."

Betsy looked at Godwin, she couldn't help it. And his face showed he was thinking what Betsy was thinking: I, too, would have ducked into a parking lot rather than encounter Irene Potter. Her face must have shown her thoughts as well, because Godwin simply bloomed with amusement, and he turned quickly and walked away.

"That man is so rude!" said Irene.

Betsy got her face under control before Irene turned back. She said, "Did you see anyone else while you were out walking?"

Irene thought. "Not close up. And not anyone I recognized. Not many people were out that night. And I wasn't looking around, I was just enjoying the
misty night air. I came down Water to Second, and up Second to Excelsior and
up Excelsior to McDonald's." She paused in the act of rolling up her wonderful
cross-stitch picture. "You know, if I had gone one block more, down to Lake,
and come up that way, I might have seen the open front door of this shop, and
it might have been me who found your sister's body. Isn't that interesting!" She
tucked the roll of cloth under her arm. "You will let me know if you want to
display this, won't you? I'll get it framed if you do."

"Thank you, yes, I'll do that," said Betsy, and watched her march out. That
woman, she thought, has no instinct for self-preservation at all.

The next day, Jill, Shelly, Godwin, and Betsy sat at the worktable
in Crewel World. Betsy was knitting—her fingers moved more swiftly now, but
not so swiftly that people might suspect her needles were getting warm from
the friction. Shelly, who was supposed to be at a teachers' conference, was
needlepointing an angel as a Christmas gift; and Godwin was doing some very
elaborate needlepoint stitches on a sampler.

Jill was in uniform, on duty, and so didn't have anything to work on. She
was drinking coffee and tickling Sophie under the chin. Sophie, purring loudly,
was draped in luxurious ease over a cushion on what Betsy had come to realize
was *her* chair. Jill had come in to have a private conversation with Betsy, but the
other two were determined to miss nothing and Betsy couldn't think of a task
that would take them to the back of the shop, out of earshot.

"I heard someone saw Joe Mickels near the store carrying the murder
weapon," said Shelly.

"Who told you that?" Betsy demanded.

"Heard it at the Waterfront Coffee Shop; that's where you go to get the
good gossip."

"But it's not true," Jill said firmly. "In the first place, no one knows what
the murder weapon is. In the second place it probably isn't an oar."

"A *broken* oar," corrected Godwin, who had decided this fact was of great
significance. "If you could have seen the way Joe behaved toward Margot, you
wouldn't be so quick to dismiss Betsy's suspicions—or the story Irene came in
here with. She said he saw her coming and he ran and hid behind his car so she
wouldn't see who he was."

"What have you got against Joe Mickels, Goddy?" asked Jill.

"Me? Nothing, but he was downright mean to Margot, you know that. He
was very angry about her thwarting his big-time plans. He bought the two lots

behind this building, you know, so whatever he wanted to build here was going to be big, really big. Probably another condo." His expressive blue eyes glanced out the front window, toward the gray condo complex across the street, then at Betsy. "Margot just hated that thing, you know," he said softly.

Betsy said, "So you think it was in part to keep Joe from putting up another condo that made her glad she could thwart Joe's plans?"

"I don't think anyone knows what Joe plans to put up on this site," said Jill.

"Well, that's true," Godwin conceded. "It could be a business block. It could be a vertical mall. But whatever it was, it was going to be a lot bigger than the current building."

"How do you know Joe bought the property behind this building?" asked Betsy.

"Because my sister's brother-in-law owned the gas station up behind here. Joe bought his place nearly two years ago, and is renting it back to him on a month-by-month basis, so he's been planning this for at least that long."

Shelly remarked, "You know, holding on to all this property all this time may have given Joe cash-flow problems. I mean, he was all set to start building this spring, but Margot wouldn't vacate."

"If Joe is going to put up a big building on this site, he can't be short of cash," said Jill. "Besides, he's collecting rent from all three shops—and the other two don't have leases, so he's getting more from them."

"But big-time financiers are always getting into trouble when they have to delay their plans," Shelly argued. "It has something to do with cash flow."

Jill made a dismissive noise. "Like you know anything about big-time financiers."

"I may not be rich, but I read," Shelly retorted. "And the *Strib* has stories all the time about big companies and rich people who get into trouble because they bite off more than they can chew, or they start in doing something big and there's a delay or a glitch. It's like one day they're rich and the next day they're bankrupt."

There was a cozy little silence as everyone contemplated Joe Mickels filing for bankruptcy.

"How far would someone like Mickels go if all that stood between him and making a lot of money was Margot?" asked Godwin, serious again.

"And if not doing what he planned meant going broke?" added Shelly.

The sober mood was broken when the shop door opened. Standing in the door was Mike Malloy in a brown tweed suit too warm for the seventy-five-degree weather. "What are you doing off patrol?" he said to Jill in a hard voice.

Jill stood, flushed a faint pink. "My coffee break," she said.

"Hit the road," said Malloy.

"Yes, sir." Jill glanced at Betsy, but Betsy was keeping her wary attention on Malloy. Jill brushed by the detective and he closed the door after her.

"I need to talk to you, Ms. Devonshire," said Malloy in that same hard tone. "Alone," he added with dramatic emphasis, just like on television. He even shrugged a little bit inside his coat as if to adjust, or loosen, the gun in an armpit holster.

That worked a lot better than Betsy's hints; Shelly and Godwin immediately put down their work and went to make busy noises in the back of the shop.

Malloy yanked out a chair—the one Sophie was in. She half fell, half jumped out of it and went square-wheeling off to join Shelly and Godwin, giving Malloy a look over her shoulder that made it clear *she* wasn't afraid of him.

Malloy sat down, leaned toward Betsy, and said in a deadly monotone, "What the hell do you think you are doing, accusing Joe Mickels of murder?"

"What makes you think I accused him of anything?" Betsy managed to keep her voice cool and calm, but she knitted when she should have purled.

"He came in and told me. I asked him if he wanted to file a formal complaint, and he said no, not if you stopped spreading it around that he's a murderer."

"I haven't been spreading it around. As a matter of fact, I didn't accuse him of anything. All I did was ask him where he was the night my sister died." She looked Malloy right in the eye. "And he lied to me, he said he was at a business meeting in—"

She tried to think. Some town with a funny name, like a fake saint.

"St. Cloud," came a voice from the back of the shop.

Damn and bless Godwin's sharp ears!

"St. Cloud," she confirmed. "But Irene Potter told me just a little while ago that she saw him in town about ten o'clock that night, and that he hurried into a parking lot when he saw her coming. She said he was carrying a broken oar with an oarlock attached to it."

"I thought you just told me you haven't been accusing Mickels of murder."

"I haven't. Irene was the one with the information. And she came in all on her own and volunteered it. If you want to accuse someone of spreading rumors about Joe Mickels, I suggest you talk to her. But I suggest you also talk again to Mr. Mickels." Again Betsy dared look the cop in the eye. "I haven't accused anyone of murdering my sister, Detective Malloy. But just because Joe Mickels is a rich man doesn't mean he's also an innocent one."

"Mr. Mickels was out of town; if Irene Potter says she saw him, she's lying."

"No, she isn't," said Shelly, loudly, from behind the shelves at the back of the store. "She's a little bit off center, but she doesn't lie."

"All right, so she saw him down by the lake with an oar in his hand. How does that make him a murderer?" demanded Malloy.

Betsy went back to her needles, purling where she should be knitting. "It means he hasn't got an alibi, Detective. He wanted my sister to relocate her shop so he could tear down this building and make a million dollars selling space in a new and bigger one. And when she refused to move, he started looking for legal ways to evict her, harassing her, not holding up his end of the lease. Talk to Mr. Penberthy, her lawyer, about the times Mickels hauled Margot into court with some stupid writ. Maybe he just got tired of it, maybe there was some kind of time limit he was operating under. You can find these things out. Why don't you go do it?"

Godwin spoke, startling them both. He was standing by the edge of the table, having come on noiseless feet up to it. "And it seems murdering Margot didn't fix things for him, Detective Malloy. Because Margot had incorporated her business, and named her sister Betsy as an officer of the corporation. So guess who stands between Joe Mickels and his big plans now?"

Betsy gulped and dropped a stitch. She hadn't thought of that.

But Malloy turned on Godwin. "In my opinion, Joe Mickels is an honest man. You can think whatever you want, you even have the right to speak up about it. But if Mickels is what you two think he is, quick to use the law for his own ends, then you maybe should worry about the libel and slander laws in this state. He was sure enough breathing fire about you, Ms. Devonshire, when I last saw him. If I was a Jeannie-come-lately thread peddler or her"—Malloy hesitated just long enough—"employee, I'd bite my tongue." He stood and suddenly his attitude gentled. "You're an amateur, Ms. Devonshire, and you're new around here. You have no idea what you're getting into, messing with Mr. Mickels. I think it's interesting that he doesn't have an alibi, and I'll check into that, but I don't think it will turn out to be important. I repeat, you would be wise to stop making accusations against him without real proof, okay?"

All Betsy could reply to that was, "Yes, sir." Malloy nodded sharp approval of her meek tone, and left.

When the door had closed on his brown suit, Godwin huffed, "He'll be sorry if he finds you dead in the middle of another fake burglary!" He sat down with a snort to resume work on his sampler.

Betsy started to laugh; she couldn't help it. When Godwin looked up at her with that innocent, limpid gaze, she laughed even harder.

But she couldn't make Shelly understand what was so funny.

Fifteen

✦

"I apologize for the short notice," said the voice of Mayor Jamison in his heavy Midwestern twang, "but things got bollixed up when Margot died. So now we have to get really moving on this thing. Can you come to Christopher Inn this evening? You'll get a free supper out of it again."

"Yes, I think so," said Betsy into the phone. "What time?"

"Seven o'clock. See you there."

Betsy didn't know of what use she would be to the committee; Margot was the driving force, she was only one of the driven. But it did occur to her to ask Shelly to stay awhile after closing and help her find the slash jacket Margot had promised to donate, since Betsy wouldn't have known a slash jacket if it jumped up and bit her. Which from its name it might.

Betsy found a big box of donated items: a table lamp, a gift certificate, a framed print. But no jacket. Shelly was the one who unzipped a garment bag in Margot's closet. "Here it is," she announced.

At first, Betsy thought it was knitted somehow, with lots of ends left loose to make it look shaggy. But no, it was some kind of red-orange cloth with small black figures printed on it, and short, multicolored fringe in curves all over—no, that wasn't it, either. "What the heck is that?" she asked, coming closer.

"It's the slash jacket," said Shelly.

"No, I mean, how is it made?"

"You take six, eight, ten different fabrics, layer them, cut out your jacket, and sew the layers together in lines, like . . . like"—she cast about for a simile—"contour farming." Her hand described curves. "When the jacket is finished, you cut through the layers between the contour lines. You line it, then you wash it over and over, until the cut edges stand up and fray. See how she used a layer of navy blue among all the reds and yellows? That gives a really interesting effect."

"It sure does. Who in the world dreamed up the idea?"

"Beats me. I've wanted to make one for a long time, and Margot told me it's easy to do, but I never got up the nerve. I mean, to take a razor to a finished garment! I'd probably chicken out and just call it quilted."

"Here, let me see it." Betsy took it off the hanger and tried it on. It fit a little snugly, and when she looked at herself in the mirror, she made a face and shrugged it right off again. "Makes me look fat."

Shelly looked as if she wanted to disagree, but honesty won out. "That *is* a drawback," she said. "And it's not as warm as a down coat would be."

"I suppose I could just hang it on the wall, like a work of art." She backed off and cocked her head, studying it. "Yes, that would be really effective on the right wall."

"Are you going to bid for it, then?"

"I don't know. How much do you think it might go for?"

"Three or four hundred, maybe more."

Betsy sighed. "Well, I guess not."

"Yeah, me neither."

"Shelly, can I ask you something?"

"Sure, what?"

"Who would you consider to have been Margot's enemies?"

"Now, that's an ugly question. But I guess the right answer would be, nobody."

"Come on, Joe Mickels has to go on the list."

"Okay, Joe Mickels."

"And Irene Potter?"

"Oh, Irene's just a little crazy, not dangerous."

"She came over here after the funeral wanting to buy Crewel World."

"Of course she did, she's wanted to open her own needlework store for years."

"So she wanted Margot out of the way, didn't she? How badly?"

Shelly was smoothing the slash jacket on the hanger. "Oh . . . pretty bad, I suppose. But she's the kind of crazy that would make a little doll and stick pins in it. I can't imagine her coming after Margot with a real weapon."

"All right, then, who would?"

Shelly hung the jacket on the closet doorknob. "I told you, nobody. Margot was a good person. She organized charity events, and got people excited to start working on them."

"There's a silly old joke: she lives for others; you can tell the others by their haunted look. Was Margot one of those, always poking into other people's business? Trying to reform people who maybe didn't want to be reformed?"

Shelly frowned. "No, that wasn't her at all. All I ever heard from people she helped were thank-yous. She was a busy lady, and she liked getting other people up off their butts. She got so much more done in a day than normal human beings, I used to wonder if she slept four hours a night or something. She kept the store going, she was involved in her church, she did a lot of volunteer work, yet she never complained about being tired. Or not a whole lot, anyway. She inspired me, so now I teach and I work part-time in the store and I'm on this one committee." She grinned, a little embarrassed. "I will say, once this committee's work is done, so am I. Christmas is coming, and there's enough work in that for me." She consulted her watch. "Oh, gosh, I've got to get home and feed the kids."

Betsy said, surprised, "I didn't know you had children."

"That's what I call the dogs. My husband got the boat, the Miata, and the condo in Chicago; I got the summer home here in Excelsior—which was my grandmother's to start with, so big deal—the Caravan and 'the kids'—two goldens and a miniature schnauzer bitch who bosses us all. Still, I figure I came out way ahead; he has the Cubs to contend with."

W hile the dogs were wolfing down their evening meal, Shelly dialed Hud Earlie's home number.

"Today Detective Mike Malloy came in and read Betsy the riot act. Remember you told me you heard she thinks Joe Mickels did it? Well, you were right. And Mr. Mickels complained to the cops and the cops are leaning on Betsy, hard."

"Yeah, well, if Betsy had said something to me, I could have told her Mickels casts a long shadow in Excelsior."

"Shoot, any of us could. But you know something? Even after he said he'd arrest her if she didn't lay off, she was asking me who Margot's enemies were."

"So you think she won't lay off?"

"You can't stop a person from thinking about something, but I don't know if she'll go around accusing people anymore. You could ask her tonight."

"What makes you think I'll see her tonight?"

"Aren't you coming to that fund-raising committee meeting tonight?"

"Oh, that. Was she invited?"

"Sure, she's on the committee, isn't she?"

"I thought she was only an add-on of Margot's. Not really official."

"Hmmm, well, I was there when Jamison called, and he asked her. Maybe they'll try to put Margot's mantle onto her."

"It won't fit."

Shelly sighed. "Nothing of Margot's will fit anyone else. That's the really sad thing about this business. I bet if it was Betsy who got murdered, Margot would have the murderer wrapped up in floss and delivered to the jail by now."

* * *

The Dick Huss vase Hud brought to the meeting at Christopher Inn was eerily beautiful. It was black glass, about fourteen inches high, shaped like a jug, down to a little neck just the right size for a cork. But it was covered with a three-dimensional flowing pattern of tiny triangles, circles, and dashes. It cried out to be touched, and Betsy complied.

"How does he get that effect?" she asked.

"He puts little pieces of tape all over it, and sandblasts the spaces away," Hud replied.

"It's beautiful," said Betsy. "Here's the slash jacket," she added, putting it on the table beside the vase. Its bright color only made the Huss vase stand out more.

"Can I talk to you?" asked Hud.

"Sure, what about?"

He led her to a back parlor. "I hear the cops are close to making an arrest."

"Where'd you hear that?"

"I also hear the perp is a burglar."

"Detective Malloy *says* he's on the trail of a burglar. But I don't think he'll arrest anyone, because I don't think it was a burglar at all."

"Of course it was a burglar, the store was trashed like only a burglar does."

"No, it was trashed way beyond that, like someone was angry at Margot."

"Angry about what?"

"I don't know. But I'm going to find out."

He looked down into her unwavering eyes. "I wish you wouldn't," he said as sincerely as he could, putting all his concern for her into the words, and he could see a bit of wavering set in.

And her reply was defensive. "But I can't just take everything Margot left behind, all that money, the shop, all her good friends, and not try to do anything in return!"

"Silly kid," he said very fondly, and pulled her into a warm embrace.

Which she immediately began to struggle out of. "Let me go," she said, and he did. She straightened her jacket and ran a hand over her hair. "Don't ever do that again," she said, and walked out of the room.

"Well, then, let me help," he said ninety minutes later, walking her home.

"How can you help?"

"I don't know. Ask me something you want to find out."

"Who hated Margot?"

"Ha!" he said, surprised. "Nobody. I don't think anyone was even mad at her."

"Joe Mickels was." How could people keep forgetting that?

"Joe Mickels was caught up in a business disagreement with her. He was doing everything he could think of to make her move out of that store. He wasn't treating her any differently than he'd have treated anyone who was in his way like that. It wasn't personal."

"You mean he'd have murdered anyone he couldn't evict legally?"

He stopped and took her by the upper arms. "Joe Mickels has been around for years. He is a very accomplished, very patient, very persistent businessman. He has never found it necessary to murder anyone before, and I doubt if his situation with Margot was any different."

But Betsy was remembering the look on Joe's face when she asked him where he was the night Margot was murdered, and the oddly long wait for his answer. There had been fear as well as fury in that face. She shrugged free of Hud's hands and continued down the sidewalk. "Who else?" she asked.

"Who else what?"

"Was mad at Margot?"

"Nobody."

"Not even Irene Potter?"

"Hey, her problem is envy, not anger. She thinks she could've run that store better than Margot."

"Hud, if Margot hadn't incorporated, what would have happened to Crewel World?"

"It would have gone out of business, I guess."

"You don't think Irene would have taken it over?"

"No. Well, she might have tried, but it wouldn't have worked, not for long. She's not a people person, which you need to be to run a successful store. And I think she might not even have tried, because on some level she must be aware that she has no people skills."

"I have people skills."

"Yes, you do. For which I am grateful. Are you going to stay in Excelsior?"

"At least for now. I kind of think I like it here."

He took her hand. "It's an even nicer place now that you're in it."

She freed her hand. "Who else?"

He sighed. "You seem to be the one with the list. Who else do you suspect?"

"Where were you the night Margot was murdered?"

"Me?" He put both hands on his chest, fingers splayed. His eyebrows were actually up under his forelock. "You're kidding!"

She had been, but his astonishment was so overdone that she frowned up at him. When she spoke, there was a crisp edge to her voice. "I know you think I'm an incompetent fool for looking into this, but I am not kidding."

He dropped his hands and sighed. "I don't think you are a fool, but I do think you are asking for trouble."

"So help me, get me into trouble. Where were you that night?"

He cocked his head at her. "I took my secretary out to dinner at the Green Mill, then went up the street and rented a movie, then went home and watched it. I put it in the car the next morning so I'd remember to take it back, and on my way to work I heard on the radio about Margot. The only part I can prove is the dinner—well, I suppose the video place will have a record of my renting *Men in Black*."

"I loved that movie."

"Me, too, but I'll never watch it again without remembering. Who else is on your list?"

She had nobody else, but didn't want him to know that. "Who is the person who knew Margot best?" she asked instead.

He drew twin lines from the corners of his mouth to his chin with thumb and forefinger. "Probably Jill Cross. Those two have been thick as thieves from the day they met."

"I'm going to repeat Mike's warning, Betsy. Stay out of this. You could get arrested. Mike's very territorial about his cases." Jill looked tired. They were at the coffee shop on Water Street; Jill was on another coffee break; Betsy had found Jill's beeper number on the kitchen phone list and arranged this meeting.

"You were Margot's best-friend," Betsy persisted. "Who was mad at her? Who was jealous? Who hated her?"

"Nobody hated her. She was an extraordinary lady with a kind heart and more energy than a dozen of the rest of us put together. You'd think, with all her activities, that someone would at least envy her, but no one did. Her loss is the whole town's loss."

"Irene envied her."

"Yes, she did. But she's crazy."

"That can be enough to set off the mob. So why aren't people out with torches demanding Irene's head? Or Joe's?"

"Because Minnesotans don't march with torches. They prefer to let the police do their job. That means Mike. He'll do it right, come up with the proof that will stand up in court. You should just get on with your life and be patient."

Betsy said, "I don't have a life. And if I did, I couldn't get on with it knowing Margot's murderer is free."

"Don't be so melodramatic!" There was a definite snap in Jill's voice.

"Then help me."

"I am helping you; I'm keeping you out of really serious trouble. I told you she had no enemies."

"Okay, then tell me what she did on the last day of her life."

"I don't know, the usual I guess—ran errands, went shopping. It was her day off. I know she went to Minneapolis, to the art museum. Check her calendar."

"Where is it?"

"I don't know. I know she has one, she called it her nag and said she'd be lost without it. But I bet when you find it, all it will have on it for that day is that trip to the art museum, and the city-council meeting that night."

Betsy nodded; she didn't remember an appointment book in Margot's purse, but she hadn't been looking for one; she'd check again as soon as she got home. Meanwhile: "Who did Margot have a fight with lately?"

"How lately?"

"Jill . . ." Betsy made two tired syllables of the name. "Forever, okay? Who had she ever been really mad at?"

Jill sighed. "Godwin, for making fun of her. That was years ago, when he thought she was just messing around with her committees. Shelly for gossiping. And Hud, of course."

"Why 'Hud of course'?"

"It's a long story. He never was a big fan of hers, you know. Maybe because she was on the board of directors of his precious museum, and she disagreed with him at board meetings once in a while. She took her position on the board very seriously, you know. And she was very bright. Hud likes women who flirt with him and let him have all the ideas. Especially if they're rich."

"Like me, I suppose?" Betsy heard the edge in her voice but couldn't help it. She was tired, too. It was late and she'd had a busy day.

"Well, maybe it's more that he gets along better with women who don't have any power over him," Jill conceded. "Because I think he likes you, so he must like some women with brains."

"But he really didn't like Margot," Betsy persisted, "just because she was on the art-museum board and therefore his boss?"

Jill took a deep drink of her coffee; she was working a double shift because a colleague was ill. "That's not all of it. Hud's second wife used to be Margot's best friend, and when he dumped her for the woman who became the third Mrs. Earlie, Margot was furious. Eleanor—that's the second wife—moved away, and Margot was depressed about that. And when the third marriage broke up after only six months, she was even madder at Hud. Every so often he'd try to be friends with Margot, and she'd get mad all over again at him."

"I suppose she thought it might have been better if Hud had just had an affair," Betsy heard herself say, and was surprised at the defensive tone. Did she like Hud that much? She rubbed the underside of her nose with a forefinger and caught Jill's sardonic look. Or was she amused? Betsy still had trouble reading that enigmatic face.

Jill said, "I think this time she was mad because he and you seemed to have hit it off."

Later, in bed, waiting to fall asleep, Betsy thought the conversation over. Margot had been furious with Hud for dumping his wife, Margot's best friend. That was interesting, but it didn't seem relevant. If anything, it might have been a motive for Margot to murder Hud, rather than for Hud to murder Margot. But not all these years later. Of course, it spoke ill of Hud, behaving that way. Hud's face, that confidence man's grin all over it, swam up before her, then Margot's face appeared, with a disapproving look. So Margot had spoken to Hud about her? How dare Margot think Betsy couldn't take care of herself!

She rolled away from the faces, seeking sleep—and after a bit, found it. In a few minutes she was dreaming that she and Jill were in a sinking boat, and she was frantically knitting a new paddle for the broken oar while Jill bailed.

Sixteen

❦

Betsy woke with a start. Something energetic was playing on the clock radio, Groucho Marx being greeted as Captain Spaulding by the gritty sound track from the old movie. Betsy had first heard that song as the theme from Groucho's TV show, *You Bet Your Life,* and had been surprised when she heard it in the movie *Animal Crackers.* Or was it *The Cocoanuts?* Never mind, it was a delightfully silly song to wake up to.

She had been surprised by KSJN's *Morning Show* because that radio station played classical the rest of the day, which in Betsy's opinion was the genuine, authentic, real stuff for easy listening. Still, she left her clock radio set to wake her to the *Morning Show*, because she was rarely annoyed by the music they offered. On the other hand, she never knew what they would play next. In this case, it was Glenn Miller's "Pennsylvania 6-5000." Betsy smiled; she could remember her parents dancing to this; it had been one of their favorites.

What was more, the sun was slanting brightly through the window, it looked to be another pretty day. On those two happy notes, she began her morning stretches. Pennsylvania stretch, stretch, stretch!

The song ended. Dale and Jim Ed began one of their faux commercials—this being public radio, and they apparently felt a need to make up for the lack of real ones. They touted a company that, for a price, thought up weird excuses for why you could not come to work. Their current offering involved a rare mildew infection, and included a scientist who would call your boss to confirm the infection and give the recipe for the powerful cleaning solution needed to wipe down anything you had touched. "This way," concluded Dale, "when you go to work the next day, not only have you convinced everyone you had a legitimate excuse for being off work, you will find your work area spick-and-span!"

And Betsy had thought California had a lock on weird!

Stretches completed, she relaxed for a bit. She felt the mattress jiggle, then lean into big-cat-size footfalls as Sophie came up alongside her. The cat fell weightily against her hip with a combination sigh and purr. The cat enjoyed these slothful morning minutes as much as Betsy did. Betsy closed her eyes and let her fingers wander through the animal's fur until she came to the special itchy place under Sophie's chin, where she paused to scratch lazily. Sophie put a gentle paw around Betsy's hand in case Betsy had any notion of moving it away. The purr became richer, deeper, deeper, deeper. . . .

Betsy was brought back from a doze by a gentle but insistent tugging at her hand. She resumed scratching.

But when Betsy tired of scratching and tucked her hand back under the covers to try for another nap, Sophie turned the movement into a game of Mouse Under the Blanket, which finished that notion.

Then, thumping along on her cast, Sophie led the way into the kitchen, where she sat pointedly beside her empty food dish. But Betsy started the coffee first. It was her sole victory in the mornings nowadays and she was determined to hang on to it.

When it was a little before ten Betsy went downstairs to open up, eager for customers.

But by noon she had added another four inches to the knitted scarf (including errors unraveled and reknit properly) and nothing to the till. Only two people had come in. One wanted something the shop didn't carry. "Try Needle Nest in Wayzata," Godwin said, adding to Betsy, "They send people to us." The other person was merely curious about Betsy's sleuthing, and she firmly put him off. As she told Godwin, perhaps he was on Detective Malloy's list of informants.

At last Betsy announced she was going to call the part-time help and tell them not to come in for the afternoon shift.

Godwin, taking down some outdated announcements on the mirror by the front door said, "Don't do that. Take a half day yourself. Margot always took Wednesdays off."

"I don't have anywhere I need to go," she objected, thinking perhaps she should give Godwin the half day and save his salary, too.

"Yes, you do."

"Like where?"

"First, you should go back upstairs, have a little lunch, and find Margot's sketchbook, the one with the red cover. I can do the needlepoint, if Margot did a graphed drawing of it. I'll work it like counted cross-stitch, only in needlepoint. It's a thousand dollars for the shop."

"Less what I'd have to pay you to do it."

"I'll do it for nothing. For the sake of the shop. For Margot."

"Oh, Goddy . . ." Betsy felt guilty for even thinking of shorting Godwin's paycheck.

"Now don't get mushy. Besides, here's where you really need to go this afternoon," he added, bringing a new flyer back to her. "Look, there's a Kaffe Fasset exhibit just opened."

"Who's Kaffe Fasset?"

He sighed and rolled his eyes. "Only one of the best needlework designers in the world. Needlepoint to cry for, knitting to die for. People who see the exhibit or read about it will be coming in to buy his patterns and it will help if you can talk intelligently about him."

He put the flyer in her hands. The front flap had a color photo of a magnificent sweater, knit in a pattern of subtle, earth-toned stripes under an Oriental-looking pattern of flowers.

"Hmmm," she said. "This is at the Minneapolis art museum. Yes, you're right, I think I need to go see this."

"Upstairs first. Go on, go right now."

Because it had been Shelly who found the slash jacket and Irene who had noticed the T'ang needlepoint horse missing, Betsy considered she, perhaps, was not the one to be looking for the sketchbook.

But she told herself sternly that since she obsessed about Margot's murder, and was therefore the sleuth, however amateur, she had a responsibility to prove herself capable of sleuthing.

Unlike Betsy, Margot had been a neat and organized person. (Already the apartment shows that, Betsy thought, and sighed.) Presumably there was a place she kept such things as the notebook she used when designing pieces. Betsy had been living in the apartment long enough to know that if the notebook were kept outside Margot's bedroom, she would have come across it by now. And she hadn't.

Therefore (Betsy smiled to herself, this was rather like a syllogism, and she'd been rather good at syllogisms), the notebook was in Margot's bedroom.

She stood a quiet moment inside the door, feeling suddenly that her sister was quite close, that this was an important moment. She stopped the shallow breaths she'd been taking and instead took a deep one, letting it out slowly.

If I were Margot, she thought, where would I keep a sketchpad on which I was designing a copy of the blue horse?

Filed away under *T'ang*, came the prompt answer.

She went to the wooden file cabinet and slid open the bottom drawer, labeled M-Z. Under *T*, she found T'ANG HORSE. The file folder was slender, containing only the handwritten note about the order for the copy Mrs. Lundgren had placed. No, wait; in the bottom of the folder were two sets of three slim packets of Madeira blue silk embroidery floss, each held together with a rubber band. They were numbers 1005, 1007, 1008, 1712, 1711, and 1710. One packet was dark, medium, and light shades of midnight blue; the other, silver blues.

By now Betsy had seen enough of needlepointers to know that a needle-pointed rose was often four or more shades of red. So why not a horse six shades of blue? She started to put the folder back, but changed her mind and kept it out.

There was no sketchbook in the file cabinet, of course; she had realized as soon as she opened it that the sketchbook was too big to fit in the drawer—Betsy had seen the sketchbook, it had a thick red cover with spiral binding across the top. Any other notes Margot had made on the original horse she'd either thrown away or taken with her to the museum, where she'd probably added a few new ones. And she'd never gotten a chance to put them back into the folder.

They were probably with the sketchpad.

Which wasn't in the closet. It wasn't tucked behind the file cabinet or the dresser, either. Or under the bed. Or under the comforter pulled across the bed.

Betsy searched the other closets, cabinets, bookshelves in the apartment with equal lack of success. She went out to the kitchen to spread a dab of peanut butter on a slice of the Excelo Bakery's excellent whole-wheat bread and do some thinking.

Betsy had overheard some conversation between Margot and a customer about using a computer to design patterns. Margot had sounded knowledgeable on the topic; maybe she did that herself.

Betsy put down her bread half-eaten and went back to the bedroom. She booted up and looked for a publishing or artwork program. The first one she found didn't have anything connected to needlework in it. The second one was for designing needlework, but there were no files in it. She searched around for a while, found no other design program, and finally summoned the word-processing program.

The computer burped and gurgled at her, and instead of a screen ready to accept text, offered something called *What Are You Supposed to Do Today?* It had a list under it, beginning with some general notes: *Betsy's birthday, October 15,* for example. Under that were specific dates. *Wed, Aug. 19, 11 am—See Hud at museum,* read the first of those entries. Under it, indented: *2 pm, Penberthy, sign papers;* and under that: *7 pm, City Hall, bring report on art fair.*

Betsy smiled. She had not been able to find a physical date book because Margot kept her appointments on her computer.

Thursday, Margot was supposed to see if Eloise was back in town and ask her if she would run the food shelf this winter. Friday asked, *Told Betsy yet?*

Betsy sat frowning at that. Tell Betsy what? She thumped the screen with a knuckle. Tell me, she thought at the screen, as if it had ESP and would respond. But it didn't.

Betsy scrolled down the screen. Margot had a date with Mayor Jamison for the Last Dance of Summer at the Lafayette Club on Friday. The date of the fund-raiser, also at Lafayette Club, was noted, and there continued a steady stream of things to be done, running right through the end of this year and into the next, including that spring art fair she'd gone to talk about at City Hall.

She pressed the exit button and the computer wanted to know if it should save the calendar, noting that no changes had been made. Betsy punched *N* for no, and on getting a blank screen asked to see a list of files.

The contents were mostly letters, including one to Mrs. Lundgren about the T'ang-horse needlepoint, saying that it would be ready Tuesday of Thanksgiving week and reminding her that the one-thousand-dollar price was due on delivery.

But there was nothing else about the T'ang project in the files.

Betsy shut down the computer and finished her sandwich before going back down to the shop, frowning with discontent.

Godwin was no help; he had no idea what might have happened to the sketches or any other notes Margot might have taken about the needlepoint project. Or what papers Margot was to sign at Penberthy's office.

"You could call and ask," he suggested.

Feeling a little foolish, she went behind the desk and phoned Mr. Penberthy. He was out, but his secretary remembered Margot coming in. "She was here to sign the incorporation papers."

Well sure; Penberthy had told Betsy that! And of course that was what Margot had meant to tell her, that she was an officer of the new corporation.

Betsy said, "Margot had this big sketchbook, a kind of tablet with a red cover. She didn't by chance leave it behind when she was there, did she?"

"Now, funny you should ask," said the secretary. "Because she did leave it behind. I had to run out of the office to catch her and give it back to her. We had a nice laugh about it, like she was getting real absentminded lately. Which of course she wasn't."

"Do you know where she went from your office?" asked Betsy.

"No. Home, I guess. She sort of waved that big pad at me and said, 'Thanks for this, I've got some work to do now,' or something kind of like that."

"She didn't say she was going straight home?"

"She said something I didn't quite catch. I said, 'Are you going home now?' and she said—well, you know how you hear something all wrong? I heard her say, 'I mean to putter around the mix,' which I know is wrong. I heard it wrong. I remember that I tried for an hour to figure out what she really said, because it kind of bothered me. Then when she was killed, I thought about it some more, because it might be important. But the police never came around asking, thank God. I'm thinking maybe I missed the last word, so it's the mixed something."

Betsy thanked her and hung up.

"'I mean to putter around the mix'?" echoed Godwin, when she repeated it to him. "What does that mean?"

"Irene Potter is next," said Betsy. She had opened her mouth to say she had no idea what Margot meant, and instead that came out.

Godwin stared at her.

"Margot was my sister, Godwin," she said. "I can understand her better than some secretary, even if she's not speaking to me."

"You are *good!* So, are you going to go see Irene instead of going to the museum?"

Betsy hesitated. "Both," she said. "The museum first, because it may be hard to get away from Irene." She picked up the file folder. "Is there anything odd about this?" she said, spilling the silk onto the desk.

Godwin came for a look. "I don't know. I'd think they were the colors for the horse, except these two families are so different."

"Would they be like samples?" asked Betsy. "I mean, there isn't enough here to do the entire horse, is there?"

"Probably not, although you get more loft from silk and so don't need as much of it as you'd need of cotton. These are more likely samples, to see which family came closer to the actual horse—Margot liked to match colors as closely as she could. But then why not a selection of yellows for the mane, or whites for the saddle? The ground was a light tan, I remember, but that wouldn't matter as much, since she wasn't matching a real wall or drapery." He checked his watch. "If you're gonna visit the museum, *and* flirt with Mr. Earlie, you'd better get a wiggle on."

"Goddy!"

"I know, I'm incorrigible."

Betsy got directions from Godwin and set off. She was halfway there before it occurred to her that she wasn't exactly dressed to kill. Oh, well, she thought, better he learns now that I'm not the clotheshorse Margot was.

The museum was perhaps a dozen blocks south and west of the Guthrie, in what had once been a neighborhood of wealthy families, and was still a long way from crumbling. Some of the fine old mansions had been converted to offices, but others held the line, stubbornly insisting that the 1880s would be right back.

The museum was built in the classical style, with lots of steps leading up to a row of massive pillars, flanking bronze doors. The new main entrance, around the corner, was a modern addition, and wheelchair-accessible.

The inside had been thoroughly renovated, too, though here and there was a room that still showed signs of having been built the same time as the beautiful old houses in the neighborhood.

The Fasset exhibit was in two rooms, one very small and the other not really large. Betsy was disappointed to discover that Kaffe Fasset was a man. She had never considered herself much of a feminist, but needlework is *so* traditionally female that while it was nice to see a woman's homely craft at last recognized as art, it would have been equally nice to have the artist be female.

On the other hand, Mr. Fasset was indeed an artist. There were gorgeous sweaters, some so enormous only an NBA star gone to fat could have worn them. Is that what makes these art? wondered Betsy. They are clothing no one can wear? Mr. Fasset favored rich earth tones of gray, mahogany, green, and gold.

The artist also did needlepoint; Betsy was intrigued by a red lobster on a checkerboard ground. His work was perfectly smooth, unmarred by errors, fancy stitches, or beadwork.

Signs everywhere warned patrons not to touch, but this was a weekday morning, and the exhibit had few visitors. Betsy took a quick peek and discovered that Mr. Fasset was not fastidious about the backs of his works. Betsy hadn't been either, when she was doing embroidery. Would it be worth her while to work really hard and gain artistic status so she might escape the criticism the Monday Bunch leveled against messy backs?

Betsy studied a knitted shawl inspired by the arum lily, row upon row of perfect curved shapes, each marked with a narrow tongue, in a harmony of colors that made her sigh with envy and covetousness. No, she would never be this good. Better to learn to be more careful with the backside of her work.

She left the exhibit and went looking for the Asian art section. One wide hallway was lined with European sculpture from the last century, which Betsy only glanced at—until she saw a small white bust of a young woman wearing a veil held in place by a circlet of flowers. She slowed, stopped. She could see a hint of eyes, nose, and mouth behind the veil, and almost instinctively reached to touch it. But her eye was caught by a hand-lettered sign asking her not to. Smudges on the veil showed not everyone pulled their fingers back as she did. Not that one could move the veil, of course; the entire thing was of marble, a three-dimensional *trompe l'oeil*. She looked for and found the brass tag naming the genius who had done this: Raffaelo Monti. When I am rich, she thought, and went on.

Her feet were tired before she found the Asian art section, up on the third floor. It was cramped between two areas being noisily renovated, and was disappointingly small. The centerpiece was a massive jade mountain carved into paths, brooks, bridges, trees, houses, animals, and people. But in the few surrounding glass cases there was no pottery horse of any color from any dynasty.

Betsy went down to the information desk on the main floor, which was manned by two middle-aged women whose manners were so open and informal that they had to be volunteers. One of them called Hudson Earlie's office, and permission given, a guard was summoned to bring Betsy up four flights to him.

She was shown into a small anteroom where a secretary said Mr. Earlie was on the phone. Hud stayed on the phone a long time—but Betsy didn't mind. Chat was better than "music on hold," and Hud's secretary was personable, as well as young, trim, and pretty. Doubtless Hud had taken her out to dinner any number of times, though Betsy was careful not to ask.

Hud's inner office was quite grand, with tall windows on two walls and an Oriental carpet on the floor. He came out from behind his desk to take her hand in both of his, pleased she had come calling.

"Nice of you to come into town especially to see me," he said.

"Actually, I came to see the Kaffe Fasset exhibit."

He smacked himself on the forehead. "Oh hell, where is my head? I should have realized that you'd be interested in that and seen to it that you got a ticket."

"It was only five dollars, Hud."

"Yes, but you're not on Easy Street yet."

"True, true." She looked around. The shelves flanking the windows held small, exquisite examples from Hud's specialty, Asian Art, and the books were also on that topic, except one called *Art Crime*.

"Do you get thieves or see a lot of fakes?" Betsy asked.

"Not a whole lot," he said. "Asian art sometimes has the same problem as art from third-world countries: provenance. Because some of it is stolen or smuggled, provenance can't be given—you know what provenance is?"

She nodded. "The paper trail of owners tracing a piece of art back to the artist."

"Or the place where it was dug up," he agreed. "So what we get sometimes is an authentic piece of ancient art with a fake provenance. It's my job to authenticate pieces that we acquire, and I've learned to look beyond the paper to the piece itself."

"Hud, where's the T'ang horse?"

If she hoped to startle him with that question, she didn't succeed. "In storage. Most of our collection is in storage, because we're renovating the Asian art exhibits, giving separate galleries to India, Korea, Islamic countries, Himalayan kingdoms"—he was counting on his fingers—"Southeast Asia, China, and Japan. Plus new lighting and better alarms. It's going to be spectacular. I take it you went looking for the horse?"

"Yes. Margot was going to redo her needlepoint picture for a customer, who offered a thousand dollars for it—a sum the shop can use, badly. I've got an employee who thinks he can do the needlepoint, so maybe we can still get the money. I was curious to see what it looks like—I don't remember more than glancing at Margot's original."

"You want me to show it to you?"

"Can you?"

Hud glanced toward his desk, where papers waited. Then he smiled at her like a schoolboy plotting to play hooky. "This will have to be quick, okay?"

"Thanks."

But as they turned toward the door, Betsy saw the one non-Asian note in the room, an umbrella stand made from an elephant's lower leg, standing by the door.

"Let me explain," Hud said with upraised hands, when her questioning gaze came back to him. "I needed something to hold my walking sticks, and they were going to de-accession that. Somehow, it ending up in a Minnesota landfill seemed worse than keeping it, though of course we can't display it. So don't look at me like I killed the elephant myself; that happened a hundred and thirty-odd years ago."

Betsy approached the object gingerly. She had heard about such things, but to actually see one was horrible—it even had the toenails—so she changed focus to the seven or eight walking sticks and the one umbrella it held. Most had brass heads, including the umbrella, which was tightly furled. "Is this your collection?" she asked.

"Part of it. I'm always taking one or another home and then coming in with a different one. I don't even know what's in there right now."

The flat-faced owl was, and another shaped like a snail. "Which one's the sword cane?"

He pulled out an ebony cane with a standard curved handle. Apart from some copper-wire inlay, it was undecorated. Hud had to pull fairly hard to get the handle to separate, which he did with an overhead flourish, and suddenly there was a length of gleaming steel waving under Betsy's nose.

"Cute," said Betsy, taking a step back. "I'm glad it was the sword or I'd be covered with whiskey."

Hud laughed and put the cane back together, and they went out of his office. "I'll be back in a few minutes, Dana," he said to his secretary as they swept by.

They took the freight elevator, a big, padded box so old-fashioned it had a human operator—a retarded man from a local group home, who loved this vehicle like Hud loved his Rolls. As it slowly clanked its way down, Hud said to Betsy, "How do you like our Guthrie Theatre?"

"Very impressive. How did you know I went?"

"You're a new face in a small town. Everyone's paying attention."

"I didn't know you lived in Excelsior."

"I don't, I live next door in Greenwood. But I eat breakfast every so often at the Waterfront Café."

Betsy chuckled.

They went up a broad hall lined with huge eighteenth-century religious paintings to an unmarked wooden door that opened with a key.

The door let into a long narrow hall, at the end of which was another door, which opened into an enormous room full of stacked wooden crates, a big stone statue of Shiva, and glass cases containing golden Buddhas, Chinese watercolors, Japanese robes, and enigmatic stone heads. "Wow," breathed Betsy, "it's like Christmas at Neiman Marcus."

Hud laughed. "Here, this way." He led her through a labyrinth formed by the rough wooden cases. At last he led her around an immense crate and pointed. "There it is."

The blue horse was inside a glass case with a brown horse and two human figures. Hud said, "As you can see, it's part of a set. They are funerary figures from a tomb in China built early in the eighth century."

He watched as Betsy slowly approached the case. The figures were on a stepped base, the male figure on the highest point in the center. But Betsy only glanced at him and focused in on the blue horse. This was so typical, thought Hud, that he was going to suggest at the next board meeting that they discontinue the postcard showing all the figures and make one of just the horse.

High but directly above the case was an air vent; it blew a chill draft down on them. He saw Betsy shiver and stuff her hands into the pockets of her blue cardigan as she moved around the case. Suddenly she stooped as if to see it from a child's angle. He could see only the top of her head, and was surprised at the amount of gray in her hair. Her face was young; she could get away with a dye job. Doubtless when she came into that money, her hairdresser would suggest it. What was it, three million? He would himself suggest some improvements to her wardrobe—that cardigan was positively shabby.

He waited, but she showed no signs of being finished. At last he cleared his throat, and when Betsy straightened he was looking pointedly at his watch.

"Sorry," she said, and they retraced the labyrinth out of the storage room.

Back in his office, she asked, "May I ask why Margot came to see you the day she died?"

"She had some idea about a proposed fund-raising campaign. She felt it was too ambitious, that we wouldn't meet our goal. She wanted me to support her at the next meeting when she voted against it."

"Did you agree to?"

"No, I told her I thought the goal was achievable. We agreed to disagree and she went off to see the T'ang horse."

"But the door was locked. Or did she have her own key?"

"No, she borrowed mine. There was talk among the board members about getting their own keys, but the staff argued successfully that the hand of authority is not the same as the hand that knows how to handle fragile artifacts."

"Yes, of course. So why, when she brought the key back, was she all upset?"

He looked at her slantwise. "Have you been talking to my secretary?"

"That's what you get for making me wait while you chat on the phone," she said archly. "But why was she angry?"

"She wasn't all that angry. Every time she went into that storage room, she snagged a stocking or her good wool skirt. She wanted to know when we'd get the renovations finished; most of our artifacts have been in storage for over a year. I told her it might be another six months; we're short of money to complete the renovations." Hud grinned at her. "I think that might have changed her mind about voting against the fund-raiser."

Betsy smiled back. "Do you remember about what time she left here that Wednesday?"

He had to think. "I'm not sure. Wait; I had an appointment at two and I made it, so it must have been fifteen or twenty minutes before that."

"Did she tell you her plans for the rest of the day?"

"No. Why?"

"I know she had an appointment with her attorney to sign the incorporation papers, but that only took half an hour. Yet she didn't get home until after

I'd closed the shop. We hardly had a chance to talk, I was getting ready to go out when she came in, and I left her changing to go to the meeting at City Hall."

"Maybe she went to a movie," Hud suggested. "It was her day off, after all." He took her by the upper arms and gave a gentle shake. "I wish you'd let this alone," he said.

"I can't, Hud. It's on my mind all the time, like one of those dumb songs that start in and won't go away. I can get busy in the shop or figuring out Margot's computer, but if I stop for just a minute, it starts in: Who murdered Margot? Who murdered Margot?"

He embraced her, and this time she let him. "Poor kid," he said. He felt her lean into him and tightened his embrace just a little.

But that only made her pull back. She said, "Hud, I understand you and Margot were not exactly friends."

"Who told you that?"

"Is it true?"

He grimaced. "Well, she was kind of mad at me, but that was a long while ago."

"Because you dumped your second wife for your third."

"I see my secretary has really been dishing the dirt." He didn't bother to sound amused this time.

"It wasn't her, someone else told me."

"You don't think *I* hated Margot, do you?"

"No, it seems to have been the other way around. What happened?"

He sighed. "I got to know Margot through my wife Eleanor. We used to go out as a foursome, Eleanor and me, her and Aaron, and we all got along swell. Then I hired Sally as an assistant and thought I'd found true love. It was like Fourth of July fireworks." He made an upward spiral with his hand. "Whoosh, whee, bang!" He dropped the hand. "Darkness." He sighed. "I was the world's greatest jerk, but by the time I found that out, Eleanor was dating a banker in Kansas City and not inclined to listen to anything I had to say. And Margot had been named to the board of directors of the art museum, which I thought for a while she maneuvered herself into as a way of getting at me. But while she never really forgave me for what I did, she was too interested in what was good for the museum to damage it in order to hurt me."

"Was she alarmed about you flirting with me?"

He felt a little alarmed himself. "Did she say something to you?"

"Kind of. Hinting that you weren't altogether one of the good guys."

He nodded. "That's fair. Because I'm not, you know."

She smiled up at him. "Yes, I suspected that from the start." He wanted to go back to that embrace, but she moved out of range, saying, "I'm keeping you from your work. Thank you for being patient with me."

"Don't forget Friday. I'll pick you up at seven-thirty, if that's not too early. I want to show you the lake at sunset."

"I look forward to that," she said, and continued toward the door. Then, just like Columbo, she turned with one last question. "Oh, how long was Margot in the storage area looking at the horse? We can't find her sketchbook, but I'll stop looking for it if I know she didn't have time to make a graph of the pattern."

He shrugged. "An hour, maybe? I'm afraid I don't know how long it takes to make a graph."

He frowned worriedly at the closed door for a moment after she left, but as he dug into the paperwork he had to work on he began to whistle. Someone was going to get kissed very thoroughly on Friday.

Seventeen

❖

Betsy retraced the route back to Lyndale and went up it, toward the towers of downtown. In a couple of stoplights she was driving past the Hennepin Avenue Methodist Church, with its circular nave and crown-like steeple, then past the Gothic St. Mark's Episcopal Cathedral, and saw ahead the entrance to 394, next to St. Mary's Roman Catholic Basilica, built in the Baroque style. If I'm going to live in this part of the world, maybe I need to start going to church, she told herself.

In another minute she was on 394, which curved around sharply and headed west.

What did it all mean? What was Joe Mickels doing in an Excelsior parking lot when he was supposed to be an hour away at a business meeting? Had he come back in time to murder Margot?

Irene Potter said she saw him, which meant she'd contradicted her own alibi of being at home doing needlework at the time of the murder. Was she so innocent she didn't realize that? Or was she astute enough to realize that someone might have seen her, and so was getting in ahead of that witness?

Hud drove a car that at first glance or in the dark looked like an American model from back in the sixties. Why hadn't she thought to ask his secretary if in fact he had taken her to dinner that fatal night? Not that there wasn't time to have gone from dinner to Excelsior and parking his convertible in a parking lot only a couple of blocks from Crewel World.

And Hud was the Asian art curator, responsible for the T'ang horse, the needlepoint representation of which was mysteriously missing.

The question was, why? Hud had no motive.

Still, it was interesting he was keeping abreast of her comings and goings. Or should she be flattered by his interest, rather than concerned?

She continued west to 100, south to 7, west to Excelsior. There, she drove around looking for Irene Potter's house, whose address she had gotten from employee records.

Irene lived in a brown clapboard house that had not enjoyed the meticulous care of the houses around it. When Betsy reached the door, she saw a clumsily crayoned sign in the window indicating that this was a rooming house with a room for rent. She knocked on the door and an elderly, sad-faced man answered it and she asked for Irene Potter.

"She ain't here," he said.

"Is this her house?" asked Betsy.

"No, it's mine. She just rents from us."

"Who is it, Father?" called an old woman's voice from the back.

"Someone wanting Miss Potter!" His voice, when he raised it, quavered.

"Let me talk to him."

A plump woman with a face like one of those dried-apple carvings came to stand beside him. She wore a faded blue dress under a clean white apron, and her dark eyes were bright with intelligence.

"You're not a policeman!" she said indignantly.

"No, I'm Margot Berglund's sister. I've taken over her shop, Crewel World. Irene sometimes worked for my sister, and I wanted to talk to her."

"She's gone out."

"So your husband was telling me. Do you know when she'll be back?"

"Not much longer, I don't think. She's at church, one of the volunteers who helps cook Meals on Wheels."

"How nice of her to do that. Do you know her very well? I take it you're her landlady."

"Yes, that's right. But I don't know her that well, though she's been with us for years. She's not one of the friendly ones."

"Yes, I'm afraid that's true. But she is very talented at needlework."

The woman smiled. "She tried to show me how, but I just didn't get it."

Betsy smiled back in kind. "Me, too. Irene isn't a very good teacher."

"Won't you come in?"

"Now, Mother—" said the old man.

"Shut up, Father." The old woman led the way, saying, "It was terrible what happened to your sister. We don't have murders in Excelsior, so this was a terrible shock. And of course it was even more terrible for you, being her sister."

"Yes, it's been a sad time." The living room had too many couches and chairs, all well used. The woman gestured Betsy to an easy chair.

"Would you like a cup of tea?"

"No, thank you," said Betsy. "Irene told me that she was out walking in the rain the night my sister was killed. In fact, she was near the shop about the time it happened."

"I know. That's why I thought it was a policeman at the door."

Betsy said, "From here to the lake is quite a walk in bad weather. Does she do that sort of thing often?"

The old man cleared his throat, clearly disapproving of the direction this talk was going. His wife shot him a look that made him decide he'd be more comfortable elsewhere. He tottered out without saying a word, but she waited until she heard a door close before turning back to Betsy.

"Miss Potter is a great one for walking. Part of it is necessity, of course; she never learned to drive. But part of it is plain contrariness. The worse the weather, the more she likes to be out in it. But I must say it agrees with her, she never gets so much as a sore throat."

"So you saw her go out that night? Do you know what time she left?"

"No, I was out myself, at my granddaughter's house. They just bought this place out in Shorewood, and it's a wreck. Needs everything, from paint to plumbing. So I was out there scrubbing and painting and watching the great-grandkids." She drew herself up a little. "Got three of 'em now."

"Congratulations," said Betsy.

"You're the one who thinks the police are barking up the wrong tree with their burglar theory, aren't you? Do you really think Miss Potter might have done it?"

"Right now I suspect everyone."

"Yes, that's probably smart, though I don't think your sister had many enemies. What were you going to ask Miss Potter?"

"If I could see some of her needlework. I've seen one or two pieces, but I keep hearing how wonderfully talented she is."

The old woman frowned in puzzlement.

"You see, I'm not trying to prove Irene murdered my sister, I'm trying to find out the truth. If Irene is innocent, I want to make use of her expertise. She's already given me some intelligent suggestions about running the shop. And my sister kept some of her work on display as an inspiration to her customers."

"I could loan you something of hers. Wait here a minute." She left the room and soon Betsy could hear heated conversation, cut off by a closing door. Then the woman was back with a square pillow. "Is this the kind of thing you want to display?" she asked, and handed it to Betsy.

The face of the pillow was divided into quarters, each containing a picture of the same house in a yard with a tree. Each quarter represented a season. In spring, a robin sang in a tree branch and tulips glowed in the yard. In summer, a child skipped rope in the yard. In fall, the leaves on the tree were a gorgeous mix of red, yellow, and orange, and a jack-o'-lantern sat on the porch. In winter, a Christmas tree decorated with tiny beads glowed in a window. The snow was done in white yarn, which had been brushed to make it fluffy. In each, the sky had been done in fancy stitches that Betsy knew had names like gobelin and Victorian step, though she did not know what names to call these skies.

There was not a misstep in the stitching that Betsy could see, and the overall effect was lovely. "This is really nice," she said.

"Her room is full of this kind of thing," said the woman. "She has a quilt stitched all over with angels. You can borrow this, if you want."

"I don't want to take it away from you. What if someone stole it?"

"Oh, likely she'd make me another. She's good about that kind of thing, though she can be very unfriendly right to your face, too. Of course, if you hit on the right subject, she'll talk your ears off."

Betsy nodded. "So I've heard. Did she ever talk to you about my sister?"

"No, not once. But your sister came to see her the day she died."

"She did?"

"Let me think. Maybe it was the day before she was killed I went to my daughter's. No, the day of because I didn't hear about the murder till the next evening, on the television news. My cousin Emily came over that Thursday, and sore as I was from the day before, we went out, so it wasn't till evening that I learned about it. It was a terrible shock, and it wasn't till the next morning it occurred to me that Miss Potter must've been one of the last people to see her alive. And it was a shame, a real shame."

"Why a shame?"

"Because Father says they went at it hammer and tongs, the two of them. He says he was in the kitchen—Miss Potter's room is over the kitchen—and while he couldn't hear any of the words, they was at it for quite a while. Then he says he heard someone coming down the stairs and he went to see, and it was Mrs. Berglund. Miss Potter, he says, stayed at the top of the stairs and hollered after her, 'You'll be sorry you talked to me like that! You'll be sorry!' But Mrs. Berglund just went on out, never looked back."

"Could I talk to him about this?"

"No, I'm afraid not. He's mad at me for not promising not to repeat what he told me to you. Says it's none of your business. He's talked to a police detective about this, and is waiting to be interviewed by him."

Joe Mickels glared up at Betsy. He was trying hard to keep hold of his temper, because angry as he was that she had come, he was more afraid of what she was going to ask. But he'd told his secretary to show her in, because he did not dare let her know of either his anger or his fear.

She came in looking tired, and he sensed at once that she was nervous, too. That made him feel he could handle her.

"I take it you are still stirring up trouble over your sister's murder," he said bluntly.

She drew herself up a little. "I am asking questions the police should be asking." He did not offer her a chair, though she seemed a little footsore. He remained seated behind his desk.

"What kind of questions?"

"For one, if you were in St. Cloud that night, as you claim, how did you manage to be seen ducking into a parking lot in Excelsior?"

"Who says they saw me?"

"Irene Potter."

"She's a loon, likely to say anything."

"Her description is a little too detailed to be a hallucination. She said she saw a man with big whiskers, carrying a broken oar and wearing a black rubber coat and a hat with the brim turned down. Do you own a black rubber coat and a brimmed hat? Is your boat missing an oar?"

Bad questions, worse than he thought. He knew lying was a mistake, so he didn't say anything at all. But she was content to let the questions hang there, being answered by his silence. At last he stood and went to the window. The sun was shining, people were going about their business. Old Mrs. Lundgren came out of the Excelo Bakery with a white paper bag in her hand.

"I should get these whiskers cut off," he said. "Not many people wear them anymore." He turned to find her looking at him with a pretty good poker face. "It was me," he said.

"Why a broken oar?" she asked.

"When I've got something I need to think over, I like to do it on the water. Bad weather don't bother me, so long as it's not a thunderstorm, and it wasn't. So I went out in my rowboat. It was so damn foggy out there that I lost my way and rowed right onto some mudflats. I didn't want to get out—you can sink up to your, uh, backside in that stuff. So I stuck the oar in and started pushing. I was stuck pretty good, I was prying hard, and the thing snapped. It's an old oar—hell, I've had that boat since I was nineteen, and that's the original set of oars. But I finally got loose and I paddled with the other oar till I found a dock I could tie up to, near the Park Restaurant. I was walking home when I saw Irene coming, the old witch. I thought I got out of her way quick enough."

"So you weren't in St. Cloud at all."

"No, that was the night before. That night I went to supper at Haskell's, then I took my boat out and rowed around. It helps me think."

"What were you thinking about?"

"You want the truth? Margot Berglund. That woman was the bane of my life till the day she died." He glared at her. "And now you've taken over, worse than her, talking about me behind my back, and all."

"I haven't been spreading rumors about you. I don't know who is repeating what I say in confidence, but they seem to be putting their own twist on it. All I'm doing is wondering out loud who murdered my sister. What time was it when you saw Irene?"

He glared harder, but she didn't back down an inch. "Sometime around ten, or a little after," he answered grudgingly. "I remember it was about twenty past when I got in the house."

"It must not have taken you long to drive home," she remarked.

"I didn't drive home, I walked. I live in Excelsior Bay Gables."

"You mean, you live in that condominium right across the street from Crewel World? I didn't know that."

"No reason you should."

"Why were you so anxious to get my sister to break the lease and move out?"

"Because it's time Excelsior had a really decent building. Are you going to insist on staying to the end of the lease?"

"I haven't decided. Did you murder my sister?"

"No, I did not. And I don't appreciate you siccing that cop detective back onto me."

"Did he come and talk to you again?" She was surprised.

"He did, said you were the one who broke my alibi."

"You shouldn't lie to the police."

"Especially in a town where everyone keeps track." He nodded.

She asked, "Did you recognize Irene when you saw her?"

"I was pretty sure it was her. That's why I ducked out."

"Tell me your version of what happened."

He did; it didn't vary much from Irene's story, so she thanked him and left.

After she was gone, he told his secretary he did not want to be disturbed, then locked the door and went into his strong room for a silver restorative.

* * *

When Betsy got back to the shop, it was going on four. Godwin was completing the sale of Marilyn Leavitt-Imblum's *Song of Christmas* counted cross-stitch graph and the yarns to complete it. "You'll need bugle beads for the candles on the tree," he was saying, leading the customer to the big metal box that held little drawers full of beads.

And Shelly was talking with a customer who was interested in using DMC floss instead of Paternayan three-ply persian on a project. "Let's see what Fiber Fantasy says is the equivalent color of Paternayan 501," Shelly was saying.

Betsy stood near the doorway a moment, thinking she really ought to go to church and thank God for competent help. And while she was there, she could apologize to Reverend John for thinking badly of him. Which reminded her, she needed to call Paul Huber at the funeral home and apologize to him, too.

The door went *bing* and she hastened out of the way. Jill came in with, of all things, an oar in one hand. She went right past Betsy, saying over her shoulder, "Follow me." She was wearing old jeans and a sweatshirt, but was nevertheless exuding cop authority, and Betsy obediently followed out the back door into the hall that led to the back entrance.

"What, what's the matter?" asked Betsy when Jill at last stopped and turned around.

"This is an oar," said Jill.

"Yes, I can see that." It wasn't broken, and so wasn't Joe Mickels's oar.

"Look at the oarlock."

Betsy obeyed, and even reached out to note how the thing was attached, which was through the oar so that it could swivel. "I can see how it might be difficult to swing it so that the spike is driven into someone's skull," said Betsy.

"And, that spike is too thick and too long to have done that injury," said Jill.

"Interesting. But I already don't think Joe murdered my sister."

"You don't?" Jill put the oar down. "What changed your mind?"

Betsy explained, concluding, "Still, it's interesting about the oar. You're sure the spike is too big?"

"The autopsy report said the spike was not more than an inch and a half long. And the injury to Margot's skull was fairly small, only an inch or so across. But that doesn't mean the weapon was that small. It depends on whether or not the weapon sank to its full diameter."

"Ugh!" said Betsy. "The things you know."

"These are things you encounter when you investigate homicides. I think Hud's right, you aren't cut out for this sort of stuff."

"Hud? When did you talk with him about me?"

"He didn't tell me, he told Shelly. Shelly told me. Didn't I warn you about her? She's the most terrific gossip I've ever known."

"And in this town that's saying something," said Betsy. "So she's the one who told Hud you and I went to the Guthrie."

"Yes, she told me he told her he wished it could have been him taking you out. Those two talk on the phone a couple of times a week."

"Hud's a suspect, you know."

"*Hud?*"

"You're the one who told me they quarreled."

"That was *years* ago!"

"Actually his motive has nothing to do with the quarrel; it's that T'ang horse. Margot went to see it on that Wednesday, and then went to see Hud upset—he says because she snagged her stockings again in that storage room and wanted to know when they'd get the new exhibit set up. That night she was murdered, the shop was ransacked, and the only things still missing are the T'ang needlepoint and her sketchbook in which she was making a new copy of it. What's more, not only does he not have an alibi, a Rolls-Royce was in an Excelsior parking lot that night."

Jill stared at her. "How do you know that?"

"Irene said she saw Joe Mickels ducking down behind a big dark car, an imitation convertible with a hood ornament. I remember those imitation convertibles, and none of them had hood ornaments. In fact the only car with a hood ornament I can remember is a Rolls-Royce—and Hud owns a Rolls that has a beautifully made convertible top, so perfectly fitted you might think it was one of those cars with the fabric top. And Joe Mickels remembers the hood ornament looked like a fairy, which pretty much describes the Rolls ornament."

Jill thought a minute. "You know, Betsy, Hud doesn't own the only Rolls-Royce in the state. Or the county, for that matter. Probably half of their owners don't have alibis. You can't go around saying this kind of thing without more proof than that!"

"I wonder how many Rolls-Royces there are in Minnesota?"

Jill frowned at her. "I don't know. I've seen a few."

"How many?"

She thought. "Two, maybe three, right in this area."

"I bet it would be interesting to call their owners up and ask them where they were that Wednesday night. If all of them but Hud have an alibi, then we'll know something of value. Say, Jill, can you really find out how many there are? Who their owners are? Where they bought their cars? Hud says he bought his at a car auction, but I wonder—could we find out where he bought it?"

"You're serious!"

"You bet your sweet bippy I am."

"The Minnesota Department of Public Safety keeps those kind of records. You can ask their computer to do sorts to get that kind of information. Like a friend of mine on the Minneapolis force was investigating a ring of snowmobile thieves. They were breaking them down for parts, but now and then they'd take the leftovers and make a new snowmobile and sell it. Jay asked them to sort out all the reconstructed snowmobiles registered in the past two years and broke the case that way."

"Can you ask for a sort of Rolls-Royces, even though you're not a detective?"

"Sure, but it will go through Mike and he'll ask me why and I'll tell him you want to know. Better you ask them yourself."

"How? Pretend I'm a cop?"

The cold look Jill gave her made Betsy wonder how she had ever mistaken any of Jill's earlier looks for chilly dislike. Jill obviously did not approve of impersonating an officer. But she replied courteously enough, "No, of course not. Automobile registrations are public information. Car salesmen line up to get lists of people who've bought more than one sports utility vehicle in the past four years, or are driving a Cadillac more than three years old. The state charges for the information, but you can get the name and address of every Rolls owner registered in the state."

Betsy started back into the shop. "Where is this department? How long does it take to get the list?"

Jill followed, the oar in her hand. "It's in downtown St. Paul. Are you really going to go and ask?"

"That's not the broken oar," Godwin observed.

"Duh-uh!" said Jill.

"What were you two talking about?" asked Shelly.

"Why do you ask?" asked Betsy. "Are you out of things to tell Hud?"

Shelly said in a hurt voice, "What do you mean?"

"I mean, it was wrong of you to tell him everything I—or anyone else—told you." Betsy flashed a look at Godwin, who had the grace to look abashed.

"*Hud?*" said Shelly. "But you're in love with him!"

"I am not in love with Hudson Earlie. I was indulging in a flirtation with him. He's very attractive, but he's not one of the good guys—you should see what he has in his office. And I think maybe he murdered my sister."

Shelly said in a faint, appalled voice, "Why do you think that?"

"Because he stole the T'ang horse from the museum and Margot found out about it."

Godwin said, "You mean, when you went to the museum today it was *gone?*"

"Oh, no, there's a horse there all right. But it's not the same horse."

Jill asked sharply, "Are you sure?"

"Pretty sure. I mean, I took those Madeira silks with me, all six of them." She fumbled in her pockets and pulled them out. "Godwin pointed out that they are really two different families of blue, one of them kind of grayer than the other. Well, the 1710, 11, and 12 are the colors that match the horse I saw. These others don't. But Margot had all six in the folder labeled T'ANG in her file cabinet."

Shelly said, "When Margot was laying out the colors, she said 1008 was the right shade of blue." They looked at her. "I'm positive, I remember it distinctly. She was putting the colors beside the framed picture and saying she remembered it was 1007."

"There, Jill; there's your proof!" Betsy said. "The horse Margot used as a model for her canvas and the horse I saw are not the same color. I think that when Margot went down there to look at the horse last Wednesday, she took the 1007 colors with her. And they didn't match the horse in the case."

Jill said, "And of course she went to tell Hud. He's responsible for the Chinese stuff."

"And Margot was murdered that night. I suspect Hud told Margot not to tell anyone else until he checked into it. But what he did was come out here and murder her. And he stole the needlepoint horse and the sketchbook, because they're evidence. Then he trashed Crewel World to make it look like a burglary."

"Wait a minute," said Godwin. "Wait just a minute." Then he himself waited until they all turned to look at him. "About those different families of blue. I've been to the museum, and I know how carefully they light those exhibits. I have a feeling they don't light the storage areas like that."

Betsy flashed on the warm lighting of the Fasset exhibit and then on the big chill storage room with its harsh overhead lights. "No, they don't."

"Well, how many of us have put on an outfit that matches beautifully in your bedroom, but when you get to the office it's like you got dressed in the dark?"

The women, frowning, nodded doubtfully.

"So of course the silks didn't match the horse! On exhibit, in storage, different lights, different colors."

Betsy stared at him, her heart sinking. What if she had made a terrible mistake?

Eighteen

❖

Hud arrived Friday evening, right on time. He paused inside the door when he saw Jill and a very tall and well-built man waiting with Betsy for him.

"I'm so sorry, Hud," said Betsy, "but Lars's car broke down this afternoon and Jill's is in the shop, too, so I said you wouldn't mind giving them a lift."

Hud looked for a moment as if he did mind, but then he shrugged and said, "Sure, why not." He was wearing a beautifully cut tuxedo—or perhaps it fit so well because he was the shape the designer had in mind.

Jill had said the dance was "dressy," and turned up in a short cocktail dress of ice-blue silk, her escort in a dark suit and tie. So Betsy felt right in her little black dress and the garnet earrings and necklace her mother had left her.

"How 'dressy' is this dance?" asked Betsy. "I mean, am I all right?"

"You look wonderful," said Hud sincerely, so she let him wrap her in her black silk coat and followed him down the stairs.

Hud put Jill and Lars into the big back seat of the Rolls and pushed a button that rolled up a window between it and the front seat—which sent the two of them into gales of laughter.

"What's so funny?" Betsy asked Hud.

"Beats me." He handed her into the car and they started off.

The drive to the club was along a back road that wound among the bays of Lake Minnetonka, through small towns and past modest cottages and the beautiful new mansions that were quietly replacing them, all set in rolling land covered with big old trees. The sun was a glowing red ball—Betsy caught herself trying to decide which shade of perle cotton would be closest and decided she was carrying this needlework business too far.

The Rolls was big and comfortable, and as smooth to ride in as Hud had said it was. "Yeah, I really lucked out with this car," said Hud when she remarked on that, and on the powerful but quiet engine.

"You said you bought it at a police auction?" asked Betsy. "How did that happen?"

"I was in Las Vegas for our annual convention about six years ago." He showed his wolfish grin. "What, you think curators should meet in Chicago? In February? Anyhow, I took an afternoon off from the doings and got lucky at the craps table. A fellow curator told me about the auction. He said there would be sports cars—he was going to bid on a Porsche 928S. I went along to see if he'd get it—he didn't—but right at the end, when most of the people had left, this Rolls Corniche came up. A cop with a great big grin bid five hundred dollars, so I bid eight, which surprised him. Then he bid a grand, and I bid twelve hundred, and we kept going up until I bid everything I'd won, which was eight thousand, two hundred dollars. Silence from the cop, who wasn't grinning anymore. So I packed my bags and started driving for home, because you don't want to be in a town where you've wiped the grin off a cop's face. And you know how you hear about how crummy English cars are? Well, this one sure isn't. It has never given me any trouble at all. It gets terrible mileage, of course, because it's so heavy. But it's like sitting on a leather couch and watching the road come at you on a big TV screen."

"Nothing like being at the right place at the right time," said Betsy. "I didn't recognize this as a Rolls-Royce until I saw the grille. I remember seeing them in England back in the sixties, and they had kind of a roll of front fender that swooped down along the side to the back fender. Very distinctive."

"I think someone around here has one of those," said Hud. "But I'm glad this is a later model. Unless people notice the hood ornament, they think I drive an older American car."

"If you don't like the hood ornament, why don't you take it off?"

"Because then it would be a Bentley, and that's not quite the same thing."

Hud laughed and Betsy joined in, because it was true, Bentleys are Rolls-Royces without the hood ornament. Once upon a time, Rolls dealerships would not sell a Rolls to just anyone. Rich commoners had to settle for Bentleys.

Interesting that Hud knew that, too.

Lake Minnetonka is big and has a complicated shoreline so the drive took a while. The lake showed itself in tree-lined bays, or in glimpses through evergreens, and even occasionally came boldly right up to the road.

They were running alongside a particularly wide bay into which the sun had nearly sunk when Hud slowed and flipped his turn signal on. They turned away from the water, past a self-consciously quaint little brown church and across a railroad line. The other side of the road was lined with a golf course. And there, awash in white lights, was the Lafayette Club.

It was not at all the modest place Betsy had expected, but a 1920s stucco palace, with an arched arcade, faux-Moorish windows, and a forest-green canvas marquee at the entrance. And a valet in a dinner jacket waiting to park their car.

The lobby was huge, with a red tiled floor and a big old antique bronze fountain. A large, live band was playing somewhere, and the three couples ahead of them checking their coats were in tuxes and long dresses.

"Oops," said Betsy, and turned to Hud. "Why didn't you say black tie?" Her glance took in Jill, who widened her eyes innocently.

"What?" said Hud. "I told you, you look wonderful."

Fortunately, when they got to the ballroom there were a number of other women who either hadn't read Miss Manners on "Proper Attire for Black-Tie Events" or didn't care. Hud took her around, introducing her to people. Some of them she already knew, such as the chief of police, whom she'd met only yesterday. His wife was an ardent counted cross-stitcher.

The band was good. It played a mix of big-band, soft rock, and standards, mixed with waltzes and, once, a polka. She danced first with Hud, who made her think she was a better dancer than she remembered, then with Mayor Jamison and attorney Penberthy, who taught her that Hud was the kind of dancer who made his partners look good.

It was a slow dance with Penberthy, and as they box-stepped around the floor, she asked, "Were you a friend of Margot's, as well as her attorney?"

"I'd like to think so," he replied, a little dreamily. He hummed a snatch of the melody.

"Did she talk to you about anything the last time you saw her?"

"Hmmm? No, I don't think so."

"Are you sure? You saw her the last day of her life. Surely you remember what people said to you when they turn up dead right after."

He loosened his hold to lean back and look into her face. "What's this all about?"

"The police are here, they're going to make an arrest," she said.

"Arrest who?" he asked, alarmed.

"I'm not supposed to say, but it's the person who murdered Margot."

Penberthy tried to look around and dance at the same time and stepped on both of Betsy's feet. "Sorry, sorry," he said. He regained his rhythm. "Is that Joe Mickels over there?" The landlord was holding a highball in one hand and gesturing sharply with the other to a trio of men.

"Yes, and there's Detective Malloy. Jill's here, too, and her date is a Shorewood cop."

"Jesus God," murmured Penberthy. "When is it going to happen?"

"I don't know, but don't worry, they won't do it in front of everyone. They're supposed to let me know when everything's set up."

"Why you?"

"Oh, I'm going to be in at the kill. In fact, I get to take the first bite."

"Jesus God." The dance ended; Penberthy assumed a patently false look of indifference and escorted her back to her date.

During a break, the mayor came by and suggested to Hud that so long as he was here he might take Betsy around and show her the features of the club, since they would be using it for the fund-raiser next month. Hud seemed pleased to get out of the ballroom, which was a trifle warm. He showed Betsy the enormous fireplace lounge (two, count 'em, fireplaces), the long screened porch that overlooked yet another bay, the dining room, the intimate café, and the indoor pool.

Betsy's opinion of the Lafayette Club racheted up another notch with every feature. The suggested cost of a ticket to the fund-raiser, she remarked to Hud, was not high enough.

"Yes, but if they pay a lot for a ticket, then they won't feel a need to buy anything at the auction."

"Oh. Yes, I suppose you're right." They were back in the café, which was deserted and dimly lit, lined with semicircular booths in red tufted leather. There was the warm smell of coffee in the air. "Here's where they make the greatest coffee in the state," said Hud. "They'll start serving it soon."

"Minnesotans sure drink a lot of coffee."

"We're probably near the top per capita," said Hud, but with an air of intimacy that did not match the topic.

She looked up at him, his smiling face, the bright hair, the broad shoulders. "Hud, did you really have to murder my sister?"

He stood perfectly still for several long seconds. "What are you talking about?" His voice was still soft, as if he hadn't understood.

"Is the T'ang horse the only thing you've stolen from the museum?"

That caught his attention. "Stolen? I haven't stolen anything!"

"Yes, you have. The Asian art collection is almost completely in storage, and has been for over a year. What better time to replace some of the artifacts with replicas? People are less likely to notice any differences when they haven't seen the originals for a long time. But Margot noticed, didn't she? She made two trips to that storeroom, the first to do her original canvas and then only a few months later to do the second. And she saw the difference right away. You said she kept snagging things while she worked on that horse, that's what made me realize that both times she saw it was in the storeroom. So it wasn't a change in lighting that made her think the horse was a different shade of blue."

"What are you talking about?"

"The T'ang horse in your collection, the one Margot made a needlepoint copy of. The horse she saw originally matched the one-thousand series of

Madeira blue silks, while the horse she saw the second time matched the seventeen-hundred series. She realized it wasn't the same horse.

"And what does one do when one suspects there has been a theft? Why, one reports it to the person responsible—that was you, wasn't it, Hud?"

He made a little noise in his throat, but no words came out.

"And you said you'd look into it right away. You probably asked her not to tell anyone until you'd checked it out, right? Then you came to her apartment that night, saying you needed to see the proof. So she got her sketchbook and took you down to the shop because that's where the original needlepoint hung. And you hit her with your cane—was it the one with the head shaped like a snail? I remembered the way the slinky little head came out of the shell on the head of your cane, and it made me wonder. But maybe it was the one shaped like a bird. What kind of a bird is that, with the pointed beak?"

"Who have you told this fairy tale to? You're going to have some explaining to do if you've told anyone, because you're making a horrible mistake."

"Whatever cane it was, you hit Sophie with it, too, but with the side, and you broke her hind leg."

"I didn't hit anyone with a cane. Anyhow, I thought you said Joe Mickels did it. Or Irene Potter. They both were near the store, weren't they?"

"Yes, but they couldn't have done it, either of them, Hud. Margot left City Hall pretty close to nine forty-five. It took her six or maybe seven minutes to walk home, so she got in before ten, but not by much. The murderer was waiting for her, but he had to talk his way into her apartment, convince her to come down to the shop, murder her, and then trash the shop. There wasn't time to do all that and still be down by that parking lot by ten-fifteen."

"Maybe Irene saw Joe on his way to the shop, before the murder."

"No, because I made that call to 911 at three minutes after eleven. Say five minutes to the shop from the parking lot, persuade Margot to come down into the shop, murder her and injure the cat, then wreck the shop, and get away before I got there at eleven—not enough time, Hud. Even if he was still in the place when I saw the open door, there wasn't enough time. The shop was *really* trashed; you must have spent a long time breaking and tearing and kicking and smashing. It must have taken you at least half an hour to do that, and more likely forty-five minutes, or even an hour.

"Both Irene and Joe described your car as the one they saw in that parking lot at a little after ten. You really should have taken that hood ornament off. Ask me how I can prove it was your car."

"You can't prove it was my car."

"The department of public safety can make up lists of Minnesota car owners broken down any way you want. Did you know there are only seventeen

Rolls-Royces in the state, Hud? And only two of them are convertibles. And guess how many owners of Rolls convertibles don't have alibis?"

"Bitch," Hud muttered. "You *bitch*!" He grabbed for her, but prepared, she ducked away.

"Jill!" she shouted, and Jill stood up on the other side of the gleaming-empty salad bar. Beside her were Lars and two more uniformed officers, one with his gun drawn.

"Hold it right there, Mr. Earlie," the cop with the gun said in a deep, calm voice.

"I tried," said Betsy. "But he wouldn't confess."

"Close enough, I think, Miss Devonshire," said another man's voice, and a heavyset man who looked like every B-movie plainclothes cop came out of the kitchen. He was the chief of Excelsior's police department. With him was Mike Malloy, handcuffs in hand.

Jill, Lars, and the uniformed cops ducked under the salad bar and approached.

"You're under arrest, Mr. Earlie," said Malloy. He reached for Hud's right arm and snapped the handcuffs onto his wrist. "For the murder of Margot Berglund. You have the right to remain silent. . . ."

Betsy had always wanted to hear the entire Miranda warning, but all of a sudden her head was swimming and someone grabbed her and the next thing she knew she was sitting sideways at the end of a booth and the room was empty, except for Jill.

"Hey," said Betsy. "Where did everyone go?"

"Down to the police station," said Jill. "They want to talk to you some more, but it can wait until tomorrow."

"That's good, I think I'm kind of talked out. Did Hud go quietly?"

"Yes."

"Too bad, I would have liked him to feel a billy club or two."

"Want to go back to the dance?"

"Oh, gosh no. But oh, and how am I going to get home? Hud brought me!"

"Want a ride in a squad car? I can arrange for you to ride in the front."

"Can I play with the lights and siren? No, sorry, I don't mean that. I think I'm still light-headed. Riding in the front—is that what you and Lars thought was so funny about riding in the back of Hud's Rolls?"

"Yes, when he rolled up that window we started reciting the Miranda warning to each other." Jill chuckled.

Betsy said, "We got him, didn't we?"

"You bet we did. Mike has a whole lot more respect for you than he used to."

"Did he order up the the list of Rolls-Royce owners like I asked him to?"

"Yes, he did. How did you know there were only seventeen of those cars in the state?"

Betsy stared at her. "There are? I just pulled that number out of the air. Wow, do you think I'm psychic?"

"No, I don't. But I do think you are damn quick on your feet. Now come on, let's go phone for transportation."

Hud wisely invoked his right to silence. And the indictment did not mention a motive when he made his first appearance in court Monday morning. So the *Strib* put the story on the first page of its Metro section, below the fold, without a photo.

But when an Asian art expert came up from Chicago on Wednesday to look at the Minneapolis art museum collection, two employees of the museum resigned without notice. They were arrested and one of them began negotiating a deal.

A week later Jill sat at the table in Crewel World. She was in uniform, drinking coffee with one hand and stroking Sophie with the other. She didn't seem too concerned that Mike Malloy might come in and run her off.

Betsy was grumbling over a piece of twelve-count aida, blunt needle in her hand threaded with scrap yarn. "I just don't get it, Goddy."

"I know, I know; but it's like purling. Just listen and be patient and all of a sudden you'll wonder what you were complaining about. Now, where do you go next?"

"I haven't got the faintest idea."

"You're about to go up, so go down here."

"See what I mean?" she demanded. "I'm going up, so I go down."

"Yes, that's right. Here," he said, pointing, and Betsy obediently stuck the needle through from the back.

Jill said, "You'd think anyone who could figure out the clues that pointed to Hud Earlie could figure out a simple thing like basketweave."

"Yeah, you would, wouldn't you?" Betsy said crossly. She stuck the needle back in again on the diagonal. "Now where?"

"Here."

"Ah, this part I get." Betsy finished the angled row and said, "Now where?"

"Now we're starting down again, so go across, here."

"Ahhh!" Betsy growled, tossing the canvas down. "To go up you go down, to go down you go across. It gives me a headache!"

"But it isn't hard," said Godwin, picking it up and putting it back in her hands. "You're saying it right, that means you know it. Just do it."

Jill said, "How's business?"

"Crazy," said Godwin. "Everyone wants to meet the person who figured out a murder. And thank God they're ashamed to admit it, so we're selling every starter kit in the place."

Betsy said, "That knitting class Margot had on the schedule is overbooked; I may have to hire Irene to teach."

"Don't do that, you'll lose all those potential customers," said Jill. "You teach it."

"Me? I can't do anything more than knit and purl. Those crossovers and knots and all are a mystery to me."

"But you're so good at mysteries," said Godwin with his famous limpid look.

"And the students will be more interested in how you solved a murder that baffled the police than they will be in how to do crossovers," said Jill.

"Are you upset that I solved it?" asked Betsy. "Is Detective Malloy?"

"I'm not upset. And I think Mike has decided you're a special kind of informant. After all, you came to him at the end."

"Of course I did! I'm not V. I. Warshawski."

"Some people think you are," said Jill. "They'll be really disappointed not to meet you at knitting class."

Betsy laughed. "You teach it, Godwin," she said. "I'll sign myself up as a student. That way we won't disappoint our clients in any way."

"Well—"

"Thanks. I'll make up the poster tonight. Say, do either of the rest of you subscribe to that newsgroup RCTN?"

"No," said Jill.

Godwin said, "Aren't they fun?"

Betsy nodded. "And long-winded. It takes forever to download their messages, but they had this thread about coffee stains on a needlepoint—"

The door went *bing* and talk stopped. A young woman wearing a maternity top she barely needed came in with an older woman who looked enough like her to be her mother. Betsy stood and asked, "May I help you?"

"My daughter may have to spend the last part of her pregnancy in bed. She can knit and wants to make a bed jacket, but she can't do complicated stitches. Can you suggest something?"

Betsy said, "Here, let me show you something." She reached beneath the worktable and lifted a wood-framed folding canvas holder up onto its surface. She pulled out a pair of knitting needles to which was attached a pale gold length of knitting. It caught the light in a very attractive way when Betsy draped it over her hand.

"Oh, that's beauti—why, look at that, Mama, it's ribbon!"

"Yes." Betsy nodded. "It's mine, and I'm just learning. If you can knit and purl, you can do it. Isn't it pretty? We have the ribbon in stock in a wide range of colors, and there are pattern books that show you how to knit with ribbon."

The older woman fingered the knitting. "You know, that *is* beautiful. It makes me want to take up knitting again myself. Do you have any alpaca wool?"

"We just got a shipment in. I've never seen such wonderful colors. We have bone and bamboo knitting needles, if you need needles. But first, let me show you the ribbon selection." Betsy started to lead them toward the back. "Oh, and do you know we have classes here? Our regular knitting class is full, but there's going to be a second one starting soon, if you're interested. Or if you want to wait until spring . . ."

Over at the worktable there was a lot of winking and nodding going on. No one had wanted to ask, but if Betsy was talking about spring classes, she wasn't going to be holding a going-out-of-business sale anytime soon.

Turn the page for your free
T'ang Horse needlepoint pattern.

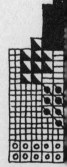

The T'ang Horse is worked in continental
stitch using three strands of Madiera silk, on
18 mesh.

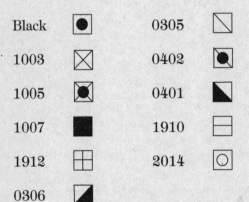

Black	⬤	0305	◺
1003	⊠	0402	⊡
1005	⊡	0401	◣
1007	■	1910	⊟
1912	⊞	2014	○
0306	◥		

Framed in Lace

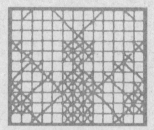

One

❖

It wasn't even Halloween, but autumn was over. Betsy sat at the little round table in the dining nook of her apartment and gazed out the back window. There was a small parking lot, with the ground beyond rising steeply through mature trees. Only yesterday the trees were ablaze with orange, red, and yellow leaves. She had planned to drive around Lake Minnetonka this weekend and take in the colors. But there had been a hard freeze last night, and now, in a light breeze, there was a Technicolor blizzard on the slope that would leave the branches bare by nightfall. Already she could see a gas station and a white clapboard house that had been hidden by foliage yesterday. The sky was clear, the sun was bright, but the weatherman on the radio had said that perhaps the temperature would break fifty by early afternoon.

Betsy, fresh from San Diego, didn't have much of a winter wardrobe. She had planned to buy winter woolens locally—Minnesota was heavily Scandinavian, and Betsy just loved their sweaters—but hadn't realized she'd need them so soon. Today she was wearing her warmest work outfit: a federal-blue cotton skirt, a bell-sleeved white blouse, and a brown felt vest with carved wooden buttons.

She looked at her watch and hastily drank the last of her tea. She put the empty cup and the plate that had held a fried egg sandwich into the sink. Sophie was already at the door of the apartment, ready to accompany her to work. The cat had a better sense of time than she did—not surprising, really. Sophie had been her sister's cat, and therefore in the business longer than Betsy had.

Like the Queen of England, Betsy "lived above the shop." She went out the door, down the stairs, and to the obscure door into a back hallway that led to the back door of Crewel World. Sophie trundled along beside her.

It was just nine-forty, and the store opened at ten, but the back door was unlocked. Betsy froze with her hand on the knob, key in the lock. The last time she had gone through a door that should have been locked, she had found her sister's body.

Sophie made an inquiring noise, and Betsy waved a shushing hand at her while she leaned forward to listen at the door. Faint conversation. One voice, a light tenor, rose to understandability: "And I'm just *so* fond of magenta, it's a warm, clear color without being *quite* so simple as red."

There was a murmur as another voice replied; but Betsy couldn't understand the words.

"That's *right!* You know, it's just *great* dealing with a customer who has a decent sense of color."

While Betsy hadn't understood the reply, she heard the pleased note in the voice, and she smiled as she opened the door into the back room. Sophie scooted through, and she closed it behind her firmly enough to be heard in the shop.

"Oh, good, now I won't have to make change out of my own pocket," said the tenor. *"Good* morning, Betsy!"

"Good morning, Godwin," replied Betsy, coming into the shop and pausing automatically. Sunlight poured between the front-window displays of counted cross-stitch patterns and needlepoint projects. It lit up the counters and tables with their baskets of wool, cotton, and silk. On one wall, the big swinging doors that held painted canvases stood open just enough to call attention to themselves. Near the front door was an old dresser painted white, its dim mirror holding advertisements for conventions and classes on knitting and needlepoint. All looked in perfect order.

The customer was a medium-sized woman in a long tweed coat, and in her hands hung a sky blue drawstring plastic bag. It had Crewel World printed on it in little Xs, as if worked in cross-stitch.

"Good morning, Mrs. Schuster," said Betsy.

"Good morning, Betsy. I was on my way to the Waterfront Café for breakfast when I saw lights on in your shop and stopped to see if I could pick up my order of magenta silk, and Godwin was kind enough to unlock the door."

"How's the project coming?" asked Betsy, going behind the big desk that served as a checkout counter.

"Very, very well," said Mrs. Schuster. Encouraged by the question and still pleased at Godwin's compliments, she pulled a needlepoint canvas from the bag. It was a square canvas of grapes and grape leaves, not quite abstract. The stitching was an appropriate and very competent basket weave. When finished and framed, it would hang in the office of a friend of Mrs. Schuster's, who vinted wines as a hobby. The grapes were being done in silk, the leaves were already stitched in various green wools.

"Oh, I like how it's turning out," said Godwin, coming to look. "You were so clever to do the grapes in silk to make them shimmer." He cocked his head. "Chalk-white wool for the background, of course."

"Yes—of course," said Mrs. Schuster, and Betsy shot him a grateful look.

Mrs. Schuster had taken up a lot of Betsy's time discussing colors and fibers for this project and had changed her mind three times about the background.

But Betsy wasn't surprised that Mrs. Schuster was quick to take Godwin's suggestion. The young man had developed a serious talent for needlework during the two years he'd worked for Betsy's sister and now for Betsy. That he was gay only added to his reputation for selecting the right color and texture for any project.

Betsy was new in town, and not knowledgeable about needlework or about running a shop. Crewel World had been her sister's, and for her sister's sake its customers were giving her every chance to climb the steep learning curve into the intricate world of needlework.

Mrs. Schuster left with her magenta silk and enough white wool to do the background of her project. As she went up Lake Street, her breath streamed out behind her. *Brrr*, thought Betsy. *And it's not even Halloween yet.*

She looked around again. The track lights were on, the front door unlocked, the needlepoint sign turned so that Open faced the street. When Mrs. Schuster had paid her bill, Betsy had put the forty dollars of startup money in the old-fashioned cash register. The hot-dust smell in the air meant Godwin had turned up the heat. Even as she turned to remind him, he was stooping to turn on the Bose radio, tuned to a classical music station. Sophie clambered up onto "her" chair, the one with a powder blue cushion that set off her white fur with the tan and gray patches perfectly. They were ready for business.

"What brought you in early?" asked Betsy.

"Oh, John was being a pissant last night, so I just went to bed early; and so I got up early, and so here I am." John was the wealthy lawyer Godwin lived with, whose support enabled Godwin to work for slave wages at Crewel World.

"Trouble?" asked Betsy.

"Oh, nothing we haven't had before. He's so *jealous*, and really, right now I'm not giving him the least *reason* to be jealous." Godwin tossed his head. He was a slender man, a little under medium height, and his wardrobe tended toward Calvin Klein Slim Fit jeans and silk knit shirts, though today, in honor of the season's change, he was wearing a brown-plaid shirt under a fine-woven Perry Ellis sweater with textured pinstripes. His short hair was an enhanced blond color, his eyes a guileless blue, his nose almost too perfect. He looked eighteen, though Betsy knew he would be twenty-six in December.

Betsy smiled at him even as she hoped there wasn't a breakup in Godwin's future. He was her best employee: knowledgeable, loyal, and reliable. He could be charming, gossipy, witty, and sympathetic in turn with customers, all in an exaggerated, self-deprecating way designed to make them remember him, talk about him, and come back for more. Betsy sometimes wondered if there was a deeper, more reflective Godwin—though she had no intention of doing an archaeological dig on his personality. He suited her, and the shop, just fine as he was.

He smiled back, and they moved with one accord to the library table in the middle of the floor. They sat down opposite one another. Betsy reached into the basket under the table, he unzipped his canvas sport-club bag, and each pulled out a project. Godwin was knitting a pair of white cotton socks. Betsy was trying to learn knitting in the round by making a pair of mittens.

Betsy found where she'd left off and, after a brief struggle, got her needles under control. Knitting with alpaca wool onto three double-pointed needles is a definite step up from stretchy polyester yarn on two single-point needles. She glanced across at Godwin who was knitting with tiny, swift gestures while looking out the window. He had turned the heel of his sock and was heading for the toe.

"Why do you knit your own socks when they're so cheap to buy?" asked Betsy after a few minutes. "And why white? I should think you'd be into argyle or at least magenta."

He laughed. "I'd *love* to wear magenta socks! But my feet are so *sensitive*, they break out in *ugly red welts* when I put colors or anything but one hundred percent *cotton* socks on them. And advertisers will say *anything* to get you to buy their products."

"Uh-huh," said Betsy, who had never been plagued with allergies.

"The weatherman says snow flurries tomorrow, did you hear?" said Godwin. "Say, did I ever tell you about our Halloween blizzard?"

"Yes, you did, at the same time you told me that I really should get going on my mittens." She had thought the famous Halloween blizzard a serious anomaly in the Minnesota weather until she, too, had heard the forecast. Snow flurries in October were apparently standard: the weatherman had been blasé about his prediction. Minnesota children must wear snowsuits under their costumes when they go trick or treating, thought Betsy.

She had been raised in Milwaukee and thought she had a good grasp of winter weather in the upper midwest, but she couldn't remember snow of any sort in October in Milwaukee. Good thing she was going to the Mall of America tomorrow on her day off. She would buy sweaters. And a winter coat and hat. And mittens. She was only halfway up the cuff of her first mitten, and at the rate she was going, she wouldn't have this pair finished until January. The only thing she didn't need by way of winter wear was a scarf. She had learned to knit by making herself a beautiful bright red scarf.

Betsy had come to Excelsior from San Diego at the end of August for an extended visit, planning to work her way through a midlife crisis. She'd been here barely a week when her sister was murdered. The police had thought Margot had interrupted a burglar in her shop, but Betsy had been convinced there was a more sinister connection between the shop and her sister's murder. She was proved right, and because of her efforts a murderer was in jail awaiting trial.

Shortly before her death, Margot had incorporated Crewel World, naming Betsy as vice-president. Now, as sole surviving officer, Betsy could do as she liked with the shop. She had thought to close or sell it, but since she had to remain in town anyway until her sister's estate was settled, and because Crewel World's customers were both friendly and insistent she not do anything hasty, Betsy was still here and Crewel World was still open. And, perhaps, dealing every day with people who had known Margot well was a way of holding onto her just a little while longer.

Betsy Devonshire was fifty-five, with graying brown hair and big blue eyes surrounded by lots of laugh lines, plump but not unattractively so. The loss of her sister was too recent to do other than weigh heavily on her heart, and the midlife crisis that had brought her to Minnesota had been triggered by an angry divorce, so the fact that at times she could smile and even laugh was proof of a resilient soul.

There was something else that helped. Margot had been the childless widow of a self-made millionaire. Since Betsy was Margot's only sibling, the estate would come entirely to her. The prospect of wealth made Betsy more of a gambler than she might otherwise have been.

At ten-thirty, the knitting became an aggravation and she put it away. "Coffee?" she asked Godwin.

"Thanks," he said. "You know, you can work on more than one thing at a time."

"I know. I'm going to try one of those little Christmas ornaments I ordered. I hope counted cross-stitch isn't as confusing to learn as needlepoint was." Betsy had long ago mastered embroidery, but only recently picked up the basics of needlepoint. To round out her understanding of her customers, she needed to venture into counted cross-stitch.

She paused on her way to the back room to stroke Sophie, who, after a hard morning of getting Betsy out of bed, wolfing down her pittance of Iams Less Active cat food, and making the long, difficult journey down the stairs and along to the back entrance, was ready for her morning nap. Perhaps it really was a difficult journey; Sophie had broken her hind leg a few weeks ago and still wore the cast, which she now arranged in what Betsy was sure was an obvious display. Sophie had quickly learned that seeing the cast excited customers to sympathy and even small treats.

I believe she'll be sorry when that leg heals, thought Betsy, bending to search in the tiny refrigerator for a bottle of V8 Extra Spicy for herself before pouring Godwin's coffee into a pretty porcelain cup.

She had barely brought them back to the table when a shadow darkened the doorway. There was an electronic *bing* as the door opened to admit police officer Jill Cross. An expert needlepointer, she was a tall woman who looked even bigger in her dark uniform jacket, hat, and utility belt. But her face below the cap was the sweet oval of a Gibson girl, and her figure, while sturdily built, was definitely female.

"Hi, Jill," said Godwin, getting to his feet. "How may I help you?"

"Trade jobs with me," said Jill in her best deadpan.

"Not bloody likely," Godwin said sincerely, then added, "Tough day already?"

"No worse than usual," she sighed, then brightened. "But I think things are improving. Betsy, can I offer you a change in plans? They're raising the *Hopkins* this morning; Lars and I are assigned to boat duty. Want to come along?"

Betsy hesitated. She didn't want to change plans; she really wanted to go to the Mall of America, where Shop Till You Drop was an actual possibility.

Godwin said, "How about you take off the morning today, Betsy, and tomorrow afternoon? I'll be okay here by myself; it's shaping up to be a slow day."

Jill said, "It must be something to watch; there's been a crowd gathering since daylight."

Betsy weakened. "Is it okay to take me along in a police boat?"

"Sure. It'll be a kind of ride-along. Except it isn't a police boat; Lars is using his own."

Jill had twice asked Betsy if she wanted to go for a ride-along in her squad car for a shift, to get a look at police work on a street level. But Betsy, needing all the time she could get hold of to learn how to run a small business, hadn't found a big enough block of time to go.

She asked, "What's the *Hopkins*, that they want to raise it?"

"You saw the *Minnehaha* before they pulled her out of the water for the winter?"

Betsy nodded. The old steam-powered boat had been raised from the bottom of the lake and restored by a local group of volunteers. It retraced part of its old route on weekends for tourists. Its shape was reminiscent of a streetcar—which was deliberate, as it had originally been one of six boats owned by Minneapolis Rapid Transit and used to take passengers to the Twin Cities streetcar terminus in Wayzata.

Besides being a wreck on the bottom of the lake, how did the *Hopkins* relate to the *Minnehaha*? "Oh, the *Hopkins* is another one of those streetcar boats!"

"Yep," said Jill. "The *Minnehaha* is doing so well that the people who restored her want to do the same with the *Hopkins*. They thought they'd have the money by next spring, but an important grant came through, and now they'll have all winter to work on her restoration."

"I hear the Queen of Excelsior Excursions are so pleased they're going to have more competition they could just spit," said Godwin. Queen of Excelsior Excursions sailed along without volunteers or grants and made a profit besides.

"They'll manage," said Jill, and to Betsy, "Want to come?"

"How long will it take?"

"They only asked for police patrol till noon, so Godwin's right that you could go with us this morning and still go shopping tomorrow afternoon."

"Then I think I'd like to see it. When do we leave?"

"I'm supposed to meet Lars down at the wharf in fifteen minutes. Better go change into slacks and a sweater. And bring your jacket, it's chilly, though not as cold as it could be. Say, did I ever tell you about the Halloween blizzard?"

"Yes, you did, but why don't you compare notes with Godwin while I go upstairs and change?"

Betsy reappeared six minutes later in an old pair of jeans and her heaviest sweater. She had a long-sleeved T-shirt on under that, and her only jacket over one arm. She hoped the boat wasn't fishy.

It wasn't. It was an immaculate flat-bottomed, flat-topped, four-seater, fiberglass, with a windshield and a steering wheel. It reminded Betsy of a '70s compact car; it was even two-toned, raspberry and cream, and its motor was hidden under a hood at the back. It being Lars's boat, he got to drive.

Lars was Jill's boyfriend, a big blond Norwegian who looked like a poster telling schoolchildren The Policeman Is Your Friend. His huge hands were callused, which surprised Betsy when she shook hands until she remembered Jill had told her he was buying a five-acre hobby farm. The notion that someone might take on the labor of farming as a hobby amazed Betsy, but Lars had done it, and he worked as hard on it as he did at being a policeman.

The boat's motor burbled deeply as they pulled away from the dock, then Lars pushed a lever and it roared, stood up on its stern, and went flying over the blue water.

Betsy shouted to Jill, "Where are we going?"

Jill shouted back, "Other side of the Big Island!" She pointed to what looked like part of the shoreline on the north side of Excelsior Bay. But as the boat went by it, Betsy saw that it was indeed an island.

As they came around to the other side, Betsy could see two barges sitting broadside to one another, each with a crane on it. Near the barges were eight or ten motorboats and a couple of sailboats, their sails furled. Lars slowed as they approached, and when the roar of his motors fell to a guttural murmur, Jill picked up a small bullhorn.

"Move back from the barges!" she ordered. "You are in danger of being struck from below! Move back from the barges!"

Heads swiveled, but nobody moved.

"Is that true?" asked Betsy. "Being struck from below?"

"There's a seventy-foot boat down there," Jill replied. "It's gonna need some room when it comes up." She spoke into the bullhorn again. "This is the police! Move back from the cranes!"

That worked. Boats started moving. Betsy looked at the slowly widening area around the barges. She could see cables running from the cranes into the water, which was otherwise undisturbed. Huge engines in the cranes whined deeply. "Is it happening now?"

"Beats me," Jill shrugged. "Our job is to keep the gawkers away until after it does."

"And then to keep them from bumping into the thing, or climbing on it, or trying to steal hunks of it for souvenirs," added Lars.

Betsy chuckled uncertainly. "People wouldn't actually do that, would they?"

Lars said over his shoulder, "Civilians do things you wouldn't believe. I was sitting in a Shop and Go parking lot so near the door the guy in the ski mask had to walk around me to get in and hold up the place. I actually sat there and watched him do it. I couldn't believe it. And guess what he said when I busted him?"

When Betsy shrugged, Jill said, "What they always say." She and Lars drawled in unison, "'I didn't dooo nuthin'!'" Then she and Lars laughed wicked, evil laughs.

The whining of the cranes went on long enough that Betsy began to realize that was the sound of their engines in neutral. Lars and Jill realized it, too, and, once they had established a perimeter, they relaxed and took turns telling Betsy stupid-crook stories. The stories were so hilarious Betsy forgot this was taking a lot longer than she thought it would.

The sun shone, the water rocked the boat. Lars and Jill removed their jackets. A couple of the motorboats went away, a new one joined the watchers. Several of the boats standing watch were of a size that looked capable of going to sea. Betsy wondered what kind of job it took to afford a cabin cruiser and yet have time to come out on a Tuesday morning to watch volunteers raise an old boat.

Jill identified some of the boats, gossiped a little about their owners. "I thought Billy'd left for Florida by now," she noted about one called *The Waterhole*.

"What, is there a river out of Lake Minnetonka that connects to the Mississippi?" asked Betsy.

"Yes, but it's not deep enough for that boat," said Jill.

"Not to mention the sudden forty-foot drop going over Minnehaha Falls," added Lars with a grin.

"Then how does he get that boat down to Florida?" asked Betsy.

"He doesn't," said Jill. "He has an even bigger boat down there."

"Is it called *The Waterhole Two*? And why *Waterhole*?"

Lars said, "Anyone with a boat will tell you that it is a hole in the water into which you pour money."

Jill added, "And a water hole is a place where animals come to drink, which is why taverns are sometimes called water holes. Billy's a party animal, and you'd be surprised how many people he can haul in that boat."

"You know something about just about every boat owner out here," said Betsy. "Is that because you're a police officer, or do you have a boat, too?"

Lars laughed. "Neither; it's because she's from Excelsior, gossip capital of the state."

"Have you lived here long, Jill?" asked Betsy.

"Third generation," nodded Jill. "My grandfather used to run the Ferris wheel at the Excelsior Amusement Park, and my mother put herself through nursing school by working at the Blue Ribbon Café at the Park."

Betsy said, "That's right, I've heard that there used to be an amusement park in Excelsior. This is a sweet little town; it doesn't seem like the kind of town for that. I mean especially years ago, when amusement parks weren't the high-class operations they are today."

"Oh, it was pretty high class," said Jill with something in her voice Betsy couldn't read.

"Did your father work in it, too?"

"He was a highway patrolman. His uncle was a deputy sheriff, and my mother's brother was an investigator on the Saint Paul cops."

"So you kind of went into the family business," said Betsy with a smile.

"It does run in families," agreed Jill. "What did your father do?"

"He worked in the engineering department of Poland and Harnischfeger in Milwaukee. They build cranes. I still catch myself looking for the P&H logo whenever I see a crane. It never occurred to me to follow in his footsteps, but when I was small I used to wish there were still cattle drives, because *his* dad was a cowboy in Utah, and I thought that was one of the great, romantic jobs. My dad used to tell some great stories about him."

"Can you ride?"

"I used to be good at it. You?"

"Oh, I don't fall off half as much as I used to." Jill looked out toward a boat drifting close to the perimeter she and Lars had established, but it stopped before crossing it. "You know what I've always wanted to do?" she asked.

"What?"

"Go on one of those cattle drives. They still have them in some places, and they allow paying guests to take part. You get your own horse to take care of and you help keep the steers in line."

Betsy stared at her. "Really? Where does this happen, in Texas?"

"They run one in South Dakota, less than a day's drive from here. Lars won't go with me."

"Gosh." Betsy's eyes became distant. The lowing of cattle, the dust of the trail, the campfire at night, sleeping under the stars . . .

"Want me to find out the details? We can go next year, maybe."

Betsy tried to make her acceptance as casual as the offer. "I'd like that very much. Thanks."

They fell silent for awhile. The sun warmed the air, the boat rocked, the motor burbled and gave off noxious fumes. Betsy began to feel a curious combination of sick and sleepy. She regretted the fried-egg sandwich she'd had for breakfast, then the seafood salad she'd had for supper last night. She was beginning to be concerned about the lo mein noodles she'd had for lunch yesterday when Lars said suddenly, "I think we're gonna see some action now. And look over there!" He pushed a lever that stirred up the motor and steered the boat toward the nearer barge.

Jill shouted through the bullhorn, "You in the blue boat, you're in danger! Move back, away from the barge!" The passengers, a man and two women, turned to look at Jill. One woman waved to show she wasn't concerned. "Move . . . away . . . from the . . . barge!" repeated Jill. "Now!"

The man shouted something at whoever was steering, and the boat began to shift around. The woman stopped waving and instead made a rude gesture.

Uh-oh, thought Betsy, and was surprised when Lars didn't go after them but only moved back himself. Then she heard a serious change in the sound of the cranes' big engines, and her attention came back to the space between the cranes. The water roiled, as if about to boil. Smoothly, as if in time-lapse film, enormous black mushrooms bloomed onto the surface. They were floats, balloons, in three clusters of three. The cranes' engines were straining now, and big drops of water drooled off the cables. Betsy realized belatedly the cables were moving.

Then, gently as dawn, a long, sleek object appeared under and then just on the surface. As it rose, water sluiced away, and Betsy could see the lines of curved boards appear, gleaming in the sun. More of the object appeared, and still more, until it was a boat about seventy feet long, canted to one side, held in place by wrappings of cable. It didn't look much like the restored streetcar boat; there were no railings, no cabin, no upper deck, just this long, narrow wooden boat.

Air horns saluted the arrival of the *Hopkins*, and only when they stopped could Betsy hear the people cheering.

Waterfalls of various sizes cascaded off the boat, and the crane operators did something so that it mostly righted itself. Three men in black diver's wet suits appeared at the edge of the far barge and dived in. They swam to the boat and helped one another aboard. They began a quick, running inspection. One picked up a large rock and threw it over the side. Then he threw a hunk of what looked like concrete, and then another rock.

"They weighed the boat down with rubble before they sank it," said Jill to Betsy. "The divers threw a lot of it overboard before it was raised, but I guess there's more still in there."

Betsy could see the divers to their waists as they moved along the boat and she deduced the presence of a deck, because otherwise they'd be out of sight. As soon as she realized that, the rubble-tossing diver went out of sight. Betsy was deducing a ladder when he straightened—he'd only bent over. He shouted and gestured to the other two divers. They came running, and more rubble was tossed. Then one leaned against the side of the boat to shout, "Police! Police!"

Lars glanced at Jill, who nodded, and Lars ran his boat alongside the big boat.

"Got something here you should look at!" the diver shouted.

"You stay here," Jill said to both Lars and Betsy. She raised her arms and was lifted over the side of the raised boat, which Betsy could now see had once been painted white. But there was lots of slime on the boards, and Jill had to scrabble for a foothold. Her light blue shirt and dark trousers were smeared by the time she vanished over the gunwales.

She reappeared less than a minute later. "Lars, there's a human skeleton under the floorboards of this thing. Looks to be adult size. Call it in." She went away again.

"Be damned," said Lars, and he reached for the radio microphone on the shoulder flap of his jacket.

Betsy rose to her feet, not sure if she did or did not want Jill to pick up the skull so she could see it. Wow, a skeleton! Had a diver from years ago been exploring the wreck and gotten trapped? Or was it a murder victim, the knife still stuck between the ribs? The boat had been filled with rubble, so the murderer must also have been a diver. Betsy had a sudden image of a man in a wet suit hauling a motionless victim down, down into the depths of the lake, finding the boat, moving hundreds of pounds of rubble—no, that was silly.

What it probably was, was a diver who found a hatch he could open and went in exploring. Then something in there ripped his air hose, and he panicked and couldn't find the hatch to get out again. Poor fellow.

She sat down, the image shifting to what the skeleton might look like now.

Sprawled and shining white, the ruins of his wet suit crumpled around him. Were there clues to his identity? A wedding ring perhaps, one with initials engraved inside it? Or an ID bracelet? She could imagine the metal, at first dimmed by algae, which would slowly yield to rubbing, and the letters would appear. And an old mystery of a disappearance would be solved at last. How exceedingly interesting!

Two

❖

Detective Mike Malloy watched the medical examiner cover the bones laid out on a metal table. Malloy had been present during the examination—it could hardly be called an autopsy—and had taken notes. Now he consulted his notes and read the important parts back to make sure he hadn't missed or misunderstood anything.

"You say the skeleton is about ninety-five percent complete," he began. "That it is a white female older than eighteen but younger than thirty-five at her time of death." He stopped to glance at the medical examiner.

"That's right," nodded Dr. Pascuzzi, a darkly handsome man.

Malloy consulted his notes again. He was a redhead with a thickly freckled face, light blue eyes, and a thin mouth. His suit was conservative, his shoes freshly but not highly polished, and he tended to think before he said anything. His career goal was to be sheriff of some rural Minnesota county, one with a really good bass lake in it; so his criminal investigations, like everything else about him, tended to be by-the-book and not splashy. He didn't like this case because it was odd and was already drawing inquiries from the media. Investigators who got known for notorious cases didn't get asked to run for out-state sheriff.

"I noticed the skull was badly damaged when I saw it on the boat, the *Hopkins*," Malloy continued. "But I thought it might've got that way banging against things under the water." He raised a pale, inquiring eyebrow at the ME.

"No, I'm sure the injuries to the face and skull happened shortly before or very soon after death. The same for the broken radius." He saw a lack of comprehension in the police investigator and said, "The smaller of the two bones in the forearm."

"Oh, yeah." Malloy searched through his notes and found the place.

"Like the other injuries," said Dr. Pascuzzi, "it happened right about the time of death."

"How can you tell that?"

"Because it happened to living bone, but there is no evidence of healing. My opinion is that it was a defense wound."

"Sure, I get it." People under attack would raise a hand or arm and it would get injured; Malloy had seen examples of that. Weird that there might be such specific evidence of something so momentary in a crime this old.

But finding it meant this was a homicide, all right; there was no other way to explain the injuries. And then, of course, there was the hiding of the body on the boat.

He continued to recite, "You say she was about five feet, two inches tall, not skin and bones or a fatso." What Dr. Pascuzzi had said was that she had been neither emaciated nor obese, but Malloy liked his English plain. He went on, "You said that when a woman has a baby, it leaves marks on her skeleton, but you don't find those marks on this one. I suppose if she was pregnant at the time of death, we could tell that?"

"Not necessarily. If she were in the first trimester, there would be no way to know."

Malloy nodded and added a little note. "You said her front teeth were broken?"

"Yes, and probably also at the time of death. I also noticed some problems with decay that might indicate she wasn't fond of the dentist. Or, perhaps, was too poor to afford proper dental care."

"So a lower-class woman who maybe had been beat up some."

"Well . . ." Pascuzzi rocked his hand to indicate doubt. "Women who are abused regularly show other signs of it, healed broken ribs or fingers. I saw no signs of that. I do think her nose might have been broken, probably while she was in her early teens, but that's all."

Still, this last severe battering to the face indicated rage or deep-seated hatred. A husband, maybe. Or a boyfriend. In either case, Malloy thought, what we probably have is an old-fashioned domestic that got out of hand. The *Hopkins* was sunk in 1949; it was possible the perp was still around. And that would for sure be a lead story on the evening news, with a camera shot of the cops rolling up to the nursing home to take him away.

Dr. Pascuzzi asked, "Want more?"

"Is there more?"

"By the look of the wear on the shoulders, elbows, and wrists she did a lot of hard labor. On the other hand, there aren't the changes to ankle and knee joints that mean prolonged squatting or kneeling. Not a char lady then, hauling water-filled buckets and kneeling to scrub floors. She might have been a farmer's wife who helped out in the dairy barn. Or a waitress, staggering under heavy trays of food. When was the boat she was found on sunk?"

"About fifty years ago."

"Not long after World War II, then. So perhaps she worked in a factory or drove a truck during the war. There are some small signs of malnutrition, not uncommon on the skeletons of people who grew up during the Depression. Apart from the nose, I find no sign of injuries or any illness that would leave its mark on bone."

Malloy grunted. That, plus the lack of dental work, was going to make positive identification difficult.

"Enough?" asked Pascuzzi again.

"For now. You'll send me a copy of your report when?"

"Couple of days. I may be able to come closer in my estimate of her age, weight, and height."

"Thanks," said Malloy and left him to it.

Malloy was right; the story of the skeleton received heavy play in the media. Small wonder that the following Monday, seven days after the discovery, the Monday Bunch gathered eagerly for its weekly meeting at Crewel World. Betsy, they knew, had been out on Lake Minnetonka watching when the *Hopkins* had come to the surface with its grisly surprise. Betsy had taken a major role in solving her sister's murder, so they were sure she had come to some marvelous conclusions about this new crime and knew things that had not yet turned up in print or on television. Thrilled to have an opportunity to hear from her in person, the women turned out in force.

The Monday Bunch was an informal group of women who loved needlework and were free at two on Monday afternoons. Some were retired, some were homemakers, some worked part-time or nights, one even arranged for a very late lunch hour. The numbers varied from week to week, rarely rising above four or five. Today, every current member was present, all eleven. Betsy had to bring folding chairs from the back.

"Did you see it?" asked Alice Skoglund, a large woman, not just plump but tall and big-boned. She had faded yellow hair well mixed with gray and a lot of jaw. Her plastic-framed eyeglasses caught the light as she looked toward Betsy. Her fingers moved mechanically, crocheting afghan squares in bright-colored polyester yarn, dropping them as they were finished into a plastic bag already bulging with them. "The skeleton, I mean."

Eyes looked everywhere but at Betsy, most at the needlework in hand. They all wanted details, too, but were embarrassed that one of their number was so open in her inquiry.

"No," said Betsy. She sat at the head of the table, where she could see the front door in case a customer came in. A cordless phone stood handy in case a customer wanted to call in an order from home. She was still working on that first mitten. Last night's flurries had melted, but under a gray sky the temperature struggled to reach forty.

"It must have been exciting out there," said Martha Winters, a pleasant-faced woman who at seventy-four worked only part-time in her dry cleaning shop, but whose eyes were still sharp enough for her to do counted cross-stitch on twenty-four-count evenweave. Flick, flick went her needle, and a chickadee had a beak.

"Oh, not so much," said Betsy. "Well, it was exciting to see the boat actually come up, but we waited a long time for that to happen."

"And when it did come up, who found the skeleton?" asked Martha's bosom companion, Jessica Turnquist. Jessica was three inches taller but twenty pounds lighter than Martha. She had a long face with large, slightly bulgy eyes, and a patrician nose over a mouth pressed thin by years of firm opinions. Jessica was crocheting a white baby blanket in swift popcorn stitch; it looked as if a cloud were forming on the table in front of her.

"Some divers. They swam over and climbed on the boat, and suddenly one of them shouted to Jill and Lars that they'd found a skeleton. Jill went aboard for a look, then told Lars to radio for help." Betsy looked at her incipient mitten, made a noise, and undid two stitches.

"Is the skeleton a man or a woman?" asked Godwin, who was working on a magnificent needlepoint Christmas stocking.

"I heard it was a woman," said Alice, the woman with the manly jaw.

"That's right," said Betsy. "Jill told me the medical examiner said that. I think I saw him out on the boat, but there were so many investigators and police and all, I couldn't say for sure. I didn't realize finding a skeleton would create such a fuss. He may even have arrived after Jill arranged for someone to bring me back to the dock, a nice man with a perfectly enormous boat."

"Any idea who?" asked Jessica, who could crochet without looking.

"I think his name was Dayton. Luke? Matt? Something like that. Very handsome and polite."

Several of the women coughed as if to cover chuckles, and Jessica said, "No, I mean who the skeleton is."

"No, there weren't any clothes or a purse or anything. Just the bones."

"How could they even tell it was a woman?" asked a very pregnant young woman named Emily, new to the Bunch. She was knitting a crib-size afghan in blue, pink, and white. "I mean, a skeleton is a skeleton is a skeleton, right?"

"Not at all," said Martha the dry cleaner. "Don't you watch The Discovery Channel? They have a wonderful show about autopsies and things. They can tell all sorts of things just from a leg bone, the age and sex and everything; and here they have the whole skeleton." Martha had curly white hair around a sweet face; that she was interested in forensic anthropology was surprising.

"Was she murdered?" asked Alice.

"Oh, no," said Godwin in his most faux-dulcet voice—for which he must hold several international records, thought Betsy, amused—"it's a suicide, obviously. She crawled under the floor boards and waited for the boat to sink so she could drown."

"Tsk," went several women, but the rest giggled. Godwin's sarcasm was part of his fame.

"When did the *Hopkins* sink?" asked Emily. "Maybe she was a leftover from the accident."

"It wasn't an accident," said Godwin. "The streetcar steamboats were sunk *deliberately.*" When Emily tried an uncertain giggle, he continued, "I'm *not* joking. They didn't need them anymore, so the company *sank* them. Happened during the roaring twenties."

"Not the *Hopkins*," said Patricia Fairland, a handsome woman in her thirties with dark hair held back by a headband. She was crocheting a lacy edging on an embroidered table runner, using a number-ten steel hook and yarn thin as sewing thread, her long, delicate fingers darting swiftly.

"Sure the *Hopkins*," disagreed Godwin, glancing up from his Christmas stocking. "They sank them all about the same time, 1920-something, when roads were tarred and everyone could afford a car, and public transportation wasn't absolutely necessary anymore."

"The other five, yes, but not the *Hopkins*," insisted Patricia. "It was sold to the Blue Ribbon Café, and they renamed it the *Minnetonka III*, painted it white, and used it to give rides to tourists until 1949. I'm a member of the Minnesota Transportation Museum, Steamboat Branch. It's in several books, about the *Hopkins*."

Betsy said, "When it came up out of the water, I could see it used to be white, not that mustard color the *Minnehaha* was restored to."

"You can tell she's new to this business," remarked Jessica with a smile, "because the rest of us would have tried to decide whether the color is closer to DMC 437 or 8325."

"Oh, DMC 437, definitely," said Martha. "You know, I remember the Blue Line buying the *Hopkins*. They painted it white after they converted the engine to run on oil instead of coal. My Aunt Esther and Uncle Swan celebrated their golden wedding anniversary with a ride on it in 1938. I'd forgotten they renamed it. I think everyone from around here still called it the *Hopkins* most of the time. My Carl used to love to watch it out on the lake. He said it was the prettiest boat he'd ever seen. It's a pity he didn't live to see it brought up again."

"Maybe he isn't dead," said Alice. "Nobody knows, right?" Blinking behind the lenses, she looked at Martha, and there was a little stir in the group; it wasn't polite to bring up old scandals when the scandalee was present.

Jessica said, "She doesn't like to talk about it."

But Martha said, "It's all right, Jess." She said to Betsy, with an air of making a statement for the record, "My husband left our house for work one summer morning in 1948 and never came home. *Some* people think he ran off with another woman, but I think he was mugged and the robber killed him and pushed his body in the lake or buried it somewhere or threw it in an empty boxcar so it got taken away. Because no trace of him was ever found. His disappearance was a great shock to me, but it happened a long time ago, and I'm pretty much over it."

"But he never knew they sank it," persisted Alice, frowning over her afghan square, "if he disappeared before it was sunk."

"I don't remember them sinking the *Hopkins*," said Martha, pausing to consider. "Maybe because it was just an old wreck they finally got rid of, not a news story. But I definitely remember Carl disappeared in July of 1948, and if the *Hopkins* was sunk in 1949, then of course he never knew." She looked around with uneasy defiance. "And yes, a woman who worked at the Blue Ribbon Café disappeared at the same time. *Some people* assumed they ran off together."

Jessica gave a sniff of support without looking up from her crocheting.

Patricia said, "There was all kinds of talk, I suppose, about Carl disappearing."

Kindly shifting the focus from Martha, Godwin said, "I hear the boat was very hard to sink. They had to fill it with stones and concrete to make it go down."

Betsy said, "That's right. Jill told me the divers said it was a real job to remove that rubble before they raised her, and I saw them throwing the last of it overboard just before they found the skeleton."

Martha, who had stopped work to think, said, "You know, it's a funny thing my not remembering them sinking that boat. I remember all kinds of other unimportant things. Like it being damaged by ice two or three years earlier. It sat against the shore over by the dredging company not far from our house. My neighbor's little boys used to fish off the back of it." She smiled at Betsy. "The younger one grew up to be mayor of Excelsior." She frowned. "But I don't remember anything about them sinking the *Hopkins*."

Patricia said, "It's interesting how everyone still calls it the *Hopkins*. Because it sailed the lake from 1926 to 1949 under the name *Minnetonka III*."

Betsy said, "I understand how you know these things, Pat, being one of the volunteers who run the boats, but how do you know so much, Godwin?"

"Because *I* am not from here and therefore am interested in local history," said Godwin loftily. Then he grinned. "Besides, John is a member of the museum, and he puts their monthly magazine in the little stack of reading material in the bathroom. They did a long article on the *Hopkins* in the last issue."

Martha chuckled. "My husband used to call the bathroom the reading room."

In the middle of the nods and laughter that remark drew, Emily began to look funny and once the ladies found she'd been having these kind of cramplike pains every twenty minutes or so, a part joyous, part worried fuss began of notifying her husband and her doctor and arranging for her to get to the hospital— all despite her protest, "But when the cramp lets up I feel just fine!" And by the time Emily was safely on her way, the Monday Bunch meeting was over.

"Godwin," Betsy said when the last woman was out the door, "why do you keep building me up so those ladies can put me down? You keep telling me how well I'm doing—"

"You are, you're doing beautifully!" insisted Godwin.

"Sure I am. Did you see how they laughed when Jessica pointed out I don't use DMC numbers to identify colors? I'm sure they all saw how I had to keep going back and picking up dropped stitches in that mitten. Thank God they don't yet realize how bad it really is; how little I know about all sorts of needlework—or running a needlework business, for that matter."

"Oh, pish-tush; I repeat, you're doing *just fine*."

"I wish I could believe that. Especially late at night, when I'm trying to fall asleep after suffering through Quicken and the checkbooks and withholding, and could just cry. But the little failures hurt, too. I thought Shelly was going to have a stroke trying not to laugh out loud when a customer asked if I thought she should do the background of her project in oriental or gobelin." Shelly was a part-time employee.

"What did you tell the customer?"

"I got out my book of stitches and looked up both stitches and said I thought the oriental would be better."

"And what was wrong with that?"

Betsy hesitated, then smiled. "Nothing. In fact, when I saw the finished project last Saturday, it was beautiful."

"See? And honey, if Shelly does something like that when I'm around, I'll remind her of the time *she* forgot to figure sales tax on a five hundred dollar order. Who cares if you *haven't* mastered every needlepoint stitch? You can do this. You *are* doing it. You *have* to do it. If you put this shop on the market, Irene Potter will buy it, and the first person she'll fire is *me*." He reached out a slender hand to touch her shoulder. "Think of it as a memorial to your murdered sister."

Betsy twitched away from his hand, not sure if he was being melodramatic. It was still too soon for her to endure casual reference to her sister's death.

"No, listen to me!" said Godwin. "I'm *serious*. You solved her murder, you are a heroine *and* a sleuth *and* a role model. You are the *happy-ever-after person;* you *can't* quit."

Betsy smiled; she couldn't help it. Godwin's charm was as warm as it was silly. She went behind the big old desk/checkout counter. "Have we got enough Madeira silks on hand?" she asked. "I see here you sold an awful lot of them to Amy yesterday."

"I wrote you a note about that. No, we don't. We should order some more right away. By the way, Shelly says we're also low on DMC pinks and blues. There should be a note from her on that desk somewhere."

"We're going to have to find a better way to keep up with inventory," grumbled Betsy, shuffling through papers to look for Shelly's note. "This business of waiting till someone notices we're running low seems awfully chancy. What if no one notices? We'll find ourselves totally out of something and screw up a big sale one of these days."

"Hasn't happened yet." Godwin was smiling again, but this time she frowned at him.

"Come on, how can we tell ahead of time what we'll run out of next?" he asked reasonably. "We notice we're running low, and we order more of it. We could increase our inventory, but that ties up money you need to pay rent and our salaries. The system we have is a good system."

"Yeah," said Betsy sarcastically, "invented by someone with nine whole weeks' experience in the retail business."

"You didn't invent this system, you inherited it," said Godwin. "Your sister used the same method. We all know to write a note when we sell enough of a product to create a shortage. The problem happens when someone forgets to write a note. Which we didn't. So, do you want me to call the order in, or will you?"

"I'll do it." She opened the center drawer and pulled out the spiral-bound address book. But before dialing, she put her hands on the open book and said, "Goddy, the Monday Bunch doesn't think I'm going to get involved in this skeleton business, do they?"

"Not once they think about it. I mean, you aren't a policeman, so it's not your job, and I didn't notice anyone coming in trying to hire you as a private eye to solve it. The last one was up-close and personal. This one has nothing to do with us, so why should we get involved?" Betsy was to remember those words in the days to come.

Three

❖

It was Halloween eve. Detective Mike Malloy was proud to know Halloween means All Hallows Eve (though he could not for twenty dollars have told anyone what All Hallows was). Therefore, he considered, the term *Halloween eve* redundant, so he corrected it in his head to *the day before Halloween*.

Appropriate to the season, he was about to meet a scientist in his laboratory, which he pictured with stone walls, gurgling test tubes, spirals of glass filled with colored liquids, and a couple of those things like old-fashioned TV antennas making thin crackles of lightning between their rods.

He knew it wouldn't be like that, not really, but it was kind of disappointing to find it was a kitchen-size room, very clean, with microscopes and a personal computer. It did smell funny, which was something, but the scientist wasn't there.

Malloy was directed by a student in a stained lab coat to an upper floor and a small, cluttered office. It wasn't a cubicle, but a real office, with walls that went to the ceiling, and a door that shut. Which Malloy did.

The man behind the desk wasn't a disappointment to Malloy's Halloween-colored imagination. Dr. Ambling had the fluffy gray hair and thick glasses of every mad scientist from every movie the detective had seen as a kid. "Ah have examined the fabric you-all sent to me," Dr. Ambling drawled—not in a thick German accent. Texas, thought Malloy, amused.

Ambling picked up two sheets of glass held together by strips of gray tape on the corners. Between the glass were four pieces of thin green fabric, three very small, the fourth roughly triangular in shape, about two and a half inches on a side. All the pieces were frayed, and there were fine threads knotted and tangled along two sides of the triangle. "The material is silk, partially edged with silk threads that may have been lace. The lace, if it is lace, was probably made by hand, and it was attached to the rest of the fabric after it was finished."

He put the glass down on a low stack of books and consulted a sheet of paper occupying a cleared space on his desk just large enough to hold it.

Mike had found a tiny, flattish, filthy, slimy thing during a search of the raised boat. A forensics expert from the state crime lab had identified it as fabric and recommended Dr. Ambling as the person to further identify it. Mike still wasn't sure if it was important, but the first thing a detective learns is not to assume something is unimportant just because it doesn't fit a theory you've been too quick to form.

"Ah," said Ambling, finding his place. "It is impossible to tell what color the fabric was originally," he continued. "The green color is from being pressed under something made of copper or a copper alloy." He looked up at Malloy through thick lenses. "Did you find it under a piece of pipe?"

"No, it was in a puddle of muddy water. But they cleared away a lot of rubble before they raised the boat and more after they got it to the surface, before they found the skeleton. We don't know where on the boat it was hidden originally."

"It was under a piece of rubble that was, or contained, some copper or brass or bronze—copper and its alloys are a good preservative of fibers. But they turn things green." He went back to the report. "Judging by the shape of the surviving pieces, the fabric was wadded rather than folded and only partly covered by the metal. The biggest piece is the only one with the edging on it."

"So what do you think, was it a dress? Or was it something smaller?" asked Malloy.

The man shrugged. "The fabric seems thin for a dress, but I don't know much about clothing from the forties. A handkerchief seems more likely, but I wouldn't testify to that as fact. It could be a fragment of sleeve, though you should check to see if lace edging was fashionable on sleeves in 1949. On the other hand, my mother used to crochet lace edgings onto her handkerchiefs. Very fine, very delicate work. That's what this made me think of. But it's only a guess; the fibers have been so stretched and pulled from the pressure of whatever was holding it down all those years, I can't see what the pattern might have been."

"Could it just be string from the fabric? Maybe it frayed a lot, from the motion of the water or something." Malloy bent over the glass for a closer look.

Ambling reached for a pencil, which he used as a pointer. "No, the fibers here and here are thicker and coarser than the rest of the fabric. And here and here and here, see? These look like knots. So not fraying, and not fringe, but trim of some sort, of a thicker fiber than the fabric, and attached to it—see, here and here. I'm quite sure these strands were formed into a pattern with deliberation. Could be crochet, but that's only a guess."

"So a woman's handkerchief, right?" said Malloy. "I mean, a man wouldn't have a silk handkerchief, would he?"

"My grandfather carried a silk handkerchief every day of his adult life. But not with lace edging, of course. For that, you'd have to go back to the eighteenth century."

"Hmmm. So a woman's handkerchief, or part of a dress. The sleeve you say? Why not the collar? That would be more likely to have lace trim."

"A collar would be doubled over, and this was hemmed, not doubled."

"Okay, I get that. This lace edging, is it silk, too?"

Ambling nodded. "Yes."

"So this was an expensive article, right?"

"Possibly, but not necessarily. You have to consider the era. Handmade at this time meant homemade, and in the forties and fifties, only poor people wore homemade clothes. Of course, silk is another matter, as is lace. Poor people didn't make their clothes of silk."

Mike picked up the glass and held it to the ceiling light. "No initials or anything," he said. "So I guess even if we identify her, we'll never know for sure if the skeleton was the person who owned this."

"Jill, you crochet and do stuff like that, don't you?"

Jill, coming out of the duty room, turned to see Mike Malloy with something flat in his hands. "No, sorry, I don't do crochet," she said politely. "But I do needlepoint, if that's any help." Malloy, she knew, wasn't the brightest bulb in the chandelier, but he was her senior in rank, so she tried to treat him with respect.

He, on the other hand, knew she was very bright and suspected she was ambitious. But he couldn't bad-mouth her the way he could male officers with ambitions to his rank and job, not in this era of hair-trigger harassment suits, so he tried to treat her with respect.

With both of them behaving contrary to their beliefs, they tended to talk like actors in a poorly written play.

"Can I show you something?" he asked, approaching with the object held out awkwardly.

"What is it?" asked Jill, not reaching for it.

"A textile expert from the university says it maybe was part of a dress or a handkerchief. It's got homemade lace edging, he says. I want to know what you think. This expert guesses it's crochet."

"Oh. Okay." Jill took the glass sandwich with both hands, careful to hold it at the edges. She lifted it so the ceiling fluorescents could shine through it. "Hard to say," she said after a few moments. "Actually," she added, lowering the glass and handing it back, "I'm not an expert on lace. But I know where to ask for experts. Want me to bring you their names?"

"Are they in town?"

"Probably. All I have to do—or you can do it yourself—is go to Crewel World and ask for Godwin. He knows just about everyone in the area who does things with fibers."

"Yeah, I should have thought of that myself."

Malloy being self-deprecating was unusual, so Jill's stiffness thawed a little. "Say, is this connected to that skeleton we found on the old *Hopkins*?" Jill had just been part of the crowd control aspect of the crime scene, she had no role in the investigation. But she was curious.

"How'd you know?"

Jill smiled. "Well, that thing you showed me is the color of algae."

"As a matter of fact, it's that color because it was under a piece of copper for fifty years—and okay, at the bottom of the lake, on board the *Hopkins*."

Jill bloomed a little bit over being right and Malloy smiled, but not unkindly. She asked, "Was it near the skeleton?"

"Not really. The skeleton was near the stern, the fabric was found more amidships, near where the engine used to be. But with all the tumbling it might've got while those divers were removing rubble, it could've started out anywhere."

"Amidships?"

Malloy's prickliness appeared. "Yes, and deck and gunwale and ladder and so forth. What of it?"

"Oh. Nothing, I guess. I thought you picked up that word talking to the divers, but I guess it's for real with you. What, you were in the navy?"

His small eyes narrowed. "Why do you ask?"

Jill shrugged. "Hey, no reason. It's just that the current owner of Crewel World is also a navy vet."

"That woman who thinks she's a detective?"

Jill wanted to remind him that Betsy had been the one who came up with the solution to Malloy's last case, and so was, in fact, able to detect. But she bit her tongue and then said, "You remember Betsy Devonshire, then. I'm sure she'll help if she can, do whatever you want."

"Yeah, I'd like that, so long as she doesn't get enthusiastic and go charging around looking for clues." Malloy sighed. "Still, thanks again for the suggestion, Jill."

When Jill took her coffee break at Crewel World a few hours later, she found that Malloy hadn't been by yet. She described what Mike had shown her to Betsy and Godwin.

"I'm surprised he's letting us in, after the last time," said Godwin.

"Hey, slow down, he's not letting you in," said Jill. "He doesn't want you to sleuth, he wants you to answer some questions about something he found on the *Hopkins*."

"What kind of lace do you think it is?" asked Betsy.

"I don't know that it's lace at all. It didn't look like anything but a tangle of threads to me. Mike said the textile expert thinks it might be crochet, though how he figured that, I don't know. But like I told Mike, I bet there are some customers at Crewel World who can look at it and know whether the expert is right or not."

"Are there lace makers around here?" Betsy asked Godwin.

"Heavens yes. Tatting and crocheting and even old-fashioned bobbin lace. Martha Winters used to make beautiful bobbin lace. And Lucy Watkins still does, and tatting besides. Patricia does gorgeous crochet work. There are probably others who do or know someone who does. And most of them are Crewel World customers, because hardly anyone who does one kind of needlework does only one kind. Even you, Miss Knit, have branched out into needlepoint. After all that complaining, I watched you do a beautiful row of mosaic this morning."

"Oh, all it took for that was learning how to interpret the illustrations in the book," said Betsy. "But I couldn't do it without the open book right there."

"Uh-huh," said Godwin, "just like the rest of us. And tell Jill how you've expanded into counted cross-stitch."

"I'm still kind of only thinking about it." Betsy continued to Jill, "Those big patterns Shelly does intimidate me, but The Stitchery catalog had some darling Christmas tree ornaments that looked about my speed, so I ordered a set."

"The little squares of animals wearing Santa Claus hats?" asked Jill.

"Yes, aren't they adorable? The set came over the weekend, but I haven't had a chance yet to take a good look at it."

"You'll like it. I'm working on my second set. I've decided to enclose one or two with some of my Christmas cards. And I'll donate one to the tree."

"What tree?"

Jill looked at Godwin, who shrugged back. Godwin said to Betsy, "Margot used to put up a little artificial tree, and her customers would make ornaments for it, and on Christmas Eve she'd take it to someone who otherwise wouldn't have a tree."

Jill misinterpreted the look on Betsy's face and said, "You don't have to do it, too. I mean, for one thing you're busy, and for another you don't have Margot's connections, so you won't know who needs the tree."

"That's not what's bothering me," said Betsy. "I feel so bad about all the things that won't get done because she's gone."

There was a little silence, then Godwin sighed noisily and asked, "What else did Sergeant Malloy say about the lace?"

"Not much. He said it might be part of a dress or a handkerchief. It's green, but that's because whatever was holding it down was made of copper or bronze, like a section of pipe. It's only about four inches' worth, going around a corner, like maybe the corner of a handkerchief or a collar point. Silk, he says. The expert, not Mike. But really, it's such a mess I don't know if even someone who makes lace could tell Mike anything useful."

Malloy hesitated before opening the door. Betsy Devonshire was okay, he was pretty sure. He had a problem accepting women as equals, and his natural cop attitude toward civilians overlay that to make him appear a male chauvinist pig. Which he wasn't, not really. But here, too, and not all that long ago, Ms. Devonshire had shown herself willing to interfere in a police investigation. So he'd have to step carefully around her, because he really wanted to use her as a resource. After all, the woman had been pretty clever coming up with the murderer of her sister. But he didn't want her poking around again because that first time was undoubtedly just luck, and if she tried again, she'd probably only scare off or corrupt a witness. So he'd have to talk kind of careful to her.

Malloy steeled himself and opened the door.

Inside the shop, Betsy and Godwin had been staring at the person standing so dark and still on the other side of the door. His head was on a level with the Open sign so they couldn't see his face, but there was a sinister tension in the stillness of his pose. And one hand was hidden in the folds of his overcoat.

Then the door went *bing* and it was Sergeant Mike Malloy. They were both so relieved that their greetings were especially warm, which made them grin at one another.

Which puzzled Malloy, who started to frown suspiciously.

"We thought you were a robber," explained Betsy, still smiling. "You were standing there like you were trying to get up the nerve to come in and demand all our money."

Mike laughed and gestured dismissively. "Heck, this is too nice a town for something bad to happen to decent people twice in a row."

"Jill was here a little while ago," said Godwin, eager to get down to business, "and she said you might come to ask us to help you with some needlework sample."

Malloy shrugged crookedly. "Well, what it is, I'm hoping you know someone who can tell me if I have an example of handmade lace here, and what kind it is." What Malloy had hidden in the folds of his coat was the glass sandwich. It now had a double seal of tape and a tag with Evidence in big red letters.

Betsy looked at it without touching it and shrugged. But Godwin took it and held it up to the ceiling just as Jill had, then over toward the front window, then close to his right eye. Frustrated, he said, "I'm sorry, it doesn't look like anything to me."

"Perhaps one of your customers could help me. Officer Cross said that everyone in the area who does needlework comes here."

"From your mouth to His ear, amen," said Betsy fervently and Malloy laughed again.

"Still," persisted Malloy, "is there anyone who comes here who is knowledgeable about handmade lace?"

Betsy said, "There are a number of local women who make bobbin lace, do tatting, crochet, and make lace in other forms. The real question is, can they look at what you have there and make sense of it? I'm worried now that Godwin says it doesn't look like anything to him, but he's not a lace maker, so maybe someone else can help. If you like, I can ask customers to take a look at your sample—but wait, I guess you wouldn't want to leave that here."

"I'm not allowed to leave it here." Malloy lifted and dropped the Evidence tag.

"Oh, I see. So how about we arrange a meeting, and you can bring it, and we'll see if someone can help."

"You'll never get everyone to agree on a time," said Godwin.

"Including me," said Malloy. "So how about I get a good picture of it, or maybe just a Xerox for a start. Then if it rings any chimes with someone, I can show the real thing to them."

"Yes, of course. Would it be all right if I taped up the photocopy? Or should I keep it in a drawer and just show it to select customers?"

"I don't see why you can't post it. I'd appreciate hearing right away if someone thinks she can help. I'll drop the copy off later today."

"All right," said Betsy.

After Malloy left, Godwin said, "You know, there are times when he seems almost human."

There's no statute of limitations on murder, and occasionally something will crop up to crack an old case. Even in solved murders, someone convicted many years ago may persuade a judge to order a new trial or a DNA test that proves him innocent, or something will be discovered during another investigation that forces the police to start over. So when it's a homicide case, the records are kept forever.

But nobody can keep records of every crime. So when Malloy wanted reports of a missing woman in the summer of 1949, the missing person reports were long gone. He went first to the public library and searched microfilm copies of old newspaper files. And found nothing, which he thought was a little strange.

Shrugging off his annoyance, he went to his first fallback location, the Excelsior Historical Society, which consisted of three seniors, all women, who met on Tuesday mornings in the vault of City Hall.

City Hall was in the basement of the volunteer fire department, a cramped space with five employees. The mayor was at his regular day job, so the highest executive present was the city comptroller. He smiled and nodded when Malloy stated his business, and Malloy lifted the flap that marked the entrance and made his way to the back of the room, where a large, thick, fireproof door let into a space almost as big as the main room. Three walls were lined with metal shelves stuffed to overflowing with wire baskets, accordion folders, boxes, and files, the official records of the City of Excelsior. The fourth wall was obscured by metal file cabinets and an old wooden map cabinet. Near these stood a scarred wooden table, at which the Excelsior Historical Society sat in session, surrounded by plats, deeds, and old tax records.

"Good morning, ladies," said Malloy. "What's on your schedule for today?"

"Good morning, Michael," said the littlest woman, who was also the oldest. "We're trying to map the location of the fire lanes. The city hasn't kept up its claim to them where they touch the lakeshore, and there's been a lot of encroachment. *Some* of it inadvertent."

This budding problem had made the news recently. When the Excelsior Fire Department was young, its pumper drew water from the lake, and so eight or ten narrow access lanes to the lake were marked off and maintained for its use. The installation of fireplugs in the '50s removed the need for the lanes. Some were turned into public access boat landings. But over the years the others blended into the lawns of the houses on either side of them. A quarrel was developing over what should be done about the lanes. Sold to the homeowner(s) who had encroached with garden or lawn? Divided equally between the properties on either side? Reclaimed by the city? Before anything could be settled, the city had to first discover just how much land was involved and where it was located.

"If I might pull you off your work for just a few minutes," Malloy said, "I'd like to know if you can tell me if there was a report of a woman gone missing in 1949."

"From just Excelsior?" asked the second oldest woman, whose name, Malloy suddenly remembered, was Myrtle Jensen.

"Excelsior and the area close by—unless you can search other areas easily," said Malloy. "And also, can you find the month the *Hopkins* was sunk? I assume it was summer, but it could have been any time there was no ice."

Myrtle pressed a crooked forefinger to her lips. "I can tell you that," she said. "It was just before the Fourth of July. I remember because Jack brought up a bushel basket of sweet corn from Illinois—ours wasn't ripe yet. We boiled it up and had a Fourth of July picnic in the backyard and a neighbor came by for an ear and said he'd seen the *Hopkins* towed out to be sunk. That was the best sweet corn I ever ate, and ever after, I associated corn on the cob with the Fourth of July, even though it's never ready up here by then. We always have to buy it from people who bring it from down south. There used to be a man who would drive to Tennessee—remember him, Lola?—he'd fill his trunk and the backseat of his car and drive all day and night and park down by The Common and sell it. I remember my dad used to put about half of our garden in sweet corn, each row planted a week later than the one before, so it didn't all ripen at once. We used to have a real big backyard garden. I remember being sent out to work in it when I was a child, weeding and picking caterpillars off the leaves. My brother's son Jimmy worked in that garden, but Jimmy's boy Adam went to college and he uses mulch and organic bug spray."

Malloy had patiently waited for her to run down, then reaffirmed the pertinent part of her remarks. "So it was July they sank the *Hopkins*."

"Didn't I say that? Yes, early July, before the Fourth, because on the Fourth we heard it had been done, so a day or two before. It was hot that day, just blazing sun. Jack set up a cauldron outside, and was miserable tending the fire. Good corn, though."

The littlest woman said, "I've got a missing person story. Trudie Koch ran off with Carl Winters, or so everyone said. Maybe he murdered her instead and ran away." Her eyes sparkled at the thought.

Malloy looked at her. "Who was Trudie Koch?"

"Waitress down at the Blue Ribbon Café. No better than she ought to be, remember, Myrt? Had a steady boyfriend, what was his name? Vern something. Mean fellow, gave her a black eye once in a while, not that she didn't provoke him something awful. She dated a lot of men, and was very easy, or so everyone said. We were surprised that she ran off with Carl, or rather, that Carl ran off with her. He had a perfectly nice wife and a good job." She looked at Myrtle. "Remember?"

Myrtle was looking thoughtful. "But that didn't happen the year they sank the *Hopkins*, did it? Those two ran off in 1948."

"I thought it happened the same summer. Are you sure they ran off in 1948?"

"Yes, because that was the year Martha had to drop out as organist and they asked me to take her place. With her husband gone, she had to run the dry cleaning store all by herself and she didn't have time for choir. I got in and stayed in. I got my gold pin for twenty years' service in 1968, see?" She touched one of two tiny round badges pinned to her dress. Malloy took a look and saw the badge said Saint Elwin's Choir and Twenty Years around its edge. A tiny gold chain led from the pin to a tiny rectangle with the year 1948 on it.

The other badge was slightly more elaborate and said Saint Elwin's Choir and Forty Years around its edge. The chained tag also read 1948.

"I stepped down as organist after I got this pin," she said, touching the second one. "My ears weren't what they used to be."

"Sorry," said Malloy, but carelessly. "Say, maybe the *Hopkins* was sunk in 1948?"

"Oh, no," said the youngest woman. She stood and went to a low shelf behind the table. She selected a slim, blue paperbound book and brought it to Malloy. "It says in here that the boat was sunk in 1949, and this book was written by the man in charge of raising both the *Minnehaha* and the *Hopkins*. He even took a picture of the *Hopkins* at the bottom of the lake."

Malloy paged through the book, which was locally published and had good black and white photographs in it. Sure enough, there was an old photo of a streetcar steamboat loaded with passengers, and another of an open hatch, this one taken under water. The accompanying paragraph said the *Hopkins* was sunk near her sisters off the Big Island in 1949.

"Anyone know where I can reach the author of this book?" he asked.

"He's with the Minnesota Transportation Museum's steamboat branch; their office is right down by the lake, in that little row of stores," said Myrtle.

"May I keep this?" he asked, displaying the book.

"For $7.95, you may," said Myrtle, producing a cash box, and the best Malloy could do was get a receipt and hope the department would reimburse him.

Four

❖

The Minnesota Transportation Museum Ticket Office and Souvenir Store was a little storefront, in a row of them behind Pizza Hut. There was a parking lot in front, and Malloy stood a minute looking at the lake across the street. A gentle slope ran down to the docks—narrow wooden walks into the water, supported on thick wooden piles—now empty in anticipation of winter. Malloy sometimes thought he would like to live in some state where winter didn't take up so much of the year. They had bass lakes as far south as Missouri, didn't they? But in Missouri, they didn't go ice fishing, did they? And Malloy loved ice fishing almost as much as fishing from his bass boat.

He turned, saw the sign, and went up and into the MTM store.

Like most souvenir stores, MTM had lots of T-shirts and sweatshirts. There were also caps, some of them the old-fashioned, high-crowned, mattress-ticking variety that yesteryear's engineers wore. There were bright-colored prints of the lake in its heyday, with streetcar boats taking on passengers in the foreground. Each boat was named after a town on the lake. There were also prints of streetcars, some in small-town settings back when Hopkins and Minnetonka were not merely suburbs of Minneapolis—though even then the main purpose of the streetcars was to take workers to the big city.

A glass case held a big model of the restored *Minnehaha*, showing the peculiar long slope of her stern. Malloy remembered seeing photographs of the Great White Fleet back in Teddy Roosevelt's time, where the ships had that same odd back end. He wondered what its purpose was.

At the far end of the store was a counter behind which a young woman with short dark hair frowned at a computer monitor.

He walked back and she looked up. "May I help you?" she asked. Her features were attractive, but she had made no effort to enhance them with makeup.

"I'm interested in learning about the *Hopkins*," he said. "What can you tell me?"

"It's no longer at the bottom of the lake," she replied with a twinkle.

"Tell me something I don't know."

"Like what?"

"When was it sunk?"

"1949."

"That's what everyone keeps telling me. Who knows that for a fact?"

She smiled. "If everyone's telling you that, then everyone, I guess. What are you looking for, an eyewitness?"

"You got one?"

She looked around. There was no one there but the two of them. "Not here in the office."

He laughed, but then produced identification, which stopped the banter as it widened her light blue eyes. Then she turned abruptly and reached for some books tucked into a shelf under the counter. "These are stories about the lake and the towns on it, and here's one about the streetcar steamboats in particular. They all say the *Hopkins*—well, it was renamed the *Minnetonka* by then—was sunk in 1949. This one even has some pictures of it on the bottom of the lake." This one was *Salvaged Memories*, the blue paperback Malloy already had a copy of.

Still, he took the books and went to a corner of the store that had a chair and looked them over. They all agreed that the *Minnetonka III*, née *Hopkins*, had been sunk on the north side of the Big Island in Lake Minnetonka in 1949.

All right, he'd accept that. He got the phone number for the author of *Salvaged Memories* and left.

Diane Bolles was sorting through a thin stack of cardboard signs when a customer came to the checkout counter. Distracted, she glanced up without at first recognizing the woman, who had a half dozen old books. "May I help you find something else?" she asked—then blinked. "Oh, hello, Shelly!"

"You must have something else on your own mind today, Diane," said Shelly Donohue.

"Well, yes, as a matter of fact, I do. I'm thinking of changing the name of my store."

"What's wrong with D. B. and Company?" Shelly looked around at the store, which looked like an old-fashioned general store in layout. There was even a penny candy counter next to the checkout. But elsewhere were silk flowers, old-fashioned tea sets, doilies, vases, jars, and over by the door a large cement statue of a frog.

"Nothing, actually. Except it doesn't describe the store."

Shelly giggled. "I don't see how you would describe this place in one sentence, much less one word."

"We sell the final touch for your decor, in the house or the garden."

"Oh. Well, yes. In fact, you put that so well, you must already be writing your new radio ad."

"Not until I get the new name." Diane picked up the cardboard squares. "May I try some out on you? I've sorted it down to these, but I don't know which one I like best."

"Sure."

"Belles Choses, which means Beautiful Choice in Italian. Or, there's Nightingale's, after the bird. Or Near Midnight—I like that one because it's romantic. You know, midnight, the bewitching hour. Or Chenille—did you know that's French for caterpillar? And last, My Favorite Year, which was my favorite this morning. This evening I'll like a different one."

Shelly said, "I like Nightingale's. The bird was a symbol of home and hope to the British during World War II, and it has a very beautiful song. I did a counted cross-stitch of a nightingale a couple of years ago for a friend who was born in England, and she just loved it."

"That reminds me. I was thinking of expanding into antique and vintage clothing. And then I found my grandmother's embroidered tablecloths and brought them in to decorate that table with the antique dessert dishes."

Shelly said, "Your grandmother made those? I can't believe you're going to sell those, Diane; they are heirlooms. The embroidery on them is wonderful; those strawberries are almost three-dimensional."

"Oh, they're not for sale, they're just decoration. But I've gotten so many inquiries from customers that I think I should add stitchery to my line." She cocked her head. "Do you still work part-time in that needlework store down on Lake?"

"Yes, I do."

"Maybe I should stop in there and ask the new owner if she can put me in touch with people willing to sell their work."

"Well . . ." said Shelly. "Actually, she probably can't help you. She's a terrific person, I really like her, but she's not only new at needlework, she's not from here." There was a subtle emphasis on that last part, *not from here.*

"Ah," said Diane.

"On the other hand, you could talk to her one full-time employee, Godwin. He knows everyone in the area who has ever done any kind of needlework. But you know something?" Shelly leaned forward in a mockery of her own posture when imparting a tantalizing tidbit of gossip. *"So do I."*

Diane's eyebrows raised in surprise, then she laughed. "Well, of course! So where do I go? Who do I see? I'm looking for vintage, antique, and new items. Not a big selection, just a few things."

"Tell you what. Let me think about it, maybe ask around. I'll draw up a list. And I think you should come to the shop anyway, meet Betsy—she's really nice.

I'll consult with Godwin. He can probably suggest some names I miss. Let's see, today's Tuesday. I'll need about a week, can you wait that long?"

"Yes, of course. I'll come by sometime next week, maybe on my lunch break."

Diane began to ring up Shelly's selections. "Do you collect old children's books?"

"No, I'm going to encourage my students to read them. I think it's helpful to expose even young children to a variety of reading experiences," said Shelly. She had a variety, all right, from the sweet and innocent *Pokey Little Puppy* to a pre-Disney version of *The Three Little Pigs* that had the wolf eating the first two.

Diane put the purchases into a bag and handed it to Shelly, who wasn't finished talking. "You know about the skeleton on the boat they raised?"

"Yes, I read about it. How dreadful for the divers, finding something like that."

Shelly nodded. "We're involved again."

"Who is?"

"The shop, Crewel World."

"I don't understand."

"You know how we solved the murder of Betsy's sister for the police, of course."

Diane started to object to that but changed her mind and only raised a mildly doubting eyebrow.

"I know the police are acting as if they solved it themselves, but they would still be looking for a burglar if it wasn't for Betsy Devonshire! She has a nose, or is it an eye, for crime solving. And so they're practically begging her to help again. They've left a big clue in our shop, and people are being asked to look at it and see if they can identify it."

"What kind of clue?"

"It's a piece of silk with lace edging, or rather a picture of it. It was found on the boat, which means it went down with it in 1949. No one has come up with anything yet, but you just watch. Of course, Betsy won't suspect you or me, because we weren't around in 1949." Shelly laughed, embraced the paper bag a little tighter, and left, not noticing the way Diane frowned after her.

The Saturday after Thanksgiving is traditionally the best day for American retailers, but for needlework shops, it's the Saturday after Halloween. That's when the procrastinators realize that unless they want to offend their mother-in-law *again* with a store-bought gift, they'd better get down to Crewel World and see if there is something that looks as if it took more than two months to finish, but doesn't.

For the first time, Betsy began to believe she could actually make a go of the little shop. Customers were waiting outside for her to open, and it was nonstop from then till closing. Fortunately, Shelly was able to join Godwin and Betsy.

Shelly was slim, not yet thirty, with long, thick, straight brown hair pulled into an untidy bun at the nape of her neck. She had beautiful eyes, intelligent and compassionate, and was a skilled counted cross-stitcher, a hard worker in the shop—but an incorrigible gossip. ". . . Linda chose that same cream-colored linen," she was telling a customer, "and frankly, I think iris-blue and purple silk would go even better for your sampler than her shades of pumpkin."

Meanwhile, Godwin was saying, "If the Ott table lamp is too small, you might want to try a light by Chromalux; it's a floor lamp, and comes already on a stand. And if you stitch in the nude—like *I* do—you'll appreciate the heat it puts out." The customer giggled, and Godwin reached for a catalog. "See, here's a picture of it; we can order it for you . . ."

Betsy stopped eavesdropping and looked at the completed piece of counted cross-stitch, Mermaid of the Pearls, lying across her hands. "Wow," she said sincerely, "this is much prettier than the picture of it I saw. Let's look at the sample mats to pick a color to match, and then we'll choose a really nice frame. You'll want to do justice to this, I'm sure."

While Betsy was writing up the order, her customer noticed the Xerox taped to a corner of the checkout desk. When Betsy saw her bend over it, she asked, "Recognize it?"

"What's it supposed to be?" asked the customer.

"Lace edging on a collar or handkerchief or sleeve. It was hauled up from the bottom of the lake, and we're hoping someone who does lace will be able to tell something about it."

"Looks like a spill of spaghetti to me," remarked the customer, taking her slip and looking at it. Betsy held her breath; the finishing, mat, and frame came to over two hundred dollars. But the customer only said, "You'll have this back in three weeks? Good, I can get it in the mail on time, then. Thank you, Betsy."

"You're welcome, Mrs. Liljegren." Betsy had thought she'd never get used to people calling her by her first name while she must address them more formally, but at these prices they could call her anything they liked.

"What's this about some lace you want identified?" asked a very handsome woman Betsy recognized as one of the Monday Bunch. She had a fistful of silk floss and a packet of needles for Betsy to ring up.

"Hello, Patricia. Detective Malloy found something on the *Hopkins* and hopes someone here can help identify it." Betsy indicated the Xerox copy taped to the desk. "It's a corner of a handkerchief or maybe a bit of a silk dress, and that tangle of string may be crochet lace."

Patricia bent over the paper, frowning. Betsy wrote the sales slip, then rang up her purchase, but Patricia didn't move. Betsy gave her a minute, then saw Godwin bringing another customer to check out. "Er-hem, excuse me?" Betsy said. "That'll be seventeen dollars and fifty-three cents, including tax. Patricia?"

Patricia said, "Hmm?"

"That'll be seventeen dollars and fifty-three cents."

"Okay."

"Excuse me, Patricia?" said Godwin politely, instead of making a wisecrack. Godwin knew which customers enjoyed him at his outrageous best and which didn't.

Patricia straightened. "I wonder why someone thinks that might be crocheted lace. It doesn't look like crochet to me, the loops are all wrong. It might be tatting, but is more likely bobbin lace."

Betsy looked at the copy. "You mean you can actually make sense of that?" She had thought the original unidentifiable, but the photocopy was even worse.

"Oh, it's definitely lace," said Patricia. "Question is, what kind? There are a number of ways to make lace, but I think I'd want to see the original before I said for sure what kind this is."

Godwin's customer crowded in for a peek but frowned and stepped back again. "I can't see any pattern to that," she said as if in complaint.

"Patricia, Sergeant Malloy is going to be *so pleased* if you can really tell him something helpful," said Godwin.

Betsy added quickly, "That is—would you mind talking to him?"

"No, of course not." She pulled her checkbook from her purse. "I'll pay for my silks and you may copy the phone number on the check to give to him." Her cheeks were pink with pleasure, her brown eyes alight. "This will be a poke in the eye for my husband, who says nothing of real value ever came out of a needleworker's basket."

Hours later, closing time approached. Betsy, near exhaustion, was trying to rearrange a basket of half-price wool so that it didn't look so picked-over. Her feet were like a pair of toothaches. Shelly and Godwin were in back, quarreling tiredly over whose turn it was to wash out the coffeepot.

The door went *bing* (Betsy gritted her teeth and swore that someday soon she was going to replace that thing), but she forced her features to assume a pleasant look and turned to greet her customer. She was a small, thin woman with dark hair standing up in little curls all over her head. She had shiny dark eyes in a narrow face and a smile as false as the leopard print of her coat.

"Hello, Irene," said Betsy neutrally—that being the best she could manage.

"I hear you've had a splendid day, lots of customers," said Irene.

"Yes, the Christmas rush has begun, it seems."

"Won't last till Christmas," warned Irene.

Irene Potter was one of the thorns on Betsy's rose. She was an extremely talented needleworker and a steady customer, but she was also opinionated, rude, hyperactive, nosy, and impatient. She thought Betsy incompetent and was watching hopefully, even cheerfully, for any sign the shop might slip into bankruptcy. Because if it did, then she, Irene, could take it over, fire that dreadful Godwin person, and run it as it should be run. Meanwhile, a mass of contradictions, she was also willing to share her considerable business and needlework expertise with Betsy. She was serenely unaware of this and other contradictions in her behavior.

"Why won't the Christmas rush last till Christmas?" asked Betsy.

"Projects done as gifts or decorations have to be bought well in advance, to be done by Christmas. Once it's too late to get the projects finished on time, they'll stop buying them."

"Oh," said Betsy. "Of course."

"Unless they are given as projects to be done by the recipients," said Godwin. "Hello, Irene."

"Goddy." Irene gave an almost imperceptible nod of her head in Godwin's direction. She was sure of a number of vicious and untrue things about gay people, so vicious she was ashamed she knew about them and so never alluded to them, even obliquely. But the knowledge made her unable to look Godwin in the eye—which was as well, because his reaction to her shame was to grin tantalizingly.

"H'lo, Irene," said Shelly tiredly.

"Why, Shelly, I thought you'd be home grading papers or something."

"Now, Irene, you know that's how I spend my Sunday afternoons, smoking and drinking and grading papers." When she was tired, Shelly could be difficult, too.

"May we help you, Irene?" asked Betsy, anxious to get this over with so she could go upstairs and sit on the edge of her bathtub and do that trick of running cold then hot then cold then hot water over her feet.

"I've come to look at that picture you have of the lace collar."

"What? Oh. It's not a picture, it's a Xerox copy. And we don't know exactly what it was part of. Sergeant Malloy left it in hopes that people can identify it." Betsy led the way to the desk.

Irene studied the copy from different angles, coming beside the desk and even behind it. Betsy, seeking a second to Patricia's opinion, was beginning to feel optimistic when Irene said, "Humph, doesn't look like much of anything to me."

Betsy sighed. "I agree, and I saw the real thing."

Irene straightened so abruptly that Godwin, who had been standing close behind her, was forced to jump backward, which he did adroitly. Irene said, "I thought perhaps I could be of significant help with your second case, as I was with the first one"—she smirked proudly, then her face fell—"but I suppose not."

"This isn't my case, Irene," said Betsy, annoyance lending strength to the assertion, which she had made several times that day. "I am not involved. I am only allowing Sergeant Malloy to leave a request for information here. He probably has also left it at Needle Nest and Stitchville and who knows where else."

"Do you mean to tell me, Irene," purred Godwin, "that there is a needlework style you can't identify? I am *stunned* to hear that, Irene, at a total loss for words."

Irene did look him in the eye then. For about three seconds. Then, silently, she turned and walked out of the shop.

Shelly, giggling, said, "Godwin, you are the limit."

"Thank you, Shelly, I try."

Five

❖

Today's Monday Bunch more resembled the usual gathering, with four present. Oddly, one of the most faithful wasn't there: Martha Winters.

Her best friend Jessica explained, "The refrigeration unit in her dry cleaning machine has been acting up for weeks, and Jeff had the repairman over at least once, but now it's broken down completely, and everyone's cleaning is going to be late. So Martha decided to supervise the replacement herself."

"Jeff's her grandson," Alice explained briefly to Betsy.

Jessica nodded. "Her grandson is careless about repairs and replacements, but you can be sure Martha's going to stand right behind that poor repairman to make sure he does it right." Jessica sniffed righteously and then added, "Oh, she said to ask if anyone knows how Emily and her baby are doing, and she'll be here next Monday." The baby blanket Jessica had been working on was nearly finished. It gleamed in soft white folds in her lap, and her crochet hook moved as rapidly as if it were attached to a machine rather than a work-thickened hand.

Alice said, "Emily's named her Morgana Jean. Six pounds, twenty inches, both at home, grandmom's there helping." She sighed and shrugged her big shoulders, fingers working on yet another afghan square.

Jessica said, "Then I'll have that pink wool, Betsy; just one skein, please. I'll embroider little pink daisies around the edge of this."

As Betsy got up to get it, Kate, a trim woman working on a complex counted cross-stitch of a horse-drawn carriage on a rain-wet cobblestone street, asked, "Have they identified that skeleton yet?"

Betsy replied, "I haven't heard anything. But Patricia is going to meet with Sergeant Malloy to take a look at the bit of silk they found on the boat. She seems to think she can tell what that tangle of thread is, or was supposed to be."

The women started talking in low voices as Betsy went for the wool, and as she came back into earshot, a sudden silence fell. Jessica's thin mouth was a mere line, Alice's complexion was a bright pink, and the other two women were trying out poker faces. *Honestly*, thought Betsy, *the way these people gossip! I wonder what they're saying about me.*

She sat down with a sigh and asked a question a customer had brought in, about how to get colors that run out of needlework (soak in frequently renewed ice water or milk, wash in Orvus, rinse copiously, roll in towels, iron dry, don't hang). Then, satisfied they were back on topic, she said she needed their advice getting started on her counted cross-stitch Christmas ornaments. She got out the kit and complained that the cloth was all one big piece, and they wanted her to leave it that way—"Is that right?"—and to baste all around the edge of it, and then across its length every four inches, and then sort the floss, making sure all the colors were there, and on and on. "When do I get to start stitching?"

"But you are stitching," said Kate in some surprise. "I almost like that part best, when you prepare your cloth and sort the colors, and start to see in your head what the project will look like, and even plan little changes you'll make and so on." Her voice had gotten dreamy at the prospect, and the women chuckled.

Betsy said, "Oh, I get it. It's like baking. You find a new recipe or a new version of an old one, and you get out the pans and line up the ingredients. You heat the milk and pour it and the sugar into the bowl, and the smell of the yeast as it starts to work is wonderful."

Jessica said a little dreamily, "Yes, it's a lot like that," and this time there was laughter.

The Monday Bunch began discussing serging around the fabric on a sewing machine or even putting masking tape on it instead of basting, and were just starting on finding the center of a pattern, when the door went *bing* and Patricia entered, Malloy close behind her. She was wearing a green plaid swing coat and her dark hair was pulled back into a ribboned clip, which made her look prosperous and responsible. Malloy was wearing a raincoat that Columbo might have coveted. "Hi, everyone!" said Patricia, looking around. "Where's Martha?"

"Not here today," said Jessica. "Why?"

"Oh, no! I told Sergeant Malloy she was our bobbin lace expert. He wants to talk to her about that little piece of fabric they found, because I told him I think it's part of a handkerchief edged in bobbin lace."

Malloy's face also showed disappointment, but Alice Skoglund said quietly, "I used to do bobbin lace."

All heads came around. Since she had joined the Monday Bunch, no one had seen her do anything but crochet endless afghan squares. She set her heavy jaw and looked back calmly.

"Well, Alice, can you look at this, then?" Patricia gestured at Malloy, who obediently put the square of glass on the table in front of Alice.

She peered at it closely for a few moments, turning it once, then said, "Have we got a magnifying glass anywhere?"

"Yes," said Betsy, and went to the checkout desk. She pawed through two drawers before finding the big rectangular one with its handle on one corner. She brought it to Alice, who bent close and used it to study the glass plates for a longer while.

"Yes," she said finally, leaning back. "This is bobbin lace."

"Are you sure?" asked Malloy.

"Yes."

"How can you tell?"

"If you pick a strand and follow it, you can see how the twists were made. And these are twisted and crossed over like bobbin lace."

Jessica asked, "How sure can you be? Couldn't it be something else? Tatting, maybe? Or crochet?"

Alice looked sharply at Jessica, then said with an air of being patient with her, "No, it's not the loop, loop, loop of crochet." She looked at the blank faces of the other women and continued, "If you found the end of this and pulled, it wouldn't all come undone, would it? So it's not crochet. And it's not tatting, I can't see anything like those circles you get in tatting. But there are twists and weaving in it, and they look like bobbin lace patterns to me." She bent over the fragment under glass again, this time so closely there was barely room for the magnifying glass. "Here, for example, this must have been ground. And here, what do you think, Patricia, the petal of a flower, maybe?"

Patricia looked, the small neatness of her a strong contrast to the large woman bent over the glass. "I see what you mean, I think."

Alice said, pointing with a thick forefinger, "But all along here, the threads have been broken. And here, see how it's pulled; this thread is thinned out to nothing here and here it's thicker and there it's thin again. Same with these. I never saw thread do that before."

She looked accusingly at Malloy, who shrugged. "It's silk, if that's any help. A textile expert says if you put animal fibers under pressure under water for a long time, they will stretch. And silk's from worms, which are animals."

Patricia, still looking at the sample, nodded. "You know, I think you're right, Alice; it's not just pulled crosswise, the thread itself is stretched, and not evenly."

Alice said, "Yes, that alone makes it impossible to see what the pattern was." She moved the magnifying glass along the fabric. "Though here, I think this was a line of picots. I don't think this was torchon. Hmmm, binche?"

"Bench?" echoed Betsy.

"No, binche, a kind of bobbin lace. Well, maybe not. It's too damaged to tell for sure." She put the magnifying glass down and sat back again. "That's all I can tell you."

Malloy said, notebook in hand, "But you're absolutely sure it's bobbin lace?" Alice nodded, and he wrote that down. "Is that a common kind of thing? I mean, lots of women knit and crochet. Do lots of women do bobbin lace?"

"No," Alice said.

"The question is," said Betsy, "did women make bobbin lace back in 1949?"

"Oh, yes," nodded Alice. "I was making it back then, and I wasn't the only one. I learned it as a child; my Grandma brought it from the old country. My mother wasn't interested, so Grandma taught me. It's very difficult to learn from a book, you just about have to have someone show you, so I doubt there's been a time since it was invented hundreds and hundreds of years ago that someone hasn't been doing it."

"So I guess the patterns have all been passed along, too," said Betsy.

Alice nodded. "Of course, you can make up your own, too. Some people make lace into pictures, like of flowers or animals or trees. You can take a picture with a nice, easy outline, like from a coloring book, and make it into lace. I once saw a Batman, the lace maker handled the cape real nice, all lines and shading. But mostly you do geometrical patterns, repeats of flowers or leaves."

"Were more women or fewer doing it back then?"

Alice considered for a bit. "Fewer, I think. There's a trend back to hand-made just now, so more women are learning how to do these things. There's someone teaching it locally. She holds a regular class at Ingebretsen's in Minneapolis."

"Is there something about the way people do this stuff," began Malloy, thinking his way slowly through the question, "so that you can tell who did it? I mean, could you identify a person just by looking at the lace they make?"

Alice nodded. "Sometimes. There are different skill levels, so if someone showed me a sample and said did this person or that person make this, and one was a beginner and the other one was experienced, that would be easy."

Patricia nodded. "Yes, that's true of all needlework."

Malloy said, "What if they were both experienced?"

"Then it would be impossible," said Patricia.

But Alice said, "Maybe not. Some people make up a pattern, or have a signature way of doing it, and if you've seen it, you can recognize it if you see it again. And some people just have a way with lace, so if you see something really well done, you might think she did it."

Malloy said, "Do you think this is a signature pattern?"

Alice frowned massively at him and said, "It was all I could do to say it was bobbin lace. I can't even tell what the pattern is, much less who might have done it."

Patricia added, "And even if she could figure out the pattern, what would that do? This skeleton you're investigating isn't a local person, so what good would it do to identify the pattern?"

Malloy said, "Because there may be a husband or a daughter somewhere who still wonders what happened to their wife or mother. We've already gotten inquiries from other law enforcement agencies about the find. We'll pass along any clues we get to the identity."

There was a little silence as this sank in, that there were people who had wondered sadly for fifty years what had become of their sister or mother.

"Hold on a minute," Alice said in a much kinder voice. "It may be possible to recreate the pattern of this lace. It will take time, but I think I can do it."

Patricia said, "Anything I can do to help, Alice, just ask."

"Thank you," said Alice, and Betsy knew suddenly how rarely Alice had felt important in this group.

Betsy asked, "Are you making any progress in identifying the skeleton?"

"Not much. The problem is, there weren't many clues aboard the boat, no shoes or clothing or a purse with a wallet, any of which would have been helpful. All we have are the bones and that piece of fabric—which might not even belong to the bones."

Betsy said, "There's a police artist in California who can put a face back on a skull. Perhaps you should contact him."

Malloy smiled. "Minnesota has an artist who can do that, too. Kerrie is, in fact, working on that task already."

Alice said, "What do you mean, put a face back on?"

Malloy said, "It's something that's been around for awhile now. She takes measurements and covers the bones with clay according to the numbers, and there's the dead person looking back at you. We've broken more than one case by showing a photograph of Kerrie's work around. It's a science, the way these artists go about this."

Kerrie held a skull between her hands and stared at the face. Although it had been cleaned, it was still faintly green. It had belonged to a woman, one who had been badly used. Pieces of bone had been glued back in place, gaps here and there filled with clay.

Who are you? Kerrie thought, directing it as a gentle question. Sometimes she got a strong feeling about the victim, once even a name, which turned out to be right. But nothing came this time.

She went to a big wooden cabinet against the wall and got a clear plastic box—the one with the red rubber stubs in it. They looked like pencil erasers cut into various small lengths, which is what they were. She also took out a fresh box of Sculpey modeling clay, and a bottle of glue.

As Malloy had said, there was a science to this business. Kerrie had gone through two intense courses in New Mexico to learn it. She would glue the markers on mapped areas of the skull to show the varying thickness of flesh at those points, then lay strips of clay between the markers. She would measure eye and ear and nose openings to determine the shape and length of the nose and ears and placement of the eyes, and as she filled in the spaces, a face would grow on the bone.

But when that was done, there was still the indeterminate to deal with: color of eyes, thickness of eyebrows, hair color and style, whether the face was habitually tense or angry or happy. No science could fill in these variables. Kerrie would keep her work on her desk, waiting to see if she'd get a flash of insight—it amounted sometimes to ESP—before completing the assignment. Sometimes it felt as if her small cubicle were haunted by the spirit of the deceased, so always, always, she handled her charges with respect and humility.

She paused again after gluing the little rubber markers to the skull, holding it cradled in both hands to ask again, "Who are you?"

But again, the answer was silence.

On Tuesday afternoon Betsy had a visitor. Before the electronic *bing* had faded his rough voice shouted, "What's this I hear?"

Betsy was behind a set of shelves that marked off a little area at the back of her shop, rearranging old stitchery magazines in date order—people *would* replace them any old how, if they replaced them at all. She was alone in the shop; Godwin had gone to pick up a shipment of fabric.

She recognized the voice; it belonged to Joe Mickels, her landlord.

"Hey!" he shouted again. "Anyone here?"

"What is it, Mr. Mickels?" she asked, a trifle impatiently, coming out from behind the shelves.

Mickels was a broad man, somewhat below middle height, with a mane of white hair and big, old-fashioned sideburns. He also wore an old-fashioned overcoat, dark gray wool with a fur collar that looked like Persian lamb—the real stuff, doubtless. Mickels would never wear fake fur, especially that of some edible animal. He was old-fashioned even beyond his years, a throwback to the unbridled capitalists of his great-grandfather's day, and as avaricious. And proud of it; that explained the coat, and the sideburns, which for him didn't date to the 1970s but the 1870s. He'd have worn spats if they were still sold, and happily sneered at frostbitten little girls selling matches, if there were any on the streets of Excelsior.

That old-fashioned arrogance showed in his voice.

"You shouldn't leave the front unattended like this; someone could walk in and steal you blind."

"The sort of person who lusts after alpaca yarn and bamboo knitting needles isn't the sort to steal them," she said. "Is that why you came in? To warn me not to leave the front unguarded?"

"It would have been, if I'd known. What I want to know is, what is this I hear about Mrs. Winters?"

"Martha Winters? What about her?" she asked impatiently. More gossip!

"Did she murder her husband?"

Betsy stared at him. "What in the world makes you ask a question like that?"

"That skeleton they found on that boat."

"The skeleton is a female."

He gestured impatiently. "*I* know that! But I heard it might belong to that woman Carl Winters is supposed to have run off with. I suppose it occurred to everyone when they found it that maybe Carl didn't run off with her, he murdered her. But now I hear they're looking for Carl's body, too; they think Mrs. Winters murdered both of them."

"Where on *earth* did you hear that?"

Mickels looked suddenly less angry, and his voice was less certain when he said, "Irene Potter told me, over at the Waterfront Café, not ten minutes ago."

"*Irene*—? And you *believed* her?"

Mickels shrugged even less certainly. "She's not wrong *all* the time. And she was a real help solving your sister's murder."

What he meant was that it was Irene Potter who supplied Joe Mickels with a badly needed alibi when he was a suspect.

Crewel World's building belonged to Mickels, who had long planned to tear it down and put up something bigger. He had been ruthlessly leaning on Betsy's sister Margot for months, trying to make her give up her lease and move out. His eagerness to dispossess Betsy after Margot's death and his fury on learning that even Margot's death hadn't broken the lease had soured any early chance of rapprochement between him and Betsy.

Now he hoped that when Margot's estate was closed, Betsy would take the money and close the shop. Struggling with the arcana of small business, Betsy often considered doing just that. Among the things stopping her was a disinclination to give Joe Mickels the satisfaction. She was aware that Mickels believed he was being mostly polite and endlessly accommodating. For example, he allowed her to live in Margot's old apartment over the shop and hadn't even raised the rent. Which he could still do, if she aggravated him enough.

So Betsy reined in her impatience and said, "Sit down, Mr. Mickels. Would you like a cup of coffee?"

Warily, he took a seat. "No, thanks, I just had one."

She sat down across from him. "Why did you think Irene was right when she told you Martha Winters murdered both her husband and that woman—I can't think of her name—"

"Trudie Koch. She was a waitress at the Blue Ribbon Café. Well, when I came into the Waterfront, Irene was there talking sixteen to the dozen with Myrtle Jensen, who—I don't know if you know her, she's one of the Excelsior Historical Society ladies. Myrtle was telling about how Sergeant Malloy interrogated her over this skeleton business, wanting to know when the *Hopkins* was sunk. She—Myrtle—sold him a history book that said it was 1949, and he wanted to know what month, and she told him it was the second or third of July." Suddenly, deftly, he put on the face of a sweet old lady and spoke in a soft, old voice. " 'I remember it was July because a neighbor came over and told me he saw it being towed out to be sunk the day before, or maybe the day before that. It was on the Fourth of July he came over, we were boiling corn in our backyard, it was simply blazing hot, my poor husband was just miserable in all that heat taking care of the fire, and we gave our neighbor an ear and he told me he'd seen it being towed out full of rocks.' "

Betsy, smiling at his clever impression, asked, "And what did Irene say?"

And Mickels became Irene Potter of the shiny eyes and malicious tongue. He said, in a skillful parody of Irene's rapid speech, " 'I've been talking to people who remember back then, and what I *conclude* is that Martha found out her Carl was messing around with Trudie and she got into a fight with Carl and hit him, and killed him, and buried him in her backyard, and then she went down to meet Trudie when Trudie got off work—in place of Carl, you see—and hit her and hid her body on the boat, which was tied up right there waiting to be towed out and sunk.' What was interesting is that Myrtle said Martha gave up gardening the year her husband disappeared, her yard went all to weeds, she said. And then she said everyone always liked Carl Winters, he didn't have an enemy in the world. He liked to flirt with the ladies, but it was all in fun, Myrtle said, and he was a hard worker, always taking on little part-time jobs in addition to his dry cleaners." Again there was a hint of old lady in Mickels's repetition of Myrtle's report.

Betsy smiled. "Well, I kind of hate to spoil everyone's fun, but it's impossible that the skeleton is Trudie's. You see, Carl and Trudie disappeared in 1948, and the *Hopkins* wasn't sunk until 1949. For another thing, I talked with Sergeant Malloy only yesterday and he didn't say a word about looking for Carl Winters's body. And, *one more* thing, if I may be so bold: What's *your* interest in this?"

"Because I used to own the mortgage on Winters's dry cleaning store. I bought it after Martha took it over, and I'm the one who brought the mortgage to her after the last payment and watched her burn it."

He seemed to think that was all the explanation necessary and turned away to look around the needlework shop—though she suspected he was not seeing the shop but its replacement. Doubtless something in steel and granite, with THE MICKELS BUILDING engraved in stone over the entrance.

At last he became aware of something in the silence and turned back to find Betsy looking at him inquiringly.

His forehead wrinkled while he did a swift dig into his memory to see where she had stopped following his chain of reason, and said, "Mrs. Winters took over the dry cleaners and ran it by herself after Carl disappeared."

But Betsy still looked at him inquiringly.

He said impatiently, "Don't you see? If she killed him, she couldn't inherit that place, not legally! I don't know who should have inherited it, but she couldn't, because you can't profit from a crime! I may have to run this through a court, and going to law always costs a fortune!"

Betsy sighed. Of course, if it was important to Mr. Mickels, it involved money.

He continued, "How sure are you about the discrepancy in the year?"

"Mrs. Winters sat in that very chair a week ago yesterday and told me and three other women that Carl disappeared in 1948. So if the history books say the *Hopkins* was sunk in 1949, then the skeleton can't be Trudie Koch's, unless the murderer saved her up for a year in his basement."

Mickels's enormous sandy eyebrows lifted, then something almost like a smile pulled his wide, thin mouth. He smacked his hand gently on the table and got to his feet. "I guess I should have known better than to believe Irene Potter. Thank you, Ms. Devonshire."

After he left, Betsy sat for awhile, thinking. Why had Mickels come to her about this? Did he think she was investigating again? Well, why wouldn't he? Everyone else did! She grimaced and went back to sorting out magazines. This one looked tattered. Look, someone had torn four pages out of it, stealing a pattern. What nerve!

But as she continued, she had trouble concentrating. Something was waving its hand from the back of her mind. What? Something about fishing from a boat.

She tried to dismiss it, but again the thought waved for her attention, and she sat back on her heels. She could picture the *Hopkins*, stripped of its superstructure, waiting to be towed out—no, pulled up onto the shore and abandoned. Ah, that was it! Martha Winters had said something about the boat sitting on the lakeshore, being used by boys as a fishing pier. How long had it sat there before being towed out and sunk? Two years or more, according to Martha. Betsy considered that. Perhaps it was something she should mention to Malloy. A murderer certainly wouldn't keep a body in his basement, but he might stuff it into the bottom of an old wreck. And if he had, it might remove that discrepancy of a year between Carl and Trudie disappearing and the boat being sunk behind the Big Island. Malloy should be told so he could look into it.

She went to the library table and phoned the police department. Sergeant Malloy was out, so she left word for him to call. But, haunted by doubt, she dialed another number.

This time, she called Mayor Jamison at his day job. "Excuse me for bothering you with a stupid question, but do you remember back when you were a kid and you used to fish off the *Hopkins*—well, I guess it was the *Minnetonka*, then—over by the dredging company?"

Jamison laughed and replied in his flat midwestern twang, "You bet! Why, has someone been telling you about the time I played hookey?"

"No—"

"Good, because I didn't start playing hookey until the third grade, and the boat was gone by then." Jamison laughed again.

Betsy, smiling now, said, "No, I wanted to ask you if you remember a terrible smell coming from that boat one summer."

"A terrible smell?"

"You know, like something died on board her."

"No, it never smelled like anything but water weed and fuel oil. We used to crawl all over the inside of that thing and come out looking like we was part mermaids and part oil riggers. Well, we did find a drowned rat in there once. And I guess it did stink. What's this all about, anyhow?"

"Nothing much, especially since you tell me you climbed all over the inside of the boat. That's right, isn't it? There wasn't a room or something below decks you couldn't get at, was there?"

"No. Anyway, there wasn't a room under the main deck to start with. Why, is it important?"

"No, no. Not from what you tell me."

"Say, listen here, are you—What?" This last query was asked away from the receiver. "Gosh, I forgot, thanks for reminding me. Betsy, I've got a meeting to get to. Talk to you later. Good-bye."

Betsy hung up, and this time when she went back to work, her mind was clear and at ease. If someone had stuffed a body into that boat while it was pulled up on shore, Jamison and his childhood buddies would have found it. She smiled to think of the sensation that would have caused in this town; no one would ever have forgotten that! She pictured the slightly shy mayor as a boy crawling around on a big old boat, tearing his clothes on rusty nails, coming home smeared with algae and traces of antique fuel oil. Perhaps he'd caught a nice bass to mollify his mother; Lake Minnetonka has long been famous for its bass.

But she was positive now; the skeleton couldn't be Trudie Koch.

The front door sounded, and Godwin came in, a bulky package in his arms, all amused about something. "Guess what I heard?" he asked. "The police are going to arrest Martha Winters for the murder of Trudie Koch and dig up her yard to see if her husband is buried there."

"How dare you go carrying outrageous tales like that?" she demanded. "Poor Martha, she's a very nice woman who probably never killed anything bigger than a fly in her whole life."

Godwin, taken aback, said, "Well, she does seem an unlikely candidate for that sort of thing, since I've never seen her lose her temper. But I heard from two different people that Malloy is going to arrest her." His eyes narrowed. "Of course, maybe she's been afraid to show her real self in case people suspected."

"Godwin, listen to me, this vicious rumor-mongering has got to stop! I don't want to hear one more word from you or anyone else about Martha Winters murdering people. It isn't true. It can't possibly be true. That skeleton can't be Trudie's." She explained the discrepancy in years, concluding, "Now you see why it can't be true, and why I want you to stop spreading that terrible story."

Godwin said with admiration, "I might have *known* you would investigate and come up with the truth. You are *so* clever! I can't wait to lay this on Irene next time I see her. I hope she comes in this afternoon."

But Irene didn't, and Godwin had to be satisfied with sharing Betsy's cleverness with other customers, though only when Betsy wasn't close enough to overhear.

Godwin had gone home, and Betsy actually had the two-sided needlepoint sign in her hand, ready to turn Closed to face the street, when Jessica Turnquist appeared outside the door, one gloved hand upraised and a pleading look on her face.

Betsy opened the door.

"Thank you, Betsy. May I come in? I really have something very important to ask you."

Betsy stepped back, but she dropped the Closed sign in place as she closed the door. "What is it?"

"You've probably heard the rumors about them arresting Martha."

"Yes, I've heard. It's ridiculous, of course."

"I'm glad you agree! Martha wouldn't murder anyone! That's why I'm here. I want you to prove it."

Betsy nearly laughed out loud. "I don't know how many times I'm going to have to repeat this. I am not a detective, I am not a police officer, I am not a private investigator. It's not my job, and I don't want the job of proving anything about anybody."

"But everyone says—"

"Everyone is wrong. Just because Sergeant Malloy asked me to ask my customers if they could recognize a bit of fabric edged with lace doesn't mean I have become a peace officer sworn to uphold the law. He put that photocopy in Needle Nest, too; why don't you go ask Pat Ingle if she'll investigate for you?"

Jessica, her eyes worried and sad, put a hand on Betsy's arm. "Because Pat Ingle wasn't the one who realized how a missing piece of needlepoint pointed to a murderer. I'm not sure why you don't want to help Martha. Perhaps it's because you're working so hard in the shop. And of course Martha isn't a relative, so you don't have the same motive you had when Margot was murdered. But please, think about it. Please. She's my very best friend and I can't bear the way the town is talking about her."

Later, pouring Sophie's little scoop of Iams Less Active cat food into her bowl, Betsy had one of those flashes of too-late insight. She *had* helped Martha! She'd proved the skeleton wasn't Trudie at all, right? Godwin doubtless had told some customers, who went eagerly to share the news with friends. For once, Betsy blessed the grapevine. By tomorrow afternoon, it would be all over town, and people would stop talking about Martha. Betsy smiled. She really had done a little deducing, and even some investigating, hadn't she? After supper she'd call Jessica and put her mind at ease.

Six

❖

On Wednesday, Diane Bolles used her lunch hour to visit Crewel World. The temperature was above freezing and the sky was sunny, so it was a pleasant walk from the Old Mill shops.

Diane was a tall, slim woman with dark hair and eyes. She wore a navy blue coat with a bright yellow scarf, a pleasant complement to the day. It was only three blocks to the bottom of Water Street, to the lake, then right on Lake for another two blocks, and she was in front of the old, dark-brick building. There were three stores on the ground floor: a sandwich shop, a used-book store, and Crewel World.

An irritating electronic *bing* sounded when she opened the door, but then she stopped short, because the shop itself was very attractive.

The first thing she noticed was how pleasantly quiet it was. Fibers are sound absorbing, and here were not only a carpeted floor, but heaps of fibers everywhere. Hanks and skeins of wool in autumn colors filled baskets of all sizes, thin wool skeins in every possible color hung from spindles on one long wall, and circular spinner racks carried floss in clusters of greens, purples, golds, reds, and other shimmering colors. Here and there were sweaters knit in complex patterns; the booklet containing the pattern was next to each, along with a selection of knitting yarns.

The shop was fairly narrow but deep. Halfway back was the checkout counter in the form of a big old wooden desk, and temptingly near the cash register were last-minute items such as packets of needles, a pretty display of little scissors, and a shallow basket of small kits marked Sale.

A hidden sound system played classical music.

Track lighting picked out items: here a sweater, there a basket of wool, over there a spinner rack of silky floss. Though Diane was not a needleworker, the colors and displays attracted her eyes ever deeper into the place. Beyond the desk were boxy shelves laden with more wool, magazines, books, and needlework accessories Diane could not imagine the use of. But she nodded in appreciation; as a fellow shop owner, she knew a good layout when she saw it.

There was a library table in the middle of the room, at which sat a slim, fair-haired man in an expensive-looking sweater, and a plump, attractive woman in a peacock-blue dress that, while a little light for the season, suited her. The woman was putting down a mitten she'd been working on; the man was looking up at her while continuing the motions of knitting a white sock.

"May I help you find something?" the woman asked.

"No, but if you are Betsy Devonshire, I'd like to talk to you."

"Yes, I am."

The woman had a pleasant smile and a look that invited questions. Diane smiled back, and said, "My husband and I own The Old Mill on Water Street."

"Ooooh," said the slim man, and to Betsy, "It's that sweet collection of gift shops halfway down Water Street."

"Yes," Diane nodded. "I also run the gift shop at the front of The Mill."

"I've looked in your window," said Betsy. "I really like that big vase, the one filled with silk roses."

"Thank you. My place is the reason I'm here. I want to add something to my line: needlework. I spoke to an employee of yours, Shelly Donohue, who said she would make a list of prospective needleworkers for me, but I see she's not here."

The slender young man said, "Oh, *you're* the one she talked to! I can tell you she's been having trouble with that list. I'm so sorry."

Betsy was looking confused, so Diane said to her, "I brought in some antique embroidery just for display, but it seems to have created a demand, so now I'm looking for needlework to sell." Diane looked around the shop. There were four or five completed pieces framed and hung on the wall, and some pillows on display in a rocking chair, but none of them impressed her as the kind of collectibles her customers might be interested in. Beyond the checkout desk hung a collection of thin doors, each slightly more ajar than the next, and attached to them were canvases painted with Santa Clauses, angels, puppies, kittens, and mottoes. Again not what she wanted—except one. "Like that garden with the gazebo, for example," she said, pointing. "That's quite nice." She walked over for a look. "I suppose the idea is to cover the picture with embroidery?"

"Needlepoint," said the young man.

"What would it cost, if I bought this stamped cloth and the yarn or floss, to have someone else do the work? I'm sure I could sell several of these a month."

The young man frowned and shook his head. "Those aren't stamped. Each one is hand-painted, and that brings us to the problem of Shelly's list. I'm sorry, but I don't think you could afford to carry a piece like that in a finished state."

Diane felt her cheeks flame. "What do you mean? I don't sell cheap things in my shop!"

"Of *course* you don't!" said the young man. "But—"

"What Godwin is trying to say," interrupted Betsy, "is that these canvases are not inexpensive to start with. Each is not only hand-painted but done in a special way to make it possible to needlepoint over it. Even so, it takes skill to do the needlepoint properly, and a fair amount of time. I believe the going rate for needlepoint is three dollars per square inch, and that's just to cover the painting in a basic stitch like basketweave." Betsy went to the swinging door set and looked at the painting Diane had liked. "That picture is twelve by sixteen, so that would be—" Betsy rolled her eyes, trying to multiply in her head.

"Five hundred and seventy-six dollars." Diane had a gift for numbers.

"All right. Fancy stitches and beadwork would cost more, and to make a really beautiful project, you'd probably want both. Add that to the cost of that particular canvas, which is two hundred and twenty-five dollars, plus wool or silk and beads, plus two hundred dollars to be finished and framed, and you're getting pretty high in cost for a piece of needlework."

"A thousand and one dollars," said Diane. "Plus materials. Yes, you're right, that is a lot of money." She bit a thumbnail and thought. "But what about something that doesn't involve hand-painted canvases? An embroidered apron, for example? Or a tea cozy?"

Betsy said, "A favorite topic among my customers is what they might charge for what they do, if they were to do it commercially. And what it comes down to is, very few people would pay that much for an apron or a tea cozy. The work my customers do is often very beautiful, as you have realized, and takes considerable time and talent. They don't do it for money, but out of love. They most usually use finished pieces as gifts for friends and family or to ornament their own homes."

The slim young man—Godwin—said, "And on a *commercial level,* people who do needlework wouldn't be excited at the prospect of doing *twenty copies* of the same project."

"Oh, but I wouldn't want twenty copies!" said Diane. "In fact, if there's just one of something, that makes it more likely to sell! Especially since, from the way you describe it, these are original works of art. And I assure you, I have customers who might be willing to pay a good price."

Godwin said, "But wait. If you're talking embroidered aprons, you're talking iron-on patterns that are *virtually identical.* If you're talking about *original designs,* then you're back up into the four-figure price. More, *lots more,* if you want an original design that is to be worked only once." He gestured airily. "And even if your customer *had* the money, it's still not something you'll be able to *provide* them, not reliably. As Betsy said, these things are made for the pleasure of working them. Putting a price on them takes away the whole *cachet.* I mean—" He dived under the table to unzip and reach into a sports bag. He came up with a large, magnificent, nearly completed stocking with a Christmas scene on it. Diane came closer, the pangs of covetousness curling her fingers. This was more like it! The scene was cleverly adapted to the shape of the stocking, crowded with a Christmas tree and part of a stair railing. Santa Claus's head was peeping out from behind the tree at the upper halves of two children coming down the stairs. The boy's Dr. Dentons were done in something that looked like brushed flannel; Santa's beard was a collection of tight curls; some of the ornaments on the tree were tiny glass or metal objects, and the garland was made of microscopic glass beads. Santa's sack and wrapped presents filled the toe of the stocking; like the little girl, they weren't done yet.

Diane reached a very gentle forefinger to touch the subtly rough surface of Santa's mitten. "Yes, something like this wouldn't last a day in my shop. Would you think of parting with it?"

"Not even *Bill Gates* could buy this from me," said Godwin. "It has taken me over *two hundred hours* to get this far. I did Santa's beard *three different ways* before deciding on French knots—there are ninety-two of them, you may count them if you like, and I can't tell you how grateful I am that only a third of his beard is showing, because I may not *ever* want to do another French knot. I haven't decided how to do the little girl's hair yet, but it will probably be something difficult and tedious and wonderful to look at. I'm sorry"—Godwin did not sound the least sorry—"but it's not for sale. It's a gift for someone I love, that's the *only thing* that makes it all worth while."

Diane turned and saw the helpless, commiserating look in Betsy's eyes. "I see," she said.

"That's not to say you couldn't have someone do a really fine embroidered or counted cross-stitch apron for you," said Betsy. "It's just that the price would make it the kind of apron you drape over a chair or hang on the wall as an ornament, not the sort you tie on to protect your clothing while you decorate cookies."

Diane smiled. "Some of my customers have kitchens with a full set of copper-bottomed pots no one is allowed to use. An apron also there strictly for show is a definite possibility." She opened her purse. "How about I leave you my card? Perhaps you can ask some of your customers if they would be interested. They can call me or just drop by."

"Certainly," said Betsy, taking the card. It had the crisp clean look of a new coin. NIGHTINGALE'S Enchanted Vintage for Home and Garden, it read. *Diane Bolles, Proprietor.* She smiled suddenly. "Maybe there will be some people interested in selling some of their projects. I have customers who complain that they just can't stop doing needlework, even though they have a closet full of things and no room left to display any more of it."

"They should rotate their work," said Diane. "That way, their eyes are always refreshed by the display, instead of getting bored and not even seeing it anymore." She had used that reasoning to increase her own sales of prints and silk bouquets.

"What a good idea!" said Betsy. "I'll suggest it; it makes my heart sink when a good customer starts in about having no more space."

"Good idea, certainly," drawled Godwin, "but *I* think Diane just shot herself in the foot by sharing it."

Diane laughed. "I've done that before." She looked around again. "You have really done some thinking in your layout."

Betsy shrugged, her eyes suddenly sad. "No, it was my sister who did this. I only inherited it."

Diane said, "I was very shocked when your sister died in that awful way. But I've heard nothing but good things about you. I'm certainly glad you were here to assist the police in solving your sister's murder. Have you always done that kind of thing?"

Betsy smiled. "Never before in my life. It was beginner's luck, I assure you. And not likely to happen again."

"Really? But I understand you are involved in that skeleton business, helping the police with a major clue."

"Not really. The police brought me a photocopy of some fabric they found on the boat, and I've been asking my customers if they can identify it. And, as it happens, just yesterday someone did. It appears to be a sample of bobbin lace."

"Oh, I saw some bobbin lace once! It was *so* gorgeous. May I see the photocopy?"

Betsy indicated the Xerox copy still taped to the desk, and Diane looked only a moment before saying, puzzled, "*This* is bobbin lace?"

"I know, it doesn't look like anything to me, either. But a customer assures me it is water-soaked bobbin lace."

"It must have been soaking for a very long time."

"Ever since that hot, dry Fourth of July in 1949," drawled Godwin, making a sort of rhyme of it.

Diane turned to face him, her eyes blank.

"Don't look at *me*, my *mother* was a toddler in 1949!"

"Hmm?" said Diane. As part of her gift for numbers, when someone said a year that came within her lifespan she automatically subtracted to see how old she was. In 1949, she had been six years old.

"I said—" began Godwin.

"You said it was a hot, dry Fourth of July," interrupted Diane brusquely. "It wasn't. In 1949, the Fourth of July was cold and wet. I remember because my Aunt Faye and Uncle James were in town and they were going to take me to the amusement park and then out on a boat to watch the fireworks, and we couldn't go because it rained all day."

Betsy said sharply, "Are you *sure?*"

"Yes, why?"

"Because our police investigator is using an eyewitness to close in on the exact day the *Hopkins* was sunk. The eyewitness says someone came to her on the Fourth of July in 1949 to say he'd seen it towed out to be sunk a day or two before—and she described the day as blazing hot."

"Then she's wrong," said Diane. "I cried all afternoon because we couldn't go, and Aunt Faye said I mustn't make it rain indoors as hard as it was raining outdoors. It rained all that day, and all evening, too, so we couldn't go see the fireworks, either. I was *so* disappointed."

Godwin said, "You were just a little kid; I bet you don't remember the year exactly. It could have been 1948, or maybe 1950."

"No, in 1948 my Aunt Faye wasn't married yet, and in 1950 my parents took me to Yellowstone. So I am absolutely sure the Fourth of July of 1949 was cold and rainy."

"Oh, my," said Betsy. "We'd better call Sergeant Malloy right away."

Malloy and his investigative partner stood in the doorway of the motel room, just looking. A uniformed officer was standing at parade rest just outside the door, the perfection of his stance slightly spoiled by the clipboard he was holding in one hand poking out from behind his back. Malloy's partner would sign in on the clipboard—Malloy had handled the skeleton, so it was his partner's turn to handle the physical inspection of this body—but neither went in just yet.

A thin, elderly man lay on his back across the bed, whose white chenille bedspread was slightly rumpled. He was wearing an old brown suit, more than slightly rumpled. His legs were off the end of the bed from about mid-calf, and his right hand hung off the bed on the near side. A semiautomatic handgun was on the floor under the hand.

A small table had a lamp on it, the lamp turned on, though it was broad daylight outside. Of course, the heavily lined curtains were pulled shut, so when the door was shut, perhaps the light was necessary.

The state crime bureau had sent a crew—"Getting to be a habit, isn't it, Malloy?" one had wisecracked—and had photographed and videotaped everything. The medical examiner was on the scene.

Malloy held out his hand for the clipboard and asked the cop, "Were you the first responder?"

"Yessir."

Everyone seemed to have signed in and out properly; Malloy gave the clipboard to his partner to sign. "Have you checked the other rooms?" he asked the cop.

"Yessir. There were only two other customers checked in last night, one up next to the office and the other down at the corner. Both checked out before nine this morning, and the room down at the end's been cleaned up already. The other one doesn't seem out of the ordinary, and none of the rest of the rooms looked disturbed."

"Did you turn any lights on when you went in here?"

"Nossir."

"Is the condition of the room now just as you found it?"

The cop came to attention before stepping around to peek in. You could always tell the ones who came to the police from the military. "Yessir."

"Who found the body?"

"Cleaning ladies. Two of them."

"Where are they?"

"In the office."

"Your witness," said Malloy to his partner and went to talk to the cleaning ladies. He detoured on his way to the unit at the end, the one also guarded by a uniformed officer. He didn't go in, just opened the door and looked. Bed mussed, one pillow used, no luggage left, towels on the bathroom floor, smell of aftershave, empty pizza box standing slantwise in the wastebasket. Nothing odd or out of place. His partner would do a more thorough search, of course.

The cleaning ladies turned out to be a pair of middle-aged women. Sitting with them on a couch, equally scared and distressed, was the owner of the motel. Her husband, she said, was at his part-time job in Excelsior.

The Hillcrest Motel, which was not located atop a hill but at the foot of one just outside Excelsior, was owned and run by an older couple. It had twelve rooms and an office along two sides of a blacktop parking lot. A small, shabby laundromat, also owned by the couple, occupied the third side. All the buildings were coated with faded pink stucco crumbling around the edges.

The cleaning partners were locals who lived just up the road. They'd worked here two years, but only while school was in. They were dressed in those aprons that cover all your clothing, even in back. These were a matching set in mint green. Patterned scarves were tied around their heads, à la Lucy Ricardo and Ethel Mertz. They had their heavy rubber gloves in their laps and they were smoking up a storm, their way of handling the fright, sickness, and excitement of this event.

They said they had knocked on the door of room seven about two, checkout time—it was now quarter after three—and when there was no reply, Lise had unlocked the door and they had seen the body and run pell-mell for the office to tell Mary to dial 911. No, they hadn't gone in, no they hadn't turned on any lights or checked to see if the man was really dead—of course he was dead, it only took one look to tell he was dead. Their little wheeled cart was still right outside the door—it wasn't? Well, they hadn't moved it, they had come right here as fast as they could and had been here ever since and did Malloy know when they might be able to finish their work and go home?

Malloy questioned them closely, but their answers were decidedly innocent. He asked if they could stay here for awhile, until the room on the end had been searched. Then they could clean it.

He turned to the owner, Mary Olsen. She said the man had checked in alone late yesterday afternoon and seemed all right, except all tired out from driving. She produced the sign-in card the man had filled out.

Malloy took it, a little five-by-six piece of thin white cardboard, and sat a few moments staring at it, because the name on it had a certain familiarity: Carl Winters. And from what Malloy remembered of the death scene, this Carl was about the right age to be the other Carl, the Carl that was Martha Winters's husband. The address on the card was Omaha, Nebraska. Hadn't run far, then. Hadn't done well, either, by the shabby suit and the tired old Chevy with Nebraska plates that was parked outside his unit. Trudie, it seemed, wasn't as valuable a partner as Martha had been.

"He check in alone?"

"Yes, and I watched his car pull up to his unit and he was the only one who got out."

"Did he make any phone calls?" asked Malloy.

She checked. "Just one, a local call."

Since he hadn't gone through a switchboard, she had no record of the number the victim had called. Malloy noted the time of the call in his notebook.

He got the names and addresses of the other two guests, then went back and stood again in the doorway and watched his partner. The medical examiner was with the body, taking measurements.

"Whaddaya think," said Malloy, "he comes home to commit suicide?"

"So you know who he is?"

"Unless he signed in under a false name, our victim was one Carl Winters, who was alleged to have run off with a waitress back in 1948, leaving his wife Martha to run the dry cleaning store and raise their son all by herself. So now he's old and sick and sorry, so he comes home, calls his wife, who tells him to get stuffed, so he suicides."

"One problem with that theory," said Malloy's partner.

"What's that?"

"This wasn't a suicide."

On his way back to the station, Malloy put in a call for Jill Cross to meet him there. She was standing beside her squad car when he pulled into the parking lot and approached at his gesture, breath gently steaming, to bend with the awkwardness imposed by a Kevlar vest and heavy winter police jacket to look in his window.

"You heard about the gunshot victim at Hillcrest?" he asked.

"Yes, I did."

"Identification on the body and the registration card both say it's Carl Winters."

"Oh, lord," said Jill.

"He made one local call after he arrived yesterday. The motel can't say to who, but it isn't hard to guess."

"So you want me to come along when you tell her?"

Malloy nodded. "It may be an arrest situation. It's not a suicide we're dealing with here, unless he had the rare gift of being able to shoot himself from across the room."

Jill stared at Malloy, who stared calmly back. She said after a bit, "We're going to arrest Martha Winters?"

"No, we're going to go talk to her. Carl Winters isn't exactly the rarest name in the world, so we're not even positive it's her husband. I'm going to go talk to her about what happened, see which way she jumps. She's not a professional criminal; if she did it, she may be waiting to tell us all about how she murdered Trudie Koch all those years ago and hid her body in that boat, and now has rounded things off by shooting her husband."

Jill was even more surprised. "I thought the skeleton couldn't be Trudie."

"Here, get in, I'm letting all the heat out through this window."

Jill came around and got in the car which, though without markings, proclaimed itself a public safety vehicle on the inside with a two-way radio and a red light with a magnet that could be stuck on the roof or dash.

Jill by now had another question. "If it is Martha Winters's husband, what brought him back to town?"

"The story of the skeleton they found on the *Hopkins*. It's been turning up in papers all across the country; I've got inquiries from as far away as Fort Meyers, Florida."

"But I thought there wasn't a connection between the body hidden on the

Hopkins and the disappearance of Carl and Trudie Koch. I thought they happened a year apart."

"Everyone thought so—except Irene Potter, whose lunatic speculations to a local columnist inspired a story about small-town gossip that apparently got picked up and reprinted. Our victim had a clipping in his wallet from the Omaha *World-Herald*. Irene would blow a gasket if she could see how she's described in that story—though the columnist was careful not to give her name. But you know how it is, even a stopped clock is right twice a day. Here, buckle up; I'll tell you the rest on our way to Winters Dry Cleaning."

They pulled out of the parking lot, and Malloy began to unwind his theory. "Around twelve-thirty today I got a call from Diane Bolles, who owns Nightingales, over in the Old Mill. She says she was talking to Betsy Devonshire and somehow the subject of the Fourth of July 1949 came up—and Ms. Bolles is as sure as she can be that it rained all day the Fourth of July 1949. I have a witness who told me that the day she heard about them sinking the *Hopkins* was the Fourth of July, and it was a blazing hot day. I called the Minneapolis public library, which keeps weather records, and guess what?"

"What?" said Jill.

"The Fourth of July 1949 *was* rainy. *But* the Fourth of July in 1948, the year Carl Winters and Trudie Koch went missing, was stinking hot. Every book about the streetcar steamboats and the raising of the *Minnehaha* I've looked at says 1949. But I wonder if maybe they're wrong, every damn one of them."

Jill said, "How did that happen, that they're all wrong?"

Malloy gestured sharply. "I wondered the same thing, but the chief says he read just the other day about that sort of thing, which happens all the time, he says. Someone researching the history of a town asks a local what year something happened, and the local says, '1949, I think,' and the author writes that down as fact, and for years after that, other history writers use his book as the source instead of asking around. The chief was about to send me out to find more people who were here in 1948 when the call came in about the body at the motel. But the upshot is, where before it wasn't possible, now it is entirely possible that the skeleton on the *Hopkins* is Trudie Koch."

Jill sat back in silence. She thought about Martha Winters, who seemed to be such a nice, quiet, competent lady. Her grandson was nice too, a good-looking young man who seemed content to take over the dry cleaning business his grandfather had founded. Jeff's father was an executive with 3M, and reportedly disappointed in the boy's lack of ambition.

Jeff had been only a year behind Jill in high school; she'd actually danced with him once or twice. And she'd sat on more than one occasion at the table in Crewel World with Martha and the rest of the Monday Bunch. It gave her an odd feeling to think she might be about to help arrest a Monday Bunch member for murder. She'd ask Malloy to get someone else, except she was the only female cop on the little force, and they needed a female cop to do this because Martha was a female.

Jill had never arrested anyone for murder. The worst arrest she'd ever made was the time she'd brought in a teen high on drugs who had thrown a plastic garbage can full of trash at her. And that had been hard because she knew the kid's parents really well.

Of course, in a small town, any arrests you made were likely to be of people you knew or at least knew about.

But Martha Winters? A murderer? That seemed impossible. Surely there was some other explanation.

"Do we have to go talk to her right now? Maybe there's some other explanation."

"Maybe there is," agreed Malloy, "but we have to talk to Mrs. Winters anyway. Tell her that her husband is a murder victim. But I kind of think she might be able to help us figure out why."

Seven

❖

It wasn't far to the dry cleaners, a small, flat-roofed building whose entire customer area was plate glass. They walked into a reek of cleaning fluid and Malloy said to the young man behind the counter, "Hi, Jeff. Is your grandmother here?"

"She's home this afternoon," the young man replied. There was no hint of reserve or nervousness in his voice. He seemed only as surprised and curious as anyone would be when the police come asking for a grandparent.

So they went without undue haste to the modest house, a two-story brick with a small front yard shaded by a towering blue spruce.

Jill saw Malloy heave a deep breath and felt for him. And herself. Martha Winters had never earned so much as a parking ticket and was a good, church-going Lutheran. If they made a slip here, the town would have their badges. Yet the questions had to be asked.

They went up the brick steps to the front door, and Malloy rang the bell. It was opened by Martha in a gray housedress and slippers. With her round, pleas-

ant face and white hair, she looked like Norman Rockwell's model of a grandmother. But when she saw Jill's uniform her hand went to her mouth. "What's
happened?" she asked. "Is it Jeff?"

"No, ma'am," said Malloy. "We just left him at the store; he's fine. May we
come in?"

"All right." Martha stepped back.

The tiny area immediately inside the door was tiled, and there was a coat
closet on the left. The immaculate living room was to their right, carpeted in a
powder blue plush that was pleasant to the feet. Most of the wall facing the
street was a box-pleated drape in a matching color, open in the center to show a
big square window. The couch was ribbon-striped, green, beige, and blue. The
recliner was vinyl in a green that didn't quite match—that's Jeff's, I bet,
thought Jill—and there was a velvet easy chair in beige. Martha sat in the easy
chair and motioned them to the couch. On the wall over the couch, pressed behind glass frames, were three ecru handkerchiefs with elaborate lace edging.

"Thanks, I'll stand," said Malloy, and Jill braked and turned to stand to the
left and a little behind him. But her eye wandered again to the handkerchiefs;
were those edgings bobbin lace?

"Mrs. Winters, do you know where your husband is?" asked Malloy.

Martha started to pretend to be surprised at the question, but discarded the
attempt immediately. "He's at the Hillcrest Motel out on Seven," she said in a
low voice.

"Did he call you from there yesterday?"

She nodded. "But I don't want to see him. I told him that and told him not
to call me again." Her lip trembled. "Is that why you're here? To talk to me
about him? I don't want to, you know. Except to ask if I'll have to divorce him,
now I know he's alive. Or will I?" Her faded blue eyes moved from Malloy to
Jill and back again. "I mean, he's legally dead, isn't he?"

"Ma'am, I'm sorry to be the one to tell you this, but we think he's really
dead. A body was found in his room this afternoon, and the driver's license we
found on the body has his name on it."

Martha sat back, and her lips began to move in a very odd way. A smile
came and went, came and broadened, and suddenly she began to laugh. Jill and
Malloy looked at one another in wonder.

The laughter quickly became hysterical, and Jill went in search of a bathroom. She found one and wet a washcloth in cold water, which she brought
back along with a small glass of water. She applied the cloth to Martha's face,
speaking soothingly to her.

"Here now, here now, it's all right, it's all right. You're going to be fine. I
want you to drink this."

The laughter caught on a sob and stumbled to a halt. Martha took the glass from Jill and took a sip, then another. "Thank you, Jill," she said at last. "I'm all right now." But her hand trembled, and her face was white.

"You sure?"

Martha nodded. She took the washcloth and wiped her eyes and mouth, then folded it carefully into her hand.

Malloy said, "What can you tell us about your husband's return?"

Martha closed her eyes. "Nothing. I was surprised, of course. I really thought he was dead." Her eyes opened. "I don't know why he came back or what he wanted. He's an old man, let's see, he must be seventy-seven—no, seventy-eight. I don't know what he thought I would say, calling me like that right out of the blue, saying he wanted to see me, would I come over. To a motel? I ask you! And I told him not to come here, either. The idea! He tried to coax me, argue with me, and I said, 'I don't want to talk to you, now or ever!' and I hung up on him." Her face changed from an echo of the indignation she must have felt to concern. "What, was he sick? I thought about it after I went to bed last night, maybe I should have listened to him, maybe he's sick and *she* left him and he's all alone . . ."

"Who left him?" asked Malloy.

"Why that waitress, what was her name, Gertrude something. Trudie, she was called. The young woman he went off with—I suppose that's true, now, isn't it? She probably left him a month after they ran off together. So what was it he died of? Heart? Cancer?"

"No, ma'am, he was shot."

Her eyes and mouth became three round Os. "Shot? I don't understand. You said he was dead."

"He is," said Malloy patiently. "He was shot to death in his room and someone tried to make it look like suicide."

"Oh. Oh! Yes, I should have thought of suicide—but you say it wasn't suicide."

"No, ma'am."

"But then, who shot him? Was it her—Trudie? Surely he wouldn't have brought her along and then called me." Her expression was verging on the indignant again.

"We don't know who shot him. That's what we're trying to determine. But before we go any further, I think we have to be sure the deceased was Carl Winters. How sure are you that the man you talked to on the phone was your husband?"

"Oh, it was Carl, all right. His voice was pretty much the same, and he talked like he always talked, kind of bossy and sure of himself. He said he had something important to tell me, he wouldn't say what it was, except it was something I needed to know. He talked just like he used to, telling me to just hush and listen to him. As if what he did to me didn't matter, as if after all these years I hadn't gotten over letting him talk to me like that!"

"Yes, ma'am," said Malloy. He reached into his coat pocket and pulled out an old wallet. "Do you recognize this?"

"No."

He opened it, found the section that holds photographs or credit cards, turned it around and held it out. "Do you recognize this?"

Jill leaned forward just a bit and saw it was an old photograph of a woman in a ruffled apron standing in front of a freshly planted evergreen tree.

Martha turned her face away. "That's me," she said. "He used to carry that photograph. He took it the day after I told him I was pregnant. He bought that tree, it's the one out in the front yard. He said he wanted it to remind him of the days before I lost my figure." Her mouth quivered. "I didn't lose my figure until Carl ran out on me." She looked toward the wallet. "Funny he kept it, isn't it?" Her eyes were hurt and puzzled.

"Do you know if Carl called anyone else but you?"

"I have no idea. I shouldn't think so, but Carl did have the capacity to surprise me." She blinked twice then said, "What are you going to do with him—his body?"

"There will be an autopsy, and then the medical examiner will give you a call and you can tell him what you want done with the body."

A very odd expression crossed Martha's face, but all she said was, "Very well."

"Have you any idea who would want him dead after all these years?"

She thought briefly. "No. Not even me."

"Well," said Malloy, "thank you very much for your cooperation. I'm going to leave you one of my cards," he added, handing it to her. "If you think of anything, please contact me. And if I have any more questions, may I talk to you again?"

"Yes, of course. I'll be at the store tomorrow morning."

Malloy was obviously finished, so Jill asked, "Martha, those handkerchiefs over the sofa. Did you do the lace on them?"

Martha nodded. "I won a blue ribbon at the State Fair with the one in the middle. I gave it up after Carl left. I was too busy with the store and raising Henry. Probably my eyes are too bad now to take it up again."

Jill went to the couch and leaned toward the middle one. "I can't imagine eyes good enough for this kind of thing to start with. I mean, look at the thread—such delicate work—oh, and look, the corner has a butterfly."

"I always put that butterfly in the lace I was keeping for my own use. It was kind of a signature."

"This is bobbin lace, isn't it?"

"Yes, why?"

"The subject came up at the last Monday Bunch meeting. Did you know Alice does bobbin lace?"

"She does? Why of course, I remember she used to. I didn't know she still did. How interesting." Martha did not sound very interested, and appeared suddenly to realize that. She stirred on the chair and said more positively, "I'll have to talk to her some time."

They did leave then. Outside, Malloy said, "Slick, Cross. I was wondering how to ask without getting her all suspicious."

"Thank you," said Jill, gratified. Compliments from Malloy were rare. She wondered if she'd get mentioned in his report. Probably not. And after all, the way Martha reacted to Malloy's questioning, it was obvious she was innocent.

For all the skull's lack of cooperation, Kerrie finished it rapidly. She got out her box of glass eyes and looked at them, and the half-formed face, for several minutes. White folks' eyes were so variable! She finally picked out a blue pair and fitted them into place, then worked the eyelids over them. She wasn't satisfied with the result and tried lowering the lids a bit, which was better but still didn't quite do it. She took the glass eyes out and put brown ones in, which was another improvement, but still not right. She couldn't think what else she could do, and sat staring at it, baffled.

She had given the lips a hint of a smile, and had found evidence of an old break in the nose and so had made it a trifle crooked, with a bump. There was a rakish air of reality in these details somehow not reflected in the eyes. She wished she were a better artist, able to capture such subtleties. She sketched eyebrows onto the forehead, hoping that would help, but it didn't, much. She colored the lips deep red—lipstick in the forties was red, red, red—and got out a selection of wigs.

Eyes were merely variable; hair was infinite in its variety. Blond, she decided, though she'd given the face dark eyebrows. What were the hairstyles of fifty years ago? Not that it mattered, all she had were modern wigs. She picked a medium-length one and tried tying it up in various ways, then finally left it loose.

She put the completed head on a shelf over her desk, sat down in her chair, and looked up at it. There was a face looking back, all right.

Who are you? she asked one more time.

And still the answer was silence. But now it was a sullen silence. The eyes said she really hated the hair.

*   *   *

Malloy got a fax of an eight-by-ten photograph of the face on Monday morning. It had the almost-real look of such re-creations, with a pleasant expression that didn't reach the eyes, which had a sullen glare.

Still, it was a whole lot better than the fractured skull he'd started with.

He took the picture along on another visit to the strong room in City Hall. The Historical Society women weren't in session today, but he would catch them later. Right now—Yes, he was right; among the books on the shelves were high school yearbooks, from back when Excelsior had its own high school.

It took some searching. He didn't know when Trudie graduated from high school or even if she had. As it turned out, she hadn't, but she'd been a cheerleader as a sophomore.

Trudie as a sophomore had been a brown-eyed brunette, her face a little plumper than the re-created face. But there were undoubted similarities; the general shape of the face, the line of jaw, and the slightly crooked nose with a bump. Both faces had a hint of the sensual, with full lips and slightly heavy eyelids. To Malloy's thinking, there were far more similarities than differences, enough to call it a match.

Identification of a skeleton from a recreated face wasn't admissible in court, but Malloy was now sure that it was Trudie Koch who had died violently fifty-one years ago, and her body hidden on the steamboat *Hopkins*, just before it was taken out and sunk. In 1948.

Malloy had thought it possible that Carl Winters murdered Trudie and fled. In fact, it was still possible. But it was also possible that someone else had murdered Trudie, someone with a hatred so deep and bitter that it reached out again to take Carl's life. And there was only one person Malloy knew about who might reserve her hatred and bitterness over that many years. He'd check further, of course, because if he was right in his surmise, it was also clear that Martha Winters was one hell of a dissembler.

The Monday Bunch meeting was in order, the chair was serving hot cocoa in honor of the first snowstorm of the season. It was very bad out, because yesterday had been very cold, so what had begun as a thin rain today froze the instant it landed on street and sidewalk. The official weather reports had predicted rain turning to snow by evening, but this hadn't waited until evening. The rain had quickly become sleet, and now was snow, the gorgeous, feathery stuff every white-Christmas-lover dreams about.

But snow over ice can be a lethal combination. The schools realized what they were faced with, and students were sent home at noon. So Shelly was present, and very pleased about it. "Two inches, they said this morning, but it turned to snow before they thought it would, and the storm system isn't moving through like they said it would, either, so now they're saying more like six, maybe seven. Late start tomorrow, I bet."

"Late start?" said Betsy.

"Schools will start late if kids have to bus from a distance. It will take awhile to clear the roads."

"If it snows six or seven inches by tonight, I bet school won't start at all tomorrow," said Betsy.

"She's not from Minnesota," explained Godwin, showing compassion for her ignorance, and there were friendly chuckles.

"I don't understand," said Betsy.

"That means," said Shelly, "that it takes a blizzard to close a school in Minnesota, and six inches isn't quite a blizzard."

"Too bad," said Betsy, having fond memories of school closings.

"Lots of accidents, however," said Jill, thinking ahead to her night on patrol. "Always are with the first storm, until people remember how to drive in this stuff."

This set off a round of complaints about Minnesota winters, with an undertone Betsy had come to recognize as boasting. "We can take it, bring on your worst," they seemed to be saying.

Betsy, who had only to walk up a flight of stairs to be home, and who had not seen snow like this for many years, ignored all that. She was filled with warm pleasure every time she looked out her window. It was so incredibly beautiful. How could these people not appreciate how magical it was to see snow falling?

A huge dump truck with a gigantic plow on its front pushed down the street. As it went by, Betsy could see little whirly motors spinning sand out from the bin in back. It spoiled the opaque whiteness of the street, but of course it had to be done.

She looked around the table. There were more than the usual four or five present—seven, in fact. The carpet under the table was crowded with discarded boots and blue plastic Crewel World bags. There was a pleasant air of anticipation among the women, which seemed focused on Betsy. Since there had never been any presiding done at these meetings, she was at a loss to know what they were waiting for.

She said, "I got in a shipment of embroidery hoops and some iron-on patterns, and it inspired me to try out some old skills." She reached into her work basket and pulled out a white apron with a fifties pattern of vegetables with smiling faces half embroidered on it. "Diane Bolles is looking for work like this to sell in her shop. Actually, she's looking for much better work than this; I won't pass this around because I know how you all are about the back." That got an agreeable laugh; the Monday Bunch thought the back of needlework should be as presentable as the front, and Betsy had never been that fussy.

"I think my mother had an apron like that," said Kate.

Jessica, who was sitting in the first chair at Betsy's right, said, "You do beautiful French knots. And you have a good eye for centering and layout of the pattern."

"Thank you," said Betsy, pleased.

Then silence fell again, and again they all seemed to be waiting for Betsy to do something, but just as she was about to cry, "What? What do you want of me?" Martha stood and lifted a big paper bag onto the table.

"We have something for you," she said. "We want you to know how much we appreciate your keeping Crewel World open. And we want to show how much we loved your sister, all of us." They all nodded solemnly. "And we came up with this way of telling you."

She opened the bag and brought out a box about twenty-four inches square and about three inches deep. It was wrapped in red foil paper and tied with golden ribbon and matching bow. She handed the box to Betsy, who stood to receive it. It was so heavy she nearly dropped it—and that gave a hint to its contents.

Her comprehension showed on her face and the women laughed softly. Shelly said, "The hardest part was finding a finisher who wouldn't automatically send it back here to you."

Betsy sat down and admired the wrapping awhile. "It's very pretty," she said. Someone handed her a pair of scissors from the basket of needleworking tools in the middle of the table, and she obediently cut the ribbon and used a blade of the scissors to open one end of the paper. The box inside was heavy cardboard, and again the scissors were needed to cut the tape.

Betsy lifted the box lid. Inside, double matted with cutouts and in a black oak frame, was a motto done in needlepoint, a fragment from the last chapter of Proverbs, which had been read to enormous effect at Margot's funeral. "Her light does not go out," it read in gold lettering on a deep blue background. Betsy did not recognize the quote at first, but then she looked at the symbols surrounding the motto and began to smile. There was a ring with a real red-glass stone ("She is worth far more than rubies"), a sheep standing in tall grass ("She selects wool and flax"), a hand grasping a kind of stick wrapped in thoroughly brushed satin stitching ("In her hand she holds the distaff"), a tiny decorated Christmas tree ("She . . . extends her hands to the needy"). There was a bright red ribbon surrounding and connecting the symbols, its meaning probably both the sashes Margot supplied to merchants and the scarlet clothing supplied her servants so they were not afraid of the cold.

"We did it as a round robin," said Martha. "Everyone in the Bunch had a hand in it."

Betsy wanted to thank them but found, to her dismay, that she was crying. The women gathered around to pat her on the back and shoulders and speak comforting words, and after awhile she realized her weeping was a more effective thank-you than anything she could have said.

When at last everyone was settled down again, and projects were brought out to be worked on, Betsy asked, "Whose idea was this, anyway?"

Martha said quietly, "Mine. But actually it was inspired by something Jessica gave me when Carl disappeared. Remember?" she asked Jessica.

Jessica bowed her head as if embarrassed and murmured, "Yes."

"When she gave that to me, it was the beginning of our friendship. She's been such a comfort to me over the years."

Jessica blushed and said nothing.

"What was it?" asked Shelly.

"It was cross-stitch, a heart with Carl's and my initials in it, and the word *Forever* underneath. All those years ago." She sighed. "I still have it."

Jessica looked up, surprised. "You do?"

"Of course. It's in my bedroom where I see it every morning first thing when I wake up. You know, though, I think sometimes I see your initials instead of Carl's. Yours is the love that proved to be the forever one."

"Awwww," everyone sighed, even Godwin.

Such a surge of emotions overwhelmed the Scandinavian breeding of the Monday Bunch, and soon after, the group decided they'd had enough and would go home.

Jessica said to Martha, "That was one of my earlier efforts at cross-stitch. What people would think if you showed it to anyone! I wish you'd let me redo it properly."

Betsy smiled. She'd heard of people going back to undo and redo work they weren't satisfied with, but not at this remove of years.

Martha said, "Oh, when I first saw it, I thought it was the most beautiful thing I'd ever seen! And it's the sentiment that still counts. And don't worry about it being seen, I'm not going to enter it in a competition." Laughing, the two friends went out together.

"We didn't get much work done, did we?" Shelly remarked.

"We'll do better next time," said Kate.

But Alice Skoglund had leaned to murmur in Jill's ear, and the two stayed behind. When everyone had left, Alice said, "Betsy, maybe you should see this, too."

"What is it?" asked Jill.

Alice, her chin even more prominent and her glasses winking with importance, brought a sheet of graph paper out of her purse and unfolded it. "I've been working on that bobbin lace pattern, and I've got a big part of it figured out." She put the sheet on the desk and said, "Here is the ground, mostly spiders." There was a pattern of solid blocks, each with thin "legs" growing out from it—twelve legs, Betsy noticed, not eight.

"And here, this was very difficult, because it's weaving and open spaces, and the outline was broken and it's not complete, the bottom portion is mostly gone. But see? A butterfly."

Jill asked sharply, "How much of this was guesswork?"

Alice replied in kind, "None of it! I just took what was there and figured it out. I didn't add anything. That's why it's not complete. Where the threads were pulled thin, I tried to think what it would look like shorter, closed up, and I only connected the broken threads in a way they most likely joined. I didn't guess, I restored." She looked defiantly at Jill.

Jill said scornfully, "And you've never seen Martha Winters's work!"

"Of course I have! Why?"

"Because she always put a butterfly into her lace."

"Are you sure? *I* never saw one."

"She has three samples hanging in her living room, and all three have butterflies, and they look a lot like this one you've drawn."

"I've never been in her living room. I saw some gorgeous stuff she made for Mrs. Allen's baby's christening cap twenty years ago, and there's no butterfly on that. And I saw the pieces she made as shelf fronts for the Sutter House restoration, and there's no butterfly on them, either."

Jill frowned, then nodded. "Okay, okay, that's right, she said she put the butterfly only in pieces she meant to keep for herself."

Alice sniffed righteously, but Jill didn't apologize.

Betsy stared at the pattern on the graph paper. Jill had told her about the butterflies in the bobbin lace that edged Martha's handkerchiefs on her wall. This was bad, this was very bad.

Eight

❖

It was a teachers' conference day, schoolchildren had the day off. But the portion for elementary school teachers ended at noon, and Shelly came to Crewel World after a hasty sandwich in the Waterfront Café.

"I, uh, wanted to see if you had any work for me," she said. She was looking very earnest—Betsy might have described her as desperate.

Betsy looked around doubtfully. The shop wasn't very busy; Godwin was seeing the first customer in an hour to the door.

"You see, there's that Carol Emmer counted cross-stitch pattern, and with the hours I put in last Saturday and my employee discount, I could buy it and the floss with just a few more hours' worth of work." Shelly glanced toward the front of the shop. "And, that front window isn't as good as it could be. I could redo that."

Betsy frowned at it. "I think it looks very nice."

"Well, then, how about I get out the Christmas decorations and put them up? There's lights for the window and some fat candles with needlepoint and cross-stitch decorations, and some artificial holly garland."

"I can't afford to buy—" began Betsy.

"No, they're in the storeroom, in a big cardboard box."

Betsy looked at Godwin, who nodded. "Well, all right," she said, wondering if perhaps Shelly needed the money for something more necessary, like groceries or car repairs. Though Shelly *was* a very avid counted cross-stitcher.

Godwin came to help her get out the box of decorations. They had been at it only a few minutes when the real reason Shelly had come to Crewel World was revealed. She asked, cautiously because of Betsy's aversion to gossip, "Did you hear about Martha Winters?"

"Hear what?" asked Godwin immediately, but then he also glanced at Betsy.

But Betsy looked inquiring as well, so Shelly burst out, "Martha is under arrest for murdering Trudie Koch!"

"Nooo!" wailed Godwin.

Betsy also made a mourning sound but said, "I guess I've been expecting that."

Godwin said, "You have? Honestly, Betsy, I don't know how you managed not to become a private eye years and years ago! You know everything before it happens."

Before Betsy could object to this, the door went *bing* and Jill, in uniform, entered. "Have you heard?" she asked.

"Shelly just told me. Was it the lace?"

Jill nodded.

"What lace?" Shelly asked.

"Were you there?" asked Betsy.

Again Jill nodded.

"How did she take it?"

"Utterly surprised. She didn't do it, Betsy, she couldn't have, or she would have been more careful what she said when Mike interviewed her the second time. He walked all around that handkerchief, and she just kept on talking, innocent as a baby chick. I had to go stand behind her, or my face would have warned her. I couldn't believe she couldn't see what he was doing."

"What was he doing?" asked Shelly.

"She said she never rode the *Hopkins*, she didn't visit it while it was aground or while it was tied up waiting to be towed out and sunk. She said she never gave away any of her personal handkerchiefs, and that she never put butterflies in any of the lace she gave away. She said that when a handkerchief would get worn out, she'd take the lace off and put it on another handkerchief. Bobbin lace lasts forever, did you know that? Mike asked if she ever missed any handkerchiefs, and she said of course she'd lost some, but mostly got them back because people knew about the butterflies. Only two she never got back. One she lost at the State Fair in 1944, and another at the Guthrie Theatre ten or twelve years ago. She was laughing about them; she was pretty sure she dropped the one in the biggest-pig display in the pig barn and was glad no one tried to bring it back to her, because you never get the smell of pig out; and the other she thinks she saw the next season, onstage, in a production of *Othello*."

Betsy smiled, then sobered. "So she didn't understand what Mike was getting at?"

"What was he getting at?" asked Shelly.

"Yeah," seconded Godwin, "what?"

Betsy said, "Alice Skoglund worked out the pattern of the lace edging on that piece of silk and showed it to me and Jill. There was a butterfly in the pattern. Martha used to do bobbin lace, and she always put her own design of a butterfly in the lace she meant to keep for herself. And the pattern Alice figured out looks an awful lot like Martha's butterfly."

"Oh, no," groaned Godwin.

Betsy continued, "And so Mike gave her every opportunity to explain how a handkerchief with a lace butterfly on it came to be on the *Hopkins*—other than that she left it there after hiding Trudie Koch's body on it."

Jill said, "And Martha said she'd never taken a ride on the *Hopkins*, or gave a handkerchief to someone who later complained of losing it on the *Hopkins*."

Shelly said, "Poor lady—but I see what you mean. If she had lost a handkerchief while hiding the body, she would have realized what Sergeant Malloy was doing, and at least tried to make up a story."

Jill said, "Of course, he didn't ask her directly, because that would have alerted her, and she might have lied. But you're right, Shelly, if she *did* lose a handkerchief about then, even more especially while moving Trudie's body, Mike's questions would have put her on her guard. But they didn't. So he thanked her and let her get back to her baking while he went and got a warrant. They're booking her now. I think she still hasn't got a clue why."

Godwin said, "Gosh, *Martha Winters* in *jail!*" He turned to Betsy. "So, what do we do first?"

Betsy frowned at Godwin and said, "What do you mean?"

"*Martha*, of course. What are we going to do about her?"

"What could *we* possibly do?"

"We can *investigate*, of course! Where do we start? Who do you want to talk to?"

Betsy said, "Are you serious?"

Shelly said, "If he isn't, he should be. The nerve of Sergeant Malloy, arresting Martha! Why, nobody with a functioning brain cell could believe she's a murderer!"

Betsy said, "He's an investigator. He'll investigate, find out she's innocent, and let her go. Meanwhile, it's awful for Martha, and I'm very sad and sorry for her, but I don't think there's anything *we* can do."

"You can help me find out about the lace," Jill said, to Betsy's surprise. "Seriously, Betsy, I'd like you to talk to some people. You would be giving me a hand here. No, no, I'm not an investigator, but Mike considers me his expert on lace, and God knows I'm nothing of the sort. I'm going to ask around, but I'd like you to ask, too; help me find out about who was making lace in 1948. And while you're about it, maybe you can find out if her pattern was hard or easy to copy."

"Oh, my!" said Godwin. "I didn't think of that!"

Shelly said, "And so long as you're asking those questions, you might as well find out who else had a reason to want Trudie Koch dead." Seeing objection in Betsy's face, she hastened on, "Since it's all tied together, isn't it? If Martha didn't murder Trudie, and of course she didn't, how *did* that handkerchief get on the *Hopkins*? Someone stole one of hers, right? Or made one just like it. Why? To frame Martha. Why frame Martha? Because if poor, dumb Malloy weren't looking so hard at Martha, even he could see who really did it."

Betsy said, "That handkerchief was left on the *Hopkins* before Mike Malloy was born."

Shelly gestured. "You know what I mean, it was so the police would think Martha did it. A frame."

"And who do you think was the author of the frame?" asked Godwin.

Shelly said, "*I* don't know. That's why Betsy has to try to find out, isn't it? But Carl Winters knew. That's why he came back, right? He learned about the skeleton on the *Hopkins,* and he knew right away who did it. He came back to tell what he knew, and that same person who killed Trudie killed him."

Godwin said, "Then I think we should start with Carl's murder; it's newer, so everyone's memory is fresher, there's more to find out, and more people to talk to."

Jill said, "There's nothing to find. The only person he called when he got back was Martha. Nobody else knew he was in town."

Betsy said, "Has she been charged with Carl's murder?"

Jill shrugged. "Not yet, though the fact that only she knew he was back in town may be damning enough. I think Malloy is going to try to tie the gun to her."

"But we *know* she didn't do it!" said Shelly. "So there must be some explanation. Betsy?"

Betsy thought while the others watched. "He phoned her from the motel, right?"

Jill nodded.

"Well, he could have phoned or written or E-mailed someone else from Omaha before he left, couldn't he? Or, he could have stopped on the road and called, or he could have gone out to supper and called from the restaurant."

"See?" said Godwin, pleased. "See? She's *so* clever! That's probably what happened. So how do we find out? What do we do first?"

Betsy said in an annoyed voice, "*We* are not going to do anything! Because *you* are going to help Shelly finish with those lights and the other decorations, which had better look as if the two of you worked hard on them. And if there is any time left after that, you are going to change the yarn in the baskets to winter colors."

"Yes, ma'am," said Shelly and she took Godwin by the elbow and led him off to the front window. But she was smiling.

Betsy said to Jill, "How about if I go talk to Alice Skoglund? She's the one who figured out that pattern from that little piece Malloy found. She couldn't be a suspect, could she? Because I don't know from lace, either, and she could tell me just about anything and I'd believe it."

"Alice, a suspect?" murmured Jill, her pale eyebrows raised. "*Alice?*"

"Yeah, yeah, okay. But I imagine she could tell me the name of at least some

of the people who were lace makers back in 1948, and who of them were famil-
iar with Martha's work." She raised her voice for the benefit of the pair up front.
"But I hope I've made it clear that I am *not* out to prove Martha isn't a murderer.
I'm just giving you a hand with some research, so you can pass it along to Mike
Malloy." She dropped her voice again. "Because at least one other person who
poked his nose into this affair got himself *shot.*"

The day was overcast, the temperature in the low thirties. There
was still some snow on the ground, and more was forecast for tonight. Betsy
rummaged through her memory and came up with memories of early-winter
snow in Milwaukee melting before more fell. But this was Minnesota, where
the snow piled up to the eaves of houses. Apparently that didn't happen in one
spectacular blizzard, it was cumulative.

She pulled the bright red muffler tighter around her neck, snuggled deeper
into the navy blue wool coat she'd finally bought at the Mall of America, and
crunched across the frozen parking lot to where her car waited, doubtless bewildered by the new viscosity of its oil.

But it started bravely, and Betsy drove off to Alice Skoglund's house, a
charming but very small white house on Bell Street, four blocks from the lake.
It had a picket fence that needed painting. Stiff, dead tops of flowers poked up
through the crusty snow to trace the curve of sidewalk to the tiny front porch.
Frowzy juniper bushes crowded the space under the front windows, whose
green trim needed paint.

Betsy rang the doorbell. There was no answer. She rang again. When there
was still no answer, she came off the porch and would have gone away but heard
an unmusical clank from around back. She followed the narrower cement walk,
stepping over patches of ice, around the side of the house. She stopped when she
saw a man in a heavy overcoat shoving something into an old-fashioned metal
garbage can, one of two. As she watched, he bent and picked up the lid, which
he replaced with a loud clank. Then he turned toward the house—and it was
Alice Skoglund.

"Hi," said Betsy, both startled and shy.

"Hello, Betsy," called Alice. "What can I do for you?"

"I—I need to talk to you," said Betsy, approaching. When close enough to
speak without raising her voice she continued, "Do you have a few minutes?"
Close up, she felt even more awkward. The coat Alice wore was a man's overcoat, her boots had low, square heels.

"I wondered when you'd come to ask me questions," said Alice. "Well,
come on in, there's coffee on the stove."

Betsy followed her in the back door, which let into a little stairwell leading to the basement, so they had to go up a step to get into the kitchen. The linoleum on the floor had been scrubbed so often for so long that the pattern was nearly worn off, and the markers for the stove burners were partly gray and partly gone. Even the walls were a very pale yellow—though that might have been the original color. White curtains with yellow stitching and a pattern of square holes near the hems covered the only window, which was over the tiny kitchen table.

"Have a seat," said Alice. "How do you take your coffee?"

"With everything, I'm afraid."

"You say that like you're ashamed of it. Why, don't you like coffee?"

"Not much, actually. I like fruit and vegetable juices, herbal teas, and cocoa, and when I have a cold, I like hot lemonade, but I'm not that fond of coffee. But everyone around here sure drinks a lot of it."

"It's a Scandinavian thing," nodded Alice. "I'm British myself, half English and half Scot. But after all those years married to a Norwegian, I got converted. I have some herbal teas around here somewhere, I can heat a mug of water in the microwave for you."

"No, don't bother. I'm fine, really. But you have your coffee." Betsy glanced over her shoulder at the hook by the back door with the man's overcoat on it. "Was that coat your husband's?" she asked.

Alice stopped in the progress of the step and a half from the stove to the table and looked at the coat as if seeing it for the first time. "No, it's mine. Bought it at a rummage sale." She sat down. "A big woman like me, with shoulders like I got, regular women's coats don't fit me. They bind under the arms and at the elbows something painful, and my wrists stick out and get chapped. I've been wearing men's coats almost all my life. Oh, once in awhile I'll find something, usually in a real ugly color or priced so it takes me all winter to pay it off. And when I do buy one, do you know I have the worst time buttoning it? It buttons the wrong way—or at least what's become the wrong way for me, for coats. Everything else I wear that buttons, I can button right the first time. But I always go to buttoning my coats from the men's side." She chuckled at herself, then took a drink of her coffee. "But you didn't come here to ask about why I wear men's coats."

"I keep hearing about bobbin lace, but I wouldn't know it if it came up and bit me on the knee," said Betsy. "Do you have any you can show me?"

Alice smiled. "Yes, I have some. You just wait, I'll go get some samples of my work. I'd invite you into the living room, but the light's better here."

Alice was gone several minutes. Betsy took advantage of her absence to look into the living room. It was nearly as small as the kitchen, and as worn, and as clean. Faded chintz curtains hung at the two windows, and a big rag rug made a shades-of-green circle on the hardwood floor. An old television set stood on a metal frame in one corner, with an upholstered chair close to it. No cable box in sight. The chair and a loveseat were both covered with afghans, doubtless made by Alice, in shades of green. On the wall were framed photographs, of Alice with a strong-looking man in a clerical collar, the man alone in front of a stone church, Alice very young in a wedding dress, and a single, sad photo of a very frail looking little girl.

Betsy saw another door off the living room start to open and scooted back to the kitchen table.

Alice came into the kitchen with a big round cushion supporting a little stack of magazines and a loose-leaf binder.

When she put the cushion on the table, the magazines and binder slid off, revealing that it wasn't quite a cushion after all, more like a flat-bottomed doughnut. It was covered in a tan fabric that looked like twill. The opening in the center held a cylinder covered with the same tightly woven fabric, and around the cylinder was a strip of paper with a pattern of dots and squares drawn in ink. The uppermost part of the pattern was clogged with dozens of straight pins, and woven through the pins was thread, dozens of threads, each stretching from the pins to three-inch wooden pegs shaped something like the bishop in unelaborate chess sets.

"Bobbins!" said Betsy. "That's why it's called bobbin lace!"

"Yes," said Alice.

"How many bobbins are there in bobbin lace?"

"It varies. This lace pattern calls for sixty-two. I've worked as many as a hundred and forty."

"Wow. I had no idea."

Coming out the other side of the cylinder and draped across the cushion was a strip of scalloped lace about an inch and a half wide, perhaps seven inches long.

"How does it work?" asked Betsy.

Alice said, "The idea is to move among the pins according to the pattern. You're only working with a few bobbins at a time." She picked up four that had been lying side by side. "You would move this one over this, then these two like this—" She moved the bobbins deftly, like a three-card monte dealer, then scooped them up and pulled the threads attached to them to the left. She reached to the back of the pattern covered with pins, plucking one and putting it at the front, pushing the newest twist of threads into position behind it.

"Then you do this—" She stopped and bent forward, peering at the pins. "No, that's wrong, I think. In fact, I think I did the last two—No, that one is— Ach, never mind!" She dropped the bobbins and pushed the cushion aside with an angry gesture, and a little wooden clatter. That immediately calmed her, and she ran her fingers across the bobbins again. "I miss that sound. When a lace maker is going fast, the bobbins chatter to her in a kind of rhythm. I used to recite nursery rhymes to the rhythm when my little Fifi was restless." She sat down heavily.

"Who was Fifi?" ·

Alice put a big hand in front of her mouth, as if afraid to let the words out. "Our little girl," she murmured through her fingers. "Phyllis Marie was her name, but I called her Fifi. She was born with a hole inside her heart. They called them blue babies back then, before they invented the surgery that could fix the hole. Because their little fingers and toes and lips were blue from lack of oxygen. She was a fighter, our Fifi. They said she wouldn't live past her first birthday, but she was four years, three months, and sixty-one days old when she died. She was our only child. I remember when they invented that surgery, it was just amazing. They had it on the *Today Show*, an actual operation. They showed the open chest, and how the doctor stopped the heart, cut it open, did a few quick stitches, then sewed the heart back up. It was fascinating, he held the stopped heart in his hand, and when he was done operating, he squeezed ever so gently, and it started beating again. That baby, they said, had been dead for the time it took them to operate, but now she was alive again, and would grow up like a normal child. It was like a miracle, that surgery—and I was *so angry!* Because they didn't dare to do that back when my Fifi was still alive, and she died. No one knew then you could stop a living heart and then start it again. It was a sin how angry I got, I think I actually hated those mothers who got their babies back healthy, and all I got was a little tombstone with a lamb on it."

Betsy could not think what to say. She was embarrassed at the naked emotions on display, and ashamed that she thought Fifi a silly name. She wanted to be big herself, and emotionally kinder, so she could gather the woman into strong arms and let her weep on a capacious bosom. She reached out and put a hand on Alice's shoulder. "I am so very sorry," she said.

"Thank you," said Alice, sniffing hard. "And I'm sorry, too, for letting go like that. I think this mess we're in is bringing up all kinds of old emotions. How about another cup of—oh, that's right, you don't drink coffee."

"Well, I do, once in a great while, but not after noon, because it keeps me up all night."

Alice smiled as one who often sits up at night and said, "Now, what else did you want to ask?"

"You said you'd show me some examples of your work."

"Oh, yes, of course." Alice opened the loose-leaf binder, which was about a third full of blank paper. "Mine isn't as fine as some." Between the leaves were samples of lace. The first piece was as delicate as a daisy chain of snowflakes. It lay almost weightless across Betsy's fingers, about seven inches of lace perhaps half an inch wide, the pattern an abstract suggestion of a blossom, repeated over and over.

Betsy smiled at it; that mere human fingers could create something so delicate and perfect was amazing.

Before she could say anything, another piece was added to the first. This one was shorter and narrower, with a curve. It was also stiffer, the pattern more dense without being less delicate, done in ecru threads, with just a few threads of palest pink and a single thread of pure green.

"How can you say your work is not fine? This is lovely." Betsy wished she could put it more strongly; the work was exquisite, delicate, like photographs of snowflakes.

Another piece was offered, this one much broader. It had lots of open spaces connected with braids or twists of thread. "This is what I think of when I think of lace," said Betsy. She experimentally crunched it up a little, seeing it gathered along the edge of a collar or running as a frill down the front of a dress. A shame such things were not fashionable anymore.

"I suppose there are all kinds of lace and ways to tell one kind from another," said Betsy.

Alice began to speak of binche and torchon, of picots and ground. Betsy nodded gamely, but without real comprehension.

When Alice ran down, Betsy handed the lace back, saying, "Why don't you make this anymore? How can you just give it up?"

"I can't see as well as I used to," said Alice. "It was hard, stopping. But I can't do the pricking of the patterns like I used to, and so I keep making mistakes. Even making lace from old patterns already pricked, I have to do it very slowly and carefully, and pretty soon I have a headache. When there's only pain and no joy in making lace, it's time to quit. So I do afghans. One day there won't be anyone without an afghan or a pair of mittens in the whole county, and I'll stop making them, too."

"So long as people keep having children, you'll never run out of little hands needing mittens. And, of course, there are adults like me, who move to the frozen north and can't learn how to knit mittens."

Alice, who had been putting the lace samples back into the binder, glanced over at Betsy. "Are you hinting for a pair?"

Betsy laughed. "Actually, I bought a pair at the Mall of America, went out to my car and started driving out of the ramp—and went right back and bought a pair of leather gloves for driving—mittens are so slippery on the steering wheel! But perhaps at the next Monday Bunch meeting you could show me what I'm doing wrong trying to knit my own. I just can't get that thumb to work."

"I don't think I'll be coming to any more meetings."

"Why not? Martha will be there—" Actually Betsy had no idea if Martha would be there; she had some kind of notion that people arrested for murder didn't get out on bail. "At least, I think she will. I don't understand why you think you shouldn't come."

"I can't face those people anymore. When they hear that Martha has been arrested because of something I did, figuring out that lace pattern, they will likely think badly about me. This is a *filthy* thing that's happened to us! I wish those people had never taken it into their heads to raise that boat!"

"No, no," said Betsy. "You can't wish a murderer to get away with his crime."

"Hmph," snorted Alice. "I imagine wherever he is, Carl Winters has more serious trouble than mere human justice."

"You are one of those who thinks Carl did it?"

"We all thought he eloped with Trudie, which almost stretched my imagi-nation to the breaking point when I heard about it. So it's not any harder to think he murdered the creature. He was a man like most men, with his off-color jokes and flirting." She pulled herself up short, closed her eyes as if in prayer, and said, "I'm sorry. I shouldn't have said that. I'm so upset." She took a deep breath and a drink of coffee, and said, "You know, I'd have bet the church he was true to his wife, because under it all he really seemed to love her. She nearly died having their boy, got an infection that took away her ability to have any more children, and Carl was there for her the whole time she was sick, practi-cally slept at the hospital for weeks. So when he disappeared and Trudie Koch did, too, I thought maybe it was a coincidence. Gossip had it they'd been seen together, laughing and flirting, but gossip is wrong at least as often as it's right. Besides, Carl was like that—and Trudie was notorious. No reputation at all."

"But now you think he murdered her?"

"What other explanation is there for his running away? And, I think the police are wrong, I think he came back and committed suicide."

"What else can you tell me about Carl? As a person, I mean."

Alice frowned. "Well, he was a member of our church, but one of those who mainly occupies a pew on Sundays—refused to serve as usher or on the board of trustees or sing in the choir, even though his wife played the organ. A hard worker at his store, very friendly with everyone who came in, good at remember-ing names. Took his boy to ball games and fishing, taught him to swim and shoot skeet. But some men didn't like the way he talked to their wives, and neither did some of the wives." Alice frowned some more, but that was all she had to say.

"What can you tell me about Trudie?" asked Betsy. "Did you go to school with her?"

There was a moment of silence, then Alice said, "All the talk going on right now about those old times, someone is bound to say something and stir this old mess up, sure as I'm sitting here. Maybe no one knows, but in a small town, people pay more attention than they ought to their neighbors, and I don't want you to hear it from someone else. I think it's time to set the record right, so I'll tell you something I haven't told a mortal soul before. I used to cry myself to sleep for shame about it."

Betsy tried to keep her face muscles in neutral while wondering wildly if she was the right person to be hearing a confession. And what she ought to do if she was sitting in a murderer's kitchen.

Alice took a big breath and began, speaking slowly. "I was always the biggest child in any of my school classes. Even when I got into high school, I was taller than most of the boys. And clumsy and goofy looking. And I wasn't very good in my studies, either, so I didn't have that to comfort me. I'd see the posters go up advertising a dance and yearn and yearn to go, but no boy would ask me, and I was just miserable.

"Then, in my junior year, Trudie Koch said something halfway sympathetic to me, and I just poured out my grief to her. She said she was going to a party where you didn't need an invitation, and there would be plenty of boys to choose among, all of them glad to see me. She said I wasn't really ugly, I just didn't know how to use what I had to best advantage. She said she'd come over and help me dress pretty for it, show me about makeup.

"I knew it was wrong right from the start, but I wasn't making any progress at all with nice boys or with being nice myself and it seemed kind of exciting, to be naughty and flagrant and welcome at a party. I followed her instructions and bought a pair of high heels and some silk stockings. I talked my parents into going out to a movie, so we had the house to ourselves when Trudie came over. She put all sorts of rouge and powder on my face, piled black mascara on my eyelashes until it was hard to keep my eyes open. She put my hair up and she pinned my good dress in a way that showed I did have a figure after all. I didn't even recognize myself in the mirror.

"We went to a house in Shorewood that was kind of isolated, and I had the first beer of my entire life five minutes after I got there. I had another to keep it company, and pretty soon I was dancing with some boy I'd never seen before in my life. He took me out on the porch and I learned a great deal about—"

Alice stopped. Her face was a red so deep Betsy was alarmed for her blood pressure, and her hands were clasped very tightly on top of the loose-leaf binder. "About life, I guess," concluded Alice lamely. "It seemed like great fun, and I became very popular for several hours. But it got later and later, and at last I began to be afraid that my parents would be waiting on the porch for me to get home. I finally persuaded one of the more sober young men to drive me back to town. I gave him an address a couple blocks from the real one, and I sneaked into our backyard and through my bedroom window. As it turned out, my parents were in bed. They had come home to a silent house and thought I'd turned in early. I was particularly attentive in church the next several Sundays, which drew the attention of a young man who was about to graduate from Luther Seminary."

Alice looked into Betsy's eyes. "We had a very happy marriage. He never knew I was only technically a virgin. I recognized two of the young men at school later, but they didn't seem to have any idea that had been me; at least neither of them ever said anything to me about it. Trudie dropped out of school a month later, and I didn't see her for awhile. I married Martin a week after I graduated, and a week after that Trudie came calling. She'd lost her waitress job and was about to be evicted and could I help her? It was just five dollars. Just this once." Alice grimaced. "It's never just once with something like that, of course. But she was careful not to drain my budget to the point where I had to tell Martin. And when she had a boyfriend with money, she'd leave me alone for months. But she'd always come back. Always. Until she disappeared. I used to pray for God to strike her dead, to open the earth so it could swallow her up, and when she vanished, I was happy for the first time in a long while. She was gone a year before I finally believed she would never come back."

She reached out and took Betsy by the wrist. "But I didn't kill her. I prayed to God to take her out of my life, but I wouldn't dare do anything myself to get rid of her; it never occurred to me to pray for the strength to kill her."

Nine

❖

Betsy went back to the shop. She thought she was maintaining a poker face over Alice's startling confession, but Godwin read something and asked, "What did you learn?"

"I can't say, for sure," she replied.

"Why?" asked Shelly.

"Because I want to talk it over with Jill first."

"Hey, I'm your friend, too, aren't I?" demanded Godwin. "You can tell me anything."

"It's not because she's a friend, it's because she's law enforcement," said Betsy, and retreated from their suddenly serious expressions. She was worried, too.

She went into the shop's little back room, where a bathroom took up half the space and the other half was crammed with a coffee machine and boxes of stock and folding chairs. She hung up her coat and put her purse in a locked cabinet. She came out, but still wasn't ready to face her employees or a chance customer. She looked around for something to do in the back of the shop. It was nearly three o'clock.

From the front she could hear Godwin and Shelly talking, their voices swift and urgent, but not loud.

Speculating, thought Betsy, *about what I learned from Alice. Thank God they don't have a clue. Poor Alice!*

Back here was a little area set apart from the front by two sets of box shelves, double sided, filled with fabric, yarns, books, and magazines. There was a small round table and two comfortable chairs on the left, where customer and employee or salesman and owner could sit and plan really big projects or a substantial increase in the credit limit.

There was a cordless phone on the table; Betsy picked it up and dialed Jill's home phone number. She got a recording, and left a message: "Jill, can you call or come over as soon as possible? I have something to tell you. It's kind of urgent." She hung up and thought about calling Malloy, but what could she tell him? She was not going to reveal Alice's secret, and it would be useless to just tell him that Alice had once hated Trudie without telling him why. No, the person she needed to talk to was Jill.

She straightened the chairs and moved some catalogs back to where they belonged. Then she decided to tackle a spinner rack near the box shelves that held counted cross-stitch patterns and supplies. The items on the rack weren't moving well—perhaps because the rack looked so disorganized, like a collection of remnants. She took the items off the rack and laid them out in various ways on the table. Scissors all together? No. Arranged in sets of scissors, needles, thimbles, patterns? No. She finally decided to treat the rack like a Christmas tree, which meant the bigger the item, the nearer the bottom it should go. She swiftly put things back on the spinner, big scissors and floss organizers on the bottom, chatelaines and smaller scissors in the middle, and thimbles and scabbard needle holders on the top row of black metal arms. That at least looked better than the original arrangement.

She was near the end of her task when she heard the sound of the front door opening, and Godwin calling gaily, "Hiya, Myrt! How's ever' little thing?"

A woman's voice giggled and said, "Now who would have thought anyone would still remember that?"

"Remember what?" asked Shelly.

But Betsy remembered, too, and, smiling, came into the front part of her shop. "It's from *Fibber McGee and Molly,*" she said.

"Who are Fibber McGee and Molly?" asked Shelly.

"It was a radio show way back when," said Godwin. "Betsy, this is Myrtle Jensen. She's president of the Excelsior Historical Society."

"Hello, Mrs. Jensen," said Betsy, coming forward. "How may I help you?"

The woman, short and very thin, wore a long wool skirt, low-heeled boots, and a plaid wool jacket. She moved briskly, but her face and hands were those of an elderly woman. She met Betsy halfway, hand extended. Betsy, leery of arthritic fingers, took it gently.

Myrtle had a small head, clear brown eyes, a tiny nose, and a wide, thin mouth. She made Betsy think of a chimpanzee. "What a pleasant store you have," she said, looking around.

"Thank you."

"I've come to talk to you about Alice Skoglund."

Betsy felt her smile vanish, and suppressed a sigh. "What about her?"

"The police are sure the skeleton they found on that boat is Trudie Koch, and I'm sure they're right. She and Carl Winters disappeared the night before it was taken out behind the Big Island and sunk. It's embarrassing how that error about the year got into all the accounts of its sinking, and we're going to prepare an errata slip to go in the books. Thank God for photocopy machines. I'm old enough to remember the days of mimeographs and ditto—that smell would give me the biggest headache! Now you just put the original facedown on the glass and punch buttons.

"But that's not the subject here. I understand the police have decided Martha murdered poor Trudie, and while it's true Martha had what some might think a good reason to do that, I don't believe for one minute that she did. She was a respectable Christian wife and mother in 1948, and it would never have occurred to her to murder some silly young woman just because her husband was canoodling with her."

"Canoodling?" echoed Betsy, amused at the term and Myrtle's lengthy way of coming to the point.

"You know. Canoodling." Myrtle rolled her brown eyes and tossed her head. Betsy nodded, and Myrtle continued, "When people hear some story from history, they tend to see just the people named in the story. They don't see all the other people who were around them, whispering in their ears, carrying tales, applying pressure, working on their own reasons for doing things. In this case, people are talking about Martha and Carl and Trudie as if they were the only people in town in 1948. And they don't pay attention to context, or make connections between stories. Like people don't realize the connection between Henry VIII and Christopher Columbus."

"What was the connection?" asked Betsy.

"Henry's first wife was Katherine of Aragon, who was the daughter of Ferdinand and Isabella of Spain, who financed Columbus's first voyage. It's also like people calling that boat the *Hopkins*. For twenty-two years, from 1926 until 1948, it was the *Minnetonka III*, owned by the Blue Line Café, the same restaurant where Trudie worked. She was a waitress there, and a very immoral person. Of course, she was popular among a certain set of people, not nice people but drinkers and philanderers. She came by her lifestyle honestly. Her mother was a tramp and her father ran off before she was born. She'd been an impulsive sort of person since before she got into high school. She had a boyfriend, a bad-tempered, jealous young man named Vern Miller, who went away to the army and came back years later married to a sweet little Japanese woman who turned out as American as any of us."

She leaned forward and said, "I understand you went and talked to Alice. Instead of just listening to what she has to say, you should have asked her some hard questions."

"Such as what?"

"Well, for example, why did she purely hate Trudie Koch?"

Myrtle nodded several times, wriggling her eyebrows, until Betsy said, "Hate is a strong word, Mrs. Jensen."

"I'm saying what I mean. I remember while it was still during the war, I saw Alice on two separate occasions looking at Trudie, and if looks could kill, Trudie would have fallen down on the spot and never moved again."

Betsy hoped her poker face worked better this time. "Have you any idea why?"

"Not one. They were in high school together, but I don't think they ever did anything together. They weren't friends, of course; Alice would never be friends with someone like Trudie. Trudie had a reputation that made all the nice girls steer clear of her. As my mother put it, Trudie was no better than she ought to be and a sight worse at times. I heard Trudie called on Alice several years later, but that may not be true because this was while Martin was being considered for pastor, so she had to be careful of her behavior."

"Martin?"

"Her husband, the Reverend Martin Skoglund. He was hired as pastor of Saint Elwin's soon after, so like I say, it may not be true that Trudie visited Alice."

"What do you know about Reverend Skoglund?"

"He was a wonderful pastor, quite wise, a good preacher. He had some old-fashioned ideas about morality, but that was expected of a pastor back then. He retired in 1987 and died five years ago, still very respected. And it was as if Alice had died, too; in a month she was forgotten by the people who'd acted like her friends and depended on her all those years. After all she and Pastor Martin had done for Saint Elwin's, it was a real shame. I always thought Alice should have gone to nursing school or become a teacher, but she set her cap at Martin, and he married her when she was barely nineteen. She was a big girl, and homely as a mud fence, but a good, good person, and they seemed very happy together, even though she was rather shy to be a pastor's wife. She never got proud, and she was a good cook, and a terrific housekeeper. It was so sad their one child died, she was a little bit of a thing, very frail, something wrong with her heart."

"Yes, Alice told me she was a blue baby."

"Yes, that's the term. I'd forgotten it. Alice turned out yards of embroidery and knit scarves and made beautiful lace. She gave most of it away or put it in the rummage sale. Half the Lutheran women in town wore her aprons or dried their dishes with her towels, the other half trimmed their dresses with her lace. And there was never a Saint Elwin's child going without mittens, not if Alice knew about it. So it doesn't seem fair, does it, that she should get cataracts and have to give up her needlework."

"Alice had cataracts?"

"Years ago, had surgery and all for it."

"She hasn't given up needlework. She comes to our Monday needlework gatherings, and she crochets afghan squares."

"I don't do needlework, and even I can crochet an afghan square. Those big hooks and the yarn in all those colors, it's not hard."

"You make it sound as if she's blind."

"No, not blind. But she can't do fine work—"

"You're wrong!" The speaker was Godwin, who had appeared as if by magic behind Myrtle's shoulder.

The old woman jumped, then gave Godwin a stern look. "It isn't polite to eavesdrop!"

"Who's eavesdropping? I'm at work right over there, and you're not exactly whispering. I couldn't help hearing what you were saying. And *I* say you're wrong about Alice. She identified the threads on that piece of silk as bobbin lace right in front of us, and she figured out the pattern, down to a little butterfly in it."

"Well, I heard about that, and I'm here to tell you she had to give up making lace twenty-five years ago because her eyes went bad on her. She had surgery, and wore thick glasses for years. Then she got lenses put right into her eyes, I don't know how they do that, and after that she got regular glasses. But I've known other women with cataracts, and no matter what the doctors do, you never get the good vision back. But on top of that, she hated Trudie Koch. I think you should wonder if she has a good reason for trying to make the police suspicious of someone else over this skeleton business."

"Have you talked to the police about this?" asked Betsy.

Myrtle nodded. "And Mike Malloy listened to me, just like he always listens to people. Then he goes and does what he likes. He's already made up his mind about this, just you watch him."

After Myrtle left, Betsy called Shelly over to join Godwin.

"All right, what do you think?" she asked.

"What do I think about what?" asked Shelly, not willing to be the one to start another round of gossip.

"What Myrtle said, about Alice Skoglund having good reason to want the police to look anywhere but at her."

Shelly hesitated. "I don't know. The things she's talking about happened before my time."

"Is Myrtle inclined to stretch the truth?"

Shelly considered this. "No. In fact, one reason she's so involved with the historical society is because she wants the facts known and kept straight. She's just curling up inside over that 1948–49 business. Irene Potter told me it's given her a whole new bee in her bonnet, about taking different collections of stories and cross-referencing them."

Betsy said, "I think she made one important point. We've been looking at Carl and Martha and poor Trudie as if they were the stars in a movie, as if everyone else were extras, there to make the place look inhabited."

Godwin said, "And as if it's history, like Columbus discovering America—not that he did, really—but as if it happened so long ago that everyone is dead. If Myrtle and Martha are still around, and Alice, who else is still here who remembers what was going on at that time?"

"Vern's still here," said Shelly. "You know, the man Myrtle said was Trudie's boyfriend. They trained him to fix jeeps in the army. He did that for them for thirty years, and then they gave him a pension and sent him home, where he opened his garage. It's Miller Motors, over on Third, near Morse. It says right on his sign, 'Since 1978'. It used to be a livery stable, his building." Shelly lifted her head a little, having made a historical connection of her own.

Betsy said, "He was in the army for thirty years, you say?"

"That's what he tells people," said Shelly. "I take my car to him to be serviced."

Betsy said, "Subtract thirty years from 1978 and you get him joining the army in 1948, the same year Trudie disappeared. And Myrtle says he was a mean and jealous boyfriend."

Godwin murmured, "I wonder if he joined up in July. *Early* July."

The three looked at one another, but before they could say anything more, the door alarm went *bing*, and Jessica Turnquist came in. She saw the trio staring at her and looked down to see if she'd come out with some private parts showing.

"Hello, Jessica," said Betsy. "I'm afraid I've caught the Excelsior Virus, which turns people into gossips."

Jessica smiled her thin smile and said, "And I'm afraid there's no cure, either. Betsy, I'd like four hanks of that hand-spun yarn I was looking at last week."

Betsy went to one of the yarn bins in the box shelves. "What color?"

"That pale yellow." Betsy got down the yarn, which was full of blibs. The yellow was an uneven and dispirited shade, a sorry imitation of the soft color onion skins produce.

Jessica shook her head over it. "I don't much like this myself, but I have a good friend who just loves sweaters made of it. It's to be her Christmas present."

"You know," said Betsy, ringing up the sale, "it's interesting how handmade has gone from meaning especially well done to meaning full of obvious mistakes, even if you have to make them deliberately. Listen, do you have to go right away? I have some questions for you."

Jessica hesitated, obviously wanting to say no, but compassion—or curiosity—won out. "If it won't take too long. I've got to go grocery shopping today. What do you want to know?"

Betsy leaned forward and asked quietly, "You knew Carl Winters, didn't you? What was he like?"

"Well, I didn't know him really well. I saw him around town, and I took my dry cleaning to him, of course. And he worked for me every August during State Fair. I used to have a food concession, and he would sell while I would cook."

"Did you really? How interesting! What kind of food did you sell?"

Jessica smiled. "Corn dogs on a stick. One of the things our State Fair is famous for is food on a stick. Steak on a stick, fish on a stick, pork chop on a stick, fried cheese on a stick, shish kabob on a stick."

Betsy laughed. "I think I've heard of that last one."

Jessica's smile had some life in it this time, and Betsy suddenly realized that she'd once been really beautiful. "You'd be surprised how much money you save not having to supply paper plates. I sold corn dogs, French fries wrapped in newspaper, and three kinds of pop in a deposit bottle. You wouldn't believe the grease inside that stand; the floor would get so slippery we had to mop it a dozen times a day."

"What was your husband's role in all this?"

"He bought the stand for me as a kind of wedding present in 1941, but we only ran it together that first year. He joined the Army Air Corps right after

Pearl Harbor, and they made him a navigator in the flying fortresses. He was killed in a mission over Germany."

"I didn't realize that's how you became a widow. I'm sorry."

"I'm more sorry we decided not to have children in case he didn't come back. We were very young but trying hard to be grown-up about things. I was so sure he would come back that I didn't mind putting off having a child."

"You know, this may seem like an impertinent question, but I wonder why it was you didn't marry again. You must have had lots of suitors."

Jessica's eyelids dropped as she simpered just a little. "Well, I did," she said. "I thought about it, but I just didn't . . . connect with anyone. And then one morning it was too late. I've had a good life anyway, good friends, a nice town to live in, my own home, my church, my needlework. It's enough."

"Did Carl Winters flirt with you?"

For just an instant those prominent eyes flashed. "I should say he did! He was notorious! 'Hiya, sweetheart, you're looking mighty fresh and tasty this morning,' he'd say. And until you put a stop to it, he'd get worse and worse. But it was never more than talk, really; he didn't mean anything by it. He loved his wife, I know that now. But at the time I felt sorry for her, even though I didn't really know her. It wasn't until Carl disappeared that we became close. She was kind of standoffish, I thought, but now I know it was because of Carl; compensating, I'd guess you'd say, for his being overfriendly."

"Would she get mad at him for acting like that?"

"She never said a word to him, not where anyone else could hear—though of course he wouldn't behave like that in front of her, that would have been going way too far. He did call her 'the ball and chain' and 'my *first* wife' and things like that when she wasn't around."

"God, I'd've murdered him," muttered Betsy.

"Yes, well . . ." said Jessica, and looked away.

Betsy said, "Now wait! You came to me and begged me to prove she *didn't* murder him!"

"No, I came to you and begged you to prove she didn't murder Trudie Koch," said Jessica. "It broke my heart to hear the talk going on around town about that. But now Carl comes back and right away he's shot dead, and it isn't suicide, the police say. So now I'm not sure what to think."

"Could it have been someone else?"

"Who?"

"I don't know. Anyone. Alice Skoglund, for example?"

Jessica's well-shaped eyebrows lifted. "I think Alice might have been the one person in town Carl didn't flirt with."

"Because she was the minister's wife?"

"No." Jessica let that stand by itself while she gathered up the bag with the her wool in it. Then she added a rather peremptory "Good-bye," and left.

"Well!" said Godwin. "Talk about *rude!* Why didn't she just come out and *say* she thought Alice was too ugly for even Carl to flirt with? Humph! I bet she was never as pretty as she thinks, not with that attitude."

Betsy thought to scold him for sneaking up, and for poking his oar in, then decided it didn't matter. Besides, she was inclined to agree with him.

A half hour later, Betsy pulled into the parking lot beside Miller Motors. The old wooden building did look like something out of a western movie, with its false front and general air of impermanence. The back of the shop was right on the edge of a gully. Betsy pulled her car up to the edge and looked over, expecting to see mechanical debris—it was, after all, so handy; just open the back door and toss. And just what one might expect of a place like this.

But the gully was clean. Down its center ran some new-looking railroad tracks. Just as she became aware of footsteps crunching on the frozen gravel of the parking lot, a low, gruff voice said behind her, "Them damned volunteers are gonna run a trolley car down there."

"What volunteers?" she asked.

"Same ones that run the trolley steamboat." The speaker was a man built approximately like a shell a battleship might fire. He was about five feet eight inches tall, with a domed head shaved bald and no hat to protect it from the chill air. His powerful, sloping shoulders and thick neck added to the gunshell effect. He was not a young man: his face was deeply seamed, and as he turned to gesture at the gully, she could see the start of a stoop as well as a thinness to his legs inside the filthy denim trousers. He wore a heavily lined denim jacket and in one large, dirty, chapped hand carried a plastic bucket full of old oil cans.

"The same ones who raised the *Hopkins?*" she asked.

"That's them." He spat, more in opinion than from need.

"Where did they put the boat after they took it out of the water?" she asked.

"Big ugly barn over on George Street. You gonna be one of·them volunteers?"

She smiled. "No. Are you Vernon Miller?"

"That's right." He spat again, less definitively. "Who are you, then?"

"My name's Betsy Devonshire. I inherited Excelsior's needlework shop, Crewel World. I was wondering if I could talk to you."

"I don't know from needlework. I do car repairs. That your car?" he nodded toward the elderly white hatchback.

"Yes, that's mine." Betsy had an inspiration. "And it needs an oil change and whatever kind of tune-up you give a car that's not used to the winter."

"Bring 'er up to the door." He nodded toward the set of double doors on the side of his building. "We'll have a look." He walked off with his burden to the row of wheeled gray garbage cans lining the other side of the parking lot.

Betsy obeyed and soon was admitted to the interior of the shop. If the floor was not dirt, it had become so thickly layered with oily dirt that it made no difference. A young man in need of serious dental work came over and listened to her story of a car bought used in San Diego and only recently driven to Minnesota.

"But I need to talk to Mr. Miller first," she said, not wanting to tell him just yet that there was no way on earth she would trust her car to this place, these people.

Miller shrugged and let her go first into his office, a room formed out of a corner of the work area with plywood and used boards. Much of its interior was taken up by a desk buried in paper, both marred by black fingerprints. There was an office chair, dirty and so broken into the shape of Miller's lower extremities she would no more sit in it than his lap, and a metal stool with a composition seat she took instead. The office was perhaps twenty degrees warmer than the shop area, so both of them unbuttoned their coats.

"What can I do for ya?" asked Miller, sitting in the chair. His eyes were small and watchful under the heavy brow.

"I'm curious about that skeleton they found on the *Hopkins*," began Betsy. "Apparently, the police are sure it's Trudie Koch."

"What's that got to do with changing the oil in your car?"

"Nothing. But I'm hoping you'll talk to me about her."

Miller shrugged his heavy shoulders and turned the chair away from her. "I suppose someone told you I was her boyfriend way back then."

"Yes."

He heaved an insincere sigh and turned the chair halfway back, glancing at her as he did so. "That was a long time ago."

"What can you tell me about her?"

"What do you want to know?"

"What was she like? Who were her friends? Who . . . who were her enemies?" She saw him start to get up and said hastily, "Please, you loved her, didn't you? You were probably the one person who really understood her. If Martha Winters didn't murder her, and I don't think she did, then who else might have done it?" He looked up at her from under that massive, frowning brow, and she tried a winsome smile along with a look of friendly, sincere inquiry.

A little to her surprise, the frown faded and he sat back in his chair. "I did love her," he said after a bit. "People didn't understand how much, because we had a lot of fights. Worst of all, I don't think Trudie understood."

"Wasn't she the understanding sort?"

"She was the kind of girl who always asked, 'What's in it for me?' She could be sweet and charming when she wanted something, and she could turn cold as—well, as January in International Falls when she didn't get it. She liked having a good time, she liked men to bring her presents, and she could be real grateful when the present was something special."

"Like money?" asked Betsy.

"No, she wouldn't take money, that was going too far. But something she could return for money was okay."

"Was this before you became her boyfriend?"

He nodded. "And when we'd have a fight, she'd go take up with someone she knew would give her things. And she made sure I knew about it."

"And I suppose that would set off another fight."

He nodded. "It sure would. Sometimes she'd pick a fight with me because she got to wanting a jacket or a hat or a piece of jewelry and I couldn't afford to give it to her. I'd blow up and say we are through, I never want to see you again; and she'd take up with a fellow who would buy it for her, but in a day or a week, I'd hear the new fellow was out on his ear. And there'd I'd be with a bouquet of flowers or some candy, saying I was sorry and would you take me back."

"And she did?"

"Every damn time. Neither of us any smarter for it."

"Why did you love her?"

He shrugged, then said, "She was smart and sassy, and real pretty. I thought she was beautiful. She had that sexy shape, like a woman oughta be shaped. And always laughing, teasing—" The frown returned, but not directed at Betsy this time. "Her last job was waitressin' at the Blue Ribbon Café. She was a waitress most of the time, once she got off the farm. Complained her mother worked her to death, but on her own she worked about as hard. Course, the money she earned on her own *was* her own. She was a hard worker. On her feet all day, but she could still dance half the night. She was a good dancer, liked to dance." He glanced up at her and something almost like a smile lightened his features. "Boogie-woogie. You ever hear of it?"

"Of course. There was swing, then boogie-woogie, then rock and roll. Where would you go dancing?"

"Different places, sometimes to a ballroom that was part of the amusement park. Huge dance floor, biggest I ever seen, it was the biggest in the midwest at one time. Lawrence Welk came there once, during the war. I went and I danced with Trudie. She was just a kid then, her ma had to bring her, but she already was giving her fits. She was a wild 'un." Smiling, he shook his head.

"Was she popular in high school?"

He nodded proudly. "Had the boys standing in line."

"I bet the other girls were green with envy."

He nodded. "Some of 'em. Some of 'em was downright mean to her about it. But it didn't bother Trudie. She'd sass 'em back, and walk off laughing. She didn't care. She just didn't care."

"Did you care?"

He looked at her, seeking suspicion, but Betsy's look only begged for a good answer. "Yeah, I cared. She was wild from the start, and I knew it, but I kept on coming. She dropped out of high school the end of her junior year, got a job, a good job in a factory, moved into a rooming house. But she flirted with the line supervisor and his wife found out, and she got fired. She said she didn't like that job anyway, and got another as a waitress, and she was always a waitress after that. She'd work six months, a year, then she'd move on. Sometimes it was the boss, sometimes it was the customers, it was never her fault. I think she'd just get bored. She knew it didn't matter; she could lose her job and turn right around and get another."

"Did she make enemies over losing her jobs?"

"I don't think so. She wasn't one to carry a grudge, and I don't think her bosses cared that much."

"But someone finally got angry enough to kill her."

"Yes, you're right. Y'know, all these years I thought she just up and left town, and that's how I thought about her, living in some other town, still waitressing, flirting with the customers. Or maybe she roped some jerk into marrying her, maybe she even settled down, had five or six kids. I used to think about her a lot for a long time. And I never quit thinking about her altogether. And all this while she was in that damn boat, a skeleton. It's like my mind got into a rut, thinking about her in some big city, sassing the customers in a café, so it's hard to change that into knowing she's been dead for fifty years, that she's forever twenty-two."

"Is that why you joined the army? Because you thought of her in some other town, flirting with someone else?"

He said, surprised, "Hell, no! I left before she went missing. We'd had another fight and I decided I wasn't gonna go crawling back this time. Besides, I wasn't gettin' anywhere in this one-horse town. So I decided to give the army a chance. I'd like to tell you we made up, that she came down to see me off and begged my forgiveness and promised to write, but she didn't. She had her pride, too, I guess. I know I did, once I made up my mind."

"So how long were you gone before she disappeared?"

He thought a long while, scratching his chin, then said reluctantly, "I guess I was still in boot camp when someone wrote and said she'd run off with Carl Winters. She'd been gone a couple of weeks by then."

"But you're sure you were in army basic training when Trudie disappeared."

"Hell, I could dig out my old service record and show it to you. My dates of service are July 3, 1948, to July 3, 1978. I got that letter, and I couldn't believe it, flat couldn't believe it. Mr. Winters was a married man, with a business and a kid and a house. I thought it was a crock, I thought she'd gone off on her own, at the most let him give her a ride to somewhere. I just couldn't believe those two had a serious love affair—and I guess I was right."

"What do you think really happened?"

"I think Trudie was flirting with him at the Blue Ribbon, just like she flirted with every man, and he took it serious. I think he waited till she got off work and tried something with her, and she slugged him, and he killed her." Miller shrugged, holding his heavy shoulders up for a bit before dropping them. "I never knew Winters, so I don't know how much that sounds like him, but it sounds a whole lot like Trudie."

"Did you come home on leave from boot camp?"

"Naw, they sent me to San Francisco, so I went right there from Kansas and had so much fun in Chinatown all my pay was gone before I reported to Presidio. The army took me in and cleaned me up, sent me to school and taught me how to repair every kind of motor there is, from motorsickle to tank. After a few wild years I started saving my pay, and a few years after that I married Miyoshi, who finished my drinking for good. Then I retired, came home, and started this business, built it from the ground up, with Japanese savvy, army money, and my own muscle. The army taught me all I know, God bless the U.S. Army."

Betsy went out to find the gawky young man leaning deep into the interior of her car. He straightened when she cleared her throat behind him. "Engine's in good shape for the mileage you've got on her," he said. "But your brakes are leaking. Better let me fix that."

"Not today," said Betsy, who was sure her brakes were not leaking; they worked fine.

"I bet you have to press kind of hard to get yourself stopped, don't you?" he asked.

"Not at all," she said firmly, going around and getting in.

He closed the hood and went to open the doors of the old garage. She noticed as she backed out that he was looking at the car and shaking his head.

That won't work either, she thought, and pulled out onto Third Avenue.

Ten

❖

It was after five when Betsy drove past her shop—darkened and, she hoped, properly locked up for the night—and went on down to Excelsior Boulevard (a prepossessing name for a narrow, unprepossessing street) to the McDonald's, where she bought a regular hamburger, a small fries, and a Sprite. She found a much-fingered copy of the Minneapolis *Star Tribune* and perused it, so by the time she left the restaurant, it was fully dark. An icy little breeze that smelled of snow flirted with the curls on her forehead. Her feet crunched on the parking lot, gritty with sand. She thought of her cozy apartment.

Oh, Lord, she remembered that Sophie was waiting at the door!

Godwin said he would push Sophie out into the hall when he closed up. Margot, he explained, did this, too, when she left before closing time. Sophie knew to go upstairs and wait outside the apartment door for her mistress to come home.

Feeling guilty for loitering over her burger, Betsy drove quickly up Lake Street to the narrow entrance to the parking lot behind her building. She let herself in the back door with her key, hustled down the back hall and up the stairs to arrive breathless in front of her door. A muzzy whiteness opened its pink mouth in complaint and greeting, a long, drawn-out cry.

"Yes, yes, Sophie, I see you, it's all right, here I am," she gasped, stooping to stroke the thick fur.

"Rewwwwwwwwwwwwww," complained Sophie. She had a high-pitched voice for an animal that weighed twenty-three pounds, not including the cast on one hind leg.

Betsy unlocked the door, Sophie shot through and ducked into the kitchen to stand beside her bowl, gleaming empty on the floor. "I'm sorry," Betsy apologized, reaching into the cabinet under the sink for the metal can that held the Iams Less Active dry cat food. She filled the little scoop and poured it into the bowl. Sophie fell to crunching her way to the bottom of the bowl with swift efficiency. One would think she hadn't eaten in a week; but Betsy had seen Godwin and two customers slip the animal tidbits.

Jill had not come to the shop nor had she called. So now Betsy checked her own machine and found a message from Jill that she would come over, but not until around nine: "Lars is taking me out to dinner."

Betsy went into her bedroom and changed from her good work clothes to jeans and a faded-pink sweatshirt with cut-off sleeves. She'd had her supper, so she filled half an hour with some housecleaning, then remembered that in the rush to get home to Sophie, she hadn't checked her mail.

She went back down the stairs to the front entrance and unlocked her mailbox with a little brass key. There were six or eight first-class envelopes—mostly the depressing kind with windows—some magazines, catalogs, and a fistful of advertising.

Back in her apartment, she began sorting. Margot was still getting mail, of course. Betsy put those aside. She would return the personal ones unopened with a brief letter explaining that Margot had died in unexpected and tragic circumstances and that she, her sister Betsy, would be at this address for at least the next six months. Doing this invariably triggered sympathy cards and even the occasional written letter of condolence, the latter requiring a thank you note. Betsy was getting used to crying over some parts of her mail.

All the catalogs were of items related to needlework. Betsy kept these in the shop for her customers to peruse. She was beginning to realize how useful they were to her in finding out what was big or popular or new—and make sure Crewel World carried it.

As she was sorting through them, a picture postcard fell to the floor. She picked it up. The picture was of the huge and ugly fruit bats in the San Diego zoo. Turning it over, she saw the message: "Going bats in Minnesota yet? I hear you have snow. Brrrrr!" It was signed *Abbey*.

Betsy sat down at the little round table in the dining nook, the mail scattered before her. Light from the kitchen shone through the window beyond the table, catching little dancing movements. It was snowing, the flakes dancing in a light wind. It was very dark out, very quiet in the apartment. If she was in San Diego, she could call Abbey and they'd go down and walk on the beach, or drive out into the desert and look up at an immensity of sky and stars. They'd talk about life after divorce, hair dyes, and estradiol versus Premarin. And the perils of dieting. Betsy felt suddenly quite alone.

Almost automatically, she looked toward the kitchen. There was leftover chicken salad in there, her favorite kind of chicken salad, with cashews and red grapes. And some of Excelo Bakery's wonderful herb bread. Betsy had a tendency to eat when she was troubled or lonely. And right now she felt both.

But just a few days ago she had gotten a glimpse of her naked self in a mirror and been appalled. Everything seemed to be puffy or sagging. Really sagging. How on earth had she let herself get like this?

So no more Quarter Pounders, no more desserts, and one day soon look into joining a health club, or do some mall walking. There was a fortune of several million dollars coming her way some time next year, and when Betsy invested in a new wardrobe, she didn't want to buy it from some mail order catalog sent to women ashamed to be seen going into the Women at Large shop at the mall.

So instead of eating a second supper, she got out the fabric, floss, and pattern for the little Christmas tree ornaments, then went to put the kettle on. Tea had no calories, she could have tea. She went into the living room and turned on the Bose, tuned to KSJN, the local public radio station. Fortunately, they weren't being experimental or operatic this evening. She listened only long enough to determine it was probably Brahms, sat back, and looked around.

The living room in the apartment was rectangular and low-ceilinged, its triple window heavily draped. The rug was a deep red on a pale hardwood floor, the walls a light cream with black baseboards. The room was furnished sparingly with a loveseat, upholstered chair with matching footstool, and some standard lamps. The low ceiling, the shaded light of the standard lamps, and the covered window made a cozy haven. Betsy had felt comfortable here from the first moment she'd entered.

But looking around reminded Betsy that while Margot had been a fine decorator and a terrific housekeeper, Betsy wasn't. She stood and debated getting out the vacuum cleaner, but decided against it. Instead, she went to the dining nook, sat down at the table, and tried again to work on the counted cross-stitch pattern. She counted very carefully with her threaded needle, both pattern and fabric, but after ten minutes a line of stitches that was supposed to join an earlier line didn't. She groaned. This was always happening! She consulted the pattern and her stitching and found the error was a dozen stitches back. She stuck the needle into the fabric and shoved it aside. Why did women insist that doing counted cross-stitch was relaxing? It was a lot of things: frustrating, aggravating, stupid, and impossible. But not relaxing.

She glanced into the kitchen but resolutely turned and went to the hall closet and got out the vacuum cleaner. She was about halfway around the living room when Sophie came out of the bedroom. Unlike many cats, Sophie had no fear of the vacuum cleaner. She got in front of it, looked up at Betsy, and opened her mouth. Betsy shut off the vacuum cleaner.

". . . ewwwwwwwwww!" Sophie was saying.

"What do you want?"

Sophie started for the kitchen, the too-long cast, designed to keep her from running or jumping, lifting her left back end up a little higher. The vet tech at the clinic described it as having "square wheel syndrome." She stopped and looked back hopefully at Betsy, then at the kitchen, but Betsy said firmly, "No."

If Betsy was giving up snacks, Sophie was, too.

Sophie limped to her cushioned basket under the window draperies. She gave Betsy a hurt look, then climbed into her basket, lying down with her injured leg pointedly on display.

Betsy felt for the animal but didn't yield. She flipped the switch on the vacuum cleaner and went back to work. It was bad enough that her employees and customers vied to see who could bring the tastiest tidbit to the cat. Betsy wasn't going to. At twenty-three pounds, Sophie was proportionately far more overweight than Betsy.

The vacuuming finished, Betsy considered dusting, but instead went to the comfortable chair with the cross-legged canvas needlework bag beside it and got out her knitting. Not the mittens, she needed something soothing. The red hat was at a section that was just knit, knit, knit—no purl to complicate the action, no increase or decrease. As she had noticed before, there was something calming about knitting. One sat down to it with a jumbled, disordered mind, started in, and after a few minutes, the pulse slowed, the fingers relaxed, the mind, like a troubled pool, settled and cleared.

She wondered if Jill would just take her word for it that Alice hated Trudie without Betsy having to say why. Betsy remembered something her mother had frequently said: "Three may keep a secret if two of them are dead." Alice had kept her secret for fifty years; it seemed a shame it couldn't be kept just a little longer, until Alice was safely dead, beyond hearing the wagging tongues of Excelsior.

And what about Vern Miller? His date of entry into the army was July 3. The *Hopkins* had been towed out and sunk with its grisly cargo on July first or second—and Trudie had been murdered the night before that. Was it what he said, an attempt to get away from a town that didn't appreciate his talents?

Or from an arrest for murder?

Eleven

❖

The kettle had been refilled, heated to boiling, and turned down to simmer long before Jill arrived a little after nine. "Sorry I couldn't get here earlier," she said as she peeled off her uniform coat, dappled with melting snow.

"But I figured I might as well change into uniform, in case this runs long. I'm still on the graveyard shift, so we have till eleven-thirty."

"How was your dinner with Lars?" asked Betsy.

"Okay. He asked me to marry him tonight."

This was said so casually, Betsy nearly missed it. "He did? What did you say?"

"I said what I always say when he asks me: No."

"Aren't you in love with him?"

"Oh, I'm mad about the boy," she said, still casually. "But he wants kids right away, and I'm not ready for that yet. Have you got English tea?"

"Yes. And the water's hot." Betsy went into the kitchen, Jill following.

Betsy used a Twinings tea bag, but heated the heavy mug with a splash of boiling water which she dumped out before putting the bag into it and pouring more water over it. Jill added sugar—two spoonfuls—and a dollop of milk.

"Bad out?" asked Betsy.

"Not yet," said Jill. She leaned against the refrigerator while Betsy made a cup of raspberry-flavored tea for herself. Jill's Gibson Girl face and her invisibly pale eyebrows made her, as usual, hard to read. And that cryptic way of talking about Lars—what was that about?

Did she want Betsy to ask questions? Or was she being cryptic because she didn't want to talk about it? Or did she think Betsy already knew enough about the two of them to understand what Jill meant?

Betsy wondered if Jill often had trouble with that enigmatic face, with people reading into it whatever they were most—or least—comfortable with. Perhaps Jill wasn't cold or unemotional at all, just reluctant or even unable to share her feelings with the world. There had been times when she'd seemed very friendly, such as that other morning on her boyfriend's boat. *Perhaps,* thought Betsy, *if I reached out a little, I'd find her easier to understand. So try to think that there is a friendly interest.*

And, actually, there must be, or why else was she here?

"Tea all right?" asked Betsy.

"Yes, thanks. You make it just like Margot."

Betsy smiled. "We both learned how from our father; he loved tea."

"With a name like Devonshire, that's not surprising."

"Yes, I suppose so. Jill, why don't you want children?"

"I *do* want children. But I want to continue in law enforcement, and when I have a child, I'll want a year or two off, and that would put my career in jeopardy. Also, I can't drive a squad while I'm pregnant, but I could manage a desk. When I make sergeant, then I'll marry Lars."

"Does he know that?"

"I've told him that, which is not the same thing."

Betsy smiled. "I see." She sipped her tea. "Is Malloy making any progress?"

"Only against Martha," sighed Jill. "How about you?"

Betsy said, "Yes, that's why I called you. I've found out something that may be important. Alice Skoglund told me that in 1948 she wished with all her heart that Trudie were dead. She told me why. She also said she didn't kill her, but she did have a good reason to. And after I called you, I discovered Vern Miller, who had been Trudie's jealous boyfriend, joined the army approximately one day after Trudie disappeared."

Jill said, "I ask you to find lace makers, and you find suspects."

"I didn't mean to, honest. Well, maybe I did go looking at Vern Miller. But all I did with Alice was ask her about her lace. She made an assumption that I was sleuthing and confessed about Trudie."

"Why would Alice Skoglund hate Trudie Koch enough to wish her dead?"

Betsy hesitated, then said, "What she told me would be nearly nothing by today's standards. But by her own, it was shocking and shameful. And Trudie was blackmailing her over it. She said she hadn't told anyone until today, when she told me. I felt so awful, listening to her pour her heart out. All that wretchedness—I had no idea. And all I wanted was for her to tell me who was making lace in 1948—oh!"

"What?"

"I forgot to ask her that." Betsy glanced at Jill and noticed a slight quiver of the shapely mouth. She smiled herself, and Jill's quiver became a genuine grin.

Jill asked, "And did Vern Miller just pour his heart out to you, too?"

"No. What happened was, Shelly said he retired from the army after thirty years, came home and opened Miller Motors. His sign says, 'Since 1978.' If you subtract thirty years from that, you get 1948. So I went to talk to him. He said he was halfway through boot camp when he got a letter about Carl and Trudie running off together. He says he didn't believe it, because Carl was a respectable businessman with a family and not likely to fall for someone like Trudie. Vern thought she might have accepted a ride from Carl to somewhere, but that's all. He said he used to think about her waitressing in some other town, sassing the customers and going home to her six kids."

"What do you think?"

"I don't know what to think. He said she used to pick fights with him whenever he couldn't buy her something she wanted, and then she'd temporarily take up with someone who would, then she'd let Vern back into her life. It sounds like it was a volatile relationship, and that can end in murder. And he did leave town at a very significant moment."

"Hmmmm," mused Jill. "You know, you have come up with two very solid alternatives to Martha. I wonder if there's a way to get Mike to look them over."

"You think I should go talk to him?"

"No, let me have a go, first. He didn't like you poking around that first time, remember? And he wouldn't listen to you until you had proof. Which you don't have, right now. He's pretty sold on Martha being the killer, you know."

"I can't believe he really thinks she did this."

"Well, look at it his way," said Jill. "Trudie works at the Blue Line Café, just yards from the dock where the *Hopkins* is tied up, waiting to be towed out and sunk. Carl is having an affair with her, he meets her after work that night in The Common, which is right there next to the docks.

"It's all over town that Carl is messing with Trudie. Think how embarrassing that must have been for Martha! It's not hard to see the obvious, that Martha comes roaring out of the darkness to smite Trudie on the head with a tire iron or a hammer—at least that's the ME's opinion.

"Now, rather than trying to stop her, Carl runs off—"

"The coward," said Betsy.

"Well, if my spouse and my lover got into a fight, I might not care to interfere. Both of them might remember who they really should be mad at."

"Oops," said Betsy.

"Right. So Carl's gone and Trudie is dead. Martha drags or carries Trudie's body onto the boat, the effort shifting her dress around so a pocket opens, or a sleeve unrolls, and her handkerchief falls out. It's dark, she's busy, she doesn't notice. And either when she's moving rubble it gets covered up, or she steps wrong in the dark, and a piece of pipe rolls under her foot, covering the handkerchief."

"But think of that big boat filled with rubble," said Betsy. "It would have been an enormous effort for a woman to move enough of it away to uncover the deck and then move it back again in order to hide the body."

"Malloy has found someone who remembers that they didn't fill the boat at the dock, but hauled maybe half of it out on a barge, since they didn't want the boat to tip over or sink before they got it out behind the Big Island."

"Oh," said Betsy, deflated.

"But there was enough that she had to clear a space, and enough that when she put it over the body, no one noticed when they tossed the rest in. It was hard work, but not an impossible task. Remember, she's scared. I'm sure you've read the stories about women who have lifted whole automobiles off their husbands or sons after the cars fell off jacks onto them. Malloy has.

"Meanwhile Carl gets into his car, drives off—"

"The *car*!" exclaimed Betsy.

"What about it?"

"All these years Martha says she thought Carl had been mugged and his body thrown into a boxcar or into the lake. How did she reconcile that notion with the fact that his car was missing?"

"His car wasn't missing," said Jill. "It was found behind the dry cleaners. I'm assuming he drove down to the lake, and then drove back again. There was a pretty fine train and streetcar service out here in those days. He left his car behind the cleaners, then caught a streetcar or a train into Minneapolis, and caught a train out of town."

"Oh," said Betsy.

"He arrives in Omaha and decides to stay awhile," continued Jill, picking up Malloy's scenario. "He finds work, tries to forget. But fifty years later, the boat is raised, the skeleton found, and a story about it gets picked up by the wire services. The story says Martha is suspected. Carl is overjoyed. At last, he can come home and tell what really happened, see to it his wife is at last punished for her deed.

"But coming back opens old memories. Maybe, he thinks to himself, he'll give his wife the same chance he took, to run off. He phones her from a nearby motel, telling her he's back and she'd better get out of town. But Martha plays it cool, asks to come and talk to him. And she's not leaving town. She goes out there with a gun and shoots him. She leaves the gun beside the body, thinking the cops will conclude it was an accident or suicide. But she's no forensic expert; she doesn't know from powder burns and angle of entry and all that sort of thing. Her hasty little plot doesn't work. She's found out; she's going to prison."

Betsy put down her cup of tea. That was very plausible. So plausible, in fact, that it might be true. Was it true? Was she on a fool's errand thinking it was otherwise?

Jill went to the pig-shaped cookie jar and lifted the lid, then turned with it in one hand. "Do you mind?" she asked.

"No, of course not. I'd love to get rid of them; I'm trying to cut back."

Jill put down the lid, selected a raisin oatmeal cookie, put it down, put the lid back on. As she did, she looked toward the dining nook and said, "That your counted cross-stitch project?"

"Yes, and I'm giving up on it. You want it?"

"What's wrong with it?"

Betsy took her to the table. "I did what everyone said I should do, I basted the edges of the evenweave, and I marked off the divisions with more basting and I folded it per instructions so now it's marked into the squares each ornament will fill. And I found the middle of the first square, and started stitching. After about ten stitches, I realized I'd counted wrong and had to frog—"

" 'Frog'?" interrupted Jill.

"Isn't that a term? I see it on RCTN all the time."

"RCTN?"

"An Internet news group for needleworkers. When they have to pull out stitches, they call it frogging. As in 'rip it, rip it.' "

Jill actually chuckled. "That's cute," she said. "I'll remember that. I've done some frogging myself." She took a big bite of her cookie and drank some tea. "You're lucky you're not working with metallics. You can pick out the little raggedy ends floss leaves on your fabric, but metallics leave a mark you can't see."

"A mark you can't see?" said Betsy, expecting a joke.

"It develops over time." Jill saw the incipient laughter on Betsy's face and said, "I'm serious. The metallic floss comes out clean and you think it's gone, but in a few days or a few weeks or even sometimes in a few months, there are these dark marks, like dirt. And on that piece you're doing, you leave some areas blank. So if you frog an area you should have left blank, pretty soon it will look like you were handling it with dirty fingers."

"Oh. All right, I guess I should be grateful that these patterns don't call for metallic. I've done this one part about four times, and there are two areas I crossed into territory I think should be blank. I'm about out of one color, and there's not a stitch of it left on the ornament."

"You'll have to buy some more."

"No, I won't. You see, *you* eventually get it right, but *I* don't; I just keep getting lost in one direction, then another. I count and count and check and double-check and still I make mistakes. And these are supposed to be *easy*. I'm giving up."

Jill picked up the patterns, which were printed all on one big sheet. "You shouldn't be having all this trouble. I've done one set of these, and they aren't all that difficult." She looked at Betsy's cloth. "Where's your gridding?"

"Gridding?"

"Yes. I hate to have you do yet more setup, but if you mark off every ten squares on your cloth and every ten squares on the pattern, it's a whole lot easier to keep count."

Betsy looked at the cloth, then at Jill. "Well, dammit, why didn't they suggest that in the instructions?"

"Because not everyone needs to grid. Especially on something as easy as these patterns."

"Sit down, why don't you? I've got a marking pen somewhere, I'm going to go get it." She walked away, muttering, "Of all the damn, dumb, stupid things. Why didn't I think of doing that myself? I'm never going to get counted cross-stitch. I don't know why I keep trying."

When she got back, Jill was looking at the color pictures of finished patterns. "I did the duck first. The one I like best is the polar bear with the Saint Lucy wreath on its head. There's a town in Ramsey County—that's where Saint Paul is—called White Bear Lake. Very nice place to live. I'll give the white bear to the tree."

"Thanks," said Betsy. She sat down with the marker and a ruler and began counting the paper pattern.

"What's this?" asked Jill after a minute, picking up the postcard. "Someone you know likes bats?"

"It's a joke. When I told my friend Abbey back in San Diego that I was moving to Minnesota, she said, 'Are you bats?' "

Jill turned the postcard over and read the message. She asked, "So, are we driving you bats?"

Betsy laughed. "Too early to tell. It sure is different here."

The wind outdoors threw a handful of sleet against the window, and Jill said, "Tell me about it."

Betsy laughed but thought she heard an invitation as well as a comment in that, so she put down her marker pen and said, "San Diego has the perfect climate, it really does. Warm all year round, but not hot in the summer. There's only about ten degrees' difference between winter and summer, so there's not a big change in the seasons like here. Even in dry season, with that wonderful ocean breeze the air is always fresh and clean, the sky an incredible blue. And then when it rains, everything flowers. It's rainy season now, so every leaf, every flower is pouring out a scent, the air is like perfume."

"Mmmmm," said Jill covetously, and Betsy wondered why she had thought Jill unemotional.

"It's a military town, a lot of sailors and marines, so by California standards, it's conservative politically. But not by, say, Montana standards. On the other hand, it's not L.A., which is dirty, crazy, only ninety miles away, and approaching fast."

"Is the ocean nice? I've always wanted to swim in the ocean."

"The water's too cold to swim in, at least for me. Even surfers wear wet suits. But I miss the beaches, especially Coronado Beach, and I miss the sun, and the fruits and vegetables being so cheap and having more varieties. I mean, I went to this great big grocery store up the road. Big as a warehouse."

Jill nodded.

"And when I looked over the fresh vegetable section, I just about cried. Apples, potatoes and onions, unripe peaches, sweet bell peppers, and four kinds of lettuce if you count iceberg. Oh, and, carrots. Pitiful!"

"Pitiful," echoed Jill, but this time her voice was dry.

"I know, I know, I can almost kind of remember my childhood, when fresh fruit all but disappeared during the winter. Still, I looked and looked and couldn't find a mango or a cactus pear . . ." Betsy sighed. "And I miss Balboa Park. There's this big tree, I love to go visit it, it's like a friend, all spreading branches like it's holding out its arms. An army could camp under it—" Betsy stopped, dismayed to find her eyes filling with tears.

Jill said, "When the money comes, are you going to move back?"

"I don't know. Yes, I do. I can't go back. It was my life for fifteen years, but my ex-husband poisoned the well for me. We did so many things together, and his college world became my world, and it's all still there. Everything I'd see or do would remind me of the pig, and he was *such* a pig. The pig." Betsy sobbed once, and took a gulp of her tea to forestall another.

"A real pig, huh?" Betsy looked up and saw Jill looking back so gravely that she had to giggle. Jill's mouth quivered, and suddenly the two of them were laughing.

When the laughter slowed enough to talk again, Jill said, "I'll take you cross-country skiing in a few weeks. I know a place so quiet and so beautiful, the air smelling of pine, you will actually start to fall in love with Minnesota."

"Yeah, I think we missed our chance to ride herd this year."

"Oh, I have a friend who has horses, so we can still ride, if you like. But I think you'd better get hardened up to the cold first. Downhill skiing, or cross-country skiing, will do it. I love both."

"How about a snowmobile ride?" asked Betsy, who wasn't big on exercise.

"I don't like snowmobiles," said Jill. "Too noisy and smelly. And some snowmobilers get drunk and try to cross the road ahead of cars and trucks. Talk about poisoning the well; those crazy snowmobilers totally put me off the sport. Especially when it got to be my turn to tell the next of kin."

"You've done that?"

"Twice. Once the jerk survived, but with about half the brains he had that morning. And that wasn't a whole lot to start with."

"Jill, why do you do this job?"

"Because it makes a big difference. It's important—no, it's essential. I always was a take-care, take-charge kind of person, and this way I can put that trait to good use."

"But sometimes it must break your heart."

"Sometimes it does," nodded Jill. She finished her tea and said, "Would there be any way to prove what day Vern Miller joined the army?"

"He says he can produce his service papers."

"Why would he still have his service papers?" asked Jill.

"Because he stayed until he could retire, and he gets all kinds of benefits, but he has to be able to produce his service record on demand. I still have mine, because if I get sick I can go to the Veterans Hospital, even though I was only in four and a half years."

"Four and a half—?"

"President Johnson extended every service person's enlistment six months during the Vietnam War."

"So I guess that makes you a veteran," said Jill with a note of admiration in her voice.

"Ha! I never got any closer to Vietnam than San Francisco, and I personally don't think of myself as a veteran. But that's not the point. Vern Miller may be the real point of this discussion. I wonder if he has a gun. I didn't think to ask. I keep focusing on Trudie Koch's murder, but maybe I should look at what happened to Carl Winters."

"I think it's likely they were killed by the same person," said Jill. "And Carl was probably killed because he knew something about who killed Trudie, or why she was killed, and came home to tell what he knew. So you're not mistaken to focus on Trudie."

"Oh, something else. Myrtle Jensen told me Alice had cataracts removed some years back, and she can't see very well. Alice said her eyes had gone bad and that's why she quit making lace—not that she couldn't, but that it was painful. That makes me wonder if she might not have fudged a little bit about figuring out that lace pattern for Sergeant Malloy. She showed me some samples of the lace she used to make. It's really beautiful, so she does know what she's talking about. Are you sure she didn't know about the butterflies in Martha's lace?"

"If she was a lace maker, I should think she knew. Martha didn't keep it a secret, and as a fellow lace maker, it seems to me Alice would pay attention to things like that. I wonder if her husband knew Trudie was blackmailing her."

"Oh, I don't think she told him. Think of the climate back then, prefifties. I bet Martin Skoglund, seminary graduate, wouldn't have married her if he knew what she'd done, so I don't think she could have told him about Trudie."

"What did she—?" Jill raised both hands. "Sorry, sorry, I didn't mean to ask. But I *am* curious."

"I know. And I'm sorry I can't tell you. Did you know Pastor Skoglund? What was he like?"

"He was my pastor while I was growing up, and as a kid, I liked him. He seemed like one of the good grown-ups, big and strong, but kind and friendly. A little bit distant, too important to be teased or to tell a joke to. Like what I imagined God to be. My mother loved his sermons, but if he was coming for a visit, she cleaned for two days and treated him like royalty."

"Yes, I see. Poor Alice; he might have been giving off unconscious messages like, 'Don't get messy,' or even 'I don't want to know.'"

"Pastors get messy stuff all the time. Other peoples' troubles are his work. Like cops. Which reminds me—" She looked at her watch and stood.

"Jill, thanks for coming over. Just talking to you helped a lot."

"I'm glad you asked me over. Do it again, any time you need to talk."

"Do *you* ever need a shoulder?"

Jill hesitated. "Once in awhile."

"Then call on me. I'm glad you're my friend, and I'd like to be one to you."

"Thanks," said Jill, and she left.

Betsy sat down with the counted cross-stitch pattern and the evenweave cloth. She finished gridding her fabric and then the pattern—a cat—then picked up her needle and threaded it with pink for the nose. It was much easier now to find the center of the fabric. She made a stitch, and another, and crossed them. She counted and stitched, and after awhile, she sat back to double-check her work. Definitely a cat's face looking back, and from under a Santa Claus hat, and exactly like the pattern. This was more like it!

But it was still a tension-making exercise, and she needed to relax her mind or she'd never get to sleep. She put the cross-stitch aside and went to the living room's comfortable chair and got out her knitting. Let's see, where was she? Here, with still two inches of knit and knit to go. That should just about do it.

But in another minute, she began thinking again about the mystery. Jill was very sure Carl's and Trudie's murders were related. And indeed, if they weren't, there were a lot of coincidences connecting them. They were both locals, they were in the midst of some kind of relationship, they had disappeared on the same day fifty years ago. Trudie had been murdered, and when Carl came back to the scene after fifty years, he was promptly murdered, too. Did they have something else in common besides that relationship? Had they been "canoodling" (to use Myrtle the historian's term) in The Common and seen someone doing something illegal? And had that someone seen them? What could someone be doing that kept alive the murderous determination to prevent its telling fifty years later? Smuggling? Hardly. Murder? No one else was murdered that night in Excelsior. Or mysteriously disappeared. Rape? Hmmm . . .

But then Carl was not murdered the same way Trudie had been. Trudie had been bludgeoned, Carl had been shot. Was that significant? Maybe there were two different murderers. No, more likely, after fifty years, Trudie's murderer was so old he simply didn't have the strength to batter Carl's head in.

Vern Miller had been surprised to hear that Carl had run off with Trudie because of the difference in their social status. Which brought up the question, what *was* Carl doing flirting with her? Not just everyday flirting, he was known for that. Everyday flirting with Trudie wouldn't have the gossips' tongues wagging so vigorously as to anger his wife.

Betsy's needles slowed. That was interesting. Was Carl genuinely taken with Trudie? Enough to risk his marriage? His business? Having lived in the small-town world of college life, she knew how important a reputation could be, and how devastating it could be to have friends and colleagues turn on you. As they had done on Hal the Pig—and, less directly, on Betsy.

No, she could never go back there.

She looked at her watch. Holy smokes, it was way past eleven! *Hey,* she thought, as she packed up her work, *this may be the answer.* Fabrics showed everything, so no snacks around the needlework. But when she got really absorbed, she didn't miss the snacks. Remembering Margot's trim figure, Betsy wondered if she hadn't stumbled onto her sister's secret to a trim waistline.

Feeling heartened, Betsy went to bed.

Twelve

❖

Betsy had a night full of odd dreams. When the radio alarm went off, instead of the strange and eclectic selections of KSJN's *Morning Show,* she got Antonín Dvořák's Symphony number eight. Occasionally the *Morning Show* remembered it was public radio and played something classical, but usually just a movement. This went on and on, the entire symphony. After awhile, she realized it wasn't the *Morning Show,* so this must be Saturday.

But Saturday is a workday for shop owners. She did not turn off the radio.

There was a heavy thump and a continued wobble of the mattress as Sophie came for her morning cuddle. She rubbed her face all over Betsy's hand until Betsy began rubbing back. The two lay in comfort for a few minutes, then Betsy got up to start the day.

By 9:30 they were through the back door into the shop. Betsy turned on lights, started the coffeepot going and the plug-in teakettle for tea or cocoa, put the start-up money in the cash register. The Christmas decorations looked nice, she noticed.

She checked the desk for notes and found she would have to order more al-paca wool, bamboo knitting needles, and little stork scissors. Godwin noted that he had sold *two* needlepoint Christmas stockings, the two underlined three times. Shelly noted that there had been inquiries about spring knitting lessons. "I think we should ask Martha," she wrote. "Show our confidence."

Betsy put the note aside.

Godwin came in just before ten looking at peace with the world. "Don't you look nice!" he said.

Betsy had worn a new wool dress she'd found on sale. It had a simple A-line skirt and was a deep cranberry color. "You like it?"

"Are you losing weight?" he asked, narrowing his eyes.

"Not yet," said Betsy.

"You should get a gold scarf to go with that dress," he said. "With a gold scarf you could take that dress anywhere." He looked around as if for eavesdroppers—though how, without the door alarm's *bing,* he could think someone might have come in—and leaned toward Betsy. "What did Vern Miller tell you?"

"He joined the army in early July, the third, to be exact."

Godwin looked genuinely surprised. "You mean, I was *right? He's* the mur-derer?"

"I don't know. I told Jill, and she's going to tell Malloy, if she hasn't already."

Godwin's smile lit up his entire body. "We did it again!"

"Did what?"

"We solved a murder!"

"We haven't solved it!" Betsy said sharply. "All we've done is supply Sergeant Malloy with another suspect to look at. We don't know that Vern Miller did it."

"Are you going to look for proof that he did?"

"I think I'm going to wait to see what Sergeant Malloy does. If Vern Miller is a murderer, I don't want to be the one to confront him about it."

Half an hour later, Shelly came in to work. Betsy told her the decorations were excellent and reminded her to mark her hours on her time card, as she was doing payroll tomorrow.

Then Betsy went into the back room to poke into cardboard boxes to see if what was written on their outsides coincided with their contents. She was standing on a chair to reach a box stacked near the ceiling when she heard a man's inquiring voice and Godwin's brief reply, then silence. She got off the chair and backed up a step to look through the open door. A slim young man was standing awkwardly in the opening between the box shelves.

"Hi, Ms. Devonshire?" he said shyly. "I'm Jeff Winters." He had light brown hair and his grandmother's faded blue eyes.

"Ah . . . hello," said Betsy. "I'm very sorry about Martha. We all are."

"I know," he said. "That's why I've got the nerve to come and ask you for an important favor."

"Of course," she said, coming out of the back room. "Anything we can do. Would you like to sit down?" His face showed signs of the strain he must be under.

"Thanks."

She sat him in one of the comfortable chairs at the little round table. "How is your mother holding up?"

"She'll be home tonight. A judge allowed bail, and I got one of those quick mortgages on the dry cleaning business for that and a good lawyer."

"Getting her home is something at least. Would you like some coffee?"

"Please. Thanks. Black." He ran thin fingers through his already mussed hair.

She went to fill two pretty porcelain cups, his with coffee, hers with a lemon-flavored herbal tea.

He took only a token sip, then put his cup down and sighed. "I know you've told people that you aren't investigating anymore because you aren't a real private eye, but—" he began.

"It's not that I don't want to help your grandmother," said Betsy quickly. "Because I do. I'm sure Martha is frightened half out of her mind, and your whole family must be suffering terribly over this."

"Yes, we're all wishing we could be braver. Except Grandmother; she's amazing."

Betsy continued, "It's funny how people seem to think I enjoy playing amateur sleuth. I don't, because I don't know how. I got involved with my sister's case because I was very angry and sad and it was my own strange way of coping with my grief. I couldn't believe she was murdered by some kid who needed a desk calculator, so I started asking questions and just got lucky."

"Yes, I understand that."

"So I hope the favor you want to ask for isn't for me to go looking for clues."

He looked at her, his face at once determined and wretched. "The problem is, the lawyer we hired says we need a private investigator to look into the case. And between posting bail and hiring that lawyer, I can't afford a private detective. I went to my dad, but he's working out some stuff of his own. You see, he was thinking his father was dead all these years, and then he heard, 'He wasn't dead after all, but now he's murdered, and the police think your mother did it' all in one sentence. It really messed him up. He isn't talking to me or Grandmother right now."

"That's very sad."

"Oh, he'll come around, but maybe not very soon, and we need to do something right away. I understand how you think you can't do anything, but you did so splendidly for your sister, I want you to try again for Grandmother. Just ask some questions, like you did the first time, and maybe it will happen again, you'll understand from the answers what really happened to my grandfather and to that other woman all those years ago."

Betsy picked up her cup of tea and took several sips while she thought what to say. She'd been lucky again already, finding out about Alice and then Vern. But that might be the end of her luck. Anyway, finding another suspect wasn't the same as proving Martha innocent. And there was another bad thing about all this.

"Suppose I do go sleuthing, and I find out things—bad things—about people? Rooting around in other people's lives can really hurt them. And if they're innocent, too . . ."

"Ignore the stuff that doesn't matter, can't you? There has to be something to find that will help, because Grandmother didn't do this. I know it. And I know you'll find it. You should start with the Monday Bunch. Those women know everyone in town, and everything that's going on, and everything that's happened, too. They've been around for years and years, most of them. And they know Grandmother better than anyone. They can tell you she didn't murder that Trudie person, or Grandfather."

"I don't know if they'll want to—"

"Are you kidding? Of course they'll want to help! Grandmother is practically the oldest member of the Bunch. The first Monday Bunch meetings were held in your sister's home, before she started Crewel World, did you know that? And Grandmother was one of the first members."

"No, I didn't know that."

"Margot used to organize trips to other towns—other states, sometimes—to buy yarn or patterns or go to conventions, and Grandmother went every time she could get away. She was devoted to your sister and just devastated by her death. She was also very proud of you for solving her murder. Please, won't you help her now?"

Again Betsy lifted the cup of tea to her lips as an excuse not to answer immediately. She didn't want an official involvement with this case. If Alice's role had to be revealed—Betsy foresaw trying to explain herself in a court of law.

But then a memory swam up, of that first Monday after her sister's funeral, when four members of the Bunch came and worked for hours to help clean up the mess in the shop left by the murderer. Martha had been the one sorting out yarn. Yes, and she had been the one who called the Humane Society and the one who designed and printed the posters asking for information about Sophie, who had gone missing. Betsy remembered what a wretched mess she herself had been, and how patient they had been with her, Jill and those four members of the Monday Bunch. They hadn't been afraid to just pitch in.

"Yes," said Betsy. "All right. I'll do what I can. But remember, I really am an amateur. You mustn't get your hopes up."

But Jeff was on his feet, extending a long-fingered hand. "Thanks! Thank you so much! I'll tell Grandmother, and she'll be so grateful and comforted."

After he left, Betsy sat back down on the chair and sighed.

"Well?!?" said a voice and she jumped.

It was Godwin, appearing as if conjured, agog with curiosity. "I just can't stand it anymore!" he said. "What's going on?"

"Jeff Winters wants me to ask some questions, see if I can find out anything that will help his grandmother's case. I said I would. Now, go away, get back to work. And please stop sneaking up on people!" she added crossly, but an indulgent smile teased her lips.

Betsy worked through the lunch hour so her employees could go out, but as soon as they came back, she left. She was hungry but had an idea she wanted to try out before she bought some lunch. She got her car out and drove up Water Street to Oak and followed it north to where George angled into it. As she made the steep angled turn back, she could see the barn belonging to the Minnesota Transportation Museum. It was more like a big, windowless shed, two stories high, made of corrugated fiberglass in an ugly beige color. Several cars had forced their way up a narrow, unplowed lane to park in front of it.

As Betsy followed suit, she went past an enormous, ancient, military-style tow truck. That must be how they got the boat over here, thought Betsy.

She got out and found a small door on the back side of the barn. It wasn't locked. She opened it, went inside, and found the entire interior was taken up by a boat. Its mustard-colored bottom rested on a big cradle built onto a trailer. She looked up and saw that the upper structure was surrounded by a kind of mezzanine built out from the walls of the shed. A set of wooden stairs led up to it.

The air was warm and smelled of freshly cut wood and varnish. Men's voices indicated there were people on the upper level working on the boat.

The boat, of course, wasn't the *Hopkins*; this was the *Minnehaha*. She knew it was pulled out of the water for the winter, but it hadn't occurred to her to wonder where it was kept.

She went up the stairs. A half dozen men in coveralls or jeans were measuring or painting or consulting a very large hardcover catalog of pipe fittings. One looked around at her. "You the new volunteer?" he asked.

"No," she said. "I'm looking for the *Hopkins*."

He laughed. "Not here, obviously. Not only because there's no room, they told us it's the scene of a crime. The police hauled it up onto the Big Island until they finish with it."

"Oh," she said, disappointed.

"You sure you aren't a volunteer? We sure can use someone to varnish the slats of the upper deck seats," he said, and stuck out a hand. "I'm John Titterington. This is Pete Weir, and that fellow in love with the catalog is Virgil Behounek, and over on the deck are Jim Hewett and Leo Eiden."

Betsy waved vaguely at the men, who nodded vaguely back and continued their labors. "Some other time," she said to Mr. Titterington and retreated back down the stairs.

I should have known, she told herself as she got back into her car and wallowed back up the lane. They wouldn't allow the public to go crawling over the boat.

And what did you think you'd find on the Hopkins, *anyhow? You're just trying to act like a real private eye, which you're not. Go do what you can, which is ask nosy questions.*

She drove back to the shop in a grump and picked up a salad with double croutons in the sandwich shop next door. The dressing she selected wasn't diet, either.

But a big special order came in that afternoon, and going through it with the customer and finding it all there, as ordered, brightened Betsy's spirits—and the big check the customer wrote helped, too.

Just before closing, the phone rang. It was Jeff Winters. "Grandmother's at home," he said, "if you want to talk to her."

So Betsy ate a hasty supper, called Jill (who wasn't home) to leave a message saying she'd be home by eight, then got back in her car and drove down Lake Street to what she called "the *other* Lake Street." At its north end, Lake Street went around a corner and became West Lake Street.

The west end of West Lake Street made another sharp turn that led it down to the lakeshore. Betsy negotiated the curve carefully, wary of ice. She'd once been a good winter driver, but that was many years ago.

Martha Winters's attractive brick house was the second from the end on this segment. A streetlight gleamed on the snow clinging to an enormous blue spruce in the front yard. Martha's driveway was gritty with sand.

Bushes beside the little porch had been covered with cloth tied close with twine. Betsy, no gardner, wondered if they were roses. She went up the brick steps to the front door and rang the bell, feeling uncertain about the conversation she was about to have.

The door opened, and there was Martha, her face pale, its folds and wrinkles looking freshly carved. "Jeff said he'd asked you to come over and talk to me," she said. "Oh, Betsy, I'm so worried! I do hope you can help me. Please, come in."

Betsy stopped on the little tiled area just inside the door and took off her coat. She glanced past Martha at the virginal blue carpet and said, "Shall I take off my boots?"

"Yes, if you don't mind," said Martha, and she hung Betsy's coat and scarf up in the little closet, then led the way into the living room. "Would you like some coffee? It'd just take a minute to make a pot."

"No, thanks. But you have some, if you like."

"No, I had three cups with my supper, which I ate in my own kitchen, *thank God,* and that's two more than I usually have in the evening. I won't sleep a wink tonight."

Martha sat down on the very front edge of a pale, upholstered chair, so Betsy started for the couch. But her eye was caught by the framed handkerchiefs, and instead, she leaned forward for a look. Sure enough, there was a butterfly, plain in the design of each corner. The lace itself was two inches wide around the center handkerchief, very elegant and rich-looking. "These are amazing," said Betsy. "Jill told me about them, but they are even more luscious than I thought. I pictured the butterflies as a subtle pattern, but they're as clear as drawings. How old is this work?"

"Years and years. I stopped making lace a long time ago—soon after Carl ran off. I had the store to mind and my son to raise, so I had to give up a lot of things."

Betsy turned and spoke from her heart. "I can't imagine the hurt his disappearance must have given you. And now this."

Martha looked up at her with wounded eyes. "Yes."

Betsy sat down. "Was he a pig before he went away?"

"A . . . pig?"

"That's the word I use to describe my ex-husband. He was a tenured professor at Merrivale, that's in San Diego, and had been cutting a swath through the undergrad women for years. I had no idea until I got a phone call from the attorney he'd hired to fight the case the university was bringing against him. Apparently, he'd dropped one student a little too abruptly in going to another, and she went to the administration. And it turned out she wasn't his first. Other women heard about it and came forward to testify—one or two actually in his favor. There were nine—nine!—willing to talk; and God knows how many weren't. I should have known, but I didn't. I mean, I met him when I was a student in one of his classes, so I really should have been more suspicious. Only I made sure he was single before I let his advances advance." Betsy looked over and saw Martha staring openmouthed at her.

"I'm sorry," Betsy said. "I came here to talk to you, not carry in the trash of my own life."

"I think perhaps you're making assumptions about Carl and me, that's what set off the confession," said Martha.

Betsy felt herself blushing. "You're right, and I shouldn't do things like that. I told Jeff and now I'll remind you, I'm an amateur. I don't know how to conduct a proper interrogation. I just ask whatever occurs to me. *Was* Carl a pig?"

Martha smiled. "He was frisky, he had a terrible reputation for it, but it was all talk. He loved to 'push the envelope,' as they call it nowadays, but he never went outside it, as far as I knew. Certainly he never ran off with anyone before."

Betsy said, "If that skeleton belongs to Trudie, then Carl didn't run away with her, either. It's even possible, I suppose, that her murder and Carl's disappearance aren't connected. I wonder if perhaps Trudie thought he was serious, and he murdered her to shut her up."

"I don't think Carl could commit murder," said Martha. "He was a scalawag, everyone knew that and was used to it. But he wasn't cruel or mean. He had a great many friends in Excelsior, and so did I; yet two women made it their business to tell me he was having lunch every day down at the Blue Ribbon and making time with Trudie. Jessie Turnquist was one of them—this was before we became close. I told her what Mark Twain said, that it takes two people to cut you to the heart: an enemy to slander you and a friend to tell you what the enemy said. Besides, I said, Carl would try to make time with a gorilla if he thought it was a female gorilla, he can't help himself. So you see, if I knew, and wasn't turning into a fishwife over it, why would Carl have to murder her?"

"Did Carl know you knew?"

"Indeed yes. I brought it up over supper that same day I heard about it. I said the whole town was talking, which hurt my feelings and might be bad for business. And he said something like, 'Aw, they know I don't mean anything.' But then he didn't come home the next night. It was late closing and I was tired, so I went to bed and didn't realize he hadn't come home till the next morning. I couldn't imagine where he'd got to. I went down to the store thinking someone had robbed the place and left him tied up in back, but he wasn't there. I called around and no one had seen him, so finally I called the police. It wasn't until that evening, when Trudie didn't show up for work, that people realized she was missing, too."

"That was the evening of the day they towed the *Hopkins* out and sank her," said Betsy.

"Yes. That's why I don't have any memory of them sinking her, because it wasn't a year later, it was the same day Carl disappeared. I was so upset about Carl, I didn't notice what was happening with the *Hopkins*. But looking back, I can see that by the time they realized Trudie had disappeared, too, the boat was already sunk. And everyone was *so sure* they'd run off together it didn't occur to anyone to think one or the other's body might be on the boat."

"The big thing we have to worry about is your handkerchief. We have to figure out who got hold of one and left it on that boat. And why."

"To make it look as if I did it, of course," said Martha.

"No, that can't be right. The boat was taken out and sunk for what was supposed to be forever," said Betsy. "If someone wanted to frame you, the thing to do would be leave the body up on shore somewhere and drop your handkerchief beside it. Why hide the body and the handkerchief?"

There was a thoughtful silence. "All right, perhaps they didn't want to implicate me," said Martha at last. "Maybe whoever dropped it didn't murder Trudie, they were just there and dropped the handkerchief by accident. Certainly I did it often enough."

Betsy frowned. "But if it was just dropped casually, then it would have floated away. It was found on the bottom of the boat, after the last of the rubble was taken out. The only reason some of it was found at all was because it was tucked away under the rubble."

"What I don't understand is how it got there to begin with. I know where all my handkerchiefs are."

Betsy asked, "How many did you have to start with?"

"One," said Martha, and she smiled at her jest. "I started making lace when I was fourteen; my grandmother showed me how. Her mother was from England and showed her how. My mother loved to knit and crochet, she made both knitted and crocheted lace."

"You can *knit* lace?"

"Oh, yes, on tiny, tiny needles. I used to know how, but once I learned the techniques, I loved bobbin lace best. My grandmother left me her bobbins. I still have them. I've thought now and again about selling them, but I'd rather wait and see if there's someone who would really appreciate them, so I could make a gift of them."

"That would be a very special gift."

"Yes, it's a pity I couldn't have more children; I'd have loved to teach a daughter how to make lace." Martha sighed, but faintly; that was an old and no longer important sorrow. "But to answer your question, I made bobbin lace edgings for nineteen handkerchiefs. Each one's a little different, but they all have that butterfly. My grandmother helped me design it. Her signature on her lace was a bee."

"Who else do you know who makes lace?"

Martha thought. "Alice Skoglund used to do very nice work. But she says it gives her a headache to do it nowadays and so she quit."

"Did you see the design Alice made from the tangled mess taken from the *Hopkins*?"

Martha nodded. "It's mine all right."

"You say you know where all your handkerchiefs are? I heard you lost two of them."

"Well, I'm reasonably sure a pig ate one and the other went into show business." She snorted genteelly and Betsy smiled, as much in admiration as appreciation of the joke. That Martha could jest in the face of danger showed she was a brave woman.

"Suppose a lace maker, one who makes bobbin lace, had gotten a really good look at one of your handkerchiefs, one you'd dropped, say. Suppose she got a chance to really study it before she gave it back to you. Could she then copy that design in some lace she made herself?"

Martha thought that over. "Maybe. She'd have to be looking at it with that in mind."

"Now," said Betsy. "Think hard. Try to remember back all those years ago. Did Alice Skoglund ever return a handkerchief to you?"

"Oh, yes," nodded Martha. "Several times. She was the Reverend Skoglund's wife, you see. And I left a hanky in church at least once a year. Sometimes the person who found it brought it right back to me. But not everyone knew about my butterfly, so they turned it in to lost and found. I distinctly remember one Sunday Alice gave it back to me saying she'd heard about my butterfly lace and so thought this was mine. We talked about lace for a few minutes. That's when I learned she was a lace maker."

"So she would have had it a whole week to study, if she wanted to make a copy," said Betsy.

"Well, yes. Oh, surely you don't think Alice had anything to do with this!"

But Betsy was thinking of the woman who even in her seventies had arms and shoulders like a man.

Thirteen

❖

Sunday afternoon Betsy went to see Alice Skoglund again, carefully choosing a time so Alice wouldn't feel obliged to feed her. "I came to talk to you about making lace," she said. "Someone told me you can't make lace anymore because you had an operation to remove cataracts and can't see well enough."

Alice grimaced angrily. "Like most gossip, that's almost sort of true. I did have early-onset cataracts. I had surgery when I was only forty-five. And it did make lace-making difficult. Not impossible, only very hard. I bought a great big magnifying glass, and ordered a lamp that sat on a stand through a catalog. But in three weeks of trying, I made four inches of lace. And it wasn't a difficult pattern or particularly fine thread, nothing like the one-twenty I used to be fond of. I can still make lace, but it's heavy gauge stuff, and I have to keep stopping and checking the pattern, and I can't see the pattern forming like I used to. When I finally realized I wasn't getting any joy out of it, I quit. I do some knitting and crocheting, but they aren't the pleasure lace-making was for me, and they aren't as easy as they once were, either. The only thing I can do real easy anymore are those darn afghan squares. I can do those practically without looking. So I make afghans and put them into fund-raisers and rummage sales and gift packages made up for people who have lost their homes to fire. That way I feel like I'm still making a contribution."

"I'm sure there are a lot of people who feel you make a great deal of difference," said Betsy. Then she screwed her courage to the sticking point and said, "You told me and Jill that you had never seen one of Martha's handkerchiefs, the kind with a butterfly on it, but Martha told me that you did, perhaps more than once. She said she left them behind in church several times, and that one time you brought it to her yourself and talked with her about lace-making."

Alice threw herself back in her chair as if poleaxed, strong chin pointed at the ceiling, eyes closed. A sound almost like a snore escaped her throat. Betsy was about to panic, thinking the woman had had a stroke, when Alice abruptly flipped forward to say, "Well, I guess I am a liar! Do you know, I totally forgot about that? She's right. I did handle one of her handkerchiefs that she had left in church. I told her she should enter it in the State Fair, it was so well done. I was a little afraid to talk to her, she was a superior sort of lady who simply ruled our choir, and I was a common sort of person, and my mother once told me I couldn't carry a tune in a bucket. But Martha was glad to talk lace with me. There weren't many women in town who still had that old skill."

"Do you remember when that happened?"

"Heavens no. Probably fairly early in Martin's career, because I got less and less afraid of women like her as time went on. I guess I didn't remember it because back when people carried handkerchiefs commonly, they were the single item most often left behind. I finally set up a table in the church hall and put items people forgot on that. People will leave the oddest things behind on those pews, we once found a set of false teeth and another time a dead fish—which of course, we didn't put out to be reclaimed. There were also a lot of umbrellas and a surprising number of single overshoes." Alice chuckled. "So it appears I did have a chance to examine the butterfly she put on the corners of her handkerchiefs. I forgot all about that until just right now."

"But," said Betsy, "perhaps unconsciously you remembered seeing it, and when you were working out the pattern on the *Hopkins* fragment, your unconscious brought it out as an example."

Alice considered this, then shook her head and said slowly, "I don't think so. I do remember now looking at the lace on her handkerchiefs—she did kind of flourish them—and thinking how beautiful it was. The work was so very fine, much better than anything I could do. But I don't remember examining the lace trim on any of them with an eye to copying the pattern. I had my own patterns."

Betsy went next to see Martha Winters. She found her in her kitchen, peeling potatoes. The heavenly scent of roasting chicken filled the air. "My son and his wife are coming over," Martha said happily. "I told them how the Monday Bunch believes in me, and how you are helping, and they decided perhaps I am not so terrible after all."

Betsy hugged her even while she hoped with all her heart that Martha's faith was not misplaced.

"I suppose you have more questions?" said Martha.

Betsy didn't want to say she was floundering, throwing herself in random directions hoping for a clue, a connection, something that would help. "A few," she said.

"Have you learned anything?" Martha asked in a low voice.

"Well, it's possible that Trudie was murdered by the man who was her boyfriend at the time. They had a stormy relationship and were in the middle of a quarrel when this happened. He joined the army right about then."

Martha beamed at her. "You are *so* good at this, Betsy!" she said.

"Well," said Betsy, "the problem is, why did he murder Carl?"

"Because Carl saw him," said Martha, surprised at her. "He saw him murder Trudie and he ran for his own life. Then all these years later, he finds out I am suspected of the murder and he comes back to testify on my behalf."

"Did he say anything to you that might show this was what he was thinking?" asked Betsy.

"Ah . . . no. As I told Sergeant Malloy, I didn't want to talk to him and pretty much hung up on him."

"Did Carl and Trudie know each other long?"

"No, I don't think so. He might have met her at another restaurant or diner when she was waitressing there, but there wasn't any talk until just before it happened. Why he picked on Trudie, why he went all the way down to the Blue Ribbon, I can't imagine. Our dry cleaning store is five blocks from the lake, so Carl would have had to walk past the drugstore fountain and two perfectly nice cafés to get there. I don't know what possessed him, I really don't. It was as if he deliberately set out to do something crazy and break my heart in the bargain."

Betsy thought about that but was even less able to make sense of it than Martha. Then she said, "Where was the Blue Ribbon Café in relationship to the lake? Was it near the amusement park?"

"It was part of the amusement park. The two men who managed it shared Christopher Inn, which had been made into a duplex for them and their families. The amusement park ran all along the lakeshore, from City Docks down past where the little ferris wheel is. They had a roller coaster and bumper cars, and a really nice merry-go-round, a big one with beautiful horses."

"Martha, did you know Trudie at all? Would you have known her if you'd seen her on the street?"

Martha nodded slowly. "Probably. This habit we have of gossiping about everyone isn't new, you know. We've always pretty much kept track of one another in Excelsior. I'm sure she must have been pointed out to me. In retrospect, I wonder if she was as terrible as everyone said, because she never took any sudden little vacations or went to nurse a sick relative in another state."

"I don't understand—oh. You mean she never went for an abortion or to have a baby. Gosh, remember when families used to do that to girls who got pregnant?"

Martha nodded. "When the father couldn't be forced to marry her, they'd send her away till it was all over, and put her baby up for adoption."

"Times sure have changed, haven't they?"

"Oh, they'll change back, probably. Nothing works, you know. We just keep trying one thing then another and then the first thing again."

Betsy sighed. "You're right, what we think of as progress is sometimes just the swing of a pendulum. But you say Trudie either wasn't as awful as everyone thought, or was perhaps more careful than most young women of her type. You've known Alice Skoglund for a very long time, haven't you? Did she have any quarrel with Trudie?"

Martha smiled. "I doubt if those two ever spoke more than three words to one another—and Trudie was in high school with Alice. That's funny, when you think about it. If Trudie were alive today, she'd be an old woman, like Alice." She made a face. "Like me. Like Jess."

Betsy said, "The older I get, the older people have to be before I think of them as old. I don't think of you as old at all."

Martha smiled faintly, taking the compliment for what it was worth. "My grandson told me that when you think of a policeman or your doctor as young, then you're getting old. I reached that stage twenty years ago. I wish I could be of more help to you." This last was said with genuine pain. "Ask me something that I can answer, something that can really help."

Betsy, floundering some more, said, "That piece of needlework Jessica made for you. Can you show it to me?"

"Of course, if you like." Martha went away and came back a minute later with a small framed object about ten by twelve inches.

Betsy took it. The pattern was a pink heart surrounded by little blue flowers—"forget-me-nots," said Martha. Under the heart, in golden letters, was the word *Forever.* Inside the heart was *MW & CW.* The *CW* was worked in gold, the *MW* and ampersand in a green that matched the tiny stems and leaves of the forget-me-nots.

"She did Carl's initials in gold because I kept insisting he must be dead. When she gave that to me, I cried and cried, I was so touched. People had been avoiding me, not knowing what to say." Martha sniffed. "They all thought he'd run off with Trudie, and I suppose they thought I was a little crazy, insisting it wasn't true. But I just couldn't believe he wouldn't write to me, explain where he was or at least try to justify what he'd done. So I was sure he was dead."

"But he wasn't dead," said Betsy.

"I know, and that puzzles me," said Martha. "He was always sure what he was doing was right, that he had a good reason, that he could make me understand. Up to then, I always had." She reached for the framed piece.

But Betsy stepped back out of reach, to take another, longer look. Her eye was becoming educated to the nuances of needlework. This piece was competently done, no fancy stitches, but no flubs or missed stitches. The piece wasn't matted; it went all the way to the frame, which was of some dark wood with a very narrow gold stripe on it. "I suppose she framed it herself," said Betsy.

Martha looked at it in Betsy's hands. "Yes, I think so. We mostly did, back then. It wasn't as if it was real art."

Betsy smiled. "You know, Diane Bolles came into my shop not long ago. She thinks needlework is valuable and hopes to sell some of it in Nightingale's, which as you know commands some stiff prices."

"Wouldn't that be nice? I know some of us have far more pieces tucked away than we have on display. There just isn't enough wall space."

Betsy smiled. "Diane said people should rotate their displays, because otherwise it becomes invisible." She hid the front of Jessica's work against her chest and asked, smiling, "What color did she do your initials in?"

Martha thought. "Let's see, the heart is pink, Carl's initials are gold . . . so, uh, blue, to match the flowers."

Betsy laughed and turned the frame around. Martha laughed, too. "Diane obviously has a point," she said.

Betsy turned it back to look some more. The *MW & CW* were worked in a simplified gothic style—and, she noticed, were not quite centered. And, now she held it so the weak winter sunlight beaming through Martha's kitchen window fell on it, the area around the *MW* and the ampersand was a slightly different shade of pink than the rest of the heart. Remembering her own difficulties, Betsy could guess what had happened. Jessica had gotten it wrong, torn it out, done it again, possibly gotten it wrong again. Whether after once doing it wrong or twice—or three times—she'd run out of pink. And Betsy knew now from her own bitter experience with embroidery that dye lots can vary, so that even buying the same brand and color number didn't guarantee a perfect match. And if Jessica was like Betsy, she didn't notice the difference until she'd redone the doggone section she'd frogged. And about then she saw the initials weren't centered.

And she said to herself what Betsy would have said: *To heck with this. I have a friend in pain who needs to see this more than I need to get it done perfectly.*

Betsy felt a sudden kinship with Jessica. Betsy's bright red scarf had at least three errors in it. She had gone back and corrected others, but these three hadn't been discovered until Betsy was at least two inches away from them. And she just didn't have the heart or whatever it was that possessed "real" needleworkers, who would undo hundreds of stitches to correct one wrong stitch. And guess what? The scarf was just as warm as if it had been knit without errors.

Besides, if people like Jessica and Betsy decided to undo and redo until they got it right, the scarf and this touching tribute might *still* be unfinished, languishing in drawers somewhere, waiting for the needleworker to get over her frustration and take it up again.

She was suddenly aware that Martha was waiting for her to continue. "I'm sorry, I was standing here woolgathering—" Betsy chuckled. "—literally, because I was thinking about knitting. Thank you for showing this to me. It's kind of an inspiration." She handed it back.

Martha looked at it doubtfully. "How can that be?"

"It tells me I should keep going toward my goal and not think so much of the process."

Martha smiled. " 'Finished is better than perfect.' You'll hear that a lot from needleworkers, though most of them take it as advice, not a rule."

"If needleworkers ruled the world, there'd be less done, but what got done would be done exceedingly well. I'll stay in touch and let you know if I find anything important or have more questions."

Monday morning there were enough customers, some with complicated questions, that noon had come and gone before Betsy and Godwin knew it. Perhaps it was because the day was sunny, a continuation of Sunday afternoon. The temperature now, at one o'clock, was forty-seven; the streets and sidewalks were wet from melting snow. "What is this, global warming?" asked Betsy.

Godwin said, "Could be. But the forecast is for much colder tomorrow." He said this with a curious sort of satisfaction. *I think he's proud of the harsh winters they have up here,* thought Betsy. *He'll actually be disappointed if we don't have at least one blizzard before Christmas.*

"How about I go get us some lunch?" said Betsy.

"Sandwich and salad for me," said Godwin. "Thanks."

She went next door to the sandwich shop and bought two chicken salad sandwiches. Instead of potato chips, she got a double order of a "finger salad," made of baby carrots, celery sticks, cherry tomatoes, and rings of sweet bell peppers—no dressing, even on the side. After eating her sandwich and enough of the crunchy stuff to feel satisfied, she washed her hands and began working the counted cross-stitch pattern again.

"Godwin, do you do the backstitching as you come to it, or wait and do it all afterward?" she asked, holding out the pattern of a raccoon, now nearly complete.

"Oh, I *hate* backstitching," he said. "So I always put it off until the end." He reached for a carrot. "These really *are* good for your eyes, did you know that? I used to have *such* bad night vision, I was actually terrified to drive after *dark.*

Then I needed to lose five pounds and started eating these things instead of candy, and one evening I was out on the road and I asked John, 'Why does everyone have their lights on so early?' Because it didn't seem dark at *all* to me."

He cocked his head and looked at her. "That's what it's like for you, isn't it?"

"Oh, I suppose my night vision is about as good as the average person's."

"No, I meant about detecting. While the rest of us wander in darkness, it's all clear as noontime to you. You've been going out talking to people, collecting clues, and now you got more of them from questioning Martha and Alice this weekend. I bet you've formulated a theory about what really happened, haven't you?"

Betsy stared at him, then began to laugh.

Godwin sat at the library table, a blank white piece of evenweave and a heap of perle cotton floss in front of him. The Monday Bunch hadn't arrived yet, and there were no other customers in the shop. The radio was playing light jazz and big band music.

He preferred needlepoint to counted cross-stitch, but he had fallen in love with a pattern and decided to try it. He was sorting the floss, smoothing the strands through his fingers, inhaling the faint scent of the fibers, enjoying the texture. His eyes were distant. The pattern, an angel in a forest watching over a fawn, called for silks on dark green cloth, the center worked in shades of dappled sunlight. But he was going to work it on white in darker colors. Except for the angel, which he would work in cream, gold, yellow, and palest green. The forest all around would be a threat of dark green, deep blue, brown, and black. Even the edges of the fawn would be darkened. A quarter stitch of white in its eye would make it look afraid, perhaps. The subtle shimmer of perle cotton would tease the eye into finding shapes of wolves or cougars. If this worked—if!—he would enter it in the State Fair next year.

He sat dreaming of blended colors while his fingers stroked and smoothed and separated.

"Godwin?"

He came back to himself abruptly, aware this wasn't the first time his name had been called. "Yes?" He looked around. It was Patricia Fairland.

"Oh, is it time for the Monday Bunch meeting already?" he asked.

"No, not yet. I came early because I wanted to talk to Betsy. Is she here?"

"No. You can ask me."

She smiled. "Are you her Watson?"

"I wish. She's playing this one very close to her chest. I know she's finding things out, she comes in excited or sad. But she won't share."

"Well, I didn't want to talk to her about this skeleton business anyway. I'm going antique hunting this weekend and I wanted to know if she could come along. She likes antiques, doesn't she?"

"I have no idea."

"I'll ask her when she comes in. Do you know where she is? The meeting starts in about fifteen minutes."

"At the nursing home out on Seven. She's starting to look for someone who would love to have a little Christmas tree."

"Oh, is she keeping up Margot's custom? How sweet! I'll have to donate an ornament." Pat turned toward the tree on the checkout desk. It already had half a dozen ornaments on it. "Which one of those is hers?"

"She hasn't finished one yet. She's doing a counted cross-stitch one. Jessica was here on Saturday and says she'll do a crocheted angel for the top, and I'm going to do a kitty in a stocking on plastic canvas."

"I'll bring mine in next Monday," said Patricia, and she went to see if any new needlepoint canvases had been put up on the doors.

The nursing home was clean, and there were cheerful paintings on the walls, but it was still depressing. Patients slumped in wheelchairs or slept in easy chairs or looked with sad, haunted eyes at Betsy as she went to the window separating the receptionist from the front lounge. Betsy explained her errand and was shown to the director's office around the corner.

The director was a pleasant woman, and her office had a real wood desk but was otherwise very modest.

"I'm Betsy Devonshire," said Betsy. "My sister Margot owned a needlework shop called Crewel World, which I have inherited. She used to offer a small Christmas tree with handmade ornaments on it as a gift to someone who didn't have anyone to remember him or her. I'd like to continue that custom."

"Unfortunately, we have a number of patients who rarely or never have visitors," said the director. "Most of them have Alzheimer's, but that doesn't mean they wouldn't like to get a present or have a visitor." She consulted a list. "But you know, we also have a patient whose mind works a little strangely, but who is quite aware and alert. She is all alone in the world. She might make an excellent candidate for your gift. Perhaps you'd like to meet her and see for yourself?"

"All right," said Betsy a little doubtfully. What could she say to someone whose mind worked a little strangely? She had no experience with this sort of person. She reminded herself not to say anything about the tree, which wouldn't be given away for weeks, and besides, she had only begun her search for a person to give it to.

She followed the director obediently and was taken to a double room. The other bed was stripped to its mattress which meant, the director said, that Dorothy didn't have a roommate at present. Betsy remembered reading somewhere that the death rate in nursing homes would give a hardened combat sergeant fits. The room was clean, with an attractive bow window, its deep shelf containing a big geranium and a plaster statue of Elvis.

"Dorothy made that in our crafts room," said the director, and left Betsy alone.

Dorothy was in bed, her blankets pulled up to her chin. She was very old and frail, exceedingly thin. She peered at Betsy fearfully. "Who are you?" she asked.

"My name is Betsy, and I've come to say hello."

"Hello. Can you take me with you when you leave?"

"Don't you like it here?"

"The food is terrible and the nurses are mean."

"I'm sorry you don't like this place. Did you really make that Elvis statue?"

"They made me make it. I wanted to make the clown, but Robert got to do that. He always gets what he wants because he's a man, and men are little tin gods. Are you the police? I think thieves work here. I can't find my glasses."

"No, I own a needlework shop. I sell knitting needles, embroidery floss, and crochet hooks."

"I used to knit."

"I'm still learning how. I made this scarf, and I'm making my first mitten."

"I made love, I made supper, I made good time with my Oldsmobile Ninety-Eight," she said.

Betsy, beginning to feel she was Alice through the looking glass, asked gamely, "Where were you born?"

"I was born at home a hundred and two years ago."

"Where's home?"

"There used to be a place in Excelsior, Minnesota, for me, a long ways from here."

"It's not so far. I live in Excelsior."

"All the people who live in Excelsior are wicked."

"Not all of them, surely," said Betsy.

"Yes, all of them. I had a son named Henry, and he got a girl drunk and scared her. I told him he was a bad boy and would come to a bad end." Her eyes filled with tears. "I didn't mean anything by it, but they played eight to the bar, Company B, and he died, a Dutchman shot him in the head in the water. Never set foot in Omaha, he was shot and drowned both together. And Alice was married to our pastor, the naughty girl. But I never told."

"It was good of you not to tell," said Betsy, trying hard to stay with the sharp curves of this discourse. "So that makes one good person, doesn't it?"

Dorothy chuckled, the tears gone as if they had never existed. "I guess so. But everyone else was bad. Vernon Miller hit Gertrude, broke her nose when she was only fifteen. The sheriff wouldn't arrest him, he was a bad sheriff. Vernon wanted to marry the girl, but she was too fast for him. She kissed all the bad men, and Carl, too. He was the worst. He pretended to be good, but he was in love with all the girls."

"Didn't you like Carl Winters?"

Dorothy nodded sagely and looked at Betsy slantwise with clever, pleased eyes. "He cheated on his mistress. He was the worst."

"You mean he cheated on his wife."

"He cheated on everyone who was a woman. He said he loved them, but he talked like a chicken, cluck, cluck, cluck, only he never laid that egg."

"Trudie—Gertrude—was his mistress?"

Dorothy chuckled. "Everyone was badly wrong. He met his mistress at the State Fair and got all greasy. They used to grease pigs and a pole at county fairs. He done her wrong with Gertrude, but he was doing Gertrude wrong, too."

"What about his wife?"

"She didn't talk to common folk like me, proud, proud, the first deadly sin. Carl wasn't proud, but he was a bad man. They were all bad."

"I don't understand. Who was Carl's mistress?"

Dorothy nodded several times. "Her husband flew in airplanes way up high in the air, but they got him anyhow. She fried hot dogs and served hot food and soda pop. She thought Carl would marry her, but they had a big fight and then he ran away."

"Who thought? Trudie?"

"Trudie thought Vern would marry her, but he joined the army, and she was mad."

"No, Vern didn't join the army until after Trudie disappeared."

"She ran away with Carl."

"No, she didn't," said Betsy. "They found her bones on a boat, the *Hopkins*."

"Ah," said Dorothy, and closed her eyes. But after awhile, she opened them again and looked sideways at Betsy. "Who are you?" she asked.

Betsy sighed. Then she remembered a simple test for brain function. "Do you know what year this is, Dorothy?"

Dorothy frowned. "It's later than nineteen ninety-seven, isn't it?"

"Yes, it is. And who is President of the United States?"

The eyes were suddenly clever and amused. "I always guess Dwight David Eisenhower, because he was my favorite."

Fourteen

❖

It was Tuesday, late-closing night. Betsy was dead tired. There hadn't been many customers that evening, but practically every one of them had been disappointed because either the shop didn't have exactly what they were looking for or Betsy couldn't answer their how-to questions. The honeymoon, she realized, was over. She shouldn't have sent Godwin home at five; his encyclopedic knowledge and indomitable good humor would have made the evening at least endurable.

Not for the first time, Betsy wondered what on earth she thought she was doing, trying to keep the shop going. She should be working for some other company, for someone who knew his or her business, someone who would give Betsy only tasks she could actually do and not make her responsible for the welfare of the entire company. Someone who would be positively aggravated if Betsy attempted to shoulder more responsibility than she'd been hired to carry.

She could sell the shop if she wanted to, she didn't have to wait until her sister's estate was settled. Margot had had the wisdom to incorporate, to name Betsy as an officer of the corporation, so that when Margot died, the shop went directly into Betsy's hands, to do with as she pleased. Why was she torturing herself like this?

She looked around the shop. It was quiet right now, the darkness outside a splendid contrast to the twinkling Christmas lights in the windows. The shop was warm with color. The track lights picked out baskets heaped with wine, amber, royal blue, and pine green wools, made deeper the patterns of the sweaters. It was all so attractive! But like all beautiful temptations, full of traps for the unwary. One saw the beautiful yarns and the finished sweaters or pillows or framed projects on the wall and wanted to have done that, wanted the admiring comments of friends when showing off a finished project. The problem came when one actually tried doing the work, because the work was arduous and difficult.

A painted canvas in the "final discount" basket caught her eye. The design was of a round basket full of balls of wool. A customer had nearly bought it awhile ago, then changed her mind, saying there was a spotted cat asleep in that basket, and she didn't like cats. Betsy couldn't see any cat, and neither could another customer consulted on the matter. That's why the canvas was desperately seeking a buyer; whoever had designed it wasn't much of an artist.

Betsy decided to put a more attractive canvas on top. She pulled the flawed canvas out and then paused to take another look at it. Here were black and white not-quite-round shapes that could almost be a black and white cat, curled tight, with some overlapping balls of yarn—was this dark purple or more black?— well, sure, here were the ears, and here the black tail overlay a white leg. What you'd do, if you wanted the cat to stand out, would be to brush the floss that you used to color the body, and maybe do a little backstitching or shading on the yarn balls, and not do that ball in dark purple but in wine or even a cherry red. Then the way the cat had snuggled itself into the basket of yarn would be more apparent. Look at how it was holding onto that green yarn, like a child with a doll.

Why, this was clever and attractive!

She'd marked the canvas down to ten dollars, which was within her own price range. Plus she got an employee discount. Let's see, how many colors would she need?

She was arranging a selection of DMC skeins on the canvas when the door went *bing* and Mayor Jamison walked in.

"Hiya, Betsy!" he said cheerily.

"Hi, Your Honor," she said, laying the DMC 321 (a rich red) next to the 821 blue—too obvious?

"How many times do I got to tell you? Just call me Odell."

"Sorry, Odell." She smiled at him. "What brings you in here? Thinking of taking up needlepoint?"

He chuckled. "Naw, I haven't got the patience for that sort of thing. I came to ask if it's true you're investigating the murder charge they've brought against Martha Winters."

"I'm trying. Jeff Winters's attorney said he needed to hire a private investigator, but he can't afford a licensed one. So he's asked me to look around and see if I can't come up with something to create reasonable doubt."

"Well, I've got kind of a weird story to tell you that may or may not help. It happened back when I was just a kid. I didn't think anything of it at the time, but now they found that skeleton on the *Hopkins*, maybe it means something."

"Odell, if you've got something you think is relevant, you should bring it to Sergeant Malloy."

"Oh, I already did that. He wrote it down and thanked me. But in the interest of fair play, I'm also telling you. What happened was, they towed the *Hopkins*—the *Minnetonka III* she was then—over to the City Docks from the dredging company, where she'd sat pulled up on the shore for years. They put a temporary patch on the hole in her bottom, which was caused by ice from a late freeze, and they were gonna take her out the next morning and sink her. I was eight years old, but I already had a notion that sinking her marked the end of an era. After all, I'd caught my first bass off her stern, y'see. So after dark I snuck out of the house and went down to see if I couldn't pry something off of her, kind of a souvenir. Now in July, dark comes after ten o'clock at night. I'd never been out that late before, except on the Fourth of July watching fireworks, and that was with my folks and about eight hundred other people.

"So here I was, all alone, sneaking from tree to tree through the park, toward the docks. There was a streetlight at the bottom of Water Street, so I could see the boat floating in the water alongside this barge, and there was this big pile of boulders and concrete chunks and old bricks heaped up on the shore. What they was gonna do was pile the rubble on the barge and tow it out with the boat, then pry off that plug on the bottom of the boat, and then pile the rubble into her to make her sink. Bein' wood, y'see, she wasn't gonna go down easy."

"So the *Hopkins* was sitting there empty."

"Oh, there was some rubble in her, maybe to test out how much they'd need, I don't know. Me an' four or five other kids had been to see her during the day, that's how I knew all that, and where she was. They'd let me climb on her, and me and some of my pals was gonna take something from her then, but they was watching too close, so we didn't.

"Well, anyhow, that night I got as far as the rubble when I heard someone on the boat. I'd talked it over with my best pal Eddie, who double-dared me to do it, so I thought maybe it was him. You know, trying to scare me so he could razz me the next day. So I come out and there's this man jumping off the boat onto the barge. I'd already said, 'Hey—' meanin' to say 'Hey, Eddie!'—and this fellow fell off the barge when he heard me. He spun around and came rollin' up the dock toward me in an awful hurry, but I was probably halfway home by the time he got to where I'd been standing, and I was in bed under the covers about forty-three seconds after that. I didn't go back, even to watch them tow her out, and so I never did get my souvenir."

"Who was it?" asked Betsy. "The man. Who was it?"

"I dunno. I didn't get a good look and didn't particularly want one. What I remember is, he wasn't fat or skinny, and he wasn't wearing a tie but he wasn't in overalls like a workman, either. I think I remember a coat or a jacket, though it was a hot summer night. He seemed big and dangerous coming up toward me, but that's because he about scared the pee out of me."

"Did he say anything?"

"I don't think so. And I didn't hear him running after me, but I was too scared to look over my shoulder to make sure."

"And you never told anyone?"

"Told them what? That I snuck out of my house and went down to the docks to steal something off a boat and got run off before I could accomplish my mission?"

"Oh, well, when you put it that way . . ." Betsy said and the two smiled at one another.

"Sure," Jamison said. "I kept waiting for the fellow to ring our doorbell and tell my folks what I'd been up to, but after a week went by and nothing happened, I figured I was safe. It all kind of faded into the background until they raised the boat and found that skeleton. Then I got to thinking, and finally decided I'd better tell someone. So, what do you think?"

"I think you saw the person who murdered Trudie hiding her body on the boat."

Jamison, suddenly serious, wiped his mouth with the edge of his hand. "Me, too. And it wasn't Martha Winters, was it?"

The store was closed at last. Betsy made sure the doors were locked and hastened up the dark and lonely street to make a bank deposit. The bank was barely two blocks away if she went by way of the post office.

Then she went upstairs to her apartment, took off her good clothes, and put on a thick flannel robe she'd bought at a consignment store in San Diego during her divorce proceedings. It was practically an antique and had been designed for a big man and so came nearly to the floor and overlapped comfortably in front. It had broad vertical stripes of gray and maroon and looked like something Oliver Hardy might have worn—and for all she knew, he had. Movie stars' castoffs were known to turn up in California consignment stores. She loved the robe; it was her "blankie," and generally made her feel comforted.

But it didn't tonight. Betsy heated a can of soup for supper and unbent so far as to feed half a cracker to Sophie, who actually ate it. Then, feeling a headache coming on, Betsy took her contacts out, swallowed a couple of aspirin, and lay down on her bed. She curled onto her side and tried to make her mind go blank. In a few minutes Sophie, purring loudly, came up on the bed and fell heavily beside her, tapping her hand in a request for a stroke.

Betsy complied, because stroking a cat is a soothing operation for the stroker as well; but tonight her mind remained a jumble of thoughts. Sophie was snuggled close beside her at about hip level. A fight over whether or not the cat was allowed on the bed hadn't lasted long; the night after coming home from the vet's, Sophie had cried piteously outside Betsy's bedroom only five minutes before Betsy got up and opened the door.

Sophie had slept with Margot. Obviously, the cat missed Margot. And so did Betsy. Why shouldn't they take comfort in one another's company during the long, dark hours of the night?

Now she stroked the cat's head and was rewarded with a deep, sighing purr.

She wondered what Sergeant Malloy was going to do about Mayor Jamison's story. Surely he would agree now that Martha wasn't the murderer. It was probably Carl Winters who Jamison had seen. Carl had murdered Trudie, hidden her body on the boat, and—being seen—fled town. Carl had no way of knowing the little boy would run home and not tell anyone. Doubtless as he shook the dust of Excelsior from his feet he was sure the sheriff or constable or policeman, at the excited direction of a small boy, was already making a grisly discovery in the bottom of the old *Hopkins*.

And that's why Martha never heard from him. He was afraid someone would see the letter or postcard and know where he'd run to. Or that Martha would turn him in herself.

So okay, that was solved: Carl murdered Trudie and hid her on the boat.

Well, then, who murdered Carl? If Carl was the murderer, surely no one would want to stop him from telling his story.

A glimmer of an idea began to lift its sleepy head from the back of Betsy's mind. She tried to discern something, anything about it, but felt herself growing less connected, drifting away . . . the cat purring . . . the new needlework project . . . who would want to murder Trudie?

Then she dreamed she was walking up Water Street toward Nightingale's, and ahead of her was her mother, dressed as if for church. Betsy ran and ran, calling, until she had nearly caught up. Then her mother turned, and it was her father who turned and smiled down at her from under her mother's best Sunday hat, the one with a veil.

Wednesday displayed a morning sky the color of old pewter, though the forecast did not call for rain or snow or sleet. It was supposed to be Betsy's day off, but Godwin had a doctor's appointment and they agreed he could take the rest of the day and Betsy would have Thursday off.

Betsy was ringing up a sale of a single skein of embroidery floss—and that was not by far the smallest sale she had ever made.

"Thank you, Mrs. Frazee," she said, handing over the blue Crewel World bag.

As Mrs. Frazee left the shop, she left the door open for Jill, in civvies. Jill wore a magnificent Norwegian blue patterned sweater with pewter fasteners over a white turtleneck sweater. Her mittens were white angora wool, and her cap matched them. She looked wonderful, and Betsy said so.

"Thanks," said Jill, blushing faintly. "I came to ask you to lunch—except, if it's all right, I'd like to buy something from next door and we can eat it while we chat."

Betsy thought she read anxiety in Jill's face. "Of course," she said. "Could I have soup and a salad instead of a sandwich?"

"Oh, for that you want Antiquity Rose, not next door," said Jill. "Their house salad is marvelous, and their soup comes with a homemade bread stick. My treat; I'll be right back."

"Wait a second," Betsy said. "How do you stand it out there with just that sweater?"

"This sweater is a lot warmer than it looks," said Jill. "Anyhow, it's not really cold out yet. It's not even freezing today." She smiled a superior smile. "Wait till January, then you'll see *weather!*"

Jill came back with a double paper sack and a friend. "You remember Melinda Coss, don't you?" she asked.

Betsy wasn't sure, but she smiled and said, "Hello, Melinda."

"Wait till you see the ornament she made for the tree!"

Melinda had a white cardboard cube in her hands, which she put on the checkout desk. She lifted out a small round ornament with a basket hanging from it.

"Oh," said Betsy, "it's a hot-air balloon, how clever!"

The balloon was made of many tiny pentagons, each covered with silk gauze cross-stitched with holly, ivy, pine, a Christmas wreath, mistletoe, a bow, or a sequin snowflake held in place with a tiny bead. In the basket underneath was a mouse wearing a crown and carrying a tiny pair of binoculars.

"Do you get it?" asked Jill, and sang, "Good King Wencesmouse looked out . . ."

Betsy laughed so hard she nearly dropped the ornament, which alarmed her into stopping. "Where did you find the pattern?" she asked, thinking how well it would sell in the shop, especially with one already finished on display.

"I made it up. I found a papercraft book that told me how to make the ball of pentagon shapes—"

"Geodesic dome!" exclaimed Jill. "I *knew* there was a name for that shape!"

Betsy said, "You should publish the pattern, Melinda. I mean, can't you just see this on the cover of a needlework magazine?"

Melinda smiled. "I've already submitted it."

"I'm afraid this won't go along when I give the tree away—if that's okay with you," said Betsy. "I want to keep this on permanent display."

"Of course, if you like," said Melinda, beaming with pleasure.

A few minutes later, Jill and Betsy were seated at the library table. The salad was great, with candied pecans and bits of orange; the soup a hearty ham and potato with an interesting blend of herbs.

"These bread sticks are wonderful," said Betsy. They were thick and chewy, with a thin crust of cheese on top.

Jill agreed, then asked, "Did Odell Jamison come to you with his story about seeing a man climbing around the *Hopkins* the night before it was sunk?"

"He sure did. What does Malloy say about it?"

"He thinks Odell saw Carl. He figures Carl came to meet Trudie and saw Martha getting off the boat and Trudie not there. He got suspicious and went for a look and found Trudie's body. Then he saw the boy—Odell—watching him and got scared and ran away. That would explain Martha's handkerchief on the boat and Carl's disappearance. Carl had no idea the boy wouldn't raise the alarm, and every reason to think they'd blame him for the murder. Then, all these years later, they find Trudie's skeleton. Carl hears about it. He's old and tired, and back home there is a business that is rightfully his, that he can sell or lease to take care of him in retirement. So he comes home, phones his wife to tell her he's back, and she, in a panic, agrees to meet him and instead she shoots him."

Betsy had been nodding through all this, finding it very believable—until the end. "Wait a second," she said. "If I thought someone was a murderer, I don't care how many years later it got to be, I wouldn't call that person and say come over and let's talk about it. And I certainly wouldn't agree to meet that person all alone in a motel room."

"Not even if it was your wife?"

"Not even if it was Mother Teresa."

"Hmmmm," said Jill.

"What does Martha say?"

"On advice of counsel, she's not talking to the police."

"Smart lady. What else does Malloy have?"

"He says the gun used to murder Carl was a World War II era semiautomatic pistol. Standard army officer issue. It was in excellent condition, with original ammo in it. Something found in an attic, maybe, tucked away with an old uniform. Not registered."

"Interesting," said Betsy. "Was Carl in the army?"

"No. He was 4F, Malloy said."

"Has he looked at Vern Miller?"

"Vern went down for his physical two weeks before he got on the bus to boot camp. At that time, their quarrel was over and she was fooling around with a new boyfriend—not Carl, someone else. Trudie was murdered the night of July first, the boat was sunk July second, he left town July third. He couldn't have known two weeks prior to that the sequence of those events."

"He knew the date he was leaving for boot camp. Maybe he went down to talk to Trudie, say good-bye, they quarreled, and he killed her."

"Malloy doesn't think it happened that way. How would Carl fit into that scenario?"

"He was the one Trudie was to meet in the park. He gets there in time to see Vern murder Trudie and hide her body. He runs because he knows the whole town knows he's been flirting with Trudie."

"Hmmmm." Jill nodded.

"What else does Malloy have?" asked Betsy.

"He found a picture of Trudie in an old yearbook and says the reconstructed face matches close enough."

"Well, that's not exactly news."

"No, I guess not. He says Carl was shot once in the chest from across the room. Nicked his heart, blew one lung all to pieces. He was sitting on the bed and fell back and died of internal hemorrhaging."

"Ugh," murmured Betsy, swallowing.

"And whoever murdered him waited until it was over, then walked to his side and wrapped his fingers around the gun, then let it fall on the floor beside his hand."

Betsy said, "Wait a second. Would bullets that old still fire?"

Jill said, "Malloy says some of the best ammo ever made was made during World War II. He says lots of gun enthusiasts look for it. He says there are markings on the casings that indicate it was made in Lake City in 1941. He says the gun had three bullets fired from the clip, but there was only one empty shell in the room and only one bullet in Carl."

Betsy said, "Ah."

"What, 'ah'?"

"Well, I didn't know ammunition could last that long, so probably whoever got the gun out didn't either. So he digs through his souvenirs of the war and finds the gun, and takes it someplace to test fire it. Who do we know who was an officer in World War II? Or a gun collector?"

"A gun collector would unload it, wouldn't he?"

"Okay, who came home from the war and put everything into a trunk in the attic?"

"Hundreds of people, probably."

"Help me out here, Jill. Who involved in this mess is a World War II veteran?"

"Vern Miller—no, he's Korea. And Vietnam. Plus he wasn't an officer."

Betsy thought that over. "Anyone else?"

"Jessica's husband was killed during World War II in a plane that got shot down over Germany." When Betsy looked exasperated, Jill shrugged. "Sorry! Those are all I know about. I suppose you can check somewhere, veterans' services or someplace; I know Malloy is doing that. Oh, I know Alice's husband didn't serve because he was a minister. Malloy's probably thinking along the same lines you are. But he also says you can go to gun shows and buy just about anything."

"Yes, but you can trace those guns, and he told you this was not traceable, right?"

"Yes."

A little silence fell, then Jill said, "Have you got anything new?"

"I was looking for someone to give the tree to, and I talked to this woman in Westwood South Nursing Home. Her name is Dorothy, and—"

"Dorothy Brown? She was my grandmother's best friend!" said Jill. "Is she still alive? How is she?"

"She's bedridden, and her mind is not as clear as it used to be."

Jill chuckled. "I don't remember her mind ever being as clear as it used to be. Of course, she was an old woman when I was a little girl." She sobered. "I should go see her someday. It's awful that I thought she was dead."

"She might not know you," said Betsy. "You know how old people get confused about modern events but remember old ones clearly? Well, Dorothy is losing old stuff, too. She said that her son never went to Omaha and was both shot and drowned by a Dutchman."

"She always says that, and she's absolutely right. Her son died in the ocean while trying to land on Omaha Beach in Normandy, shot *and* drowned, just the way she tells it."

" 'Dutchman'!" exclaimed Betsy. "That's an old word for a German. She said she is a hundred and two. Could that be right, too?"

"She was a hundred two years ago. I went to her birthday party. She knew who she was and what was going on then. They asked me as part of the entertainment to give her that little test, you know, when someone has a head injury? Do you know where you are? What year is this? Who is the President of the United States?"

Betsy said, "She told me she always guesses Dwight Eisenhower because he was her favorite."

Jill laughed. "Yes, that's what she said at the party, too. It's her favorite joke. She's not as ga-ga as people think. I really should go over there and see her."

* * *

It was Saturday. Melinda's Christmas tree ornament was as big a success as Betsy hoped it would be. She was taking the names of women who wanted to own the pattern when it was published. She would have to make sure she had enough forty-eight-count silk gauze in stock. Her own name was not on the list, of course; she was still struggling with the "easy" ornaments in the stitchery kit. Counted cross-stitch on forty-eight-count silk was not remotely within her skills at this point.

Betsy worked for awhile on the duck. Even now that she could see the picture forming on the cloth, she would still occasionally make a mistake and have to undo some stitches. And she couldn't always just unsew them, the floss would catch on something and she'd have to get out the scissors.

Finally, she just put it away and got out her knitting. She was doing another scarf, this one changing colors from blue to a blue and white mix to white and back to blue every twelve inches. She was on the seventh foot—blue—and not sure if she was going to stop there or not. If she didn't, she was going to have to do a blue/white mix, a white, and blue again so the ends would match, and a ten-foot scarf was an awful lot of scarf. Not for her to knit, for the wearer to manage. She loved knitting this; it was her favorite pattern of knit two, purl two fifty-two times with an odd stitch at either end. It made a thick, attractive pattern and she was doing it in pure wool. There were hardly any errors in it. Godwin had admired it; she hoped he had no idea it was to be his Christmas present.

Godwin was in New York with his lover, taking in a Broadway show and ice skating at Rockefeller Center. Shelly was here, consulting with a customer over some ribbon embroidery.

Betsy felt the familiar calming effect of the knitting start to take over. The customer bought her ribbon and left. Shelly came to kneel on the floor in front of Sophie and stroke her.

"When does her cast come off?"

"Monday. She's going to miss it, I think. I knew someone in California who had a dog that broke its leg, and forever after, whenever you'd scold that dog, he would start to limp."

Shelly laughed. It was very quiet in the shop; Betsy had forgotten to turn on the radio. But the silence felt good, so she didn't say anything. And Shelly didn't either, which was pleasant.

Betsy began to think about the case. "What if Odell didn't see Carl?" she asked.

She didn't realize she'd said it out loud until Shelly said, "Have you found out something new?"

"I don't know. There's just so many little things, it's hard to think of a scenario that covers all of them. You think up something that might have happened, and it seems right, but then you realize there's one little piece sticking out. Like, if Martha murdered Trudie and Carl knew it, why did he call her when he got back to town? Wasn't he afraid she'd murder him, too?"

"If he was, he wouldn't have called her, so he wasn't," said Shelly.

"But then why did he run away and not write to her or phone her? She thought he was dead."

"Maybe he did get in touch, and she was ashamed to tell anyone. Maybe he ran for some other reason than Trudie's murder. Maybe Martha was a terrible wife, jealous and mean to him, and he'd finally had enough."

"But he came back because they found the skeleton, you know. He had a newspaper clipping about the discovery of the skeleton with him."

"Oh. But what was it you were saying about Odell not seeing Carl?"

"Odell came by and told me he saw a man climbing out of the *Hopkins* the night before it was taken out and sunk. He was just a little boy, and when the man saw him, he got scared and ran home."

Shelly stood, all excited. "A man? Odell saw a man? Well, then, that's it, right? Carl murdered Trudie. Odell saw him after he hid the body. Wow! That's it!" She saw the way Betsy was looking at her and said, "Isn't it?"

"But then where did the handkerchief come from? Did Carl mean to frame his wife? Why?"

"Because . . . because he wanted to get rid of her. And in a divorce she would have gotten half his property."

"Not in 1948. And why hide the body? If you mean to frame someone, you don't put the body where it is likely never to be found."

"All right, that's right. What is it you're thinking of?"

"I'm not sure. This very old woman named Dorothy told me something important, but there's this other piece that's mixed in with the things I've already seen or heard. It keeps nagging me."

"What is it?" asked Shelly.

"That's the problem. I can't remember."

Fifteen

❖

Saturday evening the shop closed at five; Christmas hours didn't start until after Thanksgiving. Betsy changed to a pair of dark corduroy slacks and her old cotton sweater, had a quick supper, fed the cat, and left for Jessica Turnquist's house. She had called Jessica, who agreed to talk to her.

Jessica lived in the shortest row of townhouses Betsy had ever seen: three of them. They were white stucco with dark wood trim, located right down on the lakeshore off West Lake Street. A row of three garages lined one side of the driveway and there was a parking area beyond them. Jessica's townhouse was the middle one; she had left her porch light on.

A sharp breeze lifted Betsy's collar and rustled the brown leaves on an old oak tree that hadn't gotten the word that autumn was over. The air smelled of woodsmoke.

The fire was in Jessica's living room, in a small white-brick fireplace beside a pretty atrium door that was mere yards from the restless lake. The living room was not big but was interesting architecturally, with a canted ceiling and a loft, and the furniture was light and sophisticated.

"I have a friend who's a decorator," said Jessica when Betsy remarked on the decor. "Left to myself, I'd do everything in overstuffed blue brocade. Would you like a cup of coffee? Or some tea?"

"No, thank you, I just had supper."

"Is it too hot in here for you? Whenever I build a fire, it warms me up so much I sometimes have to open a window."

"No, I'm fine. The fire is nice."

"Sit down then," said Jessica, and when Betsy chose the couch, she took a beige leather chair. She touched her upper lip with a Kleenex and turned her slightly bulging eyes on Betsy. "What did you want to talk to me about?"

"About several things. What made you decide to make friends with Martha after Carl disappeared?"

"We already knew each other from church. Then Carl answered an ad I put in the paper and worked for me during State Fair for three or four years. I remember how a lot of people sort of drew the hems of their skirts away from her after—well, after Carl went away. She told several people she was sure he was dead, that a robber perhaps had thrown his body into a passing train. It seemed a strange thing to be sure of without any evidence, but it was then I realized she had loved him and missed him terribly, and she couldn't believe he'd just abandoned her. She was sure that even if he'd left her willingly, he'd at least write to her at some point. She was so sad and distressed, and no one would reach out to her, and well, it just made me angry. So I did that little needlework heart for her, whipped it up in kind of a hurry, and gathered my courage and went and rang her doorbell. Oh, she cried and cried when she opened the package! She was so grateful, and she needed someone to talk to so badly, and so I just kept going back. And over the next few weeks we found we had lots in common. She came over to my place for Saturday night supper—I had an apartment back then—and had me over for Sunday dinner. Soon it wasn't just pity anymore, we actually became good friends. And we've been friends ever since."

Betsy said, "It was good of you to reach out like that."

Jessica looked at the fire. "Thank you," she murmured. "But she was as good for me as I was for her."

"It must have been difficult for you, being a widow back then. But at least your husband died a hero. Did he win any medals?" Betsy, looking around, said, "I don't see his picture anywhere. Surely you were proud of him."

Her head lifted. "Of course I was proud of him! He was an officer, so handsome and so brave! We were very much in love, but we'd been married only a few months before he left for duty overseas. And then, when he didn't come home, and I went on to other things, he became just that small part of my life, less than a year, and less and less significant to what I was doing. Finally, I put all his things into storage. I should do something with them; I don't have anyone to leave them to, so I don't know why I've kept them."

"I understand the custom is, one of his friends packs his belongings up and sends them home. Was there a diary or anything like that?"

"No, just his uniforms and military records. And three medals, I remember them. But not that flag folded into a triangle, because that comes off the coffin, and Ed never had a coffin. But there was a long and kind letter full of little stories about Ed and his crew. I kept that, too."

"Really? Any museum or historical society would be very pleased to have something like that. Historians love letters and diaries at least as much as uniforms and medals."

"They do? Well, yes, I suppose they would. I never thought about giving Ed's things to the historical society. What a good idea. Perhaps the other families would be interested in the letter. The men were such good friends, as soldiers get to be in combat, and the stories are all about them as well. And they were all lost when the plane went down, burned to nothing. No trace was ever found, no bodies sent home to bury."

"That's why you felt sympathy for Martha, isn't it? I mean, her not having a body to bury, either."

Jessica showed that genuine smile that made her pretty. "You do understand, don't you? I remember dreaming that he came home and told me he'd missed the plane, he hadn't gone on that last mission. That was my favorite dream for a long time."

"Was there a gun in the box?"

"A gun?" Jessica looked alarmed, as if the conversation had turned an unexpected corner into unfriendly territory.

Betsy smiled her warmest. "Yes, in the box your husband's friend sent. It would have been a sidearm, a government-issue semiautomatic pistol."

Jessica's mouth pressed into a thin, disapproving line. "Oh, no. There was a what-do-you-call-it, a holster, but they don't allow guns to go by mail, it's illegal."

"Oh, yes, of course, I should have thought of that."

"Oh, there's something I have for you, so before I forget—" She got up and went to a glass-fronted cupboard whose bottom half was drawers. She opened a drawer and brought out a thin, clear-plastic bag. Inside it was a white crocheted angel made rigid with starch. "This is my donation for the tree."

"Thank you." Betsy held the bag up and twirled it very gently. "You know, my mother used to make these. I don't know what happened to the ones she gave me."

"Perhaps I can make one just for you."

"Perhaps you can show me how to make them—like showing someone how to fish versus giving him one?"

Jessica chuckled, a rich, pleasant sound. "Yes, of course, that would be better, wouldn't it? I've got a pattern somewhere. I'll bring it to the next Monday Bunch meeting."

Betsy thanked her again and left. *Oh, Jessica, you brave liar,* she thought as she got into her car. *But how can I prove it?* And then she remembered something Jill had told her. If it was true, then there was actual physical evidence, something more than mere words, which could be twisted to mean anything.

A few minutes later, she drove down the narrow lane that led to Martha's house. The road looked white in her headlights, which made her think it was coated with ice, but her tires clung obediently when she braked, and she realized it was dried salt. *Didn't the Romans used to sow an enemy's fields with salt to keep him from growing food?* she thought. *How can any vegetation survive alongside the streets and highways after a whole winter of this?*

But the blue spruce looked very healthy in her headlights, despite its proximity to the street. Betsy pulled into the driveway.

She rang the bell and Martha answered promptly, though she was surprised to find Betsy on her doorstep. "I thought it would be Jess," she said.

"Oh, if your friend is coming over, I'll leave and come back some other time," said Betsy.

"No, don't do that; she called to say you were coming to visit her, and I assumed she'd call or come over so we could talk about it." Martha smiled. "We do talk about you, you know. Come in, come in, we're letting all the heat out standing here with the door open."

Betsy came in and shed her coat and boots on the little tiled area. "Do you two always tell each other what's going on?"

"Pretty much," nodded Martha. "Anytime I get something new to talk about, I call her, and she lets me know what's going on with her. Did she tell you what you wanted to know tonight?"

"I think so," said Betsy.

"You sound hopeful. Are you actually making progress at last?" Martha's face was itself desperately hopeful.

"I think so," Betsy repeated. "It's been really hard, trying to figure something out just from what people say, or don't say. That's why I'm here. I think you can show me something that will speak for itself."

"I'll show you anything I have. What is it?"

"Would you be willing to take Jessica's heart out of its frame and frog some of it while I watch?"

". . . Frog?"

"Pull out some of the stitches."

"Why do you want me to do that?"

When Betsy explained, Martha, her face inexpressibly sad, went and got the needlework Jessica had given her.

Godwin came in Monday morning a few minutes late. He was positively agog with curiosity. "Tell me, tell me, tell me!" he demanded, slamming the door of the shop.

"Tell you what?" said Betsy, lifting both eyebrows and widening her eyes at him.

"That won't do, you clever wench; I heard all about it at the Waterfront

Café. You went to see Sergeant Malloy Saturday night and a little later he arrested Jessica Turnquist for murder. Is that not the proper sequence of events?"

"Approximately."

"Wait a minute." He hung up his beautiful camel wool coat and went to sit at the library table. "Now," he said, "begin at the beginning, and don't stop until you reach the end."

"Don't you even want a cup of coffee?" asked someone else, and he looked toward the back of the shop, where Jill and Shelly were emerging with steaming cups.

"If you've already told them, I'm going to *die*," said Godwin.

"No, we just got here," said Shelly.

"Why aren't you in school?" asked Godwin.

"Field trip sponsored by the parents, who are also supervising the children," said Shelly. "I'm off only until noon," she added, "so let's get started. You will not believe how pleased I am to be here." She put a cup in front of the chair at the head of the table and gestured at Betsy. "I understand you were positively brilliant," she added. "So sit and tell us everything."

Jill had turned back to the coffee urn and now reappeared with a cup for herself and another for Godwin. "I'd've stopped for cookies," she said, "but I didn't want to miss this, either."

Betsy sat down. "It was just a whole lot of little things that kept not adding up," she began. "If Vern murdered Trudie, where did the handkerchief come from? If Martha murdered Carl, where did she get that old, unregistered pistol? And why did it still have World War II–era bullets in it? If Carl murdered Trudie and was coming home to confess, why would someone kill him? If someone wanted that handkerchief to frame Martha, why hide it and the body on the boat? If Alice Skoglund murdered Trudie to stop the blackmail, why would she also murder Carl? I just kept going in circles, trying to decide what was and what was not important.

"One thing that didn't seem important was that a very old woman said that Carl met his mistress at the State Fair and got all greasy. Another was that Jessica's husband was an army air corps officer. But that one was very important; it was practically the key to this thing. He was the only person connected with this case who was an officer in the military, and that was important because it's officers who get issued sidearms; enlisted men get rifles. When he was killed overseas, a friend packed up his belongings and shipped them to Jessica with a nice, long letter. Jessica said she got a holster but no gun. Army-issue guns are supposed to be turned in at the end of service, but that was a rule much observed in the breach. Jessica said she'd put everything into storage long ago, and that was important, because it meant it wasn't in her house, where a visitor might come across it and steal it.

"Martha said she lost two handkerchiefs with that wonderful lace trim. One she left at the Guthrie Theatre, where it ended up as a prop. The other she lost at the State Fair. Jessica had a fried-food stand at the State Fair—that's where she and Carl got all greasy. Carl worked for Jessica there, selling battered hot dogs on a stick. Martha thought she lost that handkerchief in the pig barn, but when she came to the fair, surely she would either stop by the stand to see her husband, or if Carl wasn't working they would both stop by the stand to say hello and perhaps buy something to eat and drink. And if Martha dropped that gorgeous handkerchief by the stand, someone might have picked it up and given it to Jessica, or Jessica herself found it. In either case, she kept it."

"Why?" asked Shelly. "Didn't she know whose it was?"

"Of course she knew," said Betsy. "But she was having an affair with Carl and wasn't very fond of Carl's wife. She knew Martha was proud of those hand-kerchiefs, so it was a fun and spiteful thing to keep that handkerchief rather than give it back."

"Now, just wait one second," said Godwin. "Trudie worked in a café, so she got all greasy, didn't she? You took the word of a senile old woman who doesn't know Sleep-Around-Sue from a respectable widow."

"No, she said Carl met his mistress at the State Fair and both of them got greasy. Jessica told me she and Carl had to constantly mop the floor at her stand to keep the grease under control. Dorothy isn't senile in the ordinary sense of the word; she knows plenty. Everything else she told me was true. Her son was killed on Omaha Beach during the Normandy invasion, that same son got Al-ice Skoglund drunk at a private gathering and took liberties with her—"

"No!" said Godwin, much edified, and Shelly's eyes gleamed at this deli-cious tidbit.

"Oh, I shouldn't have said that!" said Betsy, alarmed. "So if that little fact goes beyond this gathering, I will fire both of you." And Jill looked at Shelly and Godwin with a glint in her eye that said firing might be the least of their troubles. Betsy continued, "In fact, we are going to be a whole lot nicer to Al-ice than we have been. She was very important to solving this case."

"Yes, ma'm," said Godwin meekly, and Shelly nodded, allowing the gleam to fade.

"Dorothy said Jessica's husband flew in airplanes and died in one, also true. Dorothy doesn't muddle her facts; she's just so tired of inquiries into her clarity of mind that she turns the tables on her questioners, making a joke or a riddle of their questions. While she spoke elliptically to me, she knew what she was saying and spoke only the truth.

"But," said Betsy, "I didn't know that until I talked to Jill. And even then, even if everything else she said was true, could it really be that Carl and *Jessica* were having an affair? It would explain a whole lot if it was. But how to prove it? And then I thought about something else Jill told me, and then I remembered that cross-stitch heart Jessica gave Martha, and I crossed my fingers in hopes I was right and went to talk to Martha."

"What did Jill tell you?" asked Shelly.

"That using metallic floss will leave a mark on fabric that only shows up after a long time. It kind of develops, like a photograph, into a gray or black mark. And when we took Martha's initials out of that fabric, there were black marks that spelled *JT,* for Jessica Turnquist. She had made that piece for Carl, not for Martha. The 'love forever' she stitched on that project was between her and Carl, not Carl and Martha. That's when I knew Jessica murdered Trudie."

"Now wait a second," said Godwin. "Odell saw a man running away from the boat. Jessica wouldn't look like a man no matter how you dressed her."

"Why was Jessica mad at Trudie?" asked Shelly.

"I'd've murdered both of them," said Jill.

Shelly and Godwin started at this odd confession from a law enforcement officer, but Jill only stared back. Then the three looked at Betsy to go on.

"Jessica told me she was surprised to learn how much Martha loved Carl. Carl bad-mouthed Martha to everyone, especially women he was flirting with. But I think Jessica was more surprised than average, because Carl told her he and his wife had a sham of a marriage. It's a favorite line of philanderers, more so back then when divorces were rarer. Nearly as common as 'My wife doesn't understand me.' And it's what Carl told Jessica, along with 'She says if I try to divorce her, she'll hire a private detective, which means it's possible your name will be dragged through the courts.' The truth is, he didn't want a divorce at all, because he was a businessman in a small town where his wife was highly thought of. If he dumped her for Jessica, they'd have to leave town and start over. Carl had a wife who, I think, he actually loved, and he had a healthy, intelligent son, and a successful business. I don't think he was willing to give all that up. But he wanted the thrill of a beautiful mistress, too.

"Jessica may have actually believed the lies Carl told her, or at least told herself she did. She thought Martha was a shrew who wouldn't set her unhappy husband free. But as time went on, Jessica grew impatient; if she wanted children, if she wanted to show her love openly, something had to happen. So she began to press Carl, until at last he lost his temper and they had a fight. And to show her he was not going to be bullied, he stomped off and flirted more seriously than he ever had before with someone he knew wouldn't blow him off."

"Trudie Koch," said Shelly.

"That's right," said Betsy. "Everyone noticed it; Martha scolded him about it. And Jessica was furious. She went into a tool drawer and got out a hammer—"

"How did you deduce this?" asked Godwin, amazed.

"That's from her confession," said Jill. "We both were there when Mike took it down."

"Go on, go on," Shelly urged Betsy.

"She went down to the Blue Ribbon Café close to the end of Trudie's shift and found that Trudie was already gone. The man at the counter said she was meeting someone at the City Docks at midnight. Jessica casually finished her coffee and left, arriving at the docks—which were just across the street—in time to see Trudie waiting alone. Trudie turned as Jessica came up and Jessica swung the hammer. She says she doesn't remember much of the next several minutes, which I understand is normal. Then she went out to the end of the dock and threw the hammer as far out as she could. On her way back, past the body, she dropped the handkerchief. Did I mention she brought the handkerchief with her? She told Sergeant Malloy this murder was an angry impulse, but that can't be true. She came prepared to frame Martha.

"Then Carl arrived for his rendezvous with Trudie. Jessica was waiting, and she told him what she'd done, pointing to the handkerchief and saying Martha was sure to be arrested for the murder and then, at last, Carl could divorce her and they could be married.

"Cold, cold, cold," murmured Godwin.

"She must have been crazy," said Shelly.

"Not within the meaning of the law," said Jill.

"And Carl just about went nuts. It made his previous rage seem like nothing. What on earth did she think she was doing? Martha was his wife; he loved her with all his heart; he wasn't about to see her framed for murder! Then he calmed down just a little bit and got as scared as he'd been furious; he could see that any attempt to tell the truth would involve him in a very unpleasant way. He told Jessica to go home, that he'd take care of everything. So she did. And Carl picked up the handkerchief and Trudie's body and hid them both on board the *Hopkins*. As he was getting off the boat, he saw a boy watching him. How much had the kid seen? If he'd seen Carl carrying the body out there, Carl was in big, big trouble. He ran after the boy, but he vanished into the night."

"That was Odell, wasn't it?" said Shelly.

"That's right. So Carl fled. He ended up in Omaha and worked mostly at menial jobs, scared for years he'd be located. All this while, he thought the cops were looking for him. Then, at last, he sees a newspaper article, a reprint of a humorous story about a town gossip and a skeleton. All those years in hiding, and no one had been looking for him. And now his wife—same last name, so she never remarried!—is about to be charged with murdering Trudie Koch. So of course he comes home. Maybe he can still redeem himself, pick up the remaining scraps of his former life. He checks into a local motel and he calls his wife to see if things are as reported.

"But she won't talk to him, won't let him tell her what he knows. She hangs up on him. She got over Carl Winters many years ago. But then, as she does whenever she has some news to share, she calls her very best friend, Jessica Turnquist. Martha says she doesn't know what Carl had to tell her, and Jessica says she can't imagine what it might be, either.

"But Jessica does know, of course. After all—the changes she's made in herself, her good reputation, her close friendship with Martha, her comfortable life in this town—are all about to be destroyed because of a few minutes of jealous rage cooled to ashes these fifty years.

"She hurries to that storage place and digs into the box of her late husband's military gear and takes out the gun. She drives out into the country and fires it twice to make sure it works, then she goes and knocks on Carl's door. He is surprised to see her but lets her in."

Jill said, "I wonder what they talked about? She didn't say."

Betsy said, "Maybe she tried to rekindle his old affection for her. Or did she try to scare him into promising to leave town again? But in the end she shot him. She waits until he stops breathing and then presses his still-warm fingers around the gun, lets it drop from his hand, and leaves. She thinks the police will conclude it's suicide."

Jill said, "But she doesn't know from forensics. Such as, when you shoot yourself, you leave powder residue on the wound and on your hand. Carl's body had no powder burns; he was shot from farther than the length of his arm."

"And *that's* why Jessica stopped begging you to prove Martha didn't murder Trudie," said Godwin. "Oh, my God, what a *witch!*"

Jill said, "The choice was to tell the truth and go to prison or keep silent and let Martha go to prison. Not a hard choice for her."

"What made you decide to look under Martha's initials on that heart?" asked Shelly.

"Martha had shown the needlework to me. She said it was that gift that started their friendship. Carl's and Martha's initials were in the middle of the heart, his in gold. And they weren't quite centered. And the heart was two different shades of pink, meaning it had been redone at least once. At first I thought Jessica was like me, willing to redo only so many times before deciding it was the thought that counts, not the perfection of the gift. And she was in a hurry. But after what Dorothy said, it occurred to me that maybe, originally, the heart had Carl's and Jessica's initials, both in gold. *JT* is a lot narrower than *MW.*"

"Why didn't she just throw it away?" asked Godwin.

"I don't know," said Betsy. "Maybe she was afraid someone would find it. And besides, she was trying to think of some way to really distance herself from what had happened, and really make sure no one suspected she and Carl had ever had an affair. There was Martha, so unhappy and vulnerable, and she got this idea to make friends. Turning the needlework into a gift might have seemed like a good idea."

Shelly said, "Maybe she had this evil notion of seeing something that was about her and Carl's love on display. Not in her own house, that would be dumb. So why not in Martha's house? I can see that tickling some sick person's fancy—"

"Ugh!" said Godwin. "You are making me not like Jessica at *all!*"

"Anyway," said Betsy, "she picked out her initials and cleared an area of heart around it. But she was out of both the gold and the pink she'd used originally. She had a pink that seemed to match perfectly and she had some green, so she used those. The newer pink, unfortunately, faded more quickly than the old, which kind of called attention to Martha's initials. And when Martha and I frogged her initials, we found some gray marks on the evenweave, just like Jill said there would be."

"Good job!" cheered Shelly, as if to a bright student. "Sorry, force of habit."

"So now I had real evidence of a motive," said Betsy. "I called Sergeant Malloy from Martha's house, and he came right over, bless him. I explained what I thought had happened and how it seemed to be the only version of events that didn't leave little bits sticking out. I told him that I'd talked to Jessica earlier and asked her about a military-issue gun, so that she might be trying to destroy evidence at that very moment. He drove over to her house, and she opened the door, and he smelled leather burning. By the time he got what was left of an old holster out of the fire, she was crying and telling him some nonsense about how the historical society wouldn't want an empty holster, and then that my questions had frightened her, and she kept changing her story until she finally told the truth."

"By which time she had been Mirandized twice," said Jill.

"Jessica Turnquist, hot mama and murderer," murmured Godwin, shaking his head. "It seems so unlikely. I mean, she's so *old.*"

"Someday you'll be old," said Betsy.

"Never!" promised Godwin, hand on heart.

"She did beautiful crochet work," said Shelly.

Then silence fell, a long silence, in which many memories formed them-selves into new shapes.

"I'm glad I was able to help Martha," said Betsy at last. "I'm sorry it had to be Jessica."

"She was always nice to me," said Shelly.

"I guess this confirms everyone's belief that you are a natural-born sleuth," said Jill.

"Yes, well, sleuthing doesn't put money in the cash register. Shelly, why don't you get started dusting. Goddy, bring out that shipment of wool and re-fill the baskets." Everyone stood, but nobody moved. They were all trying to think of a valedictory statement.

Jill said, "Betsy, Malloy said to thank you for your assistance, and to look for a summons in the mail."

Shelly said, "I guess Martha can fire that expensive lawyer and put what's left of the money toward the mortgage on her store. I'm going to bring some clothing to be dry cleaned, increase her earnings a little bit."

They looked at Godwin, who shrugged and said, "And since it looks like Dorothy gets the tree, I'd better make a pair of ruby red slippers to put on it."

> Turn the page for your free
> Lacy Butterfly cross-stitch pattern.

© *Design by Denise Williams*

A Lacy Butterfly

Designed by Denise Williams

After a bobbin-lace pattern

by Virginia Berringer

This pattern is worked in a combination of straight or back-stitches and cross-stitches to look like bobbin lace. Use two strands of white cotton floss on 16-count, dark blue, evenweave fabric.

First, stitch around the border of the fabric to prevent fraying.

Then, find the center of the pattern and mark it. Find the center of the fabric. (If you are making a bookmark, count up seventeen rows from the bottom of the fabric to find the last row of stitching. Mark this row, count the rows across to find the middle, and begin stitching in that place.)

Cross-stitch the head and body first, then the cross-stitch portions of the wings. Do the straight stitches (backstitching) on the wings and antennas last.

A Stitch in Time

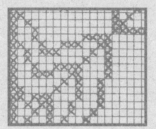

ACKNOWLEDGMENTS

I can't imagine doing this series without the help of both friends and willing strangers. Luci Zahray, toxicologist and poison guru, terrified me with how easy it is to poison someone. Chad Eschweiler knows about bankruptcy estate sales. The people of the real Excelsior, Minnesota, remain sanguine about my use of their beautiful town as my setting—and I want to add that all of these crimes and their perpetrators are entirely fictional. The members of RCTN, the Internet newsgroup, are a godsend to people as ignorant as Betsy Devonshire—and me.

On the actual writing end, I sincerely thank my official editor, Gail Fortune, and my unofficial editor and dear friend, Ellen Kuhfeld.

One

✥

John Rettger regarded the bustle and noise in his church hall with pleasure, hope, and concern. He was short, with mild blue eyes and ears that stood out beneath a circle of white, fluffy hair. He sat on a hard wooden chair, his offer to help gently but firmly refused, partly because he was the loved and respected rector of Trinity Episcopal Church, and partly because he was clumsy.

Renovation would begin after the Christmas holidays. A columbarium would be added, something that had been talked about since before he became rector over ten years ago. The library would be expanded, the administrative offices reworked and redecorated, and the long hall between the old chapel and the new church upstairs would have a magnificent hammer-beam roof and a tile floor installed.

But first, the church hall would be gutted and redone. The haphazard collection of small rooms that over the years had halved its size would be removed, and a modern kitchen installed. The antique and dangerous wiring would be replaced, the plumbing updated, the walls and ceiling repaired and repainted, the floor refinished, and new furniture brought in. The only thing unchanged would be the big, functional fireplace.

He turned from the volunteers for a moment to look at the fireplace. It had a native pink limestone surround deeply carved with apple trees—the Wealthy apple was first grown in Excelsior. Beside it was a magnificent fir tree eight feet tall, the annual gift of a Christmas tree farmer. Still on it were a few construction-paper ornaments, made by poor families in the area. Parishioners had been selecting one or two during Advent to buy something suitable for the person described on the ornament. They'd wrap their gift and bring it to Trinity by the last Sunday in Advent, which, this being Thursday, was three days off. The gifts would be delivered Christmas eve.

As Father John watched, three men came to tilt the tree, then lift and carry it up to the big hall outside the nave of the church. The instant they touched it, it shed needles as an alarmed cat sheds fur. He smiled to himself: fir tree, furry cat.

Before the renovation began in earnest, all the movables in the church hall had to be taken away. The valuable things had already been removed, and the volunteers who ran the thrift shop had emptied their area. But there were long tables (some with legs that used to fold, the rest with legs missing), a pair of grubby wing chairs, two very shabby couches, an army of bent folding chairs, assorted broken hand tools, old Sunday school texts, a half dozen dim and ugly landscape paintings in cracked frames, an enormous collection of *House and Garden* magazines, a shoe box full of broken mouse traps, on and on—things needing hauling to recycling centers or a landfill.

As the rooms had taken haphazard bites of the church hall, odd little corners had developed. Some were turned into closets or storerooms that were later closed off. The very farthest had a floor that had never been finished.

Phil Galvin, a retired railroad engineer, came from that newly reopened room. In his arms was what Father John first took to be a piece of carpet or a small rug. The smell of mildew was strong.

"What have you got there?" asked Father John, his nose wrinkling.

Phil was short and gray, but his manner was brisk and his voice loud and a little harsh, as if he had spent his life shouting orders in all weather. "I dunno. But it's probably been back in there a hundred years."

Phil looked around and saw an elderly card table still standing. He unrolled his find across it. The rug was about four feet wide and long enough to hang off both sides of the table. It reflected its wadded-up past in uneven creases. "Well, looky here! It's a tapestry! And hand stitched, too. Betcha it was done by the women of the parish."

Father John came closer. "Why, it's the Good Shepherd," he said. The tapestry depicted the Savior in a white tunic with a dark orange mantle draped over it. He was carrying a lamb on one forearm and held a shepherd's crook in the other hand. A bright metallic double halo surrounded his dark head and beard, and six grayish-white sheep huddled close to his knees, their black legs making a complicated crosshatch over the bottom of the tapestry. The design seemed unsophisticated, the figures without shading or perspective, and the background a lightly mottled tan. But every line of it was drawn boldly, by a real artist. Something about the sheep said they felt safe, and by his expression, Christ was pleased to have found the lost lamb.

"Nice, ain't it!" barked Phil. "I was wrong, it's not old, that design's too modern."

It was nice, very nice. But it was also dirty and odorous with mildew. The stitching appeared to have worn away in several places. A long strand of tan yarn hung off one edge.

Phil, his head turned sideways as he studied it, said suddenly, "Say, I bet this is Lucy Abrams's work!" He explained, "She was Father Keane Abrams's wife. Father Keane was your predecessor. She liked big needlework projects and designed some of her own."

"Ah," nodded Father John. He had never met his predecessor's wife. She had died of a heart attack the same day her husband suffered a severe and unexpected stroke. By the time Father John was called to be rector, months later, he had been greeted by an interim priest. Now, eleven years later, Father Keane still lived, but he lay helpless in a nursing home, beyond any ability to understand what had happened to him.

"*Say, Mrs. Fairland!*" yelled Phil suddenly. Father John jumped, then realized the man was summoning her, and he turned to look.

Patricia Fairland was a member of the vestry, a beautiful, talented, and intelligent person, one of those upper-middle-class women who intimidated Father John effortlessly. But apparently not Phil, by the way he'd shouted and was now gesturing impatiently at her.

She was in khaki slacks and a cotton sweater and had wrapped her hair in a complicated way with a silk head scarf. Though she had been working hard for hours, she looked fresh. She came toward them with an inquiring look, pulling off cotton work gloves.

"What's up, Phil?" she asked. "Oooh, where did you find this?"

"Back room," said Phil, pointing. "What do you think?"

"Attractive," she said. "I don't remember ever seeing it before. Moths have been at it, though. And uh-oh, it reeks of mildew. If I get a vote, mine is for tossing it."

"I think this was designed and stitched by Lucy Abrams."

"You do?" Patricia looked at it with more interest, though she didn't come any closer. "Why do you think that?"

"Well, I know she was working on a big project just before she died. She and Donna Claypool and Marge—oh, what was her name, I can't remember—and maybe some other ladies. I never saw it, and I thought she hadn't finished it. But here this is, and it's like some other designs she made. I'd look close for her initials, but it stinks pretty bad."

"Her initials?" said Father John.

"She liked to put her name or her initials or her husband or daughter's name somewhere in her work. One time she did it by crossing blades of grass so they spelled out *Lucy*. You'd never notice it unless someone told you it was there."

"That's right, I'd forgotten about that." Patricia started to come closer, then waved a hand in front of her nose and sneezed twice before she could step back out of range. "Allergic to mildew," she said thickly. "Whew!"

Phil asked her, "Still think we should toss it?"

She hesitated, then asked back, "How sure are you this is Lucy Abrams's work?"

"I'm not sure about anything except death and taxes. We can ask her daughter to confirm it, but I'll bet you a dollar she'll say it is. You sound like you're changin' your mind."

"Well, you know the parish thought the world of the Reverend and Mrs. Abrams. And mildew's not hard to get out. From here it looks like it's done in continental or basket weave, so it should be easy enough to repair. And it is a very nice piece. So yes, I am changing my vote—on a contingency. If it is her work, we should try to restore it. And if we succeed, I think it should go in the columbarium. Or better, the new library." She brightened. "*Which* we should rename in honor of Father Keane."

"Say, that's an idea!" said Phil. "I'll help you with the repairs, if I may."

"I was counting on you to volunteer."

Phil saw the look Father John was giving him and said, "I'm a pretty good needleworker, took it up when I retired."

Patricia said, "He designs and stitches steam engine needlepoint canvases. He has them all over his living room. Extremely nice work."

"Thank you, Patricia," said Phil with a little bow. "Coming from you, that's a real compliment." Phil had very old-fashioned manners.

"How much will this cost?" asked Father John. He had been increasingly alarmed at the ever-rising estimates of this renovation—the hammer-beam roof being a particularly costly item—and the reluctance of his parishioners to be as generous with donations as they were with ideas.

Patricia gave him a quelling look. "I'm sure this won't cost Trinity a cent, Father," she said. "Once people find out what it is and what our plans are for it, they'll be more than willing to contribute to restoring this marvelous find."

Father John had heard that tone of voice before. It meant that will he, nil he, this tapestry was going to get cleaned and repaired in time to hang in the Reverend Keane Abrams Library.

When Betsy came down to Crewel World on Friday morning, she saw out the big front window that it was snowing, huge flakes like the ending of a Christmas movie. Betsy sighed. It had seemed so beautiful a few weeks ago—and it was no less beautiful now. But also, she was now resentfully aware, snow had to be shoveled. Shoveling was not pretty.

Even the Christmas lights around the window didn't jingle her pleasure circuits. White Christmases should be a novelty to Betsy, who had spent many

years in California. But they were no novelty in Minnesota, which often saw
white Thanksgivings—they had, this year. This was the sixth snowfall since
mid-November. Hardly any had melted between the last three storms, so it was
really piling up. Betsy was already tired of snow.

She went to unlock the front door and let Godwin, her one full-time employee, in. He stood a moment on the plastic mat, dusting his shoulders and
stamping his feet. He was young, blond, good-looking, an expert at all kinds of
needlework, and Betsy's most valuable asset. She was ashamed she couldn't pay
him what he was worth.

He hung his beautiful navy blue wool coat up in back, and they began the
opening-up routine, turning on lights and putting the start-up cash in the register. Betsy stooped to turn on the radio hidden on a shelf half behind three
counted cross stitch books. A local station was playing all Christmas music all
the time, and Betsy kept the radio tuned to that, though at this point she was
more than weary of singing heraldic angels and Rudolph's cruel companions.

Godwin got out the feather duster and began dusting.

She looked around. "A-rew?" came a cat's polite inquiry.

"I see you, Sophie." The big white cat with the tan and gray patches had
come downstairs with Betsy and made herself comfortable on "her" chair, the
one with the blue gray cushion. The sweet-mannered animal was as much a part
of Crewel World as the Madeira silks or the eighteen-count needlepoint canvases.

"Rrrr?" trilled Sophie hopefully.

"No snacks," said Betsy, and the cat sighed and put her head down to wait
for a more malleable visitor.

Betsy went to the back room to put on the ugly but warm coat she'd found
at a secondhand store and went out to clear the sidewalk in front of her shop.

When she came back in, breathless, falling snow had already laid a thin
white cover upon her work. She went to plug in the teakettle and put the shovel
away. Godwin had finished dusting and was restocking the yarn bins.

The shop door opened—*bing!* went an electronic bell—and George Hollytree came in, feebly stamping snow off his galoshes. Betsy hurried to take his
attaché case and help him with his heavy tweed overcoat. "Hello, Betsy," he
piped in an old man's voice.

Mr. Hollytree was eighty-nine. His small, rheumy eyes were set in a pale
face as rumpled and folded as an unmade bed. His hands were roped with blue
veins and his fingers were gnarled, the fingernails thick and yellow. He was,
God help her, Betsy's accountant.

But for all his years, he looked Betsy up and down with an appreciative
smile. Betsy was plump by today's standards, but the old man would have de-

scribed her as voluptuous. More, her complexion was fresh, her clear blue eyes were friendly and intelligent. Her cropped hair had some natural curl to it, and she had recently converted its gray streaks to blond with a home coloring kit. And she was nearly forty years younger than he was, a mere child.

Mr. Hollytree walked stiff-kneed to the library table in the middle of the shop. He sat on the chair at the head of the table and opened his attaché case and brought out a very up-to-date calculator, the kind with several memories and the ability to print a tape.

"You are doing quite well keeping up with transactions," he piped, speaking slowly around ill-fitting false teeth. From a pocket in the lid of the case, he extracted a file folder with Crewel World in thick black letters on its tab. Betsy noted two other file folders in the pocket as she walked behind him, and wondered who else was keeping this man from a happy retirement in a warm climate. She sat down at his right, prepared to listen.

Mr. Hollytree had turned up a couple of weeks after her sister Margot's death. He'd explained that Margot kept computer records of sales and purchases related to the shop, and he turned them into tax records and an account of profit and loss. Frail as he appeared, he seemed to know his business. And Betsy, helplessly ignorant, had reached for his expertise like a drowning sailor grabbing at a broken spar. She had followed his instructions, and the second time he appeared, she had a computer disc ready for him. He had insisted on explaining the charts he made of her data, and though he'd been as slow and patient as he could, she understood only that so far, the shop was paying for itself.

Until today. Today, his high-pitched sigh was deeper, his shuffling of papers more snippy, his patience with her ignorance more fleeting.

"Now look here, young woman," he said at last, causing her to blush like a teenager, "what it comes down to is this: You are on the verge of spending more than you are taking in. This cannot continue. Early winter is supposed to be the best time of year for a business that serves the public, but yours is actually doing worse than last month." His mouth formed a grim line. "Unless you do remarkably well this month, this will be the third or fourth worst Christmas since I have been keeping Crewel World's books."

Betsy felt a rush of defiance. "Perhaps if we checked, we'd find the bad Christmas seasons occurred for reasons beyond the owner's control, such as a bad economy or," she rushed to add, since the economy could hardly have been hotter, "bad weather?"

The old man glared at her, then his face wrinkled alarmingly as he began to cackle. "You are Margot's sister, all right!" he crowed. "I wondered if you would ever show your spunk, or if maybe your sister got it all."

Betsy smiled. "There's far too much spunk in our family for just one of us to hold it all, Mr. Hollytree. And I'm sorry we're not doing so well right now. But I'm doing the best I can, and I don't know what changes I can make."

"Since salaries are your biggest expense, you need to cut your employees' hours. Check what your competition is charging and charge less, even if it's only a penny less—and make sure your customers know your prices are lower."

Betsy nodded. "I'll talk to my employees about working fewer hours. Perhaps, with Christmas so close, they've got all their shopping done and won't be so disappointed in smaller paychecks. And I'll look into competition prices."

"Perhaps you should hold your after-holiday sale now. That means a special advertisement, but you'll more than make it up in extra sales."

Betsy hadn't done any advertising at all, and her face must have shown that, because he said, "I thought so, when I saw no expenses for ads. Some people may think Crewel World's gone out of business because its original owner is dead. I am sorry to add another expense to your burden, but advertising always pays, especially when there's a change of ownership."

Betsy hadn't thought about that. There had been so many people who rallied around her when her sister was murdered that it never occurred to her that there were people out there who didn't know about her. What a terrible thought; once-loyal customers who had found another source of supply! Customers who might still be loyal, who might keep Crewel World in the black, if only they knew.

Oh, yes, she must advertise, tell these people Crewel World was still here, ready to serve all their needlework needs.

But how, with money already in short supply? How much did advertising cost, anyhow? Where was the best place to put it? What should she say in her ad? She didn't want to make a further display of ignorance by asking her accountant. Maybe Godwin would know.

Mr. Hollytree was making a neat stack of her copies of his report. He paper-clipped his calculator printout to it before rising. Godwin brought his coat and helped him back into it.

Betsy answered his good-byes almost absently. Crewel World's logo, needle and yarn spelling *Crewel World* in cross stitch, should appear in the ad. And how deeply could she cut the prices of—what? What bargains would be most likely to bring customers in?

Though Godwin must have wondered what she was thinking, for once he didn't ask. Instead, he went to take inventory of the stitchery books in the box shelves toward the back of the store. Such books were a big favorite as Christmas gifts, and he wanted to make sure they weren't out of the most popular ones.

When the phone rang half an hour later, he was putting an order of little scissors, thimbles, and other items on a spinner rack near the back, so Betsy put down her pencil to answer it.

"Crewel World, good morning, how may I help you?"

A mild voice said, "Good morning, Betsy. This is Father John Rettger of Trinity. Are you busy at present? I can call back."

Betsy said, "Oh, hello, Father. Unfortunately, no, we're not busy. What can I do for you?"

"I don't know if you are aware, but we're about to start a major renovation of the church hall and business offices of our church."

Betsy had seen the story in the weekly *Excelsior Bay Times*. (What would it cost for a two-column ad in the Times?) "Yes, I read about it."

"Well, we're in a great uproar, moving furniture, cleaning out storage areas, and so forth. Not surprisingly, we are finding things we thought were lost or sold or given away long ago."

"Mm-hmmm," Betsy murmured. Her eye fell on the ad she had been designing. Would it cost a great deal more to put the word *SALE* in red?

"One of the things we're going to do is expand our library. We have found a tapestry in a basement storage closet that would be very appropriate. Unfortunately, the tapestry has been damaged by moths—not very badly, but noticeably."

"Mn-hmm." A tapestry, a huge ruglike thing people hung on castle walls.

"Patricia Fairland, who is a member of our vestry, has kindly volunteered to coordinate the restoration of the tapestry. She said I should tell you that it is not woven but stitched, a distinction I am afraid is lost on me. It is about six feet long and four wide, a beautiful thing, very appropriate for the use we hope to put it to."

That wasn't so enormous. But Betsy, mindful of those extra hours she was going to have to work, said, "I don't think I'll be able to volunteer right now, this is the busiest part of—"

"Oh, I wouldn't presume to make demands on your time. I understand that as new and sole proprietor of a business, your time is very limited. No, I was hoping you would be able to make a contribution of materials for the restoration."

This, on the heels of a warning of imminent failure to break even, should have made Betsy refuse immediately. But wait—surely there would be more stories in the paper as renovation continued, and a big one on completion. If there was a photo that included the tapestry, perhaps Betsy could be mentioned as contributing to its restoration. *Free advertising,* whispered the merchant in her.

So even as she took a breath to say no, Betsy changed her mind.

But then in the second it took to change gears and say yes, Betsy had another thought.

"I'd like to see the tapestry, see what materials are required, and how much," she said, because "not badly damaged" could mean anything. "Would that be possible?"

"Oh, of course. It wouldn't be fair to ask for a donation of material without an understanding of how much and what kind. Mrs. Fairland has told me that she would be glad to come in at the same time and explain to you what is needed. I understand there is a group of needleworkers who meet at your shop, the, er, Monday Bunch? Mrs. Fairland is going to ask for volunteers from that group to do the work. I'm very pleased she has taken on this added responsibility, as I have no knowledge whatever about the needle arts. Shall I ask her to phone you? Or would you rather contact her yourself?"

"I'll call her, I have her number."

"I want you to know that we appreciate your agreeing to do this, especially since you are not a member of Trinity."

Was there a hint of rebuke in his voice? After all, Betsy had been raised in the Episcopal Church, and her sister had been an important member of Trinity. But perhaps she was being too sensitive. What she said was, "That's all right, it's my pleasure to be of service." Because it was. She enjoyed being generous— when she could afford it. And in this case she might actually injure herself by saying no and thus giving free advertising to a rival needlework shop.

Betsy worked some more on the ad, called the weekly newspaper and was shocked by their rates, but agreed a salesman might call, then made herself a cup of raspberry tea and dialed Patricia's number.

Patricia wasn't available this coming Wednesday, which, Hollytree notwithstanding, Betsy was taking off. Christmas was on the horizon, and Betsy had shopping to do. Funny how the less money she had, the longer it took to find gifts. After going through the calendar and failing to find any mutually agreeable time and day between Wednesday and mid-January, Betsy said despairingly, "I don't suppose you're free this evening?" And to her surprise, Patricia was.

Two

❖

It was dark when Betsy set off for Trinity at quarter to six, and cold. In San Diego—no, Betsy wasn't going to think about that. She lived in Minnesota now, and she liked it, really she did. If not the climate, then the people. They had taken her to their hearts when she'd come here all dispirited and unhappy, and supported her through the even worse time after her sister had been murdered. And they had encouraged her to keep her sister's needlework shop open, which introduced her to a subculture she'd barely realized existed. There were people, mostly women, who would rather do needlework than eat.

Betsy halted in the middle of the sidewalk. She could remember when she'd liked embroidery. And she could remember a time when she thought people who did lots of needlepoint or counted cross stitch were obsessed, possibly a little crazy. But now she thought about how, when she was really lost in the sweet rhythm of basket weave, she, too, was on the verge of loosing little knots that daily life tied in the back of her neck.

She started walking again, smiling at herself, until she came to Water Street. The foot of Water Street was open to Lake Minnetonka, and the north wind had a long, uninterrupted start down the length of the lake. She quickly turned her back to its bitter bite and went up Water, past the Waterfront Café and the movie theater, the bookstore, the pet store, and the imported gift shop, crossed and turned right, up the hill to the church.

Patricia met Betsy at the glassed arcade between the tiny stone church, the first church built in Excelsior, and the large building that was so modern it didn't look like a church at all. Standing next to Patricia was Martha Winters, another member of the Monday Bunch. Martha was a short woman with snow-white hair and a round, pleasant face that made her look like Mrs. Claus, an effect emphasized by the fur trim on her wine-colored coat and hat. She was an expert counted cross stitcher but did just about every kind of needlework. Though well into her seventies, Martha had an alert and vigorous manner. She still worked part time in the dry cleaners she owned with her grandson.

"Jill Cross says she will try to drop by for a while before she goes on duty," said Patricia. "Phil Galvin couldn't make it."

"All right." Phil was a regular customer, but Jill was Betsy's good friend. She was a police officer with a quiet manner that belied her strength of character—and she did exquisite needlepoint.

Patricia bent and unlocked the heavy glass door and led them into the arcade. To their left was a large room in front of the big, new church, made fragrant by a tall Christmas tree that had half a dozen paper ornaments on it. Betsy inhaled rapturously. Another reason to be glad to live in the north: Christmas trees were less of an artifice here. In this part of the world, the message they had brought Betsy's pagan ancestors—that the world in winter had not died—still had meaning.

On one wall of the hall was a row of black-framed photographs of bygone rectors. The last one had a broad, sweet face and a big nose, with white hair and intense eyes under shaggy eyebrows. His smile was sizzling enough to provoke an answering one in Betsy. On the picture frame was a little metal plate that said he was the Reverend Keane Abrams, and giving the years of the pastorship, which only amounted to seven. *I wonder what he was like as a person,* thought Betsy.

Patricia and Martha paused at the head of a stairwell to wait for Betsy. She came out of her musings and hurried after them, following them down into darkness. At the bottom of the stairs, Martha and Betsy stopped.

Patricia's footsteps went ahead, paused, and lights went on in a room off a narrow hall. Betsy and Martha walked into a severely plain and obviously elderly room with a high ceiling and a magnificent fireplace at its far end. Because the church complex overlapped the hill it was set on, the left wall had windows and there was a door at the far end leading outside.

But Betsy's eyes were quickly drawn to the only furniture in the room, a card table near a wall with a large piece of light-colored needlework draped over it.

She approached and saw, on a neutral background, a near life-size figure of Christ as the Good Shepherd, the design flat and stylized. Christ, deeply tanned and sporting long black hair and a curly beard, wore a white robe under a dark-orange mantle. A lamb rested complacently on his right forearm, and he held a crook in his left hand. Around his head was a halo of two bold lines of metallic gold, with a blue gray stripe between them. Six sheep crowded around him, their expressions benign.

The work was done in plain diagonal stitching. Martha stepped forward and laid bold hands on it, even turning a corner of it over.

"Basket weave," she said, meaning the stitching. "And whew, is it mildewed!"

"Smells awful," agreed Betsy, wrinkling her nose. "Is that moth damage?" she asked, gesturing at a spot where the stitches were missing, exposing the heavy canvas. "I mean moth larvae, don't I? It's not the moths, it's the grubs, right?"

"That's right," said Patricia, and she sneezed. "Eggscuse be," she said, and held a handkerchief to her nose.

There weren't a lot of bare places, and most were smaller than the palm of her hand. Betsy smiled. She could supply the wool to mend this with very little strain. But, "What about the mildew? No one can work on it like this. Is there a treatment we can use?"

"Sunlight is good," said Martha—surprisingly, because she owned a dry cleaning shop. "But also you can mix one or two tablespoons of sodium perborate in a pint of water and sponge it on the mildew. That will get rid of the mildew stains, too, and it's a mild enough bleach that it shouldn't hurt the colors. I'll see about treating it before we start work."

"Thanks," said Patricia.

There were footsteps, and the women turned to see a tall woman in a police uniform coming toward them, taking off her hat as she approached. Her jacket was thick, her utility belt weighty, and her gun large. Above all that was a lovely Gibson girl face surrounded by ash-blond hair, pulled back into a short braid.

"Hello, Jill," said Patricia. "Glad you could come."

"I can't stay long." Jill came up to the table. "I've been meaning to call you, Betsy. Anything you want me to bring to the party tomorrow?"

Betsy was giving a Christmas party to thank her friends and employees for their loyalty. Both Patricia and Martha were coming, so it was all right for Jill to talk about it.

"No, I have everything I need, thanks."

Jill leaned closer than Betsy had dared to examine the tapestry. "This doesn't look so bad," she said. "That ground color should be easy to match. Who's working on it?"

"So far, just me, Martha, and Phil Galvin," said Patricia.

"I'm too busy with the shop," Betsy said, feeling a slight blush warm her cheeks at this need to justify herself. "But I'll supply the wool, the needles, Febreze, anything you need."

"That's generous of you," Jill said, frowning at the bottom left corner, where a strand of tan yarn hung down. "Are you in charge, Patricia?"

"Yes, I told Father John we could do this at no cost to the church. But Betsy, I didn't tell him to ask you to donate the materials. I'm sure we could raise the money to pay you."

"Oh, that's all right. It won't break me to donate a few yards of tan wool. How old is this tapestry?" The style of the design made Betsy think of the 1950s or early '60s.

Patricia said, "Ten or twelve years. But it has never been displayed that I know of. Lucy Abrams designed it and worked on it with other members of Trinity. I called her daughter, and when I described it, she said she remembered her mother and some other women working on it shortly before she died. She said she thought it was lost, thrown away." Patricia explained to Betsy, "Father Keane Abrams was Father John's predecessor, and one of the best-loved rectors we've ever had. Lucy was his wife."

"What a character he was!" said Martha. "A diamond in the rough, certainly, but a twenty-carat diamond, at least. His sermons were down to earth, addressed to the common man, which made us refined types sit up and take notice. Pithy, that's how we described his sermons."

Jill said, "My father liked him. But my mother thought he was probably a reformed burglar who should be a chaplain down at the jail."

Patricia, laughing, said, "The first time he stepped into the pulpit, I thought, *O Lord, what have we got here?* He looked like a longshoreman or a retired boxer. But in five minutes, I was thinking how wonderful he—" She broke off, blinking.

"What?" asked Betsy.

Patricia continued, "He wasn't here long, and retired from Trinity all of a sudden, saying he hadn't felt well for awhile, and he had a massive stroke a week later at home. His wife Lucy found him and apparently tried to help him up off the floor and had a heart attack. She was found dead beside him by their daughter Mandy. It was dreadful, just dreadful. Mandy went to live with an aunt, and Father Keane has been in a nursing home ever since. Can't talk, can't walk, can't feed himself." Real tears glittered on her eyelashes.

"It was awful for her to come home to that, just awful," agreed Martha. "So sad."

Patricia said, "Father John agrees that if we restore this tapestry and persuade the rest of the vestry, he will not object to it hanging in the officially renamed Reverend Keane Abrams Library."

There was a gleam in the woman's eyes that shone through the tears. Betsy exchanged a smile with Jill and Martha, who actually winked. They all knew Patricia. Even if Father John objected, the deed was all but done.

When Betsy walked out of the church hall after the meeting, snow was coming down again, blowing sideways in a stiff wind. It stung her cheeks, flapped the skirt of her long coat around her legs, and made her walk crabwise. She staggered down to the corner of Second and Water, where it blew even harder. Her hat lifted itself, and she barely grabbed it before it went sailing out into the street. She'd seen snowstorms like this on television, after an afternoon at the beach. She unwrapped her scarf from her neck and tied it over her head.

It was a struggle, those few blocks down Water, then a lesser one up Lake to her shop and home. Once safely inside, climbing the stairs to her apartment, she was suddenly overcome with a feeling of elation, as if she'd climbed a mountain. She remembered blizzards in her youth in Milwaukee, and she found it even more exciting now in her maturity to discover they still couldn't overmatch her.

* * *

The snow stopped by bedtime, and plows must have worked all night, because by Saturday morning the streets were clear. Snow was piled along the curbs, in mountain ranges so high that from inside the shop, Betsy could see only the roofs of cars as they went by. She cleared the sidewalk yet again, adding her own peaks to the Himalayas. Then she cut a narrow passage through to the street so customers wouldn't need ropes and pitons to get to her shop.

A few minutes later, a shadow passed the front window. Betsy looked to see a woman in a wine-colored, fur-trimmed coat holding her gloved hand to her face—the wind was cutting sharply this morning. She ducked into the slightly recessed door of the shop, the hand came down, and it was Martha Winters.

"Hello, Betsy, Godwin," she said as she entered. "I've come to pick up that bellpull. Is it back yet?"

"I believe so," said Betsy. "The finisher brought a whole box of things in just before closing yesterday."

She stooped behind the big desk that served as her checkout counter and brought up a large cardboard box with a sheet of paper attached to it. She looked down the list and drew a line through a name. "It says something of yours is in here."

Inside the box, rolled up like a fire hose, was a long, narrow piece of canvas covered with eggshell stitching. The finisher had sewn on a back of eggshell linen. Betsy unrolled the piece to reveal a scattering of chickadees and cardinals sitting on branches of holly and evergreen. "Very pretty," said Betsy.

"You think so?" said Martha with a little sniff. "My daughter-in-law hinted and hinted that this was what she wanted for her dining room."

"Don't you like it?" asked Godwin, coming for a look.

"Oh, it's all right," grudged Martha. "But no beads, no fancy stitches, no zing."

"Well, right now we're in an era of rococo needlework," said Godwin. "Someday people will find this very restrained and therefore particularly lovely."

Martha smiled. "So says the maker of the Christmas Stocking That Clatters When Touched."

Godwin laughed. "The pot pleads guilty, Mrs. Kettle! Still, I can't see a false stitch in this piece. Even the tassel at the bottom is perfect."

Martha had opted for that authentic finishing touch and had made it herself from red velveteen yarn. "How much?" she asked Betsy.

Betsy consulted the order sheet in a file folder. "Sixty-five dollars, including hardware." Which meant the stiffening dowel and string, and the hook and screws so it could be fastened to a wall.

Martha got out her checkbook. Signing with a flourish, she handed a check to Betsy and at the same moment her eye was caught by a sampling of tan, buff, neutral, and cream wools. "Are these for the Trinity project?" she asked.

"Yes," nodded Betsy.

"I've told some other Monday Bunch members, and they're thrilled at a chance to do something in honor of Father Keane. Even nonmembers."

Betsy said, "I thought I'd go over on Monday and see if any of these matched."

Martha said, "I'm glad you want to get right to it. There are volunteers in the church hall today, you know."

"There are? Doing what?"

"Taking down the old kitchen and making sure nothing's left behind in the rest of the downstairs. The contractor finished another job early and will be starting our renovation on Tuesday."

"Thanks for telling me. I'll go over on my lunch break today."

Mrs. Winters left, and the one other customer said she wanted to browse, so Betsy joined Godwin at the library table in the middle of the room. He had a project of his own back from the finisher, a magnificent Christmas stocking. It was the one Martha Winters had teased him about, stiff with beading and tiny bangles, ornate with fancy stitching. The design was of two children coming down a stairway to see Santa hiding behind a Christmas tree. Santa's beard was curled into French knots, the children's pajamas were of brushed satin stitching, the wallpaper was two-color gingham stitch, and the tinsel on the tree was made of microscopic glass beads. Across the top of the stocking *JOHN* was worked with silver metallic thread.

Godwin was arranging it in a shallow box draped with silver tissue paper.

"You're not going to hang it?" asked Betsy.

"I haven't decided yet," said Godwin. "John and I exchange gifts on Christmas eve morning, because he goes home Christmas eve and stays till late Christmas day. I suppose we could hang it after he opens it, but then I'd be tempted to put something in it, and I don't want to stretch it out."

"Do you have someplace to go to celebrate Christmas?" asked Betsy.

"I just told you about my Christmas." Godwin saw the start of compassion in Betsy's eyes and said crisply, "We have our own private and very happy Christmas, and then we do something truly brilliant for New Year's Eve. So please, don't feel sorry for me."

"Don't you have parents or a brother or sister?" persisted Betsy.

"My father and mother are—well, never mind. I don't think my darkening their doorstep would brighten the holidays for any of us."

"I'm sorry."

Godwin shrugged. "Their loss."

Indeed, thought Betsy, still miffed on his behalf. She reached under the table for the counted cross stitch Christmas tree ornament she was working on. It was a hippopotamus wearing a Santa Claus hat, fifth in a series of a dozen animals she'd ordered from a catalog. Betsy had nearly decided she didn't like counted cross stitch. Those customers who claimed it relaxed them were a breed apart; for Betsy, doing counted cross stitch was aggravating, frustrating, and full of traps for the unwary.

Still, it's very attractive when it comes out right, she thought, looking complacently at the grinning hippo.

In a while she sold one skein of DMC 725 perle cotton floss to the browser and eight hanks of bright pink knitting wool to a man who had signed up for the January knitting class and was needlessly afraid someone else would buy his choice of color. His purchase reminded Betsy, and she added her own name to the class list. Rosemary had brought a finished example of the sweater she was going to teach her class to knit, and Betsy had always wondered how knitters got that twist of cable into their patterns.

Soon after the knitter left, a woman came in with a child about twelve years old and bought a yard of sixteen count canvas, two needles and a threader, a dozen DMC perle cotton colors, six needlepoint wool colors, and a copy of *The Needlepoint Book.* Betsy thought the child was the woman's daughter until the child addressed her as Aunt Jay.

"This is half your Christmas present," Aunt Jay said, handing the weighty blue plastic bag with *Crewel World* printed on it in little Xs to the beaming child. "The other half is me teaching you how to do the stitches in the book. Your present to me is your first sampler, which I will hold in trust for whichever of your daughters gets the needlework gene."

Two more customers came in to pick up finished projects, and then it was noon. Betsy put on her long, dark gray coat and the bright red scarf and hat she'd knitted herself. The hat fit a little loosely because she'd figured the gauge—how many stitches to the inch—on size six needles and then knit it on seven, but that was all right, because now she didn't get hat hair. She put the wool samples in her purse and set off for the church.

The wind had let up, the sun was shining, and it didn't feel all that cold out. No challenge to the walk today. She went into the darkened arcade, heard distant voices, and followed them down the stairs and into the hall.

A half dozen volunteers were carrying huge cooking pots and boxes of utensils, what looked like parts of an early-model gas stove, and—proverbially—an old, stained, porcelain kitchen sink. Three others carried boxes of books, coat hangers, and unidentifiable junk.

Father John Rettger was standing by the tapestry, still spread across the old table.

"Hi, Father John," said Betsy coming up from behind. He'd been concentrating so hard on the movers that her voice startled him. He shied, then laughed at himself.

"Oh, hello, Betsy! I was wondering if you'd come over today. I've been standing guard over the tapestry, because I'm afraid someone will pack it up and take it away and it'll be lost for another decade." His voice was mild, like his eyes, as if he were used to going unheard or overruled.

"Are there people who would like that to happen?" asked Betsy, surprised.

"No, no, or at least I'm pretty sure not. It's just that the contractors are coming early, for a wonder, and we're not finished moving out yet. And I don't know about you, but every time I've moved, I've lost things. Once it was volume twenty-four of our *Britannica*, Metaphysics to Norway, though all the rest of the volumes were in the box, even the annuals."

Betsy nodded. "I once lost a hamster in a move across the street. But I think maybe our cat got him. She'd had her eye on him for months."

Father John laughed, then turned to the tapestry. "Well, what do you think?"

Betsy said, "Oh, I've already told Patricia I'll supply the materials. I brought some samples of wool with me to see if anything I already have matches." Betsy opened her purse and began laying out the wool in various places on the tapestry. Just having sat in the open overnight had diminished the mildew smell significantly.

"That's funny," she said after a bit.

"What?" said Father John.

"Well, Cool Buff matches up here, but Cafe Latte matches over here. I think they must have used different dye lots. Interesting."

"What do you mean by dye lots?"

"Manufacturers stir up a big batch of dye using various ingredients. That's a dye lot. And for some reason, even though they use the same recipe, the next batch doesn't quite match the first. The label will give it the same name, but stitchers know when they are buying wool or floss to make sure the dye lot number is also the same."

"But that didn't happen with this tapestry, you say. Is that good or bad?"

"Good. It gives me more chances to match colors." Betsy continued checking, tossing the samples that matched into a little heap on Christ's mantle. Finished, she reached for them. "Uh-oh."

"Uh-oh what?" asked Father John.

"Look at this." Betsy pointed to a small area of the dark orange mantle. It was next to a gray sheep, and the mostly horizontal slice looked at first like a part of the sheep's back. But moth larvae had eaten a small section down to the canvas.

Father John said, "So you'll need to give us a few inches of that orange color, too, won't you?"

Betsy, grabbing for her sinking heart, couldn't say anything at first. As she'd already noted, color was a variable thing. It was impossible that the orange colors currently in her shop came from the same dye lot as this twelve-year-old yarn. She could feel the priest waiting for her to reply. "Sometimes it's hard to match colors," she said at last. "And if I can't match that one, we'll have to redo the entire mantle." The mantle took up a large area. It was one thing to donate a skein or even a couple skeins of needlepoint wool; it was quite another to donate enough to cover a quarter of this large tapestry. Especially done in basket weave, which by design used a lot of wool, since it was meant to stiffen the fabric on which it was stitched.

"Don't despair before you find it can't be matched," said Father John. "I've been pleasantly surprised a few times in my life."

Betsy looked to see if he was speaking ironically, but his eyes were kind and his smile genuine. She smiled back and repeated something her father used to say to her: "Never trouble trouble, till trouble troubles you."

"That's right."

"Is there a phone down here I can use?"

"Back over here."

It was early issue Ma Bell, made of heavy metal with an old-fashioned dial instead of buttons. Betsy called her shop.

"Godwin? We've run into a little complication over here. Can you bring me samples of all our orange wools? I'm looking for a color I'd call burnt orange, but bring anything from russet to red. Needlepoint, yes. What? Well, don't we have a sign that says Back in Five Minutes? Then write it on something and get over here. Fast."

While they waited, Betsy looked again at the tapestry. She knew she was still a novice at needlework, but she'd seen expert work, and this seemed very well done. The stitching had a satisfying evenness. There were no beads or metallics.

Well, except in the halo. Betsy came closer. The mildew odor was still enough to wrinkle her nose, through which she took tiny sips of air.

Between the double gold lines of halo was a blue gray, slightly sparkly area. No, it wasn't the blue-gray that was sparkly, there was a tiny design stitched over it, or in between the stitches or something. Betsy frowned and leaned over the table, holding her breath.

"Is there another problem?" asked Father John.

She straightened. "No, I'm just wondering what that is."

"I know stitches have various names, but I couldn't tell you the name of even one."

"It's not a stitch," said Betsy. "See, there are little pictures in the halo. You have to get close to see them, they're—oh, they were done separately, then stitched to the gray stitching. Appliqué, it's called. They're like little line drawings, see them? There's a clover leaf, and then some kind of animal, and then a heart or something . . ."

"Where?" asked Father John, bending beside her. "Oh, I see them. How very clever. They're attributes, I believe. See? That heart is supposed to be on fire. It's for Saint Theresa. And here, this is Saint Olaf." He was pointing to a tiny double-bladed ax.

"I don't understand," said Betsy, straightening again. "I mean, how is an ax St. Olaf?"

"Come, come, you know what I mean. For instance, that first one. If I tell you it's not a clover but a shamrock, who does it make you think of?"

"Oh!" said Betsy. "Saint Patrick."

"Of course. And the lamb is Saint Agnes, and if that's a chain, it's probably Saint Ignatius. Back before literacy was common—but also because no one knew what almost any of the saints actually looked like—when a statue or painting of a saint was commissioned, the artist could put whatever face he found inspiring on it. But then, to tell the viewer who it was supposed to be, he would add some of the symbols attributed to that saint. That's what they're called: attributes."

Betsy said, "Well, yes, of course! I remember learning about that in Sunday school. Saint Lucy was a pair of eyes on a plate, ugh! And the four evangelists were an angel, an eagle, a lion, and—what?"

"An ox. And the Trinity was a triangle or three interlocking circles. We use both here at Trinity, one overlaying the other. Not all of the attributes are for saints. Some symbolize various aspects of God or of Christian virtues. The horse means war, unless he's ridden, in which case horse and rider stand for our Lord Christ."

"So what was the idea of using attributes in this tapestry?"

"Perhaps to give it an all-saints theme as well as Good Shepherd? Hmm, this looks like a rowboat. I wonder who that symbolizes. Mrs. Abrams seems to have been something of an expert on Christian symbology—unless, unless!"

"Unless what?"

"There's an old book up in my office on Christian symbols. Can you watch over this for just two minutes?"

"Of course."

Father John hustled out of the room. Betsy traced another of the attributes with a finger. A boar? Maybe Lucy was saying something about husbands. Betsy normally referred to her ex-husband Hal as the Pig.

Hey, here was a cat, and over here was another, one sitting and the other crouching. Was that significant? Perhaps more than one person worked on this, and they forgot who was doing the cat. Here were three crowns in a tight pattern; she remembered that three crowns meant Saint Elizabeth of Hungary. Her Sunday school teacher's name was Elizabeth, and so made a point about this Saint Elizabeth's attribute. And Betsy remembered because that was her name, too. But the other emblems were hieroglyphics to her. She hoped Father John could find the book about these symbols. She rummaged in her purse for a notebook and couldn't find one, so she pulled her checkbook out of its folder and started to copy the symbols onto the cardboard back.

"Hello, Betsy," said a woman's voice.

"Hm?" Betsy said, straightening and turning. "Oh, hello, Patricia! Look what we've found! Little pictures, saints' attributes, in the halo. I'm so glad we don't have to redo this part. That would take special skills."

Patricia took a breath, held it, then leaned forward to look very briefly at the halo. She straightened and said, "Why, yes, I hadn't noticed that before. What did you call them?"

"Attributes. Father John has gone to get a book on them. I want to see who they represent. I know the three crowns are Elizabeth, and the shamrock is Saint Patrick, but here, who has a horseshoe? Isn't this interesting? Like a puzzle. And look, there are two cats. I wonder why."

But Patricia was taking two steps backward, fishing for a handkerchief in her purse. "That's very interesting and clever. I wonder what metallic she used for those, er, attributes that maintained its shine all these years? Real silver would tarnish, and anyway I don't think you could get real silver thread until fairly recently. Maybe aluminum . . . Such very fine stitching, too, looks as if it was done with a single thread."

Reminded, Betsy said, "Patricia, there may be another problem." She showed Patricia the moth-eaten section of mantle and was just starting to say something about twelve-year-old dye lots when Godwin appeared, breathless from hurry, with a dozen strands of wool in one gloved hand.

"This is what we have in stock," he said. "Hello, Mrs. Fairland," and added, "Customer waiting," over his shoulder as he turned and rushed out again.

Betsy tried each strand over the mantle. None of them matched. "See, this is what I was worried about."

"Oh, dear," said Patricia.

"Yes," said Betsy, her eyes estimating the size of the mantle. She wished she'd done what Jill had suggested, memorized the length and width of her hand, so she'd have a way to gauge size when she didn't have a measuring tape in reach.

"Now look, Betsy, if we have to redo this whole area, that will take a lot of wool, which I'm sure will be a real hardship for you. Why don't you just forget that offer of a donation? As I told you, I'm starting a drive to name the renovated library after Father Keane. He was so popular that I'm sure we'll succeed. We could even raise the money to pay for a professional restoration of the tapestry, I'm sure."

Betsy, surprised and grateful, opened her mouth to accept the offer, but to her even greater surprise what came out was, "But Martha has told the Monday Bunch, and they're all excited about the project. I'd hate to disappoint them. I'll check around for more samples—and so what if I have to supply enough for all the mantle? I hardly think even that much wool will send my shop into bankruptcy."

Patricia frowned doubtfully. "Well, if you're really sure . . ."

Betsy said, "I'm sure. Now, I'd better get back to the shop. Godwin needs his lunch break."

On her way up the stairs, she met Father John. He was carrying a thick book. "It took me awhile to find it on my shelves," he apologized. He opened it at random to display a page divided into six squares, each with a simple line drawing in it: a book pierced by a sword, a ship's wheel, a harp, a lantern, a Celtic cross, a pair of pincers. The facing page was part of a dictionary of saints' names with their dates and attributes.

"Oh, lovely!" exclaimed Betsy. "May I borrow it? I'll be working on the tapestry, and I've already written down some attributes I want to look up."

"Of course," said Father John, kindly neglecting to point out that he'd gone for the book because there were some attributes he wanted to look up himself. He handed the book over and went back to guarding the tapestry against those who might store it away so securely it was never found again.

Three

❖

"Why didn't you take her up on that offer?" asked Godwin.

"I don't know," said Betsy. "Especially since I got some really bad news from George Hollytree."

Godwin looked up from his knitting—another in his endless series of white cotton socks. "Um, how bad?"

Betsy took a deep breath but kept her eyes on her cross stitching. "He says I have to cut back employee hours and at the same time stay open longer. That means I have to work more."

"How can I work more hours? I'm already full time."

Betsy looked sideways at him. "No, you need to work *fewer* hours. *I* need to work more hours."

Godwin laughed. He laughed so hard he had to put down his knitting. When the laughter slowed, he would look at Betsy and start in again.

Betsy tried to wait him out, but Godwin's endurance was apparently bottomless. At last she said, "That's enough, Godwin," and he stopped as if she had clipped him one on the nose. "Now, why is that so funny?"

"Because, my dearest, most wonderful, and favorite living employer, you are learning both needlework and the art of owning a small business with breathtaking skill and speed, but you are a long way from accomplished at either. You may do well here in the shop all by yourself—or you may not. For example, Mrs. Hagedorn came in while you were mucking about with that tapestry to ask me if I could get her some *one hundred twelve count* silk gauze. I looked in our catalog, and sure enough it comes that high. But she also wanted to buy some needles to use in this project. An ordinary needle won't fit through the silk gauzes, so if you were here alone, what would you have told her?"

Betsy looked uncomfortable. "Well . . . I guess I would've got you on the phone."

"And if I'm not at home but in Cancun basking in the sun?"

"Okay, I'd look in that catalog that has every kind of needle you can think of."

"And it wouldn't help, unless you already knew where to look. You use the short beading needles; if you look them up, it says they are also for extremely high-count fabrics. Fortunately for you, Mrs. Hagedorn already knew that. I have ordered the silk gauze for her, but we already have beading needles in stock." Beading needles were thin as hair.

Betsy said, "Well, if she already knew—"

"But what if she hadn't known? Would you have known who to call? I would, because I know *almost* everything, including who to ask."

"Whom. All right, I know, too. I would dash upstairs and put the question on the Internet, to my favorite newsgroup, RCTN. I'd have an answer in about sixty seconds. Collectively, those people know everything."

Godwin nodded. "You're right, they do. But it's not good business practice to leave a customer alone in the shop. Admit it, boss, you need me here as much as possible. I only cost a dollar an hour more than the part-time help. Theirs are the hours you'll have to cut down on. If you can't do that, you'll have to cut some other expense."

"Which brings us back to my original question, doesn't it? Why didn't you *enthusiastically* jump on Patricia's suggestion that you back out on your offer to supply the material for the tapestry?"

Betsy said, "Because Mr. Hollytree also told me I should advertise, to let people know Crewel World didn't die with my sister. Which I am going to do. A salesman should be here on Tuesday. But if I get involved with this project, then the name of my shop will get in the paper as the supplier of materials. Before I knew we might have to replace a huge area of the thing, that seemed an easy, cheap way to get some publicity."

Godwin widened his blue eyes at her. "Then it was a *good* idea!" he said.

"Of course it was! I may be ignorant, but I'm not stupid!"

Godwin winked at her. "Honey, *no one* thinks you march with the stupid platoon, not after you beat our local police to the solution in two murder cases."

Betsy grimaced, looked for her place on the fabric, then consulted the pattern. She thought herself lucky, not bright, when it came to solving murders. But no one paid any attention when she said that. She stuck her needle in, pulled the floss through. "I was thinking of calling Picket Fence and Stitchville USA to see if they have any dark orange wool in a shade I don't have," she said, and put down her stitching again to reach for the cordless on the table.

Godwin nodded. "Another good idea."

But they didn't have anything different. Betsy was looking up more shops' numbers when a customer came in with a large cardboard box, its top folded shut.

"I'm hoping you can help me, Betsy," she said, dropping the box onto the library table. "My grandmother died a month ago, and when she got sick last spring, she said I should get her stash. But I already have a stash, and I may never get around to using this stuff."

"Are you saying you want to give it away?" asked Betsy.

"Some of it." She pulled the flaps of the box apart and began lifting out clear plastic bags filled with needlework projects, rolls of linen and Aida cloth in several colors, packets of needles, silk and perle floss, and balls of yarn. She gestured at one pile. "Look at all these needlepoint canvases! This one's stamped, but look, this one and this one are hand painted, so they're valuable. Thing is, I don't do needlepoint. And see this big bag of wool? Lots of colors but there's not more than a yard of any one color."

Betsy eyed the bag speculatively, but didn't see any dark orange.

"At least now I know where I get my squirrel nature. My mother throws leftover yarn away unless she's got another project that can use it, but I'll end up in one of those houses with paths winding among the stacks of newspapers, except my stacks will be patterns and projects waiting for me to find time to finish them, and leftover yarn and floss from projects I've completed."

Betsy said, "I hope you don't think your mother is the normal one. Almost all my customers save leftover cloth and floss." She picked up a needlepoint kit depicting a tropical sunset. The sky and sea were mauve and blue and lavender and pink, with palm trees making graceful black arcs in the foreground. She'd been to that beach, back in San Diego. But first things first: "Is there any dark orange wool? I need some for a project."

"Not in this box. If I find some, I'll bring it in. This is only a quarter of what we found. About the stash I'm keeping: Can I store everything as I found it?"

"No, you can't," said Betsy. "You need to get it out of these plastic bags and into acid-free paper or cloth bags. Fibers need to breathe."

Godwin had come over for a look. "You know," he said to Betsy, "Margot would do consignment selling once in awhile. Some of this is very nice. Like this kit, which was never even opened." Then he picked up a completed needlepoint of a white horse rearing in storm-tossed surf. "This is beautiful," he said. "Do you know Diane Bolles, down at Nightingale's? She's looking for needlework to sell." Godwin reached for something else. "And look at this, too, Betsy." He was holding an unworked canvas covered with hearts and cherubs. "It's a Patti Mann canvas. We could sell this in a New York minute."

Betsy said, "All right. Are you willing to part with some of this on consignment, Katie?"

In half an hour, Katie left for Nightingale's with a gleam in her eye. Betsy spent another half hour putting the new items out, making sure they were artistically displayed, then properly marked and listed in the notebook Godwin showed her, in which Margot had kept track of consignment items.

"Do you have a stash, Godwin?" she asked, stepping back from the Patti Mann to see if it was hung straight.

"Honey, I'm at the point where I'm throwing out *clothes* to make room. *Everyone* has stash, but we're all too enamored of SEX to quit looking for more."

Betsy laughed; Godwin meant Stash Enhancement eXperience, one of the terms invented by her favorite newsgroup. Betsy was not herself immune to the lure of SEX; she set the tropic sunset kit aside for herself.

At five they locked the front door. Godwin and Betsy straightened up the shop: washing out the coffeepot and unplugging the teakettle, shutting off the radio, running the credit card machine's total, counting the take. Betsy made out a deposit slip, which Godwin took along with the cash and checks to the bank a couple of blocks away. "See you later at the party," he said. "I'll be the one with the tie that lights up."

* * *

Betsy and Sophie went upstairs, where Betsy took a quick shower and put on her prettiest party dress, the cranberry velvet, and stroked on evening makeup, more emphatic than her daytime wear. She put on her garnet earrings and necklace, inherited from her mother.

The apartment was sparkling clean, but Betsy went around putting breakables higher or into cabinets, leaving as much flat surface as possible for plates and glasses. Sophie followed her, whining until Betsy remembered she hadn't fed her pet.

Sophie was alleged to be on a diet. She was allowed two small scoops of diet cat food a day, which should keep even a lazy cat like Sophie at a svelte seven or eight pounds. Sophie, by dint of nonexistent metabolism and a lifestyle that "Less Active" overstated, had lost three pounds, gained one back, and now held stubbornly at eighteen. The problem was, she cadged treats from anyone who approached her in the shop, and would accept any offering. Betsy had needlepointed a little sign that read, "No, Thank You, I'm on a Diet," to hang on the back of Sophie's chair, but just today, a customer, still laughing at the sign, had fed Sophie a potato chip. Betsy had thought of a muzzle, but Sophie might find it very tasty, too. And Betsy couldn't stop the Iams feedings; Sophie's diet otherwise was too unhealthy.

"You could leave her upstairs," Godwin had suggested. But the thought of the friendly, ornamental, happy creature condemned to a life of waiting for Betsy to come home was too awful.

Two hours later, Betsy took off her slippers and put on her highest heels. The apartment was beginning to smell of hot hors d'oeuvres and rock gently to the jazz piano of Ramsey Lewis. The little table in the dining nook was laden with crystal goblets, bottles of good red and white wines, and a big punch bowl filled with something pink and fragrant. Beer and soft drinks were in the refrigerator. Betsy took a ceramic pie plate out of the freezer. Last night she had overlapped alternating slices of lemons and limes in a ring in the pie plate and scattered a few maraschino cherries on top. She had put a straight-sided bowl of water in the center, poured half an inch of water into the plate, and put the whole thing in the freezer. Now she dismantled the arrangement and put the ring of frozen fruit into the punch bowl, where it would serve to chill and ornament the punch.

By the time the first tray of hors d'oeuvres came out of the oven, three couples had arrived.

Betsy loved to give parties. Godwin was there, of course, with his lover John, a tall attorney with a distinguished profile and just the right amount of gray in his hair. He looked around her apartment and then at Betsy with the amused air of the *New York Times* home/arts editor visiting Archie Bunker's house. He was obvious enough about it that Jill Cross, Betsy's police officer friend, raised an inquiring eyebrow at her when they met over the punch bowl a few minutes later. Betsy rolled her eyes to show she didn't care what the jerk thought and went to get a fresh batch of cheesy, spicy hamburgers on tiny rounds of rye bread out of the oven.

Shelly Donohue, an elementary school teacher who worked part time in the shop, came with an extremely handsome fellow she introduced as Vice Principal Smith.

Joe Mickels, Betsy's landlord, came. Betsy had an ironclad lease at a ridiculous rent on the shop, a mistake Joe's late brother had made with Betsy's late sister. Joe had made numerous strenuous attempts to break the lease when Margot had run the shop, but they had stopped when Betsy took over. She didn't know why, and it made her uneasy.

Joe was a short-legged, pigeon-breasted man with enormous white sideburns and a great beak of a nose. His winter coat with its astrakhan collar was as anachronistic as he was—Joe should have lived in the era of robber barons.

He had an attractive woman his own age with him. "Still think you're going to stay the course?" he asked Betsy with an icy twinkle.

If Betsy had the occasional tremble for herself and Crewel World, she wasn't about to show it to Joe. "We're doing fine, thank you," she said with a determined twinkle of her own and took their coats to the back bedroom.

The part-timers came with spouses or significant others. The Monday Bunch, a needlework group that met at the shop, came mostly alone. The party divided into clusters, naturally, but Betsy went casually from cluster to cluster, taking a person from the Monday Bunch to introduce her to someone in the business discussion Joe was leading, and a person from the business world to introduce to the arts discussion, and so forth, making sure everyone got a chance to meet everyone else.

The five or six on and around the couch were into politics. "Do you think Mayor Jamison will run again?" asked Peter Fairland, Patricia's husband, a state senator contemplating a run for Congress. (The mayor, typically, was in the kitchen, helping stir up a new batch of that hamburger-on-rye hors d'oeuvre.)

"I think the job is his as long as he wants it," said Godwin.

"I think it's time for a woman mayor, don't you?" asked Martha Winters, a refugee from the Monday Bunch.

Betsy paused to listen. She admired Patricia's smooth, classic exterior and wanted to see what her husband was like. Peter showed himself quick-witted and friendly, with piercing gray eyes and a great laugh. He was smooth in a practiced way, an intense listener, and Betsy found him not quite as intimidating as his wife.

Betsy left the political group to deal with a minor explosion in the business corner, where Joe Mickels was defending his latest attempt to squeeze yet more money out of a nonprofit group renting one of his buildings. "You all seem to forget," Joe growled, "that our great wealth happened *because* we use the capitalist system." Betsy asked Joe if he could help her open the sticky window in the dining nook just an inch, because it was getting rather warm in the apartment. He would have taken that as criticism of his maintenance until he recognized the look she was giving him. He came and opened the window and meekly did ten minutes of penance with the needleworkers, who were gathered around the punch bowl.

Betsy went to check on the quartet in the kitchen, who were telling favorite-pet stories while waiting for the hors d'oeuvres in the oven to come out. She stayed there only long enough to remind them that the oven ran a little hot and continued her rounds, this time bringing Mayor Jamison along.

She left him with Godwin's friend John, who was arguing probate law with Betsy's own attorney while three other guests kibitzed.

The group by the CD player were looking through the albums and not finding anything with words. "You collect only instrumentals?" asked Patricia as Betsy stopped by.

"I collect everything," said Betsy, "but I left only instrumentals out tonight, because singing competes with conversation. If you've got to have music with words, go into the back bedroom and boot up the computer; it has a CD player in it, and I put my other CDs in there."

To Betsy's surprise, Patricia went, taking another woman with her. Betsy thereafter checked the back bedroom twice. She didn't want them to get isolated, nor did she want anything messy or scandalous to happen. No fear; the first time she found four music lovers singing "Bar-Barbara Ann" along with the Beach Boys; the second time she found Jamison, retired railroad engineer Phil Galvin, and Alice Skoglund, who was a Lutheran minister's widow, looking through the book on Christian symbology.

They certainly are a moral bunch here in Excelsior, Betsy thought, remembering a couple of faculty parties from her old life in San Diego.

The doorbell rang. Had someone gone for a smoke and locked himself out? The apartment was too crowded to see if anyone was missing. She shrugged and pressed the buzzer that unlocked the door—there wasn't an intercom to ask who was there.

She opened her door to see who would come up the stairs. Her eyes widened. A handsome face appeared, tanned and smooth-shaven, with dark brown eyes, a square jaw with a cleft chin, and a mouth just begging for a pipe. It was topped with a smooth sheaf of nearly white hair with a dramatic dark streak near one temple. The head sat on broad, square shoulders, atop a torso that looked, even covered by a trench coat, to be toned and fit. The whole rode on slim, long legs.

The face looked sideways at Betsy and assumed an abashed air, a handsome comic caught with his hand in a cookie jar.

It was Hal Norman, Hal the Pig, Betsy's ex. The one who was ratted on by a college freshman after he dumped her too abruptly for another college fresh-man. Which turned out to have been a pattern of behavior dating back God knew how many freshmen, and all while married to Betsy. "H'lo, Betsy darlin'," he said. "I've come back to you."

"I—I *beg* your pardon?!?" said Betsy.

Hal began to chuckle. He bounced up the last few steps and strode quickly to her. He was smiling, which made his dimples extra deep. "No joke, darlin', it's *so* good to see you!" He would have taken her in his arms had she not stepped back inside. When she tried to close the door, he put a hand on it.

"Hey, what's the matter? Please, won't you listen for just one minute?" His voice was surprised and hurt, which amazed her.

"Who is it?" asked Jill, coming up behind her.

"It's my ex-husband."

"The one you left in California?"

"I thought I had."

"What does he want?"

"I don't know."

Hal's voice asked plaintively, "You mean you're going to leave me standing out here till the mice get round-shouldered?"

"What'd he say?" asked Jill.

"It's an old joke," said Betsy, then added to Hal, "Until they are positively hunchbacked."

"But, darlin', I don't have anyplace to stay!"

That surprised Betsy so much, she released her pressure on the door, which he promptly pushed open. She said, "You mean you actually thought you could just come here and I'd let you in? And let you stay *overnight?*"

"But why not? I drove all the way from California just to see you."

"That's too bad." Betsy started to close the door again, but he put his hand on it again.

He said in a humble tone, "You're right. I shouldn't have presumed any-thing. I should have stopped at a motel and phoned you. But darlin', the closer

I got, the more I got to thinking about what it would be like to actually see you again, talk to you face-to-face, and I just couldn't put it off another minute. Say, what's the noise? Have you got company? That should make it all right for me to come in and use your phone, shouldn't it? I need to find a motel."

"No, you can't come in. I'm having a Christmas party for my employees and some friends."

"Really? Why, say, I'd love to meet them. I understand they were a real help to you when Margot died. I'm *so* sorry about Margot, by the way. I wish I could have been here to support you through that awful time—"

The idea of Hal here during those early weeks, making himself at home in this place, helping her with the funeral—Betsy heard herself make an odd sound and heard an inquiring noise behind her. She glanced back.

Jill, reading the look on Betsy's face, immediately stepped forward to say over Betsy's shoulder, with that wonderful authority cops can summon, "There's a motel back out on the highway. You can't miss it." And she gave the door a hard shove to shut it.

Betsy said, "Thank you! I think I was about to barf on his shoes."

Jill smiled. "That message might have penetrated."

Betsy laughed. "I can't imagine his turning up here. I wonder what he really wants?"

Jill said, "Have you told anyone in San Diego about the money?"

"Oh, the money! Of course!" Betsy's sister had turned out to be wealthy. In another month or so, when probate was finished, Betsy would be an heiress. "Yes, I told three friends. I wonder who let me down and told him."

"I suppose he lost his job at the college?"

Betsy nodded. "Despite his tenure, yes, and it got into the papers, so he won't find another teaching job anytime soon. Our house was supplied by the college, so we lost that, too."

"I'm sure that if one of your friends saw him flipping burgers somewhere, they thought they were doing you a favor by letting him know his loss was even greater than he thought."

"So here he comes, playing penitent, hoping he can worm his way back into my life!"

"Worm being the operative word here," said Jill. "Is he from California originally?"

"Yes, born in Redondo Beach."

"Then he'll probably take the next bus home. Native Californians don't transplant well to climates like this."

But Betsy, as she returned to the party, wondered. Three million dollars was an excellent incentive to learn to like snow.

Four

✦

Betsy woke with a dry mouth and a headache. She opened her eyes and immediately closed them again. The bedroom was flooded with painfully bright sunlight. Why was that wrong?

Because she'd been waking to darkness lately, hadn't she? It was December in the northlands, and on workdays she awoke before dawn. Was this not a workday? Or had the clock radio not gone off? Or had it come on and she'd shut it off and fallen back asleep again?

Last night—there had been a party here last night—*that's* why she had a headache. And the party was Saturday night, so this must be Sunday. The radio hadn't come on because this was Sunday, which was lovely because even late as it surely was, she wasn't ready to get up just yet. In fact, she could feel herself drifting back to sleep again.

The mattress joggled as about eighteen pounds landed on it.

Sophie, aware by the change in her breathing that Betsy was awake, had jumped on the bed. Betsy tried to feign the deep breathing of sleep. Another fifteen seconds and it wouldn't be fake.

Too slow. There was the imperious tap of a cat's paw on her shoulder.

"Go 'way," muttered Betsy.

But this further sign of consciousness only encouraged the cat. "Reeeewwwwww," she whined, her mouth close to Betsy's hypersensitive ear. Betsy flinched and pulled the covers over her head. The cat tapped again. And again. Her normal breakfast time was long past, and she was probably genuinely hungry.

Betsy groaned—softly, softly!—and began a careful struggle to free her legs from the tangled blanket and sheet. Sophie immediately jumped off the bed and hustled toward the kitchen, where the cat food lived.

Betsy was sure that somewhere deep in the cat's soul Sophie knew she was not starving nor in danger of starving. But probably she was equally certain that this was because of her own unending efforts to keep her mistress aware that The Cat Must Be Fed.

Betsy had been running a campaign of her own to Make the Cat Wait, but so far it was a series of strategic retreats. Sophie cleverly—her laziness apparently did not include her brain—didn't approach each target directly but went for the target beyond and accepted as compromise the one she was after.

Back when Betsy fed the cat *after* she got dressed, Sophie began nagging for food before Betsy got into the shower. Betsy compromised by feeding Sophie after she showered but *before* she got dressed. Now Sophie was trying to maneuver breakfast time up to right after that first and most necessary trip to the bathroom. And Betsy had actually been contemplating feeding her before she showered. Today the cat had crossed another line: waking Betsy up. Never before had Sophie ventured to wake Betsy. She'd always waited until Betsy woke up either by herself or to the music of the clock radio. And she normally included an interval of cuddling. Not today; today The Cat Must Be Fed *Now.*

Well, no more compromising; if Betsy wanted to sleep in on Sundays, she was going to have to hold the line at feeding the cat after her morning shower.

Betsy looked at her puffy morning-after face in the bathroom mirror and smiled. The Pig had come and been sent away empty-handed. It was great how Jill had backed her up, literally slamming the door in his face. Imagine his turning up here like that, thinking he would be welcome! When it came to nerve, the Pig took the cake.

The party last night had been good, Betsy thought as she brushed her teeth. Most of the guests had departed at a respectable eleven, but a final six remained. They, with Betsy, had settled into a discussion of modern culture (what was lacking and how to fix it) that went on until nearly three A.M. Joe Mickels was proven not to be the Fascist everyone thought, and the straitlaced Patricia had unbent so far as to be amused by Godwin, who had sent John home alone when he hinted for the fifth time he was bored. Alice Skoglund told the joke about the bishop on roller skates, which set off a sidebar on religion that for a wonder actually shed more light than heat. Betsy had opened another two bottles of wine, and after her third glass had given a lecture on college faculty politics. Perhaps after the Pig's brief appearance, that was to be expected. Her guests bore it patiently, and even offered cordial thanks for a good time when at last they'd gone home.

Betsy took a quick shower, then went to give Sophie her breakfast of diet cat food. She put the kettle on.

Half an hour later, she was eating dry toast, sipping a second cup of green tea, and thinking of tackling the Sunday Crossword of the *New York Times Online.* It was a little after eleven, and Betsy was still in her striped flannel robe. The phone rang.

"Hello?" she said into the receiver.

"Hello, darlin'," said a deep, warm, oh-so-familiar voice.

"Calling to say you've got to stay on campus for another staff meeting?" said Betsy.

"Now, hon," protested the voice, but Betsy hung up so she wouldn't have to listen to the rest.

"He's still in town, you know," said Godwin on Monday morning.

"Who?" asked Betsy, checking the sky out the front window. It was gloomy, and the forecast was for snow, but so far it had held off. Perhaps the flakes would hover in the clouds until the weather system moved over to Wisconsin.

"Hal Norman, your husband."

"He is not my husband." Betsy came back to the library table and sat down.

"He's telling people he has reason to hope for a reconciliation." Godwin's tone put a twist on the words, hinting he thought this wasn't going to happen but leaving a little wriggle room because the ways of love are passing strange.

"He needs a reality check," said Betsy, picking up the hippopotamus ornament she was working on. She'd made a mistake twenty stitches back. She'd seen it half a dozen stitches ago. Realizing it wasn't an important mistake, she'd tried to ignore it; but it kept mocking her until she couldn't bear it. Frogging, it was called, when you took stitches out. She said, "No, he should fall off that pink cloud of fantasy he's been riding and break his neck."

"I see," said Godwin. "You want to know who he's talking to?"

"No," said Betsy, her needle going rip-it, rip-it. But Excelsior was a gossipy little town. Pretty soon people would be dropping by and making remarks, so perhaps it was better to be forearmed. "Okay, who?" she said.

"Irene Potter," began Godwin, but Betsy interrupted him with a groan. Of all the gossips, Irene was probably the worst. She was a fanatical needleworker, fabulously talented, but passing strange, on her way to totally weird. Perhaps because she had no social skills, she was endlessly interested in what people said and did and loved speculating aloud what their motives might be. More than anything in the world, she wanted her own needlework shop and suspected darkly that Betsy kept Crewel World open mostly to keep Irene from taking it over and running it as it should be run. Her speculations about Hal and Betsy, therefore, would not be kind.

"Who else?" asked Betsy, pinching the bridge of her nose between her thumb and forefinger, trying toward off a headache.

"I understand he bought Patricia Fairland a cup of coffee at the Waterfront Café and talked to her for about ten minutes. Left her doing that thing women do with the back of their hair. He is rather good-looking."

"Looks aren't everything," said Betsy, the voice of experience.

"But they open a lot of doors," Godwin said, the voice of his own experience. Betsy nodded. Godwin was so handsome he was almost pretty. "He talked real estate with Joe Mickels," Godwin continued—real estate was one topic on which Joe was always willing to converse—"oh, and at church yesterday morning, he expressed surprise and disappointment that you weren't there."

Betsy groaned again. "*What* am I going to do about him?"

"Nothing," said Godwin. "People are already speculating. Some think he's here because he heard about your money, others that the father of one of the co-eds he seduced has a contract out on him."

Betsy giggled and Godwin smiled. "Well, it's Irene who offered that one. If you really have to do something, sic Jill on him, why don't you? She could find an excuse to shoot him, maybe."

Betsy said, "No. I've read about what shooting a person does to the shooter."

"Not to mention the *shot,*" said Godwin, surprised.

"I'm serious," said Betsy. "I have a friend in San Diego, her name is Abbey, and she has a friend who is married to a cop, and he shot some teenage thug who was holding up a bank. He got a medal for valor, but he was suicidal for years afterward. So don't even joke about doing that to Jill."

"All right," said Godwin.

A customer came in looking for a needlepoint project and expressed disappointment that they hadn't marked down the Christmas stockings, now that Christmas was almost here.

"There's no need to mark them down," said Godwin. "Many customers give them as gift kits. And besides, it can take as long as *two years* to finish a project like this, so it isn't exactly a seasonal thing." He looked around as if to check for eavesdroppers and winked at Betsy with an eye the customer couldn't see—and then at the customer with the other eye. "However," he murmured, "we *may* be able to give you a special price on the wool or silk you select for the project, or on one of our scheduled classes on needlepoint. I *think* there's an opening in the one I'll be teaching, the one that starts the middle of January."

"Well," hedged the customer, "I always did want to learn beading, and Emily told me you do wonderful beadwork."

"I hope you will consider it. I was very impressed with that sampler you worked. You do a beautiful mosaic stitch. In another year, you'll be teaching your own class for us. Just let me get the schedule."

Her brunette and his blond heads were soon bent over the calendar on the checkout desk, and then she was writing a check.

After the woman left, Betsy got out her employee list and their schedule of hours and tried to find ways to reduce them. But she had gotten to know her part-timers. Several spent the greater part of their wages on needlework projects—a saving to the shop all by itself, even considering the employee discount. The one young woman Betsy felt she could most easily spare was newly separated from her husband and desperately needed the little Betsy was able to pay her.

"I don't want to cut any of these people," said Betsy.

"Well, what else can you cut?"

"I don't know. Maybe I can cancel my medical insurance. Crewel World pays for it, and it's very expensive."

"Don't do that," advised Godwin. "The goblins of fate are just waiting to pounce on people who cancel insurance policies."

"Well then, what does Hollytree expect me to do?" she grumbled, throwing her pencil down. It bounced on its eraser and barely missed Godwin's ear on its way into a basket of fuschia wool.

The phone rang. Godwin was retrieving the pencil, so Betsy answered it. "Crewel World, good morning, may I help you?"

"Hello, Betsy, it's John Penberthy. How are you today?"

Penberthy was Betsy's attorney, a young man of great ability with an office on Water Street.

"Except for being in danger of going broke, I'm fine, thank you. What's up?"

"This may cheer you up. I've got some more figures for you on the estate. Thanks to a healthy stock market, it looks as if the final numbers will be closer to three million than two and a half. The first million is now exempt from inheritance taxes, but the rest will be taxed at forty percent."

"Forty percent, huh?" Was that good or bad? Betsy hadn't earned the inheritance, but neither had the government.

"It also appears that certificates of deposit, money market accounts, and other assets are generating between twenty-five hundred and three thousand dollars a month, which Margot was using as income. I assume you will want to continue that, and meanwhile, the money is being put into an interest-bearing account. Not a very high interest, I'm afraid, as I'm sure you will want it to be accessible as soon as the estate is closed."

So that was how Margot kept the shop in the black, by not paying herself a salary. "Yes, please," said Betsy, stifling an impulse to shout, "How soon can I put my hands on that money?" Instead she said, "I got your last letter, where you put in writing what you told me about the stocks and bonds, and I thank you. I'm getting better at this, but I'm afraid I don't understand what you said about a silent partnership Margot was in. I can't find any record of it at the courthouse. I wondered if perhaps you were acting as her representative so her name wouldn't appear."

"Oh, no, I couldn't represent her in that way. Why don't you stop by my office today or tomorrow, and I'll show you the file? You may find it amusing."

"Is it a lot of money?" asked Betsy.

"It's an irregular income, and right now there's not much action. But it is going to pay off majorly in short order."

"What is it, interest in a gambling casino?"

Penberthy laughed, but he only insisted Betsy should be looking at the file while he explained. "If I may make one more suggestion?"

"Of course."

"I think you should consider making a will. You said there are no relatives, so it would be a shame if you died without one and the government got everything, after the time and effort we've spent keeping them from taking most of it. Name a favorite charity or give some friends a happy surprise. I will, of course, be very pleased to talk to you about it when you are ready."

"All right," said Betsy. "I'll think about it." She hung up.

After she settled back into her project, Betsy said to Godwin, "It's different when you really become rich. I mean, instead of daydreaming about it. In the dream you get huge checks every week, which you cash and spend. In the real world, there are IRAs and investment properties and nonexempt bonds and taxes. I'm just grateful I have Mr. Penberthy to help me through it all."

"Well, I'm sure he'll be equally glad to hand you a substantial bill when you start getting those huge checks," said Godwin. "And may I add just one little point of my very own? Connect the fact that you're an heiress to the money problems you are having with Crewel World. Probate's about finished, isn't it? You could have stopped paying some of your bills last month, you know. Because well before your distributor refuses to ship any more DMC cotton floss to this address, you could *buy* that distributor and fire his smelly old credit manager."

Betsy smiled. "I would love to believe that," she said.

"Believe it," said Godwin. "About money, I am always right."

Toward one, June Connor came in, her shoulders covered with snow. It had started in around noon, falling in thick, heavy flakes.

June was an attractive young woman who did wonderful counted cross stitch. "Whew!" she laughed, pulling off a knitted cap and reopening the door just enough to shake it off outside. "It's coming down out there! How are you, Betsy?"

"Fine, Mrs. Connor. How are Steven and David?"

"Very well, thank you. Impatient for Christmas to arrive, of course."

"I bet I know what brought you out in this," said Godwin with a smile. "I warned you to buy six hanks of that wool, not five."

June laughed. "No, five was enough. Barely, but enough. I came to pick up my angel—you know, the one that was being finished as a pillow."

Betsy had a sudden sinking sensation. She'd gone through the box several times to find finished projects for other customers and didn't remember seeing June's wonderful angel pillow.

On the other hand, she remembered writing up the order and packing it for the finisher, so perhaps she'd just overlooked it.

But while June's name was on the list, the pillow wasn't in the box.

When she saw the dismay on June's face, she picked up the phone and dialed the finisher's phone number. "Hello, Heidi? Betsy Devonshire at Crewel World. Fine, thank you. But we have a problem. A pillow with an angel on it, a big one, counted cross stitch—yes, the Mirabilia. You do? Oh, no! Well, can you—Oh, I see. All right, I'll call you back."

"What?" asked June.

"It's finished, and it's fine," said Betsy, to June's relief, "but it's still there. She overlooked it when she packed our other finished projects. And she says she can't bring it in until late tomorrow, she's swamped trying to finish other last-minute projects."

"But we're leaving for Florida at noon tomorrow!" wailed June. "And that pillow is a gift for my mother-in-law!"

June was a very loyal customer who spent a lot of money in Crewel World. Betsy, feeling she could ill afford to lose a good customer, said impulsively, "I'll go get it today. I mean, when the shop closes, of course. It's not that far to Heidi's place."

June said doubtfully, "It's coming down kind of hard."

"*You* drove in it to come here and pick the pillow up," Betsy pointed out. "Besides, I heard it's supposed to stop in another hour or two. You can pick it up in the morning on your way to the airport."

"Well . . . thank you, Betsy."

But the forecast changed an hour later. The front had stalled, the snow wouldn't stop now until early evening. The wind was picking up, making driving hazardous.

Godwin said, "I think you shouldn't go, Betsy."

Betsy said, "Hey, I grew up in Wisconsin. I learned to drive on ice and snow! And I've been doing fine so far."

But the Monday Bunch was more alarmed than June or Godwin.

"Betsy, it's really very bad out there," said Alice. "Already the plows aren't able to keep up, and the radio is saying road travel is not recommended."

Betsy looked out the window. In the gap she had cut in the snow lining the sidewalk, she could see cars passing by. "No one is staying home yet."

"They're not driving out in the country on winding roads in the dark," Martha Winters pointed out.

"And the roads around here can be very confusing to an inexperienced driver," added Patricia.

"Now just a goldanged minute," said Betsy. "I've been driving for nearly forty years! Heidi lives less than five miles from here. Besides, it's for June Connor, and she has spent hundreds of dollars in the shop in just the past three months. The pillow is for her mother-in-law." There was a little silence as the women thought about daughters-in-law who came to Christmas gatherings with presents for everyone but their mothers-in-law.

"Well . . ." conceded Martha, and the talk moved on to the latest patterns in *Cross Stitch and Needlework* magazine.

Godwin asked Patricia, "Have you ever bought a counted cross stitch pattern on eBay?"

"Yes, why?"

"I saw a doll house rug kit on there I really liked. And the bidding wasn't very active. Is it a good place to shop?"

Alice asked, "Where's eBay?"

"On the Internet," said Betsy. "It's like an auction house that handles just about anything you can imagine. I've looked at some things but haven't ever bid because I've heard you can get stung."

Patricia said, "I've never bought needlework items there, but I have bought antiques. I never bid on anything unless there's a picture. Do you use a computer, Martha?"

"No, I'm too old for a computer. Jeff has one." Jeff was her adult grandson, her partner in the dry cleaning business.

"Nobody's too old!" said Godwin. "I know several people who share AOL accounts with their mothers so they can stay in touch. They send pictures of the grandchildren and the grandmothers send pictures of themselves and their new husbands honeymooning in Hawaii. It's not hard to learn. I'd be glad to show you, or you, Alice."

Alice, her large face reddening, blurted, "Oh, I couldn't afford a computer," which might have caused an embarrassed silence except she went on, "Betsy, could I see some of that new floss, the kind that's a blend of silk and wool?"

Betsy said, "Of course," and brought a skein to the table. The Bunch, incorrigible fiber fondlers, handed it around and agreed the texture was marvelous. Neither computers nor the subject of Betsy driving in the snow was mentioned again.

After the Monday Bunch left, Betsy said, "Are you going to put a bid in for that rug kit?"

"Yes, but I probably won't get it. Too many things go for more than they're worth on eBay. I wouldn't even bid, except I can't seem to find it anywhere else."

"Godwin, what do you think about Patricia?"

"I like her, but I wouldn't get between her and something she wants. Why?"

"Well, I was thinking about when I get my money. I wonder if it would be a worthwhile project to buy used computers for people who can't afford them. Alice, for example. She's a lonely person, and the Internet can be a godsend for the lonesome. Patricia has lived here all her life, and she's active in her church, and I wonder if perhaps she knows other people who might benefit from a computer. But she's not the sort I'm comfortable working with, she has that kind of rich person's veneer that seems . . . I don't know, impermeable, impenetrable. Do rich people send their children to special schools to learn that attitude?"

"Well, yes. On the other hand, Patricia didn't go to one. I think she tried to marry rich, but her in-laws didn't approve of her. They thought their son was too young to marry and that Patricia didn't have the right background, so they cut him off, refused to help out, even when Patricia got pregnant before their son finished law school. Now his grandmother dotes on the boy she wouldn't acknowledge."

Betsy tilted her head. "Is any of this true, or is it just the usual Excelsior gossip?"

Godwin laughed. "It's true, really it is. Patricia used to talk about it, until her husband got into politics. Now you'll never hear a bad word about her mother-in-law. Not that it was ever all that bad, I guess. I think Patricia was just tired from the constant struggle, and Margot was a sympathetic ear—and I'm a gifted eavesdropper."

"I guess a really hard struggle can give you that veneer, too," said Betsy, feeling much more sympathetic toward Patricia and trying to put a good face on her own remarks.

A little after five, just as Betsy was locking the front door, Jill appeared, large and dark, on the other side of the glass. She was in uniform and carrying a big box wrapped in midnight blue paper with silver and gold stars on it.

"Betsy, the weatherman says the storm system is still stalled and there's a blizzard warning out from here to Fargo."

"So? I'm not driving to Fargo. Who's the present for?"

"You. It's your Christmas present," Jill said.

"Oh. Thank you," said Betsy, ashamed for the second time that day of her sharp tongue. Jill put it into her arms and Betsy was surprised at how heavy it was. She hadn't bought Jill anything remotely this substantial. "I'll take it upstairs."

"No, take it with you. It's a bunch of little things. If you skid off the road, you can open them up to keep from being bored waiting for rescue. Now I've got to get back on patrol. Good luck, and drive very carefully."

"I will. And thank you for the present." Betsy had to go upstairs to feed Sophie, who was already sitting impatiently by the apartment door, but decided it was less effort to carry the heavy box to her car than up the stairs. She took it out back to put it on the passenger seat.

Up in the apartment, she checked the map one last time, put on her heavy coat, her new leather boots, her hat and scarf, and, pulling on her driving gloves, went down the back hallway and out into the storm.

Her big mistake was probably at that first turn. She knew Route 19 turned sharply to the right, but since she was looking for a curve rather than an intersection, she went right on through.

She noticed soon after that her brakes seemed soft, but they went quickly from soft to virtually nonexistent. She had to shift down to control her speed on curves.

It was totally dark, of course, and the snow was coming down heavily, so she had to weave a bit, using her headlights to make sure she was on her own side of the road. The road's surface was a white blank, and slippery. And the bridge the map had indicated just before the turn to Heidi's house never came. This was wrong. She was lost.

Betsy was not the sort who wouldn't stop and ask for directions, but now, ready to do so, there didn't seem to be anyplace to stop and ask. When trees didn't closely line the road, she could see nothing but thick snow, blowing directly into her windshield. But surely, if there were a gas station or some other kind of store, its lights would pierce the storm. Betsy saw nothing.

After awhile, she looked at her watch. She'd been out for forty minutes, which was supposed to be the entire time of her journey. She decided to stop at a private residence if she could see one, and find out where she was. But she wasn't afraid, she told herself, only a little nervous and concerned.

She began to realize she hadn't seen another car in some while. She couldn't even see any trace of previous vehicles on the road.

She tried to think what to do. Lake Minnetonka dominated the terrain around here. It was a large lake, with an extremely wobbly outline. Some said it was a collection of bays, others said it was actually seven lakes and a couple of creeks. In either case, that meant a thousand miles of shoreline. And by now, she had no idea which part of the shore she was on.

A curve ambushed her, and as she went into it, the wind came sideways, pushing at her car like a huge, soft hand. Her brakes were useless, but she wasn't going fast, so the car spun gently. Betsy could only hold onto the steering wheel, watching the play of headlights on a whirl of white snowflakes. Then the world went upward to the left and there was a twisty, bumpy slide, then she slammed to a stop, tipped at an angle to the right.

Betsy sat still for a few seconds, trembling. Her engine was still running, no warning lights had come on, her headlights remained lit. She didn't feel any sharp pains anywhere. She was all right, everything was all right.

After a bit, she looked out the side window. She was against a pine tree. She could see the bark and branches pressed against the glass, which wasn't broken. To the rear was blackness. Forward was driving snow, piling up on the windshield even as she looked. Her wipers leaped up, smearing the view. The instant they settled back, snow piled on again. To her left was a steep slope upward, dim and lumpish and scrawled with the marks of her passage.

The road was up there, on top of that slope.

She put the car into first gear and tried to move forward, but the wheels spun. She shifted into reverse, lifted the clutch gently, and again the wheels spun. She could see nothing out her rear mirror, not even a reflection of her taillights on the blowing snow. She shifted back into first. The car moved a few inches, tires spinning. The bark of the pine tree groaned against the door. She backed up, then rocked forward again, pleased to find an old skill still existed. She put it in reverse, and lifted the clutch. There was resistance, then suddenly the car bounced hard over something and slid around the tree, tilting more obviously backward. That scared her, and she jammed on the brake pedal, forgetting it was useless. The clutch slid out from under her other foot, and the engine died.

She started it up again, but the car ran only briefly before choking and stammering. She twisted the wheel, pumping the gas pedal, then the stink of raw gasoline filled the car and instantly she turned the ignition off.

I'm okay, I'm still okay, she reassured herself.

She left the headlights on, set the emergency brake, and found a flashlight in the glove box. It had been a while since she'd needed it, and she was unhappy to discover the batteries were half dead. She opened the door just an inch. The gasoline smell was stronger outside, and snow came in with a rush, driven by the wind.

The tilt of the car combined with the push of the wind to make getting out a serious effort.

She tried to walk around the car. An old fallen tree blocked her way to the back, stubs of branches poking up through the snow. That's what she'd backed over, and apparently something sticking up had punctured her gas tank. The car's back end was buried in a sprawling evergreen bush, and the shaggy-barked pine tree was a big old monarch. She turned around and went back, looking for the skid marks she'd made coming down the slope. She found them and followed them upward, slipping and falling, until suddenly she was on the road. She turned and looked down at her car.

All she could see was a light twinkling behind curtains of whirling snow.

Betsy trudged up the road for five minutes, the dying flashlight not much help. She hadn't changed out of her work clothes before setting out for Heidi's place, and the powerful wind whipped under both her heavy coat and her box-pleated woolen skirt, chilling her halfway up her thighs. When she stopped and turned off the flashlight, she didn't see the lights of a store, a house, or a barn anywhere.

Then she turned around, and she couldn't see her headlights, either. Alarmed, she started back. The wind was strong, shoving and tugging at her as she walked. Staggering onto the slope was her only warning that she was not keeping to the road. This happened three times, and by then she was wondering if she'd gone past her car. She stopped to peer all around. An extra strong gust of wind stung her face and she turned her back to it. And there were the headlights, gleaming fitfully from down the slope. As suddenly as they appeared, they were gone again in the yellow swirl her dying flashlight's beam made of the snow flying all around her.

But having found her direction, she looked for the skid marks—they were nearly drifted over—and half fell, half slid along them back down the slope, until she reached her car. After another struggle, she got the door open enough to get back in. There, she shut off the headlights and sat in gasoline-scented darkness to catch her breath.

Now she was scared.

Five

※

"Hello, Godwin? It's Jill. Say, do you have Heidi Watgren's phone number?"

"I already called her. Betsy never arrived."

"Oh, heck."

"My very words, or nearly. I was hoping she got there and Heidi had the sense to make her stay."

"Me, too."

"Is it too soon to file a missing person report?"

"Ordinarily, yes. But this is different. I hope she has sense enough to open that box."

Betsy's stumble back down the slope had warmed her up but left her caked with snow. She had knocked the worst of it off before getting back into the car, but her coat and skirt were now damp, even wet in places. And once she started cooling off, she kept cooling right into chilled.

The stink of gas wasn't as overpowering now. Maybe most of what had spilled had evaporated or run away downhill. Was there still some gas in the tank?

She turned the key to Utilities, then turned on the running lights to make the dash light up. The gas gauge indicated a little less than a quarter of a tank. She'd had close to half a tank when she started out, and she hadn't used that much driving.

And gasoline vapor was explosive. Maybe she shouldn't try to start the car. But she was freezing, and rescue seemed remote.

Take a chance, said a small but certain voice inside her head.

She unlatched the door in case she had to get out fast, took a deep breath, held it, and twisted the key in the ignition. The car cranked strongly, but the engine didn't catch. Nor did it catch on fire.

She released the key, exhaled. After a few moments, she took another breath and cranked again.

No joy.

There was gas in the tank, and the battery was working fine. Why wouldn't it start? She twisted the key angrily, pumping the gas pedal hard and fast. Still nothing.

She sat in silence for awhile, feeling a kind of weightiness, as if the snow was piling onto her head and shoulders instead of the roof and hood of her car. The gasoline stink was strong enough to make her feel lightheaded, so she cracked the window on the passenger side. What was the correct procedure when one was lost on a back road in a blizzard, with no stores, houses, or traffic, wearing a damp overcoat, sitting with the window open in a car that wouldn't start?

*   *   *

John heard a tiny noise of scrubbing and came to investigate. Godwin was doing what he usually did when he was frustrated: cleaning the bath-
rooms. John didn't like Betsy—she sometimes took Godwin seriously, and John
liked him boyish—but here was his lighthearted boy so upset over the woman
that he was scrubbing the grout on the floor with a toothbrush. John came in to
lift him by the elbows and take the toothbrush away from him.

"Goddy, it's not like she's gone down the Colorado in a cabbage leaf. She's
in a nice warm car somewhere, listening to the radio and missing her dinner,
which she can well afford to do. She'll be found as soon as the snow stops and
they start clearing the roads."

"I know, you're right. But I do wish she'd listened to me when I warned her
about going out in the storm!"

John felt his usual reply to that complaint—"Why would anyone listen to a
silly little goof like you?"—was inappropriate. Which later caused him to re-
flect that while his relationships tended to end when there were signs of maturity, he didn't want to end this one with Godwin. Interesting.

It had been a long time—not hours, though it seemed that long.
The bones in Betsy's feet ached with cold, as did the tips of her fingers. She
wished she'd brought mittens along. Each finger in its lonesome sleeve of the
driving gloves yearned to snuggle against its fellow. Perhaps she should take
the gloves off and put her hands in her pockets. Perhaps she should get into the
backseat and huddle up under her coat, maybe go to sleep. She could escape
this nightmare for a few hours and perhaps wake to daylight and the sounds of
traffic.

No, wait, going to sleep in the cold was a very, very bad idea.

She began to move as violently as she could in her seat, stamping her feet
and waving her arms. Her feet hurt when they hit the floor, but she persisted,
and she felt the pain lessen. In a little while she was warmer. And the stirring of
her blood made her thinking a little clearer.

Perhaps it would help if she took off her coat and used it as a blanket. She
could cover that little bare section of shin above her boots that way. Suddenly
that seemed the most desirable thing in the world.

But trying to take off a full-length wool coat while seated behind a steering
wheel of a car in the pitch dark is at best difficult. And the confusing lean of the
car didn't help. During her efforts to get out of it, Betsy fell over sideways and
knocked against the big Christmas gift Jill had given her. Suddenly a light
went on over her head. There had been something significant in the tone of Jill's

voice as she suggested Betsy bring it along, "to open if you slide off the road." She reined in the wild hope that rose in her breast, even as she decided the coat could wait and went through another struggle to get it settled back into place.

She turned on the overhead light and reached for the package. She'd forgotten how large and heavy it was; it took two tries before she got it pulled close to her.

The Christmas paper looked even more glorious in the dim light, though the bow was a little crushed. Betsy took a deep breath and then rapidly dismantled the wrapping. The box inside was a sturdy grocery store refugee printed with a soup maker's logo. With trembling fingers, Betsy pulled off the heavy gray tape holding it shut.

The top item appeared to be thin aluminum foil folded into a square eight inches on a side. But it was almost as flexible as cloth, and it kept unfolding larger and larger, until it was as big as a sleeping bag. It was a space blanket; Betsy had seen them on television. They were supposed to keep people warm even in outer space. She arranged it around her shins and thighs and lap, turning it down at the top so her arms were free.

Already she was smiling. God bless Jill!

Under the space blanket was a very odd assortment of items: a bright-orange toy snow shovel with a folding handle; a pair of empty coffee cans in two sizes; a very large chocolate bar; a can of salted cashews, two bottles of designer water, a box of wooden matches; a heavy flashlight with batteries already in it; a couple of votive candles; heavy, rough-leather mittens made of sheepskin turned inside out and stuffed inside a thick knit wool hat; a ten-pound bag of kitty litter; and, still in its box, a cell phone. Under the cell phone was a note in Jill's neat printing.

Dear Betsy, I hope you are opening this in front of your Christmas tree! This is a Winter Survival Kit. Keep it in your trunk all winter and if you don't use it, eat the treats for Easter and replace them next fall. If you get stuck in the snow, dig a path with the shovel and lay down the cat litter for traction. If you still can't get out, dial 911 on the phone. (It won't activate until you use it, so it won't cost you anything if you're not having an emergency. Clever?) Tell the operator where you are, and someone will come and get you. While you are waiting: Stay with the car! Run your engine five or ten minutes every half hour to get warm, then shut it off to save gas. Get out every time you start it and clear away the tailpipe so you don't fill up with carbon monoxide. No matter what, stay with the car. Even if you run out of gas and are stuck in a place where the phone doesn't work, stay with the car. Light a candle in the smaller can. It will provide light and a small amount of heat. If you run out of water, put snow in the bigger can and melt it over the smaller one. Wrap up in the space blanket. Think cheerful thoughts. Eat, drink, and be merry. Rescue will come before you know it. Jill

Betsy's eyes stung with tears. Jill knew what a fool Betsy was; she knew

Betsy hadn't been giving this weather the respect it deserved. Betsy should have listened to her, listened to all of them warning her not to go out.

At the very least, Betsy should have put together her own winter survival kit. There had been an article about it in the paper weeks ago.

If she'd made up her own survival kit, then at least the candy bar would have almonds in it.

She smiled at this thin joke. It was the cellular phone, of course, renewing her courage. The worst that could happen now was that she'd have a whacking great towing bill. And so long as he was whacking at her wallet, maybe she could persuade the tow truck operator to make a little detour to Heidi's place to pick up that damn pillow. Betsy snorted and shook her head. Amazing! She'd gone from being afraid she was going to die to being concerned about June Connor's Christmas.

She wondered what the charge was for cellular phone service. And wait, it was possible that her car had mushed against that tree hard enough to be dented. If so, that might generate the biggest bill of all, because Betsy had a $500 deductible on her car insurance.

She tossed the shovel and kitty litter into the backseat; that solution was out. And with the smell of gas still permeating the inside of the car, she'd better not strike a match.

The directions pamphlet for the cell phone seemed daunting until Betsy realized it was printed in five languages. In short order she had the phone plugged into her cigarette lighter and was dialing, first a number to activate it, then 911, and pushing the send button.

Ring, ring, ring, ring, ring. "Nine one one, what is your emergency?" said a woman's voice.

"I've had an accident with my car. I slid off the road into a tree, and now I'm stuck."

"Are there any injured parties?"

"No. And I'm alone in the car."

"Is there another vehicle involved?"

"No."

"Where are you?"

"Don't you have one of those ID things that tells where the call is coming from?"

"All it says is that this is a cell phone."

Uh-oh. "Ah, I don't know where I am. I started out from Excelsior on Nineteen for an address in Shorewood. Let's see, I was driving for about forty minutes, and I made three or four turns. But that's not very helpful, is it?"

"No, ma'am. Can you see any landmarks?"

"No. In fact, I could barely see the road. I didn't see any lights, either, or I would have stopped to ask my way, even at a house. This may be a back road. There hasn't been any traffic for a long time, since before I skidded off it. I slid down a little slope, and I'm jammed against a big pine tree. I've been sitting here for a long time."

"Have you tried to drive out?"

"My engine won't start." Betsy had to stop at this point and swallow hard. "And, and there's a smell of gasoline, I guess I tore or punctured my gas tank. I have a winter emergency kit with me, with a space blanket and a candy bar and candles, so I'm all right for now, except I can't run my engine, and I'm scared to light the candles, and I'm getting really, really cold." Tears spilled over despite her best effort. "I'm sorry, I'm really, really sorry." Sorry for being an idiot, sorry for breaking down, sorry her last words might be to a stranger on the phone.

"Hang on, honey, you're going to be all right, we'll figure out a way to find you and get you out of there."

Betsy sniffed. "Yes, of course you will. I'm just a little scared."

"Sweetie, anyone in your situation would be scared! Now, you say you started out on Route Nineteen. When did you turn off it?"

"I didn't think I did, but I must have. The map said the road would go left so I did, except after that nothing matched the map."

"Do you have the map with you?"

"No. It was just a short trip, to pick up a pillow for someone. I never thought I'd get lost."

"I'm going to go have a talk with some people about this, so you need to hang up and be patient. I won't be long."

"All right. Oh, can you do me a favor?"

"What's that?"

"Could you notify Officer Jill Cross of the Excelsior Police Department about what's happened? She's a friend, and she'll want to be part of the rescue operation."

"Aren't you Jill Cross? That's who my phone ID says you are."

"No, she gave me this phone for emergencies. I guess she was willing to pay the first month's rent on it, bless her. My name is Betsy Devonshire."

"Oh, you're the woman who took over that needlework shop in Excelsior! I've been meaning to stop by."

"If you come by tomorrow, I'll give you a terrific buy on any item you want."

The operator said, "It's a date. Now, if I don't call you back inside of fifteen minutes, you call nine one one again and ask for me. I'm Meg Dooley."

Betsy broke the connection, turned out the overhead light, and sat for a bit in total darkness. Then it occurred to her to consult her watch in order to begin timing fifteen minutes. She pressed the button on the side of its face and it glowed its beautiful aqua color. Only seven past seven. It seemed much later than that.

The watch's face glowed a surprisingly long time after she released the button, but at last it faded to black. She sat with the phone cradled in both hands, waiting for it to ring again.

Jill called Godwin and told him what the emergency operator had told her. She told him she was going to the police station and would call him from there.

"Anything I can do?" he asked.

"Pass the word, I guess. Because all we can do right now is wait. Thanks."

She hurried out to get her car out of its garage and bully her way through the snow-clogged driveway into the street. Though she'd been aware of the weather reports, she was nevertheless alarmed at the depth of the snow and the strength of the wind.

The streets were deserted, streetlights dimmed by the thickness of snow in the air. A plow had gone down Water Street, burying parked automobiles. Drifting snow smoothed their outlines until they looked like the ghost of that carnival ride called The Caterpillar.

Jill drove up Lake Street, past Crewel World, and saw that Betsy had left a light on in her apartment over the store.

Didn't think she'd be gone that long, thought Jill. She turned onto Excelsior Boulevard, whose high-tone name belied its narrow ordinariness, and went down it to the new brick-and-stone building that housed the police department.

Jill had been prepared to like Betsy for her sister Margot's sake—Margot had been Jill's best friend for years. But her present sharp concern made her realize she had come to like Betsy for herself, for her courage and tenacity, her sense of humor, her unpredictability. Jill was braver and more tenacious than Betsy, but she was not in the least unpredictable, so it was odd that she should like unpredictable people, but she did.

I'm not going to let Betsy die. She stifled that thought, shaken that it had even occurred. She parked and hurried into the station. Of course Betsy was not going to die! What a stupid idea!

The cell phone rang, sudden and loud. Betsy, startled, flipped it onto the floor and had to scramble for it in the slush and dirt. By the time she got hold of it, it was ringing for the fourth time. She pushed the button. "Hello?" she said a trifle crossly.

"I told you not to go out on the road when it's snowing like this."

Betsy laughed. "Hi, Jill! From now on, your word is law. Are you the one coming to get me?"

"Maybe. But not right now. I'm sorry, Betsy, but we can't come looking for you because the roads are closed."

"Couldn't you send one of those big snowplows?"

"The plows are working exclusively on the freeways, trying to keep them passable for emergency vehicles. We could probably get one to come after you, if he knew where to come. But he can't just wander around, hoping he'll come across you."

There was a pause. Betsy said, "So what do we do?"

"Right now they say the storm won't move out of the area till morning. Once the storm quits, we'll turn out in strength looking for you. You'll be easy to find in daylight. Meanwhile, you just sit tight."

"Daylight? Jill, I can't sit here in the freezing dark all night!"

"Of course you can. You'll be fine, now that you opened that box I sent along."

"But—are you sure? I mean, all night? That's scary."

"Well, did you wrap up in that metallic blanket?"

"Yes. And it works. I was surprised, but it does."

"You didn't walk out on the ice and fall in the lake?"

"No, of course not."

"So you're not chilled from a soak in ice water. Is the car far off the road, or only on the shoulder?"

"I'm completely off the road."

"Good. That means you won't get squashed by accident when the plow does come through. Are you out of chocolate already?"

"No. I haven't started on it, actually."

"I think you should eat some of it now. Chocolate has lots of energy, to help keep you warm. And it has that stuff that makes you happy. What's it called?"

"I don't know. Phenyl-something."

"That's the stuff. So forget your diet and eat some. Eat a lot. You'll be warmer and you'll feel better."

"All right."

"Is the passenger compartment tight? I mean, is snow coming in, or the wind?"

"Well, you see, that's the problem. I ripped open the gas tank or something. I tried to start the engine, and it turns over but won't start, and there's a strong smell of gasoline. Does that mean it's okay to light a candle? The smell is so strong I've got a window cracked, trying to air it out."

"Hmmm, maybe you'd better not, at least right now. If the smell goes away, then you can."

"That's what I thought. But I'm cold. I'm really cold."

"All right, that makes a difference." There was a weighty pause, while Jill thought. "Have you got any idea at all where you are?"

"No. I got so lost toward the end I didn't even know what direction I was heading—and I usually have a pretty good sense of direction. I started out on Nineteen, but I missed something, I guess. Or maybe I didn't. I thought I was lost, and then I thought I was all right, but the road was curving wrong, so I guess I was lost after all. There were sharp curves where the map says easy ones, and my brakes quit working . . ." Betsy wasn't crying, but only because she had stopped talking.

Jill wasn't one to encourage people to break down. "That must have been tough," she said briskly. "How strong is that gasoline smell?"

"Well, it was pretty strong for a while, but I think it's not as bad as it was. Or maybe I'm just getting used to it. If I can't run the engine, how am I going to keep from freezing to death?"

"You're not going to freeze to death, okay? You're inside, you have a heavy coat and boots, and that blanket. You have water and something to eat. But you've got a window open and you're cold, which means you probably shouldn't curl up and go to sleep. I have an idea about how we might figure out at least your general location. You just sit back and relax, eat, drink, think good thoughts. I'll call you again in a while, okay?"

Six

❖

Godwin was sitting on the couch, asleep. The television was murmuring about cookware and flashing an 800 number on the screen. He jerked awake when the phone rang. "Yuh?" he croaked into the receiver, having grabbed it on the first ring so as not to wake John. "Yes?" he said, more clearly.

"Godwin, it's Jill. I have the phone company trying to triangulate from the car phone signal to figure out where Betsy is, but it's taking awhile. Last time I talked to her, she sounded a little sleepy. I may get called in, so I'm forming a committee to take turns calling her. Want to come?"

"Sure. Where?"

"How about we meet at Crewel World? Will you go down now and open up?"

"I'm on my way." Godwin broke the connection and stood up. He hadn't undressed; all he had to do was add a few layers.

P atricia Fairland was struggling with a bad dream. Her husband murmured "Pat?" reaching over to touch her shoulder and wake her.

"What, what? Oh, sorry, bad dream," she whispered. "Thanks, 'm okay now." She lay still until he went back to sleep, which didn't take long.

But she didn't want to reenter that dream again, so she slipped out of bed and went to the window. She lifted the heavy drape at its edge and looked into chaos. The line between air and ground had vanished into flying snow. She could see two blobs of blue-white light that were the miniature streetlights marking the gate to the pool, barely a dozen yards from the window. The lights didn't seem to have any stems, which meant the snow was drifted four feet deep right there. The big old elm beside the pool was waving its huge branches as if this were a hurricane, not a blizzard.

Nothing out in that can live, she thought, shivering. She dropped the curtain and turned her back to it. She felt a painful gratitude for the thick carpet under her bare feet, the almost inaudible hum of the furnace as it heated the beautiful house and her and the children safe asleep and her husband in the big, luxurious bed. It had been a long, hard struggle. The last hurdle had been Peter's mother, but her signal of acceptance had been buying this house as a very belated wedding gift last year.

The phone rang softly—its bell was turned all but off and could not wake people already asleep. But Patricia hurried to it anyway and lifted the receiver. "Hello?" she murmured.

"Patricia, it's Jill. We're meeting at Crewel World to help Betsy. Can you come?"

Patricia's heart leaped. It was all over town about Betsy; no less than four people had called her earlier in the evening with the news that Betsy was missing. "Has she been found?"

"Sort of. She's in a ditch out there somewhere, we don't know where, and her engine won't start. But she's got a cell phone and we're going to keep calling her. Temperatures are dropping, and we don't want her to fall asleep."

"Yes, of course. Oh, this is awful, she must be terrified! But I don't think I can get out of the driveway, much less drive eight miles to town." She gave a scared laugh. "You don't need to be trying to keep two of us awake."

"That's right, I forgot you live that far out now. So never mind, go back to bed."

"No, no, I was up anyway, looking out at the storm. And now I'm aware of Betsy's situation, I couldn't possibly sleep. I'm going downstairs to make a pot of coffee. Can you call me every so often, too, just to let me know how she's doing?"

"Sure. Say a prayer, okay?"

"Of course."

John and Godwin's house was about five blocks from Crewel World. Godwin decided walking would be safer than driving his little sports car. He bundled up, but not too much—walking in snow was hard work, and it wasn't bitter cold out. He added a light sweater to his cotton shirt, then put on his navy pea coat and covered his head with a knit hat.

It took him twenty minutes to get to the shop, even walking down the middle of the streets where the snow was not so deep. As he approached, hatless and perspiring, there was someone already waiting in the shallow shelter of the doorway. It was Martha Winters. She was wearing a long scarf that wrapped around and around, making a sloping line between her shoulders and her fur-trimmed hat, with several feet left over to wave at him.

"H'lo, Godwin!" she called. She was shuffling her feet to keep warm. That was the tricky part about dressing for weather like this. Any activity warmed you up, but standing still chilled you fast.

"Yoo-hoo!" he replied and hurried up to her. The wind altered suddenly, cuffed him from behind and then threw a handful of snow in his naked ear. The gray townhouse complex across the street stymied the gale after its rush down the lake and left it confused about its direction. The snow it carried whirled as much upward as down and likewise sideways, like one of those globes you shake to make a winter scene.

"Not a fit night out for man or beast," he opined in a W. C. Fields voice, crowding in beside Martha to unlock the door.

He'd barely gotten it open and stepped back so Martha could go in ahead of him when a deep voice came faintly: "Wait for me!"

He turned and recognized Alice's tall, mannish shape. He waved, then waited.

The snow was two feet deep in front of the door, and they tracked it in with them. December snow wasn't like January's. This snow was heavy, full of moisture. Godwin turned on the lights and hurried to the back of the store to get the snow shovel and a broom. He scooped melting snow back out and cleared the doorway while Martha swept behind him. Alice went into the back room and started the coffee.

They only cleared a space in front of the door; trying to clear the sidewalk was futile. Then Martha turned the broom on Godwin, who was covered with snow. They heard the snarl of a snowmobile. "Who is that?" asked Martha, trying to look down the street while still dusting Godwin down.

"*Whoops!*" whooped Godwin. "Watch where you aim that thing!" Laughing, he stepped halfway through an opening in the snowbank along the sidewalk and peered up the street. "Hey, I think it's Phil Galvin! And he's got a passenger!" Godwin began to wave. "Yoo-hoo, Phil-ill!"

The dark figure on the black snowmobile waved back and came though the opening to the building's driveway onto the sidewalk. The machine, a shiny black and hot pink number, came up level with Crewel World's big, lit-up window and stopped. The engine shut off.

Phil's passenger got off first. "Hi, it's me!" she said. It was Shelly Donohue. She was wearing boots that looked safe for space travel, wool pants, and a ski jacket with a hood. She was carrying a plastic drawstring bag that Godwin recognized as a Crewel World bag. The bag was bulging.

"Brought a project?" he asked.

"And some snacks," she replied.

"Good thinking," he said, waving her and Phil into the shop. Godwin realized then just how rattled he was. He hadn't brought the sport bag with his own projects in it, the one he normally carried everywhere.

At first it was fun. Betsy would call, then half an hour later one of them would call. Jill came and talked to Betsy about her boyfriend Lars's hobby farm—two of his miniature goats were pregnant, and he was going to make cheese—and about the Christmas ornaments she and Betsy had both been working on. "I even donated one of them to the Minneapolis Art Museum," said Jill. "They're putting up a tree decorated entirely with locally handmade ornaments."

Shelly talked about the medieval unit her class was doing, how the children had set up a medieval court with a king and queen and knights—some of them girls—and a magician. "I'm teaching them how to spin wool into yarn," she said. "Then we're going to try weaving."

On her turn, Martha thanked Betsy for being so clever about murder investigations and talked about the tapestry project they would be starting soon. "Everyone seems enthusiastic about naming the library after Father Keane, and we're going to stitch Lucy Abrams's name onto the canvas—once we're sure she hasn't already done that."

Alice said she was making loaves of raisin-cinnamon bread as Christmas presents, and Betsy said she often gave loaves of an Austrian bread that had blanched almonds, grated orange rind, and two kinds of raisins in it. They agreed to exchange recipes.

Phil said he was thinking of tackling an authentic aran sweater and asked Betsy if she could special order the yarn for him.

"Tell Godwin to remind me," she said.

At two, Jill became worried about using up the car battery and limited the calls to five minutes. Then she got a page from the police station, asking her to come in and relieve Emily at the switchboard.

At four-thirty, it was Godwin's turn. He talked about buying another Christmas stocking for himself, and then about his first attempt at silk gauze. "I was doing a twenty-six-count linen and making a real mess of it, remember? So I thought I was crazy to try a forty-count silk gauze, but you know something? It works! I don't even get out the Dazor, I can work it sitting by the window! Silk gauze is almost like needlepoint canvas, the holes are that obvious. I'm doing that pansy bouquet. I'm going to make it into a box lid."

"Uh-huh," said Betsy, sounding not very interested.

"Are you all right?"

"I'm just tired, I guess."

"I think it's time we marched along with the teddy bears again." He started to sing in a fair tenor, "Picnic time for teddy bears . . . Are you marching? Knees up nice and high."

After a few bars he realized she wasn't marching and stopped.

Betsy said, "I'd like something warm to drink," as if she were giving an order in a restaurant.

"Are you out of water?"

"Huh?"

"Isn't there any bottled water left?"

"I guess so."

"Well, take a sip of that."

"Okay. Are they coming soon, Godwin?"

"Very soon, I promise. The snow is slacking off, and it'll be daylight pretty quick. They'll be knocking on your car window any time."

"It's not getting light over here. And it's still snowing."

"But not as hard, right? Hang on. It'll be over soon."

"Godwin, it's never going to be over."

At five it took four rings before she answered, and she wasn't tracking at all well. Martha, near tears, was afraid her fear would infect Betsy, and Alice was openly crying. Shelly was comforting them, and Phil had fallen asleep, head down on the table, so Godwin took the receiver from Martha.

"Now listen up, woman!" he scolded. "We've been at this for too long to give up now. I called Jill, and she told me what she's been doing. A few years ago, there was a woman in South Dakota in the same fix you're in. What they did was triangulate the signal as it went through the cell phone towers, and by measuring the signal's strength at each tower, they figured out how far she was from each one. Does that make sense?"

"No. I don't know. I guess not."

"Well, it made perfect sense when Jill described it. But you have to keep talking, so they can trace the signal. All right?"

"You're lying to keep my spirits up. Nobody's coming."

"*Me? Lie?* Betsy, would I *lie?*"

"No. I don't know. I guess not."

But that was the last time she called them. They had to call her every time, now.

"Don't call me anymore," she mumbled at seven. "It's dark all the time. I'm going to die. I'm just too tired."

"Of all the nonsense—!" began Godwin, too tired himself to think clearly.

"Tell the Pig to go home and not to marry again," she said. "And I wrote this down, you get the shop. Don't forget to take inventory."

"Betsy, I'm not taking over the shop."

"Why not?"

"Because what are you going to do when you're home and safe? I don't know if I'd want you working for me. That's a joke, okay?"

"I'm not coming home. Because they can't find me. They'll never find me. Listen Godwin, you take the shop and run it, all right? And Jill gets half the money."

"Betsy—"

"Say you'll do it, Godwin. Say it."

"All right, when you die at age ninety, I'll take over the store and give half the money to Jill. I'll be twenty-nine by then and ready to settle down. That's another joke, Betsy."

"Keep the same part-timers, okay?"

"Why aren't you laughing?"

"And don't let Irene teach a class. She's a lousy teacher."

"Shall I tell her your last thoughts were of her?"

Behind him, Martha wept, "Oh, Betsy, Betsy!"

Alice shook Phil awake. "Betsy's dying, wake up!"

"She is not. Don't say that!" cried Shelly.

All four stared at Godwin, who was listening hard. "Who'll take Sophie?" fretted Betsy feebly.

"Boss lady, what is this all about? It's morning! I can actually see daylight outside, honest I can! And the snow has stopped. The sky is clear, the snow has stopped! Snowplows are already on their way! They'll be pulling up any second, and be running up and down the road, calling your name. They've got hot cocoa in a thermos with them, and you'll be just fine. And there you sit, worrying about your spoiled cat. Now stop it, okay? Just stop such nonsense. Betsy, I think we should do some foot stamps. You haven't done them in a while. Ready? If you go out in the woods today—Betsy?"

"And how can it be light where you are? It's still dark here."

"No, really, it's starting to get light, can't you see it? It's going to be a beautiful day."

"No sun here. No sun."

"Snow on the windshield," suggested Phil.

"Well, of course! Betsy, that's because there's snow on your windows. You need to roll your window down so the snow will fall off. Then you'll see it's getting light, and you can wave at the snowplow when it comes along. Roll your window down. Betsy? Roll your window down, now."

"'S too cold. Don't let 'em put her t'sleep, 'kay? Promise."

"Yeah, yeah, I promise. Roll your window down, Betsy, and you can see the sun come up. Okay?"

"In a minute." After a very long pause, "In a minute."

And that was the last anyone could get out of her. No amount of shouting, cajoling, ordering, or begging got a reply.

Jill exploded into the shop. "We know where she is!" she said, her face alive, her eyes sparkling. "A snowplow is on its way to her right now!"

"Jill," said Godwin, coming to take her by the arm, "we can't raise her. She's not answering."

"What?" said Jill. "Where's the phone?"

"Maybe the battery's dead," said Shelly, holding it out to her.

Martha, fending off despair, agreed. "These cell phones will drain a car battery right down if you don't run the engine and recharge it." Her face was pale, her eyes red-rimmed.

"She's fine!" said Jill, grabbing the phone. "Betsy, this is Jill. Betsy? Listen, they did that triangulation thing—Did you tell her about it?"

Godwin nodded.

"And Betsy, they know where you are. A snowplow is on its way to you this minute. Betsy? Betsy! *Betsy!*"

Jill turned on Godwin. "How long since she talked to you?"

Godwin looked at his watch, though he knew almost to the second how long it had been. "Twenty-seven minutes. How long till they get there?"

"Forty minutes, maybe? Less than an hour. But she's in a white car covered with snow and completely off the road. If she could flash her lights or blow her horn when she hears them coming, that would help." She lifted the phone again. "Betsy, this is Jill. We're coming to get you, but you can help us find you. Are you listening? Turn your headlights on. Do you hear me? Turn your headlights on, right now! Betsy? Have you done that, have you turned your headlights on? Talk to me, say something!"

She wasn't cold anymore, but she was muddled and very, very tired. She felt her head fall sideways, onto something hard. She thought very briefly about moving it, but it fit her ear. Besides, it was making a noise that sounded like her name, which was pleasant. She wanted to make a noise back, but she was just too tired.

The door went *bing* and everyone looked up to see someone standing just inside. The sun on the snow made a blinding halo around the figure, so they couldn't see who it was.

A mild voice said, "I heard. Is there anything I can do?" It was Father John, mufflered to the eyebrows, with an old fedora on top.

"We can't raise her," said Jill.

Godwin added, "We know what road she's on, and just about where along it she is, and the snowplow led an ambulance out there, but they can't find her. We think her car is buried under the snow. They're walking up and down the road, but it's taking a long time."

"She's dying," said Alice. "Or already dead."

"Who are you talking to on the phone?" asked the priest, approaching, hat in one hand, unwrapping his scarf with the other.

"Her, sort of," said Godwin. "The line is open, but she's not answering."

"May I try?" asked Father John, taking the receiver. "Betsy, this is Father John Rettger of Trinity." He was speaking slowly and firmly. "Can you hear me? We are going to pray for you and for your rescuers. Let us pray. In the Name of the Father, the Son, and the Holy Spirit, Amen." He crossed himself. "Our Father, who art in heaven, hallowed be Thy name. Thy Kingdom come, Thy will be done—" He began nodding hard, and gestured at the trio standing around the table, and his voice slowed further, as if to give a slow-speaking person time to catch up. "—on earth, as it is in heaven. Give us this day, our daily bread, and forgive us our trespasses, as we forgive those who trespass against us. And lead us not into temptation, but deliver us from evil, for Thine is the Kingdom, and the power, and the glory, forever and ever. Amen. Betsy, lean forward and make your horn blow." He said to Jill, "Tell them to listen for it!"

"Is she doing it?" demanded Shelly. "Is she doing it?"

Jill grabbed the mike attached to her shoulder and said, "Fifty-six ten."

"Ten fifty-six, go."

"Tell the plow to shut all engines off, tell them to listen for a car horn!"

"Ten fifty-six, copy."

Father John said, "Again, let us pray," and started in on The Lord's Prayer again. This time, both in prayer and psychic encouragement to Betsy, everyone joined in. At the end, he said, "Are you blowing your horn, Betsy?"

Godwin, standing beside him, leaned toward the priest's ear. Very, very faintly, he heard a sound that could have been a car horn blowing steadily. Or it could have been static.

Then there was a wait that went on forever—or about ten minutes' worth of forever.

Jill's radio suddenly crackled, "Ten fifty-six."

Jill lifted the microphone fastened to her shoulder and barked, "Ten!"

"They've located the car, and Ms. Devonshire. They're putting her in the emergency vehicle now. Transport will be to Hennepin County Medical Center in Minneapolis."

Jill was the only one who understood the crackling transmission, but when she translated, the room broke into cheers. People slapped one another on the shoulder or shook hands or hugged. Father John was roughly handled, but he kept grinning.

"How did you know what to do?" Jill asked, when she could be heard.

"All priests visit the dying, of course, and often, as the end approaches, the dying person will sink into unconsciousness. They don't respond when you talk to them, won't squeeze your hand when you take it. But when you start to pray, and you come to The Lord's Prayer, very often they will surprise you by suddenly joining in. If they're Christian, that is. I understand that Jewish people on their deathbeds will equally often join in on the Sh'ma—you know, 'Hear O Israel, the Lord your God is one God, and you shall love the Lord your God with all your heart, with all your soul, and with all your mind.' I wonder if there's a deeply familiar prayer in the Muslim faith that would work the same way. I know there is that statement that starts all their services, 'There is no God but Allah, and Mohammed is his prophet.' But that's rather short to rouse an unconscious person and give him or her time to join in. Perhaps there's something longer. I should look that up sometime."

Seven

❖

Betsy had little memory of what was done to warm her up, save that it was unpleasant. By the time she was able to pay attention, they had taken the noisy part away, or put her in another room, one or the other.

Then she slept for a long time.

She woke and it was night. She felt clear-headed and able to take an interest in her surroundings. A nurse came in and took her temperature and pulse and had a nurse's aide bring her a cup of cocoa. Betsy turned on the television and watched the second half of a movie with such a strange plot that the next day she wondered if it had been a dream. She slept again.

She woke famished. It was daylight, and someone brought her toast and coffee. Then a nurse came to tell her she was going home. *This sure isn't like television,* she thought, signing papers. On sitcoms, whatever brought the hero or heroine into hospitals as a patient quickly faded into the background and he or she was soon joking with visitors and/or enjoying the ministrations of kind and attentive nurses.

The nurse gave Betsy copies of the papers along with a lengthy list of things she should do (eat lightly, get plenty of bed rest) and shouldn't do (operate heavy machinery) for the next twenty-four hours. There was also a list of symptoms to watch for. If any appeared, Betsy was to call her doctor immediately.

Oh, and Betsy wasn't to drive a car for forty-eight hours.

As if, thought Betsy, whose car was, so far as she knew, still crumpled against a pine tree somewhere.

As she handed the pen back, she said, "If I'm in such precarious condition, with dangerous symptoms threatening, maybe I shouldn't go home just yet."

The nurse laughed. "No, you'll be fine recovering at home. The only people who go home well from the hospital nowadays are the doctors."

Betsy chuckled obediently and asked, "But what about my clothes?"

"They're in this closet here," said the nurse.

"Oh, no," said Betsy. "I'm not putting that underwear back on again."

"Then you'll have to call someone who can bring you fresh underwear."

Reluctant as Betsy was to have anyone but herself rummaging around in her lingerie drawer, she called Godwin at his home. Not that she would allow him to do it, but he had Jill and Shelly's phone numbers. When she got an answering machine, she left a quick message asking him to call her at the hospital—she had to consult her wrist to find out what room she was in—and then tried the shop.

"Of course we're open!" said Godwin, when he answered. "My dear, you wouldn't believe how many women woke up this morning desperate to find a Christmas gift for Aunt Mary, who never does anything but needlepoint! And, of course, there are the curious, who want to hear all about your adventure in the storm."

"Thank God for Aunt Mary," said Betsy, who then explained her dilemma. Godwin said at once, "I'll call Shelly. She's already asking if there's anything she can do."

Betsy told him to tell Shelly she wanted a complete change of clothing. "There's a spare key to my apartment in the bottom drawer of the desk," said Betsy.

"Winter break starts today," Shelly said an hour later, when Betsy asked why she wasn't at school. She had brought lingerie, jeans and a sweater, socks and walking shoes. And that ugly secondhand coat from the shop's back room, Betsy's only other winter outerwear. And a big garbage bag for the used clothes.

She walked beside Betsy as a nurse wheeled her down to the main entrance, and then left her there while she went to get her Dodge Caravan from the parking lot. The vehicle, a purple so dark it was almost black, pulled up under the wide, tall portico. Betsy abandoned the wheelchair the nurse wanted her to stay in and walked the few yards to the vehicle. Getting up and in was a problem, but Betsy gritted her teeth and managed. Shelly had turned the heat on high, it was like July in the Mojave in there. Betsy unzipped the coat.

But it was definitely December in Minnesota outside. Even the parking meters wore thick caps of snow, and every sharp angle of brick and glass and steel was softened by drapes and mounds of white. As they pulled out into light traffic, their tires chewed a brown sugar mix of snow, salt, and sand. Once they got onto 394, the lanes were already mostly clear, though about half the cars they saw wore slabs of snow on their roofs, which trailed thin comets' tails behind them.

For a wonder almost everyone was driving only forty-five or fifty miles an hour. In Betsy's experience, Minnesotans took speed limits under advisement.

They took the exit onto Highway Fifteen, just past Wayzata, where there was mostly countryside. The road was covered with snow, and the fields were a dazzle of white, with shadings of gold, pink, and lavender under the trees. Evergreens were trimmed in white, and the crotches of leafless trees were filled with snow. Not a footprint marred the surface anywhere.

"Very Christmasy," noted Shelly.

"I don't like snow as much as I used to," replied Betsy, looking at young pines bent almost double under their burdens.

"You'll get over that," said Shelly. "By the way, you won't have to cook for days, everyone's bringing something for you."

"Including you?" asked Betsy hopefully. "I just love that casserole thing you do with chicken and noodles and cream of mushroom soup."

"Casserole? Is that what you call a hot dish?"

Betsy laughed. "No, hot dish is the name Minnesotans gave to what everyone else calls a casserole."

"Well, I'm glad you like them, because that's what almost everyone is bringing. There were four lined up on the counter when I got there. Pick the ones you want for today and tomorrow, and I'll put the others in the freezer."

The road narrowed and ran between a large bay on one side, already frozen over, and a steep slope upward on the other. "Some nice houses up on top of that," remarked Shelly. "We'll have to bring you out here in the spring and show them off."

"You know, I think I've been on this road," said Betsy. "Doesn't it connect with Nineteen and take us back to Excelsior?"

"There you go!" said Shelly. "You're learning your way around."

"I thought I was," said Betsy. "But obviously, I'm not as good at navigating around the lake as I thought."

"Betsy, the way that snow was coming down, *no one* could find their way. People from out of state think we laugh at snow. We don't. We listen to the weather reports, and when a blizzard blows in like it did Monday night, we stay at home. We close schools and businesses until it's over and the roads get plowed, and if we take the kids sledding or skating, we all wear serious cold-weather gear. I can't believe Godwin and the others let you go out in that."

"What should they have done, locked me in a closet? I was going. I was sure I knew what I was doing. Besides, no one knew the storm system was going to park itself over us and keep dumping snow."

Shelly sighed. "I suppose so. But if people scold you about this, remember, they're really scolding themselves. I think it was divine providence that made Jill insist you take her present along."

Betsy said, "Have they towed my car yet?"

"I don't think so. Why?"

"Because I keep thinking about it, up against that tree, buried in snow. If Jill hadn't given me that cell phone, I'd be sitting in it yet."

Shelly had to pull over to the side of the road and hug Betsy for a minute.

Back on their way, Betsy said, "I guess it's like people who live near deserts know the rules, like to tell someone where you're going and when you'll be back, and to fill your gas tank and take a couple gallons of water along."

"Exactly. Mother Nature can be a merciless bitch. But once she gets over her tantrum, isn't it beautiful?" Shelly nodded out toward an expanse of Lake Minnetonka, where the snow piled up in exotic, glittering, wavelike drifts, the tops of which appeared to be steaming as the wind continued its work.

Betsy shivered. "It's like a dead planet."

"But it's not dead," Shelly countered. "Just wait till spring, when the land jumps up green and blooming again. I love living in a place where there are seasons; I don't think I could live in the tropics. How would you know when it's Christmas?"

"Look in the store windows or at a calendar," said Betsy, remembering Christmas in San Diego. "Listen to the radio or watch television, look at the lights on the houses next door, or—"

"All right, all right, all right," laughed Shelly. "I get your point. But look over there, isn't it just like a postcard?" She gestured toward a point of land extending into the bay, where a yellow log cabin crouched among evergreens, the snow piled like sugar frosting all around.

But Betsy was far too close to her recent adventure to appreciate the view. Nor did she like any of the other unpeopled, silver-gilt scenes that presented themselves around every bend on the road to Excelsior.

Once they got to town, that was different. Betsy looked with pleasure at the flower shop, the tiny jewelry store, Leipold's Antiques, the bakery, the pet shop, the bookstore, and Haskell's on the corner, its decorative marine pilings buried under snow. Christmas lights and decorations underlined the season. People were out, walking, shopping, greeting one another. This was lovely; this she liked. There were warm cookies in the bakery and hot cider in the Waterfront Café. One could not possibly sit down and freeze to death on a crowded street like this.

Shelly made the turn onto Lake Street, and in another block they were in front of the old redbrick building that housed the sandwich shop, the used book store, Crewel World, and Betsy's apartment over it. Home. Betsy was suddenly very tired. She sighed and reached for her purse, fumbled in it for keys.

"You go right on up and get into your jammies," said Shelly, helping her through the narrow pass in the mountain range of snow along the curb. "No one expects you to stop in the store."

"All right."

Betsy went through the door that led directly to the upstairs apartments. She walked up the stairs, Shelly close behind, and unlocked the door to her place. The first thing she saw was Sophie ambling unhurriedly toward her.

Betsy stooped and stroked the animal, who arched her back and purred. Shelly went around her into the kitchen, and Betsy heard the refrigerator door opening.

"She's been fed," said Godwin from behind her, and she rose. "Sophie, I mean," he added. She came to hug him.

"I knew someone must have taken care of her," said Betsy in a minute. "Otherwise she'd be giving orders."

Godwin laughed. "You go straight to bed, all right? Shelly's handling things in the kitchen, and I just wanted to say a quick welcome home. We're staying open late tonight."

"Who's helping down there?"

"Who isn't? Half of your employees volunteered to work for nothing! I've got them lined up until Saturday, by which time you should be able to either come to work or make other arrangements."

"You didn't accept the offers to work free, did you?"

"No, of course not. But while they're in that mood, I'm lining them up for inventory."

Betsy said, blinking away tears, "You are the best."

"Aw, shucks, no one has said that to me for years."

"Not even John?"

"Oh, well—that's different," said Godwin. And he left.

Betsy defied everyone's instructions and took a long, hot shower before climbing into bed. Sophie joined her in bed, purring loudly, snuggling close, for once seeming more interested in giving comfort than seeking it. Betsy stroked and murmured to the cat, profoundly happy and grateful to be there with her. She thought she wasn't the least sleepy, but before she knew it, she was dreaming.

She woke to the sound of someone knocking on her door. Her *bedroom* door. "Whosit?" she said, struggling with the words. Sophie padded heavily across the bed and jumped down.

"Relax, it's just me," said Jill's voice. She came in wearing her uniform, looking immense in her bulletproof vest and thick winter jacket. "How are you?"

"Okay. What time is it?" Betsy hadn't the strength to lift her arm and consult her watch.

"Almost two in the afternoon. You were asleep, I guess."

"I guess. But I'm glad you came. I was having a bad dream. Come on in. How did you get in, anyhow?"

"Your door's unlocked. Godwin is sending people up through the store. Unless you want me to tell him not to."

"No, it's all right, I s'pose." Betsy still wasn't completely awake. "What, through the shop and up the back way? Should I get up? Is there company out there?"

"No, no. Stay in bed. They're just bringing things, to judge by what's on the kitchen counters. Apparently they hear you snoring and just sneak right back out again."

"I don't snore!"

"Godwin said someone told him you were snoring, so when I came in and didn't hear anything, I decided to check on you."

Betsy sighed, "Huh. Thank you, I guess. Well, yes, thanks for checking. And Jill, thanks for that survival kit. I mean—" Betsy found, to her distress, that her eyes were watering. She tried to blink the tears away. "Thank you for saving my life. If you hadn't insisted I take that box along—" Betsy rubbed her eyes with both hands, like a child. "And all I got you was that book on hardanger you were looking at!" If Jill had come over and hugged her, Betsy would have broken down. But Jill, being Jill, only stood there, so Betsy pulled herself together again. "I'm glad you're my friend."

"I'm glad I was able to do the right thing for you." Jill smiled faintly. "Now, I've got to get back on patrol."

"Wait a minute, I thought you were on nights."

"We're working double shifts until everything's back to normal. There are still roads closed, and we've got a pair of thieves on snowmobiles hitting summer cottages around the lake. I'm cruising in a four-wheel-drive vehicle, hoping to surprise the little buggers."

So much for that serene cottage in the snow. "Good luck," said Betsy.

Someone knocked on Betsy's bedroom door again, and Betsy, who thought she'd only dozed off for a minute, opened her eyes and said, "Sorry, Jill."

But it was a man's deep, warm, familiar voice that replied, "Hello, darlin."

Betsy groaned. "Oh, no, it's the Pig."

"No, it's me, Hal, the world's greatest fool."

"You got that right." Betsy hauled herself into a sitting position again, glad she'd worn her thickest flannel nightgown to bed, and hoping her hair looked awful. "Go away, Hal." She looked at her bedside clock. It was a little past seven. She'd no idea she'd been asleep five more hours!

"Not till you let me have my say."

"Nothing you say could possibly interest me."

"There's a saying, 'Experience keeps a hard school, but a fool will learn in no other.' I've been to experience's *grad* school, let me tell you."

"It seems to me, since you're standing upright and have all your limbs and both eyes, it wasn't hard enough."

Hal's voice took on a pleading tone. "What can I do to show you I mean it when I say I'm sorry? That I've learned my lesson? What do you want from me?"

"Besides your head on a pole? Nothing. And all you're going to get from me is a hard kick to a delicate place if you don't get out of here. Now."

"Please, let's talk! I really want a second chance!"

"To what? Hurt me again? Never! If you don't leave, I'll call the police." When he didn't start immediately for the door, she picked up the bedside phone's receiver and glanced at him, fully prepared to dial.

Betsy had read in English novels about a person "going white to the lips," but had never seen anyone actually do that before. In the blink of an eye, he went from hurt and contrite to ferocious, his dark eyes blazing at her from that white face, his lips a thin slash. But he didn't say anything, only turned on his heel and walked out of the bedroom. Seconds later, she heard the door to the hall slam.

"Whew!" she said, replaced the receiver, and slid down under the covers again.

But the excitement of that visit had left her wide awake. She huffed a bit, trying to work up a sleepy yawn, but no good. So she twisted over and picked up the bedside phone again, dialed the shop.

"Godwin?" she said when he answered. "If Hal comes back, don't let him upstairs again, okay? I don't want him up here. Thanks."

She hung up and realized she was hungry—no, famished. When had she last had a real meal? Yesterday? The day before? She went out to the little kitchen and was touched to find the counter space crowded with baskets of fruit, a large selection of Excelo Bakery's cookies, and a loaf each of their beautiful herb and multigrain bread. In the refrigerator were a six-pack of Diet Squirt, a liter of V8 Extra Spicy, three brand-new quarts of milk, and four kinds of casserole—er, hot dish—plus two orders of her favorite chicken salad made with red grapes and cashews, a plastic bowl of homemade potato salad, and a whole banana cream pie. She checked the freezer and, as Shelly said she would do, there were more no-longer-hot dishes waiting in there.

This was ridiculous. And vastly touching. She stood there sniveling until cold air spilling out of the refrigerator started to chill her toes.

Then she got a dinner plate out of the cabinet and made an enormous and peculiar dinner by taking a sample of every hot dish that wasn't frozen. She washed it down with milk.

She washed the plate, glass, and fork and wandered into the living room. Normally eating an enormous meal made her sleepy, but having slept so much already, Betsy was in no mood to go back to bed. She looked around for something to do. She didn't feel up to the concentration it took for counted cross stitch. She was about to pick up the scarf she was nearly finished knitting for Godwin, when she remembered the mystery of the tapestry.

Those little symbols, the shamrock, the flaming heart, the pig. Attributes, Father John had called them, because they identified certain saints. Was there a pattern to the ones selected?

She went into the back bedroom where she had her notes, and the book on attributes Father John had loaned her. The book was there, on the computer desk, but her notes weren't. Betsy could be absentminded, moving things and forgetting where she'd put them, so she looked all around the room. No luck. She even went into the two-drawer file cabinet, though she knew perfectly well she hadn't been so organized as to make up a file folder and put the notes in there. She started to boot up her computer, then remembered she hadn't saved the notes, just printed them out.

She expanded her search to her own bedroom, then the living room. The doorbell's ring found Betsy on her knees in the kitchen, looking under the sink. She answered it warily, afraid Hal might have talked his way past Godwin again. But it was Jill.

"I saw your lights on and thought I'd check on you," said Jill, who looked barely able to stand.

"I'm feeling pretty good, but you look terrible," said Betsy. "When were you last in bed?"

Jill thought. "I can't remember, though it wasn't all that long ago. I'm just tired. Driving on icy roads after a storm like this isn't much fun."

"Have you eaten?"

"You don't have to feed me."

"Okay, how about I let one of my many friends feed you?" Betsy went to her refrigerator, brought out one of the hot dishes, and spooned half of it into a Tupperware bowl. "Here," she said, "take this home, put it in the microwave, and hit your soup button twice."

"Thank you. I didn't even think I was hungry until you started spooning it out. Then I had to keep swallowing so drool wouldn't drip off my chin. Whose is it?"

"Patricia Fairland's. It's got shrimp, pea pods, mushrooms, and three kinds of cheese."

"Golly," sighed Jill.

"It tastes as good as it smells, too."

Jill said, "Well, thanks so much. I'll call you tomorrow morning. *Late* tomorrow morning."

After Jill left, Betsy gave up her search and sat down to knit. Knit two, purl two, fifty times, with an odd one at either end of the row. There were only a few inches left to do, so she turned on KSJN and finished it to Schubert's Unfinished Symphony—she had to get out her *Learn to Knit in One Day* booklet to remind herself how to cast off—then, to the odd cadences and plaintive harmonics of medieval music, used all the colors of yarn that were in the scarf to make a long fringe at either end.

Tired at last, she went to bed and read enough of the book, which was actually called *Attributes and Symbols of the Christian Church* and was nearly a hundred years old, to put herself back to sleep.

Eight

❖

Betsy came down to her shop around ten-thirty on Thursday morning looking bright and chipper.

Godwin was explaining how to use blending filament in counted cross stitch to a customer, so Shelly hurried to intercept her, exclaiming in an undertone, "What are you doing down here? Why aren't you in bed?"

"I feel fine. I couldn't stay in bed any more without being tied down. How are things?"

"Fine, really, just fine. I'm here with Godwin, so why don't you go shopping or something?"

"I don't know if I'm up to shopping. Too much walking."

Betsy went to the library table. "But I feel odd not coming down to work. How are we doing? Has it been busy? Did that ad salesman come in? Anything going on I should know about?"

"It's been fairly busy, enough so we're glad there are two of us. We had three people waiting at the door for us to open. Godwin's just winding up the last one. And the ad salesman came in yesterday, so we showed him the ad you designed and he should call you today with prices. Are you going to advertise in all the weeklies around the area?"

"Depends on the price. Maybe only the *Excelsior Bay Times.*" Betsy leaned right, then left. "Is my project down here?"

"What, the ornaments?"

"No, the needlepoint one, the kitten asleep in the basket of yarn."

Shelly came to pull out a chair. "Here, sit down. What's it in?"

Betsy sat. "The basket with the lid." She bent again to look for it, but Shelly had already picked it up. She put it on the table, her movements hasty and her face anxious. "What's the matter, Shelly?"

"Nothing, I guess. I mean, Betsy, we were afraid you were going to die, and you still looked awful when I brought you home. I can't believe you think you're well enough to go back to work already."

"Plus," drawled Godwin as he closed the shop door on his customer, "Shelly wants that Wentzler Camelot sampler, and is afraid you'll send her home before she earns enough money to buy it."

"Goddy—!" scolded Shelly, but her face was pink. "It's not true!" she said to Betsy. "Well . . . not altogether."

Betsy laughed. "I want you to stay. I don't think I have the stamina to work a full day."

Godwin said, "I don't think you should work at all. Aren't you supposed to stay in bed until Saturday?"

"No, I'm supposed to rest until Saturday. And if I have to stay upstairs, I will start climbing the walls, which isn't very restful. I'd rather be sitting down here with you."

The shop door went *bing,* and Godwin said, "Who's sitting?"

It was Martha Winters. "Well, I'm so glad to see you up and about, Betsy," she said. "I'm here to see if you have any of those Rainbow Gallery 'Wisper' colors."

"Yes, we do," said Godwin. "They came in yesterday."

The two went off to the back. Shelly said to Betsy, "You might want to try them for your kitten. They're fuzzy, and if you brush the stitching, they look just like fur."

"Sounds great," said Betsy. "But let me figure out this stitch for the yarn first. What do you think of—"

Just then the door sounded, and Joe Mickels came in. He nodded at Betsy and said, "You should be in bed."

Betsy, beginning to get annoyed at this insistence she shouldn't be at work, snapped, "Why, do I look sick?" She had taken some care with her appearance this morning, and thought she looked at least healthy.

He frowned at her, taking her invitation seriously. "I guess not. I came by to see if your help can tell me if you're recovering on schedule. I can see that you're ahead of predictions." Joe managed not to sound pleased, but on the other hand, he didn't sound like his usual blustery self.

"I'm fine, thank you," said Betsy, frowning at him. This was the second time Joe had passed up an opportunity to bluster.

As if reading her mind, he swelled his chest and said more strongly, "You let me know right away if what happened makes you decide to move to a warmer climate, all right?"

"Yes, I'll be sure to do that," retorted Betsy, and he turned on his heel and left.

"What was that all about?" asked Shelly.

"The usual," said Betsy with a shrug.

"You know, it's odd how he hasn't gone after you like he did Margot. He was in here growling at her or serving her with some kind of legal paper practically every week for a long time."

"Maybe he has a mad, secret crush on me," Betsy joked.

"More likely it's some new trick. You watch out for him, Betsy. For Joe, everything comes down to money, and with your lease, he's losing money every day."

Betsy got out a piece of scrap canvas and consulted her book of needlepoint stitches. Someone on the needlework newsgroup had suggested the stem stitch for the balls of yarn, and though her book showed it only in straight lines, she set out to see if she could curve it just a little to make the balls look round. And maybe if she used a slightly darker shade around the edge . . .

She'd only done a few stitches when the phone rang. Godwin, who had just sold Martha four packs of hairy yarn, picked up and said, "Crewel World, good morning, how may I help you? Oh, hello, Vern!" He listened and said, "Great!" and to Betsy, "It's Miller Motors. They towed your car in and Vern wants to talk to you."

Betsy reached for the cordless on the table and pushed the talk button. "What's it going to cost me for the tow?" she asked. Miller Motors was a shabby old place, located in a converted stable, and Vern Miller was a retired army sergeant who had learned about motors by repairing tank engines. Betsy had no intention of allowing him to work on her car.

"We ain't got that figured, yet," replied Vern. "What I want to know is, who's got it in for you?"

"What do you mean?"

"I mean your brake line's been cut. Did you notice your brakes goin' soft while you was out drivin' in the snow?"

Betsy said, "Well yes, and then they quit altogether. That's why I went off the road. But I thought it was my gas tank that was punctured."

"It wasn't your gas tank, it was your gas line; it got ripped loose back near the gas tank. That was an accident that happened while you was wallowin' around that pine tree. I'm talking about your brake line. It was cut, like with a box ripper or a good pair of scissors. And you're supposed to be smart, so think: If your brakes went out while you was driving, it was done *before* the accident. Which means it wasn't an accident."

Betsy sat perfectly still for a few seconds. "You're sure?"

"You want to come and take a look for yourself? I'm tellin' you, the line was cut!"

"All right, all right," said Betsy. "I believe you." She thought, then said, "Okay, just park the car someplace. Don't let anyone touch it, and don't start any repairs; I want someone else to look at it. I'll call you back."

"Storage is twenty bucks a day."

"Fine." Betsy hung up and picked up her canvas. But she only stared at it without making any stitches.

"What?" demanded Godwin.

"Mr. Miller says someone cut my brake line."

"You mean when they were hauling it back up on the road?" asked Shelly.

"No, before I went into the ditch. My brakes failed, that's why I went off the road. He's very sure it was cut, like with a box opener, deliberately."

"Nonsense," said Shelly. "Why would someone do that?"

Godwin said, "That, my dear, is a very good question."

Shelly said, "Oh, Godwin, you don't mean—Oh, *Betsy!*"

There was a little silence. Betsy said in a small voice, "I can't think of anyone even miffed at me right now."

Shelly said, "Joe Mickels?"

Godwin said, "It's silly to think anyone would seriously want to hurt you for any reason, even Joe."

The silence fell again, then Shelly said lightly, "Who didn't you invite to your party that you should have?"

Godwin stared at her, scandalized, then started to laugh. "Yes, and you haven't held a pre-Christmas sale. That's bound to upset at least some of your regular customers."

Betsy giggled. "Maybe it's Sophie, angry because I put her on a diet."

"Yeah," said Godwin, "I can just see her sneaking out to crawl under your car and rip that puppy loose with her hind claws. That'll teach you."

"How would she know—" Betsy paused, frowning.

"What?" asked Godwin.

"How would anyone know? I mean, if it really was cut, who do I know who knows what to cut? I don't know what a brake line looks like. I don't think I know anyone who would know; most of my customers are women. Well, except Phil Galvin. Or Steve Pedersen, or Donny DePere." These were her three most faithful male customers.

"Trust me, Donny wouldn't know, either," said Godwin.

Shelly said, "You're wrong; a lot of us women know, Betsy. Remember that course, Godwin? Introducing Your Car, it was called. It was aimed primarily at women. Open U taught it four years in a row. I took the first one, and it was so great I told everyone, and a lot of women from around here signed up. Four or five of the teachers at the elementary school did. And Patricia did, she said she was sick of being taken by car repair shops. And Martha, and June, and Eloise, and Heidi, and—gosh, a lot of your customers. Mandy Abrams took it. We learned how to change the oil as well as flat tires, and we studied all the parts of the engine and transmission. It was very interesting. I kept all my notes, and I haven't felt intimidated by car repairmen since. Though I never did change my oil after that one time. I thought I'd never get my fingernails clean!"

Godwin nodded. "I think two used-car dealers went out of business while they were teaching that course."

"Only one," corrected Shelly. "And he was already notorious."

"Hmmmm," said Betsy.

"You don't think Vern is right, do you?" asked Shelly.

"Probably not," said Betsy, "but I'm going to call Mike down at the police station anyhow."

Detective Sergeant Mike Malloy, somewhat to Betsy's surprise, took her report seriously and said he would stop by Miller Motors and look at her car.

He stepped into Crewel World less than an hour later, a slender redhead with freckles spattering a thin-lipped face. "All right, what are you mixed up in now?" he growled.

Betsy said, "You mean Vern Miller was right? The line was cut deliberately?"

"Yes. You didn't discover another skeleton did you? Maybe under that old tapestry they found at Trinity?"

"No, of course not," said Betsy.

Godwin said, "What she means is, she hasn't figured out yet what her new case is about. Though obviously *someone* has."

"Goddy, go help Shelly with that customer back by the counted cross stitch patterns," ordered Betsy, and he sniffed and walked away.

"Don't listen to Godwin, Mike," Betsy said. "There isn't anything to figure out. I was thinking after I called you that if Vern is right, if the brakes were tampered with, then perhaps someone got the wrong car. People park back there once in a while while they visit someone who lives across in the condos."

Mike turned to glance out the front window at the gray eminence across the street—a large complex that blocked what once must have been a lovely view of the lake.

"All their parking is underground," continued Betsy, "and you need one of those magnetic keys to access it. So visitors have to park on the street. And with the snow emergency rules being so confusing—what are they? Something like you can only park on the even-numbered sides of the streets on odd-numbered days—anyway, people who don't want to get towed try to park off the street."

"And you're telling me someone across the street wanted to kill a visitor?"

"How would I know? I'm just looking for an alternative to the explanation that someone wants to kill *me*. Because no one does. I don't know about over there, I don't know anyone who lives over there." She smiled suddenly. "Well, except John Penberthy. And attorneys are too valuable to the law breakers to get murdered, aren't they?"

Mike laughed. "Unless they lose a case. But I see your point. Some stranger hustles back there, it's dark, it's snowing, your license plate is covered with it, and they're in a hurry. Makes sense to me." He wrote something in his notebook, tapped it to his forehead in a kind of friendly salute, and departed.

He had to sidestep out the door because someone half hidden behind an enormous plant bundled in green florist paper was coming in. The delivery man put the plant on the table and lifted a finger in a warning to wait and went back out again. When he came back, it was with a big, long white box, the sort roses come in.

"Wow, who loves you?" asked Godwin.

"They're more likely for you," said Betsy, nevertheless continuing to peel back the green paper to reveal a huge, deep, deep red poinsettia.

"Ooooh, pretty!" said Shelly. "I think that's the biggest one I've ever seen!"

Betsy began poking among the leaves for a card and found one on a clear plastic stick. It had her name on it.

She opened the envelope and found written on it, in a familiar hand, *"Remember?"* "Oh, damn," she muttered.

"Why? Who's it from?" asked Shelly.

"My ex-husband." She tore the card in half and tossed the pieces into a wastepaper basket under the table.

"Then I suppose this one's from him, too," said Shelly.

Godwin said, "It might not be. And it might not be roses, either. To fill a box that size would take two dozen roses, at least. Was the Pig one for spending big time on flowers?"

"Sometimes." Betsy sighed and opened the box. Inside were at least two dozen red roses. She picked up the card in its little envelope and opened it. In the same hand was written, *"My Love is Like the Red, Red Rose."* She sighed again, tore the card in half, and tossed it after the first.

"Maybe you should talk to him," said Shelly.

"No."

"But he spent a lot of money on those flowers."

"If they were made of rubies, I still wouldn't want to talk to him."

"Since they're only real roses, shall I put them in water?" Shelly bent to inhale the fragrance.

Betsy started to order them thrown away when she was forestalled by Godwin. "Let's give them away. A Christmas rose for every customer until they're gone."

Betsy nodded. That's a nice idea, Godwin. There's a bucket in back, Shelly. Fill it halfway with warm water, cut the bottoms off the stems, and put them in there."

"What about the poinsettia?" asked Shelly.

"Do you want it?"

"No, I've already got one."

"Godwin?"

"No, ever since I saw them growing like weeds in Mexico, I don't think of them the same."

"Me, too," said Betsy. That was what Hal was reminding her of with his card. She smiled. "I know, let's give it to—to Irene Potter. Poor lady, she spends half her salary in here, and I bet she's never gotten flowers in her life. Godwin, can you remember the company where she works?"

Godwin could. Betsy called and, handed along to the shipping department, got Irene on the line and said, "Irene, someone brought in a big, beautiful poinsettia and there's no room for it in the shop. Would you like it?"

"How much?" asked that suspicious woman.

"For free. You are one of our best customers, and I would like for once to give you something."

Irene came in from work a little after five and stood a moment staring at the plant. "It's awfully big," she said.

"I didn't think of that. It's too heavy for you to carry," said Betsy. "How about I drop it off after we close? We're open till nine tonight."

"And every night till Christmas," added Godwin with a little sigh.

"Why," said Irene, torn between suspicion and pleasure, "that's very kind of you, I'm sure. Thank you. It is a beautiful thing, and we wouldn't want it to freeze its little leaves off, would we? Which it might do if I were to carry it home. Yes, thank you. Thank you." She backed toward the door, then turned abruptly and hurried out.

"Poor thing," said Shelly. "Thinks it's some kind of prank, I bet."

When Betsy carried the big plant, wrapped again in its green paper, to the front door of the elderly boarding house where Irene lived, she was waiting in the parlor. Betsy, looking through the half-glassed front door, could also see four other roomers sitting on the two couches and three easy chairs that filled the room. But they all waited while the owner, a very old woman, answered the door.

"Why, Betsy Devonshire, how nice of you to come in person!" she said in her creaky voice. "Do come in! Irene, you have a caller, and look, she's brought you something!" This was said in a patently false voice. Obviously, Irene had told everyone about her gift.

So Betsy made a little ceremony of it, putting it on an end table and carefully unwrapping it. She said, "Irene is such a talented needlepointer that her work is an advertisement for us. I thought it would be nice to reward her loyalty and applaud her talent, so I am bringing her this little gift."

As the "little gift" was unwrapped, it spread like a red and green avalanche. The man sitting on the end of the couch beside the table had to scoot over to keep it from draping across his lap.

"Oh, my, that is just *gorgeous!*" said the landlady. "I've never seen one so large or beautiful! I just hope Irene will let it stay down here at least for tonight, so we all can enjoy it."

"Yes, of course," said Irene, and it was a pleasure watching her be magnanimous. Her cheeks were pink and her little dark eyes glowed as she raked in the smiles. She said to Betsy, "Will you come up to my room for a bit? There's something I want to tell you."

"Of course."

Irene's room was about what Betsy expected: small and inexpensively furnished. Except for the Dazor light, of course, and the magnificent needlepoint cover on the bed. Every possible surface was covered with needlepoint or with needlepoint supplies, but there was a ruthless order to everything and not a speck of dust or dirt anywhere.

Irene sat on the bed and Betsy took the only chair, which had a petit point cushion.

"I hear someone cut the brake line on your car," said Irene.

"Yes," nodded Betsy. Unlike most native plants, the Excelsior grapevine did not go dormant in winter.

"Have you thought that it might have something to do with that tapestry they found in Trinity?"

"How could an old tapestry make somebody want to commit murder?"

"Well, I've always said it was suspicious how Lucy Abrams died on the same day her husband had that stroke," said Irene. Which was probably untrue, as Betsy had never heard anything of the sort from her, or anyone else, either. "And then this tapestry, which she was working on just before she died, got put right out of sight. Now it turns up, and someone tries to murder you. I think there's a connection."

"But I'm not the one who found it," protested Betsy.

Irene leaned forward, eyes shining. "No, but you're the one with a talent for discovering murderers, aren't you?"

Nine

❖

Godwin expected to find Betsy already in the shop when he arrived the next day, Friday, at about ten minutes to ten. But he had to unlock the door and turn the lights on himself. Shelly arrived a few minutes later and, seeing Betsy was not there, said, "She's probably still in bed. I thought she was pushing it, staying till five yesterday."

"Mm-hmm," said Godwin. "Still, she didn't look tired when she left for Irene's place. I was hoping to get the morning off. I've got some errands to run. If I have to stay all day, I can't work this evening. Two eleven-hour days in a row is too much."

"Well, I'll see who's willing to work this evening," said Shelly, going to the big desk that served as a checkout counter. "Where's the list?"

"Top drawer on the left. Do you have the opening-up money?"

"I thought Betsy gave it to you."

"She must have taken it upstairs. Maybe we should call her."

"Okay, after I get someone to work this evening. Or would you rather have this afternoon off, and come back this evening?"

Godwin shrugged. "Stores are less crowded during the day, but it would be hard to come back here once I get into full shopping mode. On the other hand, fighting crowds after an eight-hour day isn't fun, either. Since either choice is vile, get who you can when you can."

Shelly was still talking to the first part-timer when Sophie came trotting out from between the box shelves that marked off an area in the back of the shop. "Wait a second, I think Betsy's here," said Shelly.

And she was. She paused in the opening, blinking blearily and looking truly ill.

"Oh, my God, what happened to you?" exclaimed Shelly. " 'Scuse me, I'll call you back," she said and hung up.

Godwin hurried to take Betsy by the arm. "Here, sit down." He led her back between the shelves to a pair of little upholstered chairs on either side of a small table.

Betsy sank gratefully into a chair. Her hair was sketchily combed, her clothing was an old pair of jeans, a faded cotton sweater, and bedroom slippers. Her complexion was pale, except under her eyes, where it was dark gray.

Godwin said, "If you feel as bad as you look, you shouldn't be down here."

"I *told* Godwin it was too soon for you to come back to work!" said Shelly, coming to look with concern at Betsy. "You obviously wore yourself out yesterday."

"No, I was still feeling pretty good right up to when I went to bed last night," said Betsy. "But I woke up sick in the middle of the night, and I've been getting sicker and sicker. I'm so sick now I'm scared to be up there alone."

Godwin said, "Then we're glad you came down. What do you think, Shelly, a delayed reaction to frostbite or whatever she got from spending the night in the cold? Or maybe to the drugs they gave her at the hospital?"

Betsy said, "No, I think it's something I ate." As if saying that reminded her, she rose and made a wobbly dash for the bathroom in the storage room. When she came back, she looked, if that were possible, even worse.

"I'm calling your doctor," declared Shelly, starting for the phone. Then she stopped and turned back. "Who is he?"

Betsy sighed. "Melody McQueen. Isn't that the silliest name? I've only seen her once, but I like her. Well, maybe twice; I think she came to the hospital. Don't call her. I'm too sick to go to the doctor's office. Do doctors in Minnesota make house calls?"

Godwin said, "I don't think so. Call her anyway, Shelly. Her phone number's on the Rolodex." He felt Betsy's forehead, which was cool and clammy. "If this is food poisoning, it's the worst case I've ever seen. What was it you ate?"

"Cashew chicken salad with red grapes, my favorite. There were two cartons of it in the refrigerator, they came with the hot dishes. I don't see how it could have gone bad so quickly. I came back from taking that poinsettia to Irene—you should have seen her, Godwin, she was so *proud* that we gave her a gift, it nearly made me cry. And you know, she said the oddest thing—" Betsy got a sudden, inward look, and leaned forward a little. "Cramps," she muttered. "There's nothing left in there, but my body still keeps trying to shove it out."

Godwin reached for her hand. It was alarmingly cold. He chaffed it gently between his own for a bit. "Have you got her doctor yet?" he called to Shelly.

"I'm on hold for her," replied Shelly.

"Change places with me, I want to talk to her," said Godwin.

Shelly came to sit with Betsy. "Have you had food poisoning before?" she asked.

"Yes, years and years ago. I think it was fish that time, not ch-chicken salad . . ." She fell silent, swallowing ominously.

Godwin called, "Betsy, Dr. McQueen wants to talk to you!"

Shelly helped her to the phone.

"Yes?" said Betsy. Between pauses of various lengths, she continued, "Yes. About ten last night. Yes. No. No. Do you really think—yes, all right. Yes, I will." Betsy hung up. "Since I can't keep even fluids down, she says I should go back to the hospital."

"I'll drive you," said Shelly.

"All right. But first go up to my apartment and get both cartons of that salad. She wants to see what kind of bug it has." Betsy reached into the desk drawer, got the spare key to her apartment, handed it to Shelly. "Bring my purse, too, will you? They're going to ask for that darn medical insurance number."

"That wonderful medical insurance number," corrected Godwin firmly. "I'm glad you listened to me when I told you not to cancel your medical insurance."

As Godwin was helping Betsy up and into Shelly's big purple SUV, she stopped and said over her shoulder, "Call Jill when you think she's up, will you, Goddy? Tell her I want to talk to her."

J ill joined Betsy in the emergency room an hour later, where she was still waiting for treatment.

"There's two heart attacks and a hand shredded by a snow blower ahead of me," said Betsy. "They say this is the usual result of a bad snowstorm."

The waiting room was large but dimly lit, with four television sets hanging down from the ceiling, all tuned to the same soap opera. The dozen people in the room bent under the sound as if being beaten.

Jill sat down on the chrome and plastic chair beside Betsy. "What do you think you've got?" she asked.

Betsy pointed to the paper bag between her feet. "I came home around ten last night and I hadn't had any supper, so I ate some of this chicken salad, and I woke up a little after midnight, very sick." She hesitated, then asked, "Can you, as a police officer, order them to test this salad for poison?"

Jill blinked and replied, "What kind of poison?"

"The kind that makes you lose everything you've eaten since the Fourth of July, makes your inside hurt like you've got ulcers, makes your fingers and toes tingle, and gives you a headache and chills."

"Sounds like bad mayonnaise to me," said Jill.

Betsy nodded. "It probably is. But Vern Miller says my brakes failed Monday night because someone deliberately cut the brake line."

Jill searched Betsy's eyes. "Does Mike Malloy know about this?" she asked.

"Yes. He checked it out and says it does look as if the line was cut. I told him I haven't made anyone mad at me lately, so it was probably somebody after someone else's car. But I don't think someone mistook my refrigerator for someone else's."

Jill touched Betsy on the arm. "You stay right here." She went back to the treatment area and used the authority of her badge to get Betsy seen right away. Then, because she could not require a test for poison on her own authority, she took the paper sack to a phone and called Malloy.

"If I hadn't seen that brake line with my own eyes, I wouldn't do this, you know," he said.

"I know. But she's really, really sick, Mike, bad enough that they're going to admit her. Besides, her doctor's having the food tested anyway, for botulism or *E. coli* or whatever."

"What kind of poison is it supposed to be?"

"She doesn't know. You're the detective, what kind of poison appears to be serious food poisoning?"

"I'll call someone at the toxicology lab."

Jill thanked him and hung up, then went to see how Betsy was doing. They'd started an IV line—she was seriously dehydrated—and were going to admit her under a preliminary diagnosis of food poisoning. Under the white .sheet on the narrow gurney, Betsy in fact looked very sick. But as they wheeled her away, Jill heard her joke to the nurse's aide, "Can I have my old room back?" Which Jill considered to be a good sign.

It was toward evening when Dr. McQueen came into Betsy's room. She was a Viking princess, nearly six feet tall with very pale blond hair pulled back into a French twist and a cool, assured manner. She was wearing a pale blue jumper over a thin white wool sweater. With her was a nurse carrying a little tray with a green cloth over it. "We'll be treating you for arsenic poisoning," said Dr. McQueen.

"Arsenic—Is that what it is?"

"Yes, and I congratulate you for recognizing the symptoms all by yourself. One of the two samples given the toxicology lab contained arsenic, and your urine sample also was positive."

"Could it be accidental? I mean, I remember reading there's some kind of poison in nuts."

Dr. McQueen replied, "Cyanide occurs naturally in peach pits and almonds. But you'd need to eat a bushel of almonds at one sitting to get sick. And in your case, the poison is arsenic, which is a mineral—an element, actually, almost but not quite a metal." Dr. McQueen gestured at the nurse, who uncovered her tray and picked up a hypodermic that looked suitable for an elephant.

"If you will roll over, please," said the nurse.

"Are—um, I mean, that's a really big needle," said Betsy.

"The dose is large," admitted Dr. McQueen, "and this is only the first in a series. Plus we have to go deep so you don't get site abscesses. The nurse will stay with you for a while after the injection, because there can be other reactions to Dimercaprol."

"Like what?" asked Betsy, allowing herself to be rolled onto her side. "Ow, ow, ow!" she added.

"You may feel a burning sensation in your mouth and throat or experience muscle cramps, tingling extremities, tightness in the chest, or nausea. You'll probably get a headache fairly quickly and may feel a little dopey."

"I already feel most of that," said Betsy, rolling back over gingerly.

Dr. McQueen took Betsy's pulse, and the nurse sat down on a chair beside Betsy's bed.

Betsy tried to relax, but alarm over possible side effects took most of her attention. And other thoughts were leaping and waving in a panicked attempt to get her attention.

Who wanted to kill her?

And why?

Two hours later, the door opened again, and a slim redhead in a dark suit, white shirt, and conservative tie came in, his charcoal-black coat over one arm. With him was Jill, in uniform.

"Hi, Malloy," sighed Betsy. "I've been expecting you."

"Have you figured out yet what you've got yourself into?" he asked, his thin mouth pulled into a little smile.

"I can only repeat that I am sure I haven't done anything to provoke this. Nothing."

Jill asked, "Are you feeling better yet?"

"Yes, the IV really helped."

Malloy hung the coat on a chair and reached into an inside pocket for a notebook and pen. He searched the notebook until he found the right page. "Only one of the chicken salads taken from your refrigerator contained arsenic. But it was enough to kill you if you'd eaten all of it."

Betsy felt a shiver run down her entire body. She had been really hungry by the time she sat down to her very late supper, but eating heartily just before bed was a guarantee of a restless night.

Not that she hadn't had one anyway.

Malloy asked, "I take it these salads were brought as gifts?"

"Yes. When I got home from the hospital, people brought me all kinds of food."

Malloy nodded. "Who brought the chicken salads?"

"I don't know."

"You mean you don't remember?"

"No, I mean it started coming while I was still in the hospital, and continued after I got home. I went to bed and to sleep. Godwin may know who brought it. He was running the shop and sent the people up. A lot of people know I love Eddie's cashew chicken, so it could have been anyone."

Malloy smiled. "Except for the ones who brought you something else." He made a note, then went back a few pages. "Jill says she remembers you told her Patricia Fairland brought a hot dish, and that Godwin and Shelly also mentioned Martha Winters, Kate MacDonald, Alice Skoglund, and Phil Galvin as people who brought food. Do you know these people?"

Betsy nodded. "Good customers. Friends, some of them."

Malloy said, his eyes amused, "What, you're so broke you're accepting charitable donations?"

Betsy rolled her eyes. "Come on, Mike. People want to do something for someone who's been in the hospital, and when they don't know what else to do, they bring food, God bless them. It was a revelation, seeing my kitchen. I didn't realize I had so many friends."

"And one enemy," Malloy reminded her. "Any idea who that might be?"

Betsy shook her head. "I told you, no."

"You sure? Nobody mad at you for any reason right now?"

She started to shake her head again, then said, "Well, my ex-husband was. But he wouldn't do anything, he's trying to get me to come back to him."

"Why?"

She frowned at him. "What do you mean?"

"Why does Mr. Norman want you back?"

"I don't know, maybe he needs someone to do his housework. But more likely it's because he found out I'm an heiress."

"You're sure he knows that?"

"I can't think why else he'd come all the way here from California to try to make up with me."

"Why did you divorce him?"

"He started it, filing for divorce after he fell in love with one of his students. But another student he'd dumped for her blew the whistle. And that started a chain reaction of whistle blowing that went back years. His true love dumped him, the college dumped him, and I dumped him."

"So things really came unraveled for him," said Jill.

Betsy nodded. "He lost his tenure, his job, his house, and me. Now he says he's learned his lesson and is very sorry and wants me to forgive him and take him back."

"And you are willing to do that?" asked Malloy.

"Remarry Hal the Pig? Not in a million years!"

"You told him that?"

Betsy, remembering the white, furious face, nodded. "He came to see me on Wednesday, trying to apologize for his behavior, and got very angry when I told him to get out."

"So he was in your apartment, then. And you exchanged words. Did he bring you a food gift?"

"He didn't say. Godwin may know."

"Did he threaten you?"

"No. He was really angry when I told him I'd call the cops if he didn't leave, angrier than I've ever seen him." She grimaced. "But his goal is to win me back, so why try to kill me?" She nodded at the enormous bouquet of mixed flowers on the shelf in front of the window. "See? Latest in a string."

But Malloy persisted, "Would he profit in some other way from your death? I mean, is there a life insurance policy he might still hold with your name on it?"

Betsy shook her head. "No. I changed the beneficiary—" She stopped.

"What?"

"I just remembered; I made Margot the new beneficiary. I'll have to change it again."

Malloy went through her current circumstances with her in some detail. "Shelly Donohue pointed out Joe Mickels hasn't gone after me like he did my sister," said Betsy at one point. "He doesn't like me, but he seems content now to wait out the lease." She frowned, remembering the last two times she'd seen him. "I think there's something on his mind, though."

"Do you know what it is?"

"No, but it's not me or the building the shop is in. It's almost like I don't matter much anymore. Otherwise, why isn't he trying to evict me?"

Malloy smiled. "You haven't heard of the law passed by our city council?"

"What law?"

" 'No building in the City of Excelsior shall exceed forty feet in height.' So he can't put up the six-story Mickels Building. I hear he's looking around for a site outside Excelsior now."

"Oh-ho! That explains it. I guess I've been too busy to notice that new law, though it's funny none of the town gossips dropped by to tell me about it. But surely they didn't pass that law just to keep Mickels from building in Excelsior?"

"No, it's this vision thing they've got hold of. There are a lot of people who live here because it's their ideal of a small town," said Malloy.

"Mayberry of the North," nodded Betsy.

"Right. They like the small-town feel, and they want to preserve it. So they elect representatives who feel the same way, and this is one way they've chosen to preserve the ambience they like."

Betsy remembered how comforted she'd felt coming down Water Street on her way home from the hospital, as if she'd stepped into a Norman Rockwell painting. "Yes, but—" Betsy began, and stopped.

"Yeah, I agree," said Malloy. "It means taxes stay high. Still, it takes Mickels off the list. What about Irene Potter?"

"What about her?"

"You know she was angry with Margot because she thought your sister was deliberately keeping her from her dream of owning an embroidery store or whatever you call it."

"Needlework," said Jill.

"And you wonder if she's transferred that anger to me." Betsy smiled, remembering the pride and delight with which Irene had accepted the gift poinsettia. "No, she's not mad at me. Though she may see me as incompetent and is just biding her time until the shop goes under, at which glorious moment she'll take over."

"Are you incompetent?"

Betsy chuckled. "In a lot of ways, yes. But I've got good help. And I'm learning fast. Irene hasn't realized that yet."

Malloy wrote something down, then went back two pages in his notebook. "A cut brake line and now arsenic poisoning. That's two attempts on your life, Ms. Devonshire."

Again, Betsy felt that chill, but all she could do was shrug helplessly. "Do you have any ideas?"

"I'm thinking you sent some people to jail charged with murder," said Mike. "Very few people are pleased by that."

"Well, yes, but both of them are still in jail."

"They've got friends and relatives."

"Oh. I hadn't thought about that. Do you know who these friends and relatives are?"

"Not yet. But I'll find out."

Jill said, "I still think it might be Joe. He was fit to be tied when it turned out Margot's death didn't give him back his building. Even if he can't build something bigger, he can at least raise the rent."

Betsy chuckled, but not wholeheartedly. It was no joke, having someone murderously angry with you.

Mike said, "But we can still eliminate people. It's someone who knows Betsy pretty well—she's still new in town, remember."

Betsy nodded. "It's also a person who knows how to get hold of arsenic—and there can't be many sources around, can there?"

Jill said, "I shouldn't think so. Do you know of any, Mike?"

"No. It's not a street drug. I know it's used in some manufacturing processes, like in preserving wood."

Betsy said, "In old-fashioned mysteries, you soaked it out of fly paper or went to a chemist and signed a poison book—but that was England in the thirties. I have no idea where you'd get it in modern America. Dr. McQueen said it also has medical uses."

Mike asked, "How well do you know Dr. McQueen?"

Betsy replied, "Not very well, why?"

"So she has no reason to be mad at you?"

"No reason at all."

Malloy closed his notebook and shook it lightly. "Still, here's a start," he said. "We'll find this crazy person, and meanwhile, we're not going to let anything happen to you. I'll arrange for an officer to stand guard around the clock."

"Wait, Mike, that'll pull an officer off every watch," said Jill. "And we're shorthanded as it is. Besides, he can't follow her everywhere—like I can. So how about you assign me? I can move in with her, and we can put out the word that she has an armed, live-in guard with a real snarky attitude."

Betsy waited for Mike to say something against that—he almost never agreed with Jill's ideas—but he didn't.

But Betsy didn't want a roommate and tried to say so politely after Joe left.

Jill replied, "All right, then we'll have to let Mike take you into custody. Do you want to spend Christmas in jail?"

"*Jail?* He can't arrest me, I didn't do anything!"

"What do you think protective custody is? His job is to enforce the law and to protect the public. You're a member of the public, and he has the power to do whatever it takes to protect you."

Betsy glared at Jill, who looked back with that serenely adamantine Gibson-girl face. So Betsy unclenched her own face and sighed. She seemed to be doing a lot of that lately.

Ten

❖

The next morning Betsy, who was feeling pretty good now her re-action to the Dimercaprol had settled down, said to Jill, "Okay, I'm ready to see what you brought from my place. How did you get in, by the way?"

Jill replied, "I called Godwin, and he came over to the shop and gave me the key to your apartment." She put a lidded basket on Betsy's legs. "In light of what's been happening to you lately, I think that key is a bad idea, so I brought it along." She held it up by its needlepointed tag, then dropped it into Betsy's purse on the bedside table.

"Then how's Sophie going to be taken care of?"

"She's in the shop. I brought her down, and her dish and some of her food in a plastic bag. You'll probably be sent home this afternoon, so not to worry."

"Was Godwin miffed at being asked to come in early? I don't like asking him to do more than he already does, which is a lot."

"It wasn't Godwin who was miffed, it was that lawyer he lives with. He treats Godwin like a boy toy, you know."

"Yes, I got a glimpse of that when Goddy brought John to the Christmas party. I wonder what will happen if Godwin starts acting more grown up?"

"Godwin will *maybe* turn twenty-three just before he dies eighty years from now."

Betsy laughed and opened the lidded basket, which sat heavily on her legs. On top was the reason: the thick old book on Christian symbology Father John Rettger had loaned her.

"What'd you bring this for?" asked Betsy.

"It was on your bedside table. I thought you were reading it."

"Well, I was, but I'm not as interested since I can't find my notes on the ta-pestry. You know, it's the darnedest thing . . ." Betsy had started to put it aside, but now paused, frowning.

"What?" asked Jill.

"Maybe I've been a dope. Did I tell you the notes I put into the computer and printed out have gone missing?"

"When did this happen?"

"Last week. Hand me my purse, will you?"

Jill did, and Betsy dug around until she found her checkbook. She opened it and pulled out the tablet of checks. "Gotcha!"

Jill said, "Now what?"

"Here are my original notes, the ones I made while looking at the tapestry. I wrote them on the back of this, then copied them into the computer. Then I added more stuff from memory and printed it out. That's what disappeared, the printout. I could kick myself for not saving it, but at least I put this back where it belonged. We can maybe start over. I suppose you've got a pen and notebook on you?"

Jill did. It was a small one, with the pages sewn in, and to be used for offi-cial business only. "But taking care of you is my official business."

Betsy paused in her search for a blank page. "It may be more official than that. Irene Potter told me I should wonder why Lucy Abrams died the same day her husband had that stroke. And it's suspicious that this tapestry went missing right about then, too."

Jill said, "If I thought a tapestry pointed to me as a criminal, I wouldn't hide it. I'd burn it or bury it."

"Yes, that would make sense. But maybe they just meant to hide it tem-porarily, and the room got sealed off, and they decided it was as good as gone. Or Lucy herself hid it."

"Why would she do that?"

"I don't know. Is there anything suspicious about her death? Did they do an autopsy?"

"I don't think so. You want me to find out?"

"Please." Jill took her notebook back, wrote herself a note, and handed it back to Betsy.

Betsy looked at the thin cardboard back of the checkbook. There was a flock of little drawings: a shamrock, then a calf or a fawn, then a heart with—something. An M? No, a heart aflame, she remembered now. And there was an ice cream cone, a candle . . . Betsy began copying the drawings into the note-book. She wished she were a better artist; it wasn't easy figuring out what her original hasty sketches were supposed to be. Of course, the original stitching wasn't always clear, either. That slanting line with the three lines coming down from its tip, for example. She remembered wondering at the time what that was supposed to be. On the other hand, "Saint Olaf," she murmured, as she copied the ax.

"Who?" said Jill, turning her head sideways to take a look at the tablet.

"Father John told me the double-bladed ax is an attribute of Saint Olaf. Like the shamrock is for Saint Patrick."

"Oh, yes," nodded Jill. "I remember those from Sunday school. The shamrock is also for the Trinity. And crossed keys are for Saint Peter. Are there crossed keys on there?"

"No," said Betsy, "but there's a single key. I wonder who that stands for. And who is the cat?" She had written "cat" rather than drawn one, and had written "2" beside it to remind her that there were two of them. That was interesting enough that she put down the pen and notebook to open the big book and search down to the section where symbols were listed alphabetically. "Ahh-hhhh, cat, cat—here. It says Saint Yvo, and it also means witchcraft. Did you know there's a witch in town?"

"Yes, but she wasn't a witch back then, she was an astrologer. And before that she was into tarot cards."

"Hmm. Then I guess Lucy wasn't telling us to hang all the witches. I remember the last item was a hangman's noose." She hadn't drawn that on the checkbook, so she drew one now on the notebook page. "There was a star, too, a Star of David, the kind you make with two triangles." She drew one of those. "I didn't copy all of the attributes on the tapestry down," she explained. "Now I think about it, there was Saint Elizabeth of Hungary." She drew three crowns, one above two. "And a horseshoe, I'm pretty sure there was a horseshoe, unless it was omega, the Greek letter. Omega is the last letter of the Greek alphabet, and if you combine it with the first, alpha, it's an attribute of God." She drew a horseshoe like an upside down U, in case it was omega. "And Father John said there was the attribute of Saint Agnes, though I can't remember which one it was."

"You really think there's a message in all this?" asked Jill.

"Maybe." Betsy looked again at the book, still turned to the section on symbols. "Did you ever know anyone named Yvo, spelled Wye-vee-oh? Maybe these attributes are members of the church back then."

"No. But there was an Elizabeth. And I think there was an Agnes. And I knew a Mr. Ives, he taught Sunday school. Is Saint Yvo the same as Saint Ives? I bet it is. Remember that old riddle: As I was going to Saint Ives, I met a man with seven wives, each with seven sacks, each with seven cats, each with seven kits."

Betsy was already looking up Ives in the section that had saints alphabeti-cally. "No, his attribute is a fountain flowing from a tomb. Ugh."

"Ick," agreed Jill.

The door opened and an attractive, dark-haired woman in a headband and beautiful swing coat came in, closely followed by three children.

Jill, who had swung to her feet in one swift movement, relaxed.

"Well, hello Patricia," said Betsy, surprised and pleased.

"Hello, Betsy," said Patricia. "We were on our way to Christmas-shop at the Mall of America and decided to stop in and see how you're doing. But I see you already have a visitor."

"That's all right, come in," said Jill, "come in and talk." She moved away to the window.

Betsy said, "I'm glad you came by. Are all of these yours?"

Patricia laughed a fond parent's laugh. "Yes, all three. This is Brent, who is eleven." She pushed forward the oldest child, a very handsome dark-haired boy with hazel eyes that looked back at Betsy—a woman in a nightgown in bed—with a warm interest that was surprising in one that age. *Knows he's good looking, too,* thought Betsy.

"And here is Edith Ann, who is nearly six." Edith Ann had her mother's light brown eyes and a gap-toothed smile. She was very thin and a little shy.

"And this is Meryl, who is three." Meryl was round and blond and ravish-ingly pretty. She smiled at Betsy from behind her mother's left leg.

"What are you doing?" asked Brent.

"Oh, I'm trying to figure out a puzzle, but I don't have all the pieces." She looked at Patricia. "I didn't write them all down, so I'm having trouble figuring out if Lucy hid her name in those attributes."

"Well, I hope you aren't straining yourself over it," said Patricia. "You should just rest and get well."

"I'll be all right in a day or two," said Betsy.

"Are you very, very sick?" asked Edith Ann, who must be named after her grandmother, because no one named a child Edith Ann nowadays.

"I was, but I'm only a little sick now," said Betsy. "I may go home today."

"That's good news," said Patricia. "So I suppose I needn't offer to bring you something."

"No, but thank you."

"I'm going to buy my grandmother a present today," said Brent. "We're go-ing to fly to Phoenix for Christmas. That's where she lives. There isn't any snow there."

"It sounds wonderful," said Betsy.

"We're going in a airplane," announced Edith Ann.

"Yes—oops, come here, Meryl," said Patricia. She went to pull her youngest off the empty bed nearer the window and continued, "My mother told me there are two ways to visit someone in the hospital. First, don't sit down, and when your feet start to hurt, go. Second, bring a small child, and when the child gets bored, go. Either way, you won't overstay your welcome. So that's it for now. Say good-bye, children."

"Good-bye, Ms. Devonshire," said Brent, offering another of his charming smiles. "I'm glad you feel better."

"Good-bye," smiled Edith Ann, who might be thin because so many baby teeth were missing. Meryl used that adorable just-the-fingers wave as her mother herded them out the door.

"Awwwww," said Betsy, when they'd gone.

"That boy of hers is a born politician, just like his father," remarked Jill, coming back to sit beside Betsy's bed.

"Phoenix, where there isn't any snow," sighed Betsy. She picked up the checkbook and finished copying her notes into Jill's notebook, then looked them over. "Phil said she also sometimes put a family member's name in her work. Maybe she had a sister named Agnes." She frowned and tapped the notebook with the pen. "How about she spelled her name with the first letter of these things?" She looked but couldn't find any symbol that started with an L. "Wait a second, I think Father John said this was a lamb, not a fawn." Betsy tapped the lying-down animal. "Now, U, U, U . . . Not here."

"Unless you're wrong about the horseshoe," said Jill. "Turn it right side up, and it's a U."

"And if the shamrock is really a clover, that's a C! All we need is a Y, now."

"Oh, Yvo, of course. But there's a lot of stretching to make it fit. Horseshoe is H, not U. Plus I know the horseshoe was upside down, or why would I think it could have been omega? Ach, this is giving me a headache." Betsy gave the notebook back to Jill and put the book on the bedside table. She lay back and closed her eyes. After a minute she asked, "What was Lucy like?"

Jill composed herself to think. "She was almost as tall as her husband—though he wasn't really tall—and very slim, with a narrow face and a long nose. She had gray hair and very nice gray eyes. She was quiet and dignified, and never said 'ain't' or 'swell' like he did. I used to wonder about them as a couple—you know, what they saw in each other. He was loud and friendly, and, now I think about it, she was probably shy. She was polite to everyone and she carried hard candy wrapped in cellophane in her purse, and sometimes she'd give one to a toddler. I remember my cousin got one and for months he kept a close eye on that purse in case it opened again when he was around."

Betsy laughed. "Did it?"

"No, she only did it once in a rare while, which made it special."

Betsy settled deeper into her pillows and said, "Go on, tell me more."

"Well, she always wore dresses, long and flowing and far out of date. She made them herself. I remember my mother talking about how well made they were. And she always wore a hat to church—and this was when nobody wore hats. She was a little too nice to join the Monday Bunch, but I admire her more now than when when I was a kid. Father Keane was more fun. But he had his dignity, too; like he never wore shorts in public." Jill smiled. "But he did have some pretty raggedy old trousers he'd put on to repair the roof or mow the lawn. And he had this straw hat with a big brim . . ." She stopped, having wandered from the topic of Lucy Abrams.

But Betsy, smiling too, said, "Go on, tell me about Father Keane now."

Jill's voice took on more color. "I adored him. We all did. He was one of those tough-guy priests, intelligent in a low-brow sort of way. He could bluster and shout, but everyone knew he was marshmallow inside. He never had any trouble with the vestry or with anyone in the congregation, which is amazing when you think about it. He was a soft touch, too; when he left, there was a scramble to rebuild some of the funds, especially the rector's discretionary fund. Not that he'd give money to everyone with a sad story, but if he thought someone was in real need, he was very generous."

Betsy, remembering that photo of the craggy face with the bright eyes and sweet smile, nodded. But she nevertheless asked a hard question. "Could he have used some of that money for himself or his family?"

"I never heard that, and you know how gossip is around here. He certainly didn't live beyond his means—the opposite, in fact. I remember Margot doing a fund-raiser to get him into a nicer nursing home, because they didn't have any savings. The church owns a rectory—that big old house on Center Street with the really huge silver maple in the front yard. It's in bad shape, and Father Keane did a lot of repairs himself to save on bills. It has five bedrooms, and Father John simply rattles around inside. The vestry keeps saying we ought to sell the place and give our rector a housing allowance. Which I wish they would; with property values what they are, the church could pay for the whole renovation just from the sale of that house. And Father John would love to live in a nice little apartment; he can't even change a lightbulb."

"I thought he was married," said Betsy.

"A widower," said Jill. "He has children, but the youngest is studying music at Julliard. I think he's actually afraid of the power lawn mower, he always hires local kids to mow his lawn. He's really different from Father Keane. I can see our old priest now, painting the windows or mowing the front lawn in that straw hat, sleeves rolled up, pants legs, too. And barefoot, with cut grass sticking to his shins. And Lucy bringing him ice tea on a tray. Some of the older members didn't think that was nice, him working on the lawn barefooted or climbing up on the roof, but those're hardly the acts of a man living high off stolen funds."

Betsy rubbed a forefinger under her nose, her sign of frustration. "Why the noose?"

"Why not?"

"Surely no saint has a hangman's noose as an attribute." She opened the book but at first couldn't find a hangman's noose. She finally found it under rope, hangman's. "It means betrayal or treason, and it's the attribute of Judas."

That set off a search for more attributes' meanings. Even the ones that had a negative symbology, like the cat, performed double duty as a saint's attribute. There didn't seem to be a Saint Amanda though, or a Saint Keane.

Then she tried to see if some combination of the initial letters of the attributes would spell Keane, or thief, cheat, or adultery, without success.

Jill said, "You know what I think? I think Lucy picked out the attributes she did because they're easy to stitch." Jill took the heavy book and opened it at random. "Look here, Saint John the Baptist's attribute is a lamb on a book of seven seals and here, Saint Lawrence's is a thurible. What's a thurible?"

"Beats me."

"I bet it's more complicated than a cat or an ax. Remember, she was working with a single strand of silver metallic on a space less than an inch square. She saw that blank blue space in the halo and thought it needed something, and an all-saints theme is nice and theological, right? And I bet you were right when you said members of the congregation have the names she picked."

"But the hangman's noose," protested Betsy.

"Oh, it was probably some kind of joke, like my grandfather calling his best friend 'you old horse thief.' But we'll never know what Lucy's joke was, because she's dead, and Keane's got the mind of a houseplant."

"We could ask Mandy."

"All right, when you get out of here, we'll do that, since it's bothering you."

Betsy smiled at Jill. "Yes, thank you for understanding. As soon as we get home." She gave the notebook back to Jill, put the checkbook in her purse, and began searching the basket for some needlework.

But it was hard to let the idea go. Soon, while pausing to count stitches, Betsy said, "We should find out if anybody else connected with the tapestry has been attacked."

"Mike already checked on that. Patricia, Martha, Phil, Father John, everyone is going about his or her daily business with no problem."

* * *

The electronic *bing* sounded, and Godwin looked up to see Malloy standing inside the door.

"Hi, Malloy," Godwin said.

"I understand you were the one sending people upstairs with food for Ms. Devonshire Tuesday and Wednesday."

"Yes, that's right."

"Do you remember the names of everyone who brought something?"

Godwin assumed a thinking pose, tilting his head back, wrapping a slim forefinger around his chin, and closing his eyes. "Martha Winters brought a hot dish. So did Shelly Donohue, Alice Skoglund, and Patricia Fairland." He spoke slowly, assuming, correctly, that Malloy was writing this down. "Katie MacDonald brought a fruit basket, and so did Phil Galvin. June Connor brought a hot dish and Annelle Byford brought a tropical fruit basket. Ellen Rose, Ingrid Leeners, and Rayne Hamilton brought hot dishes, and Gabriel Anderson brought a banana cream pie. And Betsy's ex, Harold Norman, came in and asked what Betsy liked. I said she was crazy about that cashew chicken salad the sandwich shop next door makes, and he went and brought a take-out order. But after he took it up, Betsy called and said not to let him come back up again."

"Did he come back?"

Godwin nodded. "Yes. This time he had a live Christmas tree with him, a big one. And when I told him he couldn't take it up to her, he got in my face until I told him it was her orders. Then he took his tree and went away, and I haven't seen him since." Godwin was smiling at the memory.

"It's my understanding that two people brought chicken salad."

Godwin thought. "I only remember one, the one Hal Norman brought."

"Could he have brought two orders?"

"Sure, but he didn't. I saw him with just one."

"Could someone have gone through here without you seeing him or her?"

Godwin, shaking his head, opened his mouth to say no, then shut it again. "I don't think so. I mean, I'd be helping a customer, and people would interrupt to ask me if I'd take something up to her, and I'd unlock the back door and tell them the door to her apartment was unlocked. Then, when they came back down, I'd lock the door again. I thought leaving her door unlocked was okay, because the other doors to upstairs were locked. And because I knew the ones I sent up: they were friends or good customers. That's why I know who brought what. I was careful about keeping the back door to the shop locked, and we weren't so busy that someone could sneak by. At least, I don't think so. I mean, Irene Potter came in with her Peter Ashe canvas and we got into a pretty intense discussion of stitches, and I suppose someone could have walked through during it. But that takes two coincidences, that I was distracted *and* I left the back door unlocked. Which I don't think I did."

"Did you bring her a gift of food?"

"Are you kidding? There was enough food going up there to feed an army!"

"Did Irene Potter bring something?"

"No. Nor Joe Mickels."

"I thought Joe Mickels was being a lot nicer to Betsy than he was to Margot."

"Well, it's more like he isn't doing things to harass her, like lawsuits. On the other hand, it's not like he's asking her out to dinner. He still looks at her like he looks at everyone, like we're burglars on parole."

The owner of Eddie's Sandwich Shoppe next door was a blocky, middle-aged man with dark, tired eyes and large hands in clear plastic gloves. He couldn't remember how many orders of cashew chicken salad he'd sold on Tuesday. He sold between eight and a dozen orders on any given day, it was one of his most popular salads, so probably it was between eight and a dozen.

Irene Potter? Oh, yeah, that crazy lady with the dark, curly hair. No, she hadn't bought anything from him lately.

But yeah, now that Malloy asked, his landlord was in this week, he was pretty sure it was on Tuesday. Joe came in two or three times a month, and he usually picked either the cashew chicken or the orange coconut dessert. Last time he came in, it was the cashew chicken, and that was earlier this week. Yes, he was sure.

Betsy was working on her stem stitch when the door opened. Quick as thought, Jill was on her feet, standing between Betsy and whoever came in.

It was the Viking Princess, standing very still in surprise. "Hello, Ms. Devonshire," she said over Jill's shoulder.

"Hi, Dr. McQueen. This is my bodyguard, Jill Cross."

"I see. How do you do?" The doctor nodded, and Jill stepped aside. Today she was in blue wool slacks and a white cotton turtleneck with tiny blue flowers on it. A stethoscope was slung sideways around her neck. She came to plug it into her ears and listen to Betsy's heart. Satisfied, she asked, "Feeling better?"

"Yes, thank you. Are you going to send me home?"

"Not today. We need to keep you here another twenty-four hours, monitoring your arsenic levels while we continue treatment."

"Poor Sophie," said Betsy.

"You have a child?"

"No, Sophie's my cat."

"Ah. I've heard animals become lonesome for their owners when separated." Dr. McQueen said that as if she wanted to see a study before she would believe it. "You may get up and walk the halls, if you like. A little exercise may make you feel better."

But Jill said, "Since she's here because there have been two attempts on her life, I don't think she should leave this room, doctor."

"Where does arsenic come from, do you know?" asked Betsy.

Dr. McQueen said, "It's a mineral, so you mine it. There is, or used to be, an arsenic mine in France, and there's one in New Jersey."

"Another reason we're all so fond of New Jersey." Betsy nodded and Jill laughed.

Dr. McQueen didn't crack a smile. "Hundreds of years ago it was called inheritance powder," she continued. "It's tasteless and odorless, and its symptoms can be confused with severe gastritis."

"Very reassuring," said Betsy.

Oblivious, Dr. McQueen continued, "Of course, since they developed a simple test for it, people are less likely to use it to murder. It has commercial and medical uses. It was one of the first cures for syphilis."

"Brrr!" said Jill, surprised.

"The body quickly dumps most of what you ingest, but what little remains can kill you. That's why we're giving you Dimercaprol. It's a chelating agent that apparently binds to the remaining arsenic, rendering it harmless while the body excretes it."

"Apparently?" echoed Betsy.

"Well, we know chelating agents work, we're just not sure how. Any arsenic we can't get rid of winds up in your hair and fingernails. We can dig up a body buried for centuries and find it. It was found recently in a lock of Napoleon's hair."

Betsy said, "I'm so glad you didn't have to dig me up to find out I'd been given a dose."

"That wouldn't have been me, that would have been the medical examiner," explained Dr. McQueen seriously.

When she left, Jill said, "With that sense of humor, she should have been a surgeon."

It was a shabby motel room, with a big television attached to rabbit ears instead of cable and the remote bolted to the bedside table. It had an antique microwave oven, a plug-in coffeepot, and a tiny refrigerator that leaked. Hal might have done better, but flowers here in the frozen north were expensive, and he was afraid it was going to be a long siege.

He lay back on the queen-size bed. He was familiar with the literature that portrayed Midwesterners and Southerners as inbred folk suffering from mad jealousies and inflamed libidos. He'd never thought to actually find himself among such people.

What a place this was! Excelsior, Minnesota, land of ice and snow—and people who seemed to think there was nothing wrong with living that way. Coolly polite ice people, crazily jealous when an outsider comes in and makes good. Because that was what this stuff happening to Betsy was all about, right? She moves here from San Diego and gloms her sister's money and her sister's store and her sister's friends, and they just can't stand it. Tennessee Williams would have loved it.

Someone knocked on his door. Hal rolled to his feet in one easy motion—he was in remarkably good shape for a man his—that is, he was in really good shape.

He opened the door to find a slender man a few inches shorter than himself, a redhead with freckles and very chill pale blue eyes. Something about him set off alarms in Hal's mind, but he said calmly enough, "May I help you?"

"I'm Detective Sergeant Mike Malloy, of the Excelsior Police Department. May I come in?" And suddenly he was holding up a leather folder with a badge and a photo ID in it.

Alarms now sounding loud indeed, Hal took the trouble to note that the photo and name matched the name given and face on display, then he stepped back and said, "Come in. Don't mind the mess," though the place wasn't all that messy; it was more that it was dilapidated. Hal didn't mind good furniture that showed wear, but he didn't like cheap, seedy furniture.

He sat on the bed, gesturing the investigator to the only chair in the room, a wooden armchair. "What can I do for you?" he asked.

"Were you once married to Betsy Devonshire?" Now there was a pen and a notebook in the man's freckled hands.

"Yes." Hal wanted to say more but held his tongue. He tried to look friendly, harmless, and curious—but not too curious.

"You know she's in the hospital?"

"Yes, I sent her flowers. Someone told me she got hold of some poison somehow. She's having a serious run of bad luck lately."

"It may not be just bad luck, Mr. Norman. It appears someone is trying to murder her."

"I can't believe that! She's a fine person, not the type to get involved with people who do that kind of thing!"

"Are you aware that she's been involved in the investigation of three murders since she arrived in Excelsior?"

Hal, genuinely startled, asked, "You mean, she's been a suspect?"

"No, she's taken a role in solving them."

"She has? How . . . peculiar. She never did anything like that back home."

"Well, since she's come here, she has shown a positive talent both for getting involved in crime and tracking down perpetrators."

Bewildered, Hal said, "I thought she was running a needlework store. Has she also taken out a license as a private investigator?"

"No, she's working as an amateur. How long were you two married?"

Hal, still frowning over his ex-wife's peculiar choice of spare-time activity, said, "Eighteen years. Back in San Diego, her hobbies were photography, embroidering aprons and other articles of apparel, and volunteering at the local animal shelter."

"You sent her flowers at the hospital during this stay. Did you bring her a carton of cashew chicken salad when she came home from her first stay?"

Hal nodded. "That fellow who works in the needlework store said it was her favorite. I bought it at the deli next door to her store, and he said I could bring it up. So I did."

"And she thanked you kindly, I suppose."

Hal laughed. "No, she told me to leave and never come back, and she instructed the fellow in the shop to bar me. Which he did." Hal's grin disappeared. "I hurt her badly, and our divorce was entirely my fault. I came here without an invitation, and instead of finding her heartbroken, I find she's made a new life for herself. She wants no part of me, and I can understand that. But I'm hoping that if I stick around for a while, she'll remember the good times and let me have a second chance."

"Arsenic was found in the chicken salad," said Malloy.

Hal found he couldn't breathe in. He sucked and sucked, and finally managed to get just enough air to croak, "What did you say?"

"I said, arsenic was found in the chicken salad. There was enough to have killed her twice over if she'd eaten all of it, but fortunately, she took only one small serving."

Now able to breathe again, Hal couldn't think of anything to say except, "I didn't poison the salad. I didn't even open the carton. I just brought it up and put it in her refrigerator. Why would I poison the salad?"

"Because she won't take you back. Because she left you and came here and has found, by your own description, a new and better life for herself. While you have lost your career and your new girlfriend and your standing in your community. Because she is going to inherit a great deal of money in a few weeks, which you will have no share in. And because when you came up to see her with that little offering of food, she told you to get stuffed, and you were absolutely furious. So you added your own herbal flavoring—"

"Now wait, now wait!" said Hal, an idea coming to him. "What kind of poison is arsenic?"

"What do you mean?"

"Because if you can't buy it at a grocery or drugstore, I didn't do it. I don't know anything about poisons, and I'm not familiar with what's for sale on street corners around here, or even who to ask. I certainly didn't come here expecting to poison Betsy; I came hoping to be reconciled with her, to beg her pardon and ask if she would give me a chance to prove I am worthy of her forgiveness."

"Do you have a pair of scissors or a box cutter in your possession?"

"Huh? No, I don't. I have a pair of fingernail clippers and a fingernail file. I'm doing day labor—painting the interior of houses—and cleaning up is hell on my hands. But at least it's not shoveling snow. Are your winters always like this? My God, I can't imagine living in a climate like this. I haven't been warm since I got here."

Hal could sense he was winning Malloy over, but the cop's next question showed he was still suspicious. "Do you know what the brake line of a car looks like?"

Hal gritted his teeth and told the truth—nothing else would do in his situation. "Yes, I do. But I've never so much as changed a spark plug or the oil or anything but a tire. What was she doing out in a blizzard, anyhow? I would have thought Betsy had more sense than that. After all, she grew up in this part of the country, or practically. Milwaukee is just down the road, isn't it?"

"Milwaukee is six hours south of here by freeway."

"My God, that far? Minneapolis must be practically in the arctic circle, then."

The detective grinned. "Nothing between us and the north pole but a barbed wire fence."

Relieved, Hal grinned back. When the cops started joking with you, things were going to be all right.

Eleven

✦

Jill drove Betsy home from the hospital the next morning, right after doctors' rounds. The trackless snowscape of the last ride home was now filled with snowmobile and cross-country skiing trails. The roads were wet but bare, and there were splashes of grime on the snow where it dared approach the road.

"I see two ways to go with this," Jill told her, sitting relaxed behind the wheel of her elderly Buick. "You can go into hiding—move to a new town, rent an apartment under an assumed name, and get an unlisted phone number. Run the shop by E-mail, and have Godwin send any profits to a post office box. But who knows when Mike will find out who's doing this? It could be weeks or even months."

"Or never," said Betsy.

"Or never," acknowledged Jill. "Alternatively, you can stay where you are. It may be that, having failed twice, he won't try again. For sure it will be a lot harder for him to get to you now you're aware of him and traveling with me. But if he does try again, our chances of identifying him are improved."

"So Mike thinks of me as bait?"

"No, Mike thinks of sushi as bait."

Jill knew which she wanted Betsy to choose, but shut up and let the silence last.

At last Betsy said quietly, "I'm not running."

Jill did not venture to comment on that, but she did smile, just a little.

They stopped off at Jill's apartment so she could pack a bag. They stopped in at the shop to a warm welcome from Shelly and Godwin—and Martha Winters, who had come in to buy a packet of gold needles. "I broke my last one without realizing it was my last one," she said. "Oh, Betsy, I'm so happy to see you looking well! I hope this is the end of that terrible business!"

"Thank you, me too," said Betsy. "Godwin, I've got some things to do today, but I'll be at work tomorrow, if you want to take that as a day off."

"Bless you, I do."

Shelly said, "You want me to come in?"

"Yes, thanks. And find at least one part-timer to work with me tomorrow evening, can you? I might as well start to make up for some of the time I've been away. Sophie looks comfortable. Shall we just leave her here for now? If I don't come and get her by five, just push her into the stairwell." Sophie was familiar with this procedure and would make her way up to the apartment to be let in.

"Will do. Here, take her bowl up with you."

When they got upstairs, Betsy said, "The back bedroom will be yours." It was the bigger, but it had been Margot's, and Betsy couldn't bring herself to move in there.

While Jill settled in, Betsy looked up Mandy Abrams Oliver in the phone book. Jill had told her Mandy's husband's name was Dan and they lived in Golden Valley, so all Betsy had to do was decipher GldnVly in the phone book. But there was no answer.

Betsy brewed coffee for Jill, who was a true Scandinavian in her love for that beverage, and made a cup of herbal tea for herself. The two sat and sipped and sketched out such things as who got the bathroom first in the morning, and whether the one who cooked dinner did the dishes.

That settled, Betsy asked, "Jill, what are the odds? How sure are you that you can keep me safe?"

"I'm more than reasonably sure. But you have to take some precautions. Let me drive you around, for example. Which isn't a hardship on me; I like to drive. Don't eat anything somebody else prepares for you—and that includes restaurant meals. The stuff currently in your refrigerator is a notable exception, since Mike had me bring samples of all of it in to be tested. Oh, and you've got to let me open your Christmas gifts."

"Now, *just* a *second!*" Betsy put her heart into her fake objection, and noticed with satisfaction that Jill had trouble keeping her deadpan in place.

Jill said, "Oh, I don't mind; in fact, I love opening presents so much I don't care if they're not mine."

"I always suspected you were a burglar at heart."

"Hey!" Jill's expression broke and she began to laugh. "I object!"

Betsy smiled, glad to lighten the topic, even if only for a moment and pleased to be mean to the person who insisted on talking about getting killed.

But Jill was relentless. "Speaking of opening things," she said, "let Godwin or me or one of your other employees unlock the shop in the mornings and open any orders that come in. Most important, make sure you tell people about these precautions. No need to let one of your employees get killed."

"Oh, no, I hadn't thought about that! No, Jill, I can't let other people do dangerous things for me! I couldn't live with myself if you or Godwin or one of my part-timers got killed over this. Maybe I should just cut and—No, no, *no!* I won't go into hiding! Okay, suppose I just announce loudly and often that I'm not going to open anything or eat any gift foods? Then I could go ahead and take care of it myself, right?"

"No, because someone will see you opening a box or eating the fudge some- one else made, and word will get around. You have to close that route ab- solutely. And, from now on, before you do anything, *anything,* ask yourself: Can someone possibly use this to hurt me? Could this be a trap? If the answer is yes, don't do it. It sounds awful, but I know a man who has lived like this for years, and he said it got to be a habit pretty quickly. And other people hardly notice how he is unless they already know."

"I hope I don't have to do it long enough to become a habit. I *wish* I knew why someone wants me dead!"

"Think about the why. If you figure that out, we'll probably know who."

Betsy added more sugar to her tea and stirred restlessly. "Okay, the first at- tempt was Monday. What did I do last week or over the weekend that scared or angered someone? There was the Christmas party, but I don't remember a dark look or poisonous hint from anyone. Hal came to town, but he wants my forgive- ness, not my funeral. I offered to go pick up that pillow—which reminds me—"

"Their flight was canceled, so Mrs. Connor went and got the pillow her- self."

"Good. All right, the only other new thing in my life is that tapestry. On the other hand, if it was the tapestry, why am I the only one being attacked? Lots of other people have seen it. What do I know about the tapestry no one else does?"

"The attributes?"

"No, I showed them to Father John and Patricia. I can't imagine them plot- ting together to do me in. But maybe if I talk to Mandy, she'll know something. I wonder where she is."

"Christmas shopping," said Jill. "Want to go, too?"

"Love to, but if I don't do laundry, I'm going to have to go braless tomor- row, and that's not a pretty sight on a woman my age."

Betsy found laundromats depressing. When that money finally arrived, she'd already decided, she would install a washer and dryer, then hire someone to do the laundry anyway.

Was three million enough to have "people"? She'd known someone really wealthy back in California who had people to do his laundry, take care of his lawn and garden, clean his house, cook his meals, pay his bills, decorate his Christmas tree, sort his mail, keep his calendar. That was why he always had time for the important things, like taking impulsive trips to Paris and keeping himself beautifully tanned. How absolutely lovely it would be to have people!

While Betsy was getting her laundry together, the doorbell rang. She came out with the heavy bag bumping her legs, and Jill, already at the door, gestured her back out of sight.

Jill went out on the landing and came right back to ask, "Did you order a Christmas tree?"

"No, why?"

"There's a big one coming up the stairs. A man carrying it."

"Maybe it's the guy from across the hall."

"Then why is it your doorbell he's ringing? Wait here." She went out in the hall again, and Betsy heard her call down, "Who is it?"

"It's me," said a man's voice, somewhat strained.

"Stop where you are," ordered Jill. "What's your name?"

"Who are you?" demanded the man.

"You first, mister."

"I'm Harold Norman, if it's any of your business, and I'm bringing this up for Betsy Nor—er, Devonshire."

"Wait there."

"I *can't* wait, this damn thing's heavy!"

Betsy was behind Jill by then, and she called, "What's the big idea, Hal?"

"You used to wish for a live Christmas tree, darlin', so I'm bringing you one."

Live Christmas trees had been politically incorrect at Merrivale. Still, "I don't want anything from you."

"Now don't be hasty, I—Ai!" There was a thump, a swishy sort of crash, then a series of stumbles, and finally a crunch. "Ow, ow, ow, ow, damn!" said Hal from successively farther down the stairs.

"You want to talk to him?" asked Jill.

"No."

"Then go back inside, and lock the door. I'll take care of this."

A few minutes later, Jill called out. Betsy opened the door and had to back down the little hallway to allow a large and fragrant spruce tree in, with Jill somewhere close behind it. The tree was a little crushed on one side. "He fell on it," explained Jill. "Did you really used to wish for a live tree?"

"Yes."

"Well, Hal has lost interest in this one. It seems a waste to just toss it."

"What did he say?"

"That he couldn't have it in his motel room, and with it damaged, he couldn't take it back, so the hell with it. He stuck it into a snowbank and walked off."

Betsy looked at the tree for a few moments. Apart from the damage, it was a beautiful tree.

"I'll get the stand," she said.

Though Betsy had pictured her tree standing in front of the trio of living room windows, that wasn't possible because of the broken branches. They put it in a corner, damaged side in. Betsy brought out the boxes labeled Lights and Ornaments. They strung the lights first. They were the old-fashioned, big-bulb kind. "Margot always had a real tree," said Jill. There were even two strings of the kind with a bulb hidden in a base under a stem full of colored liquid, which Betsy remembered from her childhood. They were new to Jill, however, and the look on her face when the liquid started bubbling was a pleasure to Betsy.

There were two big boxes of ornaments. But Betsy turned away from them, saying, "Laundry first."

The laundromat's windows were dripping with condensation. Four washing machines and three dryers were in use, and a girl in her mid-teens was hanging blouses and shirts on the stainless steel rod over a wheeled basket. A thin young man was deep into a Grisham paperback, and a grandmother type was futilely calling after two toddlers who ran and yelled around the place.

Jill ran a professional eye over the group and said, "I don't think any of these people are a threat."

They started two washer loads and sat down on a pair of orange plastic chairs that wobbled.

Betsy said, "Tell me what you know about Mandy."

"From back when she lived here? Hardly anything. She seemed to be just an ordinary, average kid. She's six years younger than me, so we didn't go to school together. She was about thirteen when that mess with her parents happened, and I hardly saw her again after that. As for nowadays, I already told you her husband's name is Dan, and they have a little boy whose name I can't remember. Her husband manages a garden supply center in Golden Valley. I know all this because your sister told me. Margot was involved in getting Father Keane moved to a better nursing home, so she was kind of keeping track of the family."

Betsy said, "Doesn't sound much like a murderer to me." She reached into the bottom of her laundry bag and pulled out the thick tome on Christian symbology.

"Want to see my notebook?" asked Jill.

"Yes, please."

Jill pulled it out of a pocket and found the page where Betsy had been copying her notes. "Got a new idea?"

"No," admitted Betsy. "But it hangs in my mind. If Lucy was going to put her name on there, I think she'd put the letters in the right order. And if she was going to spell something with saints' attributes, then why stick someone who was about as far from a saint as you can get at the end?"

"Maybe she just wanted to show it was the end of the line. Hanging means that, too, you know. Like newspaper reporters used to put '30' at the end of a story."

Betsy considered that. She looked at the list in Jill's notebook, squinting as if distorting her view would reveal a plan or outline or . . . something. A pig, a horseshoe, an anchor, a whip. A shamrock, a lamb, a heart, an apple, a star. An apple for a teacher. A Star of David—but Lucy didn't have a son, let alone one named David.

Jill went to move wet clothing from the washing machine into the dryer. A dog, three crowns—there used to be a British coin called a crown. It was worth five shillings. There were twenty shillings in the pound, but that didn't seem relevant here.

The cat was Saint Yvo. Why were there two of them? As Jill said, *Beats me.* Betsy put the notebook in a pocket and went to help Jill.

They'd barely gotten back to Betsy's apartment when the phone rang. Betsy answered, and it was Godwin. "Can you come down? There's someone here who wants to talk to you."

"Who is it?"

"Mandy Oliver."

"Hurray, we'll be right down!"

In the shop was a young woman with a handsome tumble of chestnut hair around a broad face set with a strong nose. She was tracing the intertwining of cable stitch on a sample sweater with a slim forefinger when Jill and Betsy came into the shop. Godwin indicated her with a tilt of his head. Betsy stepped forward and said, "Hello, I'm Betsy Devonshire. You wanted to see me?"

The young woman turned and said, "Hello, I'm Mandy Oliver, Lucy and Keane Abrams's daughter."

"How may I help you?" asked Betsy.

"May I speak with you in private?"

Betsy glanced around at Jill, who said, "Ms. Devonshire isn't allowed to meet with anyone in private right now. But I assure you, anything you tell her won't be repeated by me. Unless, of course, it has bearing on some crime."

To their surprise, Mandy turned white and would have fled if Jill, in one swift move, had not gotten to her and taken her by the elbow. "What's this all about?" Jill said.

"Take your hand off me!" said Mandy.

"No, I think you'd better stay and explain yourself," said Jill.

Mandy gave her arm one unsuccessful yank, then said, "Oh! Do you think *I* have something to do with what's happening to Ms. Devonshire?" She looked sincerely horrified. "No, no! This isn't about *that!*"

"Then what is it about?" asked Jill.

Mandy looked at Jill a considering second or two. "It's about—about my father. And that plan they're working up to hang Mother's tapestry in the Trinity library."

"What about it?" asked Jill, and Betsy came closer.

"I can't believe nobody's said something already. I really don't think they'll be happy when somebody finally does say something."

"Something about what?" said Jill.

Mandy bowed her head and said so quietly Betsy had to strain her ears to hear, "My father was a thief. He stole money from his discretionary fund, and when that was gone, he started another fund, saying it was to help poor people pay their rents in emergencies, but he kept that money for himself, too."

There was an odd noise. Betsy looked over to see Shelly staring at Mandy with big, avid eyes.

"Shelly . . ." Jill said.

Shelly gestured. "Fine, I won't say a word to anyone. But *somebody* better tell the people at Trinity, and soon. And then Patricia is just going to *die!*"

Twelve

❖

Betsy said, "But is it true? Who knew about this?"

Mandy said, "The old vestry knew, they fired Dad for it. My mother knew. She was furious. I heard her tell Dad he had to pay back the money. The church took every penny of our savings, but it wasn't enough to pay back all he stole. Dad and Mother were terrified he was going to go to jail."

"But he didn't," said Jill.

"No, he had that terrible stroke and Mother found him and had a heart attack trying to lift him off the floor. And they—the vestry—thought the scandal would be too awful, so they forgave him."

"What did your father tell you about all this?" asked Betsy.

"Nothing, he never got a chance. We moved out of the rectory into another house. It was just three days later when—when I came home from school and found them—" Suddenly she put both hands over her face and broke into noisy sobs.

"Here now, here now," said Betsy, coming to put an arm around the young woman's shoulder, removing her from Jill's grasp. "Come with me, there's a nice chair back here out of the way." She led Mandy to the area behind the box shelves. She gave Shelly and Godwin a look that warned them not to follow, then seated Mandy on one of the upholstered chairs. "Would a cup of coffee help? Or tea? Or cocoa?"

Mandy shook her head. "I-I'm sorry for losing control," she said with an effort.

"That's all right. Did your mother have a weak heart?"

"Oh yes. She'd been sick for over a year. She couldn't climb the stairs anymore, so she moved into Dad's den on the ground floor. I had to do the heavy housework, like mopping and laundry. She was taking pills, and the doctor had talked to us about a heart transplant, but Mother said she wouldn't consider it."

"And your father?"

"Oh, that came with no warning. He was fine when I went to school that morning . . ." She stared at nothing, or perhaps at what she'd walked into, coming home from high school a dozen years ago.

"I'm sorry, Mandy," said Betsy, putting her hand over the young woman's.

"Thanks," she said. "It was a long time ago, and I'd pretty much gotten over it, and then—I wish Patricia hadn't found that tapestry!"

Betsy said, "Actually, it wasn't Patricia, it was Phil Galvin. He found it in a basement room off the church hall that had been closed off. Have you any idea how it got there?"

Mandy grimaced. "Probably someone from the vestry stuck it back there. I mean, they were willing to forgive Dad, but I don't think they wanted any reminders of us around once he was gone."

"What made you decide to come to me about this?"

"Well, I remember how busy priests get when Christmas is coming, so at first I decided I'd wait until after Christmas to talk to Father John. But it's been like a balloon getting bigger and bigger inside my head. I just had to talk to someone. I called Trinity, but Father John is at a luncheon in the city with the bishop, and Patricia isn't at home, either, so at last I came here." She looked up at Betsy. Mandy was more handsome than beautiful, but there was character in that face, and her hazel-brown eyes were lovely, even spilling tears.

"You were right to come to me," said Betsy firmly. "We'll think of some way to handle this without an explosion, you'll see. Everything will be all right." She went into the bathroom and brought back some tissues for Mandy to blow her nose into.

"Oh, I don't think it will ever be all right," said Mandy. "I loved my father's church, but I joined my aunt and uncle's so I wouldn't have to face the people at

Trinity. And I joined my husband's church for the same reason. I was so sure lots of people knew, when I heard about this plan to name the new library after Dad, I was just amazed. I thought at first of not saying anything, but I knew the farther along the plans got, the bigger the mess when they found out. Shall I try again to get hold of Patricia?"

"If you like," said Betsy, "but they're getting ready to go out of town. Patricia told me they were flying to Phoenix to spend Christmas with her mother-in-law. Perhaps they've already left." She looked inquiringly at Jill, who shrugged.

"I haven't heard anything."

Mandy said, "When my father went from the hospital to a nursing home, it was as if he'd died. I thought it was because everyone knew, the way they stayed away. The nursing home wasn't very good, and it got worse as time went on. Margot—" she smiled through her tears at Betsy—"your sister was so wonderful! She held a fund-raiser to get him moved to a better place, and that shamed the bishop into finding some money somewhere so Margot didn't have to keep on raising money. But still hardly anyone came to see him." She wiped at a fresh flow of tears with her fingers.

Jill said, "But he wouldn't know anyone anyway, would he?"

Mandy nodded. "They tell me that. But I think somewhere, down deep, he's aware that something terrible has happened to him, and he wonders where all his friends went."

"Nobody visits him except you?" asked Betsy.

"Patricia comes once in a while. I don't know if you know this, but there was a time when she and her husband were really struggling. She was trying to put him through law school and worked practically till labor pains set in, and then went back to work almost the day she got out of the hospital. I remember my mother saying how tired and sad she looked, and Dad said he'd see what he could do. He said there was money in the Fairland family, and it was a shame that Peter's parents wouldn't help out. I don't know exactly what he did, but Patricia is still grateful all these years later."

"Does anyone else come to see him?" asked Jill.

"Well, Father John, of course. And Phil Galvin. Dad's grandfather was a railroad engineer back in the 1800s, and Phil loved to hear Dad talk about him. Now, Phil's the one talking, and I think it does Dad good. I don't know if there's anyone else, certainly no one else comes regularly. I kind of assumed it was because they all knew Dad was a thief."

"That tapestry your mother made for Trinity," said Betsy. "When did your mother make it?"

"She designed it before I was born, when Dad was rector at Saint Boltolph's in upstate New York. The Trinity vestry started talking about installing a columbarium, and she remembered the design and decided to make it to hang there. It took years to stitch. She called it her therapy piece. She said that doing needlework was better—and cheaper—than a visit to a shrink. She was often unhappy but would never say why. I wonder now if my father had stolen money before. I remember that other women of the parish would come over a couple of afternoons a week to stitch on it and talk. It was finished just before Dad resigned. Well, actually, it was finished a week or two before, but Mother was doing that thing needleworkers do, you know, going over it and finding missed stitches and so forth. I never saw it once we moved out of the rectory. I don't think it was ever hung in the church."

Betsy asked, "Have you talked with anyone else about it? Or has anyone come to you with questions about it?"

"No."

Jill said suddenly, "I hope the restoration project continues. The tapestry doesn't have anything to do with your father, and it's a beautiful thing, very appropriate for the columbarium."

Betsy said, "But maybe it does have something to do with Father Keane. Maybe that's what that all saints theme in the halo is about."

"What all saints theme?" asked Mandy.

"She worked tiny attributes of various saints on fabric and applied them between the double gold lines of the halo."

"She did?"

"You didn't know that?"

Mandy shook her head. "I don't remember seeing anything like that. But I was a teenager and didn't like needlework. Maybe Mother talked about it at supper three nights a week. I was full of teen angst and not paying attention to anything but myself. Then our whole world crashed in, Mother died, and Dad—well, all that would just run things like her tapestry out of my head."

"I understand. Now, this may sound like an odd question, but did your mother ever hide a message in her needlework?"

Mandy grinned. "Did you find one in the tapestry?"

"No, but I think there may be one."

"What she would usually put is just her name, my name, or Dad's name and sometimes the year into the pattern. More than once she did it by using a color barely a shade darker, so you couldn't see it unless you knew where to look. Once, she did a Noah's ark for my bedroom, and the animals coming up the ramp were monkeys, aardvarks, newts, donkeys, and yaks."

"Oh, that's clever!" said Betsy. "And were they in that order?"

Mandy frowned a little. "Of course. Why not?"

Betsy sighed. "Yes, why not? How else would you know it spelled Mandy?"

"That's right. It was clever, but some of my friends thought the newts were salamanders and the aardvarks looked a lot like pigs. Why are you asking me this? Is there a name hidden in those symbols?"

"If there is, we can't find it. Would she always put just a name?"

"When Uncle Will was young, he was a radioman in the navy. He used to send my mother letters that had some of it written in dots and dashes—Morse code. She got a book on Morse, to translate and to write some things back to him. So when she made him a scarf, she knitted a pattern down one edge and up the other that said something like Thoughts of You Are Warm as a Good Wool Scarf. If you didn't know, it was just a broken line in yellow on the green. Are you thinking she hid a message like that on the tapestry?"

"I was hoping you knew if there was," said Betsy. "There are twenty-some attributes on the halo, enough for a brief message."

Mandy shook her head. "I'm sorry, I can't help you. She must have been upset, but she never said a word, so I think she probably just picked things at random to fill the space."

"Well!" said Betsy after Mandy left. "So the sainted Father Keane wasn't such a saint after all."

"And where does that leave us?" said Jill.

Betsy replied, "I think it depends on who knew. It was only ten or twelve years ago. Surely most if not all of those vestry members are still around. I wonder why they decided not to tell the parish. There must be a record somewhere, like minutes of their meetings or something."

"If they left a record, where is it?" asked Jill. "Because this is all news to me, and I've been a member of Trinity since I was baptized. I never heard a word. Patricia's a member of the current vestry, so she certainly should know, but she's the one gung ho about renaming the library after him."

"Then they must have decided not to tell anyone," said Betsy. "And having decided that, I can see why they'd be upset if it got out now. But what I don't see is why they're coming after me." Betsy gnawed at her bottom lip. "Maybe it's Patricia trying to keep us from finding that out. He's her hero."

"But then the person to kill is Mandy, not you," Jill pointed out.

Betsy said, "She'd better act fast. Mandy will get hold of Father John or Patricia—or both—later today." She looked at Jill. "Uh-oh."

Before she could say anything more, Jill was out the door. She came back a couple of minutes later, breathing hard. "I caught her. She's going straight home and won't talk to anyone about this until we tell her she can. I asked her what she said to the receptionist at Trinity, and she only told Crystal that she'd call back."

Though Godwin and Shelly were obviously eaten up with curiosity, Betsy refused to tell them more. And to keep them from speculating together, she sent Shelly on an errand. A little Christmas tree on the checkout desk that had been decorated with donated needlework ornaments was to go to a patient at a local nursing home. "Better get that over there now," Betsy said.

Back upstairs, Betsy said to Jill, "All right, let's look at the actual attributes, copy them all down in order." She called Trinity. Father John was doing hospital calls. Betsy said to Crystal, "I've got some more wool I want to try to match to the tapestry. May I come over and see it?"

"I'm sorry, Ms. Devonshire, but I don't know where it is. It was in the church hall, but they cleared that out. I know they didn't take it with them because Mrs. Fairland called yesterday wanting to see it, and when I said it wasn't in the church hall anymore, she called all the people who volunteered to help clear things out, and none of them had moved it. Our janitor says he didn't move it, either. She's pretty upset, but I could only tell her what I'm telling you: I don't know where it is."

"Well . . . ah . . . thank you." Betsy hung up and turned, frowning, to Jill. "Remember when you said that if the tapestry had a message that accused you of something, you'd get rid of it? Apparently someone has."

Thirteen

❖

Betsy tried to call Patricia, but there was no answer. "When are they leaving for Phoenix, do you remember if she said?" Betsy asked Jill.

"No."

"So what do we do now?"

Jill looked around the apartment and said, "Finish decorating the tree?"

But while doing that, Jill, still picking at the case, asked, "Are you sure it isn't Hal Norman doing all this? There are a lot of weird men out there who decide, 'If I can't have her, no one can.'"

"I know. But don't they tend to shoot themselves after shooting their women? The Pig doesn't strike me as the suicidal type. I mean, how would the world get along without him?"

"Well, then let's call Mike and see if he's found any suspects among the friends and relations of the murderers you've unveiled lately."

Jill placed the call to Mike's pager, and when he called back, she asked if he'd developed any new suspects. "I'm afraid not," he said. "Any action on your end?"

"No, I think the word's out that she's got an armed guard. The tapestry's gone missing, and that may also be a factor."

But trying to think why someone might want her dead prompted Betsy to other morbid thoughts. She put the hot dish she'd just pulled out of the freezer into the microwave to thaw it and phoned John Penberthy at home. "I guess it's time to make out that will," she said, not very graciously.

"Do you want to come see me tomorrow?"

"I have to work tomorrow, so if you're free this evening, can you come over? Come to supper. We've got plenty to eat, if you like hot dish. Jill Cross is staying with me for a while, so there will be two of us to talk to."

"Yes, I heard about that arrangement, and I think it's a very good idea. All right, thank you, I'll be there. We've got that one asset to talk about as well. I'll bring the file."

Penberthy was prompt. He was about thirty, dark and good looking, with humorous, intelligent eyes. Under a short winter coat he wore khaki slacks, a white shirt open at the collar, and a sky-blue, V-necked sweater—his version of casual. He carried a shining old-fashioned briefcase that was probably older than he was.

Betsy had chosen a hot dish of potatoes, pork, onion, and cheese. After thawing it, she had put it in the oven to heat through. She made a salad of cucumber, tomato, endive, green onions, and herbs. That was the meal, plus seven-grain bread and milk, with coffee for dessert. Penberthy declined a slice of banana cream pie.

"Ah," he sighed at last, putting his second cup down empty. "That was delicious. My mother used to make that hot dish from leftover pork roast."

"Martha Winters made this one," said Betsy. "I only know how to mix peas and tuna with macaroni and cheese."

"Definitely not Lutheran, then," said Penberthy with a nod, and Jill laughed.

Betsy decided that was an obscure reference Minnesotans used as shortcuts to character. She also decided she didn't want to know what it said about her. She and Jill began clearing the table. "Is it a complicated thing, making a will?" Betsy asked over her shoulder.

Penberthy replied, "It can be. Depends on what you want to do. If you want to set up trusts, it definitely will be. Any idea who you want your executor to be?"

"No, but what I want is not very complicated. I want to leave Crewel World to Godwin du Lac, then split the money between Godwin and Jill Cross."

"*Me?*" said Jill, clattering plates into the sink. "Sorry."

"Well, I have to leave it to someone—"

Jill came to take the salad bowl from Betsy and said, "But Betsy, when he leaves, we'll be all alone and . . . well, I've got a gun."

Penberthy laughed hardest at that.

But when the two women came back from the kitchen, he had a thick file folder on the table. "Let's look at this first," he said.

"What is it?"

"Have you ever heard the term *silent partner?*"

"Sure. It means someone who buys shares in a company but doesn't help run it."

Penberthy said, "Yes, that's approximately correct. Your sister was a silent partner in a company called New York Motto." He opened the file folder and began handing over documents.

Betsy studied them for a couple of minutes, but then said, "I'm sorry, I don't understand what this is about. In some places it looks as if Margot owned the company, but in others it seems like it was Vicki Prentice. Who's she?"

"At the start, she was a friend of mine. She owned a small property in Wisconsin, adjoining a lake cabin your sister used to own, so Margot knew her, too."

"It was a nice place," said Jill. "But Margot sold it when the developers moved in."

Penberthy nodded and continued, "But what I'm talking about happened a few years ago. Margot had been playing the market, but it made her nervous and it demanded a lot of her time, so she wanted someplace else to put the money. I had been fooling around with futures, and she came and asked me if I wanted to do some investing for her. It's unethical for a person's attorney to enter into a business connection with her, so I introduced her to Vicki.

"Vicki was taking law courses at night while she worked as a law clerk for a lawyer during the day. The lawyer specialized in bankruptcies and receiverships, and Vicki had come up with an idea involving bankruptcy estate assets. The auction of these assets is not advertised, and often valuable assets are sold for far less than they are worth."

Betsy began to smile. "And that's where Margot put her money, into buying these assets."

"In a way. Vicki was the one who wanted to do this, but she didn't have the start-up money. Margot didn't have the time it takes to find and attend the sales and then sell the assets. So what Margot did was start a shell company, called New York Motto. Did you know the state of New York's motto is 'Excelsior'?"

"I used to, but I'd forgotten."

Penberthy continued, "Excelsior was founded by immigrants from New York."

"Really? I didn't know that. I'm going to have to research the history of this place someday."

"You'll love it," said Jill. "We have a checkered history."

"We have a varied and interesting history," corrected Penberthy. Then he continued, "Margot kept ninety-five percent of the company, selling five percent to Vicki. Vicki quit her job and dropped out of law school when she was named operating officer. Vicki hired a highly talented CPA as comptroller and other staff, mostly scouts to research bankruptcy and sheriff's auctions. New York Motto has been doing quite well since its founding. But here," he said, handing Betsy another document, "this may be of special interest to you."

It was some kind of land contract. New York Motto agreed to sell a piece of land on which was a restaurant to Joseph P. Mickels. "Joe!" exclaimed Betsy, and Jill came out of the kitchen to look over her shoulder. The legal description of the location didn't mean much until Betsy got to "City of Pinewood, in the County of Hennepin, State of Minnesota." Pinewood was another of those Hennepin county "cities" that are really small towns. In Pinewood's case, practically a village. But it was just up the road from Excelsior, on the shore of Lake Minnetonka.

Jill drew air softly through her teeth. "I know that place," she said. "The manager was a crook."

"Was this restaurant bought at one of those auctions?" asked Betsy.

"Yes, at a bankruptcy estate sale in bankruptcy court."

"And Joe is buying it from New York Motto."

"He's buying it back."

"You mean it was his? Joe went *bankrupt?*"

"Not Joe, one of his companies." Penberthy explained, "Joe plays around with a lot of different kinds of real estate. When the deal seems particularly risky, he'll start a new company and put the holding in the new company's name. That way, if it doesn't work out, the loss doesn't put a drain on any of Joe's other holdings but is confined to the corporation that owns it."

Betsy nodded.

Penberthy continued, "Restaurants are chancy businesses at the best of times. Joe put his company and its restaurant into the hands of a cousin who, it turned out, really didn't know what he was doing. And when the cousin saw it was going bad, he ran it into the ground—it's called running a bust out—and absconded with most of the money. By the time Joe realized what was going on, it was too late. The company had to declare bankruptcy.

"In legal terms, what happens when a company goes bankrupt is that it disappears and a new entity, a bankruptcy estate, is created, and the court assigns a trustee to manage it. These trustees are often overextended, handling six hundred or more cases a year. When they don't investigate the background or search the estate thoroughly for assets, they may misapprehend its true value."

Betsy, holding onto comprehension with both hands, nodded again.

"In this case, after a halfhearted search for assets—the trustee knew this was a bust-out case—the trustee ordered the property sold to pay creditors. If he'd paid attention, he would have realized that while the restaurant was deep in debt, the lakefront property on which it stood was free of liens. New York Motto's scout wasn't as careless and recommended making a bid. Joe came to the auction with a cashier's check in an amount equal to about eight cents on the dollar of the value of the property. But Vicki came with a cashier's check for twelve cents on the dollar and, when Joe couldn't raise his bid—you must have cash in hand or a cashier's check—the judge dropped his gavel and New York Motto got it. Joe was very angry, of course.

"A week later, he contacted New York Motto and expressed an interest in the property. Vicki offered him a contract for deed, and, surprisingly, he took it. What I assume is that at the time, he was cash poor, but he was sure he would be in good financial condition at the end of the purchase contract. He planned to have The Mickels Building finished or nearly finished and figured he could handle a balloon payment at the time it came due."

"Oh, a balloon payment," said Betsy, nodding more easily. She'd known several people desperately worried about balloon payments.

Penberthy smiled. "This contract offered terms that amounted to paying interest on a loan of the purchase price, with the entire principal due as the last payment."

Betsy looked at the deed, found the amount, and whistled softly. "When was the balloon payment due?"

"It hasn't come due yet. The due date is January twelve." He pointed to a place on the document.

Jill came to the table, wiping her hands on a dish towel, to ask, "What happens if he can't make the payment?"

"He forfeits all he's put into the deal, and the property reverts to New York Motto."

Jill said, "No wonder Joe was so angry at Margot! She not only kept him from putting up The Mickels Building but stood in the way of his getting a valuable property back."

"No," said Penberthy, "Joe didn't know Margot was also New York Motto."

Betsy said, "He didn't? Are you sure?"

"He never said anything to me about it."

Jill asked Betsy, "Has Joe said anything to you, anything at all, that might indicate he knows that New York Motto is now yours?"

Betsy stared at her. "You mean Joe owes *me* all this money?"

"You're inheriting the company, aren't you? I'm asking how sure you are he doesn't know about this."

Penberthy said, "I never told him. Margot and Vicki wouldn't tell him. Betsy is obviously surprised to discover this, so I don't know how Joe would have found out."

Betsy said, "If Joe knew Margot owned New York Motto, he might very well think she was holding on to her lease just so he'd lose that land." Betsy smiled wryly. "In fact, it sounds like the kind of squeeze he'd love to put on someone else, doesn't it?"

Penberthy, smiling, nodded.

But Jill persisted, "Surely when he set out to contact New York Motto about buying the land back, he would have found out who the owner was."

Penberthy said, "On the contrary. New York Motto is incorporated in the State of Wisconsin, so there is no listing of it in Minnesota at all. And in Wisconsin, the only names that appear are Vicki's and the CPA's." He was still smiling, as if Betsy surely must now see the point of a complex joke.

"What?" she asked, feeling stupid.

"You are in a position of tremendous power over Joe Mickels. You can release this information to the press and if he's stretched thin—which I think he is right now—ruin him financially. Or, under a threat to tell, make him agree to a new contract at very high interest rate. Even add some other terms. Make him agree to rename The Mickels Building The Margot Berglund Building. He may be facing financial ruin if he doesn't agree to whatever terms you dictate." Penberthy shrugged. "Or you can be kind and renew the contract under its present terms. You can even keep silent and let Vicki decide what to do—which is, after all, what a silent partner does."

"What do you think Vicki would do?"

"Let him fail to make that final payment, lose everything he's already paid into the deal plus the property, then sell the property to someone else. It's already unusual for New York Motto to hang onto a piece of property this long. Normally, they turn around almost at once and sell at a profit. Joe must have done some fast talking to get her to agree to this."

"What fast talking? Look at the mess he's in!"

Penberthy said, "But look at it from his position back then. He was all ready to put up that building. There was only this one silly, helpless widow in his way." He lifted a sardonic eyebrow at Joe's ignorance.

Jill added, "And even if he thought it was risky, this deal with New York Motto involves land that was once his. Joe operates under Will Rogers's advice: 'Buy land, they ain't makin' any more of it.' It probably caused him a lot of pain to lose that lakefront site, and he was feeling very motivated to get it back."

"I think that's an accurate assessment," said Penberthy.

Betsy said, "What do you think, Jill? If he knew, this might give him a motive to murder me?"

Jill said, "Oh, yes."

Penberthy said, "But if he knew, he would have accused Margot of deliberately trying to damage him. Margot never said anything like that. And she would have told me, because I needed to stay one step ahead of whatever he was up to."

"Still . . ." Jill said.

"Yes," Betsy said. "And it's important we find out. I want to be the one who tells him."

Penberthy said, "There is no legal responsibility to tell him anything. If it was me, and I felt he should know, I'd want to tell him long distance. From, say, Hong Kong."

Betsy snorted. Then she asked, "What's the total value of the company today?"

"You'll have to contact Vicki and ask for an accounting. I know it's been making money, but I don't think Margot was letting equity build up, she was using the money for some project or other, something charitable, I think. Here's Vicki's address." Penberthy gave her a business card.

"Thanks." Betsy asked, "When is this probate matter going to be wrapped up?"

"If you can get the information on New York Motto to me before the new year, I'd say we can finalize this by mid-January. Which is why I think we should now turn our attention to the matter for which you summoned me: your will."

He glanced up at her. She was gaping at him. "Really?"

"Really what?"

"Mid-January? That's about three weeks from now."

"I thought you'd be pleased."

"I am pleased. I'm also surprised. The way there's always one more thing to do, I thought it would be months before we got it all resolved."

"No, things have progressed very smoothly. No other heirs have stepped forward to make a claim, all the assets are found and will soon be accounted for, and there's no reason we can't make a final court appearance within that time."

Betsy sat back. "Wonderful," she murmured. And then she smiled.

Penberthy got out a yellow legal pad and prepared to take notes. "You said you want to divide your estate between Mr. Godwin and Ms. Cross," he said, writing. "Any charities?"

"Oh . . ." Betsy hesitated. Her head was spinning, and she was suddenly tired. "I—I can't think. Let's just get something on paper for now. We can revise it later, can't we? If I live." She meant that as a joke, but it came out through gritted teeth.

Through a slip in Penberthy's composure he gave her a look of such compassion she nearly threw herself on his shoulder to relieve her feelings in tears. But he was an even cooler head than Jill, and the look vanished as swiftly as it had appeared. Betsy, already leaning forward, feigned an interest in what he was writing on the notepad.

"For something as simple as what you describe," he said, "especially since it's very likely an interim will, you can just write it out in your own words."

"And then you'll turn it into legal language?"

"There's no need to do that. Holographic wills are perfectly legal. That means handwritten, not just signed. Written entirely by hand. You don't even need witnesses to a holographic will."

Betsy made a doubtful face.

"There is a case where a tractor rolled over on a farmer out in his field, and he wrote 'All to Mother' in his own blood on the tractor's fender, and it was admitted to probate. But be clear; don't attempt fancy language. A will is not subject to interpretation; it means exactly what it says." He tore off the top sheet of his legal pad, turned the pad around, and pushed it toward her. He handed her his heavy gold pen and said, "Use your full legal name."

I, Elizabeth Frances Devonshire, wrote Betsy—"I took my maiden name back after each divorce," she said—*hereby make this my last will.*

"Have you ever made a will before?" he asked.

She started to say no, then remembered. "You know, I *did* make a will, back when Hal and I got married. We each made one. You know the kind, where you leave everything you die possessed of—that sounds like you're leaving a flock of demons, doesn't it?—to your spouse." She put a hand over her mouth and stared at Penberthy.

"What?" he asked.

"I never revoked that will."

"So?"

"So *that's* what's going on here! Don't you get it? I never revoked that will! So if I die without making a new one, Hal gets everything—*everything!* That's why he's trying to kill me! Oh, my God, I've got to call Malloy this second!"

She ran into the kitchen, but before she could pick up the receiver, Penberthy called, "Wait! It doesn't work that way!"

She looked at him, hand on the phone. "What doesn't work that way?"

"The will you made probably said something like, 'to my beloved spouse, Harold What's-his-name——"

"Norman. Harold Norman."

"'To my spouse, Harold Norman, I leave all of which I die possessed,' right?"

"Yes, just like that."

"Well, he's not your spouse anymore. That will isn't valid."

Betsy let go the receiver. "Oh. Well, I didn't know that."

Jill said quietly, "I bet Hal doesn't know it, either."

Betsy stared at her. "You're right! Of course! What a jerk, trying to kill me to get something he couldn't get even if I died naturally!" She picked up the receiver, looked on the refrigerator for a business card with a badge, and dialed the number inked on it. "Mike," she said when he answered, "We've got it. When Hal and I first married, we made out those mutual wills leaving everything to one another. And I never revoked that will. Now, my attorney just told me that will became void when we divorced—which I didn't know. And probably Hal doesn't know it, either. I'll bet you ten dollars he thinks that if I die, he gets my inheritance." She paused long enough for him to ask a question. "Last I heard, three million."

She hung up and turned a harshly satisfied face to the pair in the dining nook. "There, that solves that! He'll go arrest that bastard, and I can get back to living in peace!"

Fourteen

❖

Betsy was sleeping the sleep of the just when a bumblebee flew into her dream, disordering it by trying to send a message to her in Morse code. It droned zzdah, zzdah, zit-zit-zit, zzdah, zdaaaaaaah, and then she was awake and someone was ringing her doorbell very urgently.

She flung the blankets back, and Sophie thumped onto the floor. She grabbed for her striped flannel robe and heard Jill out in the living room grumbling, "I'm coming, I'm coming!"

Betsy followed, but Jill gestured at her to move so the visitor wouldn't see her when Jill opened the door. Betsy was shocked to notice that Jill had a gun in her hand. As Jill reached for the button that released the downstairs door, Betsy hustled sideways and heard the apartment door open.

There was a thumping of hasty feet on the stairs. "Patricia!" Jill exclaimed. "What are you—?"

"You've got to get out, quick!" Patricia Fairland said. "You're on fire!"

Betsy looked around swiftly. There were no flames, and she couldn't smell smoke. She hurried to the door. "What fire? Where is it?" she asked, standing on bare tiptoes to peer over Jill's shoulder.

Patricia was nearly to their threshold. "It's around back!" She gestured widely. "I was driving by, and I saw flames reflected off the snow. Come on, come on, you've got to hurry!" Patricia looked distraught, her hair was mussed, and her swing coat was gathered strangely around her, as if she had put it on over her head, or been hugging herself inside it.

Jill reached for the door of the microscopic hall closet and Betsy backed out of her way. Jill grabbed her heavy police jacket and began shoving her feet into her boots as she pushed the gun into a pocket. "Get something on your feet!" she ordered Betsy.

But Betsy ran instead to the window at the back of the dining nook. She couldn't see straight down, but there was a bright flicker on the icy coating of the parking lot and the banks of snow that surrounded it. The flicker appeared to be coming from somewhere near the back door to the building. "Oh my God, she's right, I can see it, we're on fire!"

She turned toward the kitchen, but Jill was already on the phone, her voice urgent as she told the emergency operator about the fire.

"Come on, come on!" called Patricia from out in the hall.

"Sophie!" exclaimed Betsy, and dashed for the bedroom. The cat was standing just inside the doorway, tail up in greeting, but not wanting to join the fuss until she knew what it was about. Betsy scooped her up.

"Rowww!" objected the cat. Then Betsy's fear infected her, and she began a serious struggle to get away.

Sophie was not declawed, so Betsy ran to the bed and grabbed a pillow by the closed end of its case and shook hard. The pillow fell out, tumbling across the bed. Betsy dropped the case, grabbed it by its open end, and put the struggling animal in by pulling the pillowcase over her cat-laden arm.

Jill called, "Betsy! Let's go!"

Betsy shoved her feet into her corduroy slippers and ran into the living room, the heavy pillowcase thumping her leg. "Have you warned the others?"

"Oh, gosh!" Jill ran out, but Betsy paused long enough to yank her purse off the hook inside the closet door.

Out in the hall, Patricia was standing at the top of the stairs. "Hurry, oh hurry!" she begged, and started down.

But Jill ran across to thump with a fist on the door to one of the other two apartments. "Out, out, out!" she yelled. "Fire! Fire!"

Betsy ran to bang on the other apartment door. "Fire! Fire!" she shouted. "Get out! Get out! Fire!"

It seemed to take a long time to get a response, though it was likely only seconds. The door was yanked open, and an old man wearing only pajama bottoms stared at Betsy, his white hair standing up all around his head. "Where is it?" he asked, looking past her into the hall. "I don't see anything."

Jill was still banging on the other door, and he stared at her. "Who's she?"

"A police officer. Quick, quick, get a coat and come on!"

"Where's the fire?" the old man insisted.

"Downstairs, back door. I saw flames. Come on!"

Betsy ran to the stairs and hustled down. She stopped at the bottom. Patricia was gone, the front door left standing open. The dim night light revealed no sign of smoke, but Betsy could smell it now. Upstairs, the pair who lived in the other apartment were questioning Jill's insistence they leave right now. Betsy looked toward the back of the hall, where an obscure door let into a narrow hallway to the back door and the back entrance to Crewel World.

I shouldn't, she thought, remembering all the warnings that said get out, get out, get out. But she ran to the back door and put her palm on it. It was cool. She felt in the side pocket of her purse and found her keys. She unlocked the door and opened it cautiously. The smell of smoke was much stronger in the narrow back hall, and when she snapped on the light, there was a haze in the air. The door to the rear parking lot had a small glass insert, and Betsy could see the shifting yellow and orange of flames outside, but none in the hall itself.

The cat in the pillowcase was struggling and yelling to be set free. Outside, she could hear Patricia calling, "Help, help! Fire, fire!" Someone was coming down the stairs.

Betsy closed the back hall door. She ran out the front behind the old man, now wrapped in a purple chenille bathrobe—the siren that summons the volunteer fire department began bawling—past him and around to the front door to Crewel World. No flames in there. She unlocked the door and went in.

Patricia was suddenly beside her, grabbing her arm. "What are you doing?" she demanded.

"Fire extinguisher!" said Betsy, and handed the pillowcase to Patricia. She raced to the back storage area where a small foam extinguisher hung on the wall. She grabbed it, dodged around Patricia on her way back out. She ran to the driveway to the rear of the building.

"Stop her!" shrieked Patricia.

"Wait, wait, wait!" called Jill, coming in hot pursuit, but Betsy kept running. The ice-rutted surface of the driveway hurt through the slippers. The grit and salt-pitted surface of the parking area kept her from sliding as she stopped short. The fire was bigger than she'd thought it would be, as high or higher than the back door. It was made of log chunks—fireplace wood!—and smelled like a charcoal grill. She approached until she felt the heat of the flames, pointed the fire extinguisher, and squeezed the handle. It was stuck; it wouldn't move.

Jill grabbed it away from her. "Back!" she ordered, and Betsy retreated, but not far. Jill pulled out the little pin in the extinguisher's handle and squeezed as she stepped toward the fire.

The fire ducked under the onslaught of the extinguisher, but rebounded. It was too big for the little extinguisher to harm it. Jill moved around to a different angle, spraying white foam at the base of the flames.

Betsy became aware of approaching sirens and slithered back down the rutted driveway to the street. Cars pulled up to both curbs were disgorging men carrying yellow firemen coats. As the pumper approached, its huge engine roaring, she stepped out into the street to raise an arm and point. The men from the cars ran past her. The truck slowed, its siren cut off, then it obeyed her urgent signing, turned into the driveway and stopped. Two men bailed out.

Betsy went to check the entryway to the apartment building. There huddled the other three tenants, a young couple in winter coats and slippers hugging one another against the chill and the elderly man hiding behind them in his chenille robe and wingtip shoes on sockless feet. "Everyone all right?" asked Betsy.

"Where's the fire?" asked the man of the couple.

"Outside the back door. I don't think it's gotten inside the building yet."

Patricia hurried up, still holding the pillowcase. "Are you all right? Where's Jill?" Patricia's voice sounded harsh, unlike her normal quiet tone. Her makeup looked strange because her natural color was gone. Her hairband was a twist of black velvet and metallic gold, her earrings looked like real diamonds.

"Back with the firefighters. I'm all right." Betsy took the pillowcase from her. Sophie, hearing Betsy's voice, began complaining again about her strange confinement.

"How did it start?" asked the old man.

"I don't know."

A large blond policeman—Betsy suddenly realized it was Lars, Jill's boyfriend—came up and offered them a seat in his nice, warm squad car. But Sophie was beginning to experiment with burrowing, so Betsy went into her shop instead and closed the door. There was a faint light coming in the front window from a streetlight. She put the pillowcase on the floor. Sophie rolled it

over a few times, then pushed her way to the mouth of the pillowcase. "Ree-
ooooow!" she complained.

"Yes, your highness, I apologize for the rude treatment," said Betsy. "But
we couldn't leave you up there to die, could we?" She was trembling all over,
from cold and shock. Her voice sounded funny to her ears, so she shut up.

Sophie sat to make a single stab at putting her thick, long fur back in order.
Then she looked around. Finding the surroundings familiar, if wanting in light,
she did the familiar thing. She went to her chair, the one with the cushion on it,
jumped up, and lay down. "Reeeew," she complained again. Betsy turned a
chair at the library table around and sat down to comfort the cat. It took only a
minute to have Sophie purring as Betsy tickled her under her chin, and soothing the animal soothed her own nerves. Still, Betsy kept an eye toward the back
of the shop, expecting either flames or a fireman to come shooting through at
any second.

But neither happened. In forty minutes Jill joined her, looking smudged,
and said, "It's gonna be a real skating rink back there in a while, water all over
everything. Say, can the other tenants come in here? Lars wants to get back on
patrol."

"Of course. Shall I turn on the lights and start the teakettle?"

"Better wait till we see if the wiring is okay."

The three tenants thanked Betsy, then wandered around the dim shop,
strangers in a strange world.

After what seemed a very long while, an enormous fireman came in to declare the fire out, and the tenants followed him out, asking if they could go upstairs. Betsy turned on the lights.

They'd no more than left when Patricia came in to take Betsy by the hands.
"I just heard a fireman say this fire was *set!* Betsy, this is impossible! You have to
do something!"

"Oh, yeah?" said Betsy inelegantly, pulling back to release herself. "What
do you suggest I do?"

"Run away. Get out of town. Get dressed and pack your bags right now. I'll
drive you to the airport. You can buy a ticket on the first plane to—to anywhere. You can't stay here, you're going to get *killed!*" She'd straightened her
coat and recovered most of her color, but her eyes were frightened.

"I can't run," said Betsy. "For one thing, I don't have anywhere to go. For
another, I can't afford to go anywhere."

"I'll loan you the money—or we'll all get together and loan you the money,
the Monday Bunch will. And what about what's-his-name, your ex-husband?
He'd be glad to take you back. When I talked with him last week, he sounded so
anxious for you to forgive him. He'd do anything for you, Betsy, truly he would."

Betsy shook her head. "What Hal's been doing is attempting to murder me. Mike Malloy is going to arrest him for it, if he hasn't already."

Patricia stared at her. "He is? Arrest Hal? How do you know?"

"Because I told him to. Hal and I wrote mutual wills when we first married and never revoked them. He thinks he'll get all that lovely money I'm heir to."

"But he won't," said Patricia, a woman whose husband had a law degree. "He can't."

"That's right," said Jill tiredly. "But Betsy didn't know that until her attorney told her, and it's unlikely Hal Norman consulted with an attorney before deciding to murder Betsy."

"Oh." Patricia had gone from scared and excited to anxious and regretful. Betsy felt a stab of compassion for her. Hal was so very handsome and charming, the pig.

"Here, come and sit down. Can you smell smoke in here?"

Patricia could not have been more surprised at Betsy if she had turned into an orange. "I'm sure you can smell the smoke blocks from here," she said, and sat down on Sophie's chair, the cat barely escaping in time.

Jill said, "How did you come to see the fire?"

"I told you, I was driving by and saw the flames reflected on the ice and snow. It just happened to catch my eye."

"What were you doing in town this time of night?" asked Jill.

Patricia stared at her, and Betsy could all but see the raising of the drawbridge the rich and powerful live across. "First of all, it wasn't 'this time of night' when I came by," she said calmly. "It was only a little past midnight. I was in the Cities attending 'The Messiah.' Peter couldn't come," she added, forestalling that question. "He had a political meeting to go to, and I just couldn't face another one of those things. So I said I already had tickets—which was a lie—and went by myself." She unbent a little and said, "And I drove through town because I grew up in Excelsior, and I wanted to look at it by night, see the Christmas lights on the houses, and on the house Peter and I used to own. So I was driving slowly, and I was looking around."

Jill's cop facade melted into a smile. "Pretty in town this time of year. All right. Thank you, Patricia."

The drawbridge came back down. "You're welcome, Jill. May I go now?"

"Have you talked to the fire marshal?"

"Yes, a few minutes ago. He said I should talk to the police before I left. Will you do?"

"Yes. Did he ask you if you saw anyone leaving the scene?"

"Yes, and I told him I didn't."

"That's too bad. All right, go on home."

Patricia stood with such weariness that Betsy said, "I don't think I've thanked you for ringing our doorbell. Thank you very much. You probably saved our lives. I'm sorry they made you wait."

"Well, as they say, no good deed goes unpunished. Good night."

After she had gone, Betsy said, "What do you think?"

"I think she was driving around town because she misses living here and because she didn't want to go home to an empty bed. Her husband is starting to be seriously noticed by the political kingmakers in this state. But it's taking up a lot of his time, spending the required hours at his law office, doing the legislative thing in Saint Paul, and keeping his political mentors happy. She's attractive and correct and smart, a good political wife. But I don't think she likes the attention nearly as much as he does, and she's becoming protective of the children."

"She doesn't talk about them, does she? That's sad. That boy is handsome, and the girls are pretty. Are they very bright?"

"I hear the oldest is in a gifted program and the star pitcher on his baseball team. His parents didn't like Patricia, you know. Their son married very young and he chose a woman whose father worked in a factory and whose mother cooked in a café. And Patricia got pregnant. They stopped paying their son's college expenses, and Peter nearly had to drop out of his last year in law school. But she worked two jobs, and Peter graduated near the top of his class. He joined a prestigious law firm and became a state senator. Patricia began talking and dressing like she'd been to finishing school and insisted their first daughter be named after her husband's mother. And now there's talk about Peter making a run for Congress. His father died a couple of years ago, and his mother has decided it was all the old man's fault, that she herself has long suspected that her daughter-in-law is charming and perfectly acceptable."

Firemen brought big fans into the hall and the shop to began blowing the last of the smoke out. Betsy made an urn of coffee for them.

Joe Mickels turned up, ruffled and angry. "What's going on here?" he demanded.

"Someone tried to set fire to the building by stacking cordwood at the back door and squirting charcoal starter on it," said Jill.

"Is this another attempt to get at you?" Joe asked Betsy.

Betsy nodded, unaccountably embarrassed.

"Well, goddam it, why don't you leave town?"

"Because they might follow her," said Jill. "Here she has friends to help watch out for her, and she's on familiar ground. I don't think you want her to be put at more risk just so you don't have to fill out a few insurance forms."

"Hmph," snorted Mickels and borrowed the phone to summon someone to board up the back door.

After Mickels left, Betsy, too tired to lift her arm, asked, "What time is it?" and Jill looked at her own watch.

"Quarter to four."

The fire chief came in and said they could go up and gather a change of clothes and, if the apartment smelled too strongly of smoke and they had no place to go, a Red Cross representative would be called to find them a place to stay for a day.

Betsy went up with Jill. She stood inside it a long minute, sniffing, then said to Jill, "I can't tell if it stinks of smoke or not."

Jill said, "I think it does, but not too badly. I'm sorry about this, Betsy."

"Why? There wasn't anything you could do. I'm just glad Patricia was feeling homesick. If she hadn't seen that fire, it might've gotten into the stairwell. But I'm mad at Malloy. I thought he would have Hal under arrest by now!"

Jill said, "Maybe he does. He was probably waiting outside Hal's motel room for him to come home, and caught him with bits of firewood bark all down the front of his coat and a can of charcoal starter in his trunk."

The doorbell rang. "Now who—" began Betsy.

"Malloy, I'll bet."

It was. "Bad news, Ms. Devonshire," he said, once inside the apartment.

"What?" demanded Betsy. "Couldn't find Hal? Don't tell me you're here to take me to jail till you do?"

"No, Hal is down at the police station," Malloy said.

"Well, that's one good thing!"

"No, you don't understand. He was sitting down there telling me he loves you, he wants you to forgive him, yadda, yadda, yadda, when the fire siren went off."

That did it. Betsy was overcome by fury. She stomped across the living room and flung herself onto the love seat. "I can't stand this, I'm sick of this whole thing! It *has* to be Hal! It all made sense that it was Hal!"

Malloy said, "You had me convinced. But Hal Norman has one of the best possible alibis: he was sitting in our interrogation room telling me he had no reason to want to kill you at the very moment someone else was trying to do it."

There was a long, depressed silence. Then Jill asked, "So what do we do now?"

Mike shrugged like one who has had this happen before. "Start over. Look at everyone else. Obviously, we're missing something."

"No," said Betsy. "We've been trying to solve this by trying to see what we're missing, and that's not working. Let's look at what we do know. It can't be Hal, all right, that's one thing we know. We don't know why this is happening to me, okay, to hell with why. What else do we know? It has to be someone who knows what a brake line is. It's someone who knows where to get arsenic, and— well, I don't suppose there's any special knowledge to starting fires, is there?"

"There is, but not in this case. Pros use toilet paper, gasoline, and candles, not firewood and charcoal starter."

Betsy said, "I thought it smelled like a barbecue back there."

Jill said, "The fire marshal said he never saw an arson fire started with firewood before."

"And starting it by that back door was dumb, right?" said Betsy. "Why not start it by the front? If it had burned through the back door, it still would have had another door to burn through before it could climb up the stairs. Dumb."

"Because the back door was out of sight of passersby," said Jill. "Not so dumb."

"If it had been me," said Betsy, "I would have broken that back window, squirted the charcoal starter on the floor, and thrown a lit match in after it."

"That's what the fire marshal said," said Malloy. "Another reason he thinks it was an amateur."

"But I'm not an arsonist and I thought of it," Betsy pointed out.

"That is odd," said Jill. "What do you think, he isn't seriously trying to kill her?"

"Then what the hell is he doing?" asked Malloy.

"Maybe he's trying to scare her. Or keep her from doing something." Jill looked at Betsy. "What haven't you gotten done because of all this?"

Betsy scowled. "I haven't finished my Christmas shopping. I haven't picked up my dry cleaning. I haven't balanced my checkbook—well, I usually put that off anyway, so that's no big deal." She saw Jill was serious, so she started to think more deeply. "I need to be lining up people to help with year-end inventory. I need to figure out what goes on sale after Christmas. I'm supposed to be working more hours in the shop to cut expenses. I'm supposed to be thinking of other ways to cut expenses. What, you think this has something to do with the shop? Someone trying to make me close up?"

"Who besides Joe and Irene wants that to happen?" asked Jill.

"I don't know. Nobody."

Mike said, "So maybe he's trying to keep you from doing something else important."

Betsy said, "I'm not doing anything else important." She started to think more about that, then with a gesture sliced that thought off. "Now hold it, we're supposed to be looking at what we know. Why do people kill other people?"

Malloy said, "The usual motives are sex, money, and revenge."

Betsy smiled wryly. "Well, it's sure not sex. And since Hal has a perfect alibi, it's not money."

"Hold up on that conclusion," said Mike. "You're going to be a wealthy woman in a few weeks. If you die, who gets your money?"

Betsy looked embarrassed. "Well . . . right now it's Godwin and Jill." She had finished the hasty holographic will last night.

Blushing, Jill said, "That was all her idea, I don't want any part of it."

Malloy, grinning, said, "You can leave it to me instead, Ms. Devonshire."

Betsy lit up. "Mike, tell everyone that joke. And you, Jill, blush all over the place. Both of you, talk about my new will. If this is about the money, that should stop it."

Jill said, "But if it isn't—"

Betsy scowled but said, "Then back to what else we know. Where did Dr. McQueen say the arsenic mines were? That's the only weapon used so far that can't be found in any house in town."

Jill said, "New Jersey."

Mike said, "Arsenic *mines?*"

Jill said, "It comes out of the ground, like gold or silver."

"No kidding. Well, I don't know of anyone recently back from New Jersey. So I'll have to find out where else you could get hold of some." He pulled out his notebook and wrote that down. "Now, Ms. Devonshire, what I want to do is go over with you again everything you've done in the past few weeks. I know you already told me there were no quarrels, except with your ex-husband. But think over that period again. Anything at all strange, any new demands made on you? Any disagreements or quarrels, however minor? Have you overheard any odd conversation? Found anything that struck you as odd? Any feeling of being watched? Has anyone stolen anything from you?"

"Only something really trivial."

"What is it?" asked Mike, pen poised to write.

"I volunteered to supply the material to restore an old tapestry from Trinity Episcopal Church. I went over to look at it, and I saw some tiny pictures stitched onto it. The rector said they were attributes of saints. I recognized some of them, but a lot I didn't, so I copied most of them down, typed up notes about them, and Father John loaned me a book about Christian symbology. And the notes vanished."

"And you think someone could have taken them?"

"Well, I've looked and looked, and I can't find them. And the book I was using to look them up is still in my apartment. And now the tapestry is gone, too."

Malloy's interest sharpened. "What do you mean, gone?"

"I called over there yesterday, and the secretary said she didn't know where the tapestry was. She said it hasn't been seen since it got moved out of the church hall when they were clearing it out for the renovation."

Mike closed his notebook. "I guess I'd better go over to the church and see about this missing tapestry." He looked at his watch. "Well, in about five hours."

After he left, Jill said, "Why didn't you tell him about Joe Mickels and New York Motto?"

"Because if Joe doesn't know, then his money problems are nobody's business. You and I will go see him as soon as he gets to his office. In about five hours."

Fifteen

❖

Jill and Betsy slept for two hours after Malloy left, then washed and dressed. Jill toasted a frozen breakfast pastry. "Sure you don't want one?" she asked Betsy. "We've got time."

"No," replied Betsy. "The shots are easier to take on an empty stomach."

"How long does this go on?"

"When they can't get any more arsenic from a urine test, that will be it. Today could be the last, or it might go on into January." The thought of weeks of the painful and sick-making Dimercaprol shots depressed Betsy, and she fell silent as they got into Jill's big old car.

Jill picked her moment and pulled out of the driveway onto Lake Street. Then, sensing Betsy didn't want to talk, she snapped on the radio.

KSJN's morning show was mostly Christmas music. Odd and eccentric, but definitely Christmas music. Betsy's frown of discontent turned to dismay when announcer Dale Connelly casually noted that day after tomorrow was Christmas eve.

Where had the time gone? Betsy sighed, because she knew the answer to that. Gone to car accidents, the hospital, the doctor's office to pee into ridiculously tiny plastic cups leading to more painful injections.

Who'd be a medical technician?

Who, for that matter, would own a small business? She didn't want to go from the doctor's office to Crewel World. She didn't want to be reminded by some customer's question of how little she knew or endure the tireless chitchat of her help or Godwin's comments. She didn't want to see the stack of bills the postman would bring or argue with suppliers sold out of everything but what she didn't want. And tonight was another late closing night; she had a normal eight-hour day to get through, then another three hours of evening work. Same with tomorrow.

Most of all, she was sick of being the target of someone murderous, an unknown someone, angry for an unknown reason. Half frozen, poisoned, choking on smoke—not dead yet. Not yet.

Betsy snorted softly.

"What?" said Jill.

"Oh, I've been sitting here working myself into a foul mood, and I just thought that would be a terrible way to spend my last few hours on earth, grouchy and complaining."

"Last few hours?"

"If the assassin succeeds."

"He won't," growled Jill and set her jaw.

Betsy, looking at that grim profile, was suddenly reminded of a beer ad, hugely popular in Britain during World War II. It was just two words, a verb and the name of the brewer: *Take Courage.* She smiled and then set her own jaw.

A little after ten, Jill and Betsy were back in Excelsior, parking behind Crewel World. The back door was covered with a big sheet of plywood, so they went around front. Shelly was waiting there with a man Betsy thought she'd met before, though she couldn't place him. "This is Mr. Reynolds," said Shelly casually, sure Betsy would know him.

Jill unlocked the front door and they came in. "Whew!" said Shelly, wrinkling her nose. "Gee, you'd think there was a fire in here last night or something." Mr. Reynolds laughed.

Betsy turned on the lights. The smell wasn't strong, but it was there, like yesterday's campfire. But there was no visible smoke damage. She walked to the rear storage area, limping on the left just a little. The smell was stronger back here, and the door into the hallway had a dark gray edge. Betsy plugged in the teakettle, then reached and pulled a forefinger down the white-painted surface of the bathroom door. The finger came away dusty but not sooty.

When she came back out, Mr. Reynolds was taking off his overcoat, and Betsy, seeing the loud houndstooth sport coat he wore under it, recognized him as her insurance agent. "This keeps up," he said to her, "your rates will go through the roof." He had last been in the shop when it had been trashed by Margot's murderer.

"What can you do for us?" asked Betsy.

He looked around. "How long ago was the fire?"

"It was reported around midnight," said Jill. "It was out within an hour, pretty much."

He checked his watch. "And there's hardly any smell right now. But there were what, three closed doors between the fire and here? That's what really helped. I think you lucked out. If there had been smoke in here, you'd've lost your entire stock. Smoke gets into fibers something frightening, and it never comes out. So I tell you how we'll handle this. I'll call ServiceMaster and have them come by for a look-see. Likely they'll put in an ozone maker for a day, and that will be that. Any damage anywhere else?"

"The fire was set outside, against the back door," said Jill. "We caught it before the back door burned through. But the back door is charred, and the back hall is definitely smoky."

"Yeah, well, that's the landlord's responsibility," said the agent. "Mickels doesn't have coverage through us. What we cover for Ms. Devonshire is the contents of this store." He strode through, made some notes on a pad, and said he would call ServiceMaster. "We may be able to get them here yet today. Meanwhile, don't try any cleanup yourself; you'll only make things worse. And don't sell anything out of here until we deodorize the place." He appeared to really look at Betsy for the first time. She drew herself up straight and tried on a smile, but she didn't fool him. "You live upstairs, don't you? I think you should close the place, go upstairs, and sack out for about ten hours."

"No, I have things to do," said Betsy.

"Well, don't go far; I need to let you know about ServiceMaster. Can you give me a phone number?"

Betsy said, "You can leave a message on one of my machines. I'll keep checking."

"Oh-kay," he said, and left.

Shelly said, "Well, I guess that means I don't get any hours today, right?"

"That's right."

The phone rang, and Betsy picked it up. Godwin's cheerful voice said, "Do I get to go shopping the rest of the month?"

"My insurance agent says he may be able to get it cleaned up today. Can you come in tomorrow?"

"That's another reason I called. A case was settled out of court, so John is taking tomorrow off and wants me to go skiing with him. Can you get Shelly to come in?"

Betsy looked at Shelly, who had her hand up in a *Call on me!* gesture. "I'm sure she will. So consider yourself covered tomorrow."

"Thanks. I'll see you Friday. Oh, and Betsy . . ." There was a lengthy silence. "I guess I don't know what to say."

"That's okay, I wouldn't know what to say back, either. 'Bye, Godwin."

"So what do we do first?" asked Jill, when Shelly and the insurance man had gone.

"Let's go beard the lion."

A few minutes later, the two were climbing the old wooden stairs to the second floor of the Water Street building. At the far end of the hall they found a glass office door painted with plain black letters: Mickels Corporation. Jill went in first. They found themselves in a small room in front of a gray metal desk. A row of gray metal filing cabinets took up most of a wall. The young woman at the desk was working on a very modern computer. She glanced up and said, "May I help you?"

Betsy said, "I'm Betsy Devonshire. Is Mr. Mickels in?"

She glanced at Jill in her uniform and said, "Just a moment, please." The woman went through a back door, shutting it behind her. The door must have been a good one; they couldn't hear a sound through it. She came back, leaving the door open, to say, "Go on in."

Mickels's inner office was barely more opulent. It did have a big wooden desk with carved corners that was probably a hundred years old, but the chair behind it was an old wooden thing on casters with a back that curved into the arms. The single window overlooking the street was uncurtained. There was a wooden filing cabinet against one wall, and a low bookcase contained law books and three-ring binders. The floor was bare, and there were no pictures on the walls. A thick metal door probably led to a strong room.

Mickels sat behind the desk, his back to the window. "Ms. Devonshire, Officer Cross," he said. His white sideburns lined a very good poker face.

"Mr. Mickels," said Betsy, who had thought hard about how to approach Mickels on this, "you own the building that contains Crewel World, am I right?"

Mickels nodded, frowning a little. "You know that."

"And you know I am the sister of the founder of the company, the late Margot Berglund?"

Again Mickels nodded, his frown deepening.

In exactly the same tone, Betsy asked, "And you know that Mrs. Berglund was the founder and silent partner in New York Motto, right?"

Mickels blinked, then jumped to his feet. "*What?*" he shouted.

"I said, my sister was the owner of New York Motto."

"By God, I might have known!" roared Mickels, flinging his arms in the air. "That *bitch!* That sweet-talking, milk-faced, embroidering, conniving *bitch!*" His anger fed on itself, and the madder he got, the stronger his language became. Betsy, backing away, was further startled when the door to the outer office opened and the secretary stood in the doorway, her eyes wide.

"What's wrong?" she asked. "Shall I call—" She stopped, confused, because Jill Cross *was* the police.

"Get out!" shouted Mickels. "Just get out!"

"Yessir," she said, and went, closing the door behind her.

"I think you'd better sit down, Mr. Mickels," said Betsy, a little alarmed at the color of his face.

But Mickels was too upset to sit down. "And she told you this, so you could just keep on grinding me down!" he growled.

"No, I didn't know about it until Mr. Penberthy came to see me last night—"

Mickels exploded again, describing the attorney in atrocious language. "It was probably all his goddamned idea!" he concluded, leaning on his desk, his breathing alarmingly loud and uneven.

"Mr. Mickels, if you'll just calm down—" said Jill in her smoothest voice.

"Calm down? I ought to go and shoot him down!" shouted Mickels. "Cheat me, will she?" And he spoke again about Margot Berglund in language that exasperated Betsy as much as it embarrassed her. Jill took her by the arm and signaled with nod and lifted eyebrows that they should just stand back and let Mickels get it out of his system.

When Mickels was reduced to merely walking around and around his desk, clenching and unclenching his fingers and grinding his teeth, Betsy tried again.

"It appears you didn't know anything about this until I told you," she said. "And a good thing, too."

"What?" Mickels seemed surprised to find them still in his office.

"Mr. Mickels, someone has made three attempts on my life."

"Yes, I know." Mickels's wide, thin, mouth pulled suddenly into an ugly smile. "I wish him luck."

"You don't mean that, Mr. Mickels," said Jill.

"Don't I? Do you know what this New York Motto has done to me? Ruined me, that's what! My whole life is going to slide into the toilet in less than a month! It's not just the goddam waterfront property, it's my credit rating! My reputation as a man of business! I may have to give up on The Mickels Building, the dream of my life! All because some dotty woman wanted to sell the means to make a piddling *doily!* She's *ruined* me, d'ya hear? She—and now you, *Ms.* Devonshire, who haven't the littlest clue how to run a business! And all over what? A piddling *doily!* I hope whoever's after you squashes you like a *bug!* I hope when he finishes with you, he takes after Penberthy! Now get out of my office!" Mickels stopped to do more of that effortful breathing, his fingers working. He threw a sudden glance at his strong room, then glared at Jill. "You, take her out of here, now!"

But that glance roused Betsy's sleuthing instincts, and when Jill stepped forward, she could tell that Jill had noticed it, too. With a crack of authority in her voice, Jill said, "We're not finished talking with you, Mr. Mickels. Why don't you sit down and answer a few questions?"

Mickels stopped pacing and actually went to his chair and sat down. But it was with an effort, and he sat so rigidly that Betsy felt if she were to tap him on the shoulder he'd shatter like cheap pottery. Mickels's hands were in white-knuckled fists, and again he glanced at the strong room.

"Something in there, sir?" asked Jill.

"In where?"

"In that room behind the steel door."

"Just some records."

Betsy asked, "Records of that deal with New York Motto?"

Mickels's shrug seemed sincerely confused. "Yes."

"What else?" asked Jill.

"You can't search that room without a warrant, you know."

"I could with your permission."

"There's nothing in there."

Betsy said, "Show us."

Mickels hesitated a long while. Then, with a too-elaborate shrug, he stood and fished in his pocket for a big, old-fashioned key.

The strong room was the size of a walk-in closet. There was a small, long-legged table beside a gray filing cabinet with a combination dial on its top drawer. A huge old green safe bulked large at the back. The light came from a naked bulb hanging on a wire from the high ceiling. The cabinet and safe were open. Betsy, remembering the old game of hot and cold, watched Joe closely as Jill looked first into the filing cabinet, pulling open one drawer then the next, fingers walking quickly along the file folders. Mickels didn't show much, so Betsy said, "Maybe it's in the safe."

Jill pulled the safe door wide. Mickels tensed, and Jill, aware of what Betsy was doing, touched various papers, while Betsy played hot and hotter. When Jill touched an old metal box with a padlock on it, Mickels actually trembled.

"What's in the box?" asked Betsy.

"My coin collection," grated Mickels.

The box was extremely heavy, and Jill couldn't lift it alone. Betsy hurried to help. It made a metallic noise when it tilted, and Mickels became a white-hot statue in order not to rush to their aid.

"Open it for me?" asked Jill, after they succeeded in sliding it onto the tall table.

Mickels came to unlock the padlock with a mild show of reluctance—or was feeling so much reluctance some leaked out around the edges of his attempt to disguise it. He put the padlock on the table beside the box and stepped back.

Jill opened the box. It was nearly filled with bright silver coins, mostly half dollars, but with dimes, quarters, and dollars mixed in. The coins were loose, not in the little cardboard holders collectors use.

Betsy, puzzled, picked up a few. They were badly worn and a trifle greasy, as if from much fondling. She turned and looked at Mickels, who looked back, grim-faced.

"I don't get it," said Jill, scooping up a handful of coins. She turned and held them out to Joe.

"They're all real silver, not those cheap alloys the government issues nowadays," said Mickels, staring at them, fingers working. "They're badly worn, and of no interest to real collectors, so I bought 'em at face value. I don't know why I keep them." He shrugged stiffly, and tore his eyes away. "Anything else I can show you in here?"

Betsy, feeling she'd come to the heart of a mystery without solving it, glanced at Jill, then said, "No."

Jill closed the box and would have snapped the padlock shut, but Mickels said, "Just leave it." He turned and walked stiffly out of the strong room, and they followed. "Anything else you want to look at?" he asked, going to his chair. He put his hands on the back of it, a seemingly casual gesture, except that his grip was so tight his fingernails were pressed white.

Jill said, "Are you the one trying to murder Betsy Devonshire?"

"No."

"She really didn't know about New York Motto until Penberthy told her, you know."

Mickels nodded once, sharply. "Yes, that's probably the case." The nostrils of his big nose flared suddenly. "If I'd found out she owned New York Motto on my own, I might be asserting my right to silence and phoning my lawyer right now. But before God, I didn't know." The anger suddenly left him, and he said, with an air that seemed close to despair, "I suppose this'll be all over the business pages tomorrow morning?"

"I have no intention of sharing this with anyone, Mr. Mickels," said Betsy. "And neither does Officer Cross."

"That's something, at least."

They left him still standing behind the chair.

Out on the street, Betsy said, "What was that about the coins?"

"Beats me. But I'd say it was pretty clear he didn't know about New York Motto. Whew!"

Betsy giggled suddenly. "I haven't heard language like that since I dated a first class bosun's mate." She sobered. "But damn. All right, let's go to Trinity and talk to everyone. Find out when the tapestry was last seen, or if maybe someone walked out of the church hall with a suspicious bulge under his coat."

Things were bustling in the church office. Jill and Betsy stood a moment inside the door, taking it in. A delivery man was standing beside a stack of boxes with a local printer's logo on them, waiting for someone to sign his clipboard. A plump, sad-faced woman in a head scarf waited on a hard wooden bench, and next to her a thin, nervous man in a light jacket, far too light for the weather. Betsy was surprised to see Patricia Fairland next to him. She was staring at the floor in front of her, looking ill with worry. Betsy thought, *Maybe she's going to ask Father John to ask me to leave town.*

Two chatting women were sorting green pledge cards on a table, and the secretary was at her desk and on the phone, saying in a calm voice that no, Christmas day being on a Saturday did not mean that Sunday services were canceled. She had the receiver tucked under her chin and continued typing some text onto her computer screen as she talked. *Probably Father John's Christmas sermon,* thought Betsy.

A noise came through the floor, as of a timber being torn in half the long way, and everyone paused to look down, waiting to see if the floor was going to collapse. In the silence, Betsy realized there were other sounds of destruction from the same source.

When the floor didn't open, the secretary said to the room, "Renovation," and everyone nodded and went back to whatever they were doing.

The door to Father John Rettger's office opened, and a woman was heard saying, "But her sister was Mary two years ago, and Jessica is even prettier than Tiffany!"

Father John's mild voice replied, "But rehearsals for the Christmas pageant have been going on for weeks. We can't possibly make a last-minute substitution."

"Can she at least be the understudy?"

"We already have two understudies, and—" something like laughter appeared in Father John's voice "—I'm afraid every one of them is in very good health."

A tight-faced woman came marching past Father John into the outer office. She had a gorgeous blond-haired child about seven years old in tow. "But Mother, I don't want to be Mary," said the child in a reasonable voice.

"Of course you do, darling," replied her mother, weaving her expertly through the people and objects between them and the door to the outside hall. "We'll call the bishop."

Betsy wondered if it was in the bishop's power to make Jessica Mary. It might be worth a try; she remembered how the girls who played Mary in her childhood pageants were forever marked as special.

Father John stood in the doorway. He already looked tired, though it was still morning. His secretary hung up and started to sign to Patricia, who rose, but Betsy spoke up quickly.

"Can I just ask something first? Father, can you tell me anything about the disappearance of the tapestry?"

Father John looked blankly at her. "Did it disappear? All I know is, I brought it up to the sacristy that day I loaned you the book, wrapped it in a white sheet, and put it in one of the drawers." He looked at the secretary. "Crystal, did you take it out of there?"

"I didn't know it was in there, Father. I don't think anyone did. We've been looking for it."

Betsy said, relieved, "I was hoping you'd let me have another look at it."

"Of course. Crystal—"

But Patricia, already moving, said, "I'll get it for you, Betsy. I want to talk to you about the project anyway." She gestured at the thin man on the seat. "You may have my turn."

The man looked at the secretary, then at Father John, who nodded and said, "Hello, Hadley. Come on in."

Patricia had vanished down a short hall. She was gone barely a minute, then came back, to walk past Jill and Betsy to the secretary's desk. "Crystal, I can't find the tapestry in any of the drawers," Patricia said. "I wonder if Father John is mistaken." Her voice was a trifle thick, and she coughed. So it was a cold, not worry, that had Patricia looking ill.

"I wouldn't think so," said the secretary. "I mean, he said he wrapped it in a sheet and put it in a drawer in the sacristy, right? That's kind of specific for even him to be mistaken about, you know what I mean?"

"May I look?" asked Betsy.

"I can help, too," said Jill.

Patricia glanced at the secretary, who shrugged, then said, "Go ahead, if you like."

"Come on, Betsy," said Jill.

Jill led her down the short hall to a small room lined with wooden cabinets. There were two sets of wide, shallow drawers. One of the top drawers was pulled out, showing a green chasuble, the vestment that covers the arms and torso of a priest during the communion service.

Betsy bent and looked to the back of the drawer without seeing anything but chasuble. She closed it and pulled the next one out. It was empty. The one below that had a red chasuble.

Jill opened a vertical door and began gently pushing aside the rows of albs, the white gowns worn under vestments.

Finished with the drawers, Betsy opened a tall cabinet full of long candle holders designed to be carried in a procession. Another cabinet contained shelves with censers and other paraphernalia. A tall, narrow hanging space held stoles, the long, narrow bands hung from the neck. Next to the cabinet was a door, in the wall opposite to the one they came in by. Betsy opened it and saw it led into the chapel, which was as innocent of white sheets as the cabinets she had searched. She closed it again and opened the cabinet of albs, and checked each one to make sure Jill hadn't mistaken a white sheet for an alb. She hadn't.

Even with total overlap, it took less than five minutes to complete the search.

"What do you think?" asked Betsy.

"I think it's not in here," said Jill. "I don't know why."

"Where else could it be?"

"Beats me. It's not in the outer office, and I doubt if it's in Father John's office. You looked in the chapel and didn't see it."

They went out of the sacristy. Betsy saw another door on her right that had a small metal sign: Rest Room. It was slightly ajar, and she opened it to find the world's smallest bathroom. It had a toilet and a tiny sink. If the sink had been full size, there wouldn't have been room for the toilet.

"Find it?" said Patricia from outside the room.

Betsy turned around and said, "No."

Jill said, "Maybe someone saw it in the sacristy, realized it didn't belong, and put it somewhere else."

Patricia said, "Now that sounds very likely. I'm afraid Father John does put things down instead of away, so the staff is pretty used to picking up after him." Her voice was more indulgent than annoyed, and Betsy remembered Patricia was on the vestry.

Betsy said, "I bet Father John was kind of a letdown after the fabulous Father Keane."

Patricia frowned a little at Betsy. "Not at all. He's different, but every man is different from every other. John's kind and wise and has an amazing sense of humor."

Betsy laughed. "Good to hear someone finally say that."

"Say what?"

"Most of us women complain that men are all alike!"

Patricia started to laugh, but sneezed instead. "You're right, you're right!" she said, pulling a handkerchief from her coat pocket and blowing. "But don't tell anyone I said it, or I'm liable to be drummed out of the gender corps!"

Betsy said, "But what are we going to do? This will hold up the restoration."

"Well, nothing's going to get done during the holiday season anyway; you know that. Even I'm going out of town—but I think I told you that. We're leaving this afternoon for Phoenix. The tapestry will very likely turn up a day or two after Christmas, when it's less of a madhouse around here."

Jill said, "So you think it will be found."

"Of course! After all, it's not exactly something someone would steal. And everyone knows about it, so they aren't likely to throw it away by mistake. It's around here somewhere."

Betsy said, "Yes, I suppose you're right. Okay, I'll just wait for it to turn up. If I don't hear between now and New Year's, I'll call Father John or you."

"Thank you, Betsy."

Sixteen

❖

When they got back to the apartment, the phone message light was blinking.

Betsy pushed the Play button, and the happy voice of her insurance agent said, "Hello, Ms. Devonshire! ServiceMaster says they want to stop by with a pair of their ozone generators. Call me as soon as you hear this and let me know where you'll leave the key so I can let them in."

Jill reminded her, "Don't leave your key with anyone. Ask him when they want to come, and we'll be here to let them in."

Betsy did so, and found they would be over within the hour. Then she went into the kitchen to open a can of tuna and heat some tomato soup for lunch. "Do you think Patricia could have taken that tapestry?" she asked, handing Jill's plate to her.

"I don't know where to. You looked in the chapel, didn't you?"

"I looked through the door. But she didn't have time to go in there to tuck it back behind something, did she? She was only gone a minute, barely long enough to open a couple of drawers."

Jill nodded. "You're right. And in that short coat and slacks, she wasn't wearing it. So assume someone else got there ahead of her. We'll have to ask Father John who he told about putting the tapestry into the sacristy."

"Yes," said Betsy, "because I agree with Crystal: He was too specific about where he put it to be mistaken."

Since she'd skipped breakfast, she finished her sandwich quickly and drank her mug of soup before calling Trinity. Father John had gone out but she was told he would be back soon. Betsy left a message, asking him to call back.

The ServiceMaster man was tall and young and wore a forest-green jacket and shirt. The ozone generators were small black boxes that made a faint humming sound. "It's like concentrated oxygen," he explained. "It just eats smell."

Soon the box on the checkout desk was emitting a sharp, unpleasant odor. "Do we have to rent another box to get rid of this stink?" asked Betsy.

"No, ma'am," said the man. "An hour after you shut it off, there's no smell at all."

After he left, Jill and Betsy went upstairs, Betsy carrying a bundle of sales slips to enter them in her computer.

But she'd barely started before she was overwhelmed by a nap attack. She managed to stagger to the beautiful four-poster bed before collapsing across it and falling almost instantly asleep.

W hen the silence in the back bedroom had gone on for a while, Jill peeped in and saw Betsy sound asleep. Jill went into the closet, pulled a soft blanket off a shelf, and laid it over Betsy, who didn't stir.

Jill went back to the living room and sat down on the love seat with her needlework, but in half an hour her needle slipped from her fingers, and she dozed off.

The phone's ring yanked her awake, and she hurried to the kitchen to answer it.

"Hello, this is Father John at Trinity. May I speak with Betsy, please?"

"Oh, hello, Father. This is Jill Cross. Betsy's asleep. What she wanted to ask you was, how sure are you that you put the tapestry in that drawer?"

"Very sure. I wanted it in a safe place, but also where it wouldn't come in contact with anything else—that mildew, you know. I don't know how it got out of the drawer; I certainly didn't remove it."

"Did you tell anyone it was there?"

The priest thought for a bit. "Phil Galvin," he said. "Phil said something to me about it, and I told him where I put it."

"Anyone else?"

"I don't think so. I should have told Crystal, of course, but I didn't. Now, when I talked with Phil, it was after the Wednesday Advent service, and we weren't alone. There might have been a dozen eavesdroppers. And of course, Phil himself might have told others."

Jill nearly groaned aloud. "All right, thank you, Father. I'll pass this information along." So long as she was in the kitchen, Jill made a pot of coffee—and added coffee to the grocery list on the refrigerator—drank a cup, then went back to her needlework refreshed.

Betsy slept for three hours. She came out of the back bedroom with a grumpy face. "Why'd you let me sleep so long?" she complained.

"You looked as if you needed it."

Betsy stood still, blinking, then nodded. "I guess I did. But now I won't sleep tonight."

Jill smiled. "Wanna bet?"

Betsy yawned suddenly. "No." She lifted her head, inhaling gently. "Is that coffee I smell?"

"Yes, I'm afraid I drink it all day long."

"Well, how about I get a cup and then we'll go Christmas shopping."

"Mall of America?"

"No, that place is too big. What's near here?"

"Well, there's Ridgedale in Minnetonka."

Soon Betsy found herself standing on a mezzanine overlooking a tiled square whose center was taken up by what looked like an in-construction snow-country lodge with a big stone fireplace and plank floor. In front of the fireplace was a big wing chair, and sitting in the chair, entertaining one child at a time, was Santa Claus—the really good kind, who hangs his red coat on a hook and whose beard and stomach are real.

In a little less than two hours, her credit card still smoking, Betsy piled her purchases into the backseat of Jill's big Roadmaster for the drive home.

There is something relaxing about spending a lot of money in a short time. Betsy, still tired from last night's adventure, felt she could melt into the comfortable passenger seat. The short winter day was nearly over, and Betsy was recalled to her childhood, being driven home in the purple dusk. How comforted and at peace she had felt then—and now, with warm light from house windows making safe the coming night, and Christmas lights gleaming and twinkling—those new icicle lights were like lace edging on the eaves of houses, very pretty.

Jill had to wake her when they pulled into the parking lot.

Betsy had planned to look again at the saints' attributes after supper, but she didn't even stay awake long enough to eat.

Around eight the next morning, driving Betsy in light traffic to get her daily shot of Dimercaprol, Jill asked, "Which Christmas service are you going to?"

Betsy hadn't planned on going to church for Christmas. She didn't think much of people who went twice a year, at Christmas and Easter. Well, maybe that wasn't true any longer. It was more that she was uncomfortable with what had been her unchristian opinion of them, back when she was a regular church-goer. On the other hand, since Jill was assigned to Betsy, if Betsy didn't go, nei-ther could Jill, and it would be unkind to make Jill miss church. Besides, Father John had saved Betsy's life with a prayer, and Betsy felt a debt of gratitude. It wouldn't hurt to go. Maybe it would jump-start her back into going regularly.

So she said, "Which one do you go to?"

"I always liked the first service Christmas morning."

"All right," said Betsy. After a few minutes, she asked, "What were your other plans for Christmas before you volunteered for this?"

"Nothing much." And Jill could not be moved in any direction from that statement.

They got back quicker than usual from Dr. McQueen's office, and Betsy went to lie down until her stomach stopped doing flip-flops. But she was smil-ing; Dr. McQueen pronounced this the last shot.

A few minutes after they got back, the ServiceMaster man rang the doorbell and asked to be let into the shop to take away his ozone makers. By the time the shop opened at ten, the smell of ozone had in fact melted away, leaving nothing in its wake.

Shelly came at five after, exclaiming over the sunshine and relatively high temperature—thirty-four degrees, actually above freezing, in late *December!*—though an Alberta Clipper was predicted to blow through in the afternoon. She helped dust and vacuum and rearrange displays as the shop opened for business. It being Christmas eve, there was an urgent press of customers.

One young woman, with blond hair and a brisk air, went to the bookshelves to see what they had on blackwork. Another, a middle-aged woman in a pale gray coat, came to the desk with a Crewel World bag in her hand and a pleased smile on her face.

"Good morning, Mrs. Hamilton," said Betsy, smiling back.

"I finished it," said Mrs. Hamilton, holding up the bag, whose contents were small. Betsy rose and went behind the checkout desk.

"How did it come out?" she asked.

In reply, Mrs. Hamilton brought out a belt made of needlepoint canvas with a pattern of cats in various poses, each with a different design of coat. Made to be worked in silk or cotton floss, Mrs. Hamilton had decided to do it in beads. The canvas and beads, plus thread and the hair-fine needles, which broke or bent often, had cost over a hundred dollars. The work had taken months. And now the belt needed to be finished: washed, blocked, attached to a strip of leather, and given a good brass buckle, which was going to cost an-other eighty dollars. And the result would be a "fun" belt.

But to a needleworker's sophisticated eye, the beadwork was flawless. The texture pleasured the fingers. Betsy looked up at Mrs. Hamilton and saw she didn't need to say a word in praise; Mrs. Hamilton understood.

The woman at the bookshelves came over with her selection. "Ooooh," she said. "That's very nice. Did you make it?"

Mrs. Hamilton nodded. "Do you do beadwork?" she asked.

The woman laughed. "I can barely sew a button on. I came in to buy this for a friend who does blackwork, whatever that is. I've never been in here before. I usually buy her Christmas gift on eBay or Amazon dot com, but time got away from me, and I can't wait for shipment now."

Mrs. Hamilton said, "My daughter shops on the Internet, but I'm afraid I don't trust it. I mean, who are those people?"

"Well, there's all kinds, just like in real life. I like it because I can shop from home, plus you find things there you won't find anywhere else. Especially on the auction sites. I can search for exotic gifts and I don't get tired feet or lose my car in the parking lot. And by exercising a little care, I haven't been burnt yet."

Betsy said, "I know someone else who loves eBay. She buys antiques."

The woman nodded. "I've done that, too. I got into the glass bottles the other day and bid on two items. One was a medicine bottle from the 1800s with the pills still inside it! Of course, it came with a warning not to take the medicine." The woman laughed. "I'm Christine Schleuter, by the way."

"Betsy Devonshire," said Betsy, "and this is Mrs. Hamilton."

"How do you do?" the women said to one another.

"You aren't really going to give this to your daughter, are you?" asked Betsy, getting the conversation back on topic.

"Yes, I am. She's going to specialize in small-animal medicine, and she's always loved cats. She'll enjoy wearing this."

Shelly and Jill came to admire the belt while Betsy wrote up the order.

"You'll call when this comes back?" asked Mrs. Hamilton.

"Of course. Merry Christmas," Betsy added, as Mrs. Hamilton went out the door.

"Oops," said Jill behind her.

Betsy turned. "What?"

"Didn't you know? Mrs. Hamilton is Wiccan."

"She is?"

Shelly giggled and nodded. "She belongs to a coven in Minneapolis."

Betsy and Ms. Schleuter looked at the closed door. "Funny," said Ms. Schleuter, "she doesn't look like a witch."

"Yes, but who does, nowadays?" said Betsy. "Next time I'll wish her a happy solstice."

Toward noon, Betsy was just finishing with another customer when Joe Mickels came in. He glared at Shelly when she approached, and she retreated to a spinner rack, rearranging the floss a shopper had disordered. He looked with equal anger at Jill, who only looked back.

He should play the lead in A Christmas Carol, thought Betsy when she was finished, noting his long coat with the lamb collar, the big silver sideburns that framed his shaggy eyebrows, the arrogant nose and angry mouth. She said, "May I help you, Mr. Mickels?"

"I need to talk to you," he said, glancing again at Jill and adding, "Alone."

Jill said at once, "I'm sorry, Mr. Mickels, but she's under police protection and is not allowed to be alone with anyone."

Mickels turned as if to leave, but Betsy said, "Jill knows everything, Mr. Mickels. You know that."

Mickels looked at Jill, and for the briefest instant there was again despair. Betsy started, "Look, I'm really sorry about——"

"Sorry don't cut it," he growled.

Jill said, "I think we should send Shelly out to buy us all some lunch."

Shelly, who had been trying to eavesdrop from behind the spinner rack, came shamefacedly out.

"I can't afford to buy lunch today," she said.

"Me, either," said Betsy.

There was a pregnant pause. Jill held her tongue until Mickels with a soft groan said, "All right, I'll buy us all a McDonald's hamburger!" He took an ancient coin purse from his pocket. It was all Betsy could do to keep from laughing when she saw it. He twisted the catch open and removed with regret a ten-dollar bill. "You've got coffee here," he said, "so no drinks. Get two big orders of fries, and we'll share. And bring me my change."

"Yessir," said Shelly, not bothering to hide her grin. She grabbed her coat and hurried out.

"Do you know why the rich have money?" Mickels said to Betsy.

"Why?"

"Because they don't spend it."

"I'll take that as the good advice it probably is. Won't you sit down?" Betsy went to the library table and pulled out a chair for him.

As he came to sit down, Betsy was struck, as she had been once before, by his slightness. His wealth and arrogance made him seem large; from behind he was a scant two inches taller than she was.

Jill sat across from him, hands on the table and chair not pulled in close. Betsy sat at the head of the table, facing the door so she could see anyone approaching.

Mickels said, "I had no idea your sister was such an expert on bankruptcy estates."

"She wasn't," replied Betsy. "It was Vicki Prentice who knew how to do it. What Margot did was give her the money to start the company. Margot was a silent partner; she didn't take any part in running it. Vicki found the assets and bid on them, so even if she knew you were the actual owner of that restaurant property, she didn't know of your relationship with Margot."

"Huh," said Mickels, doubting that.

"Well, if she did, she didn't tell Margot. Because Margot didn't tell me, and I think she would have."

"Fat lot of good your ignorance did me."

"Look here," said Betsy, "acting like a sulky little boy isn't going to help. You signed that contract of your own free will, so the consequences of not making the balloon payment are your own. You're going to lose that property, along with all the money you put into making those payments."

"And I'm supposed to smile and take that?"

"There isn't anything *you* can do about it," she snapped.

He brought keen gray eyes to bear on her from under those eyebrows. "And you're going to dance on the ruins of my prosperity, right?"

"I could, if I liked. While I agree Margot was responsible for you losing that property, it wasn't on purpose. And your behavior toward her was disgraceful. I could consider the two of you even. But perhaps we can work something out."

When Shelly came back with the hamburgers, she was surprised to find the three of them talking almost cordially. But even after Mickels left, neither Jill nor Betsy would disclose what brought about Mickels's change of attitude.

Soon after lunch, Betsy sold a huge order of needlepoint, counted cross stitch, and knitting materials to a woman who was leaving for Texas in the morning, where she would spend the winter. Her loyalty to Crewel World was touching, and Betsy said as much to her while Shelly carefully added up the bill.

"You always have everything I need," the woman said, writing out a check, "and you allow me to return unused materials. And I just love your staff." She looked around the shop as if for a particular one.

Betsy said, "Godwin has the day off. I know he'll be sorry to have missed you."

"You'll wish him a happy holiday from me, won't you?"

"Yes, of course. And we wish you a happy holiday, too."

Shelly helped the woman carry her order out to her car. Betsy said, "That order should put us in the black."

Jill said, surprised, "Are you operating at a loss?"

"We might have, if she hadn't come in. In fact, we may still. I'm supposed to be working more so I can cut back on employee hours, but with all that's happened . . ."

Shelly came back in, dusting snow off her shoulders.

"*Again?*" groaned Betsy. It had clouded over without her noticing.

Shelly said, "The radio says it's only supposed to be an inch or two."

Jill said, "Be glad you live in Minnesota. If they got snow like this in, say, Atlanta, the city would be paralyzed."

"If they were getting snow like this in Atlanta," retorted Betsy, "*we'd* be fighting off glaciers."

Laughing, they looked around and saw no customers. They sat at the table to continue some projects. Shelly was knitting a minuscule cap on tiny needles to be donated to a preemie program for local hospitals. Betsy was trying out some DMC rayon floss. She liked the shimmer it gave to the snowflake she was working in counted cross stitch on maroon evenweave.

Bing went that annoying door alarm, and as she did often, Betsy promised herself a new, more dulcet-sounding one.

Jill was moving to get between Betsy and the person coming in: Hal Norman, hat in hand.

Hal said, "Betsy, I'm leaving Sunday for California. I'd like to talk to you before I go."

"We're busy here. I can't talk to you now."

"Then how about supper? Do you still like Chinese? There's a decent Chinese place here in town, the Ming Wok. I can meet you there after closing." He saw her about to refuse and said, "Or I can bring Chinese to you."

Betsy hesitated, then gestured surrender and said, "Bring carry-out for three to my apartment tonight."

"All right. Thank you." He hesitated, obviously hoping his sweet reasonableness would make her say something more, something nice, even just "You're welcome." But she didn't.

He remembered her favorite, chicken with pea pods and straw mushrooms. He also brought Mongolian beef and moo shu pork, and everyone took a little of everything.

He was attentive and humble. He had a little box of loose jasmine tea, another favorite, and brewed it for her, making funny jokes about not being able to find the tea strainer in the strange kitchen. He used chopsticks with grace, and put a series of tasty tidbits on her plate. He remarked on the tree, apparently not realizing it was the one he'd bought—or too clever to say so.

Jill sat quietly, watching and listening.

When the meal was over, he said, "There, was that so bad? Was that so difficult? Please, please, darlin'—yes, here in front of a witness—can't we work something out? It's Christmas eve, and this would be a great present, just knowing you're willing to try once more."

"There's nothing to work out."

"Are you sure? You don't act like you're still mad at me."

"I'm not mad."

"Then what's the problem?"

"I don't care."

Hal's look of charming contrition slid off his face, leaving a confused expression behind. "What?"

"I used to think up ways to get back to you, to humiliate you like you humiliated me. I was so mad at you, I got physically sick. But you know something? I got well again. It could be learning that I can stand on my own feet, run my own business. Or maybe it's the chelating agent, taking you out of my system along with the arsenic. All I know is, when I poke around for my feelings about you, I can't find any. I don't care about you anymore."

"You've found somebody else, haven't you? Don't tell me it's that little pansy down in the store!"

"Okay, I won't."

"Oh, Betsy, how could you fall for someone like that?"

Betsy giggled. "I haven't fallen for him."

"But you just said—"

"You said not to tell you, so I said I wouldn't. Now go away."

"Won't you at least accept my apology?"

"No."

"But you don't know how sorry I am!"

"I don't think you're sorry enough. I don't think you're able to be sorry for anything except yourself. Now go."

And he went. Betsy cried when he'd gone, but it was tears of relief. Jill said nothing, only handed over tissues until the storm ended.

Seventeen

❖

The first Christmas service, at 8:30, was for the children of the parish. Children formed the choir, they took the collection, the sermon was aimed at their level. Betsy found it all passable, though she had trouble with the hymns. She'd gotten too used to "O Come, All Ye Faithful" in secular settings to think of it as a hymn anymore. Father John's sermon, on looking inward rather than outward for the true meaning of Christmas, was good but hardly original. *What was I hoping for?* she asked herself, as the Eucharist came to its end. *Did I think God was going to arrange a particularly brilliant service just to tempt me into coming back again?* And then she realized that was exactly the sort of question the sermon had addressed.

After the service, the congregation scattered, rather than staying for coffee. By the eager manner of the children as they rushed for the exits, they were going home to open presents.

Betsy lingered a while in the silent nave, saying a personal prayer or two. Jill stood watch in the aisle.

The moment Betsy stood, a man's voice behind her said, "I'm glad to find you here, Betsy." She turned and saw Father John. He continued, "I hope you find here a further support for the admirable courage you've already shown in your troubles, and perhaps some comfort. It must be terrifying to have someone trying to take your life and not know why. I've been saying a prayer for your protection, a very militant prayer to Saint Michael the Archangel that has stiffened my nerve in difficult situations. 'Defend us in battle' it says, against 'evil spirits, who prowl about the the world seeking the destruction of souls.' "

"Amen," said Jill.

"I must say, however," continued the priest in his mild voice, "that I can't imagine what a ten-year-old tapestry might have to do with a current attempt on your life. After all, the woman who designed it is dead, and her husband is beyond saying anything about it."

"I assume Mike Malloy talked with you?" said Betsy.

"Yes, that's right, a few days ago. He's an interesting fellow. Catholic, of course, but not fervently so. He . . . his questions seemed rather vague."

"I'm afraid he's as baffled as we are, Father," said Betsy. "None of us understands where these attacks are coming from."

They got back to Betsy's apartment in time to listen to the Festival of Nine Lessons and Carols from King's College, Cambridge, rebroadcast by KSJN, a local public radio station. Betsy heated water for tea and the oven for some of Excelo Bakery's holiday bread, Shelly's gift to her. As usual, Betsy had to stop what she was doing when the lovely boy soprano's voice wafted up all alone, "Once in Royal David's city . . ."

Over tea and sweet, fragrant bread, Betsy said, "It's been twenty-four hours since someone tried to kill me."

Jill nodded. "And it's not like you've been sitting at home."

Betsy said, "I wonder if maybe Patricia saw something or someone, and doesn't realize it. Like in that Agatha Christie mystery, where the murderer dressed up like a postman or milkman, I forget which, and so the eyewitness said she didn't see anyone on the street, because she was looking for a chance pedestrian, not someone making his regular rounds. But the person Patricia saw realized he'd been spotted, and so he's gone into hiding."

"All right, who is supposed to be walking on our street on a winter midnight?"

"Okay, maybe not walking but driving. Someone in a police car, or a snowplow."

Jill thought about that. "I'm the only person you know who drives a squad car. And I don't think you know anyone who drives a snowplow."

"There's Vern Miller, of Miller's Motors."

"But he's the one who reported your brake line had been cut. And he hasn't shown any sign of being unhappy that you suspected him of murdering poor Trudie. In fact, I think he's proud of it. It adds to his reputation as a tough guy, having been a murder suspect."

Betsy said, "Speaking of Vern Miller: Do you think Malloy would let him get started on my car repairs? One of these days I'll be able to drive again, and I'd like to have a car."

"We can ask Malloy on Monday. What do you want to do today?"

"Can we go somewhere? I'm feeling really good, completely well, and I'd like some exercise. How about that cattle roundup you promised you'd look into back in September?"

Jill laughed. "It's a cattle drive, not a roundup. And I don't think they're doing any of that this time of year. But I did look into it. There's one in June. It goes on for a week and costs a hundred and ten dollars a night."

"A hundred and ten dollars—to eat beans and burnt beef and sleep on the ground?"

"Well, nowadays I guess it's more comfortable than that."

"I don't want a comfortable cattle drive. I want a real one."

"All right, I'll look again."

Then they opened presents. Jill expressed gratitude for the book, and was surprised to find tucked inside it a gift certificate for framing her next project. She watched with a face she could not quite keep smooth while Betsy opened Godwin's gift: a needlepoint horse in T'ang Dynasty style, done in blues, buffs, and a muted orange, matted and framed. It was very like one that had once belonged to Betsy's sister Margot.

Betsy stared at it, then at Jill. "I don't understand," she said.

"Godwin found a photo of the horse and copied it onto graph paper, then onto sixteen-count canvas."

"But Godwin can't design patterns! He told me so himself."

"I know. He struggled hard with this, and he's afraid it didn't come out as well as the one your sister designed. But he wanted to do something special for you, especially when he realized the scarf you were working so hard on was for him."

"That was supposed to be a surprise!"

"If you want to knit something as a surprise, don't ask the recipient what his favorite colors are, then knit in those colors where he can see them."

Betsy giggled. "I forgot I asked him." She reached under the tree for another gift, a long, narrow one, and showed it to Sophie, who sniffed the bow politely. Inside the wrapping was a toy fishing rod with a cluster of feathers at the end of its line. Sophie chased and leaped for the feathers and at last caught them and wouldn't let go.

There were other gifts to be given over the next week or so as chance allowed. "One thing my first husband's family taught me, to celebrate the twelve days of Christmas. All that preparation and pleasure can't be exhausted in just one day."

Jill said, "Yes, I'm going to have another celebration with Lars when this assignment is over." That nearly spoiled Christmas for Betsy, until Jill added, "I think the last Christmas I had on Christmas Day was in 1995. I'm always involved in something over the holidays. But none of them have been as pleasant as this one."

"Thank you, Jill. I don't know if that's true, but it sure makes me feel better."

Jill said, "When we get back, let's get on the Net and see if we can find a cattle drive that's more like the real ones were."

"Get back from where?"

"The arboretum. You said you wanted some exercise? There's a very pretty cross-country skiing trail I want to show you."

They weren't gone long. Betsy had seen cross-country skiers on television any number of times, and they appeared to float over the snow with smooth, dancelike movements of arms and legs. Not so in reality. Cross-country skiing is a total body workout, and Betsy, while no longer sick, was not remotely in shape for a total body workout. She lasted less than half an hour.

The two came through the door to the apartment, Jill partly supporting Betsy, for whom the stairs reawakened the ache in her back and legs. Jill helped her off with her coat and then to the chair with the footrest. "So," she said, "which part did you like best?"

Betsy started to laugh; she couldn't help it. "And I have asked you to take me on a serious cattle drive? I am out of my mind."

"Tea or cocoa?" asked Jill.

"Cocoa," said Betsy, and Jill went into the kitchen.

Betsy sighed and leaned back in the chair. "You know, though," she said, "when we found that big fallen log and sat down, and it got really quiet, that was nice. And then that fox the same shade of gray as the bushes he came out of stopped and looked toward us for the longest time. Do you know, I've never seen a fox in the wild before? Are the red ones only in England?"

"No, we have both gray and red. They're getting braver, our foxes, and moving into the cities. There's one that lives down by Lake Calhoun, only a few blocks from Uptown."

"Only one? Poor fellow, he must be lonesome. Maybe we should introduce our fox to him."

"No, the one by Lake Calhoun is a red fox. I don't think foxes believe in mixed marriages." Jill brought a mug of cocoa to Betsy. "I couldn't find the marshmallows, sorry."

"I don't have any, sorry."

They sipped in companionable silence for a while. "Jill," said Betsy, "were you hoping the person who's after me would turn up out on that trail?"

"I was hoping he wouldn't."

"Would you have shot him if he did?"

"Only if I had to."

It was Jill's turn to get dinner. While she worked, Betsy went in to check her E-mail. She sent some replies to the mail, including one to an excited Abbey in San Diego, who had once been her best friend and now at last had her very own E-mail address. Then, dinner not being ready yet, she surfed for a while. She went to eBay and found a gorgeous bronze of a Scottish terrier puppy currently going for thirty dollars. She started to register, then changed her mind. Just because she would soon be able to afford it didn't mean she should start buying things she didn't absolutely need.

Dinner was yet another hot dish, this one made with turkey. But the salad had candied pecans and bits of tangerine in it, and the dessert was lemon meringue pie. Over dinner, Jill said, "So, since you are going to buy this building, I take it you're staying in Excelsior?"

Betsy said, "I guess I am. Funny, I don't remember consciously making that decision."

"Even funnier was Joe's face when he realized you were serious," laughed Jill.

After dinner, Sophie politely played again with her new toy. That night, while the women were asleep, she dragged it far under Jill's bed and showed a blank face when Betsy wondered the next morning where it had gone.

Sunday, Boxing Day, December 26, Jill and Betsy were in the shop by eight. Signs proclaiming an after-Christmas sale were brought out of the storeroom and put into the windows. Inventory was repriced and rearranged to display the extra-special merchandise. When Godwin arrived at 9:30, they put him to work redoing the window. Shelly came in fifteen minutes later and started taking down Christmas decorations. Betsy turned on the radio and discovered the Christmas music station had gone to something extremely experimental. She retuned it to KSJN and heard the merry clarinet of Purcell's Third Symphony. Though Epiphany was eleven days away, the three kings had already come and gone.

With them all working hard, the place was ready for the sale—and set up for inventory—by noon.

"All right, that's it, I'll see you both back here Monday morning," said Betsy.

Back upstairs, Jill said, over leftover hot dish, "I don't suppose you want to try cross-country skiing again."

"I thought I'd get caught up on my computer records. We sold quite a bit Christmas eve, and I've still got sales slips from before that."

She went to the computer, finished entering sales, and returned to the living room. Jill was trying a crochet pattern, marking her progress in the book with a straight pin. Betsy walked over and plugged in the Christmas tree and stood admiring it for awhile. She wandered restlessly to the upholstered chair and opened the needlework bag that stood beside it on its little crossed legs, but she didn't take anything out.

"Something the matter?" Jill asked.

"Kind of," said Betsy. She went into her bedroom and came out with the Christian symbology book and her notes. "I keep thinking that if I look at it long enough, it'll make sense."

Jill got her notebook out, found the page on which Betsy had copied the list of attributes and, handing it to her, said, "Abraham Lincoln said that persistence is the key to success."

"He should know; he failed at a lot of things before he got to be president." She sat down at the dining table like a reluctant child preparing to do homework in a difficult subject. Like the child, she just sat for a few minutes, tapping the table with her pencil, glooming over the notes. As before, she began reordering them, trying to spell a word. Frustrated in that, she opened the book at random and found one of the pages with three pairs of line drawings. She found herself again trying to make a word from the symbols, without success, went back to her notes.

Since each attribute could represent several saints, she began ordering saints represented in columns. That she done looked the list over selecting saints, jumping from one column to another: Kentigern, Eligius, Nicholas, Eleutherius—"Well, I'll be darned, there it is!" she exclaimed.

"There what is?" said Jill.

"It's the saints they stand for! Look at this." Jill came to look over Betsy's shoulder. "The boar can stand for Saint Kentigern, the horseshoe for Eligius, the anchor for Nicholas, and another E you can get from the whip, for Saint Eleutherius."

"Keane is spelled with an A," Jill pointed out.

"Yes, but I told you I didn't write them all down. You just wait; when that tapestry shows up, there will be a symbol right there." Betsy tapped the sheet of paper. She was no longer bored and resentful.

"Then the hangman's noose *was* for Father Keane."

"I'd've used it for Hal, and she had even more reason to be furious. He betrayed his calling and his church." Betsy looked at the paper. "Just like Judas."

Behind Saint Kentigern were Saint Elizabeth's crowns, then an anvil, which could be Saint Natalia, then who was the bird? From the shape of it, perhaps a dove? Then a wolf or a dog. Was there more than just a name?

The dove was symbolic of the Holy Spirit, of John the Baptist, of Noah, of Saint Clovis and a flock of other saints, including Oswald. "This will be an O here, if this is money," muttered Betsy.

"Then the letter before it should be M," said Jill. "And where's the Y?"

"The cat, for Saint Yvo, was on here twice, so let's assume the second time was right here." Because sure enough, if the animal was a dog, it could stand for Saint Margaret of Cortona.

"I think you've done it," said Jill. "That's what this is, an accusation. I bet the word before that is 'stolen.' "

But it wasn't. "I'm missing some of them; I don't know how many," said Betsy. "There's a lit candle, and rowboat, which I think is Saint MacCald, and a chain, which is probably Ignatius, if the candle is Genevieve—*if* the word Lucy was spelling is *missing,* as in *missing money.* And above them is a cross, which can stand for Jesus, Saint Bartholomew, Saint Peter, Saint Jude, Saint Philip, Saint Andrew—no, Andrew is more like an X than a plus sign. Then Yvo's cat, then a double-bladed ax for Saint Olaf, then the Star of David, which can stand for Caspar, Melchior, or Balthazar."

Jill frowned. "Why do those last three names sound familiar?"

"They're the three kings who of Orient were. But I don't know which one this star represents."

"Maybe we're getting into random attributes here. We've got the message: Missing Money equals Keane the Traitor."

Betsy's eyes widened. "That's brilliant, Jill!"

"What'd I say?"

"Equals. That's what this thing I thought I'd only started to draw is. Two horizontal lines, that's an equals sign! Missing Money equals Keane!"

"So you've solved it, then," said Jill. "Lucy Abrams left both a name and a message on the tapestry: Her husband Keane was a thief."

The phone rang and Betsy got up to answer it.

"Hello, Betsy, this is Mandy Oliver. I hate to break into your holiday, but talking to you made me remember something, and I wanted to tell you that your problems matching the tapestry colors may be over."

"Really? What did you remember?"

"My mother had a little wooden box she kept leftover floss and yarn in. It's such a pretty box that I didn't sell it with her other things. I found it way in the back of a closet today, and in it are tan and gray and orange lengths of yarn. I think they're from the tapestry you volunteered to help restore. I'll bring them to you, if you like."

"Oh, Mandy, that would be wonderful! Can you come to the shop tomorrow? We'll be open from ten to five."

"Yes, I can come in the afternoon. See you then."

Eighteen

❖

Father John sat behind his desk, something he rarely did; but he felt this was a situation in which he needed all the authority he could command. On the other side of the desk were Betsy Devonshire, Jill Cross, Ned MacIntosh, and Howland Royce—the last two his verger and a man who had been on the vestry when the Reverend Keane Abrams was forced to retire.

"This is terrible, just terrible," said Royce. He was a frail-looking eighty and was wringing his hands, which with his arthritis looked a painful thing to do. "But when Keane offered to repay the money and resign immediately, we thought that would be the best way to handle it. He was of an age to retire and was vested in a small pension fund, which he had no access to and so couldn't use its moneys to repay what he'd taken.

"When it turned out he didn't have enough in savings to make total restitution, his wife came to us and begged us to forgive him the rest, not make a public spectacle of him in front of the parish and especially his daughter, who was just starting high school. She looked dangerously sick, and my wife, who was a nurse, had told me Lucy had a heart condition. Lucy was dead a week after we accepted Keane's resignation, and we were so scared the forced resignation triggered her heart attack that we voted unanimously to forgive the rest of the debt."

"I don't understand," said Betsy. "Had he stolen an enormous amount of money? Or were his savings that small?"

"Six of one, half a dozen of the other," said Royce. "The reason he had no savings was because he'd been paying hush money to a string of women, starting two churches back."

Father John said, "Why wasn't I told about this?"

"What good would it have done?" said Royce. "It was a private thing, and he was good as dead. No need to keep talking about what's over and done with. Or so we thought."

Ned MacIntosh said, "He should have been arrested. It's bad enough he failed to discern between his discretionary fund and the ordinary funds of the church. It's even more disturbing that he converted at least some of the church's money to his personal use. But using church funds to pay blackmail is beyond my forgiveness!"

"I'm afraid this isn't a situation in which your personal forgiveness matters much," said Father John gravely.

Royce said in his old man's voice, "I agree, this is a situation in which the church failed both him and its members. And now, because we hid the truth, we may have put Ms. Devonshire in a position of great danger. But I'm afraid that if we reveal the facts now, Trinity's reputation will be harmed, maybe the reputation of the Episcopal church. We have to decide whether we're going to tell everything, or nothing—or do something in between."

"What do you recommend, Ned?" asked Father John.

MacIntosh replied, "I say we announce that a review of Father Keane's term as rector of Trinity has revealed some irregularities in—well. Shall we just say 'irregularities,' or should we go further and say 'bookkeeping irregularities'? I don't think we should get more specific than that."

Royce said, "We'd better at least say 'bookkeeping irregularities,' or people will start to ask questions. And remember, I'm not the only person who knows the answers. There are probably eight others who have at least an inkling of why Father Keane resigned so abruptly. That's not counting the women he was paying money to, including one who was a member of this parish."

"Do you know who the local woman was?" asked Jill.

"No. Keane wouldn't name names."

"Gentleman to the end," snorted Betsy.

Royce said, "His wife knew. He told me he had to tell her when all this started to break. He used to lie about how much he was making, but the verger, that was Smith Milhaus, found a checkbook and called her, asking questions. That started things moving. I was a comptroller for Sweetwater Technologies back then, so I volunteered to audit his books. It wasn't hard to find what he'd been up to, and I confronted him. He seemed almost relieved to tell someone, poor devil."

"Who did you tell?" asked Betsy.

Royce twisted his head in a kind of shrug. "I reported to the vestry that he hadn't been faithful and was paying money—church money—to some women."

"Do you know anything about a tapestry Mrs. Abrams was working on?" asked Betsy.

Royce frowned at her. "I remember someone found it after they left and said he'd take care of it. I assume that's the one that turned up and started all this mess up again."

"Is that person still around?" asked Jill.

"No. That was old Milhouse again, and he's dead. On the other hand, three of those vestry members are still living in the area, and so are their wives. I'd like to believe nobody told anyone else, but that would be going against what I know of human behavior."

"You may be wrong," said Jill. "My parents were members of Trinity, and I was baptized here, but I never heard anything about why he quit."

MacIntosh said, "And I never heard anything, either. Come on, Royce, you must have an inkling—"

"No," said Father John. "We're not here to speculate. We're here to decide what we are going to do about our plan to name the expanded library after Father Keane. We haven't formally announced it yet, but I know Patricia Fairland has been talking about it for weeks."

"She got a real bee in her bonnet about this, didn't she?" complained MacIntosh. "She didn't used to be such a big noise in the church. Is it because her husband's gonna be the senator from Minnesota?"

"No, it's because she's not working like a dog anymore," said Royce. "She liked coming to Sunday school. It was only while she was putting her husband through law school that she quit coming to the adult education classes. She taught a class on medieval church art just a year ago. So don't blame her. It could've come from any direction. But what do we do about it? Can we say there's a rule against naming things after someone who's still alive?"

"No," said MacIntosh. "There are too many of us who know about the auditorium named for Dean Fontaine of Saint Mark's. Last I heard, he's still spending his pension money on fishing gear."

A thoughtful silence fell. At last Father John said, "Okay, there are enough people in the parish to ensure trouble if we continue with our present plan. My advice is, we announce the financial irregularities and name the chapel after someone else."

"I think we should name it after the first Native American Episcopal priest in Minnesota," said MacIntosh. "The Reverend Enmetahbowh."

"You're probably the only member of this parish who ever heard of him," said Royce. "I think we should name it after Bishop Whipple, first bishop of Minnesota."

They looked at Father John who said, "I think we should consult the membership. At least these two nominees have the saving grace of being long dead, along with everyone who knew them."

Betsy and Jill lingered after Royce and McIntosh left. "Thank you for arranging that, Father," said Betsy. "I think we've confirmed what I suspected. Mike Malloy will be in touch about tonight."

Even sitting in total darkness, there was no mistaking where they were. "The odor of sanctity," Betsy's father had called it, that mix of beeswax, incense, stone and mortar, and furniture polish. Also present was a strong scent of Christmas tree.

Betsy was sitting on a stone bench near the entrance to the new church in the wide hall, partly hidden behind the tall and beautiful fir. Beside her was Jill in an alert and patient waiting mode Betsy could only aspire to. There were other police officers hidden around the hall. One, she knew, was partly down the stairs to the basement. Mike Malloy was near the door to the hall; Betsy fancied she could see a faint light from the street glinting off his shoe. Another was inside the new church, which is why the doors to it were open—and why the odor of sanctity was carried to Betsy's nostrils. Two were inside the chapel. Elsewhere in the hall was Lars, Jill's boyfriend, and he'd brought another officer with him.

They'd been there for two hours. Betsy knew what a stakeout was, of course. But she had no idea how difficult it was to sit still for a very long time.

And what if after all she was wrong?

No, she wasn't wrong. It was sad, but she wasn't wrong.

She felt herself beginning to stiffen on the bench and began stealthily to tense and release various muscles, in her arms, her back, her stomach, her legs, her shoulders, her neck. Jill breathed, "Sit still."

Betsy started to reply, then realized it wasn't because Jill had noticed her squirming but because someone was approaching the outside door.

There was the sound of a key in the lock, then the door opened with a very faint squeak. Booted feet padded softly into the hall, paused, and then the lights went on.

Patricia whirled, but Malloy was guarding the door, his hand coming down from the light switches. "Who are you?" demanded Patricia. Her voice was thick, as if her cold lingered.

"I'm Detective Sergeant Mike Malloy, with the Excelsior Police Department. May I ask what you're doing here?"

"I'm a member of the vestry."

"And there's a meeting of the vestry at two o'clock in the morning?"

"Now look here—" she began.

"It's over, Patricia," said Betsy, and Patricia whirled again. Too bad she wasn't wearing the swing coat; it flared so prettily. "We know what was on the tapestry. I'm sure you rearranged the appliqué while you were in Phoenix so it no longer spells your name. That's it hanging over your arm. Where were you going to put it, in the rest room? That's where you hid it the first time, isn't it, on the hook on the back of the door?"

"I don't know what you're talking about," said Patricia with a faint show of puzzlement. "I found it after you left and decided to take it along and treat the mildew. I'm allergic, you know, and I couldn't work on it like it was." She started toward Betsy, her arm with the white-wrapped drape moving outward as if to hand it over, but Malloy took her by the other arm. She gave him a look that might have withered an ordinary mortal, but he only gazed back until her eyes dropped and her arm came back against her coat.

Betsy said, "You hadn't looked closely at the tapestry at first because you're allergic to mildew, but when I showed you those little symbols in the halo, you saw right away that the first three were a shamrock, a lamb, and a flaming heart, the attributes of Saints Patrick, Agnes, and Theresa, whose initials spell Pat, and you realized you were in big, big trouble."

Patricia replied, still very calmly, "What makes you think I saw at a glance what nobody else saw?"

"Because you knew Lucy liked to hide words in her stitchery, *and* you taught a course about medieval Christian art, which is all about symbology and attributes."

"And even if I recognized them, so what?"

"Because there was a message in those attributes: *Pat's boy + missing money = Keane.* Father Keane did what he could, even stealing money to help you with the cuckoo's egg you laid in Peter's nest. The boy Peter is so proud of, the grandson his mother finally approves of, isn't theirs, is he?"

"You're wrong, the attributes spell only Keane's name, that's all. Look at it, if you like." Again she held out the folded white sheet draped over her arm.

Betsy persisted, "Do you know you were not his first affair? There might even be other children."

Patricia's face reddened. "You don't know what you're saying," she said in a flat voice.

"Howland Royce, a member of the old vestry, found evidence that Father Keane had been misappropriating funds for a long time, going back years, and that he admitted he'd been paying off a string of women."

"I don't believe you," said Patricia.

"It's true, Patricia," said Jill. "I was there, too, and I heard him say Father Keane admitted it."

Patricia coughed harshly. "Well, I still don't see how that involves me. I was a young married woman trying to put my husband through law school when Father Keane quit. I don't remember hearing why. But of course, back then I barely had time to come to Sunday service, much less stay after to hear the latest gossip around the coffee urn."

"I'm sure you've noticed Brent has Keane's hazel eyes," said Betsy relentlessly. "Just like his daughter Mandy."

"Do you know what would happen to my husband if you—" She raked the hall with her eyes. "If *any* of you repeat any of this in public? Do you have any idea what my husband would do if he thought that was true?"

"What he'd do to us?" said Betsy. "Or to you? That's what this is all about, isn't it? Your son. Your marriage. Your place in this community. You were young and risked your future for what you thought was a glorious love affair. Was it because your lover swept you away with his ardor, his charm, his—what? His assurances that you were his first and only extramarital affair? But then you got pregnant. And Keane wouldn't leave his wife for you. If he did that, he would have had to give up his calling, wouldn't he? He couldn't continue being a priest after such a scandal. And at his age, it wouldn't be easy to build a new career, one that would support a wife and child. Plus his former wife and daughter. With the gauzy curtain of love ripped apart, you could see this wasn't going to work. So what to do? Your husband was still in law school and you'd agreed not to start a family until he finished. His wealthy parents disapproved of his early marriage to a woman beneath him and had cut off all aid. If any hint of the truth reached them, your bright future as wife of a wealthy attorney was dead. What a mess to find yourself in! And how sad that you're right back in it."

It was as if the whole room held its breath. "You don't know," sighed Patricia, her shoulders slumping. "It was so hard. Keane said he loved me. He said his marriage was a sham, that he had never loved anyone like he loved me in his whole life. I thought we had a special kind of love, one that excused anything. Like Abelard and Heloise, like Hepburn and Tracy. To sit in his office and hear him plan to steal—*steal!*—money to help me with the baby, was a kind of death. I wanted to say no, but Peter's part-time job paid so little, and babies are more expensive than I dreamed . . ." Patricia's voice trailed off.

"It was just easier to pretend the birth control failed between Peter and me, rather than with Keane. And it worked. Then Keane had that stroke, I thought it was the stress of the theft, and I felt so guilty. But I didn't break, I just kept going, and at last things smoothed out for us. Peter's father died, and his mother came around. She bought our new house for us—it has *three* fireplaces!—and invited us to Phoenix for Christmas.

"And then, after all this time, after all I'd gone through, all the sacrifices, all the secrets—that *wretched* tapestry! And worse, there you were, writing down the little symbols, taking that book home to look them up . . .

"I *had* to do those terrible, horrible things to you, Betsy. It was harder than you'll ever know. You're a very nice woman, working so hard and bravely to pick up the pieces of your life, I felt just awful about it. I really didn't want to, and I kept hoping you'd leave town, but you wouldn't go. But then Father John said *he* had the tapestry, and told us where it was, and I ran and got it and hung it on the hook on the back of the door of that little rest room. And I took it with me to Phoenix in a big plastic bag, and though I treated it for mildew it still made my eyes water and my nose run and I had to pretend I had a cold. But that was fine, I was so relieved, everything was going to be all right, I'd destroyed the proof. And even though now it's all coming out, oh my God, Betsy, I'm so *glad* I didn't kill you!"

"I know you took that car course and knew about brake lines, and I suppose you must have plenty of firewood for those three fireplaces, but how did you get the arsenic without giving your name? When I went to eBay, they wanted my name and address."

"I started a new AOL account under a new name. And there are places that will forward your mail. And when you buy a money order, you can put any name you like on it. I did that some while ago when Peter thought I was spending too much on antiques. I just did it for fun, buying those old medicine bottles. I suppose they had a different definition of medicine back then, because some of those old bottles have arsenic, mercury sulfate, even strychnine in them. Some come in little bottles shaped like coffins, isn't that amusing? I keep them in a locked cabinet, of course. Then when this happened, I read a book that said the thing murderers do is put just a little bit in the food to start a medical record of gastritis. I put it in the order of chicken salad and brought it up with the hot dish, and I couldn't believe how sick it made you. I was just horrified. I am truly sorry, Betsy."

Betsy fought a rising sickness by getting angry. She said tightly, "It's possible you did these things with great reluctance. I think you would have come to my funeral and wept genuine tears. But I also think you would have gone home from the funeral sighing with relief."

Patricia's smile came with sad eyebrows. "Well, yes, I suppose I would have." She turned to Malloy. "I suppose you're going to arrest me now?"

"Oh, yes, you are definitely under arrest," said Malloy. "You have a right to remain silent. If you give up the right to remain silent, anything you say can and will be taken down and used against you in a court of law. You have the right to consult with an attorney and to have an attorney present during questioning. If you wish an attorney, but can't afford one, one will be supplied to you at no cost. Do you understand these rights as I have explained them to you?"

"Yes, I do."

Malloy took the tapestry and handed it to one of the uniformed officers, saying, "Tag this and bring it to the station." Then he cuffed Patricia's hands behind her back. She took it with grace and walked out ahead of him, her head high, her face settled into a withdrawn calm.

Betsy turned away, covering her face with her hands. She said through her fingers, "Can I go home now?"

Jill replied, "I'm sorry, but you have to come with me to the station. You would not believe the paperwork we have to fill out."

"My God," said Godwin the next morning. "That is . . . *terrible!* Who would have thought Patricia was doing this? Betsy, that is just *terrible!*"

"I know, I know," said Betsy, turning her chair away from the library table to face Sophie. She stroked the cat, who lifted her head to accept the caress, exhaling a pleased purr.

Godwin continued, "How did you figure it out?"

"A collection of little things. First, she was the one who had a source for arsenic. She's an antiquer, and she uses eBay. I was amazed when I looked in the collectibles section of eBay and saw what was in some of those old bottles.

"Also, this whole thing was about the notes I made on the attributes. She stole the notes I typed but couldn't get at the originals—and only Patricia knew about them; she saw me making them on the back of my checkbook. She visited me in the hospital after the poisoning, and there I was with the original notes and the book on Christian symbology. She must have been sick with fear that I'd figure it out.

"It was the day she came to confess to Father John that Keane was the father of her oldest child that she got hold of the tapestry."

"Father John *knew?*" exclaimed Godwin.

"No, she didn't tell him. I saw her waiting to see him, looking very miserable, which I imagine she was. I thought perhaps she was worried about me, and in a way I was right. She'd tried three times to kill me, without success. She was afraid that tapestry would turn up while she was in Phoenix and that I'd see the whole set of attributes in its correct order and figure out how they spelled out an accusation against her. Her comfortable life was going to pop like a messy bubble. But then Father John came out of his office and said the tapestry was wrapped in a sheet and laid safely away in the sacristy. So she ran ahead to remove it from its drawer and hide it in the rest room, and then say she couldn't find it. She even encouraged me to take Jill along to help search for it, a very risky thing to do. But she had to convince me it hadn't been there when she went to look for it."

"Cool head."

"Oh, yes, that's why I really don't think she was trying hard enough to kill me. She's far too organized not to have gotten it right in three attempts. She really didn't want to kill me, she wanted me to stop fooling with those attributes so she could go on being the cool and competent wife of a rising politician, the respectable mother of his three children. But her boy isn't her husband's, he's the result of a passionate love affair. It's a shame it was only true love on her part; Keane was an experienced adulterer. Not that it mattered; what was important was that the secret be kept, both so her husband wouldn't find out and because Brent is the only remnant of that affair she could openly brag about and show off. I suspect Peter Fairland is not happy to learn his wonderful son is in fact not his. It may change the boy's life profoundly. Patricia did all this to prevent that happening. Having to choose between Brent or Betsy—well, out goes me."

"Bitch," remarked Godwin.

"No, she's not a bitch. She may be what my mother called a toom tabbard, an empty shell. She came from a very different background from the one she married into, and she had to rebuild herself from the ground up, casting off attitudes, behavior, and opinions that revealed her real self. Possibly there is no real self anymore, only that remade surface. So she was willing to go farther than most to retain that surface, which is all she has."

"You really do feel sorry for her!"

"Yes, I do."

"What are you, a saint?"

"No, of course not. But I can't feel as pleased over this one as the others, Godwin. I just feel a little sick." She stroked Sophie some more. "I hope Mandy is right, that there is some awareness in her father, that those tears he keeps shedding in that nursing home are not for himself but for his victims."

The door made its annoying *bing* sound and Joe Mickels came in. He marched up to the table. "Ms. Devonshire," he said in a clear but very quiet voice, "when this mess you are in is over, may I take you to dinner?"

Betsy, surprised, very nearly replied, "Whatever for?" but bit her tongue in time. "Why don't you wait until this mess is over and ask me again?" she said instead.

"Very well, I will," he declared and walked out again.

Godwin gaped after him, then at Betsy. *You* are going on a *date* with *Joe Mickels?*"

"I may," replied Betsy. "Though it's more in the way of a business meeting."

"What kind of business are you in with Joe?"

"Well, I'm buying this building from him—"

"*Strewth!*" exclaimed Godwin, grasping the front of his beautiful sweater with a splayed hand. "How did you get him to agree to that?"

"Let's just say I made him an offer he couldn't refuse." And she would say no more, which is possibly why there was a rumor flying all over Excelsior the next day that Joe Mickels had gone out of his mind.

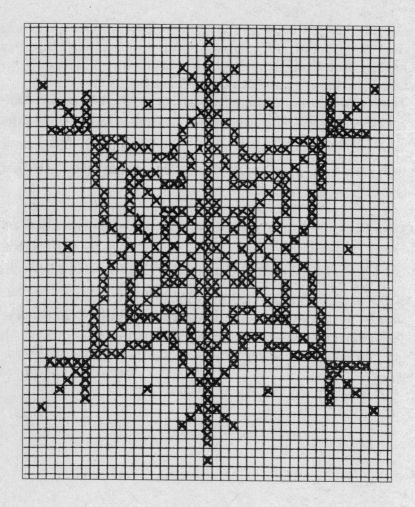

This counted cross stitch snowflake can be worked on any dark-colored evenweave fabric or canvas in white or metallic. The designer, Denise Williams, worked it on 14-count navy blue canvas with Balger #8 floss, for an interesting, sparkly effect. On that count, the snowflake is 3.5 inches across.

DIRECTIONS: Find the center of the pattern and mark it. Find the center of the fabric and begin there, making Xs as the pattern indicates. It may be helpful to grid the pattern by drawing a line with see-through marker every five or ten squares. A corresponding line may be stitched with a single thread on the fabric. (Beginners like Betsy find this very helpful!) Then pull the marker threads out when the pattern is finished.